I THE SUPREME

I

THE SUPREME

by

Augusto Roa Bastos

translated by Helen Lane

ALFRED A. KNOPF   NEW YORK   1986

THIS IS A BORZOI BOOK
PUBLISHED BY ALFRED A. KNOPF, INC.

Library of Congress Cataloging-in-Publication Data

Roa Bastos, Augusto Antonio.   I, the Supreme.

1. Francia, José Gaspar Rodríguez de, 1766–1840—Fiction. I. Title.
PQ8259.R56Y613   1986   863   85-45609
ISBN 0-394-53535-9

Manufactured in the United States of America

Published April 17, 1986
Second Printing, April 1986

TRANSLATOR'S ACKNOWLEDGMENTS

This translation would not have come into being had it not been for the light offered me by two who know the original languages far better than I: Augusto Roa Bastos and Iris Giménez.

Grateful thanks are also due Milagros Ezquerro for much way-pointing. It was her edition of *Yo el Supremo* that provided the text here used. With her kind permission, I have also used many of her notes and her Guaraní lexicon.

I also warmly thank Lee Goerner, the editor of *I the Supreme* at Alfred A. Knopf, for his enthusiasm, encouragement, and endurance.

And finally, this version of the story of the Supreme could not have been put before the reader without the generous help —in every sense—of Joan Palevsky, to whom it is dedicated.

I THE SUPREME

I the Supreme Dictator of the Republic

Order that on the occasion of my death my corpse be decapitated; my head placed on a pike for three days in the Plaza de la República, to which the people are to be summoned by the sounding of a full peal of bells.

All my civil and military servants are to be hanged. Their corpses are to be buried in pastures outside the walls with neither cross nor mark to commemorate their names.

At the end of the aforementioned period, I order that my remains be burned and my ashes thrown into the river...

Where was this found? Nailed to the door of the cathedral, Excellency. A patrol of grenadiers discovered it early this morning and brought it in to headquarters. Luckily no one had time to read it. I didn't ask you that, and it's a matter of no importance. Your Grace is right. The ink of pasquinades turns sour more quickly than milk. But it's not a page from the Buenos Aires Gazette, nor is it one torn out of a book, Sire. What books would there be around here outside of my own! The aristocrats of the Twenty Families turned theirs into playing cards ages ago. Have the houses of the antipatriots searched. The dungeons, down in the dungeons, go have a look in the dungeons. The guilty party might very well be among those rats with tangled dangling locks and foot-long fingernails. Tighten the knots in those notorious forgers' iron neckties. Peña and Molas especially. Bring me the letters in which Molas pays me homage during the First Consulate, and then later during the First Dictatorship. I want to reread the speech he delivered in the Assembly of the year '14, proposing that I be elected Dictator. His handwriting is very different in the draft of the speech, in the instructions to the deputies, in the statement to the authorities years later in which he accuses one of his brothers of having stolen cattle from him at his estancia in Altos. I can repeat what those papers say, Excellency. I didn't ask you to recite by heart the thousands of documents, dossiers, and decrees in the archives. I merely ordered you to bring me the file on Mariano Antonio Molas. Bring me the pamphlets by Manuel Pedro de Peña as well. Cantankerous sycophants! They boast of having been the Word of Independence. The rats! They didn't even begin to understand it. They think they're still masters of their words in the depths of their dungeons. But all they know how to do is squeal. They haven't shut up to this day. They keep finding new ways of secreting their accursed poison. They get out pamphlets, pasquinades, lampoons, caricatures. I am an indispensable figure for slander. For all I care they can manufacture their paper from consecrated rags. Write it, print it with consecrated letters on a consecrated press. Go print your drivel on Mount Sinai if that will unshrivel your souls, you cacogenic latrinographers!

Hum. Ah! Funeral orations, pamphlets condemning me to be burned at the stake. Bah! They're daring to parody my Supreme Decrees now. They imitate my language, my handwriting, trying to infiltrate by way of it; to get to me from their lairs. Shut my mouth with the voice that thundered against them. Bury me in words, in effigy. An old trick of tribal witch doctors. Post more guards to watch over those who labor under the delusion that they can replace me once I'm dead. Where is the file of anonymous libels? It's right there, Excellency, by your hand.

It is not wholly unlikely that those two sly scribble-scrabblers Molas and de la Peña were the ones who dictated this squib. The joke is altogether in the style of those two infamous Porteñista partisans, out to further the cause of Buenos Aires. If it is their doing, I shall immolate Molas, pen Peña in for life. One of their ignoble blind tools could well have learned it by heart. A second one written it down. A third goes and pins it to the door of the cathedral with four thumbtacks. The guards themselves are the worst traitors. Your Worship is more than right. In the light of what Your Eminence says, even the truth appears to be a lie. I'm not asking you to flatter me, Patiño. I'm ordering you to seek and find the author of the pasquinade. The law is a bottomless pit, but I expect you to be able to discover a hair in that hole. Search the souls of Peña and Molas. Sire, they can't be the ones. They've been confined to utter darkness for years now. And so? After Molas's last Outcry was intercepted, Excellency, I ordered the skylights, the cracks in the doors, the chinks in the walls and ceiling filled in with stone and mortar. You know that the prisoners continually train rats to carry their clandestine communications. And even to bring them food. You'll remember that that was how the ones from Santa Fe stole my ravens' rations for months. I also ordered all the holes and runways of the ants, the culverts of the crickets, the sigh holes of the crannies plugged up. No darker darkness possible, Sire. They don't have anything to write with. Are you forgetting memory, you of all people, you memorious lout? They may not have even a pencil stub, a little end of charcoal. They may not have light or air. But they have a memory. A memory just like yours. The memory of an archive-cockroach, three hundred million years older than homo sapiens. The memory of the fish, of the frog, of the parrot that always cleans its beak on the same side. Which doesn't mean they're intelligent. Quite the contrary. Can you state categorically that the scalded cat that flees even cold water is possessed of a good memory? No, merely that it's a cat that's afraid. The scalding has penetrated its memory. Memory doesn't recall the fear. It has become fear itself.

Do you know what memory is? The stomach of the soul, someone wrongly called it. Though nobody is ever the first to give things a name. There is nothing but an infinity of repeaters. The only things ever invented are new errors. The memory of one person alone is useless.

Stomach of the soul. That's too clever by half! What sort of soul could those pitiless, inhuman slanderers have? The quadruple stomachs of quadrupeds. Ruminant stomachs. That's where the perfidy of those successive incurable scoundrels ferments. That's where they cook up their potfuls of infamies. What sort of memory do they need to remember all the lies they've cranked out with the one aim of defaming me, of slandering the Government? A memory of cud-chewers. A ruminant's memory. Ingestive-digestive. Repetitive. Disfigurative. Sulliative. They prophesied that they would turn this country into the new Athens. The Areopagus of the sciences, the letters, the arts of this Continent. What they were really out to do with their chimeras was to hand Paraguay over to the highest bidder. The areopagites came within a hair of doing just that. I managed to get rid of them. I picked them off one by one. I put them in their rightful place. Off with you, areopagites! To jail with the lot of you, blockheads!

The worst offender, Manuel Pedro de Peña, parakeet number one of the patriciate, I disblazoned. Cured of his cock-a-hoop habits. Took him down off his heraldic perch. Caged him in a prison cell. He there learned to recite by heart, without a single mistake, the hundred thousand words in the Royal Academy dictionary, from A to Z. That's how he exercises his memory in the cemetery of words. I wouldn't want the enamel, the metal of his word-pipes to rust. Dr. Mariano Antonio Molas, Attorney Molas, or to put a fine point on it, Molas the pen-pusher, recites nonstop, even in his dreams, bits and pieces of a description of what he calls the Former Province of Paraguay. For these last surviving areopagites, the Fatherland continues to be the former province. They make no mention whatsoever, not even in the decorous euphemisms to which their colonized tongues were accustomed, to the Giant Province of the Indies, the one that in the last analysis was grandmother, mother, aunt, poor relation of the Viceroyalty of Río de la Plata, which grew rich at her expense.

It is not only the patricians and vernacular areopagites who use and abuse their ruminating memory here. The foreign marsupials who stole from the country and buried the memory of their ladronicides in the stomach of their souls do so as well. There's the Frenchman Pedro Martell. After twenty years in prison and as many more of madness he still thinks of nothing but his chest full of gold pieces. Every night he furtively removes the chest from the hole he's dug underneath his hammock with his fingernails; he counts yet again the gleaming coins, one by one, proves them with his toothless gums, puts them back in his chest, and buries it in the hole again. He then stretches out in his hammock and sleeps in bliss above his imaginary treasure. Who could feel better protected than he? This was the sort of life lived in the cellars for many years by another Frenchman, Charles Andreu-Legard, ex prisoner of the Bastille, chewing over his memories in my republican bastille. Can it be said that those didelphians know what memory is? Neither you nor they know. Those who do know have no memory. Those with prodigious memories are almost always mentally retarded imbeciles. Besides being scoundrels and very clever tricksters. Or something even worse. They use their memory to harm others, but have no idea how to do so for their own good. No comparison with the scalded cat. Parrot-memory, cow-memory, ass-memory. Not sense-memory, judgment-memory, possessed of a lusty imagination capable of engendering events in and of itself. The things that have come into being change continually. The man with a good memory remembers nothing because he forgets nothing.

The cow that my presumptive sister Petrona Regalada is allowed to keep in the yard of her house became infested with ticks. I ordered that she treat it the way this and other diseases are combated on the patrial estancias: by killing the animal. I have only one cow, Sire, and it does not belong to me but to my little catechism school. It gives just one glass of milk for the twenty little ones who come for instruction. You'll be left, señora, without the cow, and your pupils won't be able to drink even the milk of the Holy Spirit that you extract for their benefit as you dip candles. Goodbye cow, catechumens, catechesis. The ticks will devour not only the cow. They'll devour you. They'll invade the city, which already has enough to contend with, what with its plague of thugs and stray dogs. Don't you hear their rabid howls mounting, louder and louder, on every hand? Sacrifice the cow, señora.

I saw from her eyes that she wasn't about to do so. I ordered a soldier to butcher the sick animal with his bayonet and bury it. My supposed sister, the ex widow of Larios Galván, came to present a complaint. Her mind completely unhinged, the old woman swore that, even though it was dead, the cow was still mooing in muffled tones underground. I ordered the pair of Swiss forensic physicians to do an autopsy on the animal. They found in its bowels a bezoar stone the size of a grapefruit. The old woman now maintains that the hairy stone is an antidote for any poison. It cures illnesses, Sire. Especially milk fever. It tells the meaning of dreams. It foretells deaths, she says enthusiastically. She swears, moreover, that she heard the stone murmur inaudible words. Ah madness, memory in reverse that forgets its way as it retraces its path. How could anyone with an iota of good sense believe such insane things?

Begging Your Excellency's pardon, I take the liberty of saying that I too heard those words. So did the grenadier who killed the cow. Come, come, Patiño, don't you start raving too! Excuse me, Sire, with your permission I must tell you that I heard those moos-that-were-words, like human words. Voices very far away, a bit hoarse as if from a cold, gurgling words. The remains of some unknown language that doesn't want to die completely, Excellency. You're too stupid to go mad, secretary. Human madness is ordinarily extremely clever. A chameleon of sanity. When you think it's cured, it's because it's worse. It has merely transformed itself into another still more subtle madness. Hence, like old Petrona Regalada, you hear those nonexistent voices coming from a carcass. What language, may

I ask, might that excremental ball petrified in the stomach of a cow remember? With your permission, it's saying something, Your Grace. Maybe in Latin or in some other unknown tongue. Doesn't Your Worship believe that there might be such a thing as an ear for which all men and animals speak the same language? The last time Señora Petrona Regalada allowed me to listen to her stone, I heard it murmur something like . . . king of the world. . . . Of course, you scoundrel! I should have thought of that! How could that stone that addled the widow's brain be anything else but royalist? That's the last straw! Not only do those filthy Spaniards pin pasquinades on the cathedral door; they also put a stone of contagion in the belly of cows!

As much or more than false memory, bad habits silence habitual phenomena. They form a second nature, just as nature is the first habit. Forget that bezoar stone, Patiño. Forget that tripe of yours about an ear able to understand all languages in a single one. Utter madness!

I have forbidden the woman regarded as my half sister to engage in those practices of witchcraft with which she diddles ignorant, credulous fools like herself. She already does enough damage by giving the little boys who attend her school a dose of the catechism tick. I allow her to do so. Harmless mania. The Patrial Reformed Catechism and patriotic zeal will extirpate these youngsters' catechistic cyst once they've grown up.

The cursed bezoar didn't keep the cow from being infested with the tick, I told her when she came to complain. It didn't cure you, señora, of your calenture of the brain. It proved incapable of drawing the poison of dementia out of Bishop Panés. And still less capable of relieving my gout when you brought your stone here to rub it on my swollen leg for three days running. If the stone is of no use except to repeat for amusement's sake those words that it receives from a world beyond, in an unnatural language that only scatterpates and lunatics think they hear, I'm damned if I see what on earth the stone is good for!

You too have your stone, she answered, pointing to the aerolith. I don't use it for augury the way you do yours, Señora Petrona Regalada. It will end up fogging your brain, which is how your other brothers and sisters ended up. You know that the specter of madness has always haunted your kin. A more or less common family trait in those of the same blood. Bury your bezoar stone. Bury it in your courtyard. Place it at the foot of a wayside league-cross. Throw it in the river. Flush all this nonsense of yours down the drain. Don't displease me again as you did when I learned that after ten years' separation you were continuing to see your ex husband Larios Galván in secret. What is it you want from that Don Juan? He tried to deceive you. Before that he deceived the First Governing Junta. Then after that the Supreme Government. What is it you want, at your ripe old age, from that corrupt rakehell? Orphan offspring? Bastard bezoar pebbles? If not that, what? Bury your bezoar stone, the way I buried your ex husband in prison. Dip your candles in peace and enough of this foolishness!

Her eyes went blank. Characteristic cunning of madness as it outwardly feigns right reason. She began to look inward, seeking to hide herself from my presence in that perverse taciturnity of the Franças. The wretches!

Look here, Señora Petrona Regalada, for some time now the cigars you've been rolling for me have been thicker than usual. I am obliged to unroll them. To remove some of their innards. Impossible otherwise to smoke them. Make them as big around as this finger. Wrap them in a single leaf of tobacco softened in night dew and then well dried. The kind least irritating to the lungs. Answer me. Don't just stand there not saying a word. Am I speaking to a post? Have you lost your tongue along with your mind? Look at me. Speak. She has turned her head. She looks at me with the expression of certain birds that have only one expression. A face strikingly similar to mine. She gives the impression that she is learning to see, seeing for the first time a complete stranger toward whom she does not yet know whether she feels respect, scorn, or indifference. I see myself in her. A mirror-person, old França Velho sends me back my image, dressed as a woman. Beyond all ties of blood. What have I to do with blood relations? Confabulations of chance.

There are many people. There are even more faces, since everyone has several. There are people who wear the same face for years. Simple, thrifty, miserly people. What do they do with the other ones? They save them. Their sons will wear them. It sometimes happens that their dogs wear them. Why not? A face is a face. Sultan's looked very much like mine toward the last, especially just before passing on. The dog's countenance looked as much like mine as that of this woman who is standing before me, looking at me, parodying my image. She will not have any more children now. I will not have any more dogs now. At this moment our faces coincide. Mine at least is the last. In a frock coat and a tricorne, old França Velho would be my exact replica. It would remain to be seen how this chance resemblance could be used . . . *(the rest of the sentence burned, illegible).* A story just for the fun of it!

Memory is of no use here. Seeing is forgetting. That woman is standing there motionless, reflecting me. The non-face, all of a piece, fallen forward. Does she desire something? She desires nothing. She does not desire the least thing in this world, save non-desire. But non-desire too is fulfilled if non-desirers are persistent.

Did you hear how you are to roll my cigars from now on? The woman wrenches herself violently away from herself. Her face is still between her hands. She doesn't know what to do with it. As big around as this finger, eh? Rolled out of just one leaf of tobacco. Softened in night dew. Dry. The kind that draw best all the way down, till the red-hot tip gets very close to your mouth. Your breath, all nice and warm, escapes with the smoke. Do you understand me, Señora Petrona Regalada? Her puckered lips move. I know what she is thinking, flayed alive by her memories.

She is disremembering.

She is never without her bezoar stone. She keeps it hidden underneath the niche of the Lord of Patience. More powerful than the image of the Bloodstained God. Talisman. Stair. Platform. Last step. The most resistant. It sustains her in the place of certainty. Place where there is no further need of any sort of help. Obsession has its foundation there. Faith is supported entirely by itself. What is faith if not belief in things that have no verisimilitude? Seeing through a glass darkly.

The ruminant-stone has its own vigil light. Someday it will have its own niche. Perhaps, in time, its sanctuary.

In the face of the bezoar stone of the person taken to be my sister, the meteorite still has—will it ever cease to have?—the flavor of the improbable. And what if the world itself were only a sort of bezoar? Hairy excremental material, petrified in the intestine of the cosmos.

It is my opinion . . . *(edge of the folio burned)* . . . Where matters of opinion are concerned, all opinions are worse . . .

But this is not what I wanted to say. Clouds are piling up above my head. Quantities of earth. Bird with a long beak, I am unable to get any pellets out of the cup. A shadow, I cannot extract shadows from holes. I continue to wander aimlessly about, as on that stormy night that plunged me headlong into the place where the loss occurred. I thought I knew something about the desert. About dogs, a bit more. About men, everything. As for the rest, thirst, cold, betrayals, sicknesses, they all came my way. But I always knew what to do when the time came to act. As I remember, this is the worst time. If a chimera, swaying back and forth in a vacuum, can eat ulterior motives, I've been well chewed and swallowed, as compadre Rabelais put it. The chimera has occupied the place of my person. I tend to be "the very image of the chimerical." A famous joke, that will bear my name. Look up the word "chimera" in the dictionary, Patiño. *A false idea, a vain or foolish fancy, a fantastic creature of the imagination* it says, Excellency. That's what I'm in the way of being, in reality and on paper. It also says, Sire: *A fabulous monster with the head of a lion, the body of a goat, and the tail of a dragon.* They say that that's what I was. The dictionary also adds, Excellency: *Name of a fish and of a butterfly. Quarrel. Dispute.* I was all that, and none of that. The dictionary is an ossuary of empty words. If you don't believe me, ask de la Peña.

Forms disappear, words remain, to signify the impossible. No story can be told. No story worth the telling. But true language hasn't yet been born. Animals communicate with each other, without words. Better than we, who are so proud of having invented words out of the raw material of the chimerical. Without foundation. No relation to life. Do you know, Patiño, what life is, what death is? No; you don't know. Nobody knows. No one has ever known whether life is what lives or what dies. No one will ever know. What's more, it would be useless to know, once we grant that the impossible is useless. There would have to be words in our language that had a voice. Free space. A memory of their own. Words that subsisted alone, that brought place with them. A place. Their place. Their own material. A space where the word would happen the way an event does. As in the language of certain animals, of certain birds, or certain very old insects. But does what is *not* exist?

After that storm-rent night, in the deathly pale light of dawn, an animal in the form of a stag came to meet me. Horn in the middle of its forehead. Green coat. Voice part blast of a trumpet, part sigh. It said to me: It is time My Lord return to earth. I struck it a blow on the muzzle with my cane and went on my way. I stopped outside of "Nothing We Don't Have," the general store run by our spy Orrego, who was opening the doors of the place by the light of a candle. Even he didn't recognize the muddy beggar entering his establishment as the cocks were beginning to crow. I ordered a glass of cane brandy. I'll be damned, pal!, he exclaimed. Thirsty this early in the day after that downpour last night! I threw an old rusty clipped copper coin on the counter, and it bounced off onto the floor. As the storekeeper bent over I left, melting into the fog.

Excellency, a post rider has just come galloping in on a badly winded horse with this dispatch from the commandant of Villa Franca:

I beg you to allow me to describe to you in brief detail the way in which we have proceeded to observe the occasion of the funeral of our Supreme Lord. On the evening preceding that sad day the plaza and all the houses of this City were illuminated.

On the eighteenth the parish priest celebrated a solemn sung Mass for the health, success, and felicity of the individuals who make up the new, provisory, and sole de fatuo Government. When the Mass was over, the Decree was proclaimed and was received and obeyed with great sounds of rejoicing. I swore allegiance as head of this City. A short three-rifle volley was fired amid the tolling of the bells, and a solemn Te-Demus was sung.

That night the City was illuminated once again.

On the nineteenth the funeral rites were held. A cumulus three cuerpos high, adorned with mirrors, was erected. A table covered with the snow-white altar cloths that the parish priest lent for the notable occasion was placed before it. On a black silk cushion lay the crossed baton and sword, emblems of Sovereign Power. The cumulus was illuminated with eighty-four candles, one for each year of the Supreme Dictator's life. Many persons—if not all—noted his apparition amid the endlessly multiplied reflections, the very image and likeness of his infinite paternal protection.

On the twentieth a solemn vigil was sung, and during the Mass the parish priest delivered the funeral oration, developing the following theme: The Most Excellent Supreme deceased Dictator fulfilled not only the obligations of a Faithful Citizen, but also those of a Faithful Father and Sovereign of the Republic. But the oration remained unfinished for the reason that neither the multitude nor the father were able to contain their grief. Silent at first, it soon turned into wild sobs of lamentation. The Preacher descended from the pulpit bathed in tears.

On every hand there were moans, sobs, heart-rending laments. Many persons tore their hair with cries of profound pain. Paraguayan souls at their maximum intensity. The same was true of the appreciable crowd of more than twenty thousand Indians who came from both shores of the river to hold their funeral ceremonies in front of the church and mingled with the multitude. The agitation that was felt is beyond all description.

Our limited faculties did not allow us to devote more solemnity to the memory of the deceased Dictator. On the one hand, we were overcome with desolation. On the other, we felt a flood of consolation; we congratulate ourselves whenever the presence of the Supreme Lord appears or represents itself at our gatherings.

My trembling pen wrote as far as the above on the twentieth, at about six o'clock in the evening. But since very early this morning rumors that The Supreme is still alive have begun to circulate; that is to say, that he has not died, and therefore a provisory de fatuo Government does not yet exist.

Can it possibly be that this terrible commotion has profoundly altered the very meaning of the certain and the uncertain?

We beg Your Excellency to relieve us of this horrible doubt that leaves us with bated breath.

Answer the commandant of Villa Franca that I haven't died yet, if being dead means simply lying beneath a gravestone on which some stupid good-for-nothing will write an epitaph on the order of: Here lies the Supreme Dictator/in perpetual memory/vigilant defender of the Fatherland . . . et cetera, et cetera.

My absence will be the gravestone over this poor people that will be obliged to go on breathing beneath it without having died since it has yet to be born. When this happens, inasmuch as I am not eternal, I myself will have word sent to you, my dear Antonio Escobar.

What is the date of the dispatch? October 21, 1840, Excellency. I have news for you, Patiño. We have here a Paraguayan who gets ahead of events. He drops his message through the keyhole of a month that hasn't yet arrived. He leaps over all the hopeless confusions of time. The proper thing to do is to find a time for everything. One that has no end. What river's flow ever grows old? Is it possible that people like Antonio Escobar have exact and certain knowledge of something that hasn't happened yet? Yes. It's possible. There's nothing that hasn't already happened. They have their doubts but they're sure of themselves. They divine with their simple minds that the law is symbolic. They do not take everything literally as do those who speak a confused language.

I do not say unto you: This generation shall not pass till all these things be fulfilled. I say unto you: After this generation another shall come. If it is not *I,* it will be *He,* who is ageless too.

Ah, with regard to Escobar's dispatch, extend my thanks to him for the magnificent obsequies. Tell him not to let the second ones be so drenched in tears, or the hair-tearing quite so vigorous. Nor is there any need, my dear Escobar, to erect illuminated "cumuli" since my age is not measured in candles. You may spare this expense in my honor. Nor is there any need to decorate them with mirrors that give a false vision of things. Those mirrors must be the ones that were taken from the citizens of Corrientes years ago, during the siege of their city. Return them to their owners, who lost face at the time and haven't known where to look for it since.

Another thing, Escobar. Inform me immediately, before my ashes grow cold, who signed the circular notifying you of my death and the establishment of what you call a provisory "de fatuo" government. The proper term is *de facto,* which means "in fact." Although in fact what we have in this country is a bunch of fatuous fatheads. So that in your dispatch you're right and wrong at the same time.

Tell me, Patiño . . . Yes, Excellency. Do you know anything about all this? I'm completely in the dark, Sire! Nose about a little. It wouldn't be a bad idea for *us*—the two of us—to find out what's going on. It's awkward being alive and dead at the same time. Don't give it a thought, Excellency. I haven't, and that's how things like this happen. Do you suspect anyone in particular? No one, Sire. No one has ever dared go this far. I don't know who it could be, Excellency, who the guilty party might be. The truth of the matter, Most Excellent Sire, is that as far as I know I don't know anything. It just so happens that this time I don't have the least suspicion of anybody, any individual, group, or faction. If another conspiracy is afoot after twenty years of public peace, of respect for and obedience to the Supreme Government, I promise you that the guilty parties will not escape even though they hide underground. Stop picking your nasal fossae. I beg Your Excellency's pardon! Enough of that! You don't need to come to attention like that every other minute! Must I tell you so every day? Your diving in and out of the washbasin is going to turn the floor into a mudhole. We'll both drown in this bog before our enemies have the pleasure of incinerating us in the plaza. God save us, Excellency! It's not God who's going to free you of your troubles. When we're working, as I've also ordered you countless times, don't keep repeating Your Grace, Your Worship, Your Excellency, all that fancy fiddle-faddle that has no place in a modern State. Less still in this chronic state of incommunication that separates us even as it unites us without visible hierarchy. And even more so, if we are soon to be comrades in the cineratorium of the Plaza de Armas. For the time being, use Sire, if you feel it absolutely necessary to address me in some way. That won't lessen the distance between us, even if you kick the bucket. As I dictate to you, you write. Whereas I read what I dictate to you so as later to reread what you write. In the end the two of us disappear in what is read/written. Use the appropriate term of address only in the presence of third parties. For, I grant you, we must observe the formalities, save the appearances, so long as we are visible figures. Everyday words of ordinary language.

Let's go back to the pamphlet found this morning on the door of the cathedral. Where is it? Here, Sire. As you keep nibbling at your nasal conchae with your pen you keep dribbling all over the anonymous screed.

You've almost effaced the beautiful handwriting. Pass it over to me. The gachupines§ or the Porteñistas§§ who gave birth to this monstrosity haven't mocked me but themselves. Let all those termites eat each other up! This just makes me laugh all the more at their stupid self-importance and the pretension of their anonymous squibs. This paper isn't worth even one of their ears. He who uses a leaf for cover gets wet twice over. Even if they hid underneath an entire forest of pasquinades, they'd still wet themselves in their own piss. Wretched descendants of those usurers, tradesmen, hoarders, shopkeepers who used to scream from behind their counters: We shit on the Fatherland and on all patriots! We shit on the puny little republic of the Paraguayans! They shat out of fear and were buried in their own shit. The same shit those turds were born from. Blood-sucking anopheles, buzzing out their behinds and not their proboscises, like all mosquitoes. In that case, Sire, I'll be more than glad to wade through even the soiled toilet paper, coil by coil . . . Hold your tongue, you knave! I forbid you to wallow in filth playing dirty word games. Don't try to imitate the jakish japes of those culicids. I humbly beg Your Grace's pardon for my rude though involuntary irreverence. I have never allowed myself, and never shall allow myself, to fail in any way whatsoever to pay our Supreme Sire the respect due him.

Stop your whining and start looking for the perfidious scribbler. Listen, Patiño, don't you think the padres, the vicar general himself, might be the authors? You never know with the padres, Sire. They weave a very fine, very close net. The handwriting and even the signature of the lampoon, so like yours, Sire. Though it would be bad business for them to get mixed up in these fish-and-fowl affairs now that they're better off than ever. A new Government of people coming-and-going isn't in their interest. That would be the end of their bigua salutis. Well put, Patiño! I crown you king of wits. I'll will you my chamber pot. During the day, now that we've fallen on bad times again, you can wear it on your brow. Symbol of your power. During the night you'll return the alabaster crown to its usual place. In that way it will serve you twice over for different and distant uses. What's certain, Sire, is that reality has shifted place. When I read the lampoon I felt as though I had one foot touching the ground and the other dangling in the air. That's exactly what's going to happen to you. All I know, Excellency, is that I shall move heaven and earth in search of the guilty parties. I promise you I'll find the hair in the bottomless hole. Don't just chase after female-hairs as is your usual habit. Don't do like the

§Gachupines: Spaniards. (*Translator's note*)
§§Porteñistas: supporters of the cause of Buenos Aires.

fellow who opened a cupboard door one night instead of a window. And then come tell me it's dark and smells of cheese because you've stuck your nose someplace you shouldn't have, instead of nosing about where you should have. You must bring the culprit to the foot of the orange tree in less than three days. Give him his full ration of rifle bullets. Whoever he may be. Even The Supreme.

You're to make even the mutes of Tevegó speak. According to the lampooners, they go about on all fours. Give birth to mute offspring that look like dog-headed apes. With no tongue. No ears. A combination of humbug, superstitions, lies, of the sort that the Robertsons, the Renggers, those sulkers, those rogues, those ingrates wrote. The business about the people of Tevegó is true, Sire. Even though the lampoons lie, that's true. Something not to be seen or believed even with my own eyes! I refused to believe it too, Sire, till at your order I went to investigate the case with the district commissioner of Kuruguaty, Don Francisco Alarcón, and a detachment of troops of the line in that region.

After three days and nights, taking the shortest route, we arrived at the penal colony of Tevegó at daybreak. Too deep a silence. Not a site of life. There it is! the guide said. It was only after a long while, straining our eyes, that we could make out the colony sprawled out all over the countryside. In darkness still, because the sun's rays didn't reach that place that had moved its place to another place, to tell it in your words, Sire. There's no other way of explaining the very strange thing that's come about there, when there's no way of finding out what's going on. A shame not to have had your lens for far-seeing at that moment. Your star-gazing apparatus. Though on second thought, perhaps it wouldn't have worked for seeing that. I took out the little mirror that I always carry about in my pocket to signal to my travel companions. It flashed for a moment and then went out when its reflection bounced off all that motionless air that had accumulated inside the camp. You can't get into the penal colony of Tevegó, Excellency. Why not? Criminals, thieves, vagrants, scroungers, prostitutes, conspirators who escaped the firing squad in the year '21 managed to get in without much trouble. The first bands from Corrientes that I ordered taken prisoner when they invaded Apipé, Yasyretá, Santa Ana, Candelaria got in. Even mulattoes and blacks got in. You're more than right, Excellency. All I mean is that you can't get in *now*. Not because it's impossible, but because it takes so long. In your case, seeing as how you walk backwards all the time you're on duty, that doesn't surprise me. Entering there isn't entering, Sire. There are no barbed-wire fences, no palisades, no barriers, no trenches. Nothing but ashen earth and stones. First, bare stones, scarcely half a hand high, marking the line where the green of the esparto grass and the reeds ends. On the other side of this mark, nothing but ashen tanimbú. Even the light. A burned light that sheds its ash in the air and hovers there dead-still, light-heavy, moving neither up nor down. If there are people there in the distance, there's no way of telling if they're people or stone. Except that if they're people they're not moving. Blacks, quadroons, mulattoes, men, women, kids, all ashen-colored, tanimbú-colored ashes, how to explain to you, Sire, not the color of your aerolith, which is black and doesn't reflect light, but rather the color of that gritty sandstone of the ravines when there's a bad drought or those big boulders that roll down the sides of mountains. Those can't be the people that were sent here, Don Francisco Alarcón said. If they are, where are the guards? Look, Don Tikú, the guide said, if they're stones they don't need to be guarded. The soldiers laughed uneasily. Then we saw *that*. Or maybe we only thought we were seeing. Because I tell you, Sire, it's something you'd see and not believe.

(In the private notebook*)

My amanuensis, who has his thousand-and-one-nights side, has put his mercury on to heat. He is trying by every manner of means to make me lose time, to distract my attention from what is of prime concern to me. He's come out now with a weird story about those people serving out a sentence who have migrated to some unknown place while remaining

---

*An outsized ledger, of the sort that from the beginning of his government *El Supremo* used to keep track of the treasury accounts, down to the last *real*. More than a hundred of these Great Books, each with a thousand folios, have been found in the archives. In the last of them, in which the real accounts are scarcely begun, there appear other unreal and cryptic ones. Only long afterward was it discovered that toward the end of his life *El Supremo* had set forth in these folios, in a disjointed, incoherent fashion, events, ideas, reflections, minutely detailed and well-nigh maniacal observations on any number of entirely different subjects and themes: those which in his opinion were positive in the Credit column; negative, in the Debit column. In this way words, sentences, paragraphs, fragments are divided, continued, repeated, or inverted in the two columns, in an effort to strike an imaginary balance. They are somewhat reminiscent of the notations of a polyphonic score. It is well known that *El Supremo* was a good musician; or at least an excellent *vihuelist*,§ with velleities of composing.

The fire that broke out in his apartments a few days before his death destroyed the Account Book in large part, along with other files and papers that it was his habit to keep in his coffers under septuple lock and key. *(Compiler's Note.)*

§Player of the vihuela, the Spanish lute.

in the same place under another form. Transformed into unknown people who have caused their absence to take on a form there. Animals. Boulders worn smooth. Figures of stone. Fabled monsters, half-man, half-beast, that go by the name of endriagos. Patiño imitates everything. He has seen me practice the transmutation of mercury. The heaviest material in the world, it becomes lighter than smoke. Then on encountering the cold realm it immediately coagulates and turns back into that incorruptible liquor that penetrates and corrupts everything. Eternal sweat, Pliny called it, since there is scarcely anything that can absorb it. Dangerous conversation with a creature so daring and so deadly. It boils, breaks up into a thousand little droplets, and no matter how small, not a one is ever lost, for in the end they all join together to form one again. As mercury is the element that separates gold from copper it is also the one that tinctures metals, the mediator of this union. Does it not resemble imagination, mistress of error and falsehood? All the more deceiving in that it is not always so. For it would be an infallible proof of truth were it an infallible one of falsehood.

Perhaps my trust-unworthy amanuensis is only half lying. He can't yet manage to melt the quicksilver of mirrors. He lacks the forgetfulness necessary to create a legend. His excess of memory makes him ignorant of the meaning of facts. Memory of an executioner, a traitor, a bearer of false witness. Separated from their people and place by accident or by vocation, they discover that they must live in a world made up of elements foreign to them with which they believe they are conjoined. They believe them-selves to be providential figures of an imaginary populace. Aided by chance, they are sometimes enthroned in and by the stupidity of this populace, thereby making it more imaginary still. They are secret migrants and they are not where they appear to be. It costs Patiño an effort not to allow himself merely to coast downhill, to follow instead the uphill path of the telling and write at the same time; to hear the dispari-son of what he writes; to trace the sign of what his ear is taking in. To attune words to the sound of thought, which is never a solitary murmur, however intimate it may be; less still if it is the speech, the thought involved in dictating. If the ordinary man never talks to himself, the Supreme Dictator continually talks to others. He projects his voice before himself so as to be heard, listened to, obeyed. Although he may appear to be close-mouthed, silent, mute, his silence is commanding. Which means that in The Supreme at least there are two persons. The *I* can divide to form an active third who is an adequate judge of our responsibility with regard to the act that we must decide upon. In my day, I was a good ventriloquist. At present, I am unable even to imitate my own voice. The trust-unworthy scribe, even less capable. He hasn't yet learned his craft. I am going to have to teach him to write.

What were you talking about, Patiño? Of the people of the Tevegó colony, Sire. It's difficult to see that the shapes aren't stones but people. Those nomads, vagrants, conspirators, prostitutes, migrants, deserters of all kinds and sorts that in another time Your Excellency sent to that place, aren't human beings anymore either, if one is to disbelieve what one sees. Just shapes, nothing more. They don't move, Sire; at least they don't move in the same way people do. And if perchance I'm mistaken, they must move as slowly as tortoises. In a manner of speaking, Excellency: from here where I'm sitting to the table where Your Grace has the blessed patience to listen to me, for example, one of those tortoise-people shapes would take a man's entire lifetime to cover the distance, provided he hustled right along and finally made it. Because when you come right down to it, those shapes don't live like other people. They must live some other sort of life. They crawl on all fours without ever moving from the spot. It's plain to see they can't raise their hands, their backbones, their heads. They've taken root in the ground.

As I was telling you, Excellency, all those people scattered all over the countryside. Not a sound. Not even of the wind blowing. No sound and no wind. Not a single voice, man's or woman's, no baby's crying, no dog's barking, not the least sign. If you ask me, those people don't have the least understanding of what's happening to them, and to tell the truth there isn't anything that's happening. Except just being there, without living or dying, waiting for nothing, hoping for nothing, slowly sinking deeper and deeper into the bare earth. Opposite us, brush that must once have been a thicket used as a common latrine, full of cobs of maize. You know, Sire, what our country folk use them for when they relieve their bowels. Except that the stains on those cobs shone with the bright glint of cheap trade trinkets.

These people aren't dead; these people eat, Tikú Alarcón, the district commissioner, said. That was before, the guide said. We saw no maize fields anywhere about. Refuse, yes, piles of it. Old dry rags, lots of crosses amid underbrush just as dry. Not one bird, not one maize-eating parrot, not one turtledove. A coot swooped down into the hard air overarching the camp. It bounced off as if it had hit a metal plate, reeled about like a drunkard, and finally fell at the feet of our group. Its head was split open and gobs of foam came bubbling out through the slit.

Let's have a closer look, Tikú Alarcón said. The soldiers climbed down off their horses to gather up the gleaming crapcobs and stow them away in their haversacks in case they turned out to be solid gold ones. Anything can happen, one of them said. They take a walk all around the place. The same thing to be seen from no matter where. The shapes gazing at us from afar; us observing their vague outlines blurred by the smoky haze. If I may so put it, them from some time back; us from that moment, not knowing whether or not they saw us. A person knows when his gaze meets another's, isn't that so, Excellency? Well, with these people not a clue, not the slightest sign to tell us or not tell us.

Toward midday our eyes were dry from so much looking. Parboiled by the light of the sun reflecting off the shadow piled up behind. Half dead from thirst because for several leagues around all the rivers and brooks had long since gone dry. We also noted something else. The colony was getting darker, as though night were overtaking it, and it was only that the shadow was becoming denser.

A little patience, the guide said. By patiently waiting for the right moment, someone even saw a patronal festival of the blacks on the day of the Three Kings. My grandfather Raymundo Alcaraz also saw it, but he had been watching for something like three months. He used to tell how he'd even seen an attack by Mbayá Indians, when they were coming around on raiding parties with the Portuguese. A person has to have patience in order to see. You have to look and wait for months, years, if not more. You have to wait to see.

I'm going to have a look inside, the commissioner said, climbing down off his horse. The way I see it, those sons-of-the-devil don't exist; they're only pretending to. He spat and entered. After he crossed the line between the greenness and the dryness we lost sight of him. He went in and came out. According to me, he went in and came out. According to the others too. In a manner of speaking, a very quick round trip. The gob of spit that he'd hawked up hadn't even dried yet and he was back. But he came back an old man, all bent over, so that he too was practically crawling on all fours. Looking for the speech he lost, the guide said.

Tikú Alarcón, the district commissioner Francisco Alarcón, went in a young man and came out an old one, in his eighties at least; bald, bare naked, mute, more stunted than a dwarf, bent double, his skin scaly and wrinkled and hanging off him, and lizard's nails. What happened to you, Don Tikú? He didn't answer; he was unable to make the slightest sign. We wrapped him in a poncho and hoisted him across the back of his horse. As the soldiers tied him to the saddle, I took a look at the camp. It seemed to me that the shapes were dancing the dance of the blacks of Laurelty or of Campamento-Loma on all fours. My eyes were filled with tears and might have fooled me. We made our way back as though we'd been to a funeral. The dead man was coming back alive with us.

When we reached Kuruguaty, the commissioner crawled into his house on all fours. The whole town came to see what had happened. The parish priest of San Estanislao and the exorciser of the Xexueños of Xexuí was summoned. Mass, procession, public prayers, vows. They proved useless; nothing could undo the harm done. I tried the Guaykurú remedy: I gave Don Tikú's hair a good hard yank. It came off in my hands, heavier than a chunk of stone. A powerful smell of something buried.

Artigas was summoned, since people say he knows how to cure with simples. The general of the Oriental army came from his farm bringing a cartload of herbs of all sorts. Satules of melecines. A flacon of angel-water, a very powerful fragrance, distilled from all sorts of different flowers such as orange blossom, jasmine, and myrtle. He saw and treated the patient. He did for him everything that people know the Oriental refugee knows how to do. He couldn't get a single word out of him— to tell the truth of the matter, Excellency—not one sound. He couldn't force a single drop of melecine through his lips that had now turned to stone too. They laid the commissioner on his cot. Before we knew it, he was down on the floor on all fours again, like those people. They rubbed him with six taper-lengths of black wax. Don José Gervasio Artigas measured the space from the fingers of one hand to the other, which is the same distance as there is from feet to head. But he found that the measurement fitted two different men. The ex protector of the Banda Oriental shook his head. This isn't my friend Don Francisco Alarcón, he said. Well then, who is it?, the priest asked. I don't know, the general said, and went back to his farm.

The work of evil spirits!, the curé of the Xexueños of Xexuí exclaimed in annoyance. There were more public prayers, processions. The Brotherhood took the image of San Isidro the Laborer through the streets. Tikú Alarcón, still on all fours, grew older and stonier. Someone tried to bleed him. The blade of the knife broke when it touched the old man's skin, which little by little had become hotter than an oven stone.

A cry ran through the village: We must go burn Tevegó down! The Evil One lives there! It's hell! Well then, Laureano Benítez, the Elder of the Brotherhood, said gently, if this holy man could escape from hell and return, it seems to me we ought to make a niche for him. But by now the commissioner wasn't even as tall as Saint Blaise.

The following day, Tikú Alarcón died in the same position, older than a lizard. They had to bury him in a child's coffin. All right, enough of that, you insolent windbag! You sound like the lampoons. I beg your pardon, Excellency. I was a witness of this story; I brought back the preliminary inquiry made by the judge of the Township of Kuruguaty and the dispatch of Fernando Acosta, the commandant of Villa Real de la Concepción. When Your Excellency returned from the Hospital Barracks, he tore up the papers without reading them. The same thing happened, Sire, with the message about the mysterious round stone found by the thousand-some political prisoners that Your Eminence sent under heavy guard to work in the quarries of the Yariguaá. Did both things happen at the same time? No, Excellency. The stone from Yariguaá Hill, or Chair-of-the-Wind, was found four years ago, after the great harvest of '36. The story of Tevegó not a month ago, shortly before Your Eminence had his unfortunate accident. I ordered that I be sent a faithful copy of all the signs that are carved in the stone. This was done, Excellency, but you destroyed the copy. Because it was badly made, you knave! Or do you think I don't know what those rock inscriptions look like? I sent instructions as to how the copy to scale of the petroglyph should be made. Measurement of its dimensions. Astronomical orientation. I asked for samples of the material of the stone. Do you know what it would have meant to find the vestiges of a civilization thousands of years old there? Send a dispatch immediately to the commandant of the Yariguaá region ordering him to send me the stone. It will not be any harder than bringing the aerolith from the interior of the Chaco, a distance of eighty leagues. I believe, Excellency, that the stone of the Wind-Chair was used in the construction of the new garrison in the region. Have them remove it! And if it was broken to bits for the foundations, Sire? Have them all collected! I'm going to examine them under the microscope myself. Determine their age, because stones do have one. Decipher the hieroglyph. I am the only one able to do this in this country of know-it-all cretins.

Another dispatch to the commandant of Villa Real. Order him to proceed to dismantle the penal colony of Tevegó, using the troops of the line under his command. If there is a single survivor, have him sent here in chains under heavy guard. What was that you muttered? Nothing, Excellency, nothing in particular. It's just that I think that it's going to be easier to haul in the stone with its thousands of years and its thousands of arrobas than it will be to get those people out of Tevegó.

Let's get back to the matter at hand. Let's begin the cycle all over again. Where is the pasquinade? In your hand, Excellency. No, you secreting ink-slinger. On the door of the cathedral. Pinned up with four thumbtacks. A patrol of grenadiers takes it down with the tip of a saber. They bring it to headquarters. They advise you. When you read it, it leaves you with eyes bulging like a roped steer, seeing the bonfire already lighted in the plaza, about to turn us all into firebrands. You bring me the paper with the eyes of a butchered calf. Here it is. It doesn't say anything. It doesn't matter what it says. What matters is what's behind it. The sense of the non-sense.

You are to start tracking down the handwriting of the pasquinade in all the files. The dossiers of agreements, disagreements, counteragreements. International communications. Treaties. Remissory notes. Demissory letters. All the bills of Portuguese-Brazilian traders, of Oriental merchants. The piles of paperwork concerning food excises, tithes, the salt tax. Fructuary assessments. State monopoly, commercial commissions, war duties. Import-export records. Customs permits for incoming-outgoing shipments. Complete correspondence of all functionaries, from the lowest rank to the highest. Messages in code from spies, informers, agents of the various intelligence branches. Invoices of arms smugglers. Everything. The least little scrap of paper with writing on it.

Do you understand what I'm ordering you to do? Yes, Excellency: I must search for the model of the handwriting of the cathedral pasquinade, look hide and hair for it in all the documents in your archives. You're finally learning how to speak without getting lost in the clouds. This is not to be a listless search, remember. You are to go systematically through the names of the enemies of the Fatherland, of the Government, the faithful friends of our enemies. I want you to catch the most intempestive of the many pesky idiots buzzing about the streets of Paraguay, as my jingoist uncle, Friar Bel-Asshole, claims in his proclamation. Cherchez the culicid. Make him sizzle in his definitive candle-flame. Bury him in his own shit. I want to be shut of him. Do you follow me? Well then, get to work! No more mooning about. The only thing, Excellency . . . What's the matter now? It's just that the job is going to take me a certain amount of time. There are some twenty thousand dossiers in the archives. As many more in the secretarial offices of the tribunals, district headquarters, regional headquarters, frontier outposts and all the rest. Not to mention the ones on hand that are still being examined. Some five hundred thousand pages altogether, Sire. Not counting the ones that have gotten lost through your carelessness, you master of disorder, negligence, neglect. The only reason you haven't lost your hands is that you need them to eat. If I may say so, Excellency, if I may so put it with all due respect, my will never grows cold in your service, and if Your Grace so orders me, I'll find the hair in the bottomless hole, and above all those miscreants of the written rumor.

You keep saying that, but you haven't put a stop to them. The dossiers get lost; there are more and more lampooners all the time. I allow myself to remind Your Eminence that of the dossiers the only one missing is the trial of the year '20, presumably stolen by the criminal José María Pilar, your manservant, who thanks to Your Excellency's inexorable justice has already met the fate he deserved. If it wasn't for that crime that he ended up underneath the orange tree, since there was not sufficient evidence against him, it was for others no less grave. All the other dossiers are there. I might even venture to say to Your Grace, begging his pardon, that there are so many that there are even too many. You're soaked in the feet, otherwise you couldn't come up with such nonsense! Those documents, even the ones that in your misjudgment are completely insignificant, have their importance. They are sacred, since they record in detail the birth of the Nation, the formation of the Republic. Its many vicissitudes. Its victories. Its failures. Its patriotic sons. Its traitors. Its invincible will to survive. Only I know how many times it was necessary to add a bit of fox fur when the lion's skin rampant on the shield of the Republic wasn't enough to cover its ass. Go over those documents one by one. Examine them through a loupe with the eyes of a lupus, with the three eyes of ants. Even though they're totally blind they know what kind of leaf they're cutting. So as not to reduce your time on duty, recruit the horde of public scribes, scriveners, scribblers, and pen-wigglers who spend all their days scrounging themselves a living in the public squares and marketplaces. Conscript them. Shut them up in the archive. Set them to tracing the handwriting. The market women won't have their letters written for them for a few days, and the scribes won't have their mess of spicy pottage. And we too will have a few days' respite from all that written trash. How much better it would have been for the country if those parasites of the pen had been good plowmen, wielders of the hoe, field hands on the farms, on the patrial estancias, rather than this plague of letricides worse than locusts!

There are more than eight thousand scribes, Excellency, and there is only one pasquinade. They would have to take turns, one by one, so that it will take them some twenty-five years to go through the five hundred thousand pages . . . No, you knave, no! Tear the paper up into such small bits that it loses all meaning. Nobody must find out what it contains. Divide the puzzle up among those thousands of penpushers. Find a way to go about things so that they all spy on each other. The wasp-spider that has woven this web will fall into the trap all by itself. It will be tripped up by a single phrase, a single comma. The blackness of its conscience will cause it to lose its way in the delirium of similarity. Any one of them may be the miscreant; the most insignificant penman of all of them. Your order will be executed, Excellency. Although I might almost be so bold, Sire, as to say that it almost isn't necessary. What do you mean it isn't necessary, you lazy good-for-nothing? I have the handwriting of each of the documents right here at my eyetips, Excellency. And if Your Worship presses me, I would even go so far as to say the forms of the periods at the end of the sentences. Your Lordship knows better than I do that periods are never perfectly round, just as in handwriting that appears to be identical there is always some difference. A thicker stroke. A thinner one. The mustaches of the *t*'s longer or shorter, depending on how free the hand of the person who set them down. The little pigtail of the *o,* standing straight up or drooping. Not to mention the instep, the crooked legs of the letters. The columns. The fleurons. The finials. The curlicues. The campanulas capping the capitals. The morning-glory vines of the flourishes drawn in a single spiral with one stroke of the pen, which is what Your Excellency traces beneath his Supreme Name, climbing the wall of the writing sometimes . . . Enough of your scriptuary floriculture, you dimwit! I only wanted to remind Your Grace that I remember each and every one of the files in the archive. At least since Your Lordship deigned to name me his confidential clerk and actuary of the Supreme Government, in the line of succession of Don Jacinto Ruiz, Don Bernardino Villamayor, Don Sebastián Martínez Sanz, Don Joan Abdón Bejarano. Don Mateo Fleitas, the last one whom I replaced in the honor of the office, is now enjoying a well-deserved retirement in Ka'asapá. Don Mateo Fleitas lives shut up in his house, as in a dungeon, in utter darkness. Nobody sees him during the day. An owl, Sire. More hidden than the urukure'á in the depths of the forest. Only on nights when the moon doesn't come out, when its cold-fire makes his skin break out in a sort of mange like white leprosy and his eyes fill with a gummy secretion like sleep does Don Mateo come out for a walk about the village. When the moon doesn't come out, Don Mateo does. Enveloped in the cape with the red lining that Your Excellency gave him as a gift. His palm-fiber hat crowned with lighted candles. The villagers no longer take fright when they see those lights because they know that beneath that lighted sombrero is Don Mateo, out for a stroll. You'll find him down by the Pozo Bolaños perhaps, they told me when I inquired as to his whereabouts on the night I arrived in the village to look into that business of the cattle rustling.

In the pitch black of that very dark night I saw him just as he climbed up on the edge of the miraculous fountain. I saw only the sombrero floating in the air, myriad tiny little lights all aglow, which at first I took to be a swarm of fireflies illuminating the patches of thistles with their greenish light. Don Mateo!, I shouted to him in a loud voice. The sombrero crowned with candles drew closer. I say, Don Polí, what are you doing hereabouts at such a late hour? I've come to investigate the cattle-stealing from the patrial estancia. Ah, rustlers!, said Don Mateo Fleitas, now a bit of human shadow at my side. And how are things with you?, I asked him, just to be saying something. Well, as you can see, colleague, the same as always. Nothing new. It seemed as though I ought to tease him a little. What are you up to, Don Mateo—out playing bull-candle or what? I'm a little old for that, he said in his high-pitched little worn-out voice. At any rate, with those candles in your sombrero you're not going to get lost, compadre. No, no chance of my getting lost, not any more than I already am at any rate. I know these whereabouts very well. If I care to, I can go all over Ka'asapá with my eyes closed. Is it some sort of vow then? Before going to sleep, I always come down to the Pozo Bolaños to have myself a drink from the Saint's spring. There's no better remedy. Opilative. Diuretic. Let's go up to the house. That way we can talk for a bit. He put his hand on my shoulder. I felt his fingernails digging into the fringes of my poncho. I didn't even realize we'd entered the hut. He took off the sombrero and put it on top of a pitcher. He snuffed out all the candles except the stubbiest one with those nails of his of a hairy armadillo; the thumb and index one especially, Sire, as sharp and curved as knife blades. He wet the room down three times with liquid from a little squat bottle. In a trice a fragrance without an equal drove out the stuffy air reeking of old man's piss and rotten flesh that I had smelled on entering. It now smelled exactly like a garden. I looked around to see if he'd set some aromatic plants in the corners. All I could see were some shadows hovering almost motionless just under the ceiling, and others hanging in clusters from the straw thatch.

He brought a blanket out of a trunk; it appeared to be woven of wool or very soft hair, of a sort of darkish-brown color; I'd be more inclined to say a colorless color since the dim light from the candle didn't penetrate that froth that with more light would have been still less visible; the color of nothing, I suppose, if nothingness has a color. Touch it, Policarpo. I extended-withdrew my hand. Touch it, colleague—don't be afraid. I felt it with my hand. Softer than silk, velvet, taffeta, or fine Dutch linen it was. What's this fabric made of, Don Mateo? It feels like down from newborn squabs, the plumage of some sort of bird I don't know, though in fact there aren't any birds I don't know. He pointed to the ceiling: from those creatures fluttering above your head. I've been weaving this blanket for ten years now so as to give it to His Excellency on his birthday. This January sixth, if my rheumatism permits me to walk the fifty leagues to Asunción, I'm going to bring him my gift myself because I've been told that our Karaí has almost no clothes and is quite ill. This blanket is going to keep him warm and cure him. But a blanket made out of that hair, Don Mateo! Do you think His Excellency is going to use a thing like that?, I stammered, retching. You know very well that our Karaí Guasú doesn't accept any sort of gift. I know, Don Polí! But this isn't a gift. It's a remedy. There will never be a blanket like it in this world. Soft, you've already touched it yourself. Couldn't be lighter. If I toss it in the air at this moment, you and I will become old and gray as we wait for it to fall back down. Couldn't be better insulation. There's no cold can get through that weave. It can be used against the heat from outside and fever from within. This is a blanket for everything and against everything. I looked up toward the ceiling, closing my eyes. But how were you able to collect so many long-eared bats? They know me. They come. They feel at home here. They just go out for a little while perhaps as it's getting dark to have themselves a breath of fresh air. Then they come back in again. They like it here. Don't they bite you, suck your blood? They're not stupid, Polí. They know that there's not one drop of good red blood in my veins. I bring them little wild creatures; the ones that go about by night are the liveliest and have the warmest blood. The mbopís, well-fed and content, grow a hair so fine that only hands that know the feel of a feather pen, like yours or mine, can handle, spin, weave it, he said, trimming the candle with those very long nails of his. I pluck their fine silky down while they're sleeping, with a gaze and a touch as soft as silk. We're very close. But aside from the bedcover, which I won't even discuss, I suspect that one of these little creatures of mine might remedy His Excellency's ills. Some years ago now, a Dominican friar was dying here of a burning fever. The bloodletter couldn't manage to get a single drop of blood out of him with his lancet. Since the friars were certain that their sick brother was dying, they went off to bed after bidding him a last farewell and ordered the Indians to dig his grave so as to bury him in the cool of early morning. I opened the window and let out a bat I had been keeping shut up without food at the time because he'd been disrespectful. The mbopí attached itself to one of the friar's feet. When it had had its fill it flew off again, leaving the vein open. At sunup the friars came back, thinking they'd find their sick brother dead. They found him alive, chipper, almost well, reading his breviary in bed. Thanks to the medic mbopí, the friar was very soon his usual self again. Nowadays he's the fattest and most active one in the congregation; the one who is said to have given his Indian girl parishioners the most babies; but I don't pay attention to malicious gossip of that sort, occupied as I am day and night weaving the blanket for our Supreme.

Stay and sleep here, friend Policarpo. I invite you to do penance.

There's your cot over there. We have lots of things that happened in the good old days to talk about. He put the blanket back in the trunk. Don Mateo's long-eared rats fluttered and screeched up among the shadows of the ceiling, their little skull-faces veiled with signs of mourning. He slowly removed his cape, exposing his bare carcass to the air. What else do I have to do except pull the wool over the eyes of these innocents and take their hair to make clothes for our Father? Get in bed, Policarpo. He was about to blow out the candle. I rose to my feet. No, Don Mateo, I'm going to leave now. We've had a very pleasant time together. The commissioner is waiting for me. I imagine they've already caught the cattle thieves. If so, they'll have to be shot at dawn, and I must be present to sign the order. Pump those bandits full of lead!, the old man said, blowing out the candle.*

You're the most conniving chatterbox in the world. An odd bird that cackles all the time. A bird of ill omen for whom death has already

---

*Don Mateo Fleitas, *El Supremo*'s first "confidential clerk," survived him by more than half a century. He died in Ka'asapá at the age of 106, surrounded by his children and grandchildren, amid the respect and affection of the entire village. A real patriarch. He was known as *Tamoi-ypy* (First-Grandfather). Oldsters of his time whom I consulted stoutly denied, some with real indignation, the story of the "sombrero crowned with candles," as well as the life of maniacal seclusion led by Don Mateo, according to Policarpo Patiño's account. "That's malicious gossip on the part of that foul-tongued slanderer who ended up hanging himself out of sheer malice and treachery," the rhythmic but still firm voice of the present mayor of Ka'asapá, Don Pantaleón Engracia García, affirms sententiously on the recorded tape.

À propos of my journey to the village of Ka'asapá, it strikes me as not entirely beside the point to relate one event that took place. On the return trip, as I was crossing the Pirapó in flood, on horseback, my tape recorder and camera fell into the water. The mayor, Don Panta, who was accompanying me with a small escort, immediately ordered his men to divert the course of the stream. No plea or argument could dissuade him. "You will not leave Ka'asapá without your equipment," he growled indignantly. "I will not allow our stream to steal from illustrious and enlightened outlanders who come to visit us!" On being notified of what had happened, the entire population came running to collaborate in diverting the river. Men, women, and children worked with the enthusiasm of a *minga* (a voluntary collective endeavor) transformed into a fiesta. Toward evening, the lost objects appeared in the mud of the streambed, having suffered no great damage. Everyone danced till dawn to the music of my cassettes. I took off as the sun was coming up, accompanied for a long stretch of the way by the shouts and cheers of this lively and hospitable people, taking with me the voices and images of its oldsters, of its men, women, and children; of its green, luminous landscape. When he thought that the way was now clear, the mayor bade me farewell. I embraced him and kissed him on both cheeks. "Many thanks, Don Pantaleón," I said to him with a lump in my throat. "There is no name for what all of you have done!" He winked one eye at me and crunched the bones of my hand. "I don't know if it has a name or not," he said. "But since the time of *El Supremo*, these little things are a duty for us that we willingly perform when it is for the good of the country." (Compiler's Note.)

knocked on the door; who is going to die forthwith, though gradually. I haven't managed to make a decent servant out of you. You're never going to have so much material to deal with that it will shut you up. In order not to work, you invent happenings that haven't happened. Don't you think that I could be made into a fabulous story? Beyond the shadow of a doubt, Excellency! The most fabulous, the truest, the most worthy of the majestative exaltedness of your Person. No, Patiño, no. It's not possible to make stories of Absolute Power. If it were, The Supreme would be de trop: in literature or in reality. Who would write such books? Ignorant people like you. Professional scribes. Pharisaical farceurs. Idiotic compilers of writings no less idiotic. The words of power, of authority, words above words, will be transformed into clever words, lying words. Words below words. If one wishes at all costs to speak of someone, one must not only put oneself in that someone's place: one must *be* that someone. Only like can write about like. Only the dead can write about the dead. But the dead are very feeble. Do you think you could relate my life before your death, you ragtag amanuensis? You would need at the very least the craft and the strength of two Fates. Eh, isn't that so, compiler of fictions and falsifications? You smoke-collector who, deep down, hate the Master. Answer! Eh, isn't that so? Ah! Come now! Even supposing in your favor that you're playing me false in order to spare me, what you're doing is taking away from me, hair by hair, the power to die and be born by myself. Preventing me from being my own commentary. Concentrating on a single thought is perhaps the only way to make it real: that invisible blanket that Mateo Fleitas is weaving. That won't be enough to cover my bones. I've seen it, Excellency! That isn't enough. Your seeing isn't knowing yet. Your own-eyes-seeing blurs the contours of your rejuntative memory. That's the reason why you're finding it impossible to discover the pasquinaders, among other things. Let's suppose that you and one of them have gotten together. Suppose that I myself am an author of pasquinades. We talk of very amusing things. You recount stories to me. I do my accounts. You close your eyes and fall into the irresistible temptation of believing that you're invisible. On opening your eyelids it seems to you that everything is as it was before. You sneeze. Between one sneeze and another, everything has changed. That is the reality that your memory *does not see.*

Sire, with your permission, let me say, in a manner of speaking, I feel that your words, however poorly copied they may be by these hands that the earth is going to swallow up, I feel that they copy what Your Grace dictates to me, letter by letter, word by word. You haven't understood me. Open your good eye and close the bad one. Keep your ears open for the meaning of what I say to you: However much you may surpass animals in brute memory, in brute power of speech, you'll never know anything if you don't penetrate to the innermost depths of things. You don't need a tongue for that; on the contrary, it gets in your way. For that reason, in addition to the basin in which you cool your feet so as to clear your brain, I'm going to have you gagged. If our enemies don't hang you first, as they have kindly promised, I myself will make you stare straight into the sun when the minute of your hour is at hand. At the moment that its rays char your pupils, you will receive the order to pull your tongue out between your teeth with your fingers. You will then give yourself a punch in the jaw. Your tongue will fall to the ground, writhing like the tail of an iguana that's been chopped in half. It will transmit your last salutation to the earth. You will feel that you've been freed of a useless weight. You will think: I am mute. Which is a silent way of saying: I am not. Only then will you have attained a little wisdom.

I am now going to dictate to you a circular addressed to my faithful satraps. I want them too to savor the promise that their merits deserve.

To Commissioners, Commanders of Garrisons
and of Urban Militia,
Appointed Magistrates, Administrators,
Overseers, Revenue Agents, Tax Collectors
and other authorities:

The copy of the infamous pasquinade enclosed herewith is yet another testimony to the mounting outrages that are being committed by the agents of subversion. It is not merely one more of the multitude of pamphlets, libels, and every manner of attack being launched anonymously almost every day for some time now, in the mistaken belief that age, bad health, ailments contracted in the service of the Fatherland have left me prostrated. It is not merely one more of the scandalous diatribes and invectives of these convulsionaries.

Take careful note, firstly, of one fact: not only have they dared to threaten with an ignominious death all those of us who together bear the heavy burden of Government. They have now dared to commit an even more perfidious act: forging my signature. Imitating the tone of Supreme Decrees. What is their aim in so doing? To enhance the effect of this iniquitous farce among ignorant people.

Second fact: The anonymous pasquinade was found nailed to the door of the cathedral, a place heretofore respected by the agents of subversion.

Third fact: The threats contained in this decretorial mockery clearly establish a scale of punishments in accordance with the hierarchy of Government. You, who are my arms, my hands, my limbs, are offered death by hanging and burial in pastures outside the walls with neither cross nor mark commemorating your names. I, the head of the Supreme Government, am bidden to condemn myself to decapitation. Exhibition atop a pike for three days as the center of popular festivities in the Plaza. And finally, the casting of my ashes into the river as the culmination of the great patronal fiesta.

Of what am I accused by these anonymous scribblers? Of having given this people a free, independent, sovereign Fatherland? What is more important: of having given it the sense of a Fatherland? Of having defended this Fatherland since its birth against the attacks of its enemies within and without? Is that what I am accused of?

Their blood boils at the thought that I founded, once and for all, the cause of our political regeneration on the system of the general will. Their blood boils at the thought that I have restored the power of the People, in the city, in the towns, in the villages; that I have continued that movement, the first truly revolutionary one to burst forth on these Continents, even before the one unfolding in the immense Fatherland of Washington, Franklin, Jefferson, even before the French Revolution.

It is necessary to reflect on these great events, of which you surely have no knowledge, in order to appreciate the far-reaching importance, justice, and perpetuity of our Cause.

Almost all of you are servants of long standing. The majority of you, however, have not had time to study in depth these questions of our history, since all your time has necessarily been devoted to your duties. I have preferred you to be loyal functionaries rather than cultivated men. Capable of carrying out my commands. I am not concerned with the sort of capabilities a man possesses. I require only that he be capable. My most manly men are only men.

Here in Paraguay, before the Perpetual Dictatorship, we had more than enough scriveners, doctors, cultivated men, but we did not have the cultivators of fields, the sowers and growers, the tillers of the soil we should have had and now have. Those cultivated cretins wanted to found the Areopagus of Letters, Arts, and Sciences. I put my foot down. They turned into penners of pasquins and pasquils. Those who were able to save their skins fled the country, disguised as blacks. Black slaves of the plantations of calumny. Once outside the country, they became worse still, renegades who regard Paraguay from a non-Paraguayan perspective. Those who did not manage to emigrate live in perpetual migration in the darkness of their lairs. Vainglorious, vicious, vice-ridden convulsionaries, these inept intellectuals have no place in our rural, peasant society. What meaning can their cerebral exploits have here? It is more useful to plant manioc or maize here than it is to stain paper with ink writing seditious libels; more fitting to pick pests off animals itching from the tick than to scratch pamphlets that are an outrage to the dignity of the Fatherland, the sovereignty of the Republic, the honor of the Government. The more cultivated they seek to be, the less they wish to be Paraguayans. Later on there will come those who pen more voluminous libels. They will call them History Books, novels, accounts of imaginary facts seasoned to suit the taste of the moment or their interests. Prophets of the past, they will recount in them their invented falsehoods, the story of what has not happened. Which would not be an altogether bad thing if their powers of imagination were at least passable. Historians and novelists will have their lies bound in leather and sell them at a handsome price. What interests them is not recounting the facts, but recounting that they are recounting them.

For the present, posterity does not interest us. Posterity is not given as a gift to anyone. Someday it will come back looking for us. I bring into being only what I firmly command. I command only what is firmly within my power. But as Supreme Governor I am also your natural father. Your friend. Your companion. As someone who knows everything there is to know and more, I shall continue to instruct you as to what you must do in order to pursue your task. I shall give you orders, but also the knowledge that you lack as to the origin, the destiny of our Nation.

There is always time to have more time.

When our Nation was still part of the colonies, or Kingdoms of the Indies as they were called in those days, a court official appointed to hear cases that came before the Audiencia of Charcas, the Oidor Fiscal José de Antequera y Castro, saw, on his arrival in Asunción, the millstone of misfortune that had been crushing Paraguay for more than two centuries. He didn't mince words. The sovereignty of the Common Will is prior to any written law, the authority of the people is superior to that of the king himself, he declared in the Cabildo of Asunción. General stupefaction. Who is this young magistrate come down from the moon? Has the Audiencia become a lunatic asylum? We didn't hear you very well, Señor Oidor.

José de Antequera proceeded to stamp on the law, on the facts, in letters of fire, his decision as investigating magistrate: Peoples do not abdicate their sovereignty. The act of delegating it in no way implies that they will forbear to exercise it when governments impair the precepts of natural reason, the source of all laws. Only peoples who like oppression can be oppressed. This people is not one of them. Its patience is not obedience. Nor can you hope, you high and mighty oppressors, that its patience will be eternal, like the bliss you promise it after death.

The investigating magistrate did not come with the faith of the simple man who crosses himself with a sincere heart. He inquired, inspected, traced down everything. What he found revolted him. Absolutist corruption had in the end infested everything. The governors trafficked in their offices. The court allowed those who courted it to cut a wide swath, receiving in exchange their doubloons. Can I sell you the office of Perpetual Dictator? I see you hypocritically shaking your lowered heads. Well, Diego de los Reyes Balmaceda bought the government of Paraguay, for a handful of patacoons. With one kick of his foot Antequera expelled the crapulated Reyes, who went to complain to the viceroy of Buenos Aires. That's how corrupt these Kingdoms of the Indies were.

The pack of oligarchs in the cities packed Indian meat into the encomiendas. An immense barracks of cassocks, that of the Jesuits. An empire within an empire, with more vassals than the king.

In the caliphate founded by Irala, four hundred survivors from among those who had come in search of El Dorado found not the Resplendent City but the site of sites. Here. And they built a new Paradise of Mohammed in the Neolithic maize field. Cross out Neolithic. It's a word that isn't used yet. Thousands of copper-colored women, the most beautiful houris in the world, at their complete service and pleasure. The Koran and the Bible conjoined in the halfmoon of the indigenous hammock.

Antequera's war-cry roused the partisans of a communal system—the Comuneros—to rebellion against the royalist-absolutists. Blasphemies. Lamentations. Rogations. Cabals in the Cabildo. Conspiracies. Libels, satires, pamphlets, caricatures, pasquils rehearsed in those days what is happening now. The Jesuits accused Antequera of wanting to become king of Paraguay under the title of José I. A short time before they had wanted to monarchize their Communist empire by crowning the Indian Nicolás Yapuguay king of Paraguay and emperor of the mamelucos, under the name of Nicolás I. I beg your pardon, Sire, I didn't hear that part about the kings of Paraguay very well. It isn't that you don't hear. There are times when you don't understand what you're listening to. Ask Pilar the black to tell you the story. The kings of Paraguay were only fables, like Aesop's, Patiño. Pilar the black will tell them to you. Sire, as you are well aware, José María Pilar the black is no more. That is to say, he still is, but in his grave. It doesn't matter; tell him to tell you those fables. That's precisely what they're for. To be told underground and listened to astride a grave. He already told it, Sire, though in a different way, in the Truth Chamber beneath the lash. I took it to be mere bravado on the part of your former hand page and ex valet de chambre. Words sung out of tune wrung out of him by the pain. The examining magistrate himself, Don Abdón Bejarano, told me not to set down that discordant note in the record. What did the infamous black say? He declared, swore, forswore, Sire, that he was being punished and was going to be executed simply because he had wanted to be king of Paraguay under the name of José I. He said that with a grinning face and an impish devil's heart amid his snot and tears. He added other cheeky remarks that at Don Abdón's order I didn't note down in the record either. Disfortunate avowals by one accursed who discalculated. Madness of right reason. Haven't you yet learned, court secretary, that madness bares more truths than voluntary confession? Isn't it true that that clever liar tried to suborn you by offering you the office of confidential clerk in his black monarchy? Heavens, no, Sire! Isn't it true that he promised to make you consul of his Baratarian island? If that had been the case, Sire, he would have had to make Bejarano one too, and the two of us would have had to have bats in our barratry to accept. We'd have been co-confools, not co-consuls. Like Pompey and Caesar, like Your Excellency and the infamous traitor to the Fatherland the ex brigadier Fulgencio Yegros, who has already met the fate he deserved beneath the orange tree, along with the other co-conspirators.

Isn't it true that you too dream of becoming king of Paraguay someday? That would be taking chalk for cheese, Sire! You yourself always say that that would be worthwhile only if the people and the sovereign were one and the same person; but for that a person doesn't need to be a king, just a good Supreme Governor, as Your Excellency is. Yet you can see that ever since Independence, here as in the rest of America, the virus of monarchy has been floating about in the air, as much as or more so than the croup or the carbuncle that attacks cattle. Valets, confidential clerks, doctors, the military, men of the cloth. They've all caught a bad case of the itch to be kings.

Where were we? In the communal latrines, Sire. I see your mind is listening to your gut rumbling again. What I was asking you was where the last paragraph left off, you ass. I'll read you, Sire: They accused

Antequera of wanting to become king of Paraguay under the title of José I. No, no, no! That isn't what I said at all. As usual, you've mixed up what I dictated. Write slowly. Don't hurry. Pretend you have eight more days of your life left to live. Eight days could well be eighty years. There's nothing like putting off solving problems as long as possible. Better still if you have only an hour left. Then that hour has the advantage of being at once brief and endless. If a person has one good hour he hasn't had all bad ones. More gets done in that hour than in a century. The man condemned to death is fortunate; he at least has the certainty of knowing the exact hour of his death. When you're in that situation you'll know it. Your passion for hurrying stems from your belief that you're always present at the present. He who proclaims himself his own contemporary is misinformed. Are you beginning to understand, Patiño? To tell you the whole truth, not much, Sire. As I write what you dictate to me I don't grasp the meaning of the words. Occupied as I am in carefully forming the letters in the clearest and most uniform manner possible, what they say escapes me. Whenever I try to understand what I'm listening to, the line comes out all crooked. I misplace the words, the sentences. I write backwards. You, Sire, always go straight on. If I make the slightest slip, I fall into a panic, I freeze. Drops fall. Lagoons form on the paper. Then in all justice Your Grace loses his temper. It's necessary to begin all over again. Whereas if I read the text once it's signed by Your Excellency and sand has been sprinkled on the ink, it always seems clearer than day itself.

Hand me the book by that Theatine, Father Lozano. Nothing better to bring out the truth of the facts than to compare them with the lies of the imagination. This other tonsured thimblerigger had a really treacherous one. José de Antequera's most pertinacious calumniator. His History of the Revolutions of Paraguay, against the Comunero movement, against its leader. The latter was in no position to defend himself from such wicked trickery since he'd been murdered twice. Padre Pedro Lozano tried to assassinate him a third time by making a compilation of all the forgeries, frauds, and fakeries perpetrated against the Comunero leader. Just as anonymous pamphleteers are doing and will continue to do against me. One or another of those émigré scribble-scrabblers will doubtless take advantage of the impunity of distance and be so bold as to cynically affix his signature at the bottom of such clever chicaneries.

Bring me the book. It isn't here, Sire. You left it locked up in the Hospital Barracks. Well then, have them put it on bread and water, and give it a purge every day till it dies or flushes all its lies down the drain. Paí Lozano isn't here, Sire. He never was, as far as I know. I asked you to get me the Revolutions of Paraguay. They're in the Hospital Barracks, Sire. The History, you wretch! It's in the Hospital, Sire, kept under lock and key in the cupboard. You left it there at the time of your confinement.

We're still at the first crisis in the life of the Colony. A century ago now, José de Antequera comes our way, joins the fray, and there's the devil to pay when he won't surrender. The governor of Buenos Aires, the illustrious field marshal Bruno Mauricio de Zabala, invades Paraguay with a hundred thousand Indians from Misiones. Receding chin, curly hair, he places himself at the head of the repressive expedition. Five years of battles. Colossal butchery. History has not seen a bloodier struggle since the days of Fernando III, the Saint, and of Alfonso X, the Wise. With a delay of centuries, the Middle Ages arrives on the scene to wreak havoc on the forests, the men, the rights of the province of Paraguay.

In the great brawl, everyone has his eye on the mighty solar wheel minted of solid gold, the size of a cartwheel. The Saracens of Buenos Aires, the fathers of the Jesuit empire, those Goths the Hispano-Creole land grantees decapitate, disembowel the rebellion. Antequera is taken to Lima. As is Juan de Mena, his principal adjutant in Asunción. As they are being led to the scaffold astride mules, they are killed by a volley from harquebuses before the mutinous populace can free them. To make certain that they are dead, their corpses are thrown on the platform of the scaffold and the executioner chops off their heads. The first two heads to roll for American independence. A historian's vocal flourish. That doesn't mean it didn't happen. I learned from that to trust the witness of no one's eyes or ears, mine included. A hundred years in a day. A day before the century was out I closed the ring on that uprising by proclaiming in my turn in these colonies that Spanish power had reached its end. Not only the royal Bourbon rights. Likewise those usurped by the head of the viceroyalty, where monarchical despotism had been replaced by Creole despotism disguised as revolution. Which turned out to be twice as bad.

Here in Paraguay as well. Asunción was no better than Buenos Aires in that respect. Asunción, capital city. Founder of cities. Sanctuary-and-support of the Conquest, as certain royal decrees called it. An honor that dishonors it.

The oligarchs wanted to go on living till the end of time on the increase of their money and their cows. To live by being do-nothings. Scions of those who betrayed the Comunero uprising. Aristocrat-Iscariots. Those who sold Antequera for the accursed Thirty Dinars. Band of contrabanders. Band of sneak-thieves of the rights of the Common People.

Bastards of that legion of land-grantees. Lordlings of the earth and the club. Eupatrids who called themselves patricians. Make a footnote: Eupatrid means possessor. Feudal Lord. Owner of lands, lives, and vast wealth. No, just cross out the word eupatrid. They won't understand it. They'll start putting it in every other line of their dispatches, whether it makes sense or not. They're dazzled by anything they don't understand. What do they know about Athens, about Solon? Have you ever heard of Athens, of Solon? Just what Your Grace has told me about them. Go on writing: Moreover, here in Paraguay this word is meaningless. If we ever had eupatrids, we don't have any now. They've been sent to their deaths or shut up for life. Yet the genes of gens engender tenacious traitorous taints: the Gotho-Creole gens endlessly reproducing itself in the chain of Iscariot-genes. They have been, and continue to be, the judiscariots who set themselves up as judicators of the Government. For a century now they have betrayed the cause of our Nation. Those who have betrayed once will betray forevermore. They have tried, they will continue to try, to sell it out to Porteños,§ to Brazilians, to the highest bidder, European or American.

They do not forgive me for having intruded upon their domains. They have nothing but scorn for the just treatment I accord clodhoppers and bumpkins; that is how these delicate souls refer to country people. They have forgotten that the slaves of the soil were the ones who nursed their lands and their fortunes in perpetual servitude. For those lordlings of the earth, for those swaggering club-wielders, the rural populace was just one more tool for working the earth. Plowing/procreating machines. Animated equipment. Grubbing in the fields of the fiefs, humbly kneeling on weary bones to receive the sun's blazon, from generation unto generation. Without a day of rest, without a home and fireside, without anything save their worn-out nothingness.

Until I took over the reins of Government, the title of don divided the people here into lords-and-masters with a don and servants-without-one. Person-people and multitude-people. On the one hand, the caliphary idleness of the Gotho-Creole estate owners. On the other, the slave nailed to his cross. The dead-while-still-alive: field hands, farmers, ferrymen, watermen and woodsmen, rowers and growers of maté, cowherds, craftsmen, caravaneers, mountaineers. Armed slaves some of them, charged with defending the fiefs of the Creole kaloikagathoí. If Your Excellency would be kind enough to repeat that term that escaped me. Just write: Masters. Did these lords-and-masters expect the starving populace to love them as

§Inhabitants of Buenos Aires.

well as serve them? The multitude-people; in other words the laboring-procreating populace produced all the goods and suffered all the ills. The rich reaped all the goods. Two apparently inseparable estates. Equally fatal to the common good: From the one came those responsible for tyranny; from the other, the tyrants. How to bring about equality between the rich and the beggars? Don't bother your head over such chimeras!, the Porteño Pedro Alcántara de Somellera said to me on the eve of the Revolution. A vow, a pious dream that cannot be realized in practice. But don't you see, Don Pedro, it's precisely because the force of circumstances tends unceasingly to destroy equality that the force of Revolution must always tend to maintain it. No one should be rich enough to buy another, and no one poor enough to find himself obliged to sell himself. Ah, I see!, the Porteño exclaimed. You wish to distribute the wealth of a few so as to make everyone equal in poverty? No, Don Pedro, I want to bring the extremes together. What you want is to suppress the existence of classes, Señor José. There is no equality without freedom, Don Pedro Alcántara. Those are the two ends that we must conjoin.

I began to govern a country where the poor counted for nothing, where scoundrels were everything. When I assumed Supreme Power in 1814, to those who advised me, either sincerely or with hidden motives, to rely on the upper classes, I said: Gentlemen, no thank you, not for the moment. In the situation in which the country finds itself, in which I myself find myself, my only nobility is the rabble. I didn't know that around that time the great Napoleon had uttered the same or similar words. Belittled, defeated in days to come, for having betrayed the revolutionary cause of his country.

(In the private notebook. An unknown hand.)

What else have you done? . . . *(burned, the rest of the paragraph illegible).*

That coincidence with the Great Man who at every moment, in any circumstances, knew what he must do next and proceeded forthwith to do precisely that, was an inspiration to me. Something that you, functionaries and servants of the State, have not yet learned, and give few signs of being about to learn, to judge from the way you make my head swim with your dispatches full of questions, request for advice, dull-witted pondering of the least trifle. And when at long last you finally do something, I must also find a way to undo all the harm you've done.

As for the oligarchs, not one of them has ever read a single line of

Solon, Rousseau, Raynal, Montesquieu, Rollin, Voltaire, Condorcet, Diderot. Cross out all those names that you won't know how to write out correctly. Not one of them has read a single line outside of the Catholic Paraguay, the Christian Year, the Florilegium of the Saints, which by this time have doubtless also been turned into playing cards. Perched in the branches of their genealogies, the oligarchs fall into ecstasies as they leaf through the Almanach of Notables of the Province. They have refused to accept that there are certain unfortunate situations in which it is possible to preserve one's freedom only at the expense of others. Situations in which the citizen cannot be completely free without the slave being wholly a slave. They refused to accept that every true Revolution implies a change of goods. Of laws. Thoroughgoing change of the entire society. Not a mere coat of whitewash over the scaling sepulcher. I proceeded by simply going ahead. I tripped up the master, the trafficker, the whole bunch of gilded scoundrels. They fell headlong from the top of the heap to the bottom of the well. No one held out so much as a straw of consolation to them.

I promulgated laws that were the same for the poor man, the rich man. I did not scruple to have them scrupulously enforced. In order to establish just laws I did away with unjust ones. In order to create the Rights of Citizens, I suspended the rights that for three centuries have been used for the wrong ends in these colonies. I did away with the improper uses of individual ownership of property by turning it into collective property, which is only proper. I put an end to the unjust domination and exploitation to which the Creoles subjected the natural-born citizens of the country, the most natural thing in the world since the latter as such had the right of primo-geniture over the proud mingle-blooded lordlings of the land. I concluded treaties with the indigenous peoples. I provided them with arms so that they might defend their lands against the depredations of hostile tribes. But I also contained them within their natural limits, thereby preventing them from committing the excesses that the whites themselves had taught them.*

---

*In view of the frequent complaints of country people concerning the depredations and thefts that the Indians committed on rural properties in the course of their continual invasions, the Perpetual Dictator, in a long decree promulgated in March of 1816, severely criticized the ineptitude of the commandants of the troops responsible for guarding the frontier, ordering in no uncertain terms that cavalry be sent to reinforce the detachments of Arekutakuá, Manduvirá, Ypytá, and Kuarepotí; armed troops from all the frontier detachments were to organize continual patrols in the surrounding countryside so as to punish the savages for any attempt whatsoever at invasion. The same decree made the commandants responsible for any timidity they might demonstrate in

Nowadays the Indians are the best servants of the State; it is from such cloth that I have cut the most upright judges, the most capable and loyal functionaries, my most valiant soldiers.

All that is needed is equality within the law. Only rascals believe that the benefit of a favor is favor itself. Learn, once and for all: The benefit of the law is the law itself. There is no benefit, no law unless it is one for everyone.

As for myself, for the benefit of all I have no kinfolk, stepchildren, friends. The libelists throw it up to me that my conduct toward my relatives, my old friends is more rigorous. True, in the most rigorous sense. Invested with Absolute Power, the Supreme Dictator does not have old friends. He has only new enemies. His blood is not swampwater, yet he recognizes no dynastic descendance. The latter does not exist save as the sovereign will of the people, source of Absolute Power, of Absolute Being-Able. Nature does not bring forth slaves; it is man, corrupter of nature, who produces them. The Perpetual Dictatorship left its mark on the soil, freeing it by expelling from the souls of its slaves the dark stain of their immemorial submission. If there are still slaves in the Republic they no longer feel themselves to be slaves. Here the one slave continues to be the Supreme Dictator, placed in the service of the power that dominates. But there is still a certain party who compares me to Caligula and even goes so far as to rouse the specter of Incitatus, the name of the little horse made a consul by an odd whim of the simpleminded Roman emperor. Would my peregrine detractor not have done better to look into the facts rather than the fictions of history? There was, indeed, a horse-consul in the First Junta: its own president. But I did not elect him. The Perpetual Dictator of Paraguay has nothing to do with the solipedal consul

---

carrying out these measures, and ordered that all Indian invaders taken prisoner while marauding be run through with lances and their heads placed on pikes separated from each other by a distance of fifty yards, at the very spot where they had staged their invasion.

The most fearsome of the Indians who continually invaded the northern region were the Payaguaces. A people of wanderers, they roved about in hordes and dwelt in nomad encampments. Extremely treacherous invaders, they lived by cattle rustling, fishing, and hunting. There were, however, a reduced number of Indians who had their tents a little farther north of Concepción; these came with their canoes to aid the troops of the nearest detachment to pursue the errant Payaguaces. A surprise attack by some five thousand of these latter was successfully fended off at the end of 1816. They were all run through with lances and their heads, placed on pikes fifty yards distant from each other, formed an exemplary cordon stretching across many leagues of the invaded frontier region, where from that time on there reined an era of peace called by historians the Era of the Calm Heads. *(Wisner de Morgenstern, op. cit.)*

of Rome or with the bipedal consul of Asunción who ended up under the orange tree.

They accuse me of having planned and constructed more public works in twenty years than the indolent Spaniards left—a scarcely edifying example—in two centuries. I erected in the lonely wastelands of the Gran Chaco and the Banda Oriental houses, fortlets, forts, and fortresses. The largest and most powerful ones in South America: the first of all of them, the one that once went by the name of Borbón. I erased that name. I effaced that stain. What was once a mere stockade of palms and tree trunks was rebuilt from the ground up. Thus, while the Portuguese were fortifying Coimbra so as to attack us in the far north, I erected the Fortress of Olimpo as a countermove to stop them. I ordered its walls to be built of stone. Impregnable bastion. Fortified towers of a blinding whiteness against the black pirates, the black-slave traders of the Empire. Next came the Fortress of San José, in the south.*

---

*"The Fortress of San José is unquestionably the most prodigious of feats of military engineering, of unparalleled dimensions, in the whole of South America during the first half of the nineteenth century. The plan for its erection was conceived at the time of the cessation of hostilities between Brazil and Buenos Aires in the Banda Oriental, a moment favoring the invasion of Paraguay, to the point that more than once it seemed imminent. After lengthy studies and a careful concentration of means, work was begun in the last days of 1833, opposite Itapúa, at the place known as La Guardia or Campamento de San José, on the other side of the river. Two hundred fifty men, who slept at night in leather tents and shelters on the outskirts of the settlement of La Guardia, began their labors. The subcommissioner José León Ramírez, his replacement Casimiro Rojas, and the commandant of the garrison, José Mariano Morínigo, had a hand in the direction (of the operations). As the project became more ambitious with each passing day, the number of men recruited in the course of the project was never sufficient. [The 250 men who began the work eventually grew to 25,000.] The rhythm of the labors accelerated in 1837, and basically everything was finished in the last months of 1838. The Fortress, which among Paraguayans continued to be called by its original modest name, Campamento San José, and among the people of Corrientes and other provinces the Trench of San José or the Trench of the Paraguayans, had an outer wall built entirely of stone, almost four yards high and two yards thick, with a merloned profile and massive corner towers with loopholes covering all the angles of the horizon. Save for the gate that could be opened to let in convoys from San Borja, this great wall, with a deep moat running parallel to it, extended without a break as far as the eye could see, from the marshes of the lagoon of San José to the shore of the Paraná, and then described a vast semicircle measuring many kilometers that like a half-coiled monster turned back upon itself and ended once again at the river.

"An enormous mass of stone and plasterwork, reminiscent in a way of the Great Wall of China, it enclosed the troops' barracks, the quarters of commissioned and noncommissioned officers, the arms depot, and other outbuildings and storehouses, laid out in the form of a small town, with a street of fifteen row houses on each side, each room

The Town Hall, the Hospital Barracks, the reconstruction of the Capital and of numerous villages, towns, and cities in the interior of the country. All this was possible because of the first lime factory that I set up, and not by a miracle, in Paraguay. Hence and therefore, as my friend José Antonio Vázquez puts it, I introduced the civilization of lime here, on top of a past of adobe and beaten earth. Thus the patrial estancias, the patrial farms were crowned by the brilliant success of patrial lime.

From Government House to the humblest hut on the farthest border, there reigned the gleaming white of patrial lime. My panegyrist will say: The House of Government was turned into a receptacle that received the vibrations of all of Paraguay. Palingenesis of white on white. The pasquinading chivosis,§ for their part, will murmur that it was turned into the tympanum of the moans coming night and day from the captives in the labyrinth of the subterranean dungeons. Ear-Trumpet-of-Command. Receiver of sounds of a people on the march. Cornucopia of the multiple-fruit of abundance, some hymn in praise. Palace of Terror that has made an immense prison of the country, the exiled oligarchons, those migratory batracians, croak. What do I care what those deserters say! Let them taunt me, as they taunted Christ. Apology/Calumny mean nothing. They slide off the facts. They do not stain the white. White are the tunics of the redeemed. Twenty-four elders stand robed in white before the great white throne. The ONE who is seated upon it, white as lambswool: the whitest of all in the dark Apocalypse.

Here too in luminous Paraguay white is the attribute of redemption. Against this background of blinding white, the blackness in which they have clothed my figure strikes even greater fear into the hearts of our enemies. To them black is the attribute of Supreme Power. A Great Darkness, they say of me, trembling in their cubicles. Blinded by the whiteness, they fear more, much more, the blackness in which they catch the scent of the Exterminating Archangel's wing.

---

measuring five varas and a half, and the sidewalks more than a cuerda, and finally, on the outer edge, it enclosed two large corner lots or pastures separated by a dense woodlot intersected by a path that ran down to the river's edge and was lost from sight.

"In the distance, as the patrols from Corrientes prowled about the hills and the lonely expanses of the desert of Misiones, the Fortress would suddenly loom up before them, awesome, overpowering. Beyond the walls, at the very top of a towering urundey flagpole, straight as a needle and almost piercing the sky, there blazed the tri-color symbol of the legendary, respected, awesome Republic of the Perpetual Dictator." (J. A. Vázquez, *Visto y Oído* [*Seen and Heard*].)

---

§*Chivosis:* dwarfed beings who live underground; evil spirits.

I remember very well, Excellency, as though I were seeing it this minute, the time you presented the envoy of the Empire of Brazil with a puzzle. The pompedantic Correa da Cámara was unable to solve the riddle. What riddle are you talking about? Your Excellency said to the Brazilian that night: Why is it that the lion has only to bellow and roar to terrify all the other animals? Why is it that the so-called king of the jungle fears and reveres only the white cock? Since you don't know the answer, I'll explain, Your Excellency said to him: The reason is that the sun, the source and the epitome of all terrestrial and sidereal light, produces a more powerful effect, is better symbolized in the white cock of dawn, by virtue of its nature and attributes, than in the lion, king of the wild ladronicides. The lion walks abroad by night in search of prey and spoils, a bandeirante§ with a great mane and a terrible hunger. The cock awakens with the light and stuffs the lion down his gullet. Correa swallowed hard and rolled his eyes. Your Excellency then said to him: Suddenly plumed devils appear in the guise of a lion and flee before a cock. . . . Come, come, Patiño, enough of your hoary animal fables! It is not possible for us to predict what is going to happen. The roles could well be suddenly reversed and the king of the forest brigands prove savage enough to gulp down the cock. This will not happen, however, as long as the Perpetual Dictatorship lasts. If it is Perpetual, Sire, the Dictatorship will last forever and ever, through all eternity. Amen. With your permission, I am going to let go of the pen for a moment. I am going to cross myself. There, I'm done, Sire. At your orders. Valois is ready! I know your war-cry well. You've got writer's cramp in your hand and hunger pangs in your gut. Go get yourself your bean stew and make the sign of the cross over the pot.

Enough for now. The rest will come later. Send out what you already have as we go along. Take me to the chamber. To the Chamber, Sire? To my bedchamber, to my couch, to my hole. Yes, you lout, to my own Truth Chamber.

Ah bed, hated bed. You're eager for my weight on top of you, you want to be mistress of my end. Aren't you satisfied to have already robbed me of hours, days, months, years? How long, how long my person has wandered amid the immensity of your sweat-soaked straw mattresses! Prop up my spine, Patiño. The cushion first. Then those two or three books. The

§The *bandeiras* were expeditions into the hinterlands of Brazil in search of Indian slaves, land, mines and metals, and precious stones. The members of such expeditions were called *bandeirantes*. The largest number of them were Paulistas, from the colonial captaincy of São Paulo.

Statutes of Alfonso the Wise underneath one buttock. The Laws of the Indies underneath the other one. Raise my tailbone up with the Code of the Visigoths. Ah ah uy. No, not like that. Still farther. Put the Code a little lower down. There, that's a little better. I'd need Archimedes' lever. Ah, if only an unknown science could hold me up in the air. Those rings that pots hang from over the fire. Even filled with hot gas, I can't levitate like my horses. I could have a good hammock woven for you, Sire, like the ones the prisoners have in their dungeons. They feel so light in them that they even forget the weight of their balls and chains. You may be right. That's the one thing lacking. Thanks for the advice. Go have your lunch. I can hear your guts bellyaching through your ears. Eh, eh, wait a minute! Bring me the pasquinade. I want to examine it again. Hand me the magnifying glass. Shall I open the window shutters, Sire? Why, are you thinking of escaping through the window like a bird? No, Sire; just so that Your Excellency will have more light. There's no need. There's as much light under my bed as there is up at the ceiling at midday.

This filthy sheet intrigues me. I suppose you've realized that the paper of this anonymous squib hasn't been used for years. I've never seen it, Excellency. What do you note about it? Paper covered with mildew, stored away for a long time, Sire. Looking at it against the light, one can see the very fine filigree work of the watermark: a rosette of strange initials, incomprehensible, Excellency. Ask the commissioner of Villa del Pilar if that smuggler named La Andaluza has brought more reams with this mark. Tomás Gill loves to scrawl his dispatches on laid paper. Or what's more like it, lied paper. I must remind you, Sire, that Goyeneche's widow hasn't come back to Paraguay. Who's Goyeneche's widow? The captain of the boat that brought the contraband, the lady they call La Andaluza, Sire. Ah, I thought you were referring to the widow of Juan Manuel de Goyeneche, the secret emissary of Bonaparte and Carlota Joaquina, the Spanish spy who never set foot in Paraguay. After the audience that Your Excellency granted her, La Andaluza hasn't made any more trips. You're lying! I never received her. Don't turn things all hind side to. Or topsy-turvy. Check with the commissioners, frontier officials, chief customs officers, when and how more reams of this verge-paper have entered the country. And now clear out of here. Will you have lunch, Sire? Have Santa bring me a pitcher of lemonade. Is Master Alejandro to come at five as usual? Why shouldn't he? Who are you to change my habits? Tell that beard-scraper to put yours to soak. Get along with you, and good appetite.

(In the private notebook)

I think I recognize the handwriting, this paper. Once upon a time, in days long gone by, they represented for me the reality of what exists. By striking a flint spark above the sheet one could see infusoria still teeming in the ink. Parasitic fibrils. Annular, semilunar corpuscles of plasmodium. They finally formed the filigreed florets of malaria. The squib quivers with the shivers of swamp fever. Long live the ague!, the fever buzzes in my ears. The work of anopheles culicids.

Follow the trail of the handwriting through the labyrinths of . . . *(torn).*

. . . the filigreed fleuron in the vergered-perjured paper, the flagellated letters, now mark the unreality of the inexistent. In the forest of differences in which we lie, I too must guard against being deluded by the delirium of similarities. People all reassure themselves with the thought that they are a single individual. Difficult to be the same man constantly. What is the same is not always the same. **I** am not always **I.** The only one who doesn't change is **HE.** He maintains himself in the invariable. He is there, in the state of superlunary beings. If I close my eyes, I still see him, infinitely repeated in the rings of the concave mirror. (I must look for my notes on this subject of almastronomy.) It is not merely a question of eyelids. Sometimes **HE** looks at me, and then my bed rises and drifts at the mercy of whirlwinds, and **I,** lying in it, seeing everything from very high up or very deep down, till everything disappears in the point, in the place of absence. Only **HE** remains, not losing an iota of his form, of his dimension, but rather, growing, increasing by himself.

Who can assure me that I am not at that moment in which to live is to wander about all alone? That instant at which, in fact, as my amanuensis has said, one dies and everything goes on without anything apparently having happened or changed. In the beginning I did not write; I only dictated. Then I forgot what I had dictated. Now I must dictate/write; note it down somewhere. That is the only way I have of proving that I still exist. But isn't being buried in writing perhaps the most complete way of dying? No? Yes? Well then? No. A round no. Feeble will of senility. Old life burbling an old man's thoughts. One writes when one can no longer act. Writing treacherous truths. Giving up the advantages of forgetting. Excavating the well that one is. Hauling up from the bottom what has been buried there for so long. Yes, but am I sure that I am hauling up what is or what isn't? I don't know, I don't know. Doing in a titanic way what is insignificant is also a way of acting. Even if it's in reverse. The only thing

I'm certain of is that these Notes are addressed to no one. None of your made-up stories for the diversion of readers who pounce upon them like swarms of acridians. Nor Confessions (like compadre Jean-Jacques'), nor Intimate Memoirs (like those of illustrious whores or scholarly sodomites). This is a Balancing of Accounts. A plank stretched out over the edge of the abyss. My gouty leg drags itself out toward the end, to that point of balance at which plank, plank-walker, recounting and accounting, debts and debtors, facts and figures are swallowed up by the abyss. I salute you, welcome downward slope!

That idiot of a Patiño is always half-right. I didn't receive La Andaluza. I granted her an audience but I did not receive her. Receive her, Your Grace, her associate Sarratea sends word to me. This celebrated lady trader is a charming person, who couldn't be more devoted to you. She has a business proposal to make to Your Excellency that is certain to bring you lasting satisfaction, but one that can only be discussed in private because of the risks involved. Lying words of a Porteño, a liar like every other Porteño. He is trying to trick me by holding out the false promise of a huge contraband arms deal. He would have me believe that the shipment would include nothing less than all the arsenal stolen from Paraguay during the blockade of the river by pirates, plus the arms that the Paraguayan troops left behind when they went to defend Buenos Aires against invasion by the English. Even the cannons of the port, no less, and perhaps more besides.

The burned smell of the plot could be sniffed from a long way off, even before there was any sign of smoke visible. At times I like to appear to be ingenuous. Is tomorrow so important that the celebrated lady trader cannot come today, since even yesterday would seem to have been a little on the late side, I sent word to the Porteño so as to pull the wool over his eyes. Immediately the green heron with white wings of twenty meters' spread covered the seventy leagues from Villa del Pilar, where the boat had lain at anchor for two months awaiting my authorization. Gliding between the hills of Lambaré and Takumbú, it landed gently in the bay of the port, opposite Government House.

The thin silhouette of the lady-captain at the helm first entered the study through the lens of the spyglass. She is there in the mirror with her back turned. Bulrush-body. Carbine-body. Long-barreled-musket-woman. Fingers tense on the trigger of will. It was then that I wrote, nihil in intellectu, that rhetorical exercise that I copy so as to punish myself twice over, by and for the shameful bad taste provoked by the fabulary visit of this real woman. Deianira brings me the tunic soaked in the blood of the river-centaur Nessos. Nessos: Neso: Seno: anagram for breast. Amphib(i)ological creatures, mythological ones. Do you all know how the story goes? You can find it in any portable dictionary of myths. If my own wasn't devoured by the flames back then, you conscientious compiler-collector of ashes, consult pages 70 to 77; you'll find a cross marked there: Hercules falls in love with Deianira, who is already promised to Aqueloos. He fights with the latter, who has taken the form of a serpent and then that of a bull. He tears off one of his horns, which will later be known as the Horn-of-Plenty. To lose one woman is always to find plenty more. Hercules, however, is led to perdition by his victory. He takes Deianira to the hill of Takumbú, which is really Tyrinth. Which is of no great importance, since in fables such as these certain names are no more real than others. The centaur Nessos now enters the scene. He knows the fordable sites of the river and offers to take Deianira across on his shoulders. But since all these masculo-feminine deities are treacherous, Nessos the river-centaur carries her off. Hercules shoots a poisoned arrow into the abductor. Realizing that he is dying, Nessos gives his tunic soaked in blood and poison to Deianira, who in turn gives it as a present to Hercules. Here things get very complicated. Raging passion, ruthless vengeance, rending grief. For what are fables made of save such trivial misfortunes? Clad in the tunic of Nessos, Hercules writhes in his death-agony. He still has enough strength left to fell great trees at the foot of the Cerro-Léon. He makes a pyramid, a pyre amid his wrath, to the measure of his rage. He orders Philoctetes, his Policarpo Patiño, to set fire to the tree trunks over which he has spread his lion's skin, and lies down on it as though it were a bed, with his head resting on his club. The portable dictionary also says that Deianira killed herself in desperation. No; women, be they fabulary or not, do not kill themselves. They kill out of esperation. Between two moons they lose a lot of blood, but they don't die.

Ah treacherous, clever, beautiful Deianira-Andaluza! Widow of that blunderer Goyeneche, emissary of the stupid Porteños. You've come safe into port! Do you think you're going to strip me of my lion's skin so that the fatal cloth will brush my body with its black magic of monstrual-menstrual blood? Keep your transparent present. They have bought your beauty, your boldness, my death by your hand for very little money, Amazon-of-the-river. Ah, if I could populate my country with women warriors like you, though without your traitorous nature, ones who would wage war on the enemy, the frontiers of Paraguay would extend to Asia

Minor where dwelt the Amazons whom only Hercules could vanquish! But Hercules, a woman-chaser, was vanquished by women. I will not be tempted to lie with you.

Since almost my earliest days I loved a deity whom I called Star-of-the-North. More than one velleity tried to take her place by assuming other forms to deceive me, but I was never fooled. One day in my youth I asked a spirit the question: Who is the Star-of-the-North? But spirits are mute. *(In the margin):* Except for Patiño, who believes he can talk with them, merely because I made the mistake of teaching him a few rudiments of occultism and judiciary astrology. They sufficed to make him take himself, with time, for a magus. Imago. Coleopter-butterfly. Grand-Sarcophage, he has painted skulls and phosphoreal tibias on his wings in darkest mourning . . . *(margin torn).* I copied the question, in Latin, on a piece of paper. My first pasquinade, neither slanderous nor amoral, but amored, enamored, bewitched, bedazzled. I placed the note under a stone, at the top of Takumbú. If only there had been a charlatan back then to answer that question!

In any event I needed that fantasy, regardless of whether or not arms-smuggling entered into it. Standing motionless in front of the table, she casts a curious eye on the papers, the little gun rack with fifty of the rifles that she has sold me on numerous occasions, not to mention Carlón§ wine, flour, hardtack, hardware, ant-contraband that gets through the blockade of the river. She runs her hand over the meteor as she looks around out of the corner of her eye. A gentle caress of the jeopard-hawk of the cosmos. Chance-stone chained in a corner of the room giving off invisible light, a warning of minor hazards: this woman with the svelte body bare-ly trembling. She does not hide the clear intentions in the darkest corner of her mind. First-last of the Admirable Admiralasses to make an audacious attempt on my love-life. Welcome, captainess of La Paloma del Plata! Deianira-Andaluza, traffickress in arms, specious spices, lovers. Malicious gossips say that at the hour when the Mohammedan touches his forehead to the ground in prayer, the entire crew of your boat, personally chosen by you, goes to bed with you, one at a time. The meteor strips you naked as you caress it. The habit of command, of copulation. You have brought no arms for my army. Nothing but your red rag. A lure for the blunderbuss shot you intend to fire point-blank at me the moment you see me appear in the door. You draw your hand back toward

§A cheap wine from Andalusia, an imitation of Benicarló.

your waist. The Peruvian buttons of your blouse light up the slit. I take a step backward to let the sparkling gleam past. You turn your face toward the mirror looking for me/looking for yourself. You tuck in the bluish curl peeking out of your pirate turban. You are rounding the Cape of the Eleven Thousand Virgins. You lean over the sextant. You look for the rectilinear spherical coordinates; where, how to get a fix on the point that has flown off leaving you without a place in the space of the impossible; or worse still, leaving you adrift in that nonexistent space where you coexist with all possible species. A common place that blots out common sense, cancels out the very fact that you are here leaning over the sextant hoping I will receive you, searching for the right tack, the opportune moment to make me fall into the commonplace of a phrase in your stead. The easiest thing in the world; the most infallible way of making something disappear: people, animals, animate-inanimate objects. Allow me an aside between brackets: [In a drama of antiquity, I do not recall at the moment which one, there is a passage in which a conspirator-usurper is speaking with the men that he is about to send out to kill the king. The mercenaries claim that they are men, and he answers that they only go in the catalogue for men.] You are not a woman either; a specious specimen of your kind. An errant emissary of the feminine, tacking against the tide of the possible. You are no longer navigating the Paraguay River, nor cleaving the strait beneath the Magellanic Clouds. You are sailing behind things, unable to escape from a spaceless space. In contrast to the brightness of the Magellanic Nubeculae, the dark circles under your eyes have grown larger: Two coalsacks beneath the fire of your eyes rain soot down on your impersonal-person. At times they make you invisible. Ouf. No. I know that I am not writing what I want to. Let's try another tack. You have entered a dark cavern that reaches to the very center of the earth. You begin, without a word, to move about in my silenciarium. You finger, you sniff, you inspect everything. You examine the tubes, caressing/sighing. Careful there! Don't harbor false hopes, Deianira, Andaluza: Hercules has already flung himself into the flames, enveloped in the tunic. Don't start measuring my trousers' fly with my theodolite. That apparatus served me to rebuild the City that in three centuries your ancestors left more choked with filth than Augeas' stables. I demarcated, disinfected the country by cutting off with a single stroke the seven heads of the Lernoses, which could not grow back double here. The one Double is the Supreme. But you do not understand the expression be-two. You sidle up to the telescope. You remove the guantilope scrotum. You peer through the lens: You see the Southern Cross, inverted; at the same time, the mete-or, from the reverse. The needle of the compass is riveted on the stone's magnetic north. You raise the tube to its most inclined angle. If the coalsacks had not darkened the sky, you might have been able to glimpse the space, completely empty of stars, between Scorpio and Ophiucus: true hole through which our gaze can penetrate to the farthest corner of the Universe. On the table the seven watches pulse with a single beat that I synchronize each day as I wind them seventy times seven times. You are unable to cross that pulsing line, no matter how hard you push with your shoulder, with your shadow, against the spaceless space that contains you and all the other miserable species, female-phoenix of dampness. Memento homo. Nepento mulier. You feel pressed for time now. Useless for you to move the iron gnomon marking the hours on the sundial; on the face of the Acaz clock§ the shadow moves backward. Gripping the tiller, elbow bowspritted, you advance toward the table, turning into the wind which fills the edges around the door behind which I observe you. Your breathing makes the pennants flutter, your breasts quiver rhythmically, the waves of papers stir. You pick up Sarratea's letter. You toss it into the wastebasket. You shake your head to free yourself from distraction. You are under orders to kill me and you are diverting me: writing-describing what cannot happen, stubborn errand-runner, boatman of justice. Hurry up! Ah, yes, all right. You have finally decided on an end that will have no beginning. You carelessly scrawl a few words. Aha! You write first and act afterwards. You gather the ashes together first and then light the fire; well, everyone has his own way of going about things. You straighten up. You face the door. You plunge your hand amid the blouse folds. So violently that a little button pops out. It rolls along the floor and under the door, landing alongside my shoes. I pick it up. It is warm. I put it in my pocket . . . *(torn)*. You remove something from your bosom. Throw. Something bounces off the planisphere, between the constellations of the Altar and the Royal Peacock. The air in the study grows stifling. Acid odor of a musk cat. The unmistakable, immemorial odor of woman. Carnal smell of sex. Lustful, sensual, lubricious, libidinous, salacious, voluptuous, dishonest, shameless, lascivious, fornicatory. Its effluvia expand, fill the room. Penetrate the smallest interstices. Make the heaviest objects sway to and fro as on a tide. The furniture, the arms. Even the meteorite seems to float and bob in the terrible stench. It must be invading the entire city. I am paralyzed with nausea. Retching, on the point of vomiting. With a supreme effort, I contain myself. It is not merely that I smell this female odor, that I have suddenly remembered it. I see it. Fiercer than a phantom that attacks us in broad daylight, leaping

§A reference from Peter Martyr's *Décadas de Orbe Novo,* inspired by the discovery of the New World.

back and forth, to the end of those first days, burned up, forgotten, in the brothels of the Lower Town. The smell is here now. Female-Samson, she has embraced the pillars of my temperate temple. She coils her thousands of arms round the wooden columns of my unimpregnable eremitorium-erectorium. Trying to topple it. She looks at me blindly, sniffs at me, invisible. Trying to topple me. Sultan enters. Goes over to La Andaluza. Begins to sniff her from the heelbones up. The backs of her knees, her lupanarian crotch, the curve of her buttocks. The old sans-culotte dog also hangs back. He who shatters members, Desire, age-old desire flashes in his gummy eyes. He whines a little, on the verge of capitulation. But a moment later he withdraws his muzzle from those soft valleys. Lips dripping with frothy spittle. He hurls crude insults at her: "Treacherous woman! May you die of man-hunger! May you have no other roof than the firmament. No other bed than the deck of your boat. May you live amid perpetual alarms even though you bring us no more arms. May the head of your dead husband press against your thighs, a chastity chinstrap to bridle your fatal female furor. Out of here! Away with you, whore!" Eh, eh, eh. What's all that, Sultan? What's the meaning of this uncivil language of a Carbonarist dog? That's no way to treat ladies! Is that all that's to be expected of you, you cantankerous, misogynous old dog! Sultan hangs his head and goes off growling insults not to be repeated. Let's not overdo the note of lewd vulgarity here. I tend to repeat myself in this sort of excess as well. Somewhat deliberately, I expect. I exaggerate minutiae. Words are dirty by nature. Filth, excrementicity, base and ignoble thoughts exist in the mind of terati, of literati; not in words that are speakable. I apply the strategy of repetition to these notes. I have told myself: The only thing that cancels itself out is what is endlessly repeated down to the last detail. Besides, what a bunch of shit! I do and write whatever I please and however I please, since I'm writing only for myself. Why all this mirror business, all these stiff, starchy hieroglyphic texts then? Literatology of antiphonies and counterantiphonies. Of front sides and backsides. Copulation of male and female metaphors. By the horns of my crescent cock, Sultan was quite right to throw out La Andaluza, that whore!

In reality, I could throw out the whole of this little romantic interlude. In any event, I shall revise and correct it, working my way backwards. What is true and certain is that Deianira the Andalusian took off in a gust of wind. Breath of air-blot-woman swiftly disappearing; slowly turning back into La Andaluza-the-reed, followed by the eyes of Pilar the black. My valet de chambre, the indiscreet rascal, has also been spying on the scene from behind another door opened just a crack. Paler than a dead man, if the mortal pallor of a black is discernible. Vastly upset, my hand page has drifted off like a puff of smoke in the direction of the kitchen. He returns in a few moments with the maté. Water boiled for two hours, I notice at the first sip from the gourd. Did you see a woman leave the study? No, Master. I saw no one enter or leave. I've been in the kitchen all this time, preparing the maté, awaiting your orders. Go ask the guard on duty. He's back already. That scrofula can pass through several different places at the same time. Sire, none of the guards or sentinels has seen a woman enter or leave Government House while Your Grace was busy working till just a moment ago.

The rough draft of the romance in which I wish to call to mind what happened continues as follows: I fished about for the button in my pockets; all I found was an old clipped silver coin worth half a real. I went into the study. On the table the paper the woman has written on is waiting for me. In big letters, the note sings out: REGARDS FROM THE STAR-OF-THE-NORTH! I rush over to the window with the spyglass; I peer at every last corner of the port. Not a single trace of the green boat on the sheet of quicksilver of the bay. Between the Ark of Paraguay, under construction for more than twenty years, the great river rafts and other craft rotting in the sun, nothing but trembling reflections from the water. The note on the table has also disappeared. Perhaps I crumpled it up in a rage and threw it into the wastebasket. Perhaps, perhaps. How do I know? I find in its place, between two dossiers and the constellations, a fossil amaranth flower; so it is possible to go on writing something or other, for example: flower-symbol of immortality. Like stones tossed at random, idiotic phrases don't go back to where they came from. They emerge from the abyss of non-expression and know no peace till they have hurled us into it, where-upon they remain mistresses of a cadaverous reality. I know those little pebble-phrases on the order of: Nothing is more real than nothingness; or, Memory, stomach of the soul; or, I scorn this dust that I am made of and that speaks to you. They appear to be harmless. But once they are sent rolling down the slope of written words they can infest an entire language. Make it so ill it becomes absolutely mute. Leave speakers without a tongue. Make them crawl about on all fours again. Petrify them within the limit marking the most extreme degradation, a bourn from which there is no return. Monolith of vague human shape. Sown on stony ground. Hiero-glyphs themselves. The stones of Tevegó. Those stones!

So I picked up the flower. Inside the little crystallized branch the magnifying glass made it possible to see imperceptible veins. At the very bottom of the amaranth crest, peaks of infinitely tiny mountains. Substance of the fossilized aroma? A faint stench; a smell more sound than smell. Sputtering of corpuscles that have been there since BEFORE and that can be perceived only after one has rubbed the mummy-flower for a long time against the back of one's hand. Nebulae. Constellations like those of the cosmos. A cosmos turned outside in toward the infinitesimal, contracting on itself. A step away from countermatter. Confound it! Rhetoric continues to wreak its havoc. It's that I've completely lost the faculty of putting what I think or believe I remember into everyday words. If I were able to do so, I'd be cured. A harlot arrives, a strumpet sea-fox. She scatters everything that's written all about. A cruising superwhore appears. She orders you to remember to forget.

Another subject.

À propos of the History of the Revolutions of the Province of Paraguay, I mentioned the Jesuit Lozano this morning. I read the manuscript in the Hospital Barracks during my confinement because of the fall I had on my last outing. If I am to believe the witness of my senses, I must write that that afternoon I *saw* Pedro Lozano in the priest who blocked my path, down at the lower end of the Calle de la Encarnación, just as the storm was breaking. Along with the first drops darkness also suddenly fell. The sergeant on point, the scouts, the bugler, the drummer, had already gone on ahead. The priest appeared at a bend in the street, in a surplice and stole. He was accompanied by two or three acolytes carrying lighted tapers that the wind and the rain couldn't manage to put out. The fanfare of the escort was drowned out by the sound of the little bell that one of the acolytes was shaking, as terror-stricken by the sight of me as by the appearance of a ghost. The black Arabian with the white blaze strode ahead in the direction of the ringing bell, its ears quivering. The thought crossed my mind that some new plot might be lurking behind what seemed to be the bringing of the viaticum to a dying man. I was amazed at the cleverness of the scheme. They've arranged everything: pump me full of lead, and then the viaticum. No; perhaps not, another voice said within me. Isn't that the Jesuit Pedro Lozano, coming personally to place his libel against José de Antequera in your hands? The cortege of the eucharistic ambush has halted in the middle of the street, directly in front of me. It shows no signs of moving aside. It is blocking my path. Out of my way, Pedro Lozano!, I shout at him. I can now make him out clearly in the blinding flashes of lightning. Even the pores of his skin. Livid face. Closed eyes. Lips moving as he mutters the antiphon. He kneels down in the mud. At that moment I remember having read that the chronicler of the order died a century before, in the gorge of Humahuaca, as he was journeying to Upper Peru by the same route that Antequera followed on the way to his beheading. I hear once again the ringing of the little bell, muffled by the more and more violent squalls of wind and rain. The Arabian rears in fright. The acolytes run off screaming Xake Karaí! Xake Karaí! I am almost on top of the priest. What from a distance looked like the gold cover of a book is in reality the large gold pyx in which the sacred form is preserved. I give a hard pull on the reins so as to hold back the Arabian, on the point of bolting. It is then that the end of the whip, snaking amid the gusts of wind and rain, curls about the foot of the pyx, tearing it from the cleric's hands. I see him dragging himself through the mud searching for it. The strange thing is that the surplice remains snow-white. The very old stole with mourning guards, the two raveled crosses of the pectorals turn a blinding white. The Arabian leaps over the priest and into the whirlwinds of the storm. He slips and falls into a puddle, throwing me far from him. I roll in the mud in my turn, searching for some unknown lost object. Lost in two from the concussion of the fall. I find myself in the position of one who can no longer say *I* because he is not one and single, feeling himself more alone than ever in those two halves, not knowing which of them he belongs to. Sensation of having been driven to that state, cruelly deceived, thrown in the discard, tossed out like trash, chained to the mire. At that moment, beneath the Deluge, all I could do was pound on the mud with my fists like a blind man. Idiot idiot idiot! A fractured bone, a broken spinal column, a blow at the base of your skull could be responsible for this hallucination. Perhaps I didn't realize that at that moment. In discouraging situations, the truth stands in need of as much support as error. At that moment I had no support save the mud; and it was sucking me in. Amid the rain and the wind the horse stood waiting.

Give me your hand. Are you going to get up, Sire? Let me have your hand. A very great honor for this servant to have Your Excellency extend his hand to me. I'm not holding my hand out to you. I'm ordering you to hold yours out to me. It's not a reconciliation I'm proposing to you; simply a simulacrum of temporary identification.

This is a lesson. The last one. It ought to have been the first one. Since I am unable to offer you a Last Supper with the flock of Judases who are my apostles, I offer you a last-first class. What type of class, Sire? Homage to your supine ignorance in the pursuit of your duty. For more than twenty years you've been the number one secretary of the Government, my confidential clerk, the supreme amanuensis, and you still don't know the secrets of your calling. Your scriptuary gift is still extremely rudimentary. Small, even less than that, not the least. You boast of having at the tip of your eye the faculty of distinguishing the slightest similarities and differences even in the forms of periods, yet you're not able to recognize the handwriting of an ignoble pasquinade. You are more than right, Sire. With your permission I wish to inform Your Excellency that I have already shut up seven thousand three hundred thirty-four scriveners in the archive, to compare the letters of the pasquinade with the twenty thousand dossiers that add up to five hundred thousand pages, as well as all the paperwork that Your Grace has ordered me to collect for the same purpose. I have even conscripted Paí Mbatú. Even with his half-addled brain, he's the most alert and active of all the scribblers I've recruited. I'm a madman girded with wisdom and booted with patience!, the shatterpated ex priest keeps exclaiming. So bring on your files: this task is a piece of cake for me! I've put them all on hardtack and water in order to prod them and kindle their zeal. Do you remember those old Indians of Jaguarón, Sire, who refused to go on working in the tobacco manufactory, claiming they had poor eyesight? A good stew with lots of tobacco worms in it was cooked up for them, and the Indians sat down to eat. They ate every last kernel of corn, but left all the fat green marandovases untouched on the edge of their plates. I intend to do the same thing with those idlers. All I'm waiting for in order to begin the handwriting investigation is for Your Excellency to hand me over the pasquinade.

You've been my trust-unworthy secretary for more than twenty years now, and you still don't know how to secrete what I dictate. You twist and turn my words around. I dictate my circular to you in order to educate the corps of civil and military functionaries as to the cardinal facts and events concerning our Nation. I've already sent them the first part, Sire. When they read it, those ignorant beasts are going to think that I'm talking to them about an imaginary Nation. You're getting to be more and more like those pompous scribes, the Molases and the Peñas for example, who take themselves to be Solons and are no more than Scribleruses. Even when they're locked up in prison they manage to rat about filching what other people write. Don't try to imitate them. Don't use improper words that are not my style, that are not steeped in my thought. I loathe relative talent that's begged and borrowed. What's more, your style is abominable. A labyrinthine alleyway paved with alliterations, anagrams, idiosyncratic idioms, barbarisms, paronomasias such as pároli/párulis, imbecilic anastrophes to dazzle imbecilic inverts who experience erections by virtue of the effect of the violent inversions of word order, such as: Beneath the foot of the tree I fall; or one more violent still: Having Revolution firmly planted in my head, the pike winks its conniving eye at me from the Plaza. Old tricks of rhetoric that are now being taken up once again as though they were brand-new. The principal fault I tax you with is your inability to express yourself with the originality of a parrot. You are nothing but a speaking biohuman. A hybrid creature engendered by different species. A she mule—he ass keeping the treadmill of state scribery going round. You would have been more useful to me as a parrot than as a confidential clerk. You are neither the one nor the other. Instead of transcribing what I dictate to you in its natural state, you fill the paper with incomprehensible barbarisms. Pieces of mischief already written by others. You feed on the carrion of books. You have not yet destroyed oral tradition only because it is the one language that cannot be sacked, robbed, repeated, plagiarized, copied. What is spoken remains alive, sustained by the tone, the gestures, the facial expressions, the gaze, the accent, the breath of the speaker. In all languages the most forceful exclamations are not articulated. Animals do not speak because they do not articulate, but they understand each other much better and more quickly than we do. Solomon held converse with mammals, birds, fishes, reptiles. I too speak through them. He did not understand the language of the beasts most familiar to him. His heart was hardened against the animal world when he lost his seal. He is said to have thrown it away in anger when a nightingale informed him that his wife number nine hundred ninety-nine loved a man younger than he.

When I dictate to you, the words have a meaning; when you write them, another. So that we speak two different languages. One feels more at home in the company of a familiar dog than in that of a man speaking a language unknown to us. False language is much less sociable than silence. Even my dog Sultan took the secret of what he said to the grave with him. What I beg of you, my dear Sancho Pauncho, is that you not try, when I dictate to you, to artificialize the nature of the matter being dealt with, but rather to naturalize the artificiality of words. You are my ex-cretive secretary. You write what I dictate to you as though you yourself were speaking in my place in secret on the paper. I want there to be something of myself in the words that you write. I am not dictating a quanticle of claptrap to you. Mere bibble-babble. Amusing stories as false as dicers' oaths. One of those potboilers in which the writer flaunts the sacred nature of literature. Pretended high priests of letters make pretentious ceremonies of their works. In them, the characters spin fabrications out of reality or out of language. They appear to be celebrating their Mass vested in supreme authority, but in reality they are filled with turbation in the face of the figures emerging from their hands, which it is their belief that they create. Hence their office becomes a vice. Anyone who attempts to relate his life loses himself in the immediate. One can only speak of another. The *I* manifests itself only through the *He. I* do not speak to myself. I listen to myself through *Him.* I am trapped in a tree. The tree cries out after its own fashion. Who can know that I am crying out inside of it? I therefore demand of you the most absolute silence, the most absolute secrecy. For the very reason that it is not possible to communicate anything to anyone who is outside the tree. That person will hear the cry of the tree. He will not hear the other cry. Mine. Do you understand? No? All the better.

The trouble is, Patiño, that that more and more pronounced lisp of your bridled tongue is making things worse. You cover all my folios with *z*'s. Your waning power of speech is leaving them increasingly voiceless. Ah, Patiño, if your memory, ignorant of what has not yet happened, could discover that ears function like eyes, and eyes like the tongue, projecting images at a distance, as images send forth sounds and audible silence, we would have no need to resort to the slowness of speech. And still less to the clumsiness of writing, which has already set us back millions of years.

Possessed of the same organs, men speak and animals do not. Do you find that reasonable? Hence it is not spoken language that differentiates man from the animal, but rather, the possibility of forging a language to suit his needs. Could you invent a language in which the sign is identical to the object? Even the most abstract and indeterminate of objects. The infinite. A perfume. A dream. The Absolute. Could you find a way for all of this to be transmitted at the speed of light? No; you can't. We can't. The reason why you are de trop and at the same time de moins in this world in which fast talkers and charlatans abound, whereas there is a cruel lack of honest individuals. Do you understand me? To tell the truth, not much, not altogether, Excellency. Or better put, absolutely nothing whatsoever, Sire, for which I beg your most excellent pardon. It doesn't matter. That's enough of this foolishness for now. Let's begin at the beginning. Put your hoofs in the basin. Soak your solipedal bunions. Put the bucket of Alejandro the barber, the helmet of Mambrino or Minerva, anything you like, on your head. Listen. Pay attention. We are going to scrutinize together the secret of writing. I am going to teach you the difficult art of scriptuary science, which is not, as you believe, the art of tracing flowery figures but of deflowering signs.

Try by yourself first. Grasp the pen firmly. Raise your eyes. Concentrate on the plaster bust of Robespierre and wait for it to speak. Write. The bust isn't saying anything to me, Sire. Ask the engraving of Napoleon a question. Still not a word, Excellency. What reason could Señor Napoleon have to speak to me? Concentrate on the aerolith; maybe it will say something to you. Stones speak. The thing is, Sire, at this hour of the afternoon my brain is so numb I only half hear my own memory. And if you can imagine, I even feel as though my hand is going to sleep! Give it to me. I'm going to wind it up tight again. Midnight. The stroke of twelve and all is well. Beneath the white cone of the candle the one thing to be seen is our two hands, each atop the other. In order that your fading memory may rest in peace as I instill in you the magic power of specters, I shall guide your hand as though I were the one writing. Close your eyes. You have the pen in your hand. Close your mind to any other thought. Do you feel the weight of it? Yes, Excellency! It's terribly heavy! It's not only the pen, Excellency; it's also your hand . . . a real block of iron. Don't think of the hand. Think only about the pen. The pen is cold-sharp-pointed metal. The paper a hot-passive surface. Squeeze. Squeeze harder. I'm squeezing your hand. Pushing. Pressing. Oppressing. Compressing. Pressing down. The pressure melts our hands. They are but one at this moment. I squeeze hard. Back-and-forth motion. Unbroken rhythm. Stronger and stronger. Deeper and deeper. There is nothing but this movement. Nothing outside it. The iron of the point scores the paper. Right/left. Up/down.

You are writing beginning to write five thousand years ago. The first signs. Designs. Cretinographic up-and-down strokes. Islands with tall trees enveloped in clouds of smoke, in mist. The horn of a bull attacking in a cave. Squeeze. Go on. Put all the weight of your being onto the point of the pen. All your strength into each movement of each stroke. Mount it, straddle it, ride it like a stradiot. No, no! Don't dismount yet! I beg your pardon, Sire, I can't see but I feel that very strange letters are coming out. Don't think it strange. The strangest thing of all is what comes most naturally. You are writing. To write is to disconnect the power of words from oneself. To so charge that power of the word that it gradually detaches itself from oneself with everything that is one's very own and becomes that of another. The totally alien. You have just drowsily written: I THE SUPREME. Sire . . . you're forcing my hand! I've ordered you to think of nothing at all

nothing

forget your memory. To write does not mean to convert the real into words but to make the power of the word real. The unreal lies only in the bad use of the power of words in the bad use of writing. I don't understand, Sire . . . Never mind. The pressure is enormous but you almost don't feel it you don't feel it eh what is it that you feel

I feel that I'm not feeling

weight that unloads itself of its weight. The stroking motion of the pen is more and more rapid. It penetrates to the very bottom. I feel, Sire . . . I feel my body to-and-froing in a hammock . . . Sire . . . the paper has gotten away from me! It's turned the other way around! Go on writing wrong side to then. Grip the pen hard. Squeeze it as hard as though the life you don't yet have were contained in it. Go on writing

I'm going ooooon

the paper voluptuously allows its tiniest cracks to be penetrated. It absorbs, sucks up the ink of each rasp of the pen that rends it. Passional process. It leads to a complete fusion of the ink and the paper. The dusky color of the ink blends with the whiteness of the sheet of paper. The lubricious pair lubricate each other mutually. Male/female. The two of them form the beast with two backs. This is the beginning of the principle of mixture. Ah ah don't moan, you, don't pant. No, Sire . . . I'm not fucking. Yes you're fucking. This is representation. Literature. Representation of writing as representation. Scene one.

Scene two:

An aerolith falls from the sky of writing. The ovule of the point makes its mark in the place where it has fallen, where it has buried itself. Sudden embryo. It sprouts beneath the crust. Very small, it overflows itself. It designates its nothingness at the same time that it emerges from it. It materializes the hole of the zero. From the hole of the zero there comes forth sin-zerity.

Scene three:

The point. The little point is present, here and now. Set down on the paper. At the mercy of its internal forces. Pregnant with things. They endeavor to procreate themselves in the inner palpitation. They break through the shell. They come out cheeping. They settle down on the white crust of the paper.

Epilogue:

The point. Seed of new ova. The circumference of its infinitesimal circle is a perpetual angle. The forms ascend in regular order. From the lowest to the highest. The lowest form is angular, that is to say terrestrial. The next is the perpetual angular. Then the spiral origin-measure of circular forms. Consequently it is called the perpetual-circular: Nature coiled in a perpetual-spiral. Wheels that never stop turning. Axes that never break. So too with writing. Symmetrical negation of nature.

Origin of writing: the Point. Small unit. Just as the units of written or spoken language are in turn small languages. Compadre Lucretius said so long before all his godchildren: The principle of all things is that their insides are formed of smaller insides. Bone of smaller bones. Blood of little drops of blood reduced to a single one. Gold of particles of gold. The earth of little contracted grains of sand. Water of drops. Fire of sparks come together. Nature works on the scale of the minimal. Writing as well.

In like manner Absolute Power is made up of small powers. I can do by way of others what those others cannot do by themselves. I can say to others what I am unable to say to myself. Others are lenses through which we read within our own minds. The Supreme is Supreme by nature. He never reminds us of any others save the image of the State, of the Nation, of the people of the Fatherland.

Come, come, unsaddle yourself from your drowsiness. From here on write alone. Haven't you often boasted of remembering the letters and even the shape of the periods sitting on the mountains of paperwork in the twenty or thirty thousand files of the archive? I don't know if your memorative eye is deceiving you, if your lorified tongue is lying. What is certain is that in the letters that look most alike, in the periods that are apparently the roundest, there is always some difference that allows one to compare them, to verify this novelty that appears amid the foliage of similarities. It would take me thirty thousand nights plus another thirty thousand to teach you the different forms of periods. And even then we would only have started. The commas, the hyphens, the diaereses, the brackets, the dashes, the quotation marks, the parentheses that are most alike are also different beneath the semblance of similarity. The hand of one and the same person is very different when written at midnight and at midday. It never says the same thing even though a given word is the same.

Do you know what distinguishes daytime handwriting from nighttime? In a nocturnal hand there is obstinacy with indulgence. The proximity of sleep files the angles smooth. The spirals sprawl out more. The resistance from left to right, weaker. Delirium, intimate friend of the nocturnal hand. The curves sway less. The sperm of the ink dries more slowly. The movements are divergent. The strokes droop more. They tend to distend.

Daytime handwriting, on the contrary, is firm. Rapid. It spares itself useless pollutions. The movement is convergent. The strokes tend upward. An accompaniment of freely undulating curves. Above all in the flourish following the signature. Hard-fought battle between the poles of the perpetual-circle. The positive pressure is a continuous approaching-of-the-limit. The trace suddenly overflows. Floods its banks. Its obstinacy is more rigid. The resistance from right to left stronger. The loops, the double twists and bends, the doubling back, the duplicity more obdurate. It flies through the air with the greatest of ease. But in the diurnal hand as in the nocturnal the lone word is of no use except for what is useless. Of what use are pasquinades? The most shameful perversion of the use of writing! What's the point in the spiderwork that pasquinaders weave? They write. Copy. Scribble. Cohabit with the wicked word. Plunge down the slope of wickedness. Sudden full stop. Death blow to their logorrhea. The avalanche of words meeting with a sudden quiet, the wordmongers with a sudden quietus. Not the full stop of a dot of black ink; the tiny black hole produced by a rifle cartridge in the breast of the enemies of the Fatherland is what counts. It admits of no reply. It rings out. The end. Finis.

You now understand why my handwriting changes according to the compass points. According to my humors. According to the drift of the winds, of events. Above all when I must discover, search out, punish treason. Yes, Excellency! I now understand with total clarity your illuminating words. What I want you to understand with even greater clarity, my illuminated amanuensis, is your duty to discover the author of the anonymous document. Where is the pasquinade? It's right there underneath your hand, Sire. Take it. Study it in the light of the calligraphic cosmography I have just taught you. You'll be able to tell at exactly what hour of the day or night that paper was scribbled. Take the magnifying glass. Follow the trail of the trace. At your service, Excellency.

(In the private notebook)

Patiño sneezes, thinking not of the science of writing but of the roiling storms in his stomach.

I am now certain that I recognize the handwriting of the anonymous squib. Written with the contorted strength of a twisted mind. The cathedral pasquinade is too overwrought in its brevity! The same words express different meanings, as suits the mood of the person uttering them. Nobody says "my civil and military servants" save to call attention to the fact that they are servants, although the blasted bastards serve no purpose whatsoever. Nobody orders his dead body to be decapitated save someone who wants it to be someone else's. Nobody signs I THE SUPREME to as gross a travesty as this, save someone who suffers from absolute insupremacy. Impunity? I don't know, I don't know. . . . Nonetheless, no possibility is to be rejected. Um. Ah. Aha! Take a good look. Nocturnal hand, surely. The waves get weaker toward the bottom. The curves meet at sharp angles; they're trying to discharge their energy earthward. The resistance to the right is stronger. Centripetal strokes, shaky, closed to the point of muteness.

In other days I used to perform an experiment in letromancy with my two white ravens. It always gave good results. Trace a circle on the ground with a radius equal to a man's foot. Same radius as the disc of the sun on the line of the Western horizon. Divide it into twenty-four equal sections. Draw a letter of the alphabet on each one. Place a kernel of maize on each letter. I then had them bring Tiberius and Caligula. Quick pecks by Tiberius, gobbling down the kernels of the letters constituting the augury. Caligula, blind in one eye, the kernels of the letters prophesying the opposite. Between the two they always arrive at the right answer. One or the other, alternately. The two of them together sometimes. They hit on the right answer every time. Much more precise, the instinct of my vultures, than the science of haruspices! Fed on Paraguayan maize, my vulture-graphologists write their predictions within a circle of earth. Unlike Caesar's crows, they do not need to write them in the heavens of the Roman Empire.

(In the margin, written in red ink)

N.B.! Reread the Contr'Un Part One: Prefaces on voluntary servitude. The first draft is probably somewhere in the Spirit of the Laws or The Prince. The thesis: The power of intelligence is limited to the understanding of that which is accessible to the senses. When it is necessary to reason, the people can only fumble about in darkness. Especially these sorcerer's apprentices. They water their malice with the filthy spray of their sneezes. My clerk in the soul branch the most dangerous one of all. Capable of stealthily lacing my orangeades and lemonades with arsenic or some other toxic substance. I'm going to grant him a new privilege. Proof of supreme confidence: From today on, he will be the official taster of my beverages.

Well then, Patiño, did you drop off to sleep? No, Excellency! I'm trying to discover whose handwriting it is. And did you manage to do so? To tell the truth, Sire, I have my suspicions, but no more than that. I can see that the more you doubt, the more you sweat it out. Take a close look at the anonymous writing just once less. Subtle attention, mind you, eh? What name does your memory call to mind? What face, you know-it-all seeing-with-my-own-eyes? What scriptuary features? Faint suggestion of a trembling of eyelids in a chimerical little slit in the protuberances. Tell me, Patiño . . . The entire person of the trust-unworthy scribe leans forward in its weighty carapace toward what he does not yet know that I am going to say. Hopeless hope of a commutation. Terror of the drunkard staring at the bottom of the empty bottle. Tell me, isn't the handwriting of the pasquinade mine? Dull thud of the magnifying glass falling on the paper. Waterspout rising from the basin. Impossible, Excellency! Not even if I were possessed with the madness of right reason could I think such a thing of our Karaí-Guasú! One must always keep all eventualities in mind, my dear secreting-secretary. The possible is a product of the impossible. Look here, underneath the watermark, the flourish of the initials. Aren't they mine? They are yours, Sire; you are quite right. The paper, the verjured initials as well. You see? Someone is dipping into the very coffers of the Treasury where I keep the pad of paper. Paper reserved for private communications with foreign personalities, that I haven't used for more than twenty years now. Agreed. But the handwriting. What have you to say about the handwriting? It looks as though it were yours, Excellency, but it's not yours exactly. What makes you say so? The ink is different, Sire. The only thing that's copied perfectly is the hand. The spirit is someone else's. Moreover, Excellency, nobody except an out-and-out enemy is going to threaten the Supreme Government and its servants with death. You've only half convinced me, Patiño. The bad thing, the very bad thing, the very serious thing, is that someone is able to break into the Coffers, to steal the quires of watermark. More unpardonable still is the fact that this *someone* is committing the rash misdeed of pawing through my Private Notebook. Writing on the folios. Correcting my notes. Jotting down injudicious judgments in the margin. Have the pasquinaders invaded my most arcane domains? Continue the search. For the time being we'll go on with the perpetual-circular. Meanwhile prepare to wield your pen with vigor. I want to hear it make the paper moan when I begin to dictate to you the Supreme Decree with which I shall correct the decretory mockery.

By the way, Patiño, how far have you gotten with that other investigation I ordered you to conduct? Of the penal colony of Tevegó, Sire? Here is the order, all drawn up, to the commandant of Villa Real de la Concepción to proceed to dismantle the penal colony. All it lacks is your signature, Sire. No, you clod! I'm not talking about that camp of stone ghosts. I ordered you to find out what priest it was I met up with on that evening of the storm when I fell off my horse. Yes, Sire. There was no priest who was bringing the viaticum that evening. There wasn't anybody who was dying. I made absolutely certain. As regards this subject, or this great to-do, as you would put it, Sire, there were only the vaguest of romurs. The word is rumors, you rummy. Right, Sire. Malicious rumors, gossip, stories, stemming from the house of the Carísimos because of its hatred of the Government, so as to prove that your fall was a punishment from God. There was even a cheap pamphlet sneak-snaking about spreading that rumor among those with evil tongues. Your Excellency has the entire preliminary inquiry here in this dossier. You read it on your return from the Hospital Barracks. Would you care to read it again, Sire? No.

We're not going to waste more time on tittle-tattle that gossip-mongering scribes will continue to repeat in minute detail down through the ages.

So they're the ones, are they, who are going to defend the truth by means of poems, novels, fables, libels, satires, diatribes? What merit is there in that? Repeating what others said and wrote. Priapus, that wooden god of antiquity, contrived to remember a few Greek words he had heard his master utter as he was reading in his shadow. Lucian's cock, two thousand years later, contrived to speak by dint of keeping company with human beings. He had as lively an imagination as they did. If only writers could master the art of imitating animals! Hero, the dog belonging to the last Spanish governor, had more of a way with words than the best of the areopagites, despite the fact that he was a spic and a royalist. My ignorant and untutored Sultan acquired as much wisdom as King Solomon after his death, if not more.

The parrot I gave the Robertsons recited the Pater Noster in Bishop Panés's own voice. Indeed, better, much better, than the bishop, that parakeet. Clearer diction, without the showers of spit. That clever bird had the advantage of possessing a dry tongue. A more sincere intonation than the hypocritical mumble-jumble of clericletes. A pure animal, the parrot parrots the language invented by men without realizing it. Above all, without any utilitarian interest in mind. Swinging freely back and forth in its hoop, despite its domestic captivity, it preached a living language that the dead language of writers imprisoned in the coffin-cages of their books is incapable of imitating.

There were eras in the history of humanity in which the writer was a sacred person. He wrote sacred books. Universal books. Codes. The epic. Oracles. Cryptic inscriptions on the walls of caves; maxims, on the porticos of temples. Not revolting pasquinades. But in those times the writer was not a single individual; he was a people. He transmitted his mysteries from age to age. Thus it was that the Ancient Books were written. Ever new. Ever timely. Ever future.

Books have a destiny, though destiny has no book. Without the people from which they had been cut off by sign and story even the prophets would not have been able to write the Bible. The Greek people called Homer composed the Iliad. The Egyptians and the Chinese dictated their histories to scribes who dreamed of being the people, not copyists who sneezed the way you do on what you've written. A Homer-people creates a novel. Presents it as such. As such it was received. No one doubts that Troy and Agamemnon existed, in the same way as the Golden Fleece, the Candiré of Peru, the Land-without-Evil and the Radiant-City of our indigenous legends.

Cervantes, one-armed, writes his great novel with his missing hand. Who could maintain that the Gaunt Knight in the Green Greatcoat is less real than the author himself? Who could deny that his fat secretary-squire is less real than you; mounted on his mule, plodding along behind his master's old nag, more real than you mounted on the basin, awkwardly bridling your goose quill?

Two hundred years later, the witnesses of those stories are no longer alive. Two hundred years younger, readers do not know if they are fables, true stories, pretended truths. The same thing will come to pass with us. We too will pass for real-unreal beings. And having reached that pass, we shall go no farther. And a good thing it is too, Excellency!

In every country that considers itself civilized, there ought to be laws such as the ones I have established in Paraguay against penpushers of every breed. Corrupted corrupters. Vagrants. Scroungers. Ruffians, cheats and crooks of the written word. The worst poison that peoples suffer from would thereby be eradicated.

"The atrabilious Dictator has a stock of notebooks filled with clauses and conceits that he has lifted from good books. When he has an urgent need to draft a text, he goes through them. He selects the mottoes and maxims that to his mind are most effective, and proceeds to scatter them about here and there, regardless of whether or not they are à propos. All his efforts are concentrated on good style. Of good panegyrics he memorizes the rhetorical closes that most impress him. He takes dictionary in hand to vary the words. He never works on anything without it. The History of the Romans and the Letters of Louis XIV are the diurnal from which he prays each day. He has now taken to studying English with his associate Robertson in order to take advantage of the good books that the latter possesses and has collected for him in London and Buenos Aires through his associates.

"One other thing, Rev. Father, with regard to the pretended phobia that the Great Cancerberus gives every sign of having against writers, the product, doubtless, of the envy and the resentment of this man who feels the urge to be a Caesar and a Phoenix of Wit, and whose brain has been anemified by the melancholy from which he suffers.

"See, Brother Bel-Asshole, if you don't find this a most amusing story! As Your Mercy no doubt already knows, our Great Man disappears now and again for periodic confinements. He cloisters himself for months at a time in his quarters in the Hospital Barracks, making sure that the word of his retreat gets round through the use of the method of the official rumor, in other words the open State secret, so as to devote himself to the study of the projects and plans that his feverish imagination claims to have conceived in order to place Paraguay at the head of the American states. The rumor has leaked out, however, that these withdrawals to his *hortus conclusus* are for the purpose of writing a novel imitating the Quixote, for which he feels a fascinated admiration. To our novelist Dictator's misfortune, he is not missing an arm like Cervantes, who lost it in the glorious battle of Lepanto, and at the same time he is more than lacking in brains and wit.

"Other credible versions of these periodic disappearances allow one to presume that they are owed, rather, to the furtive journeys that the illustrious Misogynist makes to the houses of numerous concubines who reside in the country, with whom he has had more than five hundred natural children, having thereby pushed his record beyond that of Don Domingo Martínez de Irala and other of our no less prolific founding fathers.

"My informants have also spoken to me of one of these concubines, an apostate ex nun who is said to be his favorite. They say that this doubly impure and sacrilegious courtesan lives in a country house between the villages of Pirayú and Cerro-León. Thus far, however, no one has managed to see the Dictator's private hothouse, since it is protected on all sides by tall fences and hedges of poppies, as well as by numerous pickets of guards. The Great Man has floated the rumor that that is where he has established his artillery park.

"Publish your Proclamation to our compatriots, Rev. Father. It may come to be a true Gospel for the liberation of our countrymen from the gloomy despot to whom Your Mercy has the misfortune of being very closely related. What I set down on this paper are naked truths, which he cannot deny. He is a hotheaded man, who lays about with everything he can put his hands on in his accesses of fury. Do not fear him; it is by keeping far out of his reach that we can best combat him." *(Letter from Dr. V. Días de Ventura to Brother Mariano Ignacio Bel-Asshole.*[§]*)*

The writing mania appears to be the symptom of an uncontainable century. Outside of Paraguay, when has so much been written as in the days since the world has lain in perpetual convulsion? Not even the Romans in the period of their decadence. There is no more deadly merchandise than the books of these convulsionaries. There is no worse plague than the scribonic. Menders of lies and benders of truths. Lenders of their pens, the borrowed plumes of plebeian peacocks. When I think of this perverse fauna, I imagine a world in which men are born old. They shrink, they shrivel till they're small enough to put inside a bottle. They grow smaller still inside it, so that a person could eat ten Alexanders and twenty Caesars spread on a slice of bread or a chunk of manioc cake. My advantage is that I no longer need to eat and it matters not at all to me if I am eaten by these worms.

[§]El Supremo's nickname for Brother M. I. Velasco, one of his detractors, author of a *Proclamation of a Paraguayan to His Countrymen*, Buenos Aires, 1814.

(In the private notebook)

In the worst heat of the summer, I ordered the French Catalan Andreu-Legard brought from his dungeon to my chamber at siesta time. He made my difficult digestions more pleasant with his songs and amusing anecdotes. He helped me to take my rest, if only in sips. In five years he caught the knack of it and did his work quite efficiently, thereby paying for his meals as a prisoner without any great problems. An odd mixture of prisoner-transmigrant. Shut up in the Bastille as an agitator. On one occasion, the executioner's ax almost got him. During one siesta he showed me on the nape of his neck the scar of what might have been the fatal chop. After the storming on the fourteenth of July, he got out and participated in the Revolutionary Commune, under the direct command of Maximilien Robespierre; so at least he said or lied. A member of a section of Pikemen during the Jacobin dictatorship, he again fell in disgrace when the Incorruptible was put to death.

In prison he met and became a particularly good friend of the libertine marquis whom Napoleon had ordered arrested because of a clandestine pamphlet that the noble rakehell had circulated against the Great Man and his mistress Josephine de Beauharnais. Napoleon was the first consul. In that country they had no way of reining in the authors of pamphlets and pasquinades. There thus appeared, supposedly translated from the Hebrew, a Letter from the Devil to the Great Whore of Paris. The French Catalan assured me that although his licentious friend was not the author of this pamphlet, he deserved to be, since it was an extraordinarily corrosive one. To tell me that, to hear the ex sergeant of Pikemen, fichu comme l'as de pique, lancer des piques, was to make mention of the rope in the house of the hanged man. Tais-toi, canaille, eh! Mais non, Sire!, Legard exclaimed apologetically. I don't understand how that monstrous, sordid, fierce, evil sodomite of a friend of yours could be, as you maintain, a friend of the people and of Revolution. That is what he was, Excellency.

A revolutionary avant la lettre. Ooh la la, and what a forceful one! The most sincere conviction. Seven years before the Revolution he wrote the Dialogue between a Priest and a Dying Man, that I've just recited to Your Excellency. A year before the attack on the Bastille and in the eleventh year of his captivity, the marquis exclaims in other works of his: A Great Revolution is incubating in the country. It has grown weary of the crimes of our sovereigns, their cruelties, their profligacies, their stupidities. The people of France are revolted by despotism. The day is fast approaching when, in fury, it will break its chains. That day, France, a light will awaken you. You will see at your feet the criminals who are destroying you. You will know that a people is free only through the nature of its spirit, and can be led by no one save itself. Be that as it may, what you say strikes me as strange, Legard. There was not a single case of that sort here among the whoring oligarchons whom I was obliged to bastille. And the same goes both for the tonsured rabble and the milicasters, not to mention the cacographic bookshitters who considered themselves born of Minerva and were nothing but mongrels sired by Diogenes' dog and whelped by Erostratus' bitch. As for the great libertine, Excellency, his libertinage was more a profound task of moral liberation in all domains. In the Section of Pikemen, where his atheism brought him face to face with Robespierre. In the sessions of the Paris Commune. At the Convention. On the Hospital Commission. Even in the asylum where he was finally shut up. There you are! That licentious scoundrel was bound to end up in the madhouse! Consider the fact, however, Most Excellent Sire, that his most revolutionary political work dates from that period. His proclamation Sons of France: One last effort if you would be republicans! equals or may even surpass the Social Contract of the no less libertine Rousseau and the Utopia of Saint Thomas More. The Catalo-Frenchman disturbed my naps. He took his petty revenge with all the subtle little tricks of a man condemned to forced labor, scratching about in the sepulchral dirt of perfidy. When the marquis dies in 1814, the same year in which Your Excellency assumes Absolute Power, his holograph will is discovered among his papers in the hospice: Once it is filled in, my grave is to be sown with acorns, so that in time to come my tomb and the forest will be indistinguishable. In this way, my grave will disappear from the face of the earth, as I hope my memory will be erased from the minds of men; except for the small number of those whose wish it was to love me to the very last, and of whom I shall bear a tender memory to the tomb. His posthumous desire was not fulfilled. Nor was his outcry heard: I address myself only to those able to understand me! He lived in prison almost his entire life. Hidden away in a deep dungeon, he was strictly forbidden, by decree, the use of pencils, ink, pen, charcoal, and paper, on any pretext whatsoever. Buried alive, he was forbidden to write, on pain of death. His corpse buried, he was denied the acorns that he had asked to have planted on his tomb. They were unable to erase his memory. Later on, the tomb was opened. A profanation more perfidious still, for it was a deed performed in the name of science. They made off with the skull. They did not find anything extraordinary, as Your Excellency tells me will be the case with your own. The cranium of the "degenerate of sad renown" was of harmonious proportions, "as small as though it were a woman's." The zones that indicate maternal tenderness, love of children, were as evident as on the skull of Héloise, who was a model of tenderness and love. This ultimate enigma, following upon the others, constituted one last challenge laid down to his contemporaries. It piqued their curiosity, aroused their execration. And perhaps led them on to his final glorification. The requiem did not succeed in dimming my light enough for a good long rest. The Catalo-Frenchy knew from A to Z no less than twenty of the works of the raving pornographer, since he had served him for many years as a repository of memory; something like the listening-flowerpots that I fashion with the china clay of Tobatí and the resins of the Tree-of-the-Word. One scratches the thin little hymen-optera membrane; the needle of sardonyx and chrysoberyl awakens, sets in movement once again, sends flying out in countermovement, the words, the sounds, the faintest sigh imprisoned in the little cells and nervous membrances of the speaking-listening vessels, since the sound falls silent but does not disappear. It is there. One searches for it and it is there. It buzzes down below itself, stuck to the ribbon that is sticky with wax and wild resins. I have more than a hundred of these jars full of secrets, jealously guarded in the treasury. Forgotten conversations. Softest whimpers. Martial sounds. Exquisite moans. The mortal voice of the tortured amid the crack of whips. Confessions. Prayers. Insults. Rifle reports. Discharges of executions.

The Catalo-Gaul was of the same race as these talking-crocks. He came to my room every siesta, summer and winter, the only two seasons in Paraguay. Here he is now. Take off his shackles. The creaking of the chains made him self-absorbed, tense. He didn't begin immediately, as though it cost him an effort to unhandcuff his tongue. Come on, talk, sing, tell a story! Let's see if I can get to sleep, if you can put me to sleep. He came out with a murmur first; a certain very soft twang, half-closing his slate-green eyes. He generally started the session with one of the marquis's lascivious deliria. Ordeals of a he-goat. The faunesque satyr attacks the sex of the universe. But the din of his battering-ram, the clamor of his orgasm, is no louder than the buzzing of a fly. The incommensurable fury of lust groans, cries out, insults, implores the barren divinities, in a fly's voice. Rage of exhaustion. It appears to fill the heavens and fits in the palm of one hand. The tremendous volcano does not pour forth a single drop of its burning lava. The sails of dreams lie limp, without the breath of a breeze to swell them. Enough!

The prisoner changes theme, voice, intentions. Vast repertory. Encyclopedia of rapes, hyperbolic obscenities. He knows by heart not only these endless, mendacious, vain, profane stories, full of bad habits and vices, written by the marquis. Composed, moreover, with greater force than Holy Scripture as regards the signs, albeit weak and imponent as regards their object; so that they engender yet more avidity through the simulacrum of satiety. What is it that this turgid sodomite, this saturnal uranist is searching for? A she-God in whom to surfeit his sterile desperation? There was once, here in Paraguay, a mulatta named Erótida Blanco, belonging to the Blanco Encalada y Balmaceda de Ruy Díaz de Guzmán family. Capable of satisfying a whole regiment. Napoleon's entire army perhaps; the infernal marquis in the Bastille. Certainly not! Erótida Blanco needed a virgin forest, a cordillera, so as to copulate with a thousand, with a hundred thousand shaggy fauns at once. Enough of these profanities!

In the cells of his memory, fortunately, other voices, other stories are stored away. The palato-nasal voice began to hum the dirges of the Genevan: Man, Great Man, Supreme Man, lock up your existence within you! Remain in the place that nature assigned you in the chain of beings, and nothing can force you out of it. Do not rebel against the goad of necessity. Your power and your freedom extend as far as your natural forces. No farther. Whatever you do, your real authority will never surpass your real powers. The voice of the French-Catalan is beginning more and more to resemble that of the Genevan. Long-drawn-out r's in the philosophical tirades of the Contract, in the pedagogical harangues of the Emile. Nasals, panting-confidential in the prurient Confessions. Through the voice of Andreu-Legard, I see in compadre Rousseau an elderly child, a female male. Wasn't it he himself who spoke of a dwarf with two voices?: one, artificial, an old man's bass voice; the other piping, childlike. For that reason the dwarf always received visitors in his bed, so that they would not discover his double dolus, which is what I am doing at present underground.

I suffered a great deal, Excellency, before and after the Ninth of Thermidor, which corresponds to your Twenty-seventh of July; or perhaps to your inconsolable Twentieth of September, when everything comes to a stop round about Your Excellency. That is by no means the end of Francia however. History does not end on September 20, 1840. It might be said, rather, to begin there.

In France the Directorate is established on October 27, 1795. In 1797, Napoleon triumphs at Rivoli. The Second Directorate begins. Napoleon's expedition to Egypt. I get out, or am gotten out, of prison. I enroll as a private in the army of the Great Corsican. Palm trees are outlined against the skies of Egypt. Here too, against the burning blue Paraguayan sky. The great serpent of the Nile crawls at the feet of the pyramids. Here, the River-of-Crowns, at the foot of your chamber, Excellency. You're not getting me to sleep, Legard. What do you want me to tell you? I've been hearing the same thing from you for ten years now. Your broken old man's voice doesn't make you any younger. Let's see. Have a try with the cornucopia. Charles Legard clears his throat, tunes up his voice. To a rhythm of a habanera, such as are traditional in Bali, in Tanga-Nika, in the Spice Islands, he begins humming the Republican Calendar. Only then do I begin to grow a bit drowsy beneath a rain of garden produce, flowers, green vegetables, fruits of every sort, golden oranges, melodious melons, melonious melodies, seeds without equal, marvels of harvests. All the phases of the year, the months, the weeks, the days, the hours. All of nature with its genesic, elemental forces. The humanity of work and the work of sans-culotted humanity. Animals, stallions, mineral substances, asses and mares, horses and cows, winds and clouds, he-mules and she-mules, fire and birds, their fertilizing excrement, germinations, floreal, fructidoral, messidoral, prairial harvests descend upon me, like a fresh dew, from this horn of plenty fashioned by Fabre d'Églantine. The Festival of Virtue began to make me drop off to sleep on the seventeenth of September, a drowsy half-sleep that the Festival of Genius abruptly interrupted on the eighteenth. I sensed that I snored a bit during the Festival of Work, on the nineteenth. The Festival of Judgment, which coincided with my death or perhaps provoked it on the twentieth of September, roused me from my slumbers on the twenty-first, for the Festival of Recompense.

I can't offer you yours, Charles Legard. You sang badly. You didn't get the best out of the Horn. Perhaps the resonances of your solos have scratched it, cracked it, ruined it, betrayed it. When I am about to drop off to sleep the tip of the horn tears the membrane of sleep. I open my eyes. I observe you. Your finger gesticulates to the sound of the barbarous strains of hunters, not of tillers of the soil. I sit up. I chase you out. Do you wish to leave the country? You have twenty-four hours to do so. If you are one minute late, only part of you will make the journey. Your head will be placed on a pike in the Plaza de Marte as a lesson to those who allow themselves to make mock of the Supreme Government and do their work badly. Your memory has been the end of you, Charles Andreu-Legard. Your good memory. Your terrible memory. Goodbye and good luck!

He left with the Rengger and Longchamp pair, along with other foolhardy Frenchmen I was keeping on tap in my prison cells. I let them go because I was tired of them; they could pipe their horns elsewhere. In my time outside of time, the Republican Calendar of France was no longer of any use to me. I let the Catalan-Frenchman go without regrets. I never had any further definitive news of this errant adventurer. Vague reports reached me that he went on the rocks in La Bajada; others, that he is teaching Guaraní in a University in France.

The story of the libertine marquis of the Bastille, later transferred to Charenton Asylum, the story of his stories as told by Legard, calls to mind that of another degenerate of sad renown: the laughable Marquis de Guarany. Yet another proof of the outrageous falsehoods, wicked tricks, and diabolical machinations that Europeans and Spaniards employ to deceive, to conceal their frauds, and attempt to diminish the dignity of these peoples, the majesty of this Republic. It was in that spirit that they thought up the monstrous, or rather the ridiculous hoax of the bogus Marquis de Guarany. It is a well-known fact in Europe and America that this Hispano-European adventurer, on turning up in Spain, passed himself off as an envoy sent by this Government to the monarch of that country. The imagination lacks the instinct of imitation, whereas the imitator totally lacks the instinct of imagination. Hence the fiction and the gross lie of the impostor were soon discovered. An authority no less than the Tribunal of Magistrates of the Bourbonic court found itself obliged to pass a death sentence against this insolent trickster, which in the end was to be carried out only if he attempted to escape from the exile to which he was condemned.

Great was the damage done, however, by this cunning adventurer, to the discredit of the name of this country and the prestige of its Government. This Catalan scoundrel, who had lived in South America but never set foot in this country, claimed that his name was José Agustín Fort Yegros Cabot de Zuñiga Saavedra. Adorned with this glittering array of genteel names (the entire list of the illustrious founders of our fatherland!), he made his theatrical appearance at the Bourbonic court. He claimed he possessed an immense fortune and had donated more than two hundred thousand gold pesos to the Government of Paraguay. He arrived early in 1825, at the time when Simón Bolívar was still planning to attack Paraguay, believing that this other adventurer's scheme was also going to succeed. They had both been doomed to failure from the beginning of time. They did not know this.

From Badajoz he sent word to the court announcing that he was the bearer of a supposed commission from this Government, so important that if he were given the means he could ensure the Mother Country of the recovery of her former colonies. He demanded to deal directly with the king. The pretended powers with which he was invested allowed him, so the impostor affirmed, to stipulate in my name the following conditions: (1) Establishment in Paraguay of a government representing Spain; (2) Approval of the perfected Jesuit system holding sway (cursed wretches!) in this country already sufficiently exploited by more than a century of rule by cassocks; (3) That he, as supreme representative of the Perpetual Dictator, in his capacity as eldest-born of the House of Guarany and colonel of the Voluntary Legion of Paraguay, be placed at the head of the monarchical government of Spain with the title of viceroy; and (4) That if the king accepted these conditions, he would hand over to him twelve million duros from the public treasury of Paraguay.

Among the fictitious documents the scoundrel presented were the Declaration of Independence of Paraguay, and his appointment as supreme representative and ambassador, bearing my forged signature beneath the escutcheon with a fleur-de-lys, the Bourbonic emblem, rather than that with the palm, the olive, and the star which are those of the Republic. He cleverly saw to it that his retinue included a Yegros and a certain Brother Botelho, an honorary member of the Royal Academy of Proto-Medicine of Paraguay whom the rascal proposed as chargé d'affaires. It was all a tissue of falsehoods and falsifications. Still not satisfied even with all that, he claimed into the bargain that I had been thrown out of the Government by the Legion he commanded and been sent into exile, rowing a boat in perpetuity up and down the marshlands of Villa del Pilar de Ñeembukú.

When his villainy was discovered, the president of the Tribunal of Magistrates of Madrid decreed that he be given two hundred lashes and paraded through the streets on a donkey. The king, taken in by this farceur yet still hoping for some unforeseen turn of the cards, commuted his sentence to ten years in prison. Then another New World scoundrel, Pazos Kanki, took it upon himself to spread the story of the Spaniard's bold trick that hadn't come off. The more idiotic stories are, the more readily they are believed. The legend of the Marquis de Guarany spread throughout Europe. It crossed over to the New World. There are people who still believe it and write about it. Idiocy has no limits, above all when it goes stumbling about through the narrow corridors of the human mind.

(Perpetual circular)

The pasquinaders consider it beneath my dignity to watch tirelessly as I do over the dignity of the Republic in order to safeguard it against those eager to wreak its downfall. Foreign states. Rapacious governments, insatiable grabbers of what belongs to others. Their perfidy and bad faith have long been well known to me. It matters not whether they call themselves the Empire of Portugal or of Brazil, with their marauding hordes of mamelucos, of bands of Paulista bandeirantes whom I contained and prevented from continuing their banditing brigandage in the territories of the Fatherland. Certain of you were witnesses, you will remember, you will doubtless have heard, how the invaders struck like lightning, burning down towns, robbing people, stealing cattle. Thousands of natives were carried off as prisoners. Concerning the relations of our Republic with the Empire; concerning its underhanded machinations, snares, ruses, and wicked deeds, before and after our Independence, I will instruct you in greater detail as I return periodically to this circular.

The Pantagruelian empire of insatiable voracity dreams of devouring Paraguay as if it were a tender lamb. It will swallow up the entire Continent some day if we don't watch out. It has already robbed us of thousands of square leagues of territory, the headwaters of our rivers, the falls of our streams, the heights of our sierras lopped off with the jagged saw of boundary treaties. Thus were kings and viceroys of Spain gulled by bad governors whose women led them around by their trousers fly and whose deals both over and under the table led them around by their pursestrings. The empire of the slave-trading bandeiras invented the system of boundary markers that slither about from place to place like an immense writhing boa.

Another scapegrace–scapegoat enemy: the Banda Oriental.§ Its bands

§The Eastern Shore (of the Uruguay River). Long a bone of contention of the powers in the Plata region, it finally achieved its independence as the Republic of Uruguay.

of outlaws were the ones who helped make the shipping blockade even tighter. I have one of its principal corporals here, in safe keeping. José Gervasio Artigas, who insisted on being called the Protector of Free Peoples, threatened each day to invade Paraguay. To bring it down in fire and blood. To carry off my head at the end of a pike. When Artigas, betrayed in his turn by his lieutenant Ramírez, who rose up against him with his troops and his money, had lost everything, even the clothes on his back, he sought refuge in Paraguay. My alternative extortioner, my sworn enemy, the promoter of conspiracies against my government had the audacity to beg me for asylum. I accorded him humanitarian treatment. In a situation such as mine, the most magnanimous of governors would have turned a deaf ear to the pleas of this barbarian whose merits were such that he deserved not compassion but chastisement. I burst with generosity. Not only did I admit him and the remainder of his men. I also spent, with a liberal hand, hundreds of pesos to help him, maintain him, clothe him, for he arrived naked, with no other garment or equipment save a red coat and an empty knapsack. None of the miserable, addle-brained rebels who had placed their greatest hopes of advantages and advancements in him offered him the least charity. I gave him what he requested of me in the letter he wrote me from the gateway of San Miguel, already inside our borders.

Artigas's letter was sincere.* He was not lying when he spoke of the war against Spaniards, Brazilian-Portuguese, and Porteños. I did not fail to take this into account. If deviations in the defense of a just cause condemn many, the principles, the visionary aims of that cause contribute to redeeming, if only partially, the errant whose errors do not stem from arrogance. Plunged headlong into such anguish, such workings of fate, Artigas was a sobering example for the dupes, the rebels, those souls whose depraved ambition was to subjugate Paraguayans and impose their laws on them, to wrest away their riches, and finally to take enslaved people into

---

*"Disillusioned by the defections and acts of ingratitude of which I have been the victim, I ask you only for a wildwood where I may live. I will thus count among my laurels my having been wise enough to choose for my safe refuge the best and finest part of this Continent, the First Republic of the South, Paraguay. An ambition identical to your own, Most Excellent Sire, that of forging the independence of my country, was the cause that led me to rebel, to endure bloody battles against Spanish power, and then against Portuguese and Porteños endeavoring to subject us to a more iniquitous slavery still. A battle without respite that has cost many a long year of hardships and sacrifices. Despite everything, I would have continued to defend my patriotic aims had the seeds of anarchy not fallen on the hearts of the men under my command. They betrayed me because I refused to sell the rich patrimony of my countrymen at a sacrifice price." (Letter from General Artigas to El Supremo, seeking asylum, September, 1820.)

their service and their manufactories, so as then to laugh at Paraguay and make scornful mock of Paraguayans from the lofty heights of their pride.

I sent a detachment of twenty hussars under the command of an officer to meet Artigas. I granted him humanitarian, Christian treatment, in the true sense of the word. Granting exile to a leader in the depths of misfortune who has offered his surrender is an act not only of humanity but also one honoring the Republic. I had lodgings made ready for him in the convent of La Merced and ordered that he engage in spiritual exercises and make confession each day. I respect the opinion of others, and even though it is quite true that priests are good for next to nothing, they can at least serve to sound the sinful cares that weigh on foreigners' souls. I then granted the Oriental leader the plot of woodland he asked me for in order to go on living: not a laurel wood but one of the best plots of public land, in Villa del Kuruguaty, on which to build his house and lay out his farm, far out of his enemies' reach.

Artigas's treacherous and perfidious lieutenant insistently demanded that I hand him over to be publicly tried by the federated provinces on the charges that should rightfully be brought against him, the cynical brigand wrote me, seeing in Artigas the cause and origin of all the ills of South America. As I did not answer any of his notes, he threatened to invade Paraguay if I didn't turn his ex leader over to him. Very well then, I said, let the Supreme Savage of Entre Ríos come. He never made it. His head ended up in the cage that fate had readied for him.

Eighty leagues north of Asunción, entirely unaware of the dangers he is running, the ex Supreme Protector of the Banda Oriental works the earth that he swore to turn into untilled soil, a heap of ruins. Just look at him watering it with the sweat of his brow, rather than with the blood of its inhabitants. Today he fervently assures me of his eternal gratitude and loyalty. He praises me as the best and most just of men. The opposite of that most perverse bunch of Porteño leaders, the Rivadavias, the Alvears, the Puigrredones.

The Hydra of the Plata is in fact the only one still stubbornly bent on taking over Paraguay. Destroying it, mutilating it, cutting it off, since it has not succeeded in annexing it to the group of poor provinces being squeezed to death in its tentacles.

Period for today. It will take those saphead satraps months to read the installments of the circular if they're crammed too full of facts. They'll have an excuse now to abandon their assigned tasks altogether and devote all their time to working corks out of bottle necks.

In the fort of Buenos Aires, the new viceroy, Baltasar Hidalgo de Cisneros, readies cannons and boarding axes, no doubt believing himself still the vice-admiral of the Invincible Armada heading for the final disaster of Trafalgar. After the fort was bastilled . . . *(pages missing)*.

Here in Asunción the royalist acolytes, the Porteños disguised as Bourbonarians, Spaniards, Porteñistas prowl round the deafness of Governor Velazco. Steal into his ear trumpet. Come out through the other ear prophesying disaster. The first English invasion of Buenos Aires and the flight of Sobremonte, the viceroy, bring on a leakage of the brain that half closes his left eye. The second one, with the naming of Liniers the Frenchy as interim viceroy, makes the corners of his mouth go rigid. The captain of militias said to be my father transports barrels of wasp honey, tons of royal jelly on gun carriages to the residence of the half-deaf and half-mute governor to lubricate his larynx. Then there's the substance that the Indians of Xexuí extract from cedar, the resin of the Sacred-Tree-of-the-Word. But none of all this does any good. The aphonic governor keeps constantly chewing and swallowing these materials, which come winding out his mouth in fancy flounces and furbelows of every color as the servants watch.

The viceroy sending urgent dispatches from Buenos Aires. What's going on there? Have you all been struck dumb? Or have the Comuneros come back? The scribes waiting in the governor's study, trousers flies bulging, pens at the ready. Your father, one of those faithless-scribes, used to come to tell me the tangled plot of all the intrigues that were woven in this very place back in those days.

That morning Governor Bernardo de Velazco y Huidrobo, in an access of rage, threw out all the healers, friars, desempayenadores§ that his nephew brought to the palace in a steady procession. He dashed out into the courtyard. He spent the entire morning there on all fours, eating grass, between the gray ass and the cow of the Manger, in the place where the

§Derived from *payé*, the priest and sorcerer of the ancient Guaranís: those who undo evil spells.

governor traditionally had Nativities staged au naturel. Following along-side his master, the governor's dog Hero also pulled up weeds, cropped the grass, snapped off flowers in the flowerbeds with his teeth, in that delirium which for both was a battle against the spirits of evil. The horde of relations, servants, functionaries cautiously stole back to watch the gover-nor graze, their eyes brimming with tears. Gorged with grass, he finally rises to his feet. He goes over to the cistern. He leans over the rim. Hero abandons his florid battle. He leaps upon the governor and holds him back by the skirts of his heavy frock coat, finally tearing it off him altogether. He returns to the attack. He pulls on the seat of his breeches, baring Don Bernardo's buttocks. He leans farther and farther over the rim. My father thought, Sire, that the governor was no doubt praying for help to the soul of the Theatine who had died in the tank, many long years before, when this was still the House of the Spiritual Exercises of the Jesuits. Your father was misinformed. It was not the Theatines who erected this building. It was Governor Morphi, known as The Earless. The barber had cut off one of his ears with his razor. I beg your pardon, your mercy, the barber is said to have said to the governor. You had a fly on your ear, Most Exc. Sire. It's gone now.

The building as well was left without ears. Power of the flies. Through the hands of a barber they lop off the false handle of a governor's head. They reduce an unfinished building to brand-new ruins. Hey, Patiño, remove that fly that's fallen into the inkwell. Not with your fingers, you animal! With the tip of your pen. The way you do when you ream out your nasal fossae. Take it easy! Without spattering the papers. Done, Sire; although I take the liberty of telling you that there was no fly in the inkwell. Don't argue about truths you aren't able to see. There's always one buzzing round my ear. And then it turns up drowned in the inkwell.

The construction of the building, the roof in place, the window and door frames, walls three varas above the ground, continued in the days of the governor Pedro Melo de Portugal, who inaugurated it by pompously naming it Melody Palace, like the other melodious towns founded under his governorship on the left bank of the river. Outposts against sneak attacks by the Indians of the Chaco.

As a little boy, I used to steal into the excavation sites where they were throwing up earthen embankments against the torrents of rain, against surprise raids. I didn't yet know that I was going to enter this House and dwell in it forever. Orders and counterorders went round and round in my child's mind. I would give the workers instructions. Even the construc-tion foreman. Extend that ditch to the cliff edge. Raise that wall, bring that one a little farther in. Dig the foundations deeper. And how about filling the trenches with salt instead of sand? They appeared to pay heed to my advice, for they complied with the orders that silently issued forth from me. The tips of the picks, of the shovels, of the hoes brought to light vessels, utensils, coffers, pieces of armor, bits of bone. One morning the construction foreman, Cantalicio Cristaldo, the father of our drum major, unearthed a skull. Run off home, you son of a she-devil!, I kept insisting. Asking without asking. Mute presence. Arms crossed. Heedless of the flying dirt, the shovelfuls of earth of the diggers who were burying me little by little. Finally the skull sailed over the mounds. I caught it on the fly and put it under my altar boy's hood. Patch of red taking off into the darkness. The skull, the one that's right here. The whole earth inside of it. Impossible for there to have been room for it in the earth. A world within the world! I ran breathlessly, carrying it under my arm. Each heartbeat became two beats. Slow down a bit, don't squeeze me so!, the skull complained. How did you come to be buried here? Against my will, my boy; you may be sure of that. Here in the trenches of Government House, I mean. One is always buried somewhere after one is dead. I assure you one isn't even aware of it. What did the one who carried you on his shoulders die of? Of being born of his mother, my boy. What sort of death, I'm asking. A natural death; how else? Do you know of any other sort of death? They beheaded me because I tried to do the governor in with a shot from my blunderbuss. All because I didn't follow my mother's advice. Don't cross the sea, my boy. Don't go to the Conquest. Gold fever is dangerous. The day I left, with glassy eyes, she said to me: When you're in bed and hear dogs barking in the countryside, hide under the coverlet. Don't take what they're doing lightly. Mother, I said to her as I kissed her goodbye, there are no dogs there and no coverlets. There will be, my son, there will be. Desire exists everywhere, it barks everywhere, covers everything. And so you are now taking me under your arm to resurrection after insurrection. No, to a cave, I said to it. We were crossing the Indian cemetery of the Cathedral. What, my altar lad, you're going to bury me in sacred ground now after so many centuries? There's no need for that; don't play tricks on our Holy Mother the Church. Shhh. I muffled its voice beneath the hood. Two gravediggers were digging a grave. Is that hole for me?, he murmured again. Did you take me out of one just to put me in another? Don't worry, it's not for you; it's for a very important personage they hanged at dawn this morning. You see, my son? The sad thing about it is that in this world the powerful have the ability to hang or be hanged as they choose. Let me have a peek at the work those rustics are doing. I stopped and opened my smock a little just to please him. They're digging, he said. What's certain is that there are no gentlemen of more ancient lineage than gardeners, ditchers, grave-makers; in other words, those who engage in Adam's occupation. Was Adam a gentleman?, I asked jokingly. He was the first that ever bore arms, the skull answered in a clown's voice. What do you mean? He was never armed. He neither inherited arms nor bought them! What's that you're saying? An altar boy and a heretic? Haven't you read Holy Scripture? It says somewhere: Adam delved. How could he have delved if he didn't have arms? I'm going to put another riddle to you: Who is it builds more solidly than the stonemason? The gallows-maker. For a kid like you, that's not a bad answer. But if you're ever asked the question again, say: a grave-maker. The houses that he makes last till Doomsday.

Aren't you copying down what I'm dictating to you? I'm enjoying so much hearing you tell this droll story of the talking skull, Sire. I've never heard a more amusing one in my life! I'll copy the text about the gravediggers later, Sire; it's almost the same, word for word, as what happened in the one Juan Robertson translated in his English classes. Don't copy what's told by others; copy what I tell myself through others. Facts can't be recounted; much less twice over, and far less still by different persons. I've already drummed that thoroughly into your head. What happens is that your wretched memory remembers the words and forgets what's behind them.

For months I washed the oxiflowered skull in a cave by the river. The water turned redder still. It overflowed its banks in the flood of the year '70 which nearly carried off the melodious palace of Don Melo. When I came to occupy this house on receiving the Perpetual Dictatorship, I did it over, completed it. Cleaned the vermin out of it. Reconstructed it, embellished it, dignified it, as befits the seat that is to house a head of government elected by the people for life. I enlarged its dependencies and had them arranged differently, so that the principal departments of the State would be located within Government House. I had the old forked beams of urundey wood replaced with squared stone pillars. The overhanging roofs of the porches extended, and carved wooden benches placed beneath them; a seat and place that since then has been filled each morning with the multitude of functionaries, officials, couriers, soldiers, musicians, sailors, stonemasons, carters, farm laborers, free peasants, craftsmen, smiths, tailors, silversmiths, cobblers, shipwrights, overseers of patrial ranches and farms, Indian corregidors of villages bearing their staffs of office, freed black slaves, chiefs of the twelve tribes, washerwomen, seamstresses. The hordes of people who come all the way here to have audience with me. Each one assumes his rightful place in the presence of The Supreme, who grants no one precedence or special privilege.

The last time I had Government House redone was when I installed the meteor in my study. It refused to go through the door. One cannot expect good manners of a chance-stone from the moment it appears on the scene. It was necessary to knock out two pillars, one wall panel. Finally the aerolith took its place in the corner. Not willingly. Vanquished, a prisoner, chained to my chair. Year 1819. The great sedition was being hatched.

I filled in the cistern. If the Theatine father, the governor's chaplain or whoever it was, really threw himself into it, this must have happened in the days when the Jesuits were being cleared out of the country in 1767, so as to escape the decree that struck the fathers of the Company like a bolt of lightning, not giving them time to say either Jesus or Amen.

The mistake regarding the origin of the House of Governors as a House of Spiritual Exercises arose from the fact that the edifice was constructed with materials that were listed in the general inventory of goods belonging to those expelled, under the rubric of Royal Confiscation. So as you see, Patiño, in those days it was kings who collected a ransom from their victims. Terrorists by Divine Right.

The governors Carlos Morphi, called the Irishman, the Infamous, and also the Earless on account of the fly; and then Agustín de Pinedo; and then Pedro Melo de Portugal; all of them occupied it in that belief, even though while they were in it they did not devote themselves exclusively to spiritual exercises for the salvation of their souls.

Cause of the misapprehension: the cistern. Cretins! Nobody throws himself into a cistern in order to come out on the other side of the earth. I ordered the rim to be transported to the bishop's residence. Its iron ornament in the form of a miter, intended to hold up the pulley, delighted the bishop. But that morning Governor Velazco was still there. Leaning over the rim. His head stuck in the Mudejar arch, in place of the pulley. Lamentations, prayers of those contemplating the scene, hoping in the bottom of their hearts that the governor would throw himself to the bottom of the cistern and be done with it. Your father told me that he heard the adviser Pedro de Somellera y Alacántara mutter: Giddap there, Deaf Nell! Throw yourself into the well before it's too late!

Clutching his belly, the governor made the sign of the cross with his head. Hero had his paws around him from behind. Don Bernardo opened his mouth, trying his best to come out with the shout that wouldn't come out. What came was the big breakfast he'd eaten. The hoarse Aves, Salves, murmurs suddenly ceased. The curious vanished into the woodwork. Calmed at last, the governor returned to his study. He began to dictate a dispatch to the viceroy.

Certain malicious lies are circulating which cloud the minds of the stupid populace, so as to incline it to credulity and incite it to disobedience; rumors so absurd that they cannot make the slightest impression upon rational minds, whereas they fatally excite the bestial plebs, so that for the moment it is not possible to disabuse them. The patricians and my faithful vassals support me, are wholeheartedly behind our cause. Though I have been and shall be most zealous in my efforts to inquire into anything that may lead to the discovery of the instigator or instigators of such agitations —perhaps by turning up a letter or by virtue of some other expedient at which my aides are most expert, in particular my adviser, the Porteño Pedro de Somellera—as yet I have succeeded only in hearing stories that are widespread among the common folk, who are incapable of explaining where or how they have come by them.

Your father made a fair copy of this text that came close to braying or mooing, since that was all that Don Bernardo's voice could come out with. That afternoon he summoned me. Once we were alone in his study, he put his ear trumpet to my ear. The cavernous murmur spoke to me of those absurd rumors going the rounds among the plebs. An immense, powerful beast which must be tamed at all costs, Velazco said, even if it proves necessary to give them a taste of the cattle prod. Your uncle, Brother Mariano, very rightly advises me that it is dangerous to tell the people that the laws are not just, because it obeys them in the belief that they are just. It is necessary to tell the people that they are to be obeyed as one obeys one's superiors. Not only because they are just, but because they are superior. That is how all sedition may be averted. If it can be made to understand that, the bestial plebeity calms down, bows its head beneath the yoke. It does not matter that this is not just; it is the very definition of justice.

The power of those who govern, your uncle wisely assures me, is founded on ignorance, on the tameness and meekness of the people. Power has weakness as its foundation. This foundation is firm because its greatest security lies in the weakness of the people. Brother Mariano Ignacio, my esteemed Magistrate of the First Vote, is more than right. Consider an example, Your Grace, the governor-intendant went on trumpeting: the custom of seeing a government official accompanied by guards, drummers, officers, arms and other objects inspiring respect and fear causes his face, even if one sees it all alone, without any such escort, to inspire fear and respect in his subjects, because thought never separates his image from the cortege that ordinarily accompanies him. Our magistrates are thoroughly familiar with this mystery. All the pomp with which they surround themselves, the robes they wear, are most necessary to them; without them, their authority would be reduced to very nearly nothing. If doctors did not fill their satchels with potions and unguents, if priests did not wear cassocks, square bonnets, and long mantles, they would not have been able to delude everyone; in like manner, military officers with their dazzling uniforms, their gold braid, their dress swords, their spurs and gold buckles. Warriors shed their disguises only when they are really going off to war, bearing their arms. Fancy trappings are of no use on the battlefield. That is why our kings have not sought august adornments, but have instead surrounded themselves with guards and great ostentation. The phantom armies, the drummers who precede their cortgege, the legions that surround them make the most resolute cloaked-and-cowled conspirators tremble. It would take a very subtle mind to regard the Grand Turk guarded in his superb seraglio by forty thousand janissaries as a mere ordinary mortal. There is no doubt that when we see a barrister such as Yr. Grace in his biretta and gown, we immediately have a lofty idea of his person. Nonetheless, when I held the office of governor of Misiones, I went about all alone, without an escort, without guards. That is, I grant you, territory trod before me by the sons of Loyola, who in a hundred years managed to make of the natives a perfectly domesticated species. No José Gabriel Cóndor Kanki is going to emerge from among them. And if another Tupac Amaru were to rise up in rebellion in these lands, he would be overthrown and put to death once again, as happened in their own time to the rebel José de Antequera, the rebellious Inca, the rebels of all times and places.

Here in Asunción I took it as my rule of justice to follow tradition, with the greatest clemency possible. That is why they love and respect me. Indulgence is inherent in me. If I have not always found what is just, I at least slake my thirst in the fountain of a moderate justice. Don't you believe so, Yr. Worship? The ear-trumpet took on the form of a question mark before my eyes. I remained silent. The ear-trumpet buzzed again in Don Bernardo's mouth:

Yr. Grace, Magistrate of the First Vote, descendant of gentlemen of most ancient lineage and conquistadors of this Meridional America, as the reports on your genealogy read: of the men in this city the most conspicuous for your learning as for your zeal: you must know something about the prompters, the propagators of such absurd rumors. Tell me then, with all frankness, what you know about these specious stories. Looking him straight in the eye, I answered: If I didn't know I'd tell you, you old Bourbonian. But since I know, I won't tell you. That way we remain at peace. Nothing is changed. Neither delations nor delatations on this day of nothing and eve of much, for even though he who speaks is mad, he who listens should be sane. The ear-trumpet returned to the attack. As a worthy subject of our Sovereign you must do your part in maintaining order and harmony, public tranquillity in this province. Viceroy Cisneros has apprised me of the multitude of anonymous papers contrary to the cause of the King that are being sent from Buenos Aires to Asunción. A veritable deluge. I have ordered my adviser Somellera to investigate these subversive activities. May Yr. Grace in his capacity of Syndic-Procurator General help us.

The hint that he was dropping for me to become an informer rubbed my Eustachian tube the wrong way. I fell into a rage. I seized the ear-trumpet and stuck it in the governor's hairy ear. Heaven turns a deaf ear to the braying of bald ass!, I thundered. The governor gave a self-satisfied laugh. He withdrew his hand from my belly where he had placed it, as though to press me to cough up secrets and to stimulate evacuation. He gave me a familiar pat on the back. I knew that Yr. Worship would understand. I had no doubt that your help would be of great importance to me, my learned friend. Continue to offer it to me in honor of our beloved Sovereign. He who seeks with faith always finds, I said just to be saying something. And he, not so much in answer to the proverb as to make himself master of the situation, spread his broad velvet wing: From this cape nobody escapes! The ear-trumpet fell to the floor and disappeared amid the crisscrossing cracks. For a good while the two of us crawled about underneath the table, butting horns, heads, backsides in a sort of tauromachy on all fours. Finally, debonair, devil-may-care Hero triumphantly lifted the dripping ear-trumpet out of the spittoon and handed it to his master with a sweeping veronica.

Thus ended my last private interview with Governor Velazco, who was already on the eve of being dumped into the lonely well of dismissal.

What's that sound of a fanfare, Patiño? Your Excellency is returning from his afternoon outing. Hand me the spyglass. Throw the shutters wide open. Unfold all the tubes. Someone far in the distance is waving his arms. He's calling, shouting for help. It must be that mosquito that's stuck to the glass, Excellency. Clean it with the flannel cloth.

A sheet of quicksilver suddenly looms up. The bay, the port, the boats, thrown against the sky. The Ark of Paraguay in dry dock, almost ready to be launched. Who told you that the timbers were completely rotted? That is what the calkers, the shipwrights assured me, Sire; it's been left out in the sun, the rain, droughts for twenty years now. You're lying! The smell of hot tar, wafted this way on the north wind this very minute. The pounding of hammers. Tools ringing on the belly of the Ark. I am there directing the work, giving orders to my best shipfitters, Antonio Iturbe, Francisco Trujillo, the Italian Antonio de Lorenzo, the Indian craftsman Mateo Mboropí. I see the Ark, all red and blue. Its figurehead rends the clouds. It's real now, definite! Third reconstruction of the Ark of Paraguay. Done over, brought back to life three times. Do you see it too, Patiño? Absolutely, Sire. Where do you see it? Where Your Excellency does. Perhaps you're only trying to please me again, you base flatterer. If that were so, Excellency, the spyglass that Your Grace has before his eyes would be another base flatterer that shows you what doesn't exist.

When I succeed in reestablishing free navigation, the Ark of Paraguay will carry the flag of the Republic to sea on its topmast. Holds filled to the brim with the country's products. Look! It's sliding down the ways! It's afloat! It's afloat, Sire! Repeat it with all your strength.

oooooaaaaaat, Siiiiiiire

I see the cannons on deck. When were they installed? The cannons are on the cliff, Sire; they're the batteries defending the entrance to the port. But if the cannons aren't on the bridge of the Ark, Patiño, then the Ark isn't where it is either. No, Sire, the Ark is where Your Excellency sees it. Why has the sound of the work going on stopped all of a sudden? It was only the fanfare of the escort, Sire. That's the trouble, my dear secretary. I hear a very great silence. Order the commandants of barracks that from tomorrow on all the bands are to play once more without stopping from sunup to sundown. Your order will be executed, Excellency.

At the top of the cliff, within reach, the orange tree of the firing squads. Dry, twisted branches, the trunk nothing but a crust of ringworm.

Who is that sentry at the riverbank who's hung his carbine from one of the branches? That's the rifle, Sire, that's been stuck in the tree for a long time now. That idiot has hung his jacket, his shirt, his tie there to dry. What's the meaning of this act of indiscipline? Have him arrested. Tell the officer of the guard to put him in jail for a month on bread and water. He ought to take better care of his uniform. I can't manage to make that insouciant sentry out, Sire. I can't make out his clothes. That doesn't prove they haven't turned into a bunch of rags. Perhaps, Sire, the sentry is dressed in nothing but his birthday clothes. Give the order anyway.

(In the private notebook)

On the other side of the little Kará-Kará river, washerwomen are beating clothes on the shore. Youngsters are bathing naked. One of them looks this way. He raises his arm. He points to Government House. One of the women, crossing herself, pushes him in the water with a fillip of her finger. The black takes a ducking. The women are standing there motionless. Those people aren't fooled. They see me riding the bayard. They are not fooled. They know that this *I* is not the Supreme, whom they love-fear. Their love-fear lets them know it, while at the same time it obliges them not to know that they know it. Their fear is the only wisdom they have. To be nothing. To know nothing. Obscure sunflowers, their sorrow projects its shadow over the water. What do they know of cross-bones, of crosswords, of cross-bearing crusades. Volumes and volumes of ignorance and knowledge come out of their mouths in spirals of smoke. They are puffing immense cigars as they wield their paddles and scrub mountains of clothes white. They have laughed for months over the figurehead of the Ark that Mateo Mboropí carved in the form of a dog-viper head. If a headwind blows into the mouth, the painted monster barks with howls interrupted by fits of hoarse coughing. They laughed for years at that figure they didn't understand, at that lament they understood even less. Until nothing was left of the figurehead but a piece of jawbone.

They haven't laughed for a long time now. They know less than before. Their fear is greater. The washerwomen toss the name of a fantastic personage back and forth, from one shore to the other. Then they sing. Their songs reach me here. They come to spy, like the carrier pigeons I sent to the army. I am going, I say, to see. I am going, I say, to hear. One afternoon I went down to the river. I asked a washerwoman what she was laughing at. Her laughter turned to vast disbelief. She looked into my eyes, blinking in the face of the unknown, as though I myself had gone back to my childhood. What is the fish born of?, I ask her. Of a tiny spine that swims in the water, the woman says. What is the monkey born of?, I ask her. Of a coconut that flies through the air, she says. And the coconut tree then? The coconut tree is born of the fish, the monkey, and the coconut. What about us then? What are we born of? Of the man and the woman who took refuge in a very tall coconut tree during the Flood. That's what the Paí in the church says, Sire. But my mother was a top, on account of how sarakí she was, and my father the string that wound the top. When the two of them stopped moving I was born. That's what they say. But there's no way of knowing because the one who's born doesn't know he's being born and the one who dies doesn't know he's dying. Well put, I said and went off, leaving her laughing behind my back.

Had I been able to go down to the river this afternoon, I would have asked the washerwomen if they too saw the great flock of blind birds fall at five in the afternoon a month ago, three days after the storm. I would have asked them if they heard those birds that came from the north scream. Whatever for? They know nothing, they saw nothing, they heard nothing.

I'm not listening to the fanfare now. In seventeen minutes *He* will enter through that door. Then I will no longer be able to go on writing in secret.

The death's-head face watches me intently. It mimics my movements as I fight for breath. I dig my nails into my Adam's apple, clutch my trachea pumping emptiness. The mummy-faced specter does the same. It coughs. Its rude laughter hits me inside the top of my skull. It will go on watching me even though I manage to pay no attention to it. To ignore it. To shrug my shoulders. It shrugs its shoulders. I close my eyes. It closes its eyes. I pretend it isn't there. No; it hasn't gone away. It is watching me. Destroy it by hurling the inkwell at it. I grab the inkwell. It grabs the inkwell. Worse still if I manage to get there first. The skeletal old man would be pinned to the spot, multiplied, dancing in all the fragments of the mirror, of the circle of glass clouded with sweat. It wheels around toward the window bars. I lose sight of it. Out of the corner of my eye I see that it sees me. Monsters. Chimerical beasts. Being not of this world. They live clandestinely inside one. Sometimes they come out, standing slightly apart the better to spy on us. The better to cast their spell over us.

What do you see in that mirror? Nothing in particular, Excellency. Take a good look. Well, Sire, if I must tell you what I see, the same thing as always. The portrait of Señor Napoleon on the left. What else? The portrait of your compadre Franklin on the right. What else? The table full of papers. What else? The clipped-off tip of the aerolith with the candle-stick on top. Don't you see my face? No, Sire; only the debt's head. What debt's head? I mean the death's head that Your Excellency has always had on the table underneath the piece of red flannel. Turn around. Look at me.

Raise your head, raise those creeping eyes. When are you going to learn to look at what's right before your eyes? What do I look like to you? I always see Your Excellency in his dress uniform, his blue frock coat, his white cashmere breeches. Since he has just returned from his afternoon outing, he has on his cinnamon-colored riding pants, somewhat damp in the crotch from the horse's sweat. Tricorne. Patent leather pumps with gold buckles . . . I never wore gold buckles or anything else made of gold. Begging your pardon, Excellency, but everyone saw you and described you as looking like that, in that attire. Don Juan Robertson, for example, painted that image of Your Eminence. That's why I ordered you to burn the grotesque portrait painted by the Englishman in which he showed me in a very strange guise, a confused mixture of a monkey and a sulky girl, sucking on the immense sipper of a maté vessel that wasn't at all Paraguayan: and worse still, against a background representing a Hindu-stani or Tibetan landscape that in no way resembled our open countryside. I burned that portrait with my own hands, Excellency, and in its place I put up again, at your order, the portrait of Señor Napoleon, whose majestative figure is so like your own. I burned the portrait painted by the Englishman, but the papers we confiscated from him still exist. In them too Your Grace's likeness is portrayed. What likeness? The mien of our First Magistrate which the gringo comtemplated at the time of his first meeting with Your Worship on the farm at Ybyray. I turned round, the anglomane says word for word, and saw a gentleman dressed in black with a scarlet cape thrown over his shoulders. In one hand he was holding a maté-vessel of silver with a gold sipper of outsized dimensions, and in the other a cigar. He was carrying under his arm a book bound in cowhide with fittings of those same metals. A black youngster was standing waiting with folded arms alongside the gentleman. The face of the unknown . . . you see, Excellency, the gall of that gringo. Calling Your Mercy The Unknown! Go on, you knave, and kindly spare me your comments. The face of the unknown man was somber and his extremely piercing black eyes riveted themselves upon one with unswerving fixity. His jet-black hair combed back bared a proud forehead, and falling in natural curls round his shoulders, gave him an air at once dignified and imposing, a mixture of ferocity and kindliness; an air that drew one's attention and commanded respect. I glimpsed large gold buckles on his shoes. I repeat that I never wore gold buckles on my shoes or anything made of gold on any part of my dress. Another foreigner, Excellency, Don Juan Rengo, also saw you dressed in this fashion when with his companion and colleague Don Marcelino Lonchán, they arrived in this city on July 30, 1819, four years after the expulsion of the anglomanes. A striking figure, that of the

Supreme Dictator!, the Swiss surgeons write in Chapter VI, page 56 of
their book: That day he was wearing his regulation costume, a blue jacket
with gold braid, a mordoré cape over his shoulders, the uniform of a
Spanish brigadier . . . I never wore the uniform of a Spanish brigadier!
I would sooner have worn beggar's rags. I myself designed the attire
suitable for the Supreme Dictator. You are more than right, Excellency.
Those outlandishers, the dirty Swiss and the devilish Anglers, were very
ignorant men. They failed to realize that the uniform of our Supreme was
a uniform supreme and unique in this world. They saw only the mordoré
cape, the waistcoat, breeches and hose of white silk, the patent-leather
pumps with great gold buckles . . . Poor devils! They see in the buckles
of my shoes the insignia of my power. They can raise their sights no higher.
They see in those buckles marvelous things: Mercury's gold caduceus,
Aladdin's lamp. They could likewise paint me with the plumes of the
Bird-that-never-alights, enveloped in the cape of the Maccabee, scratching
the floor with the gold spurs of the Grand Vizier. Most assuredly, Most
Excellent Sire! That is what those outlandishers saw. How do you see me,
I'm asking you. I, Sire, see hanging from your shoulder the black cape with
the bright-red lining . . . No, you clod. What's hanging from my shoulder
is my bathrobe for the slumber of eternity fallen to tatters, the ragged
bathrobe that no longer hides the nakedness of my bones.

(In the private notebook)

The little black has floated back up to the surface, spitting out
mouthfuls of water. He bares his gleaming white teeth to the air. Great
racket among the flock of kids. The comadres go back to beating the
clothes and gossiping among themselves. Identical, the little black and the
slave José María Pilar. He was doubtless his same age when I bought him,
along with the two old slaves, Santa and Ana. I paid much less for them
in view of their advanced age and the running sores it brought on. The
old women mended and are alive. They are faithful to me in life and death.
Pilar the black, on the other hand, was unfaithful to me. I was obliged to
send him to the orange tree to cure him of his ladronicidal ills. Gunpowder
is always a good remedy for those whose ills are irremediable.
I, here, become a specter. Between black and white. Between grayness
and nothingness, seeing myself double in the trickery of the mirror. Those
who occupied themselves with the outward appearance of my person in
order to revile me or exalt me never managed to agree on the description
of my attire. Less still on that of my physical features. Not surprising, when

I don't even recognize myself in the half-breed specter looking at me! They were all held spellbound by the nonexistent gold buckles, which were just plain silver. The last pair I wore, before gout swelled my feet, I gave to the freed slave Macario, my godchild, son of my traitorous valet de chambre José María Pilar. The latter's posthumous desire was that the child be baptized Macario. I placed him in the care of the slave women. He crawled about among the ashes. I gave him the buckles to play with. Macario disappeared as a child. Vanished. More completely than if the earth had swallowed him up. He disappeared in one of those ignoble cheap novels that migrant scribes publish abroad. Macario was abducted from reality, stripped of his good nature so as to turn him into another traitor in the unreality of the written word.

The sun goes down after one last explosion that sets the bay on fire. Black, the branches of the orange tree. I continue to see it through the screen of my hand. Its branches are indistinguishable from my phalanges. Sad thoughts have dried it up more quickly than my bones. Clever caricature. Stepmother-nature, more cunning than the most cunning pasquinaders. Your imagination does not need the instinct of imitation. Even when you imitate you create something new. Shut up in this hole, I can but copy you. In the open air, the orange tree imitates my bony hand. I have more than met my match; I am unable to transplant it to these folios and occupy its place on the cliff edge. The little black is making water against the trunk; perhaps he will contrive to revive it. All I can do is write; that is to say, deny what is alive. Kill what is dead even deader. *I, orange-tree-squatting-on-my-haunches*. Skimmed of my scum as I lie on my pallet. Soaked in my own sweats-urines. Plucked clean of all my feathers, my quill falls.

Standing in the doorway, full of eyes, **HE** is watching me. His gaze is projected in all directions. He claps his hands. One of the women slaves comes running. Bring something to drink, **HE** orders. Ana looks at me with the eyes of a blind woman. I have not spoken. **HE** says: Bring the Doctor a nice cold lemonade. Mocking voice. Powerful. Fills the room. Falls on my fever. Rains down inside me. Great drops of molten lead. I turn around in the shadow streaked by lightning. I see him go off, erect, amid the storm that parts in two as he passes. Outside, night is again extinguishing the blaze of late afternoon.

Ana enters with the glass of lemonade.

(Perpetual Circular)

In July of 1810 Governor Velazco readies himself to fire off his last cartridge of time. He will graze no more; the government is fresh out of greenery, of specie. A severe drought of dinars. The ruminants of the Cabildo advise him to convoke a congress in order to decide the fate of the province. In Buenos Aires Viceroy Cisneros has been overthrown by a junta of Creole patricians. Don Bernardo already sees himself meeting the same fate amid the deplorable ferment. He hurriedly takes refuge on a warship. He discovers that the gunboat has no guns. The river has run dry. He returns to the palace and calls together the members of the clergy, military leaders, magistrates, corporations, literary types, deeprooted-uprooted citydwellers. Naturally that "immense beast," the plebs, is not admitted to the council. The conclave does not meet in the House of Government but in the obiscopal palace. A most notable circumstance that gives rise to notorious gossip. The bishop Pedro García Panés y Llorente has just arrived from the court of Joseph Napoleon. It is widely noted that he has indigestion from the surfeit of "specious rumors" that the governor has set before him as a welcome. The prelate has brought his own extravagant rumors from the other side of the pond. Moreover, the foxes of the First Junta in Buenos Aires have sent as the nuncio of the new system the oldest and most hated man in the province, the Paraguayan colonel of militias Espínola y Peña, who claims to have received orders to relieve the governor. A brilliant way of gaining adepts! And what a bad deal Revolution is for Paraguayans if it is going to consist of replacing Velazco with Espínola! The very image and likeness of what was to happen later.

Under these auspices the two hundred notables unite in the obispal hornet's nest. Unwittingly, those grotesque puppets constituted the inaugural assembly of the Fatherland: bad sometimes brings good in its train. Rebellion was already leavening the dough about to be put in the oven; but not there, obviously. So if it please you, beloved fellow citizens, the Spanish spokesman for the governor without a voice and soon to be without a vote proclaims, let us recognize the Supreme Crown Regency Council here and now by acclamation, and meanwhile maintain fraternal relations with Buenos Ayres and other provinces of the Viceroyalty. But since the neighboring Empire of Portugal-Brazil is just waiting for the moment to swallow up this precious and prized province, the Saracen counselor adds, and has its troops on the shores of the Uruguay River, it behooves us to raise an army to defend ourselves. Let us show what we are and must be, avoiding being subjugated by anyone who is not our legitimate Sovereign. This was the *argumentum Aquiles* of the partisans of the Spaniards in that emergency, Julio César writes in his Commentaries.

Nequáquam!, I said: The Spanish government has seen its day on the Continent. The governor-intendant's ear-trumpet squealed; the terrified rats of the congress squealed. The bishop latinized his mitral stupefaction. Leaning on his crosier, he pointed his pectoral cross at me with a trembling hand: Our Sovereign Monarch is still the Sovereign of the Spains and the Indies, including all its Islands and Terra Firma! Great hubbub of debarkation. I gave a sharp slap of my hand to quiet it down. Here in Paraguay, we've stowed the monarch in the ark!, I shouted. Here in Paraguay Terra Firma is the firm will of the people to make its land free, from this day forward and forever! The one question to decide is how we Paraguayans are to defend our sovereignty and independence against Spain, against Lima, against Buenos Aires, against Brazil, against any foreign power that attempts to subjugate us. On what authority are these rebellious pronouncements by the Syndic-Procurator General based?, an old country-rat squealed. I drew my two pistols. Here are my arguments: One against Fernando VII. Another against Buenos Aires. With my finger on the trigger I ordered the governor to call for a vote on my motion. He thought I had lost my mind. Ear-trumpet to his mouth, broken voice, he stammered: You promised to help me in the fight against subversives! That's what I'm doing. The sources of subversion at present are those who support Spain and Buenos Aires. He stood there blinking. His bulging eyes went from his ear-trumpet to my pistols. I demand that my motion be put to a vote, right here, I stated, with another sharp slap of my hand on the table. Many of those present thought I had shot off a pistol. The most skittish of the lot dived for the floor. The bishop pulled his miter down to his chin. The governor began flailing about like a man drowning. The machine of his supporters began working. The hall was thrown into a tumult of cries of Long live the Regency Council! The ballot-well for the vote was brought. The Saracens tossed their papers into it, yelling at the top of their lungs: Long live the Institutional Restoration of the Province! The governor recovered his voice. At that moment, as José Tomás Isasi told me later, there burst into the hall, from a popular fiesta that was being held nearby, one black behind another black who was running after a little-girl masker disguised as a little-boy clown. The bizarre dumb show turned the whole fracas into confusion worse confounded. It seems that the black doing the chasing grabbed one of my pistols; the one meant for the king. He shot at the clown, who fled, shielding himself amid the big wigs, till he fell behind the governor's chair.

I didn't see any of that. If the traitor Isasi's story was true, the entire mummery could only have been a trick contrived by the Spanish faction of the Cabildo to make sure the assembly came to nothing. Pantomime or not, I can only say that it turned out to be an excellent representation of what was being aired there.

I had left the avispal henhouse a moment before, clearing a way for myself through the flock of Spaniards flapping all over the hall. Scaring off the great bunch of brooders, capons, clerics, magistrates, inverted-transvested literary types, I went out into the street, as they remained behind making a great fuss over my two argumental pistols.

Their triumph was not to last long. I took the egg of Revolution with me in order that it might hatch at the right moment.

(*Written in the margin. Unknown hand:* By so doing, you were trying to imitate Descartes, who detested fresh eggs. He let them incubate beneath the ashes and drank down the embryonic substance. You wanted to do the same thing without being Descartes. You were not going to eat the Revolution every morning for breakfast with your maté. You turned this country into a lustral, expiatory egg that will hatch heaven only knows when, heaven only knows how, heaven only knows what. Embryo of what might have been the most prosperous country in the world. The best cock in all human legend.)

I mounted my horse. Rode off at a gallop. Breathed deeply of the smell of earth, of woodland warmed by the sun. The night was tenderly born from below. The martial drumroll of the bell-bird on the hillsides of Manorá brought a certain peace to my spirit. I loosed the reins of the horse, which quickened its pace as it headed homeward, matching it to the rhythm of my thoughts. One senses ideas coming as one senses disasters approaching. As I returned to my retreat at Ybyray I was reflecting on what had just happened; on the fact that even in the most trivial of occurrences chance enters the game. I understood then that it is only by ripping this sort of thread of chance out of the weft of events that the impossible can be made possible. I suddenly realized that to-be-able-to-do is to-be-able-to-enable. At that instant a shooting star traced a luminous streak across the firmament. Heaven only knows how many millions of years it had been wandering about the cosmos before winking out in a fraction of a second. I had read somewhere that falling stars, meteors, aeroliths, are the very picture of chance in the universe. The force of power lies then, I thought, in chasing down chance: *re-trapping* it. Discovering its laws; that is to say, the laws of oblivion. Chance exists only because oblivion exists. Subjecting it to the law of counter-oblivion. Tracing down counter-chance. Removing from the chaos of the improbable the constellation possessed of probity. A State revolving on the axis of its sovereignty. The sovereign power of the people, nucleus of energy for the organization of the Republic. In the political universe, States confederate or explode. Exactly like the galaxies in the cosmic universe.

First objective: erect hierarchy in the midst of anarchy. Paraguay is the center of Meridional America. Geographical, historical, social nucleus of the future integration of the independent States in this part of America. It is Paraguay's destiny to be the political destiny of the American continent. The black-and-white Arabian neighed a bit, pricking up his ears at this possibility that the faithful beast accepted on faith. It may be that they will win out and rule over us, I said to him, but we must try to prevent it. He gave a loud snort. Don't be afraid of your own shadow, my Thomas Moor. The day will come when you will be able to gallop in the sun without shadow or fear in this land of prophecies. He strode on, calmer now, nodding his head, bothered only a little by the metal bit that creaked between his back teeth.

I raised my head up toward the sky once again. I tried to read the book of Constellations in the light of their own lanterns. In this sphere-book that terrified Pascal, the greatest terror is that despite so much light dark chance still exists. In any event the most pensive of thinking reeds was unable to read it, not even with his ingenuous faith in God, that very short and very confused word that interposed itself between his thought and the universe: between what he knew and did not know. Tell me, compadre Blaise, you who were the first to dejesuit the Order without provincial fears, tell me, answer me this: Was what really frightened you in the infinite sphere whose center is everywhere and circumference nowhere not perhaps the infinite memory with which it is equipped? A memory whose laws the cosmos proclaims after having come forth from nothingness.

Memory without flaws. Unfailing. Absolute rigor. In the slight

breeze pervaded with the scent of mint and patchouli, the voice of compadre Blaise said: Perhaps, perhaps. Thus the man who has returned to
himself considers what he is in relation to what exists outside of himself.
You, half-breed with two souls, feel lost in this remote corner of nature.
Intoxicated by the wild aroma of an idea. You are now riding toward the
monastery of your trinitarian domain. You believe you are free. You are
riding astride an idea: freeing your country. But you also see yourself shut
up in a tiny cell writing by the light of a candle alongside the meteor you
captured and hold prisoner with you. Don't make me say what I do not
mean to say and did not say, my old Paraguayan compadrito. Learn to
judge the earth, your earth, people, your people, yourself. At their proper
worth. What is a man in the infinite? Much ado between two nothings.
In the end, what is man within nature? Nothing, compared to the infinite;
everything, compared to nothing: a middle term between nothing and
everything. The beginning and the end of all things lies hidden from him
in an impenetrable secret. Come, come, compadre Blaise, don't be a defeat-
ist! The Arabian is taking me to my farm. You are trying to lead me into
the trap of the Word/God. THAT which, as you yourself say, overflows
the sphere and hence cannot fit inside thought. Don't be less intelligent than
a horse. You were not when you spoke of concrete things such as Jesuits,
animals, insects, dust, stones. You yourself made fun of Descartes as a
philosopher. Vain and uncertain Descartes, you said. Is there anything more
absurd than to maintain that inanimate bodies have humors, terrors, horrors? That insensible bodies, devoid of life and incapable of attaining it,
have passions, which presuppose a soul? That the object of their horrors
is the vacuum? What is there in emptiness that can terrify them? Is there
anything more ridiculous? You, compadre, fell into this ridiculous error,
but you were unable to forgive Descartes for having tried to do without
God in his philosophy once He had given the world the initial kick in the
ass. You are unable to forgive him for the fact that after that he kicked
God out forever. Invented by the fear of men in the face of nothingness,
do you think that invention takes care of everything? Mind you don't leave
this factor out of your calculations, you hear?

For the moment God does not occupy my mind. The question that
preoccupies it is ruling over chance. Putting my daedal digit on the die,
the die in the dicebox. Getting the country out of its labyrinth.

(*In the margin. Unknown hand:* You dug another one. The one of the
underground prisons for those poor cats of the patriciate. But on top of
that labyrinth you built another one, deeper and more complicated still:

the labyrinth of your solitude. Playing dice with words: Your sole-étude. Your lone-age. Your long age. You filled this labyrinth of your horror of nothing, old misanthrope, with the emptiness of the absolute. Spongia solis . . . Is this the spin you gave the die so as to get the Revolution moving? Did you believe Revolution to be the mark of one-alone-entirely-on-his-own? One alone is always wrong; truth begins with two and more. . . .)

Ah you impostor of a corrector! *Raza* is something more than *azar*, § more than letters turned around backwards in a game of anagrams. My race is the constellation that I must locate, measure, know down to its smallest secrets so as to be able to lead it. I form part of it. But I must also remain outside. Observe it at a distance. Feel its pulse from within. I clench the cursed cube in one fist.

When at the beginning of the Perpetual Dictatorship I saw the aerolith fall a hundred leagues away from Asunción, I ordered that it be taken captive. Nobody understood then, nobody will ever understand the meaning of this capture of the migrant meteor. Runaway-renegade from the cosmos. I ordered it brought in as a prisoner. For months a small army dragged it over the plains of the Chaco. They had to dig down more than a hundred varas before they found it. Its magnetic field extended all around it. Impassable barrier on the only route, that of the Northern Chaco, offering any probability of its sneaking out of the country. It was via that route that the French merchant Escoffier, shut up for years in prison with other foreign swindlers, tried to make his escape. Accompanied by a number of freed black slaves, he crossed the river and entered the Gran Chaco. A black slave woman who was pregnant tried to follow them so as not to be separated from her lover. Bitten by snakes, wounded by Indian arrows, sick from fevers, the blacks died one by one until only Escoffier and the slave woman were left. The field of attraction of the meteor sucked them to the trench where some hundred sappers were excavating. The Frenchman was left no other recourse than to begin working with the others as long as his strength held out. Then he was shot to death and thrown into the hole. The slave woman gave birth to a son and went on cooking for the sappers. I might have left the meteor there in that spot; it would have been a good lookout post in that wasteland. But I preferred

§*Raza* = race; *azar* = chance.

to have it in a good safe place. It was no easy task. It cost me more than a hundred men to transport it, what with the continual struggle against savage tribes, the elements, predators, the terrible mystery of chance that refused to be reduced. Unheard-of cleverness and ferocity. Only when the slave and her son took their place at the head of the caravan did the stone appear to give in and allow itself to be led through deserts and swamps. The slave woman was bitten by a snake and died. The stone balked again, until the son of the slave, who had become the men's mascot, began to crawl and walk about by himself, the half milk-brother of the stone. They aerobaptized him Tito. He would eventually have become my best tracker, but he too disappeared from the camp one night, kidnapped perhaps by the Payaguás. The stone's passage down the river lasted longer than Ulysses' travels in Homer's sea. Longer than it took Perurimá§ to get out of the swamp that he jumped into to look for the carlos cuarto§§ that Pedro Urdemales had told him was floating on the mud. The journey lasted longer than all these fables. There was no boat or raft capable of bearing a load of ten thousand arrobas of cosmic metal. It sank entire flotillas. Another hundred men drowned during the interminable passage. The tricks and ruses that the meteor had resorted to in order not to go any farther began all over again. Hundreds of female slaves with small boys were sent; but the sense of smell of the stubborn dog of the cosmos was extremely keen; its breed, indecipherable; its laws nearly as inflexible as mine, and I was not disposed to allow that great stone to have its way, to use whims and caprices to get the better of me. In the end, the lowest water level of the Paraguay River in a hundred years allowed the troops of the line to drag it along on specially made gun carriages drawn by a thousand pair of oxen and by more than a thousand soldiers chosen from among the best swimmers in the army. It is here. Chance-meteor in chains, bound to my chair.

(*Unknown hand:* Did you believe that you were thereby doing away with chance? You are admittedly able to keep five hundred traitorous fat oligarchs prisoner in dungeons; every last one of the antipatriots and counterrevolutionaries. You could almost state with certainty that the Revolution is safe from conspiracies. Would you say the same as regards those infinite myriads of aeroliths streaking through the universe in all

---

§Contracted form, frequent in Paraguay, of Pedro de Urdemalas, the archetypical trickster.

§§A small coin worth very little.

directions? Through them chance dictates its laws annulling the vertex-quality of your Absolute Power. You write the two words with capitals to give yourself a greater sense of security. The only thing they reveal is your insecurity. Cavernous fear. You have contented yourself with little. Your horror of emptiness, your agoraphobia cloaked in black to allow you to become one with the darkness has withered your reason. Gnawed away your mind. Rusted your will. Your omnipotent power, worth less than scrap iron. One aerolith does not make a sovereign. It is here; granted. But you are shut up here with it. Prisoner. Gouty rat poisoned by its own venom. Suffocating to death. Old age, infirm-age, that infirmity that even the gods do not recover from, has you by the nape of the neck.)

Whoever you are, insolent corrector of my pen, you are beginning to annoy me. You don't understand what I write. You don't understand that the law is symbolic. Twisted minds are unable to grasp this. They interpret the symbols literally. And so you make mistakes and fill my margins with your scoffing self-importance. At least read me correctly. There are clear symbols/obscure symbols. I the Supreme play my passion cold-bloodedly . . .

you should drop that business of The Supreme, to yourself at least, in any case when you're speaking not on the surface but the subface of your much-diminished person; and above all while you're playing dice in your slippers.

. . . don't interrupt me, I said. I the Supreme play my passion cold-bloodedly in all domains. The people-man, the multitude-populace clearly understood, within its one/multiple soul, the five-year epic of the capture of the meteor. The seditious, avaricious, vainglorious, toplofty, ungrateful, slanderous, strident, cruel, violent, puffed-up, ignorant—where do you find intelligent conspirators?—attacked me furiously. They called me mad for having ordered the demented-stone fallen from heaven to be brought here. Certain of them went so far as to maintain that I carried it on my shoulders in place of my head. Excess of insolent words! But they too were after my head, searching all about at random . . .

in the old days you used to cry out in favor of sedition, and now you are crying out against it

. . . they attacked The Supreme as one single person without taking the trouble to distinguish between corporeal-Person/impersonal-Figure. The one can grow old, meet its end. The other is unceasing, without end. Emanation, immanation: magnetization of the sovereignty of the people, master of a hundred ages . . .

uneasiness of your genius. Too overwrought, what you say!

I circumcised the aerolith. The metallic clipping provided enough material to manufacture ten rifles in the State armories. The ringleaders of the conspiracy of 1820 were executed with them. Not one of them misfired. Since then it is these rifles that are used to put a period, a full stop to eversive blather. They finiquidate the infamous traitors to the Fatherland and the Government with a single shot. Because of their precision these rifles are still the very best ones I have. They don't wear out or overheat. They can get off a hundred rounds in a row. Cosmic material does not change. Once it has gone dead, it remains as cold as it was initially, after having been subjected to the highest temperatures in the universe. If I could harvest aeroliths in the same way that the country produces a double annual harvest of maize or wheat, I would long since have resolved the problem of armaments. I would not be obliged to go about begging from traders and smugglers. Each grain of gunpowder I get out of them costs me its weight in gold. They're no longer content these days to exchange arms for the country's precious woods. They demand gold coins. Idiots!

The meteoric rifles, my secret weapon. They're a bit on the heavy side. No use handing them out to weaklings. Each one of these rifles carries a charge of no less than twenty arrobas of cosmic metal. They require herculean riflemen. The only hitch is that after this meteor I was never able to hunt down another one. One of two possibilities: Either heaven is becoming more tight-fisted than Brazilian arms smugglers, or the capturing of a single meteor has abolished the unreality of chance by means of a representation at once real and symbolic. If this latter, I need no longer fear the ambushes of sheer happenstance. Then you—the one who is correcting my writings behind my back, hand that steals into the margins and between the lines of my most secret thoughts destined for the flames —are not right. You are dead wrong, and *I* am dead right: the rule over chance is going to enable my race to be truly invincible till the end of time.

This happened without taking place. At that moment, pacing along with the Arabian, face to the night sky, my mind was already made up.

At that instant I saw the jaguar again. Crouching amid the brush of the ravine, readying himself to spring, like the first time, upon the two-masted schooner anchored in the wooded cove along the river. In the shadow of the sails the crewmen were groggily sleeping in the suffocating heat of the siesta. The Arabian was already galloping at full speed toward the scent of his home ground. The farm, the house, came to meet us.

I was not going to budge from there until I had the reins of power in my hands. Tree-lookout. Solitary retreat-chapel. Hermit linked to the fate of the country, I sequestered myself in my humble dwelling to await events. They would come looking for me there. I opened my door to peasants, the populace, the people-multitude, the people-people, declared to be in a state of semiclandestine assembly. The farm at Ybyray turned into a cabildo of real councilors. This did happen by taking place.

(Perpetual circular) *

Those were the days when Manuel Belgrano came at the head of an army. A barrister, an intellectual, despite his profound belief in the cause of independence he came to carry out the orders of the Junta in Buenos Aires: round up Paraguay by force and pen it in with the other poor provinces. He came with those intentions, which in an initial ferment he must have been convinced were just. Belgrano came, heated by the wine of the impossible. As on other occasions, he also came accompanied by that legion of migrant scoundrels, the eternal partisans of annexation, which served then, which served later on, as scouts in the invasions of their Fatherland. Wine turned to vinegar.

Once he has entered Paraguayan territory, from the top of the Cerro de la Fantasma, also called by some the hill of Los Porteños, he writes to the phantom-Porteños of his Junta: I have arrived at this point with barely five hundred men, and find myself confronting an enemy numbering a good five thousand, according to some nine thousand. Since I crossed the Tebicuary not a single Paraguayan volunteer has presented himself, nor have I found any in their houses, as reports [from the renegade Paraguayan commandant José Espínola y Peña] assured us we would: this, together with the total lack of evidence of any movement in our favor thus far, and indeed quite to the contrary, their presenting themselves in such great numbers to oppose us, obliges the army under my command to state that its proper title is not that of an auxiliary force but that of an expedition to conquer Paraguay.

---

*Read the previous installments of this perpetual-circular very attentively so as to find a continuous meaning each time it comes round. Do not stay on the edges of the wheel, which are what get the hard jolts, but place yourselves, rather, along the axis of my thought, which ever remains fixed as it turns upon itself. *(El Supremo's Note.)*

A communiqué in his own hand, the Tacitus of the Plata§ records. As darkness is falling, the auxiliary-conquistador withdraws to his tent, and once he is alone with his secretary, the Spaniard Roca, he informs him in confidence of his objectives: The enemy are like flies, but in the position in which we find ourselves I am of the opinion that it would be committing a great error to beat any sort of retreat. The ones we saw this afternoon are for the most part lumpish louts; the majority have never heard the whistle of a bullet in their lives, and hence I am counting a great deal on the moral force that is in our favor. My mind is made up and I am only waiting now for the division that has remained in the rear guard to arrive so as to begin the attack.

On the following day a portable altar was erected at the top of this misleading Horeb. The chaplain of their army said the Mass for men of arms about to enter combat; according to the Tacitus, invaders and invaded were already so close, in body and in spirit, that the Paraguayan soldiers with their sombreros adorned with crosses and candles also knelt to hear it from the plain. Since it had been their belief that they were about to do battle with heretics, the Tacitus adds, citing the Despertador Teo-Filantrópico,§§ they marveled at the discovery that they were about to fight against brothers in religion. He should also have added that when the tohu-bohu of the cavalry charges began, the *lumpish louts* suddenly vanished from the backs of their mounts into thin air. These latter continued to advance like a puff of breath with empty saddles, until the dim shapes suddenly reappeared on them, bearing takuara pikes, amid a savage outcry, breaking the enemy's lines and eardrums, sweeping everything before them.

The Catholic shapes fight by slipping in and out among the ranks of the infernal legion. The invading troops' parting shots backfire on them, as the vulgar saying goes. The leader of the invasion then sends word to his dis-government: Yr. Excy. cannot have a sufficiently clear idea of what is happening; even for me it is still obscure amid the smoke of the disaster. As Yr. Excy. saw it, we had been assured that I would encounter no opposition; that on the contrary the majority of the population of this province would submit to our troops. What I have found, however, are a people who defend country, religion, and what is most sacred to them with delirious enthusiasm. Thus it is that they have performed incredible labors in order to mount their attack on me, overcoming impossibilities

---

§El Supremo's nickname for the Argentine general, statesman, and historian Bartolomé Mitre (1821–1906). Author of one of the historical sources of the novel *Vida de Belgrano*.
§§The Theo-Philanthropic Awakener.

that must be seen to be believed. Formidable swamplands, rivers in flood, immense impenetrable forests, the cannons of our artillery: all that has been nothing to them, for their enthusiasm, their fervor, and their love for their land has overcome and conquered all. What a surprise! For even women, children, oldsters, and all those who call themselves sons of Paraguay are ready to endure any and every hardship, to give all their goods, their very lives for the fatherland.

This said after two bloody battles in which he was totally defeated. The anti-Paraguayan legionnaires accompanying Belgrano and serving him as scouts, the Machaíns, the Cálcenas, the Echevarrías, the parasitical progeny of old Espínola y Peña, the Báezes and other dunderheaded annexionist adventurers, do not know how to explain to the abused-disabused Belgrano.

I have not come to destroy the rights of this province in one fell swoop, he declared as the Paraguayan horsemen were lassooing and hauling away the last cannons abandoned in the field by the invaders. I have not come to invade you, my compatriots; I have come to aid you, he protested beneath the white flag of surrender, on the shores of the Takuary. He gave his word that he would immediately leave the territory of the province and swore by the gospels never to take up arms against her again, a promise that he kept religiously. This must be said in his honor.

The Paraguayan milicasters allowed themselves to be con-vinced. After Cerro Porteño and Takuary, words did what cannons could not. The defeated leader, in reality triumphant, headed back toward his homeland. The victorious army escorted him to the spot where he was to cross the Paraná, after having held long secret meetings with him. The dimwitted Creole leaders generously acceded to everything that the vanquished leader asked for without demanding any reparations whatsoever for the immense damage caused Paraguay by the so-called liberating expedition. Cavañas, the leader at Takuary and later an infamous conspirator, did not have the shadow of a notion in his head of what was happening or of what was about to happen. But there is no denying that he had a good idea of what would further his interests. The country's principal purveyor of fine to-bacco was not expecting special privileges from the royalists now, but from the Porteñistas leading the Unitarian cause.

The uniformed owners of great estates had good reasons to seek collusion with the Porteños. The real power was no longer royal. The Spaniards had distinguished themselves by their absence in that first patrial battle. The Spanish infantry disbanded shortly after the engagement began.

Governor Velazco also fled from the headquarters at Paraguarí. In order to keep from being recognized, he hunted up a peasant and gave the man his brigadier's uniform in exchange for his rags. He also made him a present of his eyeglasses and his gold cigar holder. Then he hid himself on the heights of the Cordillera of the Orange Trees. He left the Paraguayans to get along as best they could all by themselves.

For some time they saw the gleaming uniform, fearlessly exposed in places in the thick of combat, disappearing at times and reappearing at others as though to lend the troops courage. An enigma, as much for the enemy as for the Paraguayans. They finally managed to get him to take refuge behind the lines. They were amazed at the cleverness, the bold, completely unprecedented courage of the governor, who had left his mount behind and hidden himself so well in the guise of this bearded, dark-skinned man with callused hands and bare feet. The spectacles and gold cigar holder gleamed brightly beneath the broad-brimmed hat. Cava-ñas, Gracia, and Gamarra consulted him in the beginning, making signs asking him for orders. The mute presence answered them with motions of his head, showing them all the ins and outs of how to trounce the enemy. Only after the victory, when the governor reappeared to reassume command, disguised in the peasant's clothes, did the leaders suspect the real motives of the imposture. Who are you?, Cavañas asks him. I'm the governor-intendant, commander-in-chief of these forces, Don Bernardo says haughtily, removing the broad-brimmed straw sombrero hiding his face. In person!, Gracia says with a smile. A most amusing trick, Your Grace! And where has Your Excellency been, Milord Governor?, Cavañas asks him again. At the very top of the Orange Trees, observing the evolutions of the battle. And where did you come from?, they ask the completely naked peasant, half dead with fear. I . . . the poor man murmurs covering his privates with his hands. I came . . . I just came to have myself a peek at all this pantomonium!

The thing is that it was not difficult for the Porteño leader to beguile that flock of milicaster-landowner-traders. Animula vagula conciliabula,§ he goes round honey-wording, siren-singing in Paraguayan territory before crossing back over the Paraná, offering to negotiate in order to prove that he has not come to conquer the province, nor to subjugate it as Bruno Mauricio de Zabala, working hand in glove with the Jesuits, had done in

§A reminiscence of a famous verse composed by the emperor Hadrian shortly before his death: "Animula, vagula, blandula . . . " (Little soul, errant, affectionate . . .).

days gone by. He protests that he has come with the one aim of promoting its happiness. He baits the hook with an already fried catfish; he tosses the line into the Takuary; he waits, pole in one hand, the gold key of free exchange glittering in the other. The virtue of the key is that it is aperitive; that of the hook that it hooks things. The Paraguayan chiefs, mouths wide open, were hooked. The tobacconist-chief catches sight of the nutritive fortune amid the reflections. This is good, really very good!, he comments to his acolytes. Why go on with this war if the South is our North Star? General bedazzlement. He chats endlessly with the defeated victor, who could well have been taken prisoner with every last one of his fleeting shapes. There were neither victors nor vanquished here!, Cavañas cries. Belgrano has hold of the victors by the gills of their greed. He gives proof of his magnanimity. He offers union, liberty, equality, fraternity to the Paraguayans; free trade of all the products of the province with the provinces of Buenos Aires. No more ports of entry, precise or imprecise. End of the Buenos Aires monopoly on commerce. Abolition of the tobacco monopoly. Gamarra hides the moon under his armpit. All of them eat the catfish that has turned into gleaming dorado. They all smoke the peacepipe together. The Paraguayan military leaders lick their chops, wet their fingers, and stroke the seams of their battle jackets, relishing the thought of the war taxes on tobacco and maté that can still be exacted. Over the fires of Takuary, Belgrano prophesies union and freedom. The Buenos Aires Junta will soon deprophetize him. Paraguayans and Porteños fraternize on the battlefields of Takuary still red with blood, our Julius Caesar writes. In Asunción the fear of the royalists grows. First the dispatches reporting the rout of the Bourbonic troops and the flight of the governor, and now the news of the armistice brought by messengers at full gallop. What is happening? Without waiting for an answer, the Spaniards flee from their houses in the dark of night, disguised as blacks, with nothing but the troves on their backs. They fill seventeen ships set to sail to Montevideo, where the royalists have taken a firm stand on orders from Viceroy Elío.

Bernardo de Velazco, having returned in his underclothes following his flight, was unable to prevent the armistice, much less the agreement of the Paraguayan leaders with Belgrano, captivated by his winning ways on the banks of the Takuary.

The arrival of the governor in the Paraguayan camp, Belgrano writes in his memoirs, did not have as its object putting an end to disagreements, but rather preventing the revolutionary germ from spreading. Keeping Cavañas from carrying out his salutary intentions. Likewise those of his camp, the Yegroses and the finest flower of Paraguayans. Belgrano should have been more precise: the camp of the tobacco merchants, the maté traders, and the estancia owners in uniform.

(In the private notebook)

Signing this armistice, so contrary to the aims of the annexionist invasion and the interests of Buenos Aires, was to prod a sore spot, the Tacitus of the Plata will say later on. Our sorest spot of all, Tacitus-Brigadier. You too will invade our country; and then you will begin quietly translating the Divine Comedy by invading Alighieri's Avernal circles.

You stubbornly insist, pounding the tip of your generalissimo's baton on the loose tiles of History; you are adamant that Belgrano was the real author of the Revolution of Paraguay, tossed like a torch into the Paraguayan camp. Those are your textual words. We could all have been burned to death, Tacitus-Brigadier! From May 25, 1810, on, you say, an era in which printing began to be widespread, it was easier for me to follow the march of events, consulting periodicals and the multitude of broadsheets that saw print at the time, using correlative manuscripts that I have been able to obtain to elucidate these pieces of evidence. But very shortly events grow more complicated; the press does not suffice to reflect the course of the revolution day by day, and secrecy begins necessarily to become a rule of government; but as always happens, as mystery becomes more indispensable it becomes imperative to write everything down in order to communicate, and hence the day comes when posterity finds itself in possession of even the most deeply hidden thoughts of the men of the past and can study that past better than if it had them there before its very eyes. That is what happened with me from the moment when, seeking a more trustworthy guide than the periodical press, I dug deeper into the archives of war and government, after the year '10. The first fact that I needed to throw light on was Belgrano's expedition to Paraguay, concerning which there existed very little published material worth consulting, almost all of those who had spoken of it having committed the grossest of errors . . . Ah, Tacit-Brigadier! You consider mystery to be indispensable as a rule of government. You and your capons cooked up the Triple Alliance against Paraguay in the dead of night, between midnight and cockcrow. You place all your faith in scraps of paper. In writing. In bad faith. You are one of those who believe, an honorable man who came after you will say, that when they find a metaphor, a comparison, however bad, they have found an idea, a truth. You speak, as Idrebal§ rightly character- izes you, in similes, that puerile recourse of those who do not have a mind of their own and know no way of defining the indefinite except by comparing it with what is already defined. Your weapon is the sentence, not the sword. Your historical disquisitions on the Revolution are cos- moramas, not discourses. This brought you credit, money, titles, power, this wise man says in passing judgment upon you. I can be still more indulgent toward you, for as I write this you are a mere youngster. You could scarcely have been present when Belgrano flung the "torch of Liberating Revolution" into the Paraguayan camp; in any event you would have said "firebrand of liberticide counterrevolution" since it fell into the hands of the Cavañases, the Gracias, the Gamarras, and the Ye- groses; your rhetoric of Chief-Archivist would then have been a little closer to the reality and nature of those facts that you are trying to narrate with your broad-brimmed English fedora pulled down over your eyes. This allows you to state with British phlegm, repeating that clever rascal Somellera, that the only real and immediate cause of the Paraguayan revolution was the inoculation that the Paraguayans received at Takuary. Decidedly, Tacitus-Brigadier, you give every appearance of being a veteri- narian of the remount cavalry, a penpushing quartermaster clerk. If you grant that Cerrito Porteño and Takuary were the sites of the revolutionary inoculation in Paraguay, you must also grant, as a sincere liar, that it was an artificial insemination, and that those who were really inseminated were the invaders. Beginning with the Comuneros, Paraguayan studs have gen- erously donated their sperm, and not to make candles with. In our country it's the women who make candles. What we do with our sperm is another story.

(Perpetual circular)

Before going back across the Paraná, Belgrano gave Cavañas his watch as a gift. He gave 60 ounces of gold—actually 58—to be shared among the widows, the orphans of those who had not been able to withstand the leaden arguments of the Porteños' preaching. The baggage lost, the arms destroyed, the animals killed were naturally not indemnified.

Nor was poor Belgrano indemnified on his return to Buenos Aires. Not only did his efforts go unrecognized. In the final analysis, his successes

§Anagram for the name of a historian, Alberdi, who wrote on Mitre.

went unrecognized as well. Did the brains devoid of gray matter of the Buenos Aires Junta think it a matter of little moment that the expeditionary general had been able to turn a military defeat into a diplomatic victory? His recompense: a trial by court-martial. In the same period in which Liniers, the Frenchy, was shot to death, shortly after having reconquered Buenos Aires from the English invaders. But that is a horse of another color, one too old to bear the burden of my story.

Meanwhile the impassioned echoes of Takuary, Julius Caesar again notes, arrived in Asunción, turning the news of the strange armistice in which an invading army is allowed to withdraw with maximum honors into a burning issue.

From the beginning I was the most heated critic of the Takuary accord, whereby Atanasio Cavañas's immense satisfaction had come close to making common cause with the defeated invaders. At my insistence, during these days my friend Antonio Recalde led the attack in the Cabildo against Cavañas and his absurd behavior. The members of the Cabildo unanimously demanded an explanation from him as to the real causes of the capitulation. The tobacco dealer–commandant did not give one, and indeed could not give one without condemning himself. The demand was thus left hanging in the air. Do you remember the text, Patiño? Yes, Excellency; it is the demand dated March 28, 1811. Copy out the whole thing; it is one that merits being brought to the attention of my satraps of today. Those of yesterday. Those of tomorrow.

The Cabildo in those days was the bastion of supporters of the Spanish cause, as I have already recounted; hence my long-term aims were other. The egg of Revolution was slowly incubating in the warm embers of the campfires of those bivouacs. Period. End for today of the perpetual.

Hand me that repeater watch. Which one of the seven, Sire? The one that Belgrano presented to Cavañas at Takuary; the one just now striking twelve.

(In the private notebook)

Last night I was again visited by the herbalist. Or rather, he returned to the attack. This time without his tisanes. Head drooping more than usual. A start of surprise on seeing me writing. He surely thought that I was working out my accounts in the monumentous ledger. What are you doing, Excellency? You can see very well, Estigarribia. When there's nothing else to be done, one writes. He tried to take the thread of my pulse. Hand left suspended in midair. You should rest, Excellency. Complete rest, Sire. Sleep, sleep. He went on moving his toothless gums up and down as though he were biting dust. After a long silence he ventured to wheeze: The Government is very sick. I think it my duty to ask you to prepare yourself or to make the arrangements you deem most suitable, inasmuch as your state is worsening by the day. Perhaps the moment has come to choose a successor, to appoint a designate.

He blurted all that out in a single breath. Unexpected insolence from such a puny, fearful man. Thought embodied in a mere thread of a voice. Have you spoken with anyone concerning my illness? Not a soul, Sire. Then button your lip. Absolute, total secrecy. He leaned his shadow on the meteor. Certain people, Sire, already suspect the worst. Yet they see you venturing forth for your afternoon outing on horseback as usual. Those who have grave suspicions have fewer, and those who have few have none. Through the slits in their shutters, people spy the horse as it passes by, accompanied by the escort, amid the sound of fifes and drums. They see His Excellency! Tall and erect as always in the crimson velvet saddle. How do you know whether it is really *I* mounted astride the Arabian? Your friend Antonio Recalde told me this afternoon that Your Excellency looked to be in better countenance. Bah, that old parrot is forever cleaning his beak! But you, you who are my doctor, find me in a worse and worse state. You've come to put my semi-corpse in a death-trance. How do I know you're not connivancing with the enemies prowling about on every hand, hoping to fish in a troubled river? Sire, you know my loyalty, my fidelity to Your Grace. I've never heard of such foolishness! Look, Estigarribia, you're either a stupid idiot or a scoundrel, and both at the same time. You're incapable of honoring the trust I have placed in you throughout my entire life. Are you too making mock of me? Are you too hoping for my death? In the name of heaven, no, Excellency! And is it not more despicable still for you, my doctor, to hope for it and to induce me into giving you that pleasure? Well, allow me to assure you that you are not going to have it. On the contrary, Sire, I have not abandoned the hope or the certainty that your health will improve, by the grace of God who performs miracles and brings about impossible things. I don't give a damn for the hopes or assurances of men such as you who make fun of the cross from hell to breakfast. My only thought, Sire, was that someone must relieve you of your crushing responsibilities of Government. Don't bother me with such trifles. Whoever can will take over after me. For the moment I am quite able to hold my own. Not only do I not feel worse; I feel terribly better. Hand me my clothes. I'm going to prove to you that you're lying.

See? I'm more steady on my feet than you are, than are all of those who would be pleased to see me carried out of here feet first. Death pays all debts. Retiring. Receiving your pension check in jubilation. Is that what you're after? No, Excellency! You know that that's not how it is at all. What more could all of us Paraguayans want than for you to live forever for the good of the Fatherland? Look, Estigarribia, I'm not saying I won't die some day. But the when and the wherefore are a secret I'll take to my grave with me. Death doesn't ask us to keep a day free for it. I'll wait for it sitting here working. I'll keep it waiting behind my chair as long as necessary. I'll keep it standing around cooling its heels till I've said my last word. They won't need to come round with ten-foot poles to poke at my corpse to see if I'm dead. My hair won't turn white in the grave.

I got dressed, disdaining the herbalist's help. He gesticulated, waved his arms wildly, embraced the air in his eagerness to keep a specter on his feet. He very nearly ended up on the floor. We went into the study. I wrote the note for Bonpland. Have it sent to San Borja, if he's still thereabouts. Send that courier who's swifter than lightning. If possible, have him be back here before he's left. In years past, the Frenchman's remedies at least calmed my nerves. Your treacherous herb concoctions, on the other hand, are contrabanding together with my ailments to undermine my health. What have they been able to do for my military gout and my civilian hemorrhoids? Eh, señor protophysician, what do you have to say to that? Keeping my leg, my butt in the air the whole blessed day, trying to emulate the weightless pose of holy apparitions. Thanks to you, I'm going to stick sideways in eternity's throat.

Your beverages won't make me any worse off than I am. They won't remedy my intestines hanging drying in the air like the gardens of Babylon. The bellows of my lungs wheeze like an old bronco from the weight of all the air they've had to inhale/exhale. From their place between my ribs, they've spread out over more than ten thousand square leagues, over hundreds of thousands of days. They've unleashed floods, storms, the burning-hot breath of deserts. In their natural materials there breathes a political body, the State. **HE/I**: it is our lungs that the entire country breathes through. I beg your pardon, Excellency, I don't understand this business about the lungs of **HE/I** very well. You, Don Vicente, like all the others, never understand anything. You haven't been able to keep our lungs from becoming two membranous sacs. Poor ignorant fool! Worse still, if one considers the fact that you're going to be the forebear of one of the greatest generals of our country. If you had defended my health with the strategy of cordons copied from that of the descendant of yours who defended-recovered the Chaco practically barehanded from the descendants of Bolívar, you would have already cured me. You would have been more or less of an honor to your profession. The art of healing is a martial art as well. But few families produce more than one grand cordon.

You, exalated examiner of my insides, have not managed to mend a single gutter of my aching guts. I'm so full of fistulas I leak everywhere. You come in and announce to me: The Government is very sick! Don't you think I know that? My protophysician not only fails to cure me. He kills me, he is the death of me every day. He brings me portents, presages of a protoinfirmity that's already cured. He prophesies those raging storms that cause death before it comes, after it's already passed by. He does the same thing with other patients-dying. That sentinel who guards my door buried his mother, his wife, two of his children this morning. You treated all of them. Your prescriptions have killed more people than all the plagues put together. Like your predecessors, that Rengger and Longchamp pair.

As for me, learned Aesculapius, haven't you prescribed for me in your concoctions the left foot of a tortoise, the urine of a lizard, the liver of an armadillo, blood extracted from the right wing of a white pigeon? Ridiculous folk remedies! Superstitious quackery! To get me to eat a snail you mysteriously prescribe: Imprison that son of the earth that crawls along the ground, possessed of neither bones nor blood, carrying his house about with him on his back. Have it boiled. Drink the broth after fasting. Having breakfasted, eat the flesh. If my health had depended on those poor yatytases, I would have been cured. The colic is still entranced with my entrails. And what do you prescribe in such a crucial ventral event? Nothing but pulverized turds of rats and wild guinea pigs, roasted over logs of brazilwood. Do you think I'm going to allow myself to be poisoned by such concoctions? I suspect that your mere presence makes me ill, my esteemed protophysician: seeing your curly locks, your grizzled muttonchops, the reflection of your spectacles in the shadow, your enormous skull rolling along on little cockroach feet makes me leap out of bed and into the watercloset. I shall not mention that air of surly self-importance that surrounds your immense dwarf's head: Charon rowing his funereal barque on the floor around my table, my bed, at any and all hours.

The same thing happened to me with that Rengger and Longchamp pair.* I was treated by them with unconscionable negligence. They observed my fistulas as though they were cracks in a wall. I don't know why I named you my personal physician, Don Juan Rengo, I upbraided him one time. Too bad I don't have a Corvisart at my side, like Napoleon! His magic potions allowed the Great Man to keep his intestines fresh as the

---

*Juan Rengger and Marcelino Longchamp, physicians of Swiss origin, arrived in 1818 in Buenos Aires, where they struck up a friendship with the celebrated naturalist Amadeo Bonpland. Not foreseeing his own future in Paraguay, the French savant advised his young Swiss friends to try their luck there in view of the uncertain political situation in the Plata at the time. The travelers found that the "Reign of Terror" depicted by certain observers was in reality an oasis of peace in its rigorous and rustic isolation. They were warmly received by *El Supremo,* who offered them every sort of facility for their scientific studies and the practice of their profession, despite the cruel experience he had had some years before with two other Europeans, the brothers Robertson, as will be seen. The Perpetual Dictator appointed the two Swiss doctors military physicians of barracks and prisons, in which they also acted as forensic specialists. Juan Rengger, whom *El Supremo* called "Juan Rengo" because his last name sounded like the Spanish for lame, *rengo,* and because he in fact had a bad leg, ended up becoming his personal physician. Suspecting that the Swiss were maintaining secret relations with his enemies of the "twenty golden families," the Dictator's friendship toward them eventually changed to a smoldering, growing hostility. They were obliged to abandon the country in 1825. Two years later, they published their *Historical Essay on the Revolution in Paraguay,* the first book written on the Perpetual Dictatorship. Translated into several languages, it was a great success abroad, but was banned in Paraguay by *El Supremo,* and violations very harshly punished since he considered it an insidious diatribe against his government and a "bunch of cock-and-bull stories." The first part written in French and the second in German, this book by Rengger and Longchamp may be said to be the "classic" par excellence dealing with this historical period in Paraguayan life: an indispensable "key and lantern" for penetrating the mysterious reality of an era without parallel in the world of Latin America and the even more enigmatic personality of the man who forged the Paraguayan nation with an iron will through the almost mystical exercise of Absolute Power. (*Compiler's Note.*)

morning breeze. I don't expect you to get my bile duct to flowing freely again and turn my entrails to velvet, as Voltaire asked of his physician. Nor can I drink great quantities of potable gold as the kings of antiquity did in order to postpone the moment of their last hour, as I've read somewhere. I cannot eat the philosopher's stone. I do not expect the secret of imperial tisane to be forthcoming from your herbal alchemy. But you should have at least tried a more modest dictatorial eggnog. Did I ask you to give me back my youth? Did I perchance demand that you rewind my cock, set it at its hour of yesteryear on the virile dial again? Decrepit old gaffers, bald, abject, stooped, cynical, toothless, impotent, would ask nothing else of all the deities of the universe. I expect no such thing of you, my esteemed Galen. My virility, as you know, is of another sort. It never peters out from gout. It does not decline. It does not grow any older. I conserve my energy by expending it. The deer that is chased knows a certain kind of herb; on eating it it expels the arrow from its body. The dog that chases it also knows an herb that cures it of the wounds from the jaguar's claws and fangs. You, Don Juan Rengo, know less than the deer, than the dog. A real physician is one who has survived every sort of malady. If he is to cure the French disease, stubborn itches, multiform leprosy, hanging hemorrhoids, he must first have suffered these ills himself.

You and your crony Longchamp have made a slave of me. You're the ones who have killed off half the soldiers in my army with your deadly potions. Didn't you yourselves confess as much in the libel that you invented and published two years after I expelled you from here? Were you out to defame me in return for the hospitality and all the kind attention I naively paid you? You printed in that libelous dragonflier that the temperature has a great influence on my mood. When the north wind begins to blow, his accesses of rage become much more frequent. This very damp, suffocatingly hot wind affects those who have an excessive sensibility or suffer from an obstruction of the liver or lower belly. When this wind blows continuously, on occasion for days on end, there reigns at siesta time in the towns and in the countryside a silence profounder still than that at midnight. The animals seek the shade of the trees, the coolness of the springs. The birds hide in the foliage; they can be seen to fluff up their wings and raise their feathers. Even the insects seek shelter amid the leaves. Humans become lethargic. Lose their appetite. Sweat even when not moving about, and their skin becomes dry and paper-thin. Along with all this, they suffer from headache, and in the case of persons of nervous disposition, hypochondriacal affections follow. Overcome by them, The Supreme shuts himself up for days at a time, with no communication or nourishment whatsoever, or vents his wrath on those who come within his reach, be they civil servants, officers, or men in the ranks. He then vomits out insults and threats against his real or imagined enemies. He orders arrests. He inflicts cruel punishments. At such stormy moments it would be a mere bagatelle for him to pronounce a death sentence. Ah, you pair of mendacious Swiss medics! What malicious buffoonery! First you attribute to me an excessive sensibility. Then extreme perversity that makes the north wind my prompter and accomplice. And finally, you violate the ethics of your profession by divulging my illnesses. Did you ever see me fulminate death sentences in such a state, inflict cruel punishments, as you maintain? You should have been put to death as liars, false witnesses, and cynics. You richly deserved such a fate. You received instead kind and generous treatment, even when the sultriest of north winds blew in. Likewise when the dry and pleasant south wind was blowing, which according to you is when I sing, dance, laugh all by myself, and hold endless colloquies with my private phantoms in a language that is not of this world.

Ah, unworthy compatriots of William Tell! Was it not you who advised me to expose my tricorne on a pike in the Plaza de la República so as to receive the daily homage of the populace? Had I gone along with such a cheap farce, inconceivable in this country of proud, dignified citizens, you would have been the first to subject yourself willingly to such a ceremony of submission, the mere idea of which I severely reproached you for. In the remote likelihood that, like William Tell, you had refused to be subjected to such a humiliation, you would never have been able to put an arrow through the apple placed atop my head. Yours, however, would have fallen ipso facto beneath the executioner's ax.

Ah, you hypocritical Hippocrateses! Squatting cuckoos are capable, I grant you, of laying eggs in another's nest, but not of popping out to announce the hour on the clock-face of my lower belly. I leave aside the uneven number of pills that I was to ingest at even intervals; the days of the year appointed for punctures and bleedings with leeches and tame bats; the lunar phases for enemas and emetics. As though the moon were able to govern the tides of my intestines!

Let us not exaggerate, illustrious cuckoos. I would be more inclined to say that a Pentagon of forces governs my body and the State that possesses in me its material incarnation: Head. Heart. Belly. Will. Memory. Such is the integral magistrature of my organism. What happens is that the Pentagon does not always function in harmony with the alternate seasons of flux-constipation, rain-drought, that make for copious or disastrous harvests. Neither hypochondria nor misanthropy, my esteemed meteorologists. In any event, you should have said accidia, black bile. Medieval words. A better designation of my medieval ills. I am not going to waste time in fruitless discussion. Let us get down to the facts. Do you know why birds and all other animal species do not fall ill and live out the course of their lives normally? The two Swiss Galens launched forth at the same time into a long disquisition in French and in German. No, my esteemed Aesculapii. You don't know. Well then, listen. The first reason is that animals live amid nature, which knows neither pity nor compassion, the source of all ills. Secondly, they do not speak or write as men do; in particular, they do not pen calumnies the way you do. Thirdly, birds and all animal or animated species do their business at the very moment they feel the need to. A starling flying by at a low altitude just then dropped on the crown of Juan Rengger's head a smoking skullcap. It's just as I told you, I said to the Swiss. As you saw, that starling didn't postpone the moment or choose the best place to vent his spleen, but simply did his business. Man, on the other hand, must wait until a thousand ridiculous concerns do not interfere—as is the case with me at this moment —with the regular functioning of his gut. The two of them tried again, both at the same time in their two languages, to stammer an apology. They urged me with gestures to delay no longer if I needed to go to the toilet. No, sirs; there is no need to be concerned. The Supreme Government also exercises power over its bowels. I/HE have our good weather, our bad weather within. We do not depend on shifts of the wind, the seasons, the phases of the moon. You illustrious fatheads very nearly made the North Wind the real Supreme Dictator of this country. Like this one and count- less others, you invented as many lies as you pleased about my regime, which you called "the most generous and magnanimous that exists in the civilized world," in the days when you enjoyed my favors. When I finally expelled you, the same regime became for you, far away now from this land that so kindly gave you shelter, and farther still from decency, the somber Reign of Terror that set the mold for the Robertsons' diatribes later on. The histories, the cheap fictions of every sort that scribble-starlings subsequently scrawl are nurtured on such muck. Papers befouled by badly digested infamies.

You, Juan Rengo, were the most mendacious and most malicious. You described indescribable prisons and torments. Subterranean latomies whose labyrinth of dungeons reach as far as the foot of my own chamber, copied from the one that Dionysius of Syracuse ordered excavated in the living rock. You felt pity for those imprisoned for life whose sighs console me as I listen to them in the tympanum of the labyrinth that leads to the head of my bed; for those condemned to perpetual solitude in the remote penal colony of Tevegó, surrounded by a desert more impassable than the walls of underground prisons.

"The principal object of vigilance of his despotic regime was the well-off class, although he also kept a close eye on the lower classes. His suspicious mind sought victims even among the rabble. The better to isolate individuals from this sphere who aroused his suspicions, he founded a colony on the left bank of the Paraguay River, 120 leagues north of Asunción, and peopled it in large part with mulattoes and women of easy virtue. This penal colony, which he named Tevegó, is the southernmost one in the country." (*Rengger and Longchamp, op. cit.*)

"In Asunción there are two classes of prisons: the public jail and the State prison. Though it also contains a number of political prisoners, the former serves essentially as a jail for others condemned to imprisonment and at the same time as a house of detention for those awaiting trial. It is a building a hundred feet wide, with a low roof and walls almost two varas thick. Like the typical house in Paraguay, it has but one floor, at ground level, divided into eight rooms and a patio of about twelve thousand square feet. Thirty or forty prisoners are crowded together in each room; since there is not space for all of them to sleep on the floor, they string hammocks up in rows, one atop the other. Imagine if you can some forty persons, shut up in a small room without windows or airholes; this in a country where for three-quarters of the year the temperature never goes below 100 degrees, and beneath a roof which during the day the sun heats to over 120 degrees. Hence the prisoners' sweat trickles down from hammock to hammock till it reaches the floor. If one also considers the bad food, the lack of hygiene, and the inactivity of these unfortunates, it can readily be appreciated that were it not for the health-fulness of the climate that Paraguay enjoys fatal epidemics would sweep through these dungeons. The courtyard of the jail is filled with small huts, which serve as quarters for individuals awaiting a court hearing, for those serving sentences for common crimes, and for political prisoners. They have been allowed to construct these huts because the rooms inside are not large enough. Here at least they can breathe the cool night air, though the lack of cleanliness is as great as inside the main building. Those serving life sentences go out every day to labor on public works projects. For this, they are chained together two by two, or wear only *grilletes,* that is to say leg irons, while the majority of the other prisoners drag about another sort of shackle, balls and chains called *grillos,* whose weight—twenty-five pounds sometimes—scarcely allows them to walk. The state provides a small amount of food and a few articles of clothing for those prisoners that it employs on public works projects; as for the others, they support themselves at their own expense and through the alms that two or three of them, accompanied by a soldier, go out every day to collect in the city, or that are brought to them out of charity or to fulfill a vow.

"We have often visited these horrible prisons, both for cases of forensic medicine and to care for sick prisoners. In them one sees Indian and mulatto, black and white, master and slave thrown together indiscriminately; in them all ranks and stations, all ages are commingled, the guilty and the innocent, the condemned and the accused, the public thief and the debtor, and finally the murderer and the patriot. Very often they are bound by the same chain. But what puts the crowning touch on this frightful picture is the ever-increasing demoralization of the majority of the prisoners, and the fierce joy of which they give signs whenever a new victim arrives.

"The women under detention, who fortunately are very few in number, live inside a large room and a palisade fence; within the large courtyard, where they can more or less communicate with the prisoners. A few women of a certain rank, who have attracted the Dictator's hatred, find themselves promiscuously mingled there with prostitutes and criminals, and exposed to all the men's insults. They wear balls and chains just as the men do, and not even pregnancy lightens their burden.

"Since those detained in the public jail can communicate with their families and receive help, they consider themselves most fortunate when they compare their lot with that of the unfortunates confined in the State prisons. These latter are located in various barracks, and consist of small cells without windows in damp cellars, where there is not room enough to stand upright except in the middle of the vault. There prisoners, particularly those designated as the objects of the Dictator's vengeance, may undergo solitary confinement; the others are shut up in cells by twos and fours. All of them are incommunicado and shackled, within view of a guard at all times. They are not permitted to have any sort of light, or engage in any sort of activity. One prisoner of my acquaintance managed to domesticate the rats that visited his cell; his guard hunted them down and killed them. Their beard, hair, and nails grow, without their ever being able to obtain permission to trim them. Their families are allowed to send them food only twice a day; and this food must consist only of those comestibles regarded in that country as the most ignoble, meat and manioc roots. The soldiers, who intercept them at the entrance to the barracks, search through them with their bayonets to see if there are papers or tools inside, and often keep them for themselves or throw them out on the ground. When a prisoner falls sick, he is given no help, save in certain instances at his last moments, and can be visited only during the day. At night the door is closed. The dying man is left to suffer by himself. Even in their death-agonies, the prisoners' shackles are not removed. I have seen Dr. Zabala, whom through an unusual favor on the part of the Dictator I was able to visit on the last days of his illness, dying with shackles on his feet and refused the sacraments. The commandants of the barracks have made this treatment of prisoners more inhuman still, seeking thereby to please their Chief." (*Ibid.*)

For the same reasons, viciousness and malice, you have written nothing about the punishment that best defines the rigorously just quintessence of the penal regime in this country: the sentence to life-rowing. Cowardice, theft, treason, capital crimes meet with this punishment. The guilty party is not sent to his death. He is simply kept apart from life. This sentence fulfills its object since it isolates the guilty party from the society against which his crime was committed. It is in no way opposed to nature; what it does is return the condemned man to it. The description of the criminal is sent to all the towns, the remote hamlets, all the places at the back of beyond where there is the slightest trace of human beings. It is absolutely forbidden to take him in. He is placed in shackles and set in a small boat with sufficient provisions for a month. He is told the places where he can find more supplies as long as he is able to go on rowing. He is given the order to shove off and never set foot on terra firma again. From that moment on, his fate depends on himself alone. I free society of his presence and I do not have his death on my conscience. Everything that is below the waterline of that boat is not worth the blood of a citizen. Hence I take care not to spill it. The condemned man will go on rowing from shore to shore, up or down the wide river of the Fatherland, with everything left up to his own freedom-will. I prefer to correct rather than to impose a punishment that is not exemplary. The first course preserves the man, and if he accepts it and puts his heart and soul into it, it betters him. The second eliminates him, without the punishment serving as a lesson to him or to others. Self-pride is man's most active and most intense sentiment. Guilty or innocent.

An author of our day has woven a legend about a man so condemned, who goes on rowing endlessly and finally finds the third shore of the river. I myself, in order to institute this sentence here, took my inspiration from a story recounted by a libertine in the Bastille, which a French prisoner used to recite to me over and over during the siestas of the torrid Paraguayan summer. I take what seems good to me wherever I find it. Sometimes the most depraved libertines unwittingly fulfill the function of furthering public hygiene. That noble degenerate, shut up in the Bastille, reflected in his utopia the imaginary island of Tamoraé, the revolutionary island of Paraguay, that exemplary reality the two of you calumniated.

Doubtless *El Supremo* is alluding to Sade's story *L'Île de Tamoé*, known in Paraguay a century before its publication in France and in the rest of the world thanks to the oral version of the memorious Charles Andreu-Legard, companion of the marquis in the Bastille and in the Section of Pikemen; later a prisoner of the Perpetual Dictator during the first years of the Dictatorship, as is mentioned in the beginning of these *Notes*.

The changing of the name of the imaginary island of Tamoé to Tamoraé is an unconscious, or perhaps deliberate, error on the part of *El Supremo*. The word *tamoraé* means, approximately, *may-it-so-be* in Guaraní. In a figurative sense: Island or Land of Promise. (*Compiler's Note.*)

In those days, shortly before their expulsion, the Swiss cuckoos were reduced to total silence and humility. I summoned Rengger. Look, Don Juan Rengo, you've made an herbivorous lion out of me with your herbs. What am I to do with you? I must reward you with dismissal. From this day forward you are no longer my private physician. Limit your responsibilities to not poisoning any more of my soldiers and prisoners. Thirty more hussars died yesterday on account of your purges. At that rate you are going to leave me without an army. When you perform autopsies, I have asked you to look in the region of the nape of the neck for some hidden bone in the anatomy of the cadavers. I want to know why my compatriots are unable to lift up their heads. What answer can you give me? There's no bone, you tell me. There must be something worse then; some weight that makes their heads fall down onto their chests. Look for it, find it, my good sir! With at least the same diligence with which you hunt for the rarest species of plants and insects.

As for the resplendent butterfly that has you bedazzled, the daughter of Antonio Recalde, leave her be. You know very well that all Europeans, not only Spaniards, are absolutely forbidden to marry a white woman of this country. Requests to marry are never granted, not even if rape is alleged to be involved. The law is the same for all and there can be no exceptions. You tell me that you wish to leave the country, as does your companion Longchamp. You ask me to authorize your wedding and then your departure. Impossible, Don Juan. You maintain that you're in a hurry. Haste is not a good counselor. I know that from experience. Even if this ban did not exist, it would not be a good thing to marry Miss Backward to Doctor Forward. You claim that this prohibition is absurd and is tantamount to the civil death of Europeans. Do not commit suicide then, my dear Don Juan Rengo, for you will not be restored to civil life no matter how good a doctor you may be. Find yourself one of the many pretty mulattas or Indian girls who are the pride of this country. Wed her. You'll be ahead on the deal twice over. One who knows all the ins and outs of the game can assure you of that. Let me ask you an indiscreet question. How many times have you visited the daughter of Don Antonio Recalde? Don't answer. I know. Many times. Almost every night for the last three years. This prolonged courtship, romance, love-sickness, or however you want to call it, is proof of the steadfastness of your sentiments. It also proves that if Herr Juan Rengo finds himself in a great hurry, his haste has not been wasted in mere flirtations, I presume. I am nonetheless going to allow myself to ask you another question. Have you by any chance come to know the most notable particularity of this beautiful girl? No; of course not. Unless your love is really so great that you willingly overlook this small detail. And if that is the case, I should be inclined to grant you a dispensation. I can imagine your trysts. The charming daughter of Antonio Recalde has always received you with the table and the thick tablecloth that completely hides her lower limbs between you, right? Have you happened to discover, has someone perhaps told you, what the beautiful Recalde girl's nickname is? No, you don't know, I can see that. I'll tell you. They call her Big-Feet. Huge feet. Almost an ell long and half an ell wide. Probably the biggest feet that any damsel in the world of fact and fable ever had. And the best part is that they're getting bigger still. They never stop growing. If you, Don Juan, are moon-struck enough to want to take specimens of sole-flowers not yet in full bloom back with you in your collection, I'll sign the dispensation. Go on. Think it over. Then come back and tell me what you've decided. He didn't come back. A few days later the two Swiss embarked for Buenos Aires. The Recalde girl lost out on a wedding and the country won itself two rogues less.

The protophysician isn't a bad sort. Heart above reproach. Mouth not versed in perversity. Incapable of telling a half-lie; but not able to tell a half-truth at the opportune moment either. Incapable of duplicity, he is pliable because he is softhearted by nature, so that anyone can bend his ingenuous will, by guile if not by crossing his palm with gold. A little squat jug of a man, sweating through every pore the transparent water of his immeasurable naïveté. Far from assuaging my thirst he aggravates it. When I find myself in such a state I cannot bear even this child-oldster. I vent my fury on my own pain. I abandon my body to its many sufferings. For if the pain suffered is equal to that which one is afraid of suffering, the more man allows himself to be dominated by pain the more it torments him. Physical suffering does not torment me. I can get the better of it, get it off my back, more easily than my shirt. What torments me is what happened in that storm. Pain of another sort. It sliced me clear through with a single two-handed blow of its sword; made me double by cutting me down to half my size at most, the half that is rapidly shrinking. Very shortly there won't be anything left but this tyrannosaurain hand, which will go on writing, writing, writing, already a fossil, a fossil writing. Its scales flying off. Its skin falling off. Going on writing.

I am sweating even under my fingernails. Tongue dry between my teeth. An errant going-and-coming, the attack. It spies on me, lies in wait for me.

The herbalist observes me intently. Head hanging down because of that secret bone in the nape of the neck that prevents Paraguayans from holding it erect. Thinking that the demolition is taking its course. Complete rest! Sleep! Sleep, Sire! You know very well I can't sleep, Estigarribia. Sleep is the concentration of inner heat. Mine no longer produces any evaporation. My thought is the waking dream of a hairy, corporeal material. Visions more real than reality itself. Perhaps the moment has arrived to choose a successor, appoint a designate! Is that all that comes to your mind? Is that the final homage you're coming to pay your young patient? I'm only in the twenty-sixth year of my infirm-age.

I can't choose a designate, as you say. I didn't choose myself. The majority of our fellow citizens elected me. I couldn't elect myself all by myself. Could someone replace me in death? Well then, no one can replace me in life either. Even if I had a son he could not replace me, inherit my place. My dynasty begins and ends in me, in **I-HE**. The sovereignty, the power with which we find ourselves invested will return to the people to which they imperishably belong. As for my few personal assets, they are to be divided in the following manner: the farm at Ybyray to my two natural daughters residing in the Home for Orphan and Foundling Girls; from my uncollected emoluments, which amount to the sum of 36,564 silver pesos, 2 reales, a month's pay to be given to the troops of the barracks, forts, border posts, and frontier customs, both in the Chaco and the Región Oriental. To my two old women servants 400 pesos, plus the maté vessel with the silver sipper to Santa; to Juana, who is so old now she's as curved as a jug handle, my chamber pot, which is rightfully hers since she has handled it every day and night with more than selfless devotion during all the time that she has been in my service. To Señora Petrona Regalada, said to be my sister, 400 pesos, plus the wardrobe stored away in the trunk. The rest of my uncollected emoluments are to be distributed to schoolmasters, master and apprentice musicians, in the amount of one month's pay each, not forgetting the little Indian musicians who play for all they're worth in the barracks bands both in the Capital and in the interior. I wish those little Indians to be well dressed and fed: they are the ones who are the best, the most disciplined, thanks to their natural sense of rhythm. It is my wish that they be endowed with instruments as splendid as those of any white or half-breed. Those who have belonged to my escort since they were youngsters are to be provided with new fifes and drums, and if there are any reales left over, they are to be divided among those who must now be far advanced in years, with no way of meeting their needs by their own means. My guitar is to go to Maestro Modesto Servín, organist and choir director of Jaguarón, with the expression of my very warmest affection.

I will all my optical and mechanical instruments and other laboratory equipment to the National Polytechnical Institute, and my entire collection of books to the Public Library. The remainder of any of my private papers that may have survived the fire are to be totally destroyed.

But please know, Don Vicente, that despite the rumors going round, despite what you yourself predict and desire, I haven't yet given you the pleasure of departing this life. Have you some idea at least of where I'll end up when I die? No. You don't know. In the place where things not yet born are.

Céspedes Xeria, the vicar general, has also offered to hear my last confession and administer the sacraments. I have sent word to him that I shall make my last confession by myself. He who holds his tongue keeps his soul. Mind your tongue and keep your soul. And mind you don't repeat what we've talked about here. Don't allow rumors about my illness to circulate. A shoe has a sole and its tongue says nothing. Do likewise. Be tough as shoe leather and you'll be around for a long time. Remember, Don Vicente, that you too in your green years were an ear of corn being eaten up by grubs, and that if you escaped with your life it was because I brought you into Government service by appointing you State apothecary. I can't complain, I grant you, about the rectitude of your life since then. But don't do with my life what you did with yours: going about telling everybody, in the streets, in the houses, about your youthful indiscretions, and above all the lamentable fact that that lively young creature who sucked all the sense out of you died in your arms. The excesses of her nymphomania would have done her in sooner or later, perhaps even sooner in the arms of some other lad better endowed than you. You maintain that you made your public confession in order to serve as an example to others. Nobody learns anything from inside somebody else's head. One man's madness is never the same as another's. From now on, shut your door to the visitations of repentance.

And now, as to the subject of my illness, clam up, eh? Not a word. It's my affair. Your life depends on it. Out of here. And don't come back till I call you.

On the day following the installation of the Junta, ex Governor Velazco's dog left Government House before his master. That realist-royalist pooch understood immediately what the Spaniards couldn't get through their heads. More intelligent than the new contingent of Porteñistas. He decamped with the dignity of a royal chamberlain, his functions having been taken over by my dog Sultan, a sort of Jacobin sans-culotte with long hair and a short temper. Out with you, he barked, hastening Hero's retreat. Booming, commanding voice. We'll be back, Hero sputtered. Astride your granny's Turkish saddle!, Sultan shot back. Saber between his teeth, he mounted guard at the palace door. I'll have you hanged, you Spic dog! That will not be necessary, my esteemed plebeian peer. I've made the gallows already. The guillotine has already lopped off my head three times. I myself don't remember it very clearly. I hope, citizen Sultan, that you don't catch the mal-de-horror. The first thing to go is one's memory. Do you see this length of sword planted in my back? I have no idea how long it's been there. Perhaps the English buried it in me when I fought at my master's side during the reconquest of Buenos Aires. Or during the siege of Montevideo. I don't know where. Out with you, you fraud! Out! Hero looked at him without resentment. You're right, Sultan. Perhaps it's all but a dream. He pulled the rusty sword from his bones. He thrust its shadow firmly in the ground after pushing down hard on it twice and went out limping. Outside there awaited him the immensity of the unknown. Poor Sultan! You don't know how good one feels on finding oneself another. I've finally found someone like me, and that someone is myself. Heaven be praised! God is my Father and everybody else's uncle. A thousand worse things could happen to me. Dying a non-Christian death, without the aid of confession, of the holy oils. What has happened to you is nothing in comparison with what hasn't happened to you. But it's of little use to you to be a Christian, Hero, if you don't have a few clever tricks up your sleeve. Giddap! On your way, and skip the prophecies.

Old, mangy, filled with a strange happiness, he soon adjusted to his new egalitarian life. Neither ups nor downs. He who has two has one. He who has one has none, he said to himself. He did not lie down atop the tombs of the royalists hanged in the conspiracy that had hatched in order to teach realists a lesson. He took to wandering about the streets, the marketplaces, the public squares. He would tell stories he made up for whatever small change people would give him. Enough so that he always had leftovers left over. He never lacked guts. Which for a street-corner storyteller turned out to be food for his fables. He ended up as a guide for blind Paí Mbatú, an ex curé of ex sound mind, though still a right clever rascal, who also lived in the marketplaces on public charity.

Fascinated by the talents of the ex canine of royalist persuasion, the brothers Robertson bought him for five ounces of gold.* Paí Mbatú refused to seal the bargain with the stingy Englishmen for less. For perhaps the first time on the soil of the New World, a half-mad Creole imposed his conditions on two subjects of the greatest empire on earth. They asked my permission to bring him to the English classes. One dog more or less won't matter around here. Bring him. That was how Hero returned to Government House, thereby fulfilling his promise. Which was not at all to Sultan's liking, for he felt displaced by the intruder during our evenings. The stories of the Thousand and One Nights, the tales of Chaucer, the fanciful embroideries of the English deans transported him to regions out of this world. Each time he heard words such as king, emperor, or guillotine, Hero gave an alarmed growl. Illiterate, plebeian, Sultan, scornfully turned his back on him. Habit,

---

*Juan Parish Robertson arrived in Río de la Plata in 1809, in the group of British merchants who had come to Buenos Aires shortly after the Invasions that opened its port to free trade. He was then seventeen years old. He took up lodgings in the house of a well-known family. Madame O'Gorman was one of his principal protectresses. The young Scottish entrepreneur frequented forthwith the most prestigious circles, managing to become friends with Viceroy Liniers. He was present at the May Revolution "as at a picturesque staging of the desires for freedom of the Porteño patriots," he states in one of his Letters. Three years later his brother Roberto joined him. They undertook together what was for them the "great adventure of Paraguay." The Robertsons repeated their exploits in Asunción, with even greater success, in every domain, than in Buenos Aires. They could count here on the protection of El Supremo, who praised them to the skies but ended up expelling them in 1815. The Robertsons boast in their books of having been the first British subjects to come to know Paraguay, after having penetrated the "Chinese wall" of its isolation, concerning which they put forward a novel interpretation. (Compiler's Note.)

more than memory, took him afar to do his barking, making the rounds of all the barracks, one by one, and out to the very last guard post of the city.

Not everything is a question of memory. Instinct is a surer guide in the realm of the indistinct.

The two green men with red hair arrive at the usual hour. Hero the dog is with them. Sultan goes to the door to receive them. Come into the study, gentlemen. Distinct coolness toward the street jongleur. A certain fear makes him shrink at the sight of the sans-culotte cancerberus. Have a seat wherever you like, gentlemen. He points to the armchairs. You there, over in the corner, he mutters over his shoulder to Hero. Have you taken a bath by any chance? Oh yes, in rose water, Señor Sultan! Have you brought any fleas with you? Oh no, Most Excellent Señor Dog! I never take them out. They have weak lungs, the poor little things. I'm afraid they'll catch cold. They might catch distemper, tonsilitis, heaven knows what. The climate in Asunción is most unhealthy. It is full of germs. I bathe them in my own bathwater. I shut them up in a little Chinese lacquer box that was specially made for the little creatures and brought to me from Buenos Aires by Don Robertson, and it's bye, babies, bye, I'm off to spend the evening at The Supreme's. They're very obedient. They've learned perfect manners. Isn't that so, Don Juan? I intend to make them the best-trained trick fleas in the city. Into the corner with you! Nobody asked you anything! Hero curled up in a ball against the great bulk of the aerolith. Age-old, a century young, he begins to sniff in the stone the odor of the cosmos, wrinkling his nose slightly.

Ten pounds of brandy are heating in a caldron on the fire. Pilar the black perfumes the room with incense. He sprinkles powdered varnish on the clouds of steam. Sultan opens the door to the aqueduct and lets me in. I enter with a sheet of red-hot copper, and the room glows with celestial lights. Multicolored sparks. Objects levitate a palm's breadth in the air, surrounded by an ethereal halo. Good evening, gentlemen. Don't get up. The two men turn red; their hair, green. They glide gently in their armchairs to the floor. Their foremouths move in relief. Good evening, Excellency! Time stands still for a moment in the tail of the dogs. Bring the beer, Pilar. Here he is, back already from the cellar with the demijohn. He pours the foaming liquid into the glasses. What's certain is that, between the conjugation of English verbs and my groping and fumbling efforts to translate Chaucer, Swift, or Donne, the Robertsons came around for five years to drink my invidious fermented brew. I wasn't going to uncork a fresh demijohn each week in honor of those perfidious green-go-homes. The letter from Alvear, head of the Buenos Aires government in those days, was the drop that made the swill run over. Up to that point they'd drunk it. Juan Robertson brought the shipment of beer himself on one of his voyages. It cost me good patacoons. I never get gifts from anyone. They downed the beer without ever being able to finish it, since its volume kept increasing with the foam from the fermentation. Isn't there some way at least to put a lid on the tankards till the next lesson, Excellency?, Guillermo, the younger and craftier of the two, belched, laughing fit to kill and spitting out a couple of live flies. No, Mister William, here in this country even the most humble remains are precious to us. We're very poor, hence we can't give up even our pride. But, sir, to drink this is to snatch up Hades itself and drink it to someone's health, the younger of the Robertsons said in English with a hearty guffaw. Pe kuarú haguä ara-kañymbapevé, peë pytaguá, I joked in turn. What's that, Excellency? As you can see, our Guaraní still isn't very good. Very simple, sirs: May you piss my beer till the end of time, you greedy fools. Ah, ha, ha, hooo . . . Your Excellency! Always joking! After razing hell and drinking it to the health of someone they were fond of, the two merchants might well go on pissing my beer till Judgment Day. Tankard in hand, Juan Robertson hummed to himself his favorite little ditty:

> *There's a divinity that shapes our ends,*
> *Rough-hew them how we will!*

Between sips of the pestilential bubbles, Juan Robertson kept gurgling this pet refrain of his over and over. Acid bubbles of vaticination. Does a person's voice dream of what is possible and real? Does it dream without the dreamer's dreaming? Things have happened to me, long after they were sung about, without my having noticed the warning. The secret hides its knowledge. Without knowing it, Juan Robertson was humming what was going to happen to him at La Bajada. But I always sense something real, in the realm of the visible or audible, in an individual who sits leaning to starboard with half his backside in the air, the position the Englishman briefly assumed from time to time back then, the very one that I am in at this moment without being able to change it. His mind elsewhere, absent, Juan Robertson was bleating that idiotic prelude to himself, apparently lost in his calculations of profits and losses. That wasn't what he was doing. Yet that was it exactly. Calculations of profits and losses in the Book of his Fate. Better that way. Negative balances in the Credits are clearer than positive balances in the Debits.

Prodigious imagination, Excellency! In the open mouth of the younger of the Robertsons there formed an immense balloon of foam that could not decide whether to go up or down. He punctured it with the nail of his little finger. Once his voice was uncorked, he went on burbling enthusiastically about the canine jongleur. Hero's memory is amazing! Last night he said: I'm going to compose a little thirty-page novella. It doesn't need to be any longer than that to describe episodes of the most incontestable utility since they are born of the soul of a renegade to his class, or rather of a convert. . . . I must reflect a bit on this difference that condemns me or exalts me, depending on the mirror. . . .

Hero gulped down the rest of the tankard, looking at me out of the corner of his eye, the uncouth creature. I ordered Pilar the black to fill our glasses again. Hero was again straining my incredulity with his guttural gypsy cant. As in a congress of Babelic polyglots, the Anglomane was translating in fits and starts what Hero was growling. His red mustache full of foam was marking to a hair the cadence of his phrases: He is speaking of Nit . . . Mother of Mothers, who is at once male and female. Scarab, vulture, in her female part. Woman of the black sphere, who has her double in the man with the head of a pelican . . . The Hispanic dog's chant, translated by the Scottish merchant, reminded me of Leonardo's bestiary: The pelican loves its offspring. If it comes back to the nest and finds that they have been bitten by serpents, it tears its breast open with its beak. It washes them in its blood. It restores them to life. Is it not *I* who am the Supreme Pelican in Paraguay? Hero interrupts himself, gives me a sarcastic look through his cataracts: Your Excellency loves his offspring the way the mother-pelican does; she caresses them so fervently she kills them. Let us hope that your blood of a father-pelican will bring them back to life on the third day. Should that come to pass, Most Illustrious Sire, your pelican image will be celebrated by patriotic analists. The eunuchs of the Eucharist will have it embroidered on their capon-copes. The Old Ones will trap it in mirrors. I did not deem it the proper moment to answer the dog's beastly sarcasms. I had the impression that the others had not heard. Juan Parish went on translating: . . . Mother of the black sphere has her double in the sky, likewise a lamb vulture, at once male and female . . . Where did you get that from? It doesn't matter where I got it from! Perhaps from the Canticles of Alfonso the Wise, king of Castile and León, who, incidentally, offers in his Siete Partidas an excellent definition of a tyrant: that is to say, that man who chooses to act pro bono suo, thereby turning a rule that was a right into a wrong. That man is to be deemed a tirant, the wise king said, who, using the progress, wellbeing, and prosperitie of those he governs as a praetext, replaces the cultus of his people by that of his owne person, becoming thereby a fereful and fallacious pelican. His diabolical cunning turns those very men he doth claim to liberate into slaves. He transforms them into fishes. He stuffs them into the reddish pouch that hangs beneath his insatiable beak. He spits out only the prickles of the sort that grow on thistles, cacti, every manner of spiny species. But what is worst about tirants is that they are weary of the people, and hide their cynicism behind shamed apologies for their nation. In the face of the innocence of their vassals they feal guilty, and endeavour to corrupt one and all with their own leprosie . . . It's plain to see that street life has taught you a great deal, Hero, but for the moment I'm not asking you to recite your little tyrannicidal fables. Don't play Tupac Amaru here. You'll end up quartered. I'm asking you about that fable of the lamb vulture, the one that's at once male and female. I want to know where you got it from. What does it matter? I could have gotten it from the books of the Cabala, from the Koran, from the Bible, from the Gentiloquio of the Marqués de Santillana, from the draft that creeps in around the edges of the doors. Language is the same everywhere. As are fables. There is no fixed point allowing us to judge. It seems to me that they did not come from men's written words, but from their spoken ones, which preceded writing. But that is of little moment, since it is less important to know the origin of things than it is to know their end. Everything exists through symbols. One merely changes fantasies. Our two eyes engender a single vision. A single book, all books. But each thing gives off a certain effluvium at once like and unlike all others. An exhalation, a breath of its own. Those who know most, see most, are always the blind. Those with the sweetest voices, the mute. Those with the keenest hearing, the deaf. Homer! O mere repeater of other blind men and deafmutes! Man's principal malady is his insatiable curiosity regarding things he cannot know.

It's quite obvious, I said to the green men. This dog is as taken as my amanuensis Patiño with the notion of gilding metals, silvering mirrors, clouding them with the vapor of his breath. Hero was left speechless. Come, gentlemen, it's absurd to hang on the mystifications of a dog! Worse still, the ex canine of the last Spanish governor!, Sultan growled, baring his dislocated jaw. Shall I chase this insolent dog out of here, Excellency? Kick him out, drive him out with my sword? No, leave him where he is without being there, and you just stay quietly where you should be and aren't, unconsulted, uncultivated Sultan. Taking advantage of the interruption, the Robertsons and Hero drained their glasses with a smug little smile.

Gentlemen, what this dog is relating is an old story. From age-old books, including Genesis, we know that in the beginning primitive man was male/female. No race is perfectly pure. Every hundred years and a day, or rather, every long hundred-year day, male and female incarnate themselves in a single being that gives rise to all creatures, events, things.* It brings them forth out of a terrible pact and a principle of intermixture. The elders of the tribes here also know, without having read Plato's Symposium, that each one was originally two. Perfect types of dual men. Individuals all of a piece. Whole and complete. Fixed species. Many. Inheritance assured indefinitely through the union of the best and the best. Till thought tore them loose from nature. Separated them. Divided them in two. They continued to believe they were a single one, not knowing that one half was seeking the other half. Irreconcilable enemies in the impulse which the Man-of-Today calls love. The twins were not born of a mother; the so-called Mother-of-Mothers, so the indigenous payés who know their cosmogonies say, was devoured by the Blue-Jaguar that sleeps beneath the hammock of Ñanderuvasú, the First-Great-Father. The twins were born of themselves and engendered their mother. They inverted the idea of maternity, mistakenly considered to be the exclusive gift of women. They canceled out the difference between the sexes, so dear and so indispensable to Western thought, which can operate only by pairs. They conceived, or rediscovered the possibility, not only of two, but of many, of innumerable sexes. Though the man is the reasonable sex. Only he is capable of reflection. Hence, too, only he is called upon, destined, condemned to render an account of his unreason. How is it possible that we

---

*In his *History of Eternity,* Jorge Luis Borges, citing Leopoldo Lugones (*The Jesuit Empire,* 1904), notes that in the cosmogony of Guaraní tribes the moon was considered to be male and the sun female. In the same note he writes: "In the Germanic languages, which have grammatical gender, the sun is feminine and the moon masculine."

In another of his works Borges informs us: "For Nietzsche, the moon is a tomcat (*Kater*) that travels about on a carpet of stars and, also, a monk." A limited, symmetrical mind would immediately ask itself: What about the sun? How did Nietzsche conceive of the sun? A *she-cat sun?* A *nun-sun?* What sort of carpets did he see her traveling on? *El Supremo's Notes* hint that he solved the riddle propounded by Nietzsche. He settled the question once and for all by propounding a riddle of his own, having to do with historians, writers, and pests that infest libraries: "An insect ate words. It thought it was devouring the famous song of man and his firm foundation. But the larcenous bookworm learned nothing from having devoured words." (*Compiler's Note.*)

should have a single progenitor and a single mother? Can one not perhaps be born of oneself?

The only serious maternity is that of the man. The one real and possible maternity. I was able to be conceived without woman by the power of thought alone. Do people not credit me with two mothers, a false father, four false brothers, two birthdates? Does all this not prove beyond doubt that these many stories are without foundation? I have no family; if indeed I was really born, which has yet to be proved, since only what has been born can die. I was born of myself and *I* alone have made myself Double. (*El Supremo's Note.*)

Yes, certainly, Excellency, but . . . I would venture to say that the pleasure principle enters into it. The wise principle of the preservation of the species! Supreme bliss! Ah! Oh! Ouuu! Is it not so? Very, very nice! Agreed, Mister Robertson. But an infinitely assured species does not mean immutable species. All right, Excellency, but . . . Pardon me, Don Juan. There is not a *single species* of men. Do you know of, have you heard of the other possible species? The ones that were. The ones that are. The ones that will be. Beings come from living roots; they are born only when their path forks. Which is not a happenstance. It is only our dim understanding that believes that chances rules everywhere. Nature never tires of repeating her trial efforts. Nothing that in any way resembles a divine or pantheistic lottery, however. If One grows and keeps on growing immeasurably in and by itself, the Many will disappear. One alone will remain. Then this One will again become Many. Are you suggesting, Excellency, getting along by oneself . . . as best one can? The green men with red hair looked at me with a sly gleam in their eye. What could they know of my double birth or disbirth? I riveted my gaze on them until it transpierced the nape of their neck: I merely said that all things are ruled by the rigorous necessity of a terrible impact and a principle of fusion. Man is an idiot. He doesn't know how to do anything without copying, without imitating, without plagiarizing, without aping. It might even have been that man invented generation by coitus after seeing the grasshopper copulate. Ah, Excellency, let us grant then that the grasshopper is a reasonable animal. She knows what is good and what is practical. If I were the first man I wouldn't be the last to imitate her. I'd even learn to sing the way she does. Make the most of your summer, Don Juan. I could see him once again at Doña Juana Esquivel's country house, next to mine at Ybyray. I could see Juan Parish, not as a victorious grasshopper, but rather as the victim of that old nymphomaniac. Woman of the black sphere. Scarab, vulture in her female part, who made the green lamb of Scotland her "double" on earth.

Shhh, shhh, I beg your pardon, Excellency! Hero is recounting something on that very subject this minute. As I was speaking, the rude ex regalist bow-wow hadn't stopped talking, so that my words were counterpointed by the muffled harmonics of the dog's growls. Merely to contradict everything I said, even in the realms of languages and unknown, forgotten myths. I put on the earpieces. Hieroglyphic voice of the dog. Half-drunk voice of his English interpreter: Hero is recounting a Celtic legend. Two creatures who form one. The old hag confronts the young hero with an enigma. If he deciphers it, that is to say, if he responds to the repulsive old woman's advances, on awakening he will find in his bed a young and radiant woman who will enable him to obtain kingship . . . Dear Hero, we can't hear you very well. A little louder. Couldn't you go a little more slowly? The canine shook his head disdainfully and went straight on, in Spanish this time, ending the joke: The repulsive old woman, or the beautiful girl, has been abandoned by her people during a difficult migration as she was giving birth . . . A little more beer, please. From that time on the woman wanders about the desert. She is the Mother-of-the-Animals who refuses to deliver them into the hands of hunters. Anyone who chances to meet her in her bloody rags is so terror-stricken that he feels an irresistible erotic impulse. Infinite desires to copulate . . . To hide away in an immense fornicatory forest. To drown himself in a seminarial sea. A state that the old woman takes advantage of to rape him, rewarding him with abundant game. In that case . . . I laughed heartily, interrupting the storyteller. Ah, you're finally in a good humor again, Excellency! As a matter of fact the night has turned cool and pleasant with the south wind. Odd that it should begin to blow at midnight. Perhaps the north wind has stopped blowing at the hour when ghosts walk abroad. Ah, caprice of the winds! And of ghosts, I added, to hide my uncontainable bursts of laughter. What are you laughing at so heartily, Sire? Oh, just a bit of nonsense, Don Juan! I suddenly remembered our first meeting, that afternoon in Ybyray.

In his *Letters*, Juan Parish Robertson describes the encounter as follows:

"On one of those pleasant Paraguayan afternoons, after the wind from the southeast has cleared and refreshed the atmosphere, I went out hunting in a quiet valley, not far from Doña Juana's house. I suddenly came upon a small dwelling, clean and unpretentious. A partridge flew up. I fired, and the bird fell to the ground. Good shot!, a voice at my back exclaimed. I turned around and saw a gentleman of about fifty, dressed all in black.

"I apologized for having shot off the gun so close to his house, but with great kindness and extreme courtesy, typical of the simple, primitive hospitality of the country, he invited me to sit down on the veranda and smoke a cigar and had the little black bring me a maté.

"The owner of the house assured me

that there was not the least reason to apologize, and that his lands were at my disposal whenever I wanted to divert myself with my shotgun in those parts.

"Through the little portico I spied a celestial globe, a large telescope, a theodolite and various other optical and mechanical instruments, which caused me immediately to infer that the figure before me was none other than the gray eminence of the Government himself.

"The instruments confirmed the rumors I had heard concerning his knowledge of astronomy and his practice of the occult sciences. He left no doubt in my mind on this head. Here you have, he said to me with an ironic smile, motioning with his hand in the direction of the dark laboratory-study, my temple of Minerva, which has fed so many legends.

"I presume, he continued, that you are the English gentleman who is in residence at the house of Doña Juana Esquivel, my neighbor. I answered that that was indeed the case. He added that he had intended to visit me, but that the political situation in Paraguay, particularly with regard to his person, was such that he found it necessary to live in great seclusion. There was no other way, he added, to keep people from putting the most sinister interpretations on his most insignificant acts.

"He ushered me into his library, a closed room with a very small window, so shaded by the very low-hanging roof of the veranda that it barely allowed the dwindling light of late afternoon to filter into the room.

"The library was ranged along three rows of shelves running the width of the room and might have contained some three hundred volumes. There were several voluminous Law books. As many more on mathematics, experimental and

applied sciences, some in French and Latin. *Euclid's Elements* and a number of tomes on Physics and Chemistry were lying open on the table with marks between the pages. His collection of books on Astronomy and general Literature occupied an entire row. The *Quijote,* also lying open in the middle, in a handsome edition with a purple page marker and gold galloons on the cover, lay on a stand. Voltaire, Rousseau, Montesquieu, Volney, Raynal, Rollin, Diderot, Julius Caesar, Machiavelli formed a choir just beyond it in the shadow which was beginning to grow darker.

"On a large table, more like a treasure galleon than a study table, were great piles of dossiers, sheets of paper with writing on them, and trial records. Several volumes bound in parchment were scattered about on the table.

"The Dictator took off his cape and lit a candle that did its feeble best to light the room, though it appeared to be used ordinarily to light cigars. A maté vessel and a silver inkwell adorned the other end of the table. There were neither rugs nor straw mats on the tile floor. The chairs were of such an antique style that they appeared to be prehistoric pieces that had come from some excavation. They were covered with old hides or incrustations in an unrecognizable material, almost phosphorescent, on which strange hieroglyphs, similar to rupestrian inscriptions, were imprinted. I tried to lift one of these chairs; but despite my every effort I did not manage to move it one millimeter. The Dictator then came to my aid, and with his affable smile levitated the heavy curule with a slight gesture of his hand. He then caused it to descend in the precise place I had wordlessly chosen in my mind.

"Open envelopes and folded letters were scattered all about the floor of the room; one could not say in disorder, but in accordance with a certain pre-established order that gave the atmosphere, *from below,* a slightly sinister and incomprehensible air.

"A large earthen jar for water and a pitcher stood on a rough wooden tripod in one corner. In another, the Dictator's saddles and riding gear gleamed in the half-light.

"As we talked together the little black began to pick up, slowly, with studied gestures and as though imbued with the importance of his task, the half-boots, the slippers, the shoes that were scattered about everywhere, without, as I have said, their disturbing the more profound and unalterable order of a pre-established system that ruled the atmosphere of the humble, meticulously neat little dwelling located so idyllically amid the trees, giving every appearance of being inhabited by a being who loved beauty and tranquillity.

"From the outside, perhaps from the enclosed yards or pens in the back, the sound of shrill squeals, as of hungry rodents, began to reach my ears, growing louder and louder.

"My attention was instantly arrested, for those squeals were so muffled, so hideously concerted, that they seemed to me to be coming from some subterranean cave, if not from beyond the grave.

"Only then did the Dictator, who had not ceased pacing the room from one end to the other as we conversed, halt in his tracks too.

"He summoned another of the heavy chairs with a clap of his hands and sat down in front of me. On noting my look of utter surprise at the more and more audible concert of squeals, he reassured me, with his odd smile: It's suppertime in my rat nursery. He ordered the little black to go tend to them."

Ah! You behaved like a gentleman in this hospitable land! You repaid as best you could the interested hospitality of the octogenarian damsel of Ybyray.* When I withdrew from the Junta because of my war

---

*"The site of Doña Juana Esquivel's house was absolutely splendid; the landscape that surrounded it was no less so. One saw magnificent woods of a rich and varied green; here the bare plain and there the dense brush; murmuring springs and brooks cooling the ground; orange groves, fields of cane and maize surrounded the white manor house.

"Doña Juana Esquivel was one of the most extraordinary women I have ever met. In Paraguay, women are generally old at forty. Doña Juana, however, was eighty-four, and though her skin naturally was wrinkled and her hair snow-white, she still had a vivacious look in her eye, a ready laugh, and an active body and mind to testify to the truth of the dictum that there is an exception to every rule.

"She lodged me like a prince. There is in the Spanish character, especially when enhanced as in this instance by South American abundance, such a magnificent conception of the word 'hospitality' that I allowed myself, through particular demonstrations of courtesy and reciprocal favors on my part, to comport myself in many respects in precisely the same manner as Doña Juana. In the first place, everything belonging to her house—servants, horses, food, the products of her estate—were all at my disposal. Then, if I happened to admire anything that she possessed—her favorite pony, rich filigree work, choice specimens of ñandutí, dried fruits, or a pair of splendid mules—they were conveyed to me in such a way that it made acceptance of them inevitable. Because I had remarked that it was very pretty, a

with the military, I was the involuntary witness of that other less silent, albeit more intimate, war, staged in the rural Troy of my neighbor Juana Esquivel. I heard at all hours the din of her well-nigh secular salaciousness. I saw her chasing you along the veranda, amid the greenery, up and down the stream. Her battle-hardened Fallopian tuba sounded the charge, in sunlight and shadow, with energy enough to annihilate an entire army. The old lady's cries of pleasure ruptured my Eustachians. The two of you made the trees shake, the water in the river boil when you dived into it naked. Doña Juana's ardor made the white-hot heat of afternoon siestas last far into the night. She brought the cool night dew to the boiling point. A fog with the taste of acid drifted across the land bathed in moonlight. It crept into my hermetically sealed house. It kept me from concentrating on my thoughts, on my studies. It disturbed my solitary contemplation. I was obliged to give up my favorite occupation: taking out my telescope and observing the constellations. I saw the gaunt cicada of an old hag drag herself across the grass, moaning, enveloped in a long tail of smoke. You

gold snuffbox was brought to my room one morning by a slave, and because one day my eye had chanced to fall on it, a diamond ring was placed on my table with a note that made its acceptance imperative. Nothing was cooked in the house save what was known to be to my liking, and though I endeavored by every possible means to compensate her for her costly courtesy and at the same time to give her clear indications that I found her generosity quite overwhelming, my efforts proved to be entirely in vain.

"I was hence of a mind to abandon this overhospitable mansion when an incident occurred. Unbelievable, yet absolutely true. It changed my subsequent relations with this singular woman, and placed them on a better footing.

"I was very fond of the mournful airs sung by Paraguayans to the accompaniment of a guitar. Doña Juana knew this, and to my vast surprise, on returning from the city one afternoon, I found her trying, under the direction of a guitarist, to sing, in her cracked voice, a plaintive love-lament and accompany it on the guitar with her dark, bony, wrinkled fingers. What else could that dirge have been? What could I have done in the face of that spectacle offered me by a woman

in her dotage save to give a hint of a mocking smile, thereby risking offending the lady's sensibilities? 'For the love of God,' I said, 'fourteen years after you should, by every natural law, be in your grave, how can you turn yourself into an object of ridicule for your enemies or an object of pity for your friends?'

"The exclamation, I confess, even though addressed to a lady eighty-four years old, was not gallant, for where age is concerned, what woman can bear a reproach of this sort?

"It was immediately apparent that Doña Juana possessed all the weakness of her sex in this regard. She flung the guitar to the floor. She brusquely ordered the singing teacher to leave the house, threw the servants out of the room, and immediately, with a sort of fierceness I did not believe her capable of, she stunned me with the following words: 'Señor Don Juan, I was not expecting such an insult from the man I love,' placing extraordinary stress on the last word. 'Yes'— she went on—'I was ready, as I still am, to offer my hand and my fortune to you. Why would I have learned to sing and play the guitar if not to give you pleasure? Why have I studied, what have I thought of, for whom have I lived in the last three

Don Juan, the Young hero of the Celtic legend, were powerless to decipher the enigma that the repulsive sorceress compulsively propounded to you, varying it each time. Each time you waited for the next rape, knowing beforehand that your recompense would never take the form of seeing the old woman turned into a radiant damsel. You can't complain, however, since she did reward you after all—by bringing you exceptional good luck in hunting doubloons, if not turtledoves.

I have a bad memory, Don Juan. I don't remember which writer of antiquity it is who speaks of an Old Woman-Devil, armed with a double set of teeth, one in her mouth, the other in her sex. Here in Paraguay too, where the devil is a woman for the natives, certain tribes worship this succubus. What is the meaning of the vulva-with-teeth if not the devouring nonengendering principle of the woman? Juan Robertson gave a slight shudder. Don't those teeth fall out, Excellency, when the woman grows old? No, my dear Don Juan. They become harder, even sharper. Is there something you're afraid of? Has something unpleasant happened to you? I don't think so, Excellency. In any event, Don Juan, I think you ought to know how the Indians conjure away these risks. They begin to dance, night and day, around the devil-woman. They dance madly, and make her dance and leap and cavort too. At sunrise on the third day, two things can happen: The fangs fall out and the floor of the Ceremonial House turns white with them. The men then run after those teeth that hop from one place to another, trembling, hanging from the umbivaginal cord, till they fall motionless, turned into dry coconut, thistle, tuna cactus thorns. They gather them up and throw them in a big fire where it takes three more days for them to be entirely consumed, as meanwhile they fill the brush with a thick, viscous, acrid smoke, as befits their origin and condition. It may

---

months save for you? And is this the recompense I receive?'

"The very elderly lady's show of emotion at this point was a curious combination of pathetically impassioned suffering and ridiculousness as, dissolving into tears and sobbing with indignation, she gave vent to her feelings. The spectacle was a novelty that took me by surprise and alarmed me more than a little on the poor old lady's account. I therefore left the room and sent her servants to her, telling them that their mistress was seriously ill; and after hearing that it was all over, I went to bed, not knowing whether to feel pity or to smile at the tender

passion that a young man of twenty had awakened in a lady of eighty-four. I hope that the story of this amorous adventure will not be attributed to a sense of vanity. I recount it simply as an example of the well-known aberrations of that most ardent and most capricious of all the gods: Cupid. There is no age beyond reach of his darts. Octogenarian and green youth alike are his victims; and his caprioles tend to be all the more extravagant when outward circumstance—age, habits, decrepitude— have conspired to make the notion of his access to the heart incredible and absurd." (*Ibid.*)

also happen that the lower-teeth of the woman do not fall out. Convulsed and driven out of their minds, the men-dancers are turned, to their misfortune, into what we call sometics or he-whores here. Once they have met with this disaster, they are condemned to the most humiliating duties. It is best to be forewarned against such contingencies. Suddenly, without his having foreseen it, the cleverest of men may find himself sitting on the horn of a bull, swaying back and forth. Fi, fi, fo, fum! Watch out for the devil-woman, Englishman!

Juan Robertson put his hands between his legs. His body wrenched into an arc as he retched. The reek of beer filled the room. Even the dogs turned up their noses. Hero glanced all about, scowling. Sniffed in every direction. Judging from the salacious stench, Excellency, it would appear that we've been invaded by more than a hundred thousand devil-women! Possibly, Hero, possibly. I don't smell a thing. I have a head cold. The pooch went over to the Englishman, who was arched over fighting his stomach cramps, his head drooping on his chest, his elbows digging into his groins. As consolation, Hero muttered without conviction: You'll soon be better, Don Juan. It's just an attack of moral colic. And he added in English so that I wouldn't understand: Fucking awful business this, no, yes, sir? Dreamt all night of that bloody old hag Quin again. . . . I ordered Pilar the black to throw some pellets of incense and liquidambar and another pint of brandy on the red-hot copper plate. The beautiful colors drove away the bad odors. Go to the kitchen, Pilar, and ask Santa to fix a tisane of flowers of fennel, mistletoe, white mauve, and yateí-ka'á. The bluish skulls of the Robertson brothers were dimly visible amid the aromatic smoke and the sparks. Hero and Sultan, half-asleep, disdainfully offered their backs to each other. Except that they flew into a rage when Candide and his manservant, the Tucumán mulatto Cacambo, arrived in Paraguay to fight for the Jesuits. This empire is a marvel!, Cacambo exclaimed excitedly, trying to trick his master. I know the way and I'll take you there: the padres own everything and the peoples have nothing. It's a masterpiece of reason and justice. Uncontainable joy. Sidereal optimism. Sultan was all confused. He thought he was in a Paraguay that had been disjesuited forever, and here were two suspect-looking foreigners taking off for that vanished kingdom with which some people dare compare mine. The clatter of their mounts' galloping hoofs resounded in the shadow of the room. The entire kingdom as well. Brought back to life, intact, present. A giant honeybear-hive, an anthill three hundred leagues in diameter with a hundred fifty thousand Indians inside. The father provincial entered, his spurs striking sparks from the floor. He recognized Candide immediately. They embraced affectionately. Sultan and Hero, the pair of them one, maddened, enraged, attacked walls, doors, and windows, Bulgar-fashion, roaring louder than a hundred dragons and dog-serpents. Powerless in the face of this immense, iridescent soap bubble. Amid columns of green and gold marble, cages full of parakeets, hummingbirds, cardinals, colibris, all the winged creatures of the universe, Candide and the father provincial peacefully lunched on a table service of silver and gold. Songs held the senses suspended. Birds, cithers, harps, fifes, suspended in the music-air. Cacambo, resigned, was out in the splitting sun eating grains of maize from a little wooden bowl with Paraguayans squatting on their heels amid the cows, the dogs, the lilies of the field. Candide, what is optimism?, the mulatto from Tucumán shouted from a distance, a rifle shot away from the green marble bower. As far as I can tell, Candide answered him, it's maintaining how well everything is going when everything is manifestly going very badly. Amid the wine fumes, the father's face did not appear to register anything. Hero and Sultan flung themselves upon the tonsured general of the Theatines. Let's put an end to this hurly-burly, I said to the Robertsons, busy chasing a colibri across the page for the fun of it. If you've begun reading the story to kill time, imagine that it's lying dead now beneath the weight of such phantasmagorias; either that or the dogs kill us and gobble up our buttocks as well, leaving us only the credulous half of our rear ends, the incredulous half of life. Young Robertson placed the plumule of the colibri between the pages of the book and closed it. The two of them rose to their feet, feeling their backsides as an augury, and good night, Reverend Father Provincial, oh I beg your pardon, I mean Excellency.

À propos of the "rat nursery" that *El Supremo* did in fact maintain for experimental purposes at his farm in Ybyray, let us look at another example of the method employed by Dr. Días de Ventura and Brother Bel-Asshole to vilify and defame him by distorting the facts. The fragments that follow have been extracted from the already-mentioned private correspondence between these two rabid enemies of the Perpetual Dictator.

"Rev. Father and friend:

"I am already moved, before the fact, by your future *Proclamations of a Paraguayan to His Countrymen,* in which with your admirable art of persuasion you will convince them that they must rebel and end this era of shame and sorrow before it is too late.

"Perhaps in this monstruary of facts you may find a use for the Dictator's latest mad idea, concerning which he is maintaining the strictest secrecy. Imitating the prisoners who tame rodents in the dungeons (so I have been informed confidentially), he has set up an immense rat nursery at his country house in Trinidad. He has there rounded up every species of rodent known in this country. He has posted two or three deafmute slaves to guard the nursery. José María Pilar, his little black valet, is the one who keeps watch on the watchmen. His trust in the little black and his innocence are perhaps, in the Dictator's opinion, sufficient guarantee against any sort of perfidy. But it is out of the mouth of babes, slaves though they may be, that truths are forthcoming: those that on occasion take the form of symbols or parables.

"From high up in a tree lookout, the little black—I have it from most trustworthy sources—performs his assigned mission of observing and noting down point for point all the movements of the thousands of rodents. The Dictator frequently comes out to the estate in person to verify the data. According to the rumors that are circulating, based on the little black's own accounts, the Great Man has turned the nursery into a strange laboratory. He there engages in experiments in crossbreeding and above all in observations of the crowd behavior of this impressive mass of sharp-toothed mammifers. Feeding at the ringing of a bell; maneuvers, as though the rodents were military troops; matings; even long periods of starvation during which the bell sounds the tocsin so frequently that it drives this multitude of rats and mice mad; all this, I tell you, Rev. Father, leads one to suspect that the diabolical Dictator tries out there, in that sort of rough draft in vivo, those methods of government of his through which he is bestializing our peasants.

"The latest experiment goes beyond all the limits that a respectable person in his right mind can imagine. Imagine, Yr. Grace: something truly demoniacal! The Dictator has ordered the kit of a female cat to be shut up in absolute darkness from the very moment of its birth. For three years, the time that has passed since the Dictator assumed absolute power, the kit has been kept in total solitude and isolation, completely removed from contact with any other living species. The cat, now an adult, was removed in a leather sack from its place of hermetic confinement and taken to the nursery. There, beneath the blazing sun, the cat was let out of the bag and thrown in among the thousands of starving rodents as the little black rent the air of the siesta hour with earsplitting peals of the bell. Imagine, my friend, the scorching sunlight suddenly burning the eyes of the cat accustomed to utter darkness since its birth. The light blinds it at the very instant it first sees it! Well-fed in its nocturnal cave, it also fails to recognize the ancestral enemy species that surrounds it and attacks it fiercely, so that in the space of seconds it is reduced to tiny splinters of bone that are carried off in all directions in the midst of this frightful witches' sabbath. Is this not, Rev. Father, something truly satanic?

"The greatest strength of one who governs resides in the perfect knowledge of those he governs, the Dictator said in his inaugural speech. Are we Paraguayans, or at least our countrymen who have been unable to escape the hydrophobic dog, condemned to the fate of that poor cat born in a dungeon? May Yr. Grace use all this to sound salutary warnings in his *Proclamations.* Your devoted friend and humble servant *Buenaventura Días de Ventura.*" (*Compiler's Note.*)

Shut up in my last-quarter, I rubbed the skull with a flannel cloth at night. Only later, much later, did it begin to take on a faint shine. It gave off a sort of rose-colored sweat from the heat of all the friction. I'm the one that's doing the rubbing, but you're the one that's doing the sweating, I said to it. I kept rubbing, in complete darkness. Night after night for nine moons. Only then did it begin to give off minute sparks. It's beginning to think already! Light-heat. Everything known. Everything white. Heart panting in my mouth. All white/all black. Tremendous tremulous happiness! Things typical of a child flying solo-to-solo. Or rather: things typical of a child still unborn incubating in the cube of a cranium. Any receptacle will do, even the dead head of one who has gone down the drain and ended up in a coffin, victim of an unexpected illness or a long-awaited old age. Better still, one who has simply remained buried underground. But I was a non-born, lying hidden by my own will within the six walls of a cranium. The memories of the adult man that I had been weighed heavily on the child that was not yet, freighting him with leftover fears. Fear not!, I said to him to raise his spirits. It is men of profound culture who bury themselves the deepest. They yearn to return to the nature they have betrayed. To return, out of fear of death, to the state that most resembles death. Something like forced confinement in a prison, a dungeon, a police station, a penal colony, a concentration camp. I didn't think all of this then, in the stifling shadow of the garret. I imagined it, I will imagine it later.

Being born is my real idea . . . (*burned, the rest illegible*).

How long can a man lie in the earth before he rots? That depends, if he's not rotten before he dies he'll last some eight or nine year. And if he's a good Christian and dies the day of his death rightly and properly, he may hold up till Judgment Day, maybe. Be raised from the dead by God's voice alone. Ever'body knows that, little Jo. My name isn't Jo. Yes, child. From taitá Adam to Our Lord Jesus Christ, that's what it's always been. Joshua. Or Adam. Or Christ. Can a man lengthen his life, machú Hermogena Encarnación? If he's not guilty of his own death, he doesn't shorten his own life. A man begins to grow old the day he's born, little Jo. His old age keeps forever creeping backwards there in front of him. But where you ever seen anybody alive what doesn't shorten his life voluntarily? Don't nobody know how to desert this miserable lot.

The nanny turned her back to me as she rubbed her kinky hair, the nape of her neck, her back, her breasts with turtle-fat. Stop asking so many questions, Master Josué, and come rub me round my middle. I'm an old woman and my hand lacks the reach and the strength. She stretched out on the floor. I began distractedly rubbing the bundle of wrinkles, thinking about the skull, as the nanny, her mouth glued to the floor, hummed:

> . . . I'll never die
> without knowing why why
> why
> why
> yai yai yai . . .

How long do you think this skull's been buried? Heavens above! What in the world are you keeping that for? All skulls are mad. Why is that, machú Encarna? Because they've no brains, of course! This death's head, she said, turning it round and round in her ashen-colored hands, has been buried for nine thousand one hundred twenty-seven moons. When the moon comes round again, it will go off and die yet again. Hi, hi! Better, if you want my bad advice, to take it to the cemetery ery ery. Tell me, machú Encarna: was it the head of a man or a woman? Of a man, of a man. Look here at the cock crest. A most distinguished gentleman, he was. Smell tells. The more cality the owner had in life, the worse smell he has after he's dead ead ead. In other days he had a tongue, he could sing:

> When I was young
> strumming my guitar
> strumming my guitar
> I spent my time
> spent and spent
> avá avá *§
> avá avatisoká **§§

*§*Avá:* in Guaraní, Indian.
**§§*Avatisoká:* stick or pestle.

The gentleman's tongue is now in the power of milord the worm. Hi hi hi! Ah, sir, if you've lost your good judgment you won't last till Judgment Day! Hi hi hi! All those bones will be good for, my child, is a game of ninepins ins ins. They won't even be good for that. Now that I've had a good look at it, I see it was an Indian's head. The song said so. There's nothing like singing to show a person what's what. Look here: the mark of the leg iron on the bone, the cleft left by the hairband. Throw it in the river of the Payaguá guá guá. Throw it away, my little master, it could bring you a big handful of bad luck! Yai yai yai! The nanny's voice echoing back and forth between the six walls: That's no toy for a child!

I wasn't a child. I wasn't one yet. I wouldn't ever be one again. The nanny, laughing: When you sucked my tit I didn't feel your mouth. What you need is to exist in your natural being.

Ah fortune what misfortune
when the she-ass wants to the he-ass can't . . .

Laughter. White in black. Your mama got you off to a bad start from the very first, little Jo. Worse still when there's two mothers in the picture. Be still, Hermogena! I didn't have a mother!, I said, but the nanny had flown out the window, leaving only the resounding echo of her laughter of a bird of ill omen.

I see myself exploring by the light of a candle the armature of bone. First globe of a world that fell into my hands. Small dungeon where the thought of a man was imprisoned. No matter whether he was an Indian or a great lord. Greater than the terrestrial globe. Empty now. Who knows. Bah! Idle subject. Living imagination imagining dead imagination. No empty space anywhere. Anyway, what is there about emptiness that can terrify anyone? Those who are terrified of the image that they themselves have created are children. I place the candle inside the skull. The spongy transparency affords a hint of the now-vanished labyrinth of matter. Stains. Mere traces in the whiteness of the rotunda. I measure, I mark, I survey all that is within my compass. Radii, diameters, fissures, angles, cells, orbital nebulae, temporal circumvolutions, occipital, equinoctial, solstitial zones, parietal regions. Places of great brainstorms. Bottomless holes. Craters. Lunar globe. Ancient cranium. Oldster's skull or a youngster's. Ageless. The metopic suture divides it into two halves. Childhood/ Old Age. Now that I repose in my great age without having emerged from the infancy that I never had, I know that I must have a beginning without ceasing to be an end. Given three or four lives or perhaps a hundred on this thankless earth, I might have been able to get somewhere. Know when I went too far or not far enough. Know what I did badly. Know, know, know! Though we already know from the Scriptures that knowledge increaseth grief.

In the crypt-cryptorium of the Gothic pagoda of Monserrat we students read in secret the books of the "libertine" authors, sitting on skulls that had been robbed of their authority centuries before. In the light of the candles placed on their graves, amid the flutter of bats and the miasmas of death, those books of the "anti-Christs" held for us a strange flavor of new life.

Long afterward, Brother Mariano Bel-Asshole passes on to his friend Dr. Ventura Días de Ventura the following confidential report on his nephew's days as a student:

"The resolute youth very soon becomes one of the first in his class. His total concentration on his studies permits him to advance more rapidly than his classmates. In two years he completes two curricula for the degree of bachelor of arts, at the end of which he sits for an examination in Logic and three entire branches of Philosophy, graduating with a Licenciate in Law and a Master of Arts degree. He crammed a volume of Aesthetics into his head which made him a visionary. Latin is his strong point. He speaks it to perfection and writes in that language his essays and studies, his love letters, and all the clandestine pasquinades with which he bombards the Students' Quarters and the Rector's Residence.

"When the new pupil was admitted into the Boarding School we did not yet foresee that this fifteen-year-old adolescent would become in the course of time the protagonist of one of the most terrible political dramas of South America.

"The Rector gave him the accolade in the Secret Hall of the Community. The students embraced the newcomer from Asunción as a sign of charity and welcome. All of us kissed the dark and taciturn Judas on both his cheeks crusted with pimples. We kissed his hands that later would cuff all those of us who helped him and aided him, in the realm of the temporal as in the realm of the eternal.

"Nervous and irascible temperament. Withdrawn. Not at all communicative. Arrogant, rebellious, toward Masters and fellow students alike. Does nothing to gain their sympathy, but commands their respect nonetheless thanks to his intelligence and tenacity. In the classroom and outside, his strong personality makes a vivid impression. The memory of his mischievous pranks and exploits long lingers in the traditions of the Cloister. With respect to his fellow students, he takes especial pleasure in dominating them, and succeeds in so doing because he is bold, self-willed, intrepid in his plans and their execution. He frequently comes to blows with them and threatens them with a dagger that he carries about on his person at all times. But it is his courage that causes his fellow students to respect him. A number of anecdotes prove this.

"Inside the church of the Company (which he called the 'Gothic Pagoda') there was a deep subterranean passage that ran through a good part of the city and came out at its other end in the building known as the Old Novitiate. That cellar containing numerous tombs of saintly and illustrious men also contained cells for the application of corporal punishment. The students were in the habit of stealing into this catacomb to hold their revels and carouse. The scholarship student from Asunción acted as leader of these forays, preceding the others with a lantern. One night he induced one of his companions to accompany him. Frightened to death but urged on by his pride, as the lad confessed later, he started down the gloomy passageway. Halfway through it, a skull appeared amid the tombs, blocking their way. The companion stumbled over it and fell to the ground, half terrified to death. The impetuous roisterer then unsheathed his rapier and plunged it repeatedly into the eye sockets of the skull. The subterranean passage rang with the cry of a wounded animal. The weapon came out dripping with blood, to the great terror of the other lad, who witnessed the macabre scene as though in a nightmare, he said. With a kick of his foot the ringleader sent the skull flying into the wall, as a rat ran off amid the bits of bone scattered about on the ground. This episode won the Paraguayan pupil a somewhat sinister reputation, and made his influence on the others all the greater.

"During one of the student outings to the countryside round the city, at the recreational villa of Caroyas, he carved his name on an inaccessible boulder on a hill. Much later, a bolt of lightning split the stone in two and destroyed his mark, but his name remained indelibly engraved on the desk that had been his, since he had carved it with a knife point so deeply that the strokes cut all the way through the log.

"On another occasion he forced a companion to swallow the stones of several peaches because the boy had stolen fruit from him. He was already known around the school as *El Dictador,* a prophetic nickname that proved to be only too apt, going beyond the limits of the Royal College at that stage of his juvenile education. In the *Private Book* on the students of the College, the Rectors, Fathers Parras and Guittian, confirm that he is much taken by the diabolical doctrines of those anti-Christs appearing in legions in France, the Low Countries, or those in the North. An indefatigable reader of these new Books of Chivalry, not just of Romances, or of Vain or Profane Stories such as the Amadíses and others of this nature, he steeped himself in the Macchiabellian ideas whose arm is to build an atheist society on the abomination of man without God.

"The rebel ringleader was therefore expelled from the Royal College and obliged to continue his studies at the University as a day student or one at liberty (though in this case a *libertine* one would be the more exact term) until he completed them and received the mortarboard *in utroque juris* of Doctor in Sacred Theology and Philosophy, at the hands of Saint Albert himself.

"Yet another injustice was committed, for which I bear a double share of the blame, as professor and as relative. The expulsion of the aberrant disciple should have been total; his punishment, exemplary. How many tyrants, how many sinister personages who have un-leashed torrents of blood and tears might we have been spared had they been crushed in time, when the young viper first begins to raise its poisonous head! These avernal ophidians are marked from birth by their triangular heads. I was weak enough to intercede on my nephew's behalf. I not only defended him, offering myself as the guarantor of his future moderate comportment. I also paid a financial debt he owed the College. And finally, exposing myself to even greater derision and as punishment for my sins, I acted as his sponsor at the graduation ceremony.

"If anything further were needed to model the image of his horrendous character, it suffices to add one more fact that casts a revealing light on his innermost secrets, from deep within his twisted mind. Around the time of his expulsion, he received the sad news of his mother's death. A grievous occasion for any well-born man of normal sensibilities. It did not, however, make the slightest impression upon him. Do you think, my dear friend Ventura, that the Dictator gave signs at any time of being in the least affected? Far from it! The wellsprings of filial love, of which even animals give proof, having dried up in his soul, he did not even appear to be aware of the distressing event. Rather than grief and mourning he manifested, on the contrary, a total insensibility, striking even more defiant poses and making even more arrogant remarks against Masters and fellow students. Finally, I could tell you of countless similar instances, but it is only pinned on the end of a fork that one could do this monster justice, and I fear that you may grow as weary of reading me as I am of digging about in such obdurate and ignominious material," Brother Mariano concludes his long letter to Días de Ventura. (*Compiler's Note.*)

The rector summons me. He orders me to prostrate myself before his chair, and putting his arm about my shoulder speaks paternally in my ear in confessione, caressing the lobe of my other one with his silky fingertips: What deeply pains us and disturbs us is the venom of sedition and atheism that the books and the ideas of those libertine impostors that all of you are reading in secret are insinuating into your minds. The devil, my son, is prompting the pages of those deicidal and regicidal books. Spitting on the Holy Books his execrable slaver of exotic doctrines. But, your paternity, the God that all of you have brought to our America, binding to his service the mitayo and yanacona§ gods of the Indians, is exotic too. Don't be a heretic, my son! No, reverend father. We simply want to know what is new, and not just keep parroting the Paternicas, the Summa, the maxims of Peter Lombard. You still want to destroy Newton with syllogisms and all you can do is patch your decrepit theological bastion with other odd bits of old shoe leather. We, on the other hand, are endeavoring to make *everything new* with the help of masons such as Rousseau, Montesquieu, Diderot, Voltaire, and others as good as they are. Omnia mecum porto,

§Indians in the service of Spaniards in colonial days were called *mitayos* and *yanaconas.*

reverend father, and if I carry everything that is mine about with me, those new ideas form part of our new nature. You can't confiscate them unless you wash our brains out with muriatic acid. Rebellious pig! The round rectorial gob of spit hit me square in the eye, rinsing it out. I noted that my powers of vision were all the better for it. Paradoxes of washing not properly done. When a hard rain falls, men get smeared with mud and pigs are left nice and clean.

I have an old skull in my hands. I am searching for the secret of thought. At some point the greatest secrets are in contact with the smallest. This is the point that my fingernail traces on the bone. Lustravit lampade terras. After much groping about, I believe I have now located the throne of will. The locus of language beneath this mushroom of aphasia. Here, the forgotten screen of memory. Standing motionless, what were once power plants of movement. The senses, vanished; the power of reason that makes us miserable; the conscience that makes cowards of us all because it makes us know that we are cowards and miserable.

I turn the calcareous ball between my hands. Valleys, dark depressions where Capricorn gambols. Horns in flames. Mountains. A mountain. Shadow of a mountain. The top still emits a vague phosphorescence. It goes out. I withdraw the smoking candle. I enter. There is no horizon other than the bone underfoot. I slowly drag myself toward the precise point that does not divagate. Great darkness. Great silence. Not even an echo answers my shouts in the concave dungeon. Sound of footsteps. I leave in a hurry.

Betrayal by the nanny. Ambush. Heelbones of the artillery captain of the king's militias. Creaking of the door. The man they say is my father, the Paulista mameluco, is here, immense, imposing, swarthy-skinned. Loud voice, very high, heard from ground level. It takes a long time to reach me. Thundering cannon blast: Miserable! Jogar-se jôgo da bola con un cráneo humano! Haverem vergonha malnacido! Vai'mbora ahora mismo a enterrarlo en la contrasacristía de la Encarnación!§ Then you're to go to confess this profanation to the senhor cura! Nanny says, sir, that it's not a Christian head but an Indian one. Throw it into the river then! Black with rage, the captain of militias makes his exit with such a hard slam of the door/fillip of his finger that it nearly splits my head in two. The skull

§"Wretch! Playing ninepins with a human skull! Aren't you ashamed, you ill-born creature! Off with you this minute: go bury it behind the sacristy of Encarnación!" (As here, whenever *El Supremo* has his father speak, it is in a bastard language, half Spanish, half Portuguese.)

has rolled off into the darkest corner. It is there, some ten paces away, bobbing its head. Pleading. Pleading. Pleading, it too, to return to earth. White, disborn, not-finished. All white in the little milky shadow it casts about it in the darkness. Supplicant pleading for memory. Penitent having forgotten what is habit among the living. Dust begging to return to dust. It drags itself over to me. Take me away! Bury me again! It sways drunkenly back and forth. I'm nothing but the skull of a rakehell whore-son! It is weeping through its empty eye sockets. Come, come, you ungrateful rascal! This is no time for tears. If you were weak-willed whilst you lived, be strong-hearted whilst you're dead. Don't try to fool me. I'm no numskull: I know you for the true skull that you are. You're not a libertine whoreson, as is the individual who claims to be my progenitor. Ah you, son, you don't know anything because you haven't been born yet. Nanny told me you were the skull of an Indian. No, my boy, no! If that were so, how is it that I speak the Old Castilian of Castilla la Vieja? With a La Mancha accent, to boot. Naturally thou art not a past master of the art of sounds of language. Were it otherwise, thou wouldst know it to be a veridical truth that I am a sly rascal. I nursed my reputation as a liar so as to tell the truth with impunity. Nannies are bitches whose lies are like beeches: their fruits aren't good for anything but fattening pigs. In the name of charity, bury me, throw me in the river! A very dark place where I can hide my shame! Standing there before it, amid the ringing that fills my battered head, I dimly hear its silence begging me, begging me, begging me. I pick up the gray flowerpot. All grays are reaching the same level as in the beginning. There where the fall began. Quicksilvered gray is situated between white and black; white reduced to the state of darkness. The buzzing fills my skull and comes out my ears, my mouth, the eye sockets of the dark whiteness I am cradling in my arms. Everything known: White. Everything past: Gray. Everything finished: Black. The nanny's song comes to my lips. I allow it to screech out between my clenched teeth, my mouth pressing against the bone of the penitential-pestilential skull. What's the matter now? I'm suffering mightily, my boy! My feeling of guilt has undone me. My mother said to me one day, with glassy eyes: When you're in bed and hear the dogs barking in the countryside, hide under the coverlet. Don't take what they're doing lightly. The white ball began shivering again. Come on, skull, forget such tripe! Forget your mother. Think of something serious; I need you to think of something serious. You're beginning to bore me with your melancholy humor. You were much more amusing when you asked me riddles or made fun of the grave-diggers. I shut it up in a box of noodles, which I then hid in the attic amid the rusty junk that the captain of militias had stored up there.

For some time the Paulista whoreson was to leave me in peace. He departed shortly thereafter on one of his inspection tours of the posts of Costa Abajo and Arriba, to distant Fuerte Borbón. I now had precious time and absence of time at my disposal. I set up camp in the attic. I took the box to the darkest corner of the garret. Sitting before it I began watching the whitish mass through the little glass circle, without the hours passing by or seeing the day drawing to a close. I felt it was night when the darkness grew denser within me. I then got the skull out and took it to bed with me. When the dogs began to bark I put it underneath the coverlet; its jaws were trembling with fear, its parietals damp with icy sweat. Everything white underneath the bedclothes, giving off in the darkness that lividity, that humidity that were not of this world. I hounded it with questions. Tell me, you aren't really the skull of a libertine whoreson, are you? Tell me it isn't true! You're the skull of a most distinguished gentleman! Answer! A yawn. Less and less memory. Less and less desire to speak. When it slumped over sideways I knew it was dead-asleep again. Mute, deaf, white, burning in the whiteness: the skull. Icy. Sweaty. Dreaming of me. Dreaming of me so intensely it made me feel I was inside its dream. Its body full of thinking members was stretched out alongside my body. Tired of searching, with my hands, with my feet, for that body clinging to mine without touching me, tired of sounding that depth in vain, I too finally fell asleep beneath the shroud of the sheets. The effort not to fall asleep put me to sleep. Sleep overcame me, but only for an instant. In less than a second I woke up again. Perhaps I've never slept; not during that time or any other. Just as now, I pretended to be sound asleep. I watched his sleep closely. I kept on the lookout for his awakening, his slightest somnambulic movement, which was not merely opening his eyes, stirring, clacking his tongue from the bitter taste of saliva fermented by the miasmas of the protonight. Hanging by this tremulous thread, I nonetheless was always just a moment too late. It was necessary to begin all over again from the beginning, to start from the end. Bring into phase between the two that infinitesimal fraction of time that separated us more than millennia. Listen to me! I lowered my voice till it matched his silence. Don't you think that by adding a second pitch to our roofs we might come to an understanding? It may be that with two counterposed angles our thought would fly farther and faster. Couldn't it be that if they met, your death and my life would be shed down two different slopes? I was begging now: I want to be born in you! Don't you understand? Make just a slight effort! What would it cost you anyway? My child's tears mingling with his silence, the sweat that flowed from him in a thin, ice-cold stream. But even if that were possible, he finally chattered, you'd be born so old that before you were born you'd already be in death again, without ever really being able to get out of it. You don't understand! You don't understand, you old skull! You've the addled pate of an old Castilian. Poor Spain! When will it be able to get out of the Middle Ages with a breed of idiots like you! The only thing I'm asking you is your permission to incubate in your incubus-cube. I don't want to be engendered in a woman's womb. I want to be born in a man's thought. Leave the rest to me. Okay, kid, if that's all you want. Why do you keep pestering me so? Good Lord! Get out through whatever hole you please and stop trying my patience! There won't be all that great a difference; take it from somebody who knows all about holes.

From then on the skull was my mother-house. How long did I stay there gestating myself by my will alone? From before the beginning. Intense heat. Burning surfaces. Contractions. Circumvolutions of matter in combustion fall on me without burning me. Inundate my non-being. Submerge me in air-without-air. Primal fire. Isn't that how native food is cooked? Isn't that how savages are engendered, with no need of a mother? And less still of a progenitor?

Infinite silence. More than in the cosmos. It enters, knocks hard, resounds in the bone. The bone resounds in the imagination. Floor, vault, cupola vibrate then. Even the shadow vibrates. Gray-white, smoke-black. Between the two, depending. We are not one. We are not two. *He* is gone now. I am not yet *I*. I feel the universe pressing down on me, aging me inside the skull. Come on, hurry up!, the skull-lender gibbers. Or are you going to brood inside there for an eternity and a bit more of the one after? I'm coming, I'm coming, calm down! I rub my hands over the damp calotte. I caress it, dripping with sweat. Embryonic matter. Perhaps I feel its hair growing. There's that anyway; a sign, an indication. At last: hair growing! It grows and grows till it fills all the first-quarter. It envelops me. It asphyxiates me. Heat. Darkness. Viscous matter. A cord burning in my mouth. Mouth sewn shut. Eyes sewn shut. A voice of thunder: Lázaro veni fora!§ Didn't I tell you to bury that skull? Its bad smell tenerem house turned into dump heap. Rotten Indian head! Throw that skull into the river! Otherwise I mesmo will throw you in with it!

I come out again. Draw back. The little construct disappears. Up and away! Faster! White in the whiteness, the cupola ascends. The light grows fainter. Everything grows darker at the same time. Floor. Wall. Vault. The temperature of matter in a state of ignition-ebullition is going down. It rapidly descends to the minimum. Around zero. Instant at which the

§Bastardized Portuguese: Lazarus, come forth.

blackness appears again. The black point. It grows. It's me, crawling. Hallucination. The shadow of the Paulist or Marian mulatto from the January River, the dark silhouette of the captain of militias astride the skull palpitating in the white tremor of its last contractions. What kind of a fix is this you've gotten me into, you little devil! The captain of militias astride a young lad of twelve, who has aged thirty or three hundred years inside a skull without having been able to be born. Which may seem odd if we think that things begin/end; if it is thought that death is the only remedy for the yearning for immortality to which the door of the tomb bars the way. Since mine has already been barred it will have to be reopened now in order for the dream to be explained. By whom? Explained by me alone, for me alone. No; that may not be how it is. A person's life doesn't end. No; or perhaps yes. What's a man's thought, hidalgo or whoreson? Must be son-of-something. Is there something born of nothing? Nothing. What is life/death? What is this mystery that divides and divides into other infinite mysteries, I keep asking myself. Hanging from a branch, the whore-nanny can't teach me/peach on me now. The reason behind the mystery is mystery itself. I know that nowhere else is there anything similar to what has happened to me. It is not necessary to dream to discover once again that white point lost in whiteness, in the deepest depths of black. The Great Whiteness is immutable/mutable. It doesn't end. It keeps engendering itself, over and over, from blackness.

I put the skull in the noodle box. I took it to that place of the future already past for me, to which others will take the box with my skull. The house, the street, the entire city were filled with a stench of death. With slow steps I headed toward the cliffs. I squatted on my heels to rest for a moment beneath the orange tree, leaning the box against the trunk. Struck by the sun, the glass circle flamed. Nothing could be seen inside it. I went on down; or rather, I went on not knowing whether I was going up or down.

Complete rest. Sleep. Sleep. Sleep. The protophysician's voice comes to me from far away, from an immeasurable distance. For this once, I take his advice. I pretend to sleep. I feel that someone is spying on me. I play dead. I open the door of my tomb a crack. I draw the tumulus open. It parts with a gritty granite sound. I open my eyes. I practice the simulacrum of my resurrection by raising myself up. Before me, He-who-is-sleepless. He-who-is-ageless. He-who-is-deathless. Keeping watch. Watching.

(Perpetual circular)

I withdrew to my observatory in Ybyray. I saw how the politically inept Takuary leaders, banded together now and summoned to Government House by the Porteño Somellera, were about to complete the capitulation, handing over all of Paraguay, tied hand and foot, to the Buenos Aires Junta. I therefore decided to put a stop to it. Glowing with happiness, Don Pedro Alcántara, a good spy for the Porteños, was in a fever of activity. Beguiled by the extravagant idea that I would help them, all of them called upon me as one to lend my aid. Urgent pleas. When to their misfortune I appeared at the barracks that morning of the fifteenth of May, Pedro Juan Cavallero received me at the door: You no doubt know, my dear doctor, that we've tried the bull with the cape and he's turned out to be very docile. Yr. Grace is the only one who can lead us in this emergency from here on. As we were crossing the courtyard I asked him: What are the plans? What is being done? It has been decided that the shipowner José de María is to be sent posthaste by boat to inform the Buenos Aires Junta of what has happened, the captain answered.

Somellera was at the guard post putting the finishing touches on the dispatch. I tore it out of his hands. This dispatch is not to be dispatched, I said. If it were, the proud Porteños would be overjoyed. Out of the question. We have just emerged from one despotism and must proceed with the greatest caution if we are not to fall into another. We are not going to transmit our tacit recognition of the Buenos Aires Junta in the tone of a subordinate to a superior. Paraguay does not need to beg for anyone's aid. It need depend only on itself to ward off any aggression. I then turned to Somellera, who was watching me closely, an irritated chameleon. As a polite hint, I said to him gently: You are no longer needed here. I would even go so far as to say that you're in the way. Each one must serve his own country in his own country. The same boat that was to take the dispatch will transport you without further delay. Sire, I must take my family with me, and the dry river is innavigable. You leave first. Your family will then leave the moment there is free traffic on the river again. The group of annexionists were profoundly disappointed and discountenanced. Their faces fell, leaving them only their masks. That was what I had intended.

Just to see what he would do, that capitulator of a Cavañas was asked to come from his estancia in the Cordillera. Come, word was sent to him, rally to the cause of the Fatherland. Come join us patriots gathered together with the troops in the barracks. He had the effrontery to answer that he would come only if Governor Velazco summoned him. But Velazco had been dismissed from office, without having a say or a bray in the matter. Shortly thereafter he will end up in jail along with Bishop Panés and the most conspicuous of the Spaniards who keep tirelessly conspiring. The other leaders of the capitulation at Takuary also vanish into thin air. Gracia flees to the north in search of support from the Portuguese: that's how much courage he showed under pressure! Gamarra answers that he will join the cause only on the condition that nothing ever be done to bring down the Sovereign. He even had the brass to write it with a capital letter. Sovereign idiot! He wanted to make the Revolution without rising up against the sovereign: like making a maize cake without maize.

The rest of the milicaste, apparently faithful, was weighing the situation with a surreptitious thumb on the scales. Ever since the establishment of the First Junta, the milicasters had sought at every moment to shake the Government so as to obtain with threats not the good of the country but anything that tickled their fancy. Instead of occupying themselves with public affairs they spent their time gambling, parading, partying, devoting themselves to carousing. The Pompeys and the Bayards of the Junta got tangled up in their own spurs, in their ineptitude. Dudes. Knights of the lasso and bola who'd lost their seat. Braggarts, no doubt of that. Coxcombs. Beribboned billygoats, corseted in resplendent uniforms. Proto-heroes of their country gleaming with sweat saw themselves already shining with glory in what they believed to be the mirror of History. They promoted themselves to military ranks whose insignia they adopted, getting themselves up in disguise after the fashion of the ex governor, now as brigadiers, now as colonels of Spanish dragons. Back in the days of the Colony they were already noted for such military virtues. The procurator Marco de Balde-Vino, an inveterate Porteñista, said of them in his report to Lázaro de Ribera: Events have left us as an eternal monument the intolerable blows inflicted upon the Patriots reduced to serving and financing the militias which have become the worst plague of the Province.

They trafficked in everything in order to meet the expenses entailed by their boundless passion for ostentation, now that in addition to being milicasters they were heads of government as well. Thus, in order to satisfy their ridiculous mania, they freed State prisoners after exacting fat sums in return for this dereliction of their duty. As they had little notion of what national Independence, civil or political Liberty meant, they allowed their subalterns to commit countless arbitrary acts throughout the land. Especially in the countryside, the principal theater of their violent excesses.

In Ykuamandijú, a captain of militias who had distinguished himself by his revolutionary zeal endeavored to explain to the peasants what Liberty was. He reeled off a seven-hour discourse to them, speaking of everything without saying anything. The village priest then wound up the harangue by saying that Liberty was simply Faith, Hope, and Charity. After that the two of them went down, arm in arm, to get drunk at the district post, from which there were forthcoming orders of arrests, violent abuses, the most iniquitous vandalage, all in the name of the supernatural virtues they had just proclaimed.

To administer was to imprison, to sequester anonymously, sometimes causing suspicion to fall on others as authors of the outrage; to condemn or free, for a base price, as hatred or greed demanded. The word patriotism was mouthed; in its name everything was permitted; it sanctioned any and all passions, crimes, acts of savagery.

In that time of beginnings that was how things were. The troops, in very nearly their entirety, were made up of the most ignorant men, the worst felons in the country. Murderers, known criminals let out of prison. Unpunished, omnipotent in uniform, they considered themselves possessed of the right to insult, to humiliate the most peaceable citizens in a thousand ways. If a peasant forgot to doff his sombrero as he passed by a soldier, they cropped his hair with their sabers. Later on, I was the one who was said to have introduced this contemptible custom of salutation by baring the head, which in and of itself is not so much a sign of respect as it is a mutilation. Symbolic decapitation of the one saluting. In this land of twenty-four suns the sombrero-pirí forms part of the person. There was no way of eradicating this humiliating habit in our fellow citizens wrapped in straw inside their immense sombreros.

The behavior of the officers was worse than that of the men. Without the least respect for their functions, their rank, they became involved in disputes between peasants, settling them with bullets when their arguments or their patience gave out. Since almost all the commissioned and non-commissioned officers were related to the chiefs of the Junta or of the principal barracks, the latter tolerated their most scandalous misdeeds.

I tried in vain from inside the Junta to curb these excesses. Discouraged by my futile efforts to oblige my companions in the Government to comport themselves with greater moderation, I withdrew twice more from their midst. I cleared out and watched them from a distance. Affairs of state came to a standstill. Equerries sat in the curules in the absence of their drunken masters. Strike out curules. Strike out equerries. Put: Seated in the chairs of the Junta, the stableboys of the proto-fathers of their country did not conduct the affairs of state any worse than they. There was no way they could have been any worse. Dispatches were not dispatched. The loot they collected from their co-ladronicides was divided fairly among them. Just as all of you share and share alike today. Strike out that last sentence. I don't want them to have the distinct feeling that they're already sitting in the prisoner's dock.

The times that I abandoned the fatuous fops of the Junta, they themselves asked me to return. My cousin, Fulgencio-Pompey, the effulgent president, the Junta member Cavallero-Bayard, the scribe-pharisee Fernando Mora-torium wrote me. What's the date of the note, Patiño? August 6, 1811, Sire: Entirely persuaded of your generosity of heart, we have no fear of appearing fearlessly bold in addressing the present plea to you, and inasmuch as our knowledge is quite inferior to our zeal, we have been able to discover no other step that we might take save to implore Yr. Grace to take your place once again at the helm of our vessel, which the present ignorant storm has carried off. Otherwise the Fatherland is lost and all else with it. Your ever affectionate comrades.

Turning aside for a moment from his festive tourneys, the president of the Junta proposes, in his illiterate hand and with a friendly clap on the back: Let us try, my dear compatriot and kinsman, to settle matters between us so that you may again pilot the ship of State amid these ill winds that threaten to cause all our endeavors to founder.

My other relative, Antonio Thomas Yegros, commander-in-chief of the armed forces, addresses me as Venerated Sire, as though I were a pre-late: The chaplain who is the bearer of this missive has offered to go to your residence to inform you of the decision arrived at today with regard to your return among all the officers and the Junta. Break through this sort of barrier that stands in the way of that possibility and your duty to return to the Junta to lead us. If you really love your country, illustrious kinsman, you will awake at dawn tomorrow in this city, and all of us will receive you in triumph, amid general rejoicing. You will have time later to mend the roof of your house, the cause of your absence, once you are beneath that of the Government. Your most affectionate kinsman q.s.m.b.§

I didn't even answer them.

Cavallero-Bayard insists in a note of the . . . Four days later, Sire, dated the 10th of August: Your withdrawal to your farm, due to your need to put your house in order, has moved me deeply, both because of the particular affection that I feel for you, and because great works that have been begun under your particular influence and direction may not be able to be completed and given the crowning touch.

Come, come, you bunch of rascals! All this after so many dire conminations, denunciations, fulminations!

Plea from the Cabildo: the General Staff and the People clamor for your reincorporation as a member of the Superior Governing Junta. This body begs you, with sincerest affection, admiration, and respect for the authority of your talents as Conductor. Because it believes firmly that in the present storm and anguish that threaten, your appearing here in the place that is rightfully yours will be the Iris that will bring peace and calm.

For that worthless lot floundering about amid their interests, their fears, their ineptitudes and mutual mistrust, my return to the Junta had turned into a problem of meteorology and navigation. This was confirmed on Monday, November 16, when I reincorporated myself with the Junta, amid a terrible storm and a pouring rain. The Cabildo in plenary session hastened to congratulate me, unanimously acclaiming me with the agnomen of Storm-Pilot, which the multitude chorused with inconsolable rejoicing, since the greatest good fortune is often a near mis-fortune.

My first withdrawal from the Junta, one month and ten days after its constitution, was occasioned by the incident provoked against me by the military; or more exactly, by an attempt at blackmail on the part of men who availed themselves of their arms, believing themselves possessed of the right to do so not by virtue of the cause to be defended but out of sheer caprice and willfullness. The milicasters were seated on their bayonets, as we still say today; and not only the milicasters but also their servile civil minions. In the palace intrigues, the knaves shamelessly flaunted their scarlet hose.

They said I was guilty of crimes against society. Subversive promoter

§Variant of the traditional formal close q.b.s.m.=*que besa su mano* (who kisses your hand).

of innovations, divisions, confrontations. Look you, milords of the military and the aristocracy, it does not suffice to call things by any name you please. Authority, power should not be used in support of slanderous imputations, I upbraided the joker-mandarins of the Junta through the intermediary of the Cabildo, which had intervened in the row.

Why call the one who proposes that this provisory and useless Junta be replaced by a genuine Government, originating in a General Congress in which all the citizenry is represented, the author of divisions, of innovations? Why tax with subversion the one who proposes that authorities be elected by genuinely popular assemblies?

Quite to the contrary, honorable councilmen, as you yourselves have proclaimed, it is a well-known, proven fact that the weight of the office of dean-member and secretary-counselor has been borne entirely on my shoulders, not only since the establishment of the Junta but since the Revolution itself. I shall always look with indifference upon my being so named, since my one aim was to lend my services, to the best of my abilities, to the Fatherland, taking upon myself alone all those posts and burdens. You are doubtless well aware that the other members of the Junta have not shouldered the weight of so much as a single feather.

It is not necessary to call to mind the violent, reprobate, and crafty means that were employed to bring about my withdrawal, and the subsequent dismissal from his post of the other member, the presbyter Xavier Bogarín. The Junta, composed of only three members, was no longer legitimate or competent. No one in his right mind, no one acquainted with the persons and the circumstances, could possibly imagine it to be the sense of the Congress that the reins should be handed over, even in such a case, to three absolutely untried, untutored individuals; in a word, three completely inept and ignorant individuals. If it so happened that they obtained such a position, it was through the intermediary of this senior member, whose departure they provoked, inasmuch as their aims and interests were not exactly those of the Revolution and Independence of the country.

It is only hesitant and uncertain authorities who can cause division and fail to end those that may arise. Only those who fear to be judged fear Congresses. Innovations in and of themselves have nothing about them that cannot be properly channeled by upright citizens for the good of the country. For if certain of them are harmful, others of them are good, even excellent. Wasn't our Revolution itself a great innovation, indeed the greatest of all? And the most brilliant as well. The most just. The most necessary of all innovations.

Neither liberty nor anything else can endure without order, without rules, without a unity, brought into harmony within the nucleus of the supreme interest of the State, of the Nation, of the Republic, inasmuch as even inanimate beings preach to us the lesson of rigor. Were this not so, the freedom for which we have made, are making, and will continue to make the greatest sacrifices will lead to unbridled licence, which will reduce everything to confusion, discord, disorders, disturbances. A theater of desolation, of weeping and gnashing of teeth, of the most horrendous crimes, such as even now are occurring, so that the only pole star of the powerful would appear to be the violence of those on the top against those on the bottom. We cannot oblige our citizens to sleep in peace with a river on the rampage. You alone, as officers of the General Staff, named by the Governing Junta, paid by it in the country's money, are not the people. By acting in this fashion, you are, rather, the counterpeople. By your very profession as military officers, you ought to be the first to set an example of faithful performance of your duties; of respect for the dignity of the Junta; of decency and honor to citizens, protecting those who are most defenseless, ignorant, and humble, those who have been taught to welcome blows as though they were a blessing from God.

To the hobgoblins of the Cabildo I replied very clearly: The threatening, dictatorial tone of the officers who have arbitrarily established themselves as the counterpower of the Junta cannot be ignored. Can you assure me that from this day forward they will not raise their hand or commit their usual wicked deeds? That they will keep the arms in their hands merely as adornments? And their heads on their shoulders?

I am entirely prepared to serve the Government, the country, the cause of its sovereignty and independence provided that the armed forces submit to the rigorous discipline required by the tranquillity, the unity, the good order, and the defense of our Nation.

I am a partisan of proceeding without compromise or hesitation. Supporting the principle of authority by imposing on the military a rigorous obedience of the will expressed in the Congresses. Any weakness on the part of the Government endangers the Independence of the Fatherland, whose foundations are not well cemented yet.

The Revolution can expect no aid from a counterrevolutionary army. There is no understanding or agreement possible with this army of battle-cattlemen, of uniformed mercenaries, ever prepared to make their own interests alone prevail. We cannot command or beg such militias to place themselves in the service of the Revolution. Sooner or later they will destroy it. Every genuine Revolution creates its army, since it is itself the people in arms. Without their own spurs, the best fighting cocks end up as capons. And as everyone knows, you can always make a cock into a capon, but you'll never get a cock from a capon, or even a cock crow, except in falsetto.

That was the last thing I said, but not the last thing I did.

The cardboard figures of the Junta became more and more unsteady. In the Yegros mansion, band, orchestra, elegant soirées, roistering, revelry, night after night.*

Upright citizens of city and countryside come to my dwelling in the countryside to complain. Come, think a moment, I say to them. Who is Don Fulgencio Yegros? An ignorant gaucho. What is there about Don Pedro Juan Cavallero that's any better? Nothing. And yet the two are leaders invested with supreme authority, who like the other military myrmidons insult you by their vain pomp, which would be laughable were it not so deplorable. What are we to do, Sire, in such a situation? At the opportune moment I shall tell you what is to be done to conjure these ills. They went off filled with confidence.

Last night, after the meeting of the Junta, we were visited by a number of foreigners. Juan Robertson reported that he had received letters from England from his brother. According to him, the Emperor Alexander of Russia has entered into an alliance against Napoleon. The British Empire has sent a great number of warships and munitions to its ally, the Muscovite Empire. I'll be damned!, Fulgencio Yegros exclaimed, with the same excitement as Archimedes climbing naked out of his bathtub shouting Eureka!, after having discovered the method for determining the specific weight of bodies. I'll be damned!, the archidiot president of the Junta muttered. May a good steady blow from the south bring all those warships up the Paraguay River to the port of Asunción! How can such a stupid animal possibly govern the Republic?

Cavallero-Bayard orders the mayor arrested because he neglected to place a red carpet on his seat in the cathedral on All Sans§ Day, and a second time on the day of the two Sans, his patrons.

As in Proverbs, the trash in uniform continues to throw money down the drain. It is hell-bent to stir things up. Kick up a rumpus. All excited

---

*"The pantomime continues, to the great discontent of the people, who are beginning to murmur," Colonel Zavala y Delgadillo writes in his *Journal of Memorable Events*.

---

§A seldom-used plural of Santos, Saints.

by the fiesta of violence, the unbridled sensuality of authority, the intoxication of power that turns the heads of those of weak character. They are tottering and making the Government totter with their extravagant behavior. I shall not have anything to do with these gentlemen who hold the cause of the Fatherland in so little esteem. I have exhausted my patience and the means at my command, however, trying to teach them and rescue the least bad ones, the better to serve our cause. I have spoken to them in every possible tone of voice; I have endeavored to get them to read at least a few paragraphs of the Spirit of the Laws. Read this, my dear Don Pedro Juan. I'm not a reader, the chief of the general staff replied. I'll read it to you then. Listen to this idea of Montesquieu's regarding the concept of a federative republic: If a model of a fine republic were needed, I should choose the example of Lygia. I don't know where Lygia is, the ignorant clod says with a yawn. It doesn't matter where that country is, Don Pedro Juan. The important thing is its system of government based on an association of cities or states with equal sovereignty and rights. We have only one city here, he says, being deliberately obtuse. Yes, I say to him, but there are other cities that are trying to subject and enslave us. No, sir, that shall never come about. Better to die than to live as slaves. Well, Don Pedro Juan, I am gratified to hear you say that. But the best part of all, as Montesquieu also says, is that we can live as free men by putting our Republic in order. Perhaps better than in Lygia. Look, doctor, you know all about books and scholars. Why don't you look after all this nonsense yourself? If you think it's a good idea, write this Señor Monteswhoever. We could offer him a little post as a paid secretary of the Junta, to put our papers in order. Impossible to understand each other. Like looking for wisdom teeth in a rooster. I slammed the door in the face of the Junta once again and went back to my farm.*

Pleas for my return began to rain down for the second time the moment I withdrew to Ybyray. From Buenos Aires, General Belgrano himself writes me with the sincerity that my fellow members of the Junta are lacking. He addresses me as his dear friend: I feel I must tell you that I find it most regrettable that you are thinking of private life in the dire circumstances in which we find ourselves at present. Return to your rightful occupation; life is nothing if freedom is lost. Take heed of the fact that it lies exposed to many dangers and demands all manner of sacrifices if it is not to succumb.

---

*He withdrew twice from the Junta, Julio César confirms. The first time from August, 1811, to early October of the same year. The second time from December to November. (Compiler's Note.)

Those are the words of an upright man.

I will not say that it was on the advice of Belgrano, but rather on that of my own conscience, whose dictates are the only ones I obey, that I came to return to Asunción on that morning of the sixteenth of November, almost a year after my withdrawal from the Junta, amid the storm that had broken during the night.

The day before, after arising from my siesta, something happened that caused me to make up my mind. Awake, I *saw* this dream-vision: My rat nursery had turned into a caravan of men. I was walking at the head of this teeming multitude. We reached a column of black stone, in which a man was buried up to his armpits. Superimposed on the image of the man was that of the rifle buried up to the middle of the barrel in the orange tree of the executions by firing squad. The man buried up to his armpits in the stone reappeared immediately. Black too, and of the size of the trunk of an old palm tree. He had two enormous wings and four arms. Two of the arms were like a man's. The others like the legs of jaguars. A bristling mane of hair, like a horse's tail, whipping wildly about his head. Before my mind's eye was Ezekiel's vision of the four beasts or angels; the figures with the face of a lion on the right, of an ox on the left, and the four faces of a man, but also of an eagle, growing larger and larger as they came forward one by one, each in its rightful turn. The man buried in the stone was totally unlike this. Stuck fast there, he appeared to be crying out to be dispetrified. The caravan behind strained and squeaked.

I was now fording the raging torrents of a stream, breasting the wind and the rain astride my black-and-white Arabian. Stained dark red with mud from head to foot, I entered the chapter room. A dripping specter, I strode forward, to the stupefaction of a handful of town councilors and scribes. Prior to resuming my post in the Junta, I told those watching openmouthed, I have come to attest in the Cabildo that I am doing so only in defense of the integrity of the Government.

With airy step, despite his tubby belly crossed with gold chains, La Cerda came forward, the craftiest schemer in all of Asunción. During my absence he had contrived to usurp my post as adviser-secretary. He held out his hand to me. I left it hanging in midair. It's a sight for sore eyes, my dear dean, to see you here again after so long a time. I gave the rogue a piercing stare; not only had he tried to steal the post from me but he had also done his best to imitate the details of my dress. He tipped his tricorne and let the folds of his garnet cape fall. He felt obliged to come out with one of his usual stupid witticisms: It is quite evident, señor dean, that the Red Sea of our rivers has not parted before you! Never mind, I answered him cuttingly, it will soon close behind you. I shall accompany you, doctor, to the throne of the Junta, he insisted, not turning a hair, parting the cape and allowing the gleaming gold buckles of his knee breeches and shoes to show. No, Cerda, I prefer to go alone. Go bid your comadres farewell and pack your bags, because you are to leave immediately. We don't want any foreign panders and thieves here in Paraguay.* The tricorne rolled onto the floor. La Cerda bent over to pick it up. I turned my back on him and headed for Government House. My clothes gave off a red steam in the sudden sun that appeared against the sky, magically causing the high wind and rain to cease. I crossed the Plaza de Armas, followed by a growing crowd acclaiming my name. When I came back, I was another man. I had learned a great deal at my farm-lookout in Ybyray. The retreat had brought me closer to what I was seeking. From that point on I would yield to nothing and to no one opposed to the holy cause of the Fatherland. All my conditions were accepted and duly recorded to ensure strict compliance: total autonomy, absolute sovereignty of my decisions. Training, under my command, of the forces necessary to

*Commentaries of Julio César: La Cerda at no time acted as secretary of the Junta. It would appear that he was the confidential agent of Fernando de la Mora [another of the members of the Junta]; since neither the latter nor Yegros nor Caballero gave proof of any great attachment to the work of government, he [Cerda] became their factotum. He was a picturesque character, from Córdoba, famous for being the compadre of half the people in the country, something that makes a man highly respected in Paraguay. The influence of compadrazgo§ on the development of our political life should be studied some day.

He [El Supremo] gave evidence of a profound antipathy toward his colleague de la Mora because he regarded him as responsible for certain steps taken during his absence to unite Paraguay and Buenos Aires, and in particular for the loss of the additional article of the treaty of October 12, a circumstance that the Buenos Aires Triumvirate seized upon in order to impose an unjust tax on Paraguayan tobacco. Mora was eventually expelled from the Junta on the grounds of the concrete charges that the senior member brought against him; in particular for "the removal and loss of the aforementioned extremely important document, during the time that I had absented myself from the Junta, in connivance with the Cerda individual, who is neither a citizen nor a native of this country, the longstanding and intimate friend and confidant of the aforementioned Mora. On the latter's instructions, Cerda took home with him a number of extensive files of documents from the Secretariat, among them the aforementioned additional article. A young man given to drink, usually in a total state of inebriation even in the meetings of the Junta, he also found himself charged with the crime of being a spy and an informer on behalf of the Triumvirate of Buenos Aires, in the person of Dr. Chiclana, keeping it informed of the activities and resolutions of our Government." Mora and Cerda were thus devoured in a veritable feast of beasts.

§Compaternity (fr. M. L. + com pater): the intimate ties between godparents of a child, or between them and the child's parents. By extension, the term compadre (fem. comadre) also means bosom friend, crony.

see that they were obeyed. I demanded that half of the armament and munitions stored in the depots be put at my disposal. From the people-multitude I picked the men who formed the skeleton organization of the army of the people. An even more invincible support than that of cannons and rifles in the defense of the Republic and the Revolution.

(In the private notebook)

The parody of the obsequies decreed by the vicar general, the gloomy prophecy of the herbalist have brought to a paroxysm the pasquinerian insurrection. I knew those chatterboxes weren't going to shut up. More diatribes, caricatures, and threats have dirtied the façades. I should have ordered them to be painted over with tar, rather than with the patrial whitewash that those panders of subversion besmirch in such cowardly fashion. We are back to the days of grand punchinellery.

Day before yesterday, the obscene figures in waspwax, appearing at dawn opposite the windows of Government House, representing my decapitated effigy. The head resting on the belly. An immense phallus-cigar thrust in the mouth. I managed to see the insulting simulacrum before it melted in the heat of the red-hot fire lighted by my careless guards. They were so horror-stricken that one of them fell into the fire. Embracing the figure embrasing him, become a blazing firebrand. The flames set off the cartridge in the rifle slung across his shoulder; the projectile embedded itself in the frame of the window from which I was witnessing the parody of my inhumation. They are trying their hand at intimidation through the sort of jiggery-pokery used elsewhere. They are boldly attempting to delude the ignorant people through the use of violence. To provoke terror. But terror is not the product of such idiotic intrigues. Such methods may have been effective in other countries where the anarchy, the oligarchy, the synarchy of apatriots has enthroned despots. Here the generality of the people is embodied in the State. Here I can affirm with perfect reason: I-am-the-State, since the people have made me their supreme potestate. Identified with it, what fear can we feel? Who can make us lose our judgment, our senses with such punchinullos' tricks?

I pardon certain errors. Not those that threaten to endanger the order in which those who wish to live in dignity live. I do not tolerate those who seek to undermine the untouchable, the inviolable system on which the order of society, public peace, the security of the Government are firmly founded. I cannot coddle those enemies who bore from within. The most dangerous miscreants. The hair on their heads bristles with hatred. Hatred muffles their voices. It leaves them only the cowardly, the wretched courage to rush at me amid the shadows, pen at lance rest, stick of charcoal in hand. The perverse man liveth with a perverse mouth. He cannot look the sun in the face. He ever moves about behind his shadow. He does not deserve the pride of belonging to the most prosperous, independent, and sovereign country on the American continent. Pride that the very last, the most ignorant of free peasants of this Nation feels. The very last mulatto. The very last freedman.

Despite everything, I tried sometimes to help them. Throw them the end of a rope. Save them. Haul them back to the shore of the human. They refused my aid. They are filled with fear. Fear is terrified of everything, even of that which could alleviate it.

It is madness to lose one's reason. The delirious hatred of these sons of the Great Sigillaria, their impotent ambition has dried up their very last atom of gray matter. They threaten to thread my head on the flagpole of the Republic. The Scrutinium Chymicum of my cremation is the least they ask. To ask more would be to ask less. Since they can't burn me in person they burn me in effigy, making me smoke my own phallus. Dress rehearsal again. Ouf. Ah. I'm tired of their clowning. I don't intend to answer them. Nothing enhances authority so much as silence. My patience has a very wide turning circle. I must also shelter you, you threepenny troublemakers. Castrati with your egg-souls cut off. Pamphletary band of incubi/succubi guerrillas. Debauched legion of seven-month eunuchs. You champ at the bit of Government and leave your decayed milk teeth imbedded in it. Effeminate phantoms. You shave your secret parts to get hair to make your paintbrushes. Corrupters of the public peace, of social peace. I shall not take the trouble to have you thrown in the river in a sack, Roman-style, along with a monkey, a cock, and a serpent. Secret agents of those who block navigation, you have no need of a safe-conduct pass to seek wider horizons downstream. The offspring of bad stock, I shall imprison you in the stocks, a good counselor for cooling heads seeking to inflame other people's. The more you execrate me, the more authority you lend my cause. The more you justify my command. You are my best propagandists. You band of pasquinist serenaders: I'll break your guitars over your heads. Music is only for people who understand it. I am not going to treat you with the scruples of the proverbial Friar Phlegm. What do you think, you scoundrels? Do you think that the reality of this nation to which I gave birth and which

gave birth to me accommodates itself to your phantasmagorias and hallucinations? Conform to the law, you layabouts and loafers, you airy-fairy
merry-andrews! The world as it ought to be. The law: the first pole. Its
counterpole: anarchy, ruin, the desert which is the non-house, non-history.
Choose if you can. There is not a third world beyond. There is not a third
pole. There are no promised-lands. Less still, much less are there such for
you, you virtuosos of rumor, you artful farters, you buzzing ball-less bees!
I'll have you know that once and for all, you worthless know-nothing
turds, you sepals of shit in bloom!

They take no respite and give me none. The malady plagues me from
within and from without. Spreads throughout the city. Contaminates.
Infects. Not sleeping releases in the air the salamandrine virus of sleepless
sickness. Worse than cattle carbuncle. Plague of the general. By day, not
even the flight of a fly. Silence turned topsy-turvy. Those lying in wait
hold their breath from dawn to dark. Only then does the buzzing of the
ground beetles begin. Scrabble of scarab-feet. Flutter of bats. Slithers of
scales. The night is peopled with ghost-sounds. I am the spyglass, the
telescope through the windows. Nothing. Not even a shadow. The houses
leave white stains on the darkness. Milky way raised by me amid the trees.
Whiter than the cloud of our galaxy amid the clouds. The sentries' cries
come from another world. Suddenly a shot. Howls. They multiply. Fill
the night. All the dogs in Paraguay bark at the nightmare of darkness. Then
the silence rides at anchor once again. Silhouettes enveloped in black
ponchos loom up. Shaggy feet wrapped in sheepskin. They prowl about,
glide past the houses of the enemy. They search about in the aisles of the
churches, in the little squares, in the alleyways, in the tortuous back streets,
in the ditches. I know that they will see nothing, find nothing, despite their
instinct and their hunters' flair. They will hear nothing through the cracks
of doors and windows. The night is vaster, more monotonous than the day.
It plunges them into another life. They think they see something. A
sulfurous exhalation zigzagging along the ground. They retrace their steps
immediately. Too late. Farther on, music of a sidewalk serenade. They
hasten there. Window shutters closed. Only the memory of the sound
beneath the eaves. The furry-feet hear nothing, see nothing. They spit out
vulgar insults. They suck their decayed wisdom teeth. They spit. They
stand there blinking in the slurry of their spit. That's all they're good for.

Here in my bedroom, the muffled tick-tock of the watches, among
them the one Belgrano presented to Cavañas at Takuary. The faint flutter
of moths in the books. The stealthy minute hand of the wood borer in the

timbers. Every so often the weary sounds of the cathedral bell, marking not hours but centuries. How long a time I haven't slept! Everything is repeated, in the image of what has been and will be. The infinitely great and the infinitely small. Absolutely true that there is nothing new under the sun, and this very sun the repetition of innumerable suns that have existed and will exist. The ancients knew the sun was two thousand leagues distant and were surprised that it looked to be two hundred paces away. They knew the eye could not see the sun if the eye were not somehow a sun itself. More than necessary to know how not to fall sick, to make oneself invulnerable to everything. According to the Jesuit Montoya, the Indian chieftain Avaporú chewed the magic herb of the Yayeupá-Guasú§ he sneezed three times and became invisible. So that even if I were dead I wouldn't be, since I would be my repetition. Only the shell of my first soul would be broken or dead after having incubated the others.

Tell me about this, I ordered the Nivaklé chieftain. Tell me everything you know about it. The native witch doctor's face turns darker still. The coals of his eyes float back to the surface for an instant amid wrinkles stained red with paste from the bija tree. Speak! Wildcat leans on his staff of office and through his closed mouth there comes a murmur that seems to be traversing his body from somewhere very far away. Chasejk, the interpreter, translates. All beings have doubles. Garments, tools, arms. Plants, animals, men. This double appears to men's eyes as a shadow, reflection, or image. The shadow all bodies project, the reflection of things in water, the image seen in a mirror. We may call it a shadow, though it is made of a more subtle material. Hence the shadow of the sun covers objects but does not conceal them. The reflection of water does not allow fish to hide themselves completely. Shadows are identical to the beings they duplicate. They are very thin, more-than-transparent. They cannot be touched. They can only be seen. But not always with the eyes of the face, only with the inner eye that thinks. Thus the shadow is the image of each being. All beings have doubles. But the double of the human being is one and triple at the same time. Sometimes more. Each one of these souls is different from the others, but despite their differences they form a single one. I tell the interpreter to ask the Nivaklé if that is like the mystery of Christianity: a single God in three different Persons. The sorcerer laughs dryly, without parting his lips puckered with tattoos. No, No! That's not how it is with us, the men-of-the-forest! The first soul is called the egg. Then comes the little-soul, located in the center. Completely surrounding the egg is the shell or hide: the *vatjeche*. Hard bark that protects the

§Yayeupá: Let's-Eat-Everything-Up.

soft-soul or pith. As the egg is the soul of the body, the shell is the soul of the egg. Neither of them can see or touch the other. They are formed by something that is less than the wind, since wind can be felt, while these two souls have nothing that can be seen or touched. They can pass through the hardest things. They never bump into anything. When a person blows his breath on another person's face, that person feels it. The egg and the shell are thinner than breath. The third soul is *vatajpikl:* the shadow. Soul of the shell that "has something." There are many people who see the shadow of a person who has recently died wandering about his tomb. Its likeness to the body "that isn't there any more," to its past movements, to its manner of being that is no more is so perfect that the boy gives the appearance of continuing to exist. But this wandering soul is completely empty; it has nothing at all inside. For us the body is more important than the souls, because the body is the origin of the souls. Without a body souls do not exist, though they survive after its destruction. This is the thought of the Old Ones. There are no words to explain this, but they, the Old Ones *know* that there are several souls in one: the egg soul, son-of-the-soul, or little-soul; the shadow cast by the sun; the reflection in water, the image in the mirror; the shadow cast by the sun around midmorning or midafternoon; the shadow of the sun when it falls on the back of the body moving forward; the shadow of the body when the sun is at the highest point in the sky; the shadow cast by the light of the sun filtered through clouds; the shadow cast by the light of the moon; the moon itself through the clouds. But of all of them, the principal ones are the three souls that are the support of the health and life of man. Their task is to keep him healthy, without ailments or miseries, with vigor and energy. That is their office; the sacred office that only the three together can fulfill. If any of the three is missing, the egg-soul for example, the incomplete man will go on, fulfilling his obligations, but his head and body will ache continually. Sign that the little-soul is no longer there. It has departed. The sick man may go on living. If he does not undergo a cure in time, the missing part of his being makes it easier for evil spirits to steal the other two. These evil spirits are the *chivosis* or dwarf creatures that live underground; deformed souls of newborn babes and dead children. There below, these creatures torture the stolen shadows. They drink maize beer and amuse themselves by torturing them, like those perverted Indians who administered torture in the cellars of the Great-White-Lord. Several *chivosis* get together and between them they cruelly twist and bend the stolen souls double. Then the body suffers the tremors of one-being-dead-continually. Ask him, Chasejk, if he can cure me. He says no, Excellency. He says that he sees Your Lordship's inside as being entirely empty. Nothing there but bones, he says. The three souls have already departed. All that's left is a fourth one, but he doesn't see it. Tell him to look, to try to see. The shadow is more difficult than the egg. He says that he has no power over it; that he is unable to see it. He says, Excellency, that even if he were to blow till he had no breath left, the helpful spirits of the cure couldn't penetrate the emptiness-without-a-soul of the body now. He could blow and spit till his mouth dries up and falls off. The great stone of death has fallen inside and there is no way to get it out now. That's what the Nivaklé says, Excellency.

So that I too, according to the diagnostic powers of this agnostic savage, have soul-eggs that are all broken. All he sees is emptiness amid the bones. But emptiness is still something; everything depends on what a person makes of it. No? Yes. The pamphleteering fetuses of the *chivosis* are twisting the wet rag of my body underground. They're drinking maize beer. They keep on twisting me, their pockets bulging with calumnies. They drink more beer. They throw me into the fire. My body smolders in the tremors of being-dead-continually. But they won't put an end to me. I'm water that boils outside the pot, a schoolgirl will say of me. Being dead and remaining on my feet is my forte, and even though for me it's all a return trip, it's always adios and onward, and I never come back, right? Right! Do trees grow downward? Do birds fly backward? Does a word that's spoken get wet? Can all of you hear what I don't say, see clearly in the dark? What is said is said. If you only listen to the half of it, you'd understand the double. I feel like a fresh-laid egg.

What else do you have there among all that paperwork? The widow of the sentry José Custodio Arroyo, who was burned to death yesterday, has presented a petition to Your Mercy. What is it the widow wants? That we resuscitate her husband as a reward for the grave dereliction of duty he committed by leaving his post?

With all respect and veneration for the Supreme Government I declare, the widow declares: that I have the dead man lying in his coffin in my house without being able to bury him, and that with the heat of this season the stench has invaded the entire district of La Merced. For which reason, the neighbors are raising a great fuss and rumpus. They want to see him buried once and for all. The parish priest of Encarnación, Supreme Sire, absolutely refuses to say the prayer for the dead and to allow my deceased, Your Excellency's servant, to receive Christian burial. I don't mean to say under the floor of the church, as would only be fitting and proper, but at least behind the sacristy where all Christians are buried. May the priest say why he refuses to intone the interment. The Reverend Father claims that my deceased José Custodio was a double-dyed atheist and Mason. He also claims that for that reason it is no mere happenstance that he was seen amid the troop of demons dancing with infernal savagery around the great fire that swallowed up the Supreme. I don't mean to say that, so I'll take it back and say what I meant to say: around the fire that my deceased José Custodio lit so as to burn the sacrilegious figure of our Supreme Karaí Guasú, meeting his death with his arms clasped about him, that is to say, not the Supreme in person but only his wax image, burning to a crisp in the fire when he fell upon it.

That is what the parish priest claims, when I know better than very well that my deceased José Custodio did so solely and with all his soul because he was trying to save that image that to us is sacred, because it represents our Karaí, made with evil intentions by those who wish to make mock of the Supreme Head of Government, and hence will meet with eternal damnation, if it be the will of God and Most Blessed Mary.

As a consequence of all this, the neighborhood, in league with the

Paí, accuses me of being a witch. They continually take the Most Holy One, though forbidden, out in street possessions, amid lamentations and prayers. They also take out the image of Our Lady of the Assumption, which has been placed in the keeping of Doña Petronita Zavala de Machaín, as perpetual guardian of the Virgin, also forbidden.

They have brought from all over everywhere women specially chosen to weep and to pray, more than a thousand of them. They have lighted bonfires of palma-Christi and male-laurel in front of my house and on many streets, saying that it's to drive away the bad spirits that according to them come out of the body of my José Custodio. They shout at me and insult me, on and at the hour.

I hereby declare that last night several individuals and women of my acquaintance, dressed in habits of the Tertiary Order, forcibly entered my house. They tied me up and veiled my face with rosaries of the Fifteen Mysteries. They dragged me to the shore of one of the rivers of fire that rage down the street and the ditches like the torrents of storms with their tongues of water. They also hauled along the coffin with the deceased inside and tied me on top of the lid with ropes. They would have thrown us into the ditch that the fire was coming out of, so that my José Custodio would have burned up—God save us!—for the second time after he was dead, and I for the first time before dying. This happening would have happened if the guards hadn't arrived just in time to save us with their rifle volleys.

All this matters little to my deceased, who is already dead, or to me, who am still alive, and I would have asked for nothing from our Supreme Dictator. But I have twelve sons, and the biggest of my little ones is barely fifteen. He is the drummer in the Hospital Barracks band. I am a washerwoman, but what I earn from the dirty laundry of the people up there above isn't going to be enough for me and my little chicks to live on.

But this too doesn't matter very much to me, Supreme Sire. What matters a great deal to me, more than anything, is that because of the slander and malice of wicked people, I am unable to offer Christian burial to my much-lamented deceased. Nobody knows what a good, kind soul poor José Custodio was. One of the Lord's own. It's not the same to bury him in the yard of our hut or dump him into the river, even though the man that served our Supreme with utter loyalty and died through and in the service of the Fatherland and the Government was an Arroyo.

Arise, señora. What is your name? Gaspara Cantuaria de Arroyo, at your service, Yr. Excellency. Arise. I cannot allow any Paraguayan, man or woman, to kneel before anyone, not even before me. Go, with my condolences. Your wishes will be fulfilled.

Has she gone, Patiño? Who, Sire? The widow, you clod. She hasn't been here, Excellency. Your Mercy refused to grant anyone an audience. I've merely been reading the widow's petition, Sire. You're such an idiot you don't know that persons, things, aren't real. Wake up for once and for all from that sort of besotted bewitchment that makes you continually miss out on what's going on. Don't you sense all the misery of the general? People whose life is rife with difficulties, ripe with discouragements. The poor, the only ones who have a pitiful love of uprightness. Trees that gather dust. If they weren't able to breathe at least a sigh, they'd suffocate. I've found out, Excellency, that this matter involves a long-standing enmity between the priest and the Arroyos because they refused to pay the baptism tariffs for their twelve children.

Inform the parish priest of Encarnación of my sovereign will and decree:

He is to declare where the soul of the late José Custodio Arroyo ended up. If he finds him in hell, he is to leave him there. Should this prove impossible to verify, he is to proceed immediately to give the corpse sacred interment, after a funeral with the body lying in state. Without charge. Pass the dossier on to the vicar general. Order is also hereby given to transport the priest of Encarnación to the penal colony of Tevegó.

Supreme Decree:

Pay 30 ounces of silver to the widow Gaspara Cantuaria de Arroya as a compensation for moral and material damages. Plus a pension of six pesos, two reales for each son until the eldest attains his majority. On so doing, he will join the Hospital Barracks Band as a musician with the rank of corporal.

By the way, in order that the bands of the entire country may again deafen the air with their martial sonorities as I have ordered, take note of the following order to be forwarded to the Brazilian traders in Itapúa: 300 brass bugles and an equal number of bronze-plated ones; 200 cornets-à-pistons; 100 oboes; 100 horns; 100 violins; 200 clarinets; 50 triangles; 100 fifes; 100 tambourines; 50 kettledrums; 50 trombones; two gross of music paper; 1000 dozen treble and bass guitar strings, to replace the previous shipment that fell into the water during the crossing of the Paraná through the carelessness and negligence of the transporters.

Of these instruments a complete set is to be given to the Indian musicians making up the band of Infantry Battalion No. 2, directed by

Maestro Felipe Santiago González, which is to be rehabilitated and enlarged to a complement of one hundred places. The soloists Gregorio Aguaí, oboe, Jacinto Tupaverá, trumpet, Cristano Aravevé, violin, Lucas Araká, clarinet, Olegario Yesa, fife, José Gaspar Kuaratá, tambourine, José Gaspar Jaharí, triangle, members of the orchestra that paid the last tribute at the funeral, are to be retired with the pension due them.

What have you found out about the theft of the 161 flutes stolen from the organ in the choir of the temple of La Merced? I have here, Excellency, the report of The Hon. Ecclesiastical Judge and Vicar General Dn. Roque Antonio Céspedes Xeria: In view of the gravity of the sacrilegious theft, I resolved to threaten the presumed thieves and their accomplices with all the weight of the machinery of State, but as of this writing this has produced no results worth communicating to Your Excellency. Despite such threats and that of excommunication which I decided to fulminate *post mortem,* the only thing that has come to light is that the musician Félix Seisdedos (who is called that because in fact he has six digits on each hand and each foot; organist of the suppressed convent of La Merced, servant and slave of the deceased presbyter O'Higgins) is presumably the one who sold the flutes to the silversmith Agustín Pokoví as scrap lead. This too has not been possible to verify, Excellency, since Pokoví the silversmith died shortly after the theft, of an attack of apoplexy, and the aforementioned slave and organist Seisdedos drowned in a river in flood, on the very same day as the storm in which Your Excellency had the accident. Pede poena claudo!§ Our investigations are now leading us in the direction of the public schools, since I have received reports that secret bands of flutists have been formed among the pupils of the said establishments. I submit this information to Your Excellency without waiting to acquire more, in the belief that its prompt arrival may best befit the action that Your Excellency may deem desirable to pursue in order to halt the spread of this evil.

Order the investigation of the robbery not to be pursued, Patiño. Add to the list of musical instruments that I have already dictated to you the quantity of 5000 small piccolos, which are to be distributed to each one of the pupils of the public schools. I order, furthermore, that in each one of them bands of piccolo players be formed from among the most gifted pupils. From this day forward, theory and solmization are to be included in the school curriculum.

What else? Corporal Efigenio Cristaldo, musician, humbly presents

§End of last verse of Horace's Book III, Ode ii: "Punishment on limping feet."

to Your Excellency a petition to retire from the post of drum major that he has held for thirty years. He maintains that his age and bad health no longer permit him to fulfill his obligations with the capacity demanded by his duties. He asks permission, on the other hand, to resume his labors as a farmer, especially as a planter of royal water lilies in Lake Ypoá. Do you see, Patiño, how infirmity disturbs men's activities even more than death? At the very moment that I am sowing the seeds so that thousands of musicians will spring up in this country of music and prophecy, the dean of drummers, the very best of my drummers, the one who made of his instrument the very sound box of my orders, wants to retreat into silence. Why? To cultivate victoria regias in the muddy water of the lake! What victories are there without drummers? Summon him. This is a problem that he and I must resolve between us.

What else? Petition from Josefa Hurtado de Mendoza, who asks for the restitution of the landed property that belongs to her in consequence of the division of her husband's estate. An afternoon of widows, musicians, flutists, drummers, of any wretched devil that takes it into his head to come here to wag his tail at the wrong moment! Have you looked into the antecedents of the case? Yes, Excellency. The Judge of the Court of Appeals has ruled in her favor. Isn't that plump widow dripping a little candle fat your way, Patiño? In the name of Heaven, Sire! The widow Hurtado de Mendoza is merely asking that justice be done. My sovereign decree then: If there's nothing furtive going on and it won't leave the late Mendoza hurting, the petition is granted.

What else? The widow Noseda seeks Your Excellency's permission to take the cargo of maté she is carrying through to Itapúa. More widows! Where are the certificates of payment of the sales tax on foreign merchants, the fractuary contribution, the war duty, the state monopoly, all the taxes required by law? They are not included in the dossier, Excellency. They are still under consideration. Listen, you immeasurable scoundrel. Raise your eyes! Don't sneeze. That Noseda widow, who has a face harder than leather and stone, is in the process of pulling strings with you: you're her compadre from way back. She's your old bosom pal. No, I swear that's not true, Excellency! All right then. We'll handle Señora Noseda with silk gloves. Write: The widow Noseda, traderess, is to be given what she has asked for: Let her bring in her cargo if her hold is empty, but if it's full don't let her bring it in. For her belle-lettristic contrabandistic legerdemain, the petitioneress is to be charged a fine of three thousand pesos, to be paid to the Treasury in specie.

Your favorite can't complain, Patiño. Some years ago I levied a fine of 9539 silver pesos against the mulatto José Fortunato Roa, a secret agent of the Porteñistas, for a similar shady deal he tried to put over on me, in connivance with his ladroni-sociate Parga. I, Most Excellent Sire . . . You for now will take care of those dossiers while I make a note of other notes. No road is all bad if it has an end.

What about those rings for the boats? Ah, yes, Excellency. The carter who was bringing them drowned in the Pirapó, which had overflowed its banks in the recent rains, trying to get to the other side. What I'm asking you about is the iron rings. They've already arrived at their destination, Sire. The commandant of the town of Yuty, near the place where the cart went down, the driver was drowned, and the whole cartload was lost, gathered all the inhabitants together and they decided to change the course of the stream that had turned into a raging river. Even the lepers from the lazar house worked. In three days and nights the rings were high and dry again. A hundred horsemen rode hell for leather to deliver the rings to the Deputy of Itapúa.

Send a dispatch to that useless official:

To the deputy of Itapúa, Casimiro Roxas:

On receipt of this dispatch, you will immediately carry out the following orders:

(1) It is absolutely necessary to speed up the construction of the barges. The flotilla must be ready before the month is out. I am sending Trujillo to direct the work. He knows precisely where to place a cannon, how to secure the breeches, just as I myself showed him, so that the recoil doesn't capsize the vessel.

(2) I am also sending marine gun carriages, one hundred in number. Another hundred land ones. I shall see about sending whatever else is needed later. More details concerning all of this will be forthcoming in the Sealed Confidential Instructions that will be sent to all military commanders. The idea is that this war fleet will contribute, when the proper moment arrives, to breaking the blockade of the river and freeing navigation. I myself shall arrive shortly to organize the preparations for defense. I shall lead the troops myself and direct operations in accordance with a plan that I have drawn up. I am going to keep a strict accounting of what there is on hand and what is spent; and with regard to equipment I am not going to pay those insatiable Brazilian traffickers the exorbitant prices you people show on your lists. Not one grain of powder will be bought for more than it is worth.

(3) Tell the commander of the garrison that in order not to ruin the horses for good by giving them time to put on fat this summer, it is necessary to put them to work in the fields with extra bastos§ under their work harnesses. Tell him also that he may continue to cut wood till the first quarter of the moon, which will be on Friday. He is to sort the wood cut into two parts: in one, the logs that can be used for the construction of the boats; in the other, those which are to be traded off to the Brazilian and Uruguayan smugglers for arms. In your reports and dispatches, omit the *don,* which is no longer customary.

(4) What about Señora Pureza? Has she already arrived there? Have you offered her asylum, cordial hospitality, as I ordered you to do in my previous dispatch? Treat her with all the respect that so eminent a lady deserves, for the country owes her many services that I alone have any knowledge of. You need not play high and mighty with her or launch into those lofty diatribes of yours which in your stupidity you fondly believe enhance your authority. Authority that is not yours, but merely conferred upon you as a deputy of the Supreme Power.

(5) I have received many complaints about you from the Brazilian traders. Rage, no matter how justified, is something one should never tolerate in himself. For nursing anger against someone is the same as allowing that person continued control of our thoughts, our feelings. The least moments. That is a lack of self-sovereignty. The height of stupidity in fact. Plant this bit of advice beneath your bush of kinky hair. Let it take root there and flower one day in thoughts, in useful actions. My dear Roxas, do as duty commands you.

(6) Send numbers of the Buenos Aires Gazeta. The last one you sent me was six months old. Pay a surcharge, even if it is for back copies. Pamphlets, any sort of publication that comes out there. I have read that Rosas is beginning to be favorably disposed toward me, which might mean something, if only astute flattery on the part of the Restorer so as to win time and win me over now that Lavalle's army is pressing him hard. That wet rag of a Ferré is again governor of Corrientes. The Correntinos deserve him. Verify the truth of the story that the liar Rivera has been offered the command of the army against Rosas and Paz the one-armed has been put at the head of its troops.

(7) Ask Spalding, the Englishman on the other side, to send me the promised book by the Robertson brothers on my Reign of Terror, along with their Letters on Paraguay. I want to see what new villainies those two scoundrels come up with after a quarter of a century. For those lies bound

§*Bastos:* padding.

in leather you may pay up to a hundredweight of maté. One more if there are two volumes. Haggle. To my mind, those miserable lies in print are worth no more than a pair of hemp sandals. In any case, don't go beyond the two hundredweight in all. If it's not a deal, to hell with Spalding the Englishman, the two Scots Robertsons, the British Empire and every last one of its miserable subjects.

(8) Tell agent León to order in good time another shipment of toys to be distributed to children at Epiphany. The toys will be paid for this time in specie by the Treasury, out of my uncollected salary. The caravan of carts bringing the gun carriages and the cannons can bring back on their return the bundles and crates of toys, a detailed list of which follows.

(9) See what you can do to improve our secret service in the area outside our borders for which you are responsible. To make it more rapid, more effective, more secret. As it functions at present, I am the last to know what's going on. Especially now that I have embarked upon a project of vast proportions. On this head you will find further details in the sealed Confidential Instructions.

(10) Sound out Señora Pureza as to her relations in Río Grande, the Banda Oriental, Entre Ríos. Don't say anything to her yet. As usual, you will only muddy the waters. The best thing would be to invite her in my name to journey to Asunción to talk with me. Don't inform her of the reasons. If she finds the prospects of such a journey pleasing, provide her with the means of transport, along with a proper escort. The old coach of the governors, it seems to me, is still around somewhere thereabouts after having been abandoned in Itapúa by those Robertson rascals on their journey to Misiones. Put it back in good enough shape so that Señora Pureza may use it. Should she decide to avail herself of it, advise me beforehand that she is coming.

(11) Increase to three the number of relay stations for the Asunción-Itapúa courier service. One in the town of Acahay; another on the Tebikuary-mi River; the third at the confluence of the Tebikuary and the Pirapó. Have rafts made for the transit of heavy cargo across the two largest rivers. Assign to these points the best rower-raftsmen you can recruit there. Send people from the leprosarium at Yuty to look after the equipment, the installations. You will furnish one head of cattle daily, plus provisions and military uniforms, both to the raftsmen and to the river patrols. Likewise to the crews for storing, repairing, and maintaining the matériel.

(12) I do not understand, my dear Roxas, why you should suddenly say in a report that you need clothing for the battalion. Here where I am, I'm not able to finish uniforming more than a thousand recruits. The only three tailor shops, with three tailors and twenty seamstresses, can't get the

job done, even though they're working in three shifts. Hence these recruits haven't yet been able to pass in review, though they have been duly instructed and are ready to join the troops of the line. Let those others wait their turn; and if they are really in such great need of clothing, let them get along as best they can, because at the moment I am occupied with other extremely important matters besides providing fancy traps for the troops. And what is that business of mixing uniforms all about? You know very well, or should know after twenty years, that the issue uniform is a blue jacket with facings whose color varies according to the branch of service. White breeches. Yellow cording in the back seams distinguishes Cavalry from Infantry. Round leather hat with tricolor cockade and the inscription *Independence or Death* above. Another larger one over the heart on the tunic. If these details are neglected, the units will be unable to maintain order in the first real hand-to-hand combat. Battalions, squadrons, companies will be all mixed up. Each one will attack, open fire on his own. As happened to Rolón in his skirmish with the Correntinos.

The carts bringing the gun carriages will also bring those articles of clothing that are ready at the moment. Perhaps everything, outside of the cravats, which will come later.

Itemized toy order:

- 2 figures of uniformed generals on horseback, each one on a cart with four small wheels, the figures ten inches tall.
- 6 uniformed officers, also on horseback and likewise on a cart with 4 little wheels each, 7 inches tall.
- 770 figures of uniformed grenadiers, 6 inches tall, 10 of them with bugles.
- 10 figures of uniformed drummers with their drums, and springs to make them play, in assorted sizes from 5 1/2 inches on up, each one mounted on a box containing the spring.
- 1000 figures of a sentry in his box, which he enters and leaves by means of a spring, the figures 3 inches tall.
- 600 little cannons 3 1/2 inches long, on gun carriages.
- 12000 rifles with barrels 12 1/2 inches long, painted in different colors.
- 100 bugles painted in different colors, 13 inches long.
- 20 figurines of women 6 1/2 inches tall, dressed in white and playing guitars, each standing on top of a box containing the spring.

20 strolling actors with their women partners, waltzing in a ring placed on a box with the spring inside, 5 inches tall.

20 figures of women sitting on chairs playing the piano, 9 inches tall, placed on top of boxes containing the spring.

40 young girls squatting on their heels on boxes 3 inches tall, each of them feeding two baby birds.

30 young girls 3 inches tall on boxes with a spring training their puppies.

30 young girls 3 inches tall on boxes with a spring, each one feeding one baby bird.

400 figures of women 4 inches tall, dressed in colors, with their children in their arms, standing on boxes containing the spring to make them walk.

50 young girls seated on bellows, with their little birds on their skirts, 2 1/2 inches tall.

120 women 6 inches tall holding their little ones by the hand with a spring.

200 women dressed as field hands 9 1/2 inches tall.

7 friars 3 1/2 inches tall, standing on bellows (barefooted).

4 old men measuring 3 1/2 inches, each one preceded by a she-mule loaded with fruit, on boxes with a spring.

80 children sitting in a hammock.

77 Guaikurús on horseback, each one with lances 3 1/2 inches high.

20 colored jaguars 3 1/2 inches high and 7 1/2 long, placed on bellows.

20 cats 2 1/2 inches tall on bellows.

20 baby rabbits on bellows.

20 foxes with a rooster on top of each of them, placed on boxes with springs 9 inches long.

60 wooden noisemakers 3 inches long, 1 1/2 wide.

(In the private notebook)

I pick up the mummy-flower of amaranth once again from among the papers. I rub it on my chest. Once again the faint fetor arises from its depths; an odor, more like a sound than an odor. Magnetic irradiation that communicates its waves directly to the brain. Feeble current that has been there since BEFORE. Fossil-aroma in appearance only. Nebula outside of time, of space, propagating itself at a fantastic speed in several simultaneous, parallel times and spaces. Convergent-divergent ones. Objects do not possess the aspects that we find in them. I hear with my entire body what the waves are whispering electrically. Accumulated radiations vibrate in the amaranth-tympanum. The screen of memory turns around backwards, projecting infinite instants in reverse. Scenes, things, events, superimposed without dissolving one into the other. Projected sharply. Momentum. Luminous wave. Continuous. Constant. One need only take shelter behind a mirror to look without being destroyed. Although the shock of this infinitesimal ray of energy, more terrible than that of ten thousand suns, might shatter the world of the mirror to bits. The mirror of the world.

The sun's rays beat down on the little two-master in which we are sailing toward Córdoba. The river flowing back to its sources. Not a breath of a breeze. The fore-and-aft sail hangs limp from the gaff. The water stinks of the slime of sun-baked banks. Gleaming amid the reflections. I can clearly make out each one of these reflections. I *see* what is going to happen in the next instant or a century later. The boat moves through a floating field of victoria-regias. The round black silk buttons suck in the light, breathing out a smell of funeral wreaths. I pick one of these buds. I open the warm ball. Inside the polished, ivorine sphere, I discover what I am looking for. Round mirror of cold bluish-gray dots, blinking in the center of silky lashes blacker than a raven's wings. As darkness descends, the buds sink beneath the surface to sleep underwater. They float back to the top of the water at dawn, but even beneath the noon light, as at this moment, their plumage remains nocturnal. Complete innocence. I can catch hold of time, begin over again. I choose at random one of those instants of my childhood that unfold before my closed eyes. I am still deep within nature. After erasing the last word from the blackboard, my hand has not yet arrived at writing. My child's mind takes the form of things. I seek my oracles in the signs of smoke, fire, water, wind. The swirls of dust blow their mathematical powder in my eyes. The baculus makes it way along alone, very slowly. The jaculus shoots through the air, swifter than an arrow. I go row-row-rowing in my boat. I consult here and there those natural nests where what-is-not is nesting. Prognostications. Prophecies. I make water on the muddy water. The trembling of the little waves is yet another source of predictions that have already come true. When events, the most trivial of occurrences, do not happen as one has seen that they will, it is not that the things-that-are-signs have been wrong. It is the reading that one makes of these prophecies that is mistaken. It is necessary to reread, to correct every last hair of error. Only thus, at long last, when one no longer even expects it, does the keen blade suddenly appear, and, gliding along it, behind the last drop of sweat, a first drop of truth. The only one who could say this without lying would be the last man. But who is to know who that final man is if humanity itself has no end? And if this is how it is, couldn't it be that there is no humanity as yet? Will it ever exist? Will it never again exist? What an inhuman humanity our poor humanity is if it hasn't even begun yet!

Why is it you want to hang up your drum, Efigenio Cristaldo? I'm old, Your Excellency. I don't have the strength it takes to get the sound out of the hide that's needed for a Proclamation, a Decree, an Order, an Edict. Especially in the escort of your Excellency. You know I no longer go out. Well, Supreme Sire, that may be why I can't get the sound to come out either. I'm older than you are and I'll go on beating the drum for the Government, whether or not the sound comes out. What's most audible isn't what's heard the best, Efigenio. I'll go on beating as long as there's a pulse of life left in me. Your life will be a long one, without a second, Most Excellent Sire. No one can replace Your Grace, whereas I can be replaced by any of those young thumpers that I myself taught. I take the liberty of recommending most particularly the trumpeter Sixto Brítez, who comes from the Cerro Ñanduá in Jaguarón. He's the best horn in the Escort Battalion, but his forte is the drum. He was born to be a drummer, Supreme Sire, and there's nobody better. He knows how to fill his belly, his chest with wind, and beat out any drumroll you can think of. It can be heard for a league and more away, when there's no wind. Above all after a big blowout in the mess hall when he's gotten filled up on bean stew and eaten an entire calf's head all by himself. I don't need any recommendation from you, Efigenio, especially one for that notorious glutton, who has another vice as well: putting his hand in his trousers fly when he's on parade so as to enjoy sniffing the sticky stink on his fingers as he marches along. What does he mean by stealthily whiffing his prepucial effluvia? What does he mean by doodling with his fife as he plays the trumpet? He's already earned himself any number of whacks for that nasty habit. A special pair of trousers, with no fly, was made for him. It now has all the inside seams of the pockets ripped out. It's lucky for him that he's going to be a good second lieutenant in the war against the Triple Alliance. A future hero may be forgiven certain present vices.

Policarpo Patiño worked here among these papers till his last day, copying his own death sentence. Your father, a master mason, worked stone till the last day of his old age. It was his calling, Excellency, as yours is to be Supreme Governor. Everyone is born for a different calling, Sire. If that's so, isn't yours playing the drum? A person never knows, Excellency. So you want to give up on the job now? Maybe you too think I'm the Defunct Supreme. I've never thought that and I never will, Excellency! I merely allowed myself to ask Your Grace to relieve me of the duty I can no longer fulfill, because I'm old and because the drum is getting farther and farther away from me. In our brief relations with existence everything depends upon our having more or less kept up the rhythm, Efigenio. Look at this, Supreme Sire. What is it? The callus the drum has formed on me as it rested on my chest. As big as the hump of a zebu, as hard as a rock. It takes lots of whacking, with very long sticks, Sire, and even so the sound that comes out is very weak. All the sound that didn't come out must be buried in that bump. You've been humping along too long on the job, Efigenio. I see you've gotten hunchbacked. So you too have your stone to bear, eh? Well then, what occupation do you think would suit you now? What I've wanted very much to be ever since I was a little boy is a schoolmaster, Sire. And you've waited thirty years to tell me so? I would have waited even longer, Excellency, if I'd been able to go on serving as a drummer without the inconvenience of this hump that's appeared on my chest, besides the one I'm carrying around on my back. In the petition that you've presented you say you want to go back to work as a farmer and grow giant water lilies in Lake Ypoá. That's also true, Sire. But the office I was born for is that of schoolmaster. You didn't ask for my good offices for that in your petition. I didn't have the courage, Most Excellent Sire, to propose myself for a charge as high as that of schoolmaster, even though the two things to my mind are the one and only reason for which I was brought into the world. I say this without meaning to belittle in the slightest the honor of having served under the direct orders of your Excellency. I have taught the little Indian musicians here; but the only thing they need to learn are the strokes of the first letters. All the rest, which is the part that's most important, they already know by the time they come here from the wilds where they were born. Enough! You are relieved of your post as drummer which you held on sufferance for thirty years. Sufficient unto the day the sufferance thereof. Go off to your aquatic flowers. Give my most affectionate best wishes to those buds that float back to the surface at the break of dawn with a very soft sound not to be found among the seven notes of the scale. Look at those flowers with my eyes, if you can. Touch them with my hands, if you can. You will see that the sieve of those velvety floating wheels gathers in many clouds. Moses would have liked to be born in one of those little baskets. Take that tricorne hanging on the hat rack with you. Put it on your head. Come on. Put it on! Pick up that petrified flower that's on the table, there next to the skull. Put it underneath the tricorne. Higher. Right next to your scalp. There, there. Press down harder. Antenna the equal of that of blind insects. In it you will hear the voice that goes on and on. The bit of coal that one is oneself is a little live ember of the whole. Uuu, ah. What a long time has gone by, or else none at all! Where are you, Efigenio? Can you hear me? Not very well, Excellency! Your voice sounds as though it were coming from underground! Not from underground but from inside a can of noodles! Wheeeere aaaaare yoooouuuuu? Here in the lake, amid the green sieves with their black silk buds! You don't seem to be in sound health either, Efigenio. Haven't things been going well with you of late? Living my lot, fighting every step of the way, Sire! I can't complain! Children soon grow old! Flowers too! There isn't time for a body to notice anything. I so attest and go on my way!

Communication with the ex-drummer is interrupted. Tin is not a good conductor. You are old. I am Old. The Old Ones were. The Old Ones are. Sounds are not. The Old Ones will be. Not in the spaces or the time that we know but in the time, in the unknown spaces that circulate amid the known. Their hands grip the throats of the living. But they do not see them. They cannot see them. They cannot see them *yet. (Unknown hand):* You can only spy on them in the dark . . . *(torn, burned).*

. . . wait patiently because they will reign here again. They are the Old Ones because they are wise. You must not ask questions, the Voice-of-Before says to you. You must not ask questions because there is no answer. Do not try to get to the bottom of things. You will not find the truth that you betrayed. You have lost yourself after having caused the failure of the very Revolution that you sought to make. Do not try to purge your soul of lies. All this prattle is futile. Many other things you have not thought of will go up in smoke. Your power has no power over them. You are not you but others . . . *(the following folio missing).*

(Perpetual circular)

A sloop loaded with bales of maté, one of the many lying rotting in the sun of (since) the Revolution, was given permission to set sail, on condition that Pedro de Somellera, who had been expelled from the country, leave aboard it. He embarked with his entire family, his European furniture,* huge trunks. Immense cages full of hundreds of monkeys, animals of every kind, strange beasts, rare birds. Others as well: a number of Porteño agitators, lesser heads who had never ceased contriving plots to bring about the intervention of Buenos Aires against Paraguay, were also placed on board in shackles amid the bales of maté and the cages. Along with the Córdoban Gregorio de la Cerda.

The sloop departed so heavily laden that it wallowed in the water. A zoo, a botanical garden, an overstocked game preserve. On the cliffs

---

*In 1538, fighting against the squalls of Magellan, the Genoese pilot León Pancaldo was obliged to turn back from the Strait of the Eleven Thousand Virgins. His ship, the Santa María, had its holds full of a fabulous cargo of goods destined for the newly wealthy conquistadors of Peru. Bad luck continued to dog him. He arrived in Buenos Aires when very ill winds were blowing. Dying of hunger, the members of the expedition headed by the First Adelantado had ended up eating each other. Under the governorship of Domingo Martínez de Irala in Paraguay, the remains of the deserted city were concentrated in Asunción, thereby making it the "shelter and support of the Conquest." Pancaldo's magnificent treasures were also transported to this city, thereby permitting the conquistadors to furnish and adorn their rustic seraglios with exquisite pieces worthy of true caliphs. From 1541 to the Revolution (and even long afterward) there was traffic in León Pancaldo's merchandise in Asunción; thus Spaniards who barely had strings for their bows possessed daggers with beautifully worked handles, opulent fox-fur jackets, velvet doublets and hose. In humble straw huts it was not rare to find, alongside indigenous aópoí (very primitive cotton cloth), precious fabrics, satin curtains, pomegranate cushions, inlaid chests and credenzas, dressing tables with cut-glass mirrors, beds with baldaquins and curtains embroidered in gold thread; chaises longues, footstools, and ottomans of very fine tapestry, indiscriminately mingled with rough benches and stools carved by the natives for their masters. This situation long obtained among Creoles and mestizos, the *sons of the earth.*

The shipment of furniture and goods that Pedro de Somellera took with him from

above the port a great crowd of patrician ladies and others of mixed blood had gathered to bid farewell to the *omni compadre,* bringing with them an enormous flock of his godchildren. As the sloop cast off its moorings, the comadres burst into tears. Scenes of despair. Silk tunics were rent, hooped petticoats raised to wipe noses and to dry tears, the comadres' cries and lamentations rivaling those of the female parrots and monkeys setting sail.

I expelled la Cerda at a somewhat later date, when I returned for the second time to the Junta. In the event, it is of little moment that we are shipping him out for the time being aboard the sloop together with Somellera and the rest of his annexionist associates.

This did not put an end, however, to the clandestine efforts to recover power through a counterrevolution. On the morning of September 29, 1811, a headquarters company under the command of Lieutenant Mariano Mallada came out of the barracks hauling two cannon behind them, beating drums and making the streets ring with cries of Long live the king! Long live our Governor Velazco! Death to revolutionary traitors! A trick contrived by the idiots of the Junta. A simulated restorationist uprising. Many Spaniards nibbled the bait; a number of them swallowed the hook. At that moment the reserve troops came out of the barracks and arrested the agitators.

Because of the stupid way in which the whole scheme was planned and executed, the insurrection came to nothing. Having received an urgent message, I left the farm and went down to the city. The performance in the plaza was just beginning. I arrived just as they were shooting and hanging one of Velazco's servants, Díaz de Bivar, and a Catalan storekeeper by the name of Martiní Lexía. Cut down those corpses and enough of this bloodshed!, I thundered. The soldiery, excited by the smell of blood, calmed down. In the middle of the plaza, sitting tall in the saddle on my sweat-soaked horse, my presence commanded respect.* The inept farce

---

Asunción doubtless had its origin in the traffic in Pancaldo's treasure to which the *perpetual-circular* refers. One of those authors of fictionized history who proliferate in Paraguay, where history itself is a museum piece or something stored away in an archive, took it upon himself to reconstruct the inventory of what was taken out of Paraguay by Don Pedro. It is an impressive catalogue. It would have taken an entire fleet to transport the shipment, not just one small sloop that set sail with its waterline below the surface in those days when the river had very nearly run dry. The inventory would have it, moreover, that Don Pedro stuffed his monkeys, dogs, pigs and other animals full of gold and silver coins before his departure; taking such specie out of the country was rigorously prohibited and severely punished at the time. *(Compiler's Note).*

*"His appearance was imposing. Enveloped in his black cape with a scarlet lining, his eyes flashing, his silhouette standing out against the clouds, he was the very image of an avenging Archangel; his voice resounded more powerfully than the trumpet's

came to an abrupt end. Later on, certain newsmongering scribblers dared to accuse me of directing it from behind the scenes. Had this been so, I would have staged things on a grand scale. As I did later. Not this ridiculous burlesque of unleashing an entire army to murder a grocer and one of the ex governor's grooms.

They cut down the hanged men amid the general horror. Suddenly the crowd of Spaniards, armed with clubs and antique harquebuses, broke into an uproar once more, with enthusiasm this time. Delirious joy. Everyone dissolved into paeans of praise, and as one recognized me as their liberator. The women and the oldsters wept, blessed me. Some of them knelt and tried to kiss my boots. A splendid triumph for the a-cephali of the Junta! Mounting this grotesque farce in which I appeared as the savior and ally of the Spaniards! Wasn't this what they had aimed at from the beginning?

In the end the parody of restoration favored the cause of Revolution, enveloping it at the beginning in a cloud of smoke. For the time being it was advisable that *I,* its director and civil head, should appear to be the arbiter of the conciliation to be effected between the forces in contention for the institutionalization of the country. I will do so, I proclaimed, on the basis of minimal coincidences of views, so that none of the parties or factions will lose its identity and individuality. (*In the margin:* This was a half truth; as far as "minimal coincidences" were concerned, there were none at all; the entire truth would have been to speak of "minimal connivances.") I was going to maneuver them on the game board in accordance with the deliberate and inflexible strategy that I had resolved to follow. Chance began to collaborate with me. I had gotten rid of Somellera the bishop, la Cerda the knight, and other Porteño pawns, who incidentally had cleaned out the State coffers. I wasn't going to stop till checkmate, with or without a sipper. You of course are not familiar with the royal game of chess, but you are past masters of the plebeian game of truque. So pretend that I said: until I have the ace of swords in my hand and break the bank.

The majority of the wealthy Spaniards ended up rotting in jail. An orderly man, it was not *I* who had given this order for disorder. Ransom of the prisoners at least had the advantage of contributing a goodly sum of doubloons to the State treasury; not to mention other confiscations, expropriations, and fines that the circumstances demanded as just restitution.

---

blare," a witness of the period, the Hispanophile colonel José Antonio Zavala y Delgadillo writes in his *Journal of Memorable Events.*

While the friars rebuked the officials of the Junta and the general staff, as the plumifer Pedro de Peño concluded in his notes to the other felon-scribe Molas, they blessed me roundly. I was the magnanimous Doctor who had been brought into the light of day and suckled by the brothers of the Pious University of Córdoba.

In the city first of all, and then throughout the province, it was bruited about that *I* had opposed the plan of the members of the Junta whereby the prisoners taken as hostage, including the bishop and the ex governor, were to be shot to death en masse. The families of the prisoners came to me seeking justice and protection.*

Somellera and Cerda departed. Belgrano and Echevarría arrived. At less than a snail's pace. Not as invaders this time, but on a mission of peace. This mission was well calculated, the Tacitus of Buenos Aires relates, to negotiate with a naive and suspicious people such as the Paraguayans, as strongly inclined to mistrust as it is easy to delude. On this mission Belgrano represented candor, good faith, loftiness of character. Vicente Anastasio Echevarría cleverness, knowledge of the ways of men and things, easy and persuasive eloquence. I saw in this jackanapes only a varicose, viperine tongue; I heard in him only the tumult of his out-landish ideas peeking out of his reptilian eyes. Belgrano, on the other hand, was a man of much greater worth than the description of him by the Tacit Brigadier. A transparent soul, that of this man unacquainted with evil, peeping out through the pupils of his clear blue eyes. A man of peace condemned to be different from what he was in the depths of his being.

The two emissaries not only did not complete or complement each other, as the Tacit Budgereegah maintains; they in fact got in each other's way and canceled each other out. The situation of their country made it

---

*"At this time he acts in a concilia-tory manner. He wishes to inspire general confidence, to be the man of order, to attract the goodwill of the pro-Spanish faction. He even changes his ways. He becomes amiable, affable. He is visited in his office by many ladies of the aristocracy, among them Seño-ras Clara Machaín de Iturburu and Petrona Zavala de Machaín, whose husbands are also in prison, to ask him to expedite their trial. He listens to them most courteously, grants their request, and bids them fare-well 'with great consolation,' according to what Petronita's father reports in his *Journal of Memorable Events*. The unsocia-ble attorney has become very civilized. Power changes men so much! He does not even notice that the youngest of his lady visitors is his old love. Has he forgotten? Has he forgiven?" (*Commentary of Julio César*.)

"After an unfortunate love affair with Clara Petrona, the daughter of Colonel Zavala y Delgadillo, who rejected his suit out of hand, he is not known to have had other love affairs or courtships. Affections occupied little space in the frigid soul of this man, absorbed in accomplishing one funda-

imperative for them to bring about a supposed reestablishment of concord with ours, the apple of discord of the extinct viceroyalty. It was not peace and genuine accord, however, that the successive governments of Buenos Aires were seeking. The truth was that the poor Porteños were having a very bad time of it. One government followed another in the vortex of anarchy. The one at dawn could not be certain that it would last till dark. Being in doubt, they kept their valises all packed and waiting at the door. Outside their borders things were not going any better. After the disaster of Huaqui, the Spaniards had again taken possession of Upper Peru. The Portuguese-Brazilians had occupied the Banda Oriental militarily. The royalist squadron controlled the rivers. Buenos Aires enjoyed, before Asunción, the pleasures of a blockade and isolation.

At this moment I don't remember if it was Rivadavia the wooden-headed or Saavedra the great stone face who conceived the idea of sending General Belgrano and the shyster Echevarría with instructions to insist that Paraguay submit to the rule of Buenos Aires. Failing that, to attain at least the union of the two governments through a system of alliance. Always "union," and any pretext would do! Annexation at any price! The Revolution in Paraguay had not been born to be a thing of mends and patches. *I* was the one who cut its brand-new swaddling clothes to measure.

Belgrano and Echevarría had to endure a long wait in the purgatory of Corrientes. Before their visit, on July 20, 1811, the Junta had sent to the Buenos Aires government whose turn had come round a note that firmly expressed the ends and objectives of our Revolution. I said that no Porteño would ever set foot in Paraguay again until Buenos Aires fully

---

mental purpose. To penetrate it one needs a ladder and a lantern." *(Commentary of Justo Pastor Benítez.)*

"Strange universe, that of this man who is said to have possessed an obdurate heart, like that of Quintus Fixlein, completely untouched by the flames of passion, for the only seductions to which he yielded were his occupations. Others firmly maintain, however, that it was endlessly set on fire and was sensible to those Andalusian eyes that still gleam brightly unto the tenth or twelfth generation. The thought comes to mind that in such cases it must have burned like anthracite, as it is said that his eyes gleamed in his face of an urubú.[§]

There are vague rumors to this effect.

"Poor Supreme! A pity that there was not a pair of these eyes with sufficient intelligence, depth, and soul to have taken him captive permanently, turning him into a virtuous paterfamilias. Is there, moreover, any certainty that the young, dark, harebrained, vivacious young woman living a disorderly life, who twenty years later was selling flowers in the streets of Asunción, was a daughter of El Supremo? Nothing but shadows, shadows, shadows. Words, words, words!, Hamlet, the melancholy prince of Denmark, said through the mouth of our Shakespeare." *(Commentary of Thomas Carlyle.)*

[§]Black vulture. From Tupi *uru* (bird) + *vú* (eat).

and expressly recognized its independence and sovereignty. End of August. The reply was held up deliberately. I deliberately prolonged the wait of the emissaries at the Gate to the South. I repeated the entire score of the note for the benefit of the Porteños. Once colonial domination has been abolished, the tenor of it went, the representation of supreme power devolves upon the Nation in its entirety. Each people then considers itself free and has the right to govern itself freely by itself. From this it follows that, inasmuch as the peoples have reassumed their original rights, they are all on equal terms with respect to each other and each one is entitled to look to its own preservation. A hard bone for the proud Porteños to swallow. There were other barbs in the note: Anyone who might imagine that it is Paraguay's intention to abandon itself to an alien power and allow its fate to depend upon the sovereign will of another would be deluding himself. Were it to do so, it would have gained nothing, harvested no fruit of its sacrifice other than to trade one set of chains for another and change masters. By virtue of the very fact that Paraguay recognizes its right, it does not seek to do any other people the slightest injury, nor is it opposed to whatever is fair and just. It is firmly resolved to unite with that city and others in a confederation, not only to preserve a mutual friendship, good harmony, free commerce and communication, but also to found a society based on principles of justice, equity and equality, as a true Confederation of autonomous and sovereign States.

With the fishbone stuck fast in his gullet, Tacitus the Brigadier had no other recourse than to concede the fact: This was the first time that there had resounded in the history of the American continent the word *Federation,* so famous later in its civil wars, its constituent congresses, its future destinies. This celebrated note may be considered to be the first act of Confederation proposed in the Río de la Plata.

Paraguay thus freely offered the Porteños this idea that could resolve all its problems at one stroke. It projected, for all of America, before any other people, the form of its future destiny.

The Junta sent a dispatch to Belgrano, stranded in San Juan de Vera de las Siete Corrientes: We solemnly assure the honorable envoy that it is only the necessity of a complete and happy conclusion of past differences that impels the Junta to prolong this forced halt in his journey until his government understands and adheres to our sincere proposals and our sacred pledges, which are and ought to be identical. We also solemnly profess a sincere friendship, deference, and loyalty toward our brother peoples; generous valor against armed enemies; contempt and punishment for traitors. These are the sentiments of the Paraguayan people and of its

Government, one and the same as those they expect and await on the part of Buenos Aires. In this regard, the honorable envoy may be certain that the moment we have received a favorable reply from his government, we shall take particular satisfaction in facilitating the journey of the mission and its arrival in this city.

[*(In the margin):* The catfish of Takuary had turned into a prickly bone. The fish is born of a thorn. The monkey of a coconut. Man of the monkey. The shadow of Christopher Columbus's egg wheels round and round above the Land of Fire. The shadow is not more difficult than the egg. The shadow flees before itself. Everything eventually gets to where it's going. Merely to be on the way is already to be arriving.]

The reply from Buenos Aires came crawling back. It accepted unconditionally everything that had been demanded of it, and gave its solemn word to do even more than had been required of it. The plenipotentiaries arrived. As they stood in the prow of the boat, the sun set their splendid regalia afire in the spring morning. Magnificent reception. The twenty leading families at the top of the cliffs. Thousands of curious humble folk deafening the air as they banged away on their drums, big and small, as at festive bullfights in black and mulatto encampments.

The assembled Junta bade them welcome amid cannon salvos and rifle volleys. General Belgrano stepped forward toward the officers. After exchanging a military salute, the ex adversaries of Takuary gave each other a lingering embrace, murmuring furtive messages in each other's ears. Amid the cries of the multitude we set out for Government House in the ex carriage of the governors. A broken rim obliged us to bow to each other at each turn of the wheel. Rigadoon of nodding heads and smiles. On passing through the Plaza de Armas, the newly arrived visitors saw the gibbets. Skinny starved canines were licking the bloodstains of the storekeeper and Velazco's groom. Echevarría turned and with a wicked gleam in his eye asked me: Are these stage props for the reception? I disliked that man's face the moment he made his entrance upon the scene. Amalgam of pedantic schoolmaster and black bird of tribunals. A plain chicken done up in fancy dress. A monocular chicken. Any creature of the animal kingdom except a man to be trusted. No, doctor, this was the setting for another performance. The thing is that in Paraguay time is so hard-pressed that it slows way down, mixing up facts, shuffling things about, misplacing them. Fortune is born here every morning and by noon it's already an old lady, according to an old saying that's new and true all over again each day. You see that over there. No. It no longer exists. It has become an apparition. I see, I see, the chicken-plenipotentiary said, half-closing his one eye. Exhausted by a terrible mental effort, he wiped his crest with a particolored handkerchief. The general, very sparing of words, very serious, nodded at each thump of the wheel.

There comes forth from the souvenir-pen another reception that I shall offer the envoy from Brazil, fifteen years later. I can allow myself the luxury of mixing up the facts without confusing them. I thus save myself time, paper, ink, and the trouble of searching through almanacs, calendars, dusting shelf lists. I don't write history. I make it. I can remake it as I please, adjusting, stressing, enriching its meaning and truth. In the history written by publicans and pharisees, they invest their lies at compound interest. Dates to them are sacred. Particularly if they are erroneous. To those rodents, error consists precisely of gnawing holes in documented truth. They turn into rivals of moths and rats. As for this perpetual-circular, the order of the facts does not alter the product of the factors.

On August 26, 1825, Antônio Manoel Correia da Cámara,* envoy of the Empire of Brazil, is conveyed to Government House in the same carriage in which I am riding with Belgrano. I naturally do not accompany him. The district commander suffices for such a task. A battalion from the regiment of mestizos and mulattoes escorts him. The maximum honor I can offer this fine-feathered fool who has made so bold as to omit the title of *Republic,* to which our country is rightfully entitled, in his request to enter Paraguay. I am observing him from the window of my study. Bunches of heads are milling about in the empty spaces along the main street. The populace rushes to the corners as the gold-braided visitor, jingling with decorations, passes by. From the carriage the friend of Sultan Bazajet ceremoniously waves his plumed hat. Flag of truce negotiations. The hordes of people push and shove each other to get a closer look at the imperial envoy. There are no loud cheers or acclamations. Curiosity blunted by instinctive apathy. I know what is behind it. Red shadows. The

---

*"Parallel to the mission from Buenos Aires [the reference is not to the mission of Belgrano and Echeverría but to that of Juan García de Cossío] is the Brazilian one of Antônio Manoel Correa da Cámara. An extraordinary character. No one better suited than he, thanks to his life straight out of a novel, his taste for adventure, to write the dramatic chapter of an entry into isolated Paraguay; his journey, his stay in Asunción and Itapúa, his negotiations in the capital, make for a story of the most absorbing interest. A warrior in India, a combatant in Portugal, a traveler in Turkey, a revolutionary in Río de Janeiro, an intimate friend of José Bonifacio, a devotee of the muses, pounding on the gates of a cloistered Paraguay to reveal the Sphinx. Such was the man chosen for such a mission." *(Commentary of Julio César.)*

common horde cannot help but see in the Man-who-comes-from-afar the Brazilian kambá:§ descendant of marauding bandeirantes, arsonists, thieves, slave traders, rapists, throat-slitters. The broken wheel rim decapitates him with each thud. The greetings fall in the dust. When the trumpet of the escort falls silent, angry buzz of boos and jeers can be heard. Muffled catcalls: Kambá! Kambá! Kambá-tepotí! How different from the welcome given Belgrano!

I have arranged not to receive Correia yet. Let him wait a while longer. I do not extend my hand hastily. I want to have a very good idea of what it is the empire wants, what it is that its scatterbrained strawman is prepared to hand me in exchange. Let him be taken to his lodgings. From the black carriage a white hand agleam with sparks reaches out, waving the plumed hat to right and left in greeting. The crowd observes the spectacle, forming part of it without participating in it. From deep within the black calash, the Man-who-comes-from-afar advances, surrounded by the atmosphere of his carnival in Río. Useless theater. Tinseled trappings, propped up by the non-visible. He is preceded by a shaking shindy of black batuque§§ dancers wearing necklaces. Tumblers, capoeiras§§§ brandishing their clubs stained red. Not enough. Not red enough. Not as red as real blood. Perhaps it suffices to simulate it beneath the marginal sun of Brazil, to the west of Africa. The incendiary sun of Asunción is another matter. Continually beating straight down, splitting stone. The glare bares, betrays, bleaches out the treasures of this cardboard carnival. Blurs the dancing girls, the capoeiras. The white hand against the black lacquer of the carriage clutching the ibis of the hat. Royal-heron. Bird-of-Paradise. Alchemical buttons. Colored sequins. Wear more if you like. Pile on as much as you please. To me it will be mere theater. To me the imperial envoy is just another messenger boy. An empty-headed suitor come to seek my hand. But I don't give my hand away to anyone.

At times the carriage in which I accompany Belgrano and the carriage bearing Correia pair off. They advance backwards, rolling along together for a stretch. Unite. Form a single carriage. We are all going along together, ceremoniously saluting each other at each hard jolt. The break in the wheel rim forces agreement upon us as we nod in concert. Each one

§A black, especially a Brazilian soldier in the War of the Triple Alliance.
§§*Batuque:* an African dance (Brazilian).
§§§*Capoeiras:* ruffians skilled in the *capoeira* technique of attack, similar to jiu-jitsu (Brazilian). Cf. also Brazilian *capoeiro:* chicken thief.

firmly says no while appearing to say yes at every second and fractions thereof.

Buenos Aires has sent Belgrano to negotiate a union or an alliance with Paraguay. The Empire of Brazil has sent Correia to negotiate an alliance, but not union with Paraguay.*

Antônio Manoel Correia da Cámara descends from the carriage in front of the accommodations reserved for him. The figure of the typical Brazilian macaque stands out against the whiteness of the wall. I study it from my window. Unknown animal: lion in front, ant behind, pudenda inverted. Leopard, more pard than leo. Illusory human form. Its most amazing particularity, however, lies in the fact that when the sun strikes it, it casts the shadow of a human being and not that of its bestial figure. Through the spyglass I observe this monster that the Empire is sending me as a messenger. Pasted to his mouth, a fixed enamel smile. Gleaming gold tooth. Platinumed wig down to his shoulders. Eyes half-closed, scrutinizing his surroundings with the cautious duplicity of the mulatto.** He is one of those who see the grain of sand first. Then the house. The Brazilian-Portuguese, this sly trickster, is here to build a house on sand, even though he hasn't come yet. Or perhaps he's already come and gone back where he came from. No. He's here, since I see him. The past comes to life again in the object-holder of the memory-lens. What a splendid plumed hat!, I hear the secretary of the Treasury murmur at my side. Get to work, Benítez, and leave off your quips and cranks and wanton wiles.

(In the private notebook)

I am the final judge. I can decide how things will go. Contrive the facts. Invent the events. I could prevent wars, invasions, pillages, devastations. Decipher those bloody hieroglyphs that no one can decipher. To consult the Sphinx is to risk being devoured by it without being able to

---

*"Correa himself requested, demanded this mission, for he was anxious to conclude a Paraguayan-Brazilian alliance in order to crush the Plata in the inevitable war that it will wage with the Empire in the Banda Oriental." *(Ibid.)*

**"Tall, fair-haired, piercing dark brown eyes, erect and intelligent head, slightly aquiline nose with marked indications of energy and will; in short, a fine figure of a man. Grave, circumspect, self-contained, formal gestures. Fashionably dressed, with the diplomatic elegance that he has acquired in old European courts." (Porto Aurelio, *Os Correa da Cámara*, Anais, t. II. Introd.)

unveil its secret. Guess it and I devour you. They are coming. Nobody walks about simply because he wants to and because he has two legs. We glide along in a time that is also bumping along on a broken wheel rim. The two carriages roll along together in opposite directions. Half going forward, half backward. They separate. They graze each other. Their axles creak. They draw farther and farther apart. Time is full of cracks. It leaks everywhere. Scene without a break. At times I have the sensation that I have been seeing all of this forever. Or that I've come back after a long absence. To resume the viewing of what has already happened. It may also be that nothing has really happened except in this image-writing that goes on weaving its hallucinations on paper. What is entirely visible is never seen entirely. It always offers something else that must be looked at further. One never sees the end of it. In any event the club is mine . . . I mean this pen with the memory-lens imbedded in the pommel.

This is a cylindrical pen of the sort manufactured by prisoners serving life sentences in order to pay for their food. It is evident that this object is not a product of the unaided imagination of the prisoner, but was made according to precise instructions. It is of white ivory, a material not available to prisoners. The upper end is shaped like a small spatula: it bears an inscription blurred by traces of years and years of nibbling. "What's the use of one tooth biting on another?" was one of El Supremo's favorite expressions. "To blur inscriptions by the superimposition of other more visible, though more secret, ones," He himself would have answered himself. The lower part of the pen ends in an ink-stained metal plate, alveolated in form, and integumented. Mounted in the hollow of the cylindrical tube, scarcely larger than a very bright point, is the memory-lens that turns it into a most unusual instrument with two different yet coordinated functions: writing while at the same time visualizing the forms of another language composed exclusively of images, of optical metaphors, so to speak. This projection is produced by means of orifices along the shaft of the pen, which lets in the flood of images in the manner of a microscopic camera obscura. A device on the inside, probably a combination of mirrors, causes the images to be projected in their normal position, not inverted, in the spaces between the lines, amplifying them and endowing them with movement, in the same fashion as what is today known as a cinematographic projection. I believe that at one time the pen must also have possessed a third function: reproducing the phonic space of writing, the sound-text of the visual images; which could have been the spoken time of those words without forms, of those forms without words, that allowed El Supremo to conjoin the three texts in a fourth intemporal dimension turning around the axis of an undifferentiated point between the origin and the extinction of the writing; that thin shadow between tomorrow and death. Trace of invisible ink that nonetheless triumphs over the word, over time, over death itself. El Supremo was extremely fond of constructing (he himself speaks of the squint of his fancy) such contrivances as the little mother-of-pearl club, the meteoric-rifles, the flowerpots-that-listen, the infinitesimal calculus abaci fashioned from coconut seeds, the flying-messengers, looms able to weave even curls of smoke ("the cheapest wool in the world"), and many more inventions that are spoken of elsewhere.

Unfortunately the sensitive mechanism of the memory-pen is partially broken, so that today it writes only with very thick strokes that tear the paper, effacing words as it writes them, endlessly projecting the same mute images stripped of their sonorous space. They appear on the paper with a sharp break in the middle, like rods submerged in a liquid; the upper half entirely black, so that if they are figures of persons they give the impression of being hooded. Shapes without faces, without eyes. The other half beneath the line of the surface of the liquid is diluted, forming a range of watery grays. Patches of colors, once vivid no matter what their tone, with each and every point of a dazzlingly bright visibility, grow fainter and fainter as they scatter in all directions, all equally motionless. An optical phenomenon that could only be defined as frozen movement in absolute stillness. I am certain that beneath the lactescent, kaolinic water, the images retain their original colors. What must turn them gray to the point of invisibility is the blindingly bright light that most probably still persists in them. No acid, no water can burn them, extinguish them. The alternate possibility is that they have turned the other way around, thus showing the necessarily dark side of the light. I am also certain that the images retain underwater, or whatever that gray plasma may be, their voices, their sounds, their spoken space. I am certain. But I am unable to prove it.

Through the workings of chance, the souvenir-pen (I prefer to call it memory-pen) ended up in my hands. The "little mother-of-pearl club" is in my possession, to do with as I please. The marvelous instrument belongs to me! I realize that to say this is to say a great deal. It seems incredible even to me, and there are many who will not believe it. But it is the absolute truth, even though it may give every appearance of being a lie. Anyone wishing to dispel his doubts has only to come to my house and ask me to show it to him. It is here on my table watching me continually with the nibbled tooth of the upper end, biting me with the memory-eye imbedded in the pen. It was given to me by Raimundo, nicknamed Loco-Solo,§ great-great-great-grandson of one of *El Supremo*'s amanuenses. I practically wrested it away from my old grade-school classmate, whom I visited more or less assiduously in the hovel he lived in, on the Jaén near the Military Hospital, the former Hospital Barracks. In his last days, Raimundo never left his miserable dwelling except to go in search of the meager provisions he needed to stay alive, and most importantly the brandy and narcotic herbs that he consumed in great quantities. Every so often I would drop in with a few bottles of *Aristócrata* cane brandy and cans of corned beef. We would remain for hours in silence,

§An indirect homage paid to Raymond Roussel (1877–1933), one of the most unusual figures in French literature, like Lautréamont a precursor of the surrealists and the Nouveau Roman, entirely unrecognized in his own lifetime. His many works include a novel entitled *Locus Solus* (1914).

not looking at each other, not moving, till night made our two shadows one. Raimundo knew my avid, my secret desire to possess his treasure. He pretended not to know it, but I knew that he knew, so that between the two of us there was frankly no secret. That is how things had been since the year 1932, when we first met each other in the República de Francia Primary School. Benchmates in the sixth grade. First boys' section. I remember it very well because that year the city was full of band music and patriotic songs. The war with Bolivia broke out in the Chaco. The mobilization that took even dwarfs to the front began. To us the war was a never-ending fiesta. If only it would last for a lifetime! We played hooky and went down to the port to say goodbye to the recruits. Farewell, you future te'ongués (corpses)! Go and don't ever come back, you poor dummies!, Raimundo shouted to them. Watch it, it'll be our turn some day!, I said, digging my elbows in his ribs to shut him up. It's already been our turn and we got screwed! Just look at how many wars there have been and we've been screwed every time. And here we are, still stuck in school with those fucking books! But they're not going to ship me off to the Chaco, even though they come begging me on their knees! I'm going to take off for Africa! Why Africa, Loco-Solo? Because I want strong impressions, not that shitty little war with the Bolís. Balls on that!

When it came time for examinations that year, I helped him out on the written tests. I took the orals, the anals for him. The whole works. From the first subject to the last. The school was already a brothel. The schoolmistresses burning with patriotic ardor, furiously writing letters to their wartime adopted sons, and us cheating like mad on the exam. Without budging from his seat, Raimundo got a ten, whereas I, who'd worked my ass off for the two of us, came out with a three. As compensation, as a consolation prize, he showed me, for the first and only time, the fabulous pen that the great-great-great-grandson of Policarpo Patiño had "inherited" through a complicated tangle of little strokes of luck, above and beyond the right of an amanuetic dynasty: Here the thing is, he said. I barely managed to touch it. He immediately grabbed it out of my hands. I'll buy it from you, Raimundo!, I almost shouted. Not even if I were mad!, Loco-Solo said. I'll sell you what I dreamed last night if you like, but not this. Not even if I were dead! The tips of my fingers itched from the mere touch of the little mother-of-pearl club.

On the eve of the Exodus that began in March of 1947, I went to visit Raimundo for the penultimate time. He was nothing but skin and bones now. In a little while they're going to be able to make buttons out of you, I said to him jokingly. He looked at me with his bloodshot eyes of a man with his throat slit, blinking in the swollen pockets of his eyelids. Hee! Hee! That's exactly what's awaiting me in a very short while, he said, and then after a long silence: Look, Carpincho,§ I know you all too well, and I know that you're a heartless disheartened monster. Disarm-

---

§A common nickname in the Río de la Plata region. A *carpincho* (capybara) is a very large rodent, principally aquatic in habit, living on the margins of lakes and rivers. It has a coarse coat, partly webbed feet, and no tail. It is hunted both for its fur and for its edible flesh.

ingly unarmed. For a long while now, or to put it a better way, from all eternity and even a little while before, not only since the bench in the República de Francia School and our whoring around in the brothels of the Calle General Díaz, but even a while before being born. The only thing you want is the Pen of *El Supremo*. Your mouth is watering. You wet your head just thinking about it. It melts your brain and your hands tremble more than my hands of a drunkard, of an epileptic, of a taker of güembé powders and the cocaine that the nurses give me, that you yourself bring me. You've courted me, besieged me, helped me to die with a patience more stubborn than love. But love is only love. Your desire is something else. That desire, not of what I am but of what I have, has chained you to me. It has made a slave of you, a dog that comes to lick my hand, my feet, the floor of my shack. But there is no friendship, love, or affection between the two of us. Nothing more than that desire that doesn't allow you to sleep, or live, or dream of anything but *that*. Day and night. I don't envy you. You're much worse than I am. Think for a minute, Carpincho. I was born slowly and I've also been a good while dying. What's done is done. Through my own will. Some seek death and don't find it. They want to die and death escapes them. They have the teeth of a lion but they're like women. Women who don't know they're whores. You're one of them. But much worse perhaps. Very bad times await you, Carpincho. You're going to become a migrant, a traitor, a deserter. They're going to declare you an infamous traitor to the country. The only recourse left you is to go on to the very end. Not stop halfway. Go on whittling the stick down to a point. He

fell silent, panting, exhausted not so much perhaps by the effort to speak as by the effort to observe a silence that had now been broken. His lungs eaten away by phthisis made more noise than a cart full of stones. He dumped out a great clot of blood against the wall. In a dwarf's voice he went on: At least another century of bad luck is going to rain down on this country. You can smell it in the air already. Many people are going to die. Many people are going to go away and never come back, which is worse than dying. Though it doesn't matter all that much because people are like plants in this country. You kick the dust and for every one that isn't there any more five hundred others spring up in the same spot. What matters is something else . . . but at this moment I don't remember, I forgot what I was going to tell you. I tried to interrupt him. He raised his hand: No. Carpincho, don't worry about me. The soldiers are going to shut me up in the asylum because they say that besides setting a bad example here around their hospital, I stink up the place. Maybe so, but what about the whores in the brothels all over the neighborhood? I'm the only Angel of the Abyss around here. The Exterminating Lazarus. The families of the officers who were confined screamed to high heaven. They've sent letters to the president, the archbishop, the chief of police. But I'm not going to go to the asylum. They're not going to take me to the asylum, not even over my dead body. Not even if I'm dead. I'm Loco-Solo. I'll be Loco-Solo to the very end. They won't shut me up in the asylum! I'd rather bury myself in the stream that carries away the used cotton swabs, the dirt and filth of the Military Hospital, the bloody rags of the whores, their aborted fetuses . . . Another gob of spit smoked as it hit the adobe bricks. I don't know if I'm going to get through the night. I know I'm not going to make it through. Up there in the crawl space of my shack, just below the roof, inside a tin tube is the Pen. Grab it and go straight to the Devil with it. It's not a gift. It's a punishment. You waited a long time for the time of your perdition. I'm going to be free tonight. You're never going to be free again. And now leave, Carpincho. Grab the Pen and clear out in a hurry. I don't want to see you again. Oh, wait a sec. If you manage to write with the Pen, don't read what you write. Look at the white, gray, or black figures that fall to the sides, between the lines and the words. You'll see terrible things heaped up in bunches in the dark that will make even the trees rotted by the sun sweat and scream. . . . Look at those things while the dogs in the countryside howl in the middle of the night. And if you're a man erase with your blood the last word on the blackboard . . . What word, Raimundo?

He spoke no more. He turned his back encrusted with dry sores from writhing about on the earthen floor in the attacks of convulsions, the violent hallucinatory spasms brought on by the coca and the drugs. Raimundo's spectral silhouette was gradually reduced to that bent back of his that was looking at me. But I was the one contemplating my own back. Beneath the worn skin like tree bark crisscrossed with inscriptions and lines scratched out, the vertebras deformed by arthritis were pointing their parrot beaks at me. Was that spine, whiter and whiter in the darkness, which

was my own spine and was sticking me in the eyes, going to start sweating and screaming? I heard myself breathe at half throttle. From the other side, the death rattle grew louder and louder with that sound of dry leaves that the threat of a storm wrests from the dead calm of summer.

Only much later did I happen to learn that Raimundo died that night, as he had foreseen. His whole life long, or at least as long as I knew him, he had cultivated a taste for his own death along with his fear of death. They found him after he had been dead for several days. His body was blocking the door, which in life he had never locked since there was no bolt or key. That corpse of a man like the dead body of a bird was so light that the wind alone blew one leaf open. The smell of Loco-Solo came out through the opening, since that was all that could come out of him now; it spread the news that he had now interned himself in his own Asylum. Taken his place in the tales of the hospital quarter. Cured in absentia. Transformed into that double sobriquet that became the name for all time of the fatally misleading legend of a man.

Some say they buried him in the cemetery of the Military Hospital, which seems unlikely given the rigid rules of the military. Others say the corpse was thrown into the river. This seems more natural somehow, being in accordance with Loco-Solo's own wishes. There would not have been any great difference between the two ceremonies, however. *(Compiler's Note.)*

As I write it projects its gaze between parentheses. Raises it to another power. Intervention of all the angles of the universe. Interversion of all perspectives concentrated in a sole locus. I write and the tissue of words is already crossed by the chain of the visible. Damn it! I'm not talking of the Word nor of the Holy Spirit transverberated! That's not what I mean at all! Not at all! Writing within language makes every object, present, absent, or future, impossible. These notes, these spasmodic notations, this discourse which refuses to discur, this visible-speaking artificially fixed in the pen; more precisely, this crystal of aqua micans imbedded in my memory-penholder offers the roundedness of a scene visible from all points of the sphere. Machine encrusted in a scriptorial instrument allowing things outside of language to be seen. By me. Only by me. Since the visible-speaking will be destroyed by what is written. The sap of the secret will go up in smoke, leaving not a rack behind. No matter that the little migratory mother-of-pearl club will go on reflecting the sunny beaches of the shipyards on the shore of the river where the Ark of Paraguay is being constructed. It captures the shouts, the sounds, the voices of the shipfitters, the craftsmen, the oily gleam of the sweat of the black workers. Their untranslatable expressions, their interjections, their vulgar exclamations. Sudden silence. Inaudible sound that palpitates. What meaning can plays-on-words have in the face of that? Saying, for example: Paradise is a lofty, flowering, well-peopled dwelling place where the just become choruses of castrati. Or, the cock of winter stamps its feet angrily when dawn is late. Or as Bertoni, the expert on Indians, states, the belief that the son descended exclusively from the father and merely passed through the body of the mother, transformed the mestizo into a terrible enemy. Or, the people are brutalized by means of their own memory.

To say, to write something has no meaning whatsoever. Straining your guts does. The crudest little fart of the humblest mulatto who works in the shipyards, in the granite quarries, in the lime mines, in the gunpowder factory has more meaning than scriptorial, literary language. There, that, a gesture, the movement of an eye, spitting in the palms of the hands before grabbing the adze again: that means something very concrete, very real! What meaning can writing have, on the other hand, when by definition it does not have the same sense as the everyday speech of ordinary people?

(Perpetual circular)

In the meeting room the president of the Junta has no idea what to do with the empowerments and credentials of the Porteño envoys. He finally pockets them, and twirling his mustaches says to Belgrano: You may begin your peroration, señor general.

Buenos Aires has no intention of subjugating the peoples of the viceroyalty, Belgrano begins by saying, and naturally offers the most ample satisfaction to Paraguay for having sent the military expedition to aid its cause. It feels well recompensed for its sacrifice by the revolution of the Fourteenth of May and the establishment of the new government. It is necessary now that Paraguay join and obey the central government since it is imperative to form a center of unity, without which it will be impossible to draw up and execute plans conjointly. The Portuguese threat is serious, and it is directed not only against Buenos Aires but also against Paraguay. The only means of containing the prince of Brazil within his boundaries lies in the conformity of the opinion, conduct, and action of Paraguay with that of the government of Buenos Aires. The provinces must join forces in the face of the common enemy, and the withdrawal of Paraguay would be a disastrous example for all of them. All of the interior, that is to say the provinces that constituted the former viceroyalty, is represented in the present government of Buenos Aires. Only deputies from Paraguay are missing, and their incorporation is a matter of urgency. (Applause from the pack of the Junta. I remain silent. Imperturbable silence.)

Don Fulgencio endeavored to reply. He groped for words, leaning for support on the jingle of his spurs as he pawed the ground. I intercepted his stammerings in midair. I said: To begin with, honorable envoys, the aforementioned expedition was not to aid us but to invade us, as is recognized in the act of capitulation signed at Takuary. That is true, Belgrano granted at that point. He admitted as much again later in his

Memoirs: This error could only have been the product of hotheads looking solely to their immediate interests, for whom nothing was difficult because they were incapable of reflection and acted in ignorance. Well, general, let us lay this dreary episode aside and pass on to another point, sir, the most urgent and most important one: Paraguay is no longer a province. It is an independent and sovereign Republic to which your Junta has granted full recognition. The viceroyalty is an ugly word, sirs. An immense corpse. We are not going to waste time restoring this fossil. We are in the midst of seeing our countries born of the provinces that in the Kingdoms of the Indies were reduced to mere colonies of an oppressive power. Neither oppressors nor servants there be / there where reign union and equality,§ even schoolchildren sing here in this country. Paraguay has offered Buenos Aires the plan for a Confederation, the one form that will make this confraternity of free States viable, without union meaning annexation. The pettifogger Echevarría stuck his oar in, ad-umbrating the idea that an ad-referendum treaty providing for the incorporation of Paraguay and the sending of its deputies might well be concluded, where-upon it would be submitted to a congress for its approval. I can assure the honorable envoy that the congress will neither applaud nor approve this ad-referendum treaty. We can do nothing behind the backs of the people and their sovereign will. Less still submit to it an idea that will oblige it to submit once again to a foreign power. Do you have the instructions written in Mariano Moreno's own hand well in mind? Clear and definite. Straight to the point. Union presupposed for him establishing *perfect order* in Paraguay, removing the Cabildo and the authorities, putting in their place entirely trustworthy men, and expelling suspect citizens from the country. The fiery tribune of your May, gentlemen, decreed: If there is armed resistance, the bishop, the governor, and all the principal instigators of resistance will die. No, gentlemen; these ideas of death and destruction must not be revived. We are endeavoring to put Paraguay in perfect order without all that ceremony and bloodshed, in accordance with our own ideas and needs; independently, and not in obedience to instructions or orders from outsiders.

Echevarría pecks at the deliberation with his forked tongue. Dia-logues of the deaf. Of dead men. Of half-deadmen. Speeches. Counter-speeches. Belgrano is silent now, his eyes closed to the present. He surely remembers Moreno's impassioned instructions, point for point. It was with that man, not with that pedantic impostor Echevarría, that I would have

§Verses from Paraguay's present-day national anthem.

liked to discuss at that moment the principles of the Social Contract as applied to our countries. But the spectral monarchical crown coveted by the Porteño "re-publicans" has already crushed him beneath its weight and buried him in sea-slime. For the time being I am obliged to put up with the stupidities, the shadow-plays, the absurdities, the extravagances of the Porteño pettifogger.

For the moment, I conclude, Paraguay is entirely occupied by the organization of its public administration and its armed forces. It cannot commit them to any objective save its own defense. Threatened internally by the Spanish faction and externally by the Portuguese army, it must confront these dangers with every means and every resource it possesses. Be sufficient unto itself. Not count on foreign non-aid. The captious negotiations entered a faintly promising fourth phase, though I for my part regarded them as having been already knocked into a cocked hat. I had already stored them away in the attic along with other useless junk. If they come rapping at your door with mischief in mind, I said to myself, answer them with the key. It was necessary to go on waiting awhile longer however; to see this inconsequential farce through to its ultimate consequences. October 12, the Day of the Race, was set for the final discussion and the signing of the treaty.

The guests are the object of delicate attentions on the part of the leading families. Many fiestas in their honor. Levees, soirées, parties carrées, libations, celebrations, invitations. With the president of the Junta at the head, the Porteñistas jig for joy. They plan a great military parade, to be held on the same day as the signing of the treaty. The most conspicuous partisans of "union" visit Belgrano and Echevarría assiduously. Nothing good can come of these clandestine meetings, despite the discreet surveillance I order. The listening-flowerpots surreptitiously installed in the meeting places pick up alarming gossip. I therefore decide to accompany the guests personally, everywhere, at all times. Belgrano especially. I become his shadow, though I won't say I follow him to the door of the toilet (every place has become suspect), or that I turn into the guardian angel of his sleep, because I must also draft the text of the treaty. Word for word. Detail for detail. The treaty is my splendid louse-cap; my head never hits the pillow. I close my eyes neither by night nor by day. Thinner than a vine shoot, in the shadow of my single leaf I can slip in anywhere. Press the juice from whatever grapes suit me. The greenest ones are quite ripe enough for me.

The project of Buenos Aires, under pressure from the new British or
French tutors to achieve the unity of its interests, will end up as no more
than a rodeo, a roundup of vast Paraguayan domains, with the Porteños
running the show. I address myself to the door. On the other side of it
the general is making his ablutions. He doesn't answer me. I hear the sound
of water splashing in the washbowl. The meek cattle of the provinces
eating the salt set out for them in the basin by the English, I say. He doesn't
hear me. The splashing grows louder. The general must think he is still
crossing the Paraná and then the Takuary in flood, in a leather boat, on
his expedition to Paraguay. So then, my dear general, you came to invade
us mounted on a dead cow!, I venture jokingly. What dead cow?, he asks,
coming out of the dingy cubicle. A smiling sheik beneath his towel-turban.
You were saying something about a dead cow, my esteemed dean? Just a
bit of antic salt, my dear Don Manuel; a trifling joke. As the French say,
Vive la bagatelle! Vogue la galère! I was remembering your boat. Boat?
The boat made of cowhide that you crossed the rivers in. The story you
told me about it last night at the party was most amusing! Well, in any
event that dead cow saved my life!, the general says, returning the ball to
my court. Waggish familiarity. I don't know how to swim even in sand.
That boat was splendid. Imagine that, general! And it was only the hide
of a Paraguayan cow! Belgrano laughed good-naturedly. If Pascal had
come with you in that leather boat, he wouldn't have said what he did:
Rivers are roads that move and take you where you want to go. The turban
fell off his head. As a matter of fact, Pascal never came here except in the
form of a boat. What's this story you're telling me, my esteemed dean?
You'll remember, general, that in the middle of the last century Voltaire
set himself up in business and freighted out a ship named the *Pascal* to make
war on the Jesuits. The *Pascal* was then chartered by the Spanish government, which used it as a troop transport in the fight against the patriots.
A somewhat cynical genius, Voltaire; a burning ambition to make money.
His greed made of him an armateur-philosopher. He was taken in by the
legend of El Dorado. He sent Candide to Paraguay, and I later took the
latter's manservant, the mulatto Cacambo from Tucumán, into my service,
thereby freeing him from the written word. I don't understand, he said,
shaking his head. I took him out of the book, that's all. Cacambo had a
good time of it with me. He had my confidence. He betrayed it, naturally,
since it's in mulattoes' blood to turn traitor. The general went on laughing,
his funny bone tickled by my seriousness, doubtless believing that I was
telling him another myth.

Bowlegged Echevarría comes along and butts into the conversation. Look, señor dean of the Junta, Paraguay's refusal to become part of the United Provinces of the Río de la Plata means purely and simply the continuation of the policy of isolation that has been established here. Not at all, señor jurisconsult. Paraguay did not isolate itself of its own will. It's as though you were to maintain that if we walled you up in this bathroom you would remain there for the sheer pleasure of it and claim that it was the best of all worlds. Come now, Doctor Echevarría! Would you allow yourself to be isolated in this way? Would you say, truthfully, that you did so of your own will and accord? It is the governments of the ex viceroyalty that have taken control of the river by barring the port, ever since the Revolution that freed our countries from the power of the oppressor. Buenos Aires now comes along offering us peace, union, and free trade. Is this offer in accord with the attitudes and the conduct of a State that arrogates to itself the role of gendarme in relation to the others, and above all to a free, independent, and sovereign State such as Paraguay? No, a thousand times no, señor jurisconsult! Didn't the Junta of Buenos Aires send General Belgrano here with troops to subjugate this country? We have already had sufficient discussion and explanation of this error, which is not the error it appears to be. We preferred, señor dean, not to become involved in side issues. You are one of the most enlightened intellectuals of our America. Why waste time over the past? Look, doctor, here in Paraguay the most enlightened man we have is the city lamplighter. He lights and extinguishes five hundred thousand candles a year. Even he knows that the future is our past. Let us trim our candles too, and look alive. Let us speak of the future. Why, certainly. With great pleasure. With the greatest pleasure. That is precisely the point I wish to come to. I think, señor dean, that you are given to making plays on words, and we are in the midst of discussing very serious things here that pressingly demand our serious attention. We are in accord on that point, most illustrious doctor. Such is the curse of words: an accursed game that obscures what it is seeking to express. Above all, señor dean, if we do not observe the formalities of an elementary urbanity. Is the bathroom door a proper place to ensure that all our disagreements will come out in the wash? We are in accord on that point, doctor. Let us proceed to the salon d'a-grément.

What advantages was the Porteño pettifogger trying to gain by his petulant digressions? He wanted to speak of the future. Grand, solemn words. Naturally, that unseemly go-between was interested in winding up the cloudy affairs of the mission as soon as possible so as to be able to get around to still shadier affairs. He was eager to propose the sale of the

Foundling Press to the ignorant a-cephali of the Junta. Contrabanding among scoundrels.

As for us, honorable envoys, the North Star of the Paraguayan Revolution is to cultivate the prosperity of our native soil or be buried beneath its ruins. Irrevocable decision. There is no power on earth that will make us change conviction or course. If they bar the river, we shall walk on water. You, honorable sirs, can prevent this. Among all of us we can avoid the worst and attain the good. Turn the word *Confederation* into a useful reality. You have already taken much land and much water away from Paraguay. You shall not take away its fire or its air. Echevarría's greenish jawbone searched for the support of his fist. Belgrano's white silhouette cloaked itself in shadow.

Let us speak clearly, gentlemen. If a center of unity is to be formed, that center can be none other than Paraguay. Nucleus of the future confederation of free and independent States. Why should Buenos Aires not incorporate itself with Paraguay? Model-center of the States that are to confederate. It has been that from the beginning of colonization. With even more reason it ought to be that from the beginning of decolonization. Its driving force. Not only because it is *already* the First Republic of the South; but also because its merits have always entitled it to be so. The first uprising against feudal absolutism took place in Paraguay. The hierarchies that are responsible for the events of history place Asunción above Buenos Aires: Mother of Peoples and nurse of cities, as it says in some idiotic letter-patent of the crown, which in its own way, no matter how idiotic, nonetheless expresses a truth. When Buenos Aires lay in flaming ruins, Asunción reconstructed it. And now Buenos Aires aims to deconstruct us. That merely shows what the misuse of a single letter can mean when the reality of the facts is riddled with errors! Buenos Aires, my friends, is a great error in itself. A great ruminant stomach drooping from a port. With Buenos Aires at the head we risk being swallowed alive. Fatal predestination. Brother Cayetano Rodríguez, my old professor at the University of Córdoba, writes me: You do not know, my son, that the name of Buenos Aires is reviled in all the disunited provinces of Río de la Plata!

This is no mere happenstance. As early as the days when, in the light of new ideas, we reflected on the destiny of this part of the Continent in the underground passages of the gothic pagoda of Monserrat, we saw with noonday clarity what was going to happen. Some of my fellow students, now members of the Junta, know this as well as I do. When the city dominates the countryside, the supposed Revolution turns into a theater of discord and disturbances. That is what happened here with the disaster that befell the Comunera Revolution. The patriciate of the capital betrayed it. When the Common People, the people as a whole, regains power, Revolution takes over. It then commits the error of handing it over to "enlightened" intellectuals, to the hierarchs of the patriciate. Then the people are defeated. Its natural heads are decapitated; the liberation movement destroyed.

Here in Paraguay the forces of Revolution lie in the free peasants, in the rural bourgeoisie aborning. A sort of "Third Estate," albeit incapable as yet of governing directly in the form of a revolutionary parliament. Incapable as yet of following the fight for independence through to its ultimate consequences.

In Buenos Aires the Revolution is being made by the Girondins among the commercial bourgeoisie of the port. Its best and greatest efforts do not go beyond preserving the system of the viceroyalty, along with a handful of reforms that will tend to crystallize once again in a monarchical crown. A Creole one this time. Its most "enlightened" intellectuals are out of touch with the popular masses, as are the toplofty military chiefs who head the Junta.

The general rose to his feet. He began to pace once more from one wall to the other. He shook his head. I do not agree with what you say, Sire. I am not a merchant. Nor are you. You love your people. I too love mine. We are unfortunately in the minority, general. It depends on us whether the majority of the people will side with us. Didn't Cornelio Saavedra accuse Mariano Moreno of being an evil Robespierre who advocated exaggerated principles of liberty, impracticable theories of equality? He then segregated this sect of false Jacobins-in-a-lather who were trying to foment, according to Don Cornelio, a rabid democracy in perpetual ferment, destined to subvert religion, morality, and our traditional way of life. At this point Moreno was sent to go soak his head in the depths of the sea.

Vicente Anastasio Echevarría was gravely taking notes. Instead of sipping he was blowing into the bombilla of the maté vessel that the little mulatto Pilar was serving him. No, not that way, doctor. Difficult to suck/breathe at the same time, isn't it? His eyes rolled. He didn't know what to say. Look, gentlemen, at times it pleases me to be naive, though not as naive as it would appear. I am absolutely certain that you have come to ask me to give Buenos Aires the rest of what has already been given it. He who gives and gives is left with nothing left. In such a situation, the one recourse left me is to lock the door from the inside. Keep the keys. Erect a chain of fortresses from Salto to Olimpo. Keep open only those loopholes that are in the country's interest. This is what I shall do. It's already done. Accomplished.

It is my understanding however, señor dean, the pettifogger insists insidiously, that Your Excellency is merely one of the members of the Governing Junta of Paraguay. Here, señor jurisconsult, more than a Junta on parade we have a Revolution on the march. I am the Director of the Revolution. Traitorous Thermidorian coups threaten us at every step of the way. An iron hand is needed to conjure them. Hence you needn't waste your time with figureheads. If my words do not suffice to bare the facts to you, events will bear me out. Victorious on the battlefield, my dear friends, Paraguay does not decline to sign an accord. But it refuses to be defeated by a treaty. The Junta, the entire Cabildo as one applauds my words. By offering you the bases of a Confederation, I am opening doors to you that can lead to a solution at once nationalist and Americanist. Equable. Fraternal. In the general interest. This is to speak of the future in the most concrete terms possible. Let us not cast dice to determine our destiny. Let us share it equitably, and not waste our time in equitation competitions. Let us not accept the iniquity of inequity. Let us all put our money into a kitty without its turning into a sackful of cats. Let us seek as one the best path. It is quite sad enough to see ourselves reduced to bottling up our accords-disaccords in words, notes, documents, counter-documents. Locking up facts of nature within signs against nature. Papers can be torn up. Can be read between the lines, and even between the lines between the lines. Millions of meanings. They can be forgotten. Falsified. Stolen. Trampled on. Not facts. They are there. They speak louder than words. Let us bend our every effort to shaping the Confederation. But I see no other possibility of establishing it save through a truly popular and revolutionary process.

As we ride on horseback along the King's Highway and through the lower town, the inhabitants of the city throng into the streets cheering. General Belgrano smiles and waves, enveloped in the halo of his image. A living saint in a general's uniform. We ride through the streets of Asunción, not amid a hostile multitude of sons of Jews, but a people of fervent devotees; the sons of this red South American Jerusalem: our Earthly Jerusalem of Asunción. Echevarría, ill at ease, his pettifogger's soul making the varices of his tongue burn: Without the axis of a center of order such as Buenos Aires, and without a proper fixed orbit, that constellation of free and independent States that you proposed, señor dean, will be stillborn and formless. Look, illustrious doctor, neither you nor I must oppose what is inscribed in the nature of things. Look, contemplate this simple people, eager like all peoples for liberty, for happiness; just see how it is beginning to stir in the heat of its fervor! Those real beings, those possible beings are questioning us, acclaiming us, clamoring for us, imposing their innocent mandate upon us: we who are still probable beings, with as yet no fathers or mothers, mounted proudly on our ideas which are dead ideas if we do not lead them along the path to becoming realities. Those beings are alive. They are applauding us but they are also judging us. Awaiting their turn. Coming round the circle once again. Look, doctor, contemplate those black, callused hands! They are waving, turned completely white by the bright blazing sun! They want to make of us their Roman candles. They are trying to set us off with their fervor. In the light we cast but a shadow, give off only smoke. I don't quite understand what you mean, señor dean. You needn't understand me, Doctor Echevarría. Understand them. As General Belgrano already has.

We are shouting to each other amid the tumult without hearing each other's words, merely seeing their emptiness shape our mouths. I am accustomed to not having doctors understand me, Doctor Echevarría. Your Tacitus will say that this doctrine of Confederation is destined to be exploited in a sinister fashion in the wilds of Paraguay by the most barbarous of tyrants. He maligns me. He maligns the two of you, speaking of your total blindness, of your total deafness. That word, set down in a treaty, taking on visible form, your Tacitus says, was soon to arouse all the people of Río de la Plata, furnishing a basis for anarchy and a banner to the political and social dissolution that will compromise the success of the revolution and annihilate social forces, even though it is later changed into the constitutional form synthesizing the elements of organic life of our peoples. Your Tacitus with his faulty syntax recognizes it and denies it at the same time, having learned his lessons under English colonial tutelage. This is not the cloth we ought to be cutting to make the coat that will fit all of us well. If such a thing comes about, such a coat, despite what Tacitus the Brigand says, will pass from hand to hand, turned into a magician's bag of tricks and in the end nothing but a bloody, stinking rag. Your image of the coat, señor dean, is very graphic. But like every image, illusory, deceiving. We are not dealing in images or in coats, but in political realities. We are not tailors. We are men of ideas. We must govern and establish laws, as the wise legislators of antiquity realized. Excuse me, doctor, but the congress of Buenos Aires or of Tucumán wouldn't dream of meeting in antiquity. You wouldn't want the Confederation to age two thousand years even before it was born. Nowadays, señor jurisconsult, in this sack of cats of our colonized provinces, we "enlightened" intellectuals, as you proclaim, must first establish institutions in order that they in turn may make laws, may educate men to be men and not jackals snatching what belongs to others. Apply your art of persuasion, your clever mind, your knowledge of men, of things, not to impugn our motives but to oppugn the intrigues in which the enemies of our independence are seeking to trap us. It is not giving our people the honor due them to consider them born for endless subjugation and slavery. Take a good look at this people that is acclaiming us, that believes in us *still*. Do you believe that they are fervently pleading with us to turn them back into slaves for a minority of the privileged to exploit for their own private benefit, as their foreign masters have always done heretofore?

I rejoined General Belgrano at a gallop, for he was dangerously skirting the edge of the cliffs of La Chacarita, where once upon a time the huts of the parish of San Blas had perched. Stay away from there, general! That's treacherous ground! Because of the danger of landslides! Don't worry!, he answered me, galloping across the precipice. I know when I'm on firm ground and when I'm on ground that will give way! Naturally. The general is right. When he came to Paraguay the first time he was obliged to form his army from levies on the people-multitude. Living beings. Powerful. Profound natural wisdom. Alike everywhere under like conditions and like destinies. From among these people were conscripted the men who went to Buenos Aires to help combat the English invasions, shortly before you came to invade us, general. That is true, my esteemed dean. The Paraguayans lost their men, their arms, their limbs, their courage, their lives on the battlefield in that first patriotic crusade against foreigners. Then my troops too came to Paraguay on an auxiliary mission. When they realized that the Paraguayans did not realize that the expedition wasn't against them but against the Spanish power that still reigned in these parts, my soldiers preferred defeat with honor to the false glory of continuing to shed the blood of brothers.

The conversation was becoming weighty. Freed of gravity, horsemen ought to be sparing of words. Saddles do not permit highflown disquisitions. Except on steeds such as mine, fed on the clovercarburant and aeromobile alfalfa that I cultivate on my experimental farms. Above all the black-and-white and the bayard, the heartiest eaters, on which Belgrano and I were mounted. A night of feeding on this forage produces, in the process of digestion, enough volatile gas for a flight of several hours. Aristotle derived animals from air. Leonardo made contrivances that flew, stealing from the birds the secret of propulsion and the plan of their wings. Julius Caesar fed his horses on seaweed, thereby imbuing them with Neptunian vigor. Basing myself on the principle that heat is simply a levitating substance more subtle than smoke, source of energy of matter, I outdid the Stagirite and the Florentine: instead of making mechanical and aerodynamic devices, I contrived the idea of cultivating thermic pastures. Magically useful food/thought. Factories of natural forces of incalculable possibilities for the perfecting of animals and the progress of human genetics. Construction of the super-race by means of nutrition. Alpha and Omega of living beings. Here you have the Eldorado of our miserable real condition. Don't you think, general, that the plankton stored up in the oceans could be the solution? Inexhaustible nurseries of energy! I am not acquainted with the sea, but I know that that is possible. You people are on its shores and should begin these experiments. In secret, since otherwise they might bring on a war with cattlemen and butchers, arouse an even more inexhaustible craving on the part of the avaricious merchants of the port for their pound of flesh.

We were now galloping amid the clouds on our montgolfier mounts. The red map of the city looked an even brighter red from on high. The green of the groves more green. The palm trees more feathery and graceful, dwarfs, tiny little dwarfs. The shadows of the ravines darker. The setting sun spread liquid fire over the bay, over the houses crowded together on the hillsides. Oh, what a beautiful landscape!, Belgrano exclaimed, breathing in deeply. He raised up a little in his saddle. What has happened to Echevarría? I was unable to hide my smile of satisfaction. I could see the meddlesome secretary riding along among the gullies formed by torrents and floodwaters. Look at him down there, general! At the very bottom of the Bajo. Lost in the depths of the Lower Town! How too bad for Don Vicente Anastasio!, he said pityingly. Missing this spectacle! Really bad luck, general. Your secretary is riding Fulgencio Yegros's nag, one that's only good for riding at the ring and sprint races on the straight and level.

Let's take our aerostatic Bucephali down. What do we do? Do we prick them somewhere? Do they have some sort of escape valve? No, general. Everything happens naturally. Your terror is groundless. They're thermic beings. When their gas gives out, the horses touch down again on terra firma. It all happens very naturally. The twilights in the west are incomparable at this season of the year. Look, general.

Free for once of the presence of the shyster secretary, I began harping once more on my pet subject: What happened to the viceroyalty twice in a row would happen to Paraguay only once. During my lifetime at least. Belgrano blinked, not understanding. The English, my dear general, invaded the Plata in a typical pirate expedition in order to get their hands on the flood of tax revenues from Chile and Peru that had poured into the port of Buenos Aires. Isn't that so? That's how it was, señor dean. Some five million silver patacoons, more or less, isn't that right? More or less, yes. The viceroy ordered the treasure to be transferred elsewhere and hidden. The money fell into the hands of English pirates. It was shared equally among commodores, generals, brigadiers. The remainder was sent to his Britannic majesty. Angel-Saxon probity. Leaders and officers of the invaders are lodged in mansions of the respectable classes. Freedom of worship and of trade with the pirate country begins. The patriciate takes a great fancy to the scented soap that comes from London. Meager compensation for the Porteños. Naturally the tide of fragrant lather never reaches the rabble inland. Blacks, mulattoes, and gauchos smell nothing but the growing ferment of their discontent.

The pillaging operation became a political undertaking. In view of the ease with which a handful of determined men, without exaggerated scruples, laid their hands on such rich booty, the English undoubtedly thought they could replace the Spaniards as the governing power in the Colony, even though their rule would have to be disguised under the name of "protected independence."

Meanwhile the coffers with the patacoons for the archons' annuities were paraded through the streets of London. Pomp and circumstance. A delirious multitude, very different from the one cheering you down there. The chariots transporting the product of the plundering are drawn by picturesquely adorned horses. They bear banners and inscriptions in gold letters: TREASURE! BUENOS AYRES!! VICTORY!!! Do you see them? Here they come, amid a fanfare of bagpipes and drums!*

If we deal with South Americans as merchants and not as enemies, we will reinforce localist tendencies; in this way we will end up with all of them in our pocket, the ruling powers of the British Empire thought/ adopted as their policy, thereby setting their descendants in New England a brilliant example. Despite all this, despite the May Revolution, despite all the feelings of spite, the New Governing Junta promised not only to

---

*These fragments regarding the first invasion of Buenos Aires in 1806 by British troops under the command of Beresford and under the leadership of Popham and Baird have been culled from the rough notes jotted down by *El Supremo* in the first years of his government. Although he does not quote or mention the Robertson brothers (nor do they do so in their own writings), it is evident that young Juan Parish Robertson, "direct witness" of events, both of the arrival of the flood of treasures in London and of the beginning of the British domination of Buenos Aires, was the obliging informant of *El Supremo* during his stay in Asunción. In these notes there are very precise references —true or not—to both significant and trivial facts, such as the sums that fell to Baird, Popham, and Beresford when the pirate booty captured in Luján, after the flight of the Spanish viceroy, was divided. *El Supremo* notes, for example: "The conquest of the Dutch colony of the Cape appears to have whetted the appetite of the English." And then: "Baird's share was 24 thousand pounds (to be precise, 23 thousand pounds, five shillings, ninepence), Beresford's more than eleven thousand, Popham's seven thousand;

give the English protection. It would do much more. Thus the "indirect domination" of Río de la Plata, or "protected independence," was abundantly assured in the hands of the new masters. Isn't that true, general? Belgrano had swallowed a bit of coarse-grained cloud that made him cough. I know, my dear general, that you did not attempt to cover up all these facts, but instead openly resisted them. I also know that you went to the Banda Oriental in repudiation of the invaders. Your sense of honor refused this dishonor. Through a friend I have there, in the Chapel of Mercedes, on the Uruguay River, I know that you suffered in those days. I also know that during the brutal acts of savagery on the part of the British you did not remain idle, as befitted your patriotism. Later on they forced you to come here.

I in my turn was witness of the events/counterevents that brought about your expedition. After my retreat to my farm in Ybyray I observed them intently, as you did after yours to Mercedes. Nonetheless, I was more fortunate than you. Thrice over: fortunate that your penetration of our borders ended in a more than prompt withdrawal; fortunate that I am now your friend; fortunate that I am galloping with you through the blue of this Paraguayan sky. The honorable head of a mission of peace, you, general, have come to propose to Paraguay not the aberration of a "protected independence" but an egalitarian, fraternal treaty. An addicted reader of Montesquieu, of Rousseau, as I am, we can readily agree in principle to model the project to attain the freedom of our peoples on the ideas of these masters. You, general, are one of the very few Catholics to whom the Pope gave license, in the most liberal terms, to read any and all manner of condemned books, even those that are heretical, with the exception of those on judicial astrology, obscene works, libertine literature. I will not say that the Contract and other avant-garde books contain all the wisdom we are lacking in order to proceed with infallible judgment and wisdom. It is quite enough if we arrive at a meeting of minds as regards the principal ideas. Points of departure in the struggle for the independence, freedom, and prosperity of our countries. It is in this spirit that I am drawing up the draft of the treaty that we are to sign tomorrow.

---

each one of them was able to buy himself a country seat with his part." But at the same time he does not fail to note that during this same period, at the other end of the continent, Miranda, using British money [which allowed him to hire mercenaries and buy arms], was endeavoring to win the "independence" of Venezuela. "What is all this shit?" *El Supremo* exclaims indignantly. "In August of 1806, Miranda lands at La Vela. He finds no one there. The patriots flee from the liberators, believing them to be pirates. In September, the English land in Buenos Aires, and there the pirates sack it in the guise of liberators!" *(Compiler's Note.)*

. . .

The long caravan of those carrying their children in their arms slowly files past the holy water font for the ceremony of baptism at which General Belgrano is acting as general godfather. They have collectively asked him to do so. He has accepted the imposition with his usual natural goodness, and now the procession of parents, both legitimate and natural, has reached him. They deposit in his arms thousands of offspring that, by virtue of the waters, become godchildren of the general and their fathers and/or mothers compadres and comadres. He has been standing alongside the font, in the atrium, for hours now. The cathedral, leaning like a latter-day tower of Pisa, threatens to topple over at any moment. The mother church creaks, groans threateningly through the countermouths of its cracks and crannies. Nothing daunted, Belgrano goes on holding the babies over the round Jordan. The first one was María de los Ángeles, just born. José Tomás Isasi and his wife shed tears over their little bundle from heaven kicking amid yards of lace.

On the stage set up below the Cabildo, a performance of Phèdre* is given. Petrona Zabala is admirable in the role of the daughter of the king of Crete and of Pasiphaë. It is as though she is the wife of Theseus in person, incestuously enamored of her stepson Hipólito Sánchez. In the scene in which, overcome with remorse, she hangs herself on Mount Venus with her own girdle of a virgin queen, the verisimilitude of the real borders on hallucination. From the top of the cliffs, seated beneath the orange tree, we contemplate that slender, endless body. Spectral whiteness oscillating on the black mirror of the water amid the gleaming torches. Hair ruffled by the wind veiling her face.

---

*It was not *Phèdre* but *Tancrède* that was performed that night, the only work for the stage known at the time in Paraguay. *(Compiler's Note.)*

Fourth recess of the thirteenth session, adjourned at the request of Echevarría, sweating, in a bad humor, turning up his nose at the maté vessel passing from mouth to mouth. The president of the Junta has had a basketful of maize cakes brought in. Everyone is sucking and eating greedily. Nothing but the sound of mouths, the slurp of the sipper in the foam. Just to be saying something, I bring up yet again the rebuilding of Buenos Aires, whose aim is the recasting of Paraguayans. Always a good subject. At least it keeps me from having to listen to one of my kinsman Fulgencio's stupid jokes, which he has been giving signs for some time now of perpetrating. In 1580, almost forty years had gone by since the disappearance of the port city. The last huts burned down, overrun with grass which covered the ashes and erased it from the map. How much we would all have gained, gentlemen, if the slate had been left as it was, wiped clean! But Asunción, prolific mother of peoples and cities, was born to nurse suckling pigs. The founders of the second Buenos Aires left from Asunción. Governor Juan de Garay decided to establish a port in Río de la Plata in order to link Spain to Asunción and to Peru. So the standard for levying a work force was raised. The town crier went through the streets to the sound of trumpet and drum summoning all inhabitants who wanted to join in the undertaking. Those enlisted numbered 10 Spaniards and 56 native-born. They left Asunción accompanied by their families, their cattle, their seed, their tools for working the land, their hope. Garay and his companions go downriver by boat. Others go overland, driving 500 cows along with them. A fair-sized herd, right? A fine nursery. On June 11, 1580, the second birth of the port-city takes place. Everything goes smoothly. Harmoniously. The epic is over. It's never one and the same man who kills the wild beast, dresses the hide, and lines the cape. Mustn't skip the liturgy of the foundation. The governor whacks at the grass with his sword, as ancient custom prescribes. Garrido the notary speaks in a solemn, cavernous voice. The good Basque Garay smiles to himself. His smile is reflected in the blade of his sword. See how chronicographers invent details. Buenos Aires is definitively founded. Cabildo. Scroll. Cross. Its plan, on parchment. Just a flat stretch of open ground. There was no need for all that fancy-dancing, Larreta said. Perpendicular streets are traced, north to south, "easte/weste." A plain, straightforward checkerboard. Sixteen blocks along the riverfront, nine deep. Six blocks to the Fort, lined with Adam's-apple trees. Three convents. Main square. A hospital. Land for the small farms of the settlers. The young city is already creeping, becoming a prattler. The same never-ending story. Among the fifty or so Paraguayan sons of the earth there is a Paraguayan daughter of the earth, Ana Díaz. The pettifogger gives a suck on the sipper and chuckles. What are you laughing at, señor jurisconsult? Oh, nothing, señor dean. Your tale of the second birth, as you call it, more than two centuries ago, suddenly made me remember the homage rendered that woman, Ana Díaz, not long ago by the Paraguayan ladies who reside in Buenos Aires. A fine colophon for the story of the foundation! Tell us about it, Doctor Echevarría, Fulgencio Yegros says. The other takes his time. He takes a long sip from the bombilla, till the belly of the maté vessel complains that it's running dry. Well, the pettifogger says, the Paraguayan ladies' homage to Ana Díaz had an unexpected ending. No, no!, the members of the Junta cry. Begin at the beginning! There wasn't one, really. Just that the resident ladies began searching, very early in the morning, even before the sun was up, for the plot of land that Juan de Garay awarded Ana Díaz as one of the founders of the city. They wanted to pay her homage at the same hour at which Garay supposedly gave that founding fillip with his sword. The hundred-some patrician ladies wandered all morning and all afternoon amid row houses, salting-houses, drinking-houses and foggy vacant lots in search of the Paraguayan woman's piece of phantom ground, without losing heart in the face of the freezing wind from the estuary. As night was falling, they reached the place where, according to the barely readable maps, the domain they were looking for was located. All they find there is a shabby, broken-down house, a combination convent, salting-house, and general store. One of the ladies, a friend of mine, the reason why I don't mention her by name, climbed up on top of a pile of refuse and began the speech in honor of the occasion. She was continually interrupted by men of all sorts who kept entering the building as others, drunken, boisterous roisterers, came out. When my friend, the lady giving the speech, solemnly called out the name of Ana Díaz three times, a rather scantily clad woman appeared in the doorway. That's me, what is it you ladies lookin' for?, she said that the woman inquired in a strident voice. The house of Ana Díaz, the lady answered. We've come to render her homage. I'm Ana Díaz, the lady. This is my house, and as it happens it's my birthday, so jes' come right in. The ladies were horrified. Wait a sec though, till I call my pals and my neighbors, so they can live it up a little too. You've doubtless already guessed what sort of house it was: a vulgar Temple of Eros, the pettifogger added, feeling obliged to explain what was already clearer than day. A noisy herd of some hundred or so men and women, including musicians with their instruments, appeared. The ladies consulted the map again. There was no doubt about it. This was the place; fate, that joker, had put another Ana Díaz there. Nonetheless the discourse was resumed, with renewed warmth but a different emphasis. My friend was so eloquent and so overcome with emotion, or so confused, that in a short while meritorious matrons and meretricious maidens were embracing each other in a flood of tears, as the musicians struck martial chords to serve as a background for this ceremony of unforeseen and unrepeatable feminine confraternity. The Porteño pettifogger lied as usual. Gross falsehood. Insidious invention. Anything to contradict me and check the course of the Treaty galloping along at full tilt in the steam of the maté. My investigations of the incident did not even remotely confirm it. On the plot of land awarded Ana Díaz by Garay, there is no such Temple of Eros, only a common, ordinary saddlery.

During the night the president of the Junta came to consult me as to whether, in view of the sudden paralysis in both hands with which Echevarría had been stricken, the day of the signing ought to be postponed. Look, cousin, if the two envoys don't sign the treaty, the Buenos Aires Junta can always play that old game of claiming later that it is thereby null and void, Fulgencio Yegros says confidentially. Look, you who know all the ins and outs of cozening, we've set tomorrow, October 12, the Day of the Race, as the Day of the Signature. The treaty will be signed tomorrow. Pass confirmation of this along to the other members of the Government. Is the treaty drafted, cousin? Every last word. Fair copy. Definitive text. It will not be corrected. May we read it? You'll hear it tomorrow; less work that way. Leave that part up to me. You see to your parade. Arrange things so that it starts when the trumpet sounds, so that the ceremony of the signing ends the negotiations and we can bid our guests farewell with all the honors. And be good enough to have La'ó-Ximó, the healer of Lambaré, brought here immediately. Send him to me the moment he arrives.

Echevarría has reluctantly agreed to hold his two arms out above the straw mat, with his face turned to the wall. His clenched fists stand out against the stains of old blood on the esparto. La'ó-Ximó, a skinny skeleton of a man yet possessed of the strength of a bull, has been struggling for some time now to relax those hands tensed in a death grip. Frictions, massages, lightning blows capable of splitting a chunk of marble in two. All to no avail. La'ó-Ximó's bald pate drenched with sweat gleams amid the candles; a little stream trickles down from his pigtail onto the bundle of nerves at the nape of his neck. He turns to me: Sire, it's a simple case of apava, in other words paralysis. But the kuruchí, in other words the knot of the gnarl, is not in the hands. It's located at a certain point in the celebrum. It's the mark of a point from which there is no return. This man can still return; the trouble is, he doesn't want to. So you have your points too, eh, La'ó-Ximó? Yes, Sir, it's a point. I'm going to see where it is. I'm going to burn him a little and the leaves of his hands will open again. He inspected, sniffed the two fists, pore by pore. He suddenly stopped at the point of the paragraph, the article, the clause. Over the flame of a candle he softened a mixture of artemisia, benjamin, and liquidambar, and formed two little balls. He crushed one of them in the juncture between the thumb and the index finger of the right hand; the other in the center of the metacarpus of the left hand. He lit a little stick of incense and brought it close to the poultices. The combustion finally melted them and volatilized them into smoke, vapor, odor. The hands slowly opened. A sort of gradual resurrection. Little by little the fingers regained the ability to move. There you are, Sire, La'ó-Ximó says. Echevarría gazes at his hands, glowering; he suspects that he has had others attached to him that aren't his. He moves them reluctantly. As he gathers together his straw mat, his potions, his needles and little sticks, La'ó-Ximó says to me in Payaguá dialect in a low voice: Wanting to go on being sick, the sick man has gotten well without meaning to, through the opilative power of Santa Librada and the Great-Grandfather La'ó-Xé who-binds-and-unbinds what kills. At the door I throw him a coin. It remains suspended in the air. La'ó-Ximó catches the silver colibri of the carlos-cuarto and puts it in his guayaka.§ Be careful, Sire! That foreigner's hands are full of tongues! Don't worry. Off with you. His figure cuts a corner and disappears.

Another solemn meeting of the Junta and the Cabildo. I read the Treaty aloud in a calm, deliberate voice. I regulate the decibels of the acoustic volume, underlining the most important parts: Article One: Inasmuch as Paraguay finds itself in urgent need of aid in order to maintain

§*Guayaka*: pouch (Guaraní).

an effective and respectable force for its security and in order to confront the machinations of its enemies within and without, the tobacco of the Royal Treasury on hand in the province will be sold and the proceeds credited to Paraguay, to be invested in the aforementioned object or an analogous one. Article Two: It is established that the food and municipal taxes previously paid to Buenos Aires on each hundredweight of maté imported from Paraguay are henceforth to be collected in Asunción, to be applied specifically to the object set forth in the preceding article. Three: It is hereby provided that foreign duties will be collected at the point of sale. Article Four: The department of Candelaria, situated on the left bank of the Paraná, is hereby declared included within the boundaries of Paraguay. Article Five: In view of the independent status retained by Paraguay, the Junta of Buenos Aires will not in any way oppose the implementation and execution of the other measures passed by the Governing Junta of Paraguay, in conformity with the provisions of the present Treaty, both contracting parties desiring to strengthen still further the ties and obligations that unite and ought rightfully to unite them in a Federation. Each of the parties pledges for its part not only to cultivate a sincere, firm, and perpetual friendship, but also to offer aid and cooperation, mutually and effectively, with every manner of assistance, as the circumstances of each permit, whenever required by the sacred end of annihilating and destroying any enemy that may attempt to oppose the furtherance of our just cause and common freedom.

Thunderous applause greets the end of the reading. There is no further discussion. We all come forward to sign the double-tenor papyrus intoned without a single false note. Everyone wants to be the first to sign. A moment before, I have been obliged to drag Eschevarría out of his lodgings, still protesting that his hands are not his hands. Come on! Hurry up! They're your hands, your very own hands! No more of this . . . ! I pull him. I push him. I row and tow him, haul and heave-ho him, a heavy barge of bad faith. I shoot him across the Plaza full of horses. He sees Belgrano affixing his signature with an air of great satisfaction; he has no other alternative than to sign himself. Everyone highly satisfied. The envoys because they have obtained, if not the much-desired union, a close alliance; the military leaders of the Junta because they have arrived at an accord with the Porteños; I because I have prevented domination by Buenos Aires. In his chronicle, the Tacitus of the Plata will later severely reproach the envoys for having yielded to Paraguay's demands by agreeing to a federal league without obtaining the slightest advantage in return. Everyone speaks in accordance with the promptings of his particular mad vision. The Devil take the Tacitus of the Plata! Off with him! All of us here are as happy as larks! More shouts of Long Live the Holy Federation! Ovations. Applause. Even Echevarría claps his usurer's hands for all he's worth. The roar of applause swells and dissolves into the thunder of cavalry.

From the dais erected on the Plaza de Armas we witness the parade. The two thousand five hundred horsemen of Paraguay and Takuary ride by in combat formation, giving their coursers free rein. Arms dipped in salute to Belgrano, who beams with pleasure at this anteposthumous honor. Fulgencio Yegros and Pedro Juan Cavallero, that is to say half the Junta, at the head of the parade. Sound of a fanfare. The closed formation then breaks up into a thousand fanfaronades. Simulated charges, attacks, hand-to-hand encounters. Horses and horsemen divide in two, with a horseman-half and a courser-half coming back together a moment later, galloping on like centaurs. Individual feats multiply, yet maintain their nature of a collective choreorganization. Two troopers mount the same half-broken horse; suddenly one of them dismounts on one foot on one side, the other on the other; they cross over, changing from foot to hand, doing a scissors on the back of the galloping mount. Ten horsemen ride along standing upright on a line of chargers alternately saddled and barebacked. They alight, run alongside their mounts on foot, and unsaddle them without slackening their pace. The saddles fly through the air. In the wink of an eye, they saddle them up again, but now the ones riding bareback are the ones on the mounts. They set one foot on the ground, with the other hooked in the stirrup, snatch up off the ground lances that they have tossed a hundred yards in front of them. Look, general; I don't believe any country has horsemen that can surpass Paraguayans in the art of equitation. Indeed, señor dean, these figures that they are executing are amazing! They're well done, it's true, Echevarría mutters, but in the province of Buenos Aires I've seen riding exhibitions that would have amazed you, señor dean. There are gauchos in the Migueletes Regiments who can harness their nervous Frisians using nothing but their teeth. Others who, between two horses with one foot in each saddle, take off at full spur when retreat is sounded, carrying a man, whom we take to be a comrade wounded in battle, off with them in their arms. Another gaucho standing atop the first one keeps shooting his harquebus or his crossbow to cover the retreat of the three. I knew an equestrian from Bragado who put his trained mount through all sorts of exercises, dances, and contredanses. Between the saddlepad and his knees, and between the stirrup and his big toes, he placed little silver coins. They never fell off, as though they had been nailed to those spots more firmly than the coins sewn to the leather of his belt. The secretary's wrinkled hands had been let loose to allow their tongues to graze in the pastures of a purple erudition. Who could stop him! I remembered La'ó-Ximó's warning. He was shouting louder and louder in the midst of all the din: In the East Indies the principal honor was to ride an elephant, not a plebeian horse. The second, to ride in a coach drawn by four oxen with monumental horns. The third, to ride a camel. The last category, if not to say the last honor or practically a dishonor, was to ride a horse or be driven in a cart pulled by a single jade. A writer of our time says he saw that, in those regions of extremely ancient culture, worthy individuals ride oxen fitted with rawhide saddles, stirrups, and bridles, and adds that they are pleased and proud to ride such mounts. Ah well, my esteemed Echevarría, speaking of such matters, you no doubt know that in the war against the Samnites, Quintus Fabius Maximus Rutilius, seeing that on the third or fourth charge his cavalry had nearly defeated the adversary, ordered his soldiers to let go of the bridles of their steeds and charge at full spur; with no obstacles to hinder them as they galloped through the enemy lines, where the troops lay all about on the ground, they cleared the way for the infantry, which consummated the bloody rout. Quintus Fulvius Flacus used the same tactic against the Celtiberians: Ib cum majore vi equorum facietis, si effraenatos in hostes equos immittitis; quod saepe romanos equites cum laude fecisse sua, memoriae proditum est . . . Detractisque fraenis, bis ultro citroque cum magna strage hostium, infractis omnibus hastis, transcurrerunt,* as Livy describes it. More or less, esteemed doctor, what happened at Cerro Porteño and Takuary. Echevarría, a shifty one, changes the subject: in ancient times the Duke of Muscovy performed the following ceremony with the Tartars when the latter sent him their ambassadors: He came out to meet them on foot and presented them with a glass of mare's milk. If on drinking it a single drop fell on the horses' manes, the duke was obliged to lick it up with his tongue. Well, my dear Echevarría, you haven't yet licked the manes of these victorious horses. Nor have you, señor dean, offered us the glass of mare's milk that the Duke of Muscovy offered the foreign ambassadors. On the contrary, señor secretary; you drank down half of it and spilled the other half on the manes of the Junta's horses. What happened is what happened

---

*In order that the shock may be more impetuous, let go of the bridles of your coursers. It is a maneuver whose success has oftentimes honored the Roman cavalry . . . The moment the order is heard, they unbridle their mounts, cut through the enemy troops, break all the lances, retrace their steps, and wreak terrible carnage.

This fragment from Livy can be found copied out in like manner in the *Combat Manual for Cavalry Forces,* among the numerous works on tactics and strategy also owed to *El Supremo's* own hand. *(Compiler's Note.)*

to Croesus on traversing the city of Sardis. He found a meadow in which there was a multitude of serpents. His horses ate them with a will, which was a bad omen for his undertakings. Almost all of them were lamed hand and foot, according to the account by Herodotus of Halicarnassus. We call a horse whose other parts are as perfect as its mane and ears, not to mention, naturally, its testiculary parts, whole and complete in every way, a caballo entero. Other horses are only half horses, and geldings not horses at all. See, look, watch that!, Belgrano exclaimed, reining Echevarría in before he could come out with another imminent stupidity. A spectacle truly phantasmagorical. The sort of dazzling darkness spread by the sun's fire falling from directly overhead at midday is suddenly rent. A single clap of thunder makes the earth tremble. Two thousand five hundred horses ride down upon us, amid whirlwinds of dust. Horses alone. Saddled or bare-backed. No sign of horsemen. Compact mass. Geometric exhalation of steeds. They thunder past the reviewing stand, sweat-stained, bearing lances between their teeth. Completely unbridled. When finally our eyes grow accustomed to this unreal charge, they gradually make out the cross of the barebacked steeds, or above the empty saddles doll-sized horsemen no bigger than a man's foot: in reality it is the crossed feet of each horseman. Look at that, Echevarría! That was the mystery of Takuary! How was a person to shoot at those tiny cruciform figures? How was a person to imagine that those X-shapes were the Paraguayan horsemen upside down! By the time we realized, they were right side up again, pressing us hard with their lances and machetes! Not to have seen that, general!, Echevarría stammered, biting his fists.

Silence of three shadows. Three times silence in the shadowness of the study. They have been sitting there for a long time. It cannot be said that they are in good countenance. But in order to put a good face on things, the only recourse is to recall all the vexations of the past. My apologies, noble sirs. Your mercies' patience must be sorely tried by these buffooneries. Forget them, I beg you. What we must remember is the good of our countries. We must reflect on what we have agreed upon. Weigh the justice of our pact, to the last grain. See to it that what has been said, written, covenanted, signed is fulfilled. You two in your country, through your government, backed by the sovereignty of the people in their honor-able legislative assemblies. I in turn shall do the same here. Or better put, consider it done already, since my will represents and realizes by delegation the invincible will of a free, independent, and sovereign people.

The two shadows do not answer. The flight of a blowfly distracts them. Are you gentlemen with me or not? Yes, señor dean, we are here, Vicente Anastasio Echevarría says, straightening up on his seat again. I rise from mine. Take Benjamin Franklin, steel-engraved, down from the wall. The Porteño pettifogger gazes, frowning, at the inventor of the lightning rod. Manuel Belgrano opens his eyes. This, my friends, is the first democrat of these new worlds. The model that we must imitate. Forty years from now, our countries may have men like him. If and when, naturally, the great country of the north continues to produce men like Franklin. If it does, we may enjoy in the future the freedom for which we are not prepared today. By some misfortune, it may so happen that North America will not produce more men of the stamp of the inventor of the lightning rod and that in our countries the lightning bolt of anarchy will strike down our best men. It may so happen that they will invent the Big Prod up there and that down here we'll all die of the croup, carbuncle, and tick, like the cattle in our fields. We must take care not to fall into the hands of master-butchers. Echevarría raised his hand full of grasping fingers: You are not very optimistic, señor dean. On the contrary, doctor, I replied. I am highly optimistic, but not amnesiac. A minimum of memory is indispensable in order to survive. The destruction of this faculty brings on idiocy, and we here in Paraguay do not drink the black cardamom coffee that brings Berber forgetfulness, but maté infusions and kidney-bean tea that help to preserve memory, and the good and bad memories within it. We have oftentimes seen the face of misfortune here. Now we want to see, forevermore, the face of fortune, even though it may cost us a fortune to see it. And so you see, I am clearly optimistic. True optimism is born of the center of sacrifice. Free of all selfish calculation, eh? Ah! He who sacrifices himself gives himself totally, and the sacrificer is the one who loses his life. Remember that, Doctor Echevarría. Franklin knew it. Thrifty spirit who husbanded his visionary energy, carefully hoarded his rigorous discipline down to the last cent. Faith, confidence, charity, hope, freedom. A peer of yours, among your equals, right, general? He did not listen to me very attentively, lost in the delicate central solitude of his thoughts. Compadre Benjamin was optimistic even about death, I said. At the age of twenty-three he had already composed his epitaph with words of the Office. I've copied it on the back. Read it, doctor. The pettifogging voice stammered:

> The body of Benjamin Franklin, Printer
> (like the cover of an old book,
> its contents torn out and stripped
> of its lettering and gilding),

lies here, food for worms;
but the work shall not be lost,
for it will (as he believed)
appear once more in a new edition,
revised and corrected by the Author.

Would that we all might write our epitaphs with words as simple and wise, no? Although if I were to write mine I would not waste more than four letters:

I'm O.K.

General Belgrano smiled. I offered him the portrait, which he accepted with emotion. The copper discharge-wire of the minuscule lightning rod affixed to the very top of the engraving coiled round the feet of the pettifogger, hobbling him and volting him over. He rose to his feet, half-charred with wrath, thundering imprecations. I placed in his spidery fingers a manuscript history of Paraguay. Take it with you as a souvenir. Have it printed if you like, but don't condense it, all right? The reality of this country is richer than what is bound together in these in-folios. The future is even more so. May we keep it safe from lightning.

The bushy-haired Don Benjamin, on the general's chest, winked an eye at me. I raised my eyes to Belgrano's face. I saw reflected in it, through dark images, the din of future disasters. I heard him sweating blood. Elephantine§ agony of his Garden of Oblivion: *Ay Patria mía!* Muffled thunder of the infernal cavalcade that makes the American earth tremble. Murmurs of tongues tormenting the man who is vanquished. Mouths that create mudslides of false witness. I could see myself. Even though the years of your life were three thousand or ten times three thousand, no one lives any other life than the one he loses. The longest and the briefest span are equal. The present belongs to everyone. No one loses either past or future, for no one can be deprived of what he does not possess. The reason why, compadre Marcus Aurelius, according to you, we all keep finding ourselves buttoning up in another man's house, at the wrong moment. I bet my last wisdom tooth against the gravedigger's shovel that eternity doesn't exist. What? Still not enough? All right then, I bet the false half of my skull. That's piling it on a little thick! Come on, calm down. I keep getting all

§Allusion to the disease that killed Belgrano, a malady resembling leprosy that turns the sufferer's skin into a thick, wrinkled hide like an elephant's.

excited for nothing in these no-limits games, forgetting that every card's a joker.

General Manuel Belgrano looks at me with his very bright eyes. He shakes his head. Somewhat sadly. He takes a few steps toward me. We stretch out our hands in silence.

Almost the moment he returned to Buenos Aires, the pettifogger Vicente Anastasio Echevarría made a deal under the table with the members of the Junta to sell the printing press of the Foundlings, the only one in existence at the time in the sluice of Buenos Aires. The first American edition of the Social Contract was printed there, in Mariano Moreno's translation. A relic. That sly shyster of an Echevarría not only tried to sell the press; he also offered Moreno's library, at what amounted to a clearance-sale price. All this confirmed my suspicions as to what tasty morsels it was that the pettifogger and the members of the Junta were nibbling on in their conciliabules; what the real motives had been behind his pressing hurry to return home.

My ex brother-in-law Larios Galván, secretary of the Junta, writes to him: We naturally accept the press for the agreed sum of 1800 pesos. In order to deliver the money to Yr. Excellency, kindly inform us if there is anything else to pay, and if the machine will arrive with all the necessary equipment. Please be kind enough also to send us a memorandum concerning the library of the late Doctor Don Mariano Moreno, informing us of the price, so as to be able to conclude its purchase. We will take at whatever price everything dealing with public law, politics, belles lettres, as well as curiosa, rare jewels for bibliomanes; above all those of great material value because of their beautifully crafted bindings in precious metals and materials. Cost will not be a consideration.

When I learned of the plot, I put my foot down and stopped all negotiations. My obligation as syndic-procurator general was to block the shady press deal. I did so. Moreover, I also nipped the other deal in the bud, the one having to do with Don Mariano's books, which he wouldn't be reading anymore in any event. I dictated the cancellation of the whole fraudulent affair to that rogue of a Larios Galván: For the moment, we regret not being able to take the press and the books, but with the enlightenment we already have here, we have no need of more or better.

The lasso-and-bola contingent of the Junta, the areopagites of the Twenty Families cried out that this was a great loss for the country's culture. It's one for your purses and your knavish intentions!, I threw back in their faces. As long as I am able, and have the power, I shall not allow clandestine acts of larceny. My broom swept clean. Hens have slim pickings on a well-swept floor. But at that point they upped the ante. Having lost out on the Foundling Press, they founded the Exposed Gamblers' Gaming House. With the remains of the wooden press of the Jesuitic settlements, the patrician gamesters found a way to set up a press to print playing cards. Those wretches gone to wrack and ruin brought from the town of Loreto, where it lay buried, the wrecked type that had been the ruin of the civilization of the Indians. They brought from Buenos Aires the master printer Apuleyo Perrofé. Very soon, and also very clandestinely, his first fine handiwork came rolling off the press and began to circulate. It soon flooded the country, which was left without books, almanacs, manuals of devotion. Apuleyo fed even the files of the archive of the Junta through the machine.

Perrofé's impressions were very nearly perfect. The most famous cardsharps of the era were unable to tell the faces from the backs of the cards, just as a person can't tell one egg from another. Dissimilarity creeps into man's works all by itself. No art can arrive at a perfect resemblance. Similarity is always less perfect than difference. It is as if nature made it a rule not to repeat its works, making them different each time. Perrofé, however, made his at once alike and different. He knew how to gloss, polish, and color the backs and even the faces of his cards so carefully that the most consummate gamester was always fooled as he saw them slip and slide in and out of the hands of his adversaries in the deal. Apuleyo's decks of cards fooled even me. With the same perfection he composed and illuminated in miniature Bishop Panés's Breviary; a book which at his death passed into the possession of the State; it is now among my rarest curiosa. It is so curious, Sire, that the last time I saw it it was completely blank. It is not rare for books to turn white with age, Patiño; especially if they are Books of Hours. The letters grow weary, become blurred, disappear. It's the same with them as with mercury, eh? You know that, eh, don't you? The more it is worked together, compressed, divided, the more it slips away and scatters all about. The same thing happens with all things. Subdividing them into subtleties accomplishes only one thing. It multiplies the difficulties. Increases the uncertainties. Augments the contention. Everything divided indefinitely becomes confused and is finally reduced to dust. That is what that accursed Apuleyo Perrofé did. Only after years of searching and raids was the Government able to put its finger on the clandestine press. I can still see the moment, Sire, when the hangman pushed Perrofé, with his neck in the noose, off into the air with a kick in the rear. A midget of a man, rounder than a butterball, the body of the master printer swayed back and forth till it almost burst inside his clothes full of bright-colored mends and patches. In the strong wind sweeping the plaza, the hanged man soon began to deflate. Coveys of cards came sailing out of his particolored clothes and soon filled the entire city. People immediately thought of the hundred thousand butterflies that are traditionally let loose every year in homage to your Excellency, on the auspicious anniversary of your birth. But in the silence that followed, since no one heard cannon salvos, nor sounds of the hundred bands of musicians from the barracks, nor the din of street bands of blacks, coloreds, and mulattoes, the populace finally realized that it was not the day of the Three Magi. The execution of the criminal magus, maker of cards, was ended. They cut down the corpse. All they found was the empty sack of clothes, burst open at the bottom, out of which there had poured the rain of cards, images of saints, pictures of naked women, first communion cards. Despite this exemplary punishment, despite the fact that the security forces had outdone themselves in the exercise of vigilance, Most Excellent Sire, there has been more gambling than ever since then in Asunción, in all the cities, towns, villages, garrisons, outposts; even in the most remote guard house and the most wretched hut in the country, even in the Indian camps there is gaming, Sire. It is useless to send the forces of the law and order to clean out the wicked gamblers. The next minute they're right back at the cards, playing for all they're worth as though nothing had happened. Even the guards are starting to try their luck in the gaming dens. When I was talking with Minister Benítez one time before he too fell in disgrace, he told me that if he had been First Magistrate, he would not have prohibited gambling or ordered Perrofé hanged. What I would have done had I been El Supremo, he said to me, would have been to legalize gambling and name Apuleyo Perrofé administrator general of the State Gambling Enterprise. A sort of vast patrial gambling den, covering the entire country through the intermediary of agencies and branches of the Internal Revenue Service installed in the tax collectors' offices and even in barber shops, Benítez said. There are already patrial farms and estates, but the tax on gambling would have produced much more wealth than all of them put together; more than the sales tax, tithes, the state monopoly, the fructuary contribution; more than stamped paper, import and export tariffs, taxes on salaries and emollients, and the war tax. A fructuary tax on gambling, ex Benítez said, would have constituted the major source of revenue for the coffers of the State, for the well-being and prosperity of the people. It would have turned a collective vice into a superior civic virtue by turning the secret plague of gaming back into a multitude of public services, by making of it the purest source of National Savings. The passion for gambling, the ex minister went on enthusiastically, is the one thing that does not die in man's heart. That's what he said, Sire. Gambling isn't like fire, he said. It's not the son of two pieces of wood who, the moment he's born, devours his father and mother, as among the tribes nor, as among Christians, the fire born from tinder and flint, or from a mere match head; the fire that serves to make the stew for supper, to burn off and fertilize the fields, to burn away scrub in the forest. . . . And also, Patiño, to cremate our corpses, the fate that awaits us in the pasquinade. My, Excellency, that was something that escaped Benítez! We're not going to escape the fire, Patiño. It's not by sneezing all over the place the way you're doing now that you're going to put out the fire that is to consume us later. I beg your pardon, Most Excellent Sire. I can't stop sneezing. It must be my way of raining. Especially in August, which is a month of rains and head colds. What Benítez added, Sire, is that neither fire nor gambling should be forbidden. Their utility lies within their very nature, and their own prohibition as well. The first thing that everybody learns about fire is that it mustn't be played with, he said. The last, that it's used for cooking food. That's all well and good, ex minister Benítez said, but to stop games of chance would be playing with fire, and besides, they're more useful than fire because they bring the poor man money. Hence gaming cannot be prohibited. It would be a cruelty. . . .

(Noted in the margin)

That idiot is right on one point. Our first *knowledge* of fire gives rise to a social prohibition. This is thus the real basis of the respect for flames. If the child brings his hand close to the fire, his father gives him a fillip on the fingers. The fire does this without any need to hit out. Its language of punishment is to say *I burn*. The problem to be solved is deliberate disobedience . . . *(remainder of the folio burned).*

Gaming should not be prohibited, Benítez said, Excellency. The passion for gambling is the only one that does not die in man's heart, he repeated. The more it is fanned by the wind of necessity, the higher its flames blaze, the more it illuminates the soul of the man in need. Apart from the last phrase that you doubtless culled from somewhere as usual, isn't all the rest of this little discourse on the pros born of the cons of gaming something you trumped up yourself? Isn't it true that you're quite fond of peeking at the pips yourself? In the name of heaven, Excellency! Have my tongue cut off, my mouth sewn shut if I lie!

A clever cardsharp's idea, that one of ex minister Benítez's to impose a fructuary tax on gambling. Other governments have made of their countries veritable gaming houses where the people rob each other, trick each other, kill each other, exactly as gamblers do.

Here in Paraguay they didn't win. I beat them. I destroyed their advantages as clandestine gamblers by forcing on them the counteradvantage of knowing that they're miserable sharpers. I know the mark of each card they play. I know what books they've been ripped out of. I hear the gallop of the steed of cups.§ I hold the four aces. The ace of clubs in my hands, the staff of my power. The ace of gold in the coffers of the State. The ace of cups in which to offer gall and vinegar to traitors. The ace of swords to lop off their heads. This is my game of truque. In it I play the trump card cold-bloodedly, without tricks of any sort. In the end, out of the black intentions of that shyster Echevarría there came to light clear, very clear things.

§Card in the Spanish suit of *copas* (cups) with the figure of a horse.

I come back to Correia da Câmara. In this same place, fifteen years later, I am with Manoel attending the performance not of Tancrède but of Gasparina. Its author, my liaison officer Cantero, aide-de-camp of the imperial envoy, whom I have placed at his service not so much to serve him as because it serves my purpose, has taken on the task of writing the play and staging it. We are no longer spectators of the theater of tancredulity but of incredulity. Gasparina is a woman wearing a liberty cap who, according to the author, represents me and the Republic. She is not incarnated by Petrona Zavala, but by a sculptural Payaguá girl who appears onstage with nothing on but the eyelashes, tattoos, and paint of all colors that make a mask of her face. Correia da Cámara outdoes himself in praise of the work. I know that it is really meant for the indigenous actress. Dazzled by her, he cannot take his eyes off her. He devours her with a gaze clouded by the gleam of desire. The Republic advances to the center of the stage to be crowned by the Great Sorcerer, wearing a tricorne and a frock coat. Scales in one hand, Sword in the other, the Republic halts beneath the throne canopied with palms against which an imposing prop lion is leaning on two paws. The Republic turns, slowly and majestically, toward the audience. She stands firmly on her scissored legs. The two blades spread slightly apart. Pubis shaved completely bare. Bathed in broken reflections, patches of light. Phosphorescent flashes—achiote, bija, orellana, tapaculo, urukú§—turn it into a black sun. Likewise her mouth. Two beacons of intermittent light. One half necessarily black, the other necessarily gray. Correia runs his tongue over his lips. A born pedant in all his expressions, he exclaims: That Woman-who-comes-from-the-forest appears to be enveloped in a dazzling, primordial visibility. In her the visible and the invisible are one and the same. At once nocturnal and solar in each one of her movements; even when she mimes absolute immobility. Profound secret. Inviolable secret. Only in certain seraglios of Barbary have

§Names of plants of the dye-producing Bixaceae family. Cf. English annatto, bixin, orellin.

I seen the like, Excellency. That woman, Excellency, is a meteorite from out of the protonight! Look! Look! She is splitting in two! She is motionless yet parting night from night. Dividing in two! Two bodies and two faces in a single body, a single face! The rustic author, señor consul, has attempted to represent in Gasparina both the natural-Woman and the Republic. Well, he has succeeded, Excellency, and at this moment I proclaim him greater than Racine himself! The dialogue is idiotic. It must be patiently sat through. The envoy has promised, in the name of the Empire, to send rifles and cannons. El cargamento mais grande do mundo! That's what really interests me. It doesn't interest me to waste saliva on the plumed Cariocan/Rio Grandese consul. Our saliva cleans and heals over our wounds yet kills the serpent, I say to the macaque, imitating him. As Correia devours the Woman-who-comes-from-the-forest with his eyes, her naked body swaying back and forth beneath the liberty cap, as the devout worshiper of the muses quavers choked phrases, I observe the extreme left of his mouth; that is the corner of it that is moving and pronouncing the aforementioned words, half in Spanish, half in Portuguese. The rest of his mouth remains motionless and closed. A recourse of courtly liars, of imperial envoys. Thanks to long years of practice they arrive at the point where they can split their lips and their tongue into independent sections. Articulate simultaneously phrases intermingled with different voices and intonations. The left half is now curling up like a horse's lip, baring his teeth without carrying along with it in its undulations the right region, which remains closed and impassive in the counterphrases. I know that trick. I myself have learned to double-tongue. To fugue my voice. To superpose ventriloqual voices through tightly closed lips. Child's play for me. Art that this bungling imperial buffoon has not mastered. He is trying to convince me that the empire is offering Paraguay its alliance simply to protect it from being ambushed by Buenos Aires. He knows my sore spots: I know those of the empire. What the latter in fact is seeking is precisely the opposite: seizing the Banda Oriental, crushing the Plata. Eventually swallowing up its "ally." Not much. A mere nothing. I allow the envoy to mouth words as long as he likes. I'm the one who is holding the hook. I pay out more line to the gold fish of the empire. Meanwhile I get my hands on a copy of all his secret correspondence with French and English spies. Then I give a quick jerk. I reel the emissary in to the shores of my demands, and refuse to let him go till he assures me that my terms will be met. Full, irrevocable recognition of the Independence of Paraguay. Return of usurped territories and cities. Indemnification for the incursions of bandeiras. New boundary treaty erasing the crucificial frontiers imposed by the bull of the Borgia pope and the Treaty of Tordesillas. Arms and ammunition in exchange for lumber and maté.

Look, señor consul, you will put down in writing everything you've promised. I take your words as though they issued from the very mouth of your emperor himself. What is pledged in them is the honor of the empire. Eh eh ah. Mais claro, absolutamente verdade, Excelencia! Você va a tener el cargamento de armas mais grande do mundo!§ I trust the arms will arrive soon, I say to him, and imitating him: Que sabe faz a hora nao espera acontecer. Os amores na mente as flores no chao/ A certeza na frente/ A historia na mao.§§ Eh? Eh? Certissimamente, Excelencia! Certissimamente! When will the shipment come, seor consuleiro? Embora embora, que esperar nao é saber,§§§ I buzz in his ear. Certissimamente!, the consul's voice zoomed from left to right. Sucking motion with the Y-piston of the linguageral.§§§§ There is also the question of those drifting limits that we must tie down, eh, seor cónsul? The waterfalls. The dam sites. Above all those damned sights fixed on Paraguay by the Imperio mais grande do mundo. Eh. Eh. Eh. Ah! Ah! Ah! Certissimamente!, the flustered farceur went on muttering out of both sides of his mouth. Ah y ah y ah, and this time I expected the titles of the respect due the Republic and the Supreme Government. I remind you that this is not play-acting. What we agree upon with the empire will not be a reason for applause but for solid signatures on the dotted line. Honest and honored. From one cordillera to the other. Certissimamente, Excelencia! When I saw that the commissional commissure was going to slip something in my ear, I raised my hand: Você va a pedirme§§§§§ to send the Woman-who-comes-from-the-forest to your lodgings after the performance, isn't that right? You want her to repeat in private the scene where she does the splits, isn't that it, seor conselheiro? You are a genius, Señor Perpetual Dictator of the Republic of Paraguay! You have the gifts of a thaumaturge and a seer. The cleverest of mind readers! Sheer telepathy! Look, my esteemed telepath Correia, how to convey to you that I cannot prostitute the Republic by bringing her to your dark room! No, da Cámara, that lovely naked body will not touch your raw hide. Would I ask you to bring the empire

§Naturally, absolutely true, Excellency! You are going to have the biggest arms shipment in the world! (As *El Supremo* notes above, the envoy's language is half Spanish and half Brazilian.)

§§The man who knows goes straight ahead, doesn't wait for things to happen./ Lovemaking in mind, flowers fallen to the floor./ Certainty ahead/ The whole story well in hand. (A Brazilian popular song.)

§§§Right away, right away, for waiting isn't knowing. (Another verse from the song.)

§§§§*Lingua* (tongue, language) + *geral* (common, general), Portuguese.

§§§§§You're going to ask me.

and put it in my bed? Frankly, no. The least that can be said on the subject, seor consuleiro, is that it's not right, right? Nada beim! Os amores na mente/ As flores no chao, eh? no? Certissimamente tein razón,§ Excellency! Well then, we'll go on talking together in Government House tomorrow, because the play is ended now. I see Minister Benítez coming in with the imperial envoy's plumed hat. Don't you know, you knave, that you are not to accept gifts from anyone? Return that featherduster to the person who tried to suborn you with it! This extravagant farce is going to cost you a month's arrest.

§You're more than right.

In the same place where Echevarría is sitting on October 12, 1811, witnessing the parade and biting his nails, I seat the third Porteño envoy, Nicolás de Herrera, two years later. A congress of more than a thousand deputies has established the Consulate by acclamation. I occupy Caesar's seat; Fulgencio Yegros, Pompey's. My first cousin, ex president of the ex First Junta, is now in second place, behind me.

In Buenos Aires, on the fall of the Triumvirate, a supposed Supreme Power in Formation sends the ill-tempered tomcat of a Herrera to me. He has arrived in Asunción in May. Bad month for Porteños. He has been waiting since then for me to receive him. I have put him up in the Customs warehouse. Most suitable accommodations, this shed for suspect goods smelling of contraband. The emissary cat sits there with eyes that have itchy fingers. He gives vent to his frustration, meanwhile, by sending his government confidential notes heavily embroidered with fancied reasons for misconfidence.*

---

*"They are diverting me with delaying tactics. They are keeping me practically interned in the Customs shed. I am told that I shall not be received until after the congress and the change of government, but no one knows when this famous congress is to meet. The one thing certain is that Porteños are more detested here than Saracens. If the congress declines to send deputies and war is declared against it, half the province will rise up in arms. . . . The gray eminence of this Gover^mt, a greater and greater tyrant, with a People more and more a slave, has no other object than to win time and enjoy without let or hindrance the advantages of independence. This man imvued with the maxims of the Republic of Rome is ridiculously attempting to organize his Gover^mt on that model. He has given me proofs of his ignorance, of his hatred for Buenos Ayres, and of the inconsistency of his principles. He has persuaded the Paraguayans that the province by itself is an Empire without equal, that Buenos Aires flatters it and courts it because it needs it: that on the pretext of union it is endeavoring to enslave the continent. That force has been used to make peoples send their representatives: That all our adbantages are supposed ones: And his bitter rivalry is transpirant even in his reply, since he has never recognized me as enboy of the Supreme Executive Power of the Provinces of the Río de la Plata, but only as a Deputy of Buenos Aires; nor is any other authority attributed to Y^r. Ex^cy." *Memorandum from*

He is now seated in the same place once occupied by Echevarría. Forming with him the second person of a single traitorous non-person. A while back, I permitted him to attend the Congress in order to present his pretensions. The answer was no, no, and no, to every last one. I told him that Paraguay has no need of treaties to defend its liberty and maintain fraternity with the other States. These are natural laws and sentiments of its constitution. Two months later he will go off with empty hands. Without a union, without an alliance, without a treaty, with only the pair of new shoes and the poncho with sixty stripes offered him out of public funds to replenish his wardrobe and footgear, completely worn out in his vain comings and goings. It was only with the greatest of difficulties that he managed to save his skin on being attacked by the citizens on account of his arrogant behavior at the congress.

There he is, under heavy guard, witnessing, peeved and aggrieved, the parade that he supposes I have ordered in his honor and by way of apology, without realizing the real ends that it is intended to serve.

My plan being to seat like individuals together, I place the Porteño Herrera next to the Brazilian Correia da Cámara, our well-known Brazilian envoy. In those days we did not yet know him, since it will be just over ten years before he makes his appearance in Paraguay. My favorite diversion is to put two scorpions together in the same bottle. Two of a kind easily turn into a trey. So let's put another Porteño scorpion in the bottle. This third one, that wood-borer of a Coso, like that crab Herrera and that fox Echevarría, is much given to letter-writing. This third man in, Coso García* complains to me of his clients in Buenos Aires. At the

---

Nicola de Herrera to the Executive Power, November, 1813.)

"The deputies were already so irritated that they considered the proposal insulting. Taking advantage of this mood, the Gover^{mt} persuaded them to reject it out of hand. The congress having received my message, a great tumult arose and the Deputies swore they would kill me if I made a move to join them, and had a priest not ascended to the pulpit to calm the multitude, I would have died, inevitably, ignominiously." *(Ibid.)*

*The person here referred to is Juan García de Cossio, sent in December, 1823, by Bernardino Rivadavia, the head of the Por-

teño government. He will be no more successful than the previous envoys. Cossio complains that *El Supremo* behaves toward him in the most obdurate and uncivil manner. The latter for his part, Julio César comments, never explained the reasons that lay behind his attitude; in his voluminous correspondence with his delegates, in which he dealt at length with all internal and external questions, he never once referred to García Cossio, to his mission, or to his notes. According to Juan Francisco Seguí—secretary to Vicente Fidel López—the fundamental objective of the Cossio mission was to negotiate an alliance with Paraguay in view of the imminent struggle with the Empire in the Banda Oriental. *(Anais, t. IV, p. 125.)*

same time he flatters me with Porteño shamelessness. I don't know why all these rascals think they are going to be able to ruin Paraguay with epistolaries. To the devil with them.

Here in this world I put them in the bottle. Three scorpions. Four. However many you like. They intertwine their tails, their pincers, secrete their venefic juices. Shake the bottle well. Expose it to the night air till all the creatures therein cool down altogether. The poison then becomes a benefic potion. To be taken on an empty stomach, at dawn. Homeopathic doses. At the same hour, regularly. Continuity-simultaneity is the best thing to remedy obstructions of all sorts.

Nicolás de Herrera, Juan García Coso, Manoel Correia da Cámara, master diplomat-scorpions with degrees to prove it, serve me as a diuretic. They tried to use me. I used them.

By his behavior Correia shows that he is still brooding, still fearful. He always walks sideways. Shows only one eye, one cheek, one hand, one leg, half a heart, no head. Crab figure. One can't tell if he's walking backward or forward. Double heels. The only difference is that the feathers of his hat and the hair all over his body have grown longer. On his ermine cape, in the middle of summer, the black stain of his intentions is spreading

---

The communications from Cossio to *El Supremo*, as far from the other Porteño and Brazilian envoys subjected to the purgatory of being kept endlessly waiting, were numerous. In this "torture by hope," the "tiresome pests and bothersome beggars" gave vent to their frustration in pleading, bitter, or melancholy missives.

For each of the 37 notes sent from Corrientes to Asunción, Cossio was obliged to make the couriers a present of 6 ounces of gold, a complete outfit and set of riding gear, which included everything from the horse's reins to the rider's spurs, plus a horn flask filled with 10 liters of raw rum. In February, 1824, Cossio informs his government from Corrientes that *The Supreme Dictator* has not yet answered and that the messengers have not returned. Nothing. Not a sign of them. The earth appears to have swallowed them up. Cossio voices this sad reflection: "And this silence, so far removed from both the Law of Nations and Civilization, is manifest proof, naturally, that he has no intention of departing in the slightest from that conduct on which he has fixed his entire attention within the singular isolation in which he finds himself. All this despite reminding him of the successful joint undertakings of the two countries in the War of Independence and the threat which the ambitious aims of the Holy Alliance and the possibility of an expedition of reconquest represent at this time for America." On March 19, 1824, Cossio again writes to *El Supremo*. His message concludes: "Paraguay is doing itself harm inasmuch as it has ceased to sell its maté, its tobacco, and its lumber; its commerce is falling off because of the closing of the rivers and the lack of foreign markets. Moreover, the government of Buenos Aires is alarmed by the opening of a port to Brazil, and requests that it be granted a facility identical to that granted the Portuguese, even though it be circumscribed to a single Point." At the bottom of this communication there is a note of *El Supremo*'s, written slantwise in red ink: "We're finally going to hear some good music!" *(Compiler's Note.)*

across his back, in the form of the map of the empire, also folded down the middle. Only the half that is spreading toward the west is visible. For now, half an inkstain trailing after the bandeiras. We'll see later on.

Possible interference from Buenos Aires is an obsession with Cámara. This suits my purpose. He suspects that Coso will use underhanded tricks to block my negotiations with the empire. He also fears that the Porteños and the Porteñistas of Asunción will stage an attempt on his life. Last night, during dinner, he told me of the plot that is being hatched against him. He directly accuses the government of Buenos Aires of wanting to murder him. Just look at the letter, Excellency, from Doctor Juan Francisco Seguí to Bonifacio Isaz Calderón that my agents have managed to intercept. The Emperor has appointed as his emissary to the Paraguayan government a hair-brained idiot who is in Montevideo at present, about to depart for Asunción. It is advisable that he be surprised en route and taken to Buenos Aires where he will be received as he deserves, or that he be assassinated somewhere in the middle of the Countryside, if possible by some Peasant who would like to earn himself Six Thousand pesos. Or if not that, a good dose of arsenic in his soup. Is that letter authentic, Correia? Certísimamente, Excelentísimo! It's not something made up? Não é! It's a very real letter! Don't worry, my dear doomed sir! You are now eating in peace and quiet with me, and I assure you that this soup of well-pounded meat, which we call so'yo, is the healthiest and most nutritive soup in the world. Take some of it, without thinking twice about it. In Paraguay you're under safe cover. Certíssimamente, Excelencia! Mais me he salvado só por un pelinho!§

I decided, then, to combine these festivities into a single one. And since we're on the subject of carousing, let's start off with the celebration in Asunción that inaugurated these festive excesses, even before Independence. Let's go back a little way. My association with crabs has left my notes riddled with atavistic vices.

What is deplorable about all popular fiestas is that they always smack of a circus, a trap. Lion cages ready and waiting. The poor people come running to divert themselves, forget their penury, roar at the top of their lungs to banish the cares of their humiliated existence. How? At the spectacle of petty lords on the boards. Anything serves as an excuse. The least little trifle. The fall of an ingrown nail on the toe of the foot of a monarch. The anniversary of the birth of a delphine menarche. The fall

§But I've been saved by a hair!

of an empire. The rise of another to replace it. The birthday of a favorite. The signing of a treaty. Anything. The people flock to these costly and miserable chimeras. They are taken in by them, their spirits sent skyrocketing all for nothing by fancy fireworks displays. They are robbed of hours of their labor. Money that belongs to the State is wasted. It is as though the miseries that ensnare them can be kept hidden only by arousing collective fanaticism. But what is to be done about it, what is to be done? It is the oldest custom in the world, dating from the Romans. Someday we will go back to living austerely in catacombs like the first Christians. All in cages, the tigers, the emperors, the consuls, the fine gentlemen. Meanwhile let the people live. Kill bad habits little by little.

Decidedly, the worst of all as far as pretexts go: dates. This one of October 12, the Day of the Race, one of them. In the square boxes of calendars they appear to be immortal. They rule the illusion of reality. Luckily time, on paper at least, can be compressed, saved, done away with.

1804

The queen's favorite, Manuel Godoy, Prince of Peace, has accepted the honorary office of Perpetual Councilor of the city. Asunción is the first Capital in the kingdom of the Indies to merit such a distinction. The symbolic reception of the Prince of Peace in the City Hall is the occasion for the aforementioned festivities. The most sumptuous within memory. They begin with a great seventy-four-cover banquet, on silver plates, offered by the detested governor Lázaro de Ribera y Espinoza de los Monteros.* At the head of the table, propped up by a tall gold goblet, the favorite Manuel Godoy; that is to say, his portrait draped with garlands. Beneath an immense wax seal the royal letter-patent that consecrated him as Grand Conjoiner. From the portrait he greets us with slow gestures, his

---

*"Early in 1795, Lázaro de Ribera was named military and civil Governor and Intendant of the royal Treasury of Paraguay. Before journeying to the seat of his government he married a lady of high lineage, María Francisca de Savatea, thereby establishing ties to the aristocracy of Buenos Aires. One of his sisters-in-law was the wife of Santiago de Liniers [the future viceroy]. Ribera need yield precedence to none of his great predecessors [in the governor's chair] —Pinedo, Melo, Alós—and in many respects he may well have been their superior. He sank deep roots in the land of the Guaranís, knew its suffering and miseries, and held his hand out to the helpless and the poor. He pointed out, prophetically, that the great port for Paraguay was Montevideo, and anticipated the greatness of the Plata, writing: 'The Provinces of the Viceroyalty of Buenos Aires will attain great opulence once it becomes easy to extract the raw materials that must cross the Ocean to revive and strengthen the Manufactories of the Pen-

fingers weighed down with rings. After the banquet, which lasts six hours, the Prince of Peace is borne off in a carriage drawn by eight black stallions and eight white mares, to the sound of the band of musicians. A corps of young soldiers escorts the galley. Behind it come the governor and the bishop in another galleon. On foot, the officers on the staffs of the regiments, the editors on the mastheads of the daily papers, the holders of the title of corregidor, the leading aristocracy. A very large contingent of regular and irregular clergy. How dignified an era that was!

On the Campo de Marte four triumphal arches have been erected. On one of them, that of Immortality, the portrait adorned with flowers and memorial wreaths of palm and laurel has been solemnly placed. The entire square and the neighboring cluster of houses bedecked with banners and streamers. The balconies of adjacent buildings occupied by ladies of highest rank and gentlemen of the second and third. Fustian rascals proudly posing in their fustian capes and doublets.

At night the streets, the public buildings, the residences of leading citizens are illuminated. Sprays of fireworks sparkle overhead. The sky a garden of fleeting andromedas and aldebarans.

From the triclinium he occupies on the platform in the plaza, Lázaro de Ribera waves the baton of his office and directs all the movements, continually stroking the curls of his powdered wig, like an orchestra leader irritated by the raggedness of the horns. The Prince of Peace on the other hand looks very pleased with himself in the portrait, lightly touching, nonchalantly caressing the horns of a royal stag.

From the mansion of the municipal councilor Juan Bautista de Hachar there appears a barouche, to the accompaniment of violins, tambourines, and flageolets. On arriving in front of the portrait, the occupants, costumed for the stage, descend and play Tancrède. María Gregoria Castelví and Juan José Loizaga [grandfather of the traitorous triumvir who will store my skull away in the attic of his house] shine in the roles of the Crusader and Clorinda. Ten thousand people attend the performance.

The novenary of festivities goes on without interruption. Bullfights.

---

insula.' He believed in the future of Paraguay, because of its fertile land, its abundant harvests, its rivers that irrigate it and place it in contact with the world." *(Note by Julio César.)*

"Despite his ardent and impetuous char-acter, vainglorious and impatient in the face of every obstacle, and despite his aristocratic lineage, Lázaro de Ribera was one of the most enlightened Spanish officeholders in this part of America in the twilight years of the eighteenth century." *(Comment. of Father Furlong, cited by J.C.)*

Gala mounted maskers, with choruses of musicians, tilt the lance in dances and contradances, as in the tourneys of antiquity. Fifty horsemen, disguised as Saracens and Indians on steeds with resplendent trappings, vie in riding at the ring. Threaded on the silver barb by the winner of the round, the ring is offered on his lance, with a gallant bow, to his fiancée, to the damsel he is courting, or to his loftily proud spouse. They catch it up by the loop of ribbon and drop it down the cleft of their low-cut gowns. With a childish gesture, without realizing it, they are miming the ceremony of Restoration. Not of the monarchy, not if we are in the period when the monarchy reigns supreme, certainly! Restoration of that-which-is-lost-once-and-only-once. Royalty. Virginity. Nobility. Dignity. Even though there are those who, losing them once, regain them twice over.

With haughty nonchalance Lázaro de Ribera says to the bishop: Resurrection is a completely natural idea, don't you believe so, Your Reverence? The bishop nods with a self-satisfied smile. Quite so, Your Excellency. It is no more extraordinary to come back to life once than it is to create the same thing twice.

Lázaro de Ribera's dazzlingly beautiful daughter leans over to him without taking her eyes off the tourney: What was it Your Worship said, if I may ask? Nothing, daughter. Nothing that might interest you at this moment when the fiesta is so splendid it suspends the senses. Look at that native rejoneador§ galloping this way at full tilt! In fact, standing atop a chestnut mount stripped completely bare and gleaming with sweat, the horseman, plumed and tattooed in the manner of the ka'aiguá or people of the wilds, is coming toward the governor's box. Slender-waisted, giant-tall, completely drenched with sweat. Tail of a comet sweeping the mount along in its dizzying course. The aboriginal horseman's nakedness is covered with nothing except a sort of cache-sexe or loincloth of a fabric that gives off opaque reflections. He is carrying at arm's length, threaded onto an extremely long coconut spine, the ring that leaves the trace of its red edging suspended in the air. The chestnut steed, without bit or bridle, slows down, advancing now with dancing steps. Its hoofs do not follow the beat of the musicians, but echo other sounds audible only to the horse and its rider. Its nostrils breathe out a rose-colored breath that expands at enormous pressure. The two jets of breath hit its flanks with their compact mass. They levitate the comet-tail, project it backwards, giving it the awesome appearance of a fabulous animal. Head of a horse and a jaguar. The funalia

§Lanceman (a term still used for a bullfighter on horseback).

or destrarii of the Romans would have appeared to be insects by comparison with this Indian hippocentaur!, the erudite bishop raves deliriously. The ancients called such steeds desultorii equi; of their horsemen united as one with them they said . . . But now Lázaro de Ribera is rising to his feet, beet-red with anger, shouting to the guards and whetting his baton-sword on the air: In the name of Beelzebub! Who is this insolent infidel who dares to be so bold! Guards! Constables! Harquebusiers! The hippocentaur with the double head of a man and a jaguar abruptly reins in before the platform. Rearing. Hoofs pared down to claws pawing the air. The human part of the fabulous animal bows and drops the ring in the lap of the governor's daughter. Shoot, shoot, you louts!, the governor's voice, breaking with wrath and terror, orders. In the sudden silence he has lost all control of himself. Shoot, you monstrous miscarried musketeers!, his voice cries out. The shots finally rang out. The keen whistle of the bullets could be heard. The native's teeth gleam amid the smoke and dust. His tattoos give off a phosphorescent glow in the dusk that is beginning to fall. With the same coconut spine he rakes his coppery skin from throat to crotch. He pulls the wax casque from his head, baring his hair tonsured in a spiral-crown. Amid the flurry of feathers, adornments, scales, insignia, he has the appearance of an Adam-Christ of the wilds. Almost albino, so pure white is he. Snow-white skin. Snow-white eyes. Nazarene beard of the jaguar-Christ. The mysterious chief of the most warlike, the fiercest mountain tribes of the Upper Paraná is come! Chieftain, sorcerer-prophet of the Ka'aiguá-Gualachí.§ Neither the conquistadors nor the missionaries were able to subjugate them. Beneath him his mount too has now been transformed, into a pure-blue jaguar. Tongue, jaws blood-red and dripping, ivory fangs. The spots of its coat shine with a metallic gleam in the sunlight. This growing legend is there in the middle of the plaza, in front of the governor's box. His daughter contemplates in ecstasy what to her is little less than an Archangel. A real, true apparition.

The bishop has knelt down, pointing his pectoral across at the dazzling apparition. Vade retro Satanas! The governor screams orders, cries that seem like rat squeals amid the jaguar's roars. As another shot rings out, the legendary aborigine snaps his fingers. With one bound the jaguar leaps above the heads of the terrified crowd. Turned into a real meteor, a real comet now. It crosses the river and is lost from sight in the sky as it heads for the cordilleras to the East.

The ring in the form of a serpent biting its tail grew larger and larger

§An earlier name for the Axé-Guayakí.

in the lap of the governor's daughter.* It soon enclosed the girl, her crazed father, the bishop, the municipal councilmen, and members of the clergy within its circle. The virgo-viper continued to grow larger and larger. It covered the plaza, the buildings and their balconies crowded with women of the aristocracy. At the same time the metal of the ring, resembling ytterbium, the hard metal of virgin land, grew softer and softer, turning into a squamous-viscous material. The scales flew off and remained suspended in the air, lighter than fleece-of-the-virgin. Suddenly the huge serpent burst into iridescent particles. There was a great commotion in the official box. The governor's daughter lay on the carpets covering the platform, bleeding profusely. Her white hoop skirts had taken on the color of the crimson edging of the ring. The crowd broke into a cry of superstitious terror: God's Punishment! God's Punishment! Amid the uproar, the governor and the bishop had a heated argument as to whether the doctor or the viaticum should be sent for.

The Prince of Peace and Great Conjoiner stepped out of the Portrait, crossed through the arch of Immortality, and embraced the dazed Lázaro de Ribera. Very good, very good, my dear governor! A real fairy tale! Allow me to congratulate your daughter for her marvelous performance in the role of the swan. It takes one's breath away! The swan-killer is something that has always sent me into sheer delirium! That strange assassin who murders swans in order to hear their last song! Ah ah ah! Unutterable, immeasurable, imponderable marvel! The queen's favorite bent over the serpent's head. Look, just look at this! An animal retains in its eyes the image of the person who has killed it, until decomposition sets in! And now, my dear Lázaro, I shall return to the portrait, the Great Conjoiner said. Let the performance go on.

The festivities went on until the tenth day and one more.

*"Shortly after the arrival of Lázaro de Ribera in the Province, a terrible event occurred. In the district of Villa Real, one hundred fifty men armed themselves on the pretext of rebuking the Indians for having broken the peace pact, took one of their camps by surprise, and killed seventy-five Indians who had surrendered and were defenseless. All of them were bound by their waists to horses called 'cincheros'; all of them died from blows with flint-edged wooden machetes, sabers, and lances. This entire testimony can be found in the records of the five court hearings held. The person principally responsible was the Commander José del Casal. The barbarous act took place on May 15, 1786. Ribera had assumed the governorship on April 8. Commander José Antonio Zabala y Delgadillo was named judge in the case.

"The slaughter, with undertones of the death of Tupac Amaru in Cuzco, the dominant note being the quartering by horses, caused a tremendous stir throughout the Province. Thanks to his influence and his wealth, Casal escaped punishment." (Julio César, op. cit.)

Nonetheless, a short time thereafter, the

The official account of the Municipal Council regarding these festivities states: "This province will never be able to point to a more brilliant era than the present. Until very recently its power was illusory and precarious; its commerce, full of obstacles and hindrances, stagnant; its treasury, without solidity; its defenseless frontiers, violated; its resources, though fecund, existent in name only; and the festivities staged in homage to the Prince of Peace, when he accorded this Cabildo the high honor of accepting appointment as its Councilman and Perpetual Conjoiner of Greatest Preeminence and Authority, its Zealous Defender and Sublime Prince of the Royal Secret, are a striking testimony to this brilliant present of power, prosperity, and grandeur."

The Annals and Chronicles of Memorable Occasions of the Province of Paraguay, which record down to the very last detail the events of a monotonous and monotonal era—nuptials, baptisms, demises, last rites, first communions, obsequies, funerals, novenas, illnesses, kitchen recipes and even herbalist formulas to increase or neutralize the generative vigor of couples—likewise describe the aforementioned festivities with a wealth of details. They say noth-

ing, however, concerning the strange episode played out between the daughter of the governor and the winged Axé-Guayakí horseman, which is the name ethnologists today give to the tribe of those once known as Ceratos, Ka'aiguás, Barbudos, Gualachís, and various other names.

Nor does the *Diary of Memorable Events,* maniacally and minutely detailed, contain the slightest allusion to the event related by *El Supremo.* It is necessary to go back to the hoariest chronicles of the Colony to find any suggestive traces. Du Toict, 1651, speaks of the Gualachís: "Savage people whose ferocity surpasses that of the barbarians of the Guayrá. Probably anthropophagous, they live by hunting and eat every manner of vermin, though the staple of their diet is honey from wild bees, for which they have a real passion. They were never subjugated by the conquistadors, much less subjected by the Missionaries to the advantages of our holy religion so as to inseminate them with Christian humanity. Nor do I believe they ever will be. A common characteristic of this tribe is the light color of their skin, which has given rise to the absurd myth of their European descendance. On the contrary, they are the

ethnocide Casal fell into disgrace. As is evident in the documents pertaining to the case, José del Casal y Sanabria tried by every means possible to persuade *El Supremo* (who at the time was practicing as a lawyer, held no public office, and had no official influence whatsoever) to undertake his defense. "Among all the popinjays who defend cases," the Indian-killer writes to the judge, "he is the only one who can get me out of this quagmire. I have offered him half my fortune, and more besides, for such note-

worthy service. But all my efforts have been in vain. Not only has the proud barrister stubbornly refused to sponsor my cause, thereby leaving me helpless and defenseless; he has also dared to heap calumny upon my actions against these savages of the wilds by claiming, as is public and notorious fact, that he would not move a finger in my favor for all the gold in the world, when, on the contrary, as God and our Most Exc. Sr. Gov.nor know, I acted as I did only for the good of all of society." *(Compiler's Note.)*

wildest of the savages that people these wild regions. They have been ruled since time immemorial by a famous cacique, a sorcerer and a terrible tyrant whose subjects attribute to him the gift of immortality. They have spread abroad the no less absurd legend that he is not only immune to the arms of the Europeans, but can also change appearance at will thanks to the strangest metamorphoses imaginable, and even make himself invisible. They say he travels about his domains by land or by air mounted on a blue jaguar, one of the zoomorphic myths of their cosmogony." *(Account of the Caaiguá People, passim.)*

I have endlessly checked not only the correspondence of Lázaro de Ribera

(the governor who ordered the one copy of the *Social Contract* that existed in Paraguay to be burned), but also his genealogical and biographical references. These documents all agree that the incendiary governor had two daughters: one by his legitimate spouse and the other by one of his Indian mistresses. One of these daughters died at a very early age; the other reached puberty, and if the Prester John is not lying, it would appear that she even reached old age. I have not been able, however, to determine with certainty which one of them it was. In the oral tradition, on the other hand, there exists the myth of the swift horseman who stole the daughter of a *Karaí-Ruvichá-Guasú*, a *Great-White-Chief. (Compiler's Note.)*

On the eleventh day, encouraged by the visible signs of confidence and support on the part of the Prince of Peace, Lázaro de Ribera signed decrees confining the Indians to encomiendas and abolishing the exemption from military service granted tobacconists: his two obsessive aspirations. He had finally been able to realize them, thereby thwarting the royal will.

1840

Congresses. Military parades. Processions. Theatrical performances. Equestrian tourneys. Parades. Masquerades of blacks and Indians. Feasts of patron saints. Double burial rites. Triple funerals. Conspiracies, many. Executions, very few. Apotheoses. Resurrections. Lapidations. Multitudinarious jubilations. Collective grief (only after my disappearance). Festivities of every order. Yes, all taking place in perfect order. And yet there are pasquinaders who dare to present the Perpetual Dictatorship as a dark, despotic, oppressive era! For them, yes. For the people, no. The First Republic of the South turned into a Reign of Terror! Archvillain archliars! Is it not obvious to them that on the contrary it was the most just, the most peaceful, the most noble era, that of most perfect well-being and felicity, the period of greatest splendor enjoyed by the Paraguayan people, as a whole and in its totality, in all of its wretched history? Did it not deserve it after so many sufferings, hardships, and misfortunes? Is it this that plunges my old enemies into such darkness and gloom? Is it this that fills them with hatred and treachery? Is it this that they accuse me of? Is it this that they do not forgive me and never shall? I'd be really done for if I needed their absolution! For the moment, the memory of the people-multitude, the five or six commonest senses, testify, bear witness in my favor. Don't you have eyes to see, ears to hear, you consignatories of calumnies and stupidities?

For the moment, the first testimony. Don't you hear the martial sounds that dizzy even the deafest ears? I am proud of having made Asunción the capital with the greatest number of bands of musicians in the entire world. There are exactly a hundred of them thundering in the city right this minute, almost in unison. With only an infinitesimal difference of tone, rhythm, key, adjusted with mathematical precision. Endless rehearsals. Infinite patience of maestros and players until they achieve the production of sounds, syncopations, and silences in relief. Stereophonic volumes (not stercophonic ones, as with the buzzing of the swarms of pasquinaders) make of the vault of heaven their resonance box and of the earth and the air their natural media of propagation. As if the elements themselves were the bands of musicians. The instruments fall silent and the conic sections of silence continue to vibrate, full of martial music. Parabola of sound that survives itself circularly, like light, at that point where the circle opens and closes at the same time. Listen. The fanfare of the same, sole, and only parade that I offered the mob of imperial, directorial, provincial, conspiratorial envoys. To compensate the country. Years 1811, 1813, 1823.

The plenipotentiary envoys of Buenos Aires, Herrera and Coso, and of the Empire of Brazil, Correia, superposed. Transposed to the dimension upon which I oblige them to gaze. Sitting on each other's knees. In the same place though not at the same time. Look, observe: I am unfolding before you the parade that covers the first two decades of the Republic, including the last decade of the Colony. Distinguish the illegitimate from the legitimate. The pure from the impure. Ugly is beautiful, the beautiful ugly. Be stupefied, you stupid fools. See the limits. The lines dividing the waters. This side and the other side of the real. Royalty of reality emitting sparks in the haze of the paper between the lines of ink. Thorn pen, enter their eyes and ears. And you, distinguished guests, fix in your retinas, in your souls, if you have such a thing, these ugly/beautiful visions. The earth has bubbles just as water does, Echevarría says airily. But they've disappeared. No, my dear doctor. The bubbles are still there. If you don't see them breathe them. Invisible respiration is also corporeal. If you stop breathing you die, isn't that so? Nunca he visto una mañana más hermosa!,§ Correia exclaims. Do those beings we're seeing really exist?, the Brazilian asks. Herrera, who once shook hands with Napoleon, answers him, humiliated, full of rancor: Don't you see they're phantoms? They must have given us some harmful root to eat, of the sort that makes one's reason a prisoner. Correia shudders. Don't worry, my esteemed guests. A real fear is less to be feared than an imaginary one. To think of a crime is still an imaginary thing. To commit it is already a very natural thing. Didn't you know, gentlemen, that the only thing that exists is what does not yet exist? Echevarría's squint eyes blink in Correia's farsighted ones. Coso's cat whiskers twitch on the toad face of Herrera, who has swallowed his old skin. I beg your pardon, noble sirs. Your role in events has been noted down in a register whose pages I shall read all the days of my life. Whatever happens, time and circumstances will help sort out the difficulties. For now, let us not miss the parade.

The two thousand five hundred horsemen of Takuary parade past. My illustrious cousin Yegros, very pale at the head of the cavalry troops. He is already tied to the trunk of the orange tree. He has confessed his treason. It has cost him a great deal, and he has done so only after having had his hundred twenty-fifth taste of the lash. The Truth Chamber works miracles. He has shown great repentance. I had no other recourse than to have him shot to death twenty years ago. The best thing about his life was the way in which he took his leave of it. He died in the attitude of someone who suddenly realizes that he must throw away his most precious treasure as though it were a mere bauble. To think he was someone in whose ingenuousness and stupidity I had placed a certain trust! Ah ah ah! There is no such thing as an art enabling us to read in a face the evil of the soul hidden beneath that mask. He is galloping along amid the best horsemen passing in review. On his chest the wounds of the execution gleam as brightly, if not more brightly, than the decorations earned at Takuary. The latter speak of honor; the former of dishonor. It is the same with Cavallero-Bayard. The seven Montiel brothers. A number of others. Almost all the conspirator-cavaliers among the sixty-eight condemned men executed beneath the orange tree on July 17 of the year '21.* Pale and gallant, they

§I've never seen a more beautiful morning!

---

*"Day of terror, day of sorrow, day of mourning! You will forever be the anniversary of our misfortunes! O fateful day! If I could but erase you from the place

stand out at the head of the squads as they simulate a charge. Weightless. Disembodied. Free now of the sin of ingratitude. Washed clean of their lack of love of the Fatherland. They cross the light lens so swiftly, pulled so hard by the centrifugal force of time, that the winged act of remembering them is too slow to catch up with them.

I have my visitor-plenipotentiary-negotiator-spies seated on the porch of the cathedral. Not a drop of water to raise to their parched lips. Not a drop of air to breathe into their lungs. The fiery sun is melting their marauder-negotiator brains. The parade of the troops is endless. The artillery pieces pass, drawn by mules. Infernal racket. Correia da Cámara is swelling up more and more. His splendid costume has burst like a balloon, revealing, through the tatters, bits of skin crawling with flies sipping in libation the liquid of blisters along with his sweat. Nicolás de Herrera is in no better shape.* I see him fighting inside his skin against the torment of the heat. Brain befuddled. Tongue thick as a doormat. The parade seems fine to me, señor dean, but what I don't quite understand is your stubborn resistance to union with Buenos Aires.

Correia da Cámara has had to be tied to his chair with the ornamental cordons of the banners and his own braided aiguillettes. An augur, the sun casts the animalesque shadow of the imperial envoy before.

The mirage of the parade enlarges, tenses its arc of reflections. The

---

you occupy in the harmonious round of months!" (Note by the Argentine publicist Carranza to *Outcry of a Paraguayan*, addressed to Dorrego and attributed to Mariano Antonio Molas in his *Historical Description of the Former Province of Paraguay*.)

In the *Outcry* the Porteño leader Dorrego was again entreated to invade Paraguay. *(Compiler's Note.)*

*"As in a nightmare I saw those endless companies of dark specters pass by, their weapons gleaming in the blinding sunlight. The din, the clatter of hoofs seemed to me to grow gradually fainter. Cannons, strange catapults, complicated war machines passed by without a sound. They appeared to fly, to glide along a foot above the ground.

"Beneath a yellow baldachin, which was the canopy of the Most Blessed Sacrament in the processions of yesteryear, the Caesar-Consul, seated in the high-backed curule that makes his scrawny figure look even more sickly and ridiculous, smiled enigmatically, inordinately pleased at the effects of his triumphal spectacle. Now and again he looked to each side out of the corner of his eye, and at such times his features took on an expression of insane self-importance.

"A very tall catapult, at least a hundred meters high, advanced without a sound, propelled by its own automotive force, probably a steam engine. Powerful jets of water projected beneath this immense bulk of wood a veritable cushion of gaseous exhalation, making it lighter than a feather. That was the last thing I saw. At midday I fainted and was taken to my lodgings at the Customs House." *(Unpublished note of N. de Herrera.)*

girandole of whirling visions spins faster and faster. The embroideries of the tambours take on a more and more dizzying rhythm. I keep Correia from fainting or falling asleep. Pilar the black screens him with a feather fan. Every so often he moistens his face with orange blossom and damascene rose water. In place of the plumed bicorne, an immense straw sombrero, giving off perfumed vapor, covers his head.

I have used mirages on other occasions with equal effectiveness. In the north, with the Brazilians. In the south with Artigueñians, Correntinos, Bajadeños, Santafesinos. My leaders receive thorough instruction in the mechanism of refractions. When the enemy attacks in desert terrain or in swamplands, they order a retreat. They cause their troops to flee deliberately. The invader presses on, pursuing them through burning hot sands or bogs. Hidden amid the dunes or the bulrushes, the Paraguayans leave the image of their army reverberating in the sands or the swamps. It thus becomes at once imaginary and real in the distance. False perspectives forge the miracle. The invaders advance. Lying in ambush, the Paraguayans wait. The invaders shoot. The Paraguayans play dead on the distant screen. The invaders fling themselves upon the "cowardly Guaraní enemy." Everything has disappeared. For many days, many leagues, the same illusion tricks the invaders. Dumbfounded by this incomprehensible sorcery and asking themselves how the Paraguayan footsoldiers or their horses of smoke and fire, however swift they may be, can disappear instantaneously, taking their dead with them. This fight against phantoms exhausts the invaders, who are then surrounded by the Paraguayans descending upon them from all directions in a howling avalanche. Their adversaries are destroyed in the wink of an eye. They die, taking with them in their eyes the vague horror of a terrifying apparition rendered even more diabolical by its irony.

This ruse never fails. All it takes is good training and the precise sense of parallaxes and angles of light that these men possess in the darkest depths of their instinct. They would not even need arms, since the shock effect of the bloody farce is more deadly than that of rifles. In the circle of its action every word creates what it expresses, the Frenchman used to say, feeling suddenly miraculous as he clutched his pen in the attitude of a magus twirling his magic wand. I don't feel that sure of myself with my little mother-of-pearl club released from its prison. Just in case, I provide my soldiers with rifles and cartridges. Only a few all the same, ones who are in on the game. Only a very small number of the infantry's muskets are real arms; those carried by the point men who are closest in the line of march to the official flag. The rest imitations, wooden rifles. Like the cannons carved out of trunks of timbó, the smoke-tree that has the color of iron and the weight of smoke. My secret arms! As for the troops, the men who have been parading for thirty years now number less than three thousand. They pass before the reviewing stand at a martial pace. They turn at the corner of La Merced. March down the block lined with Adam's-apple trees. Disappear from sight in the depths of the Lower Town. Pass by the samu'ú-peré tree, a palo borracho stripped bare. Arrived at the cemetery and the church of San Francisco in the Tikú-Tuyá quarter. Then start back via the King's Highway, return to La Merced, and pass by the reviewing stand once again, exactly as before. The farthest distant are already coming back round.

The imperial envoy's resistance is extraordinary. Superhuman. Anthropoidal. He won't last much longer. He's already collapsing. This makes three days and three nights now that he hasn't slept, what with the festivities in the streets and the preliminal negotiations at Government House. Last night, after the performance in the Theater of the Lower Town, the blacks' handkissing in homage to him began as dawn was breaking, and the sun was high in the sky by the time it ended. African blood found occasion for heathen celebration. They danced endlessly before the emperor's portrait, placed in a forest of triumphal arches. And now the din of the military parade will not cease till sundown.

Correia da Cámara's head is dangling from its gold-braided restraints. Useless whole, complete in its own way. Every so often, he still straightens up for a brief moment. Tries his best to laugh at the situation. Laughter that does not come from the lungs. For long intervals he remains silent. Tongue hanging out, dribbling a flower the color of milk. I cast a sidelong glance at him. The same figure as at the beginning: Just one eye. Face in profile (though completely boldfaced). Body in profile. One arm. One leg. Trembling a little each time the troops pass by, shivering with intermittent fever, on the verge of sunstroke.

The complete circuit takes one hour and six minutes, following the diagram of the parade that I have laid out down to the last quarter of a hair. Hence during the twelve hours of the parade they have managed to round off exactly twenty-six years in this motus perpetuus of their marching. Minuscule, punctilious little men advanced in seven platoons and a single direction at an equally motionless pace. Red dust. Magnetic vibrations of the reverberations. Monotonous tread of the infantry. Look at that, Correia. Doesn't my army seem as large, as well armed as Napoleon's? The imperial emissary doesn't answer me. A green aqueous humor drips from the drooping lips, dribbles down the chest, spatters the iridescent jacket.

I have few friends. In all truth, my heart is never open to the present friend but to the absent one. We embrace those who were and those who are not yet, no less than those who are absent. Among them, General Manuel Belgrano. There are nights when he comes to keep me company. He is arriving now, with no burden of cares, of memories. He enters with no need for me to open the door for him. I do not see him so much as feel his presence. He is here, present at my absence. There is not the slightest sound to announce him. He is simply here. I turn over on my side in thought. The general is here. Monstrously swollen, not so much from hydropsy as from suffering and sorrow. Floating half a span above the floor. Occupying half and a half of the non-room. My swollen leg the rest of the space. With no need to squeeze over to make room for each other we occupy in time a greater place than the limited one that space grants us in this life. Good evening, my dear general. He listens to me, answers me, after his fashion. The nebula-person stirs a little. Are you comfortable? He informs me that he is. He gives me to understand that, despite our dissimilarities, he feels at ease alongside me. What I appreciated most in men, he murmurs, wisdom, austerity, truth, sincerity, independence, patriotism . . . Come, general, all is accomplished now and compliments have no place here. But as you were remarking, our dissimilarities are not that great. Submerged in this darkness, we are indistinguishable. Among the non-living absolute equality reigns. Thus the weak and the strong are equal. As things have turned out, general, I would rather have lived the life of a field hand. Remember, Excellency, the general consoles me, citing Horace's vain consolation: Non omnis moriar.§ Ah, Latin quotations!, I think. Maxims not good for anything besides funeral orations. The thing is, no one ever manages to understand how our deeds survive us. Both those who firmly believe in the beyond, and those who, like us, believe only in this world here below. O altitudo!,§§ my guest said, and his words bounced

§I shall not wholly die (Odes, III, 30).
§§O heights sublime!

off the stones . . . udo . . . udo . . . udo . . . When the echoes of the versicle had died away amid the buzzing of the flies, the silence of the depths returned to us. I only hope, general, that you did not end up in despair at the thought of your May, while I, despairing of our May that lacked all thought, bent my every effort to make a true revolution of it. Do you remember that you yourself advised me to do so in a letter? The memory carries great weight. The memory of works accomplished is weightier than the works themselves. Our egg-souls communicated with each other without need of a voice, of words, of writing, of treaties of peace and war, of commerce. Strong in our supreme weakness, we went to the very bottom of things. Wisdom without boundaries. Truth without limits, now that there are no longer limits or boundaries.

To console himself for his defeats, he began writing his Memoirs. One notes in them how the revolutionary idea ferments, germinates, falls beneath the shadow of foreign economic domination. Belgrano, one of the first proponents of free trade in South America, says nothing of his participation in the schemes to found monarchies which, according to the learned Porteño doctors, were to further the cause of free trade. Fools beguiled by soap bubbles!

I think I understood your thought, general. He does not answer, lost in the deepest of silences. Perhaps he is praying. I hunch up a little so as not to disturb his prayers. I am not about to ask him at this point what the reasons were behind his chimerical projects to restore monarchies in these wild lands. My immense guest hated anarchy as I did. Since the troublemakers, the blathering idiots, the cynical politicasters had not yet proclaimed any dogma, any form of government, confining themselves to splitting each other's throats to win power, my friend General Belgrano was beguiled into seeking the center of unity in the principle of monarchical hierarchy. But while the so-called republicans of Buenos Aires wanted to place a queen or a foreign king on the throne, Belgrano aspired only to a modest constitutional monarchy. The monarchist re-publicans were negotiating with the Bourbonarian Carlota Joaquina. Any mercenary infante purveyed by the dominant powers of Europe would do. It was not by chance that the Rodríguez Peñas and the other Porteño monarchists held their secret meetings in the Vieytes soap factory. There are certain stains no soap can withstand. Yet what reproach can be leveled against you, my esteemed general? You did not attempt to set up a theocratic monarchy in the American world that had half liberated itself from monarchs and theocrats. You did not attempt to establish a Roman, Pampa, Ranquel, or Diaguita-Calchaquí papacy. You spoke only of placing a descendant of the Incas on the throne of the Creole monarchy, the brother of Tupac Amaru,

an octogenarian who was wasting away in the dungeon of his imprisonment for life in Spain. Was this what your fellow citizens never forgave
you, general?

Through your silence, I contemplate the beginning of your agony,
nailed to your cross at the Cruz Alta relay post for fourteen long station-
months, even before the viacrucis of your pilgrimage began. You were
spared neither afflictions, hardships, nor humiliations. You wanted to reach
Buenos Aires to die. I'll never make it now!, you complain. I have no way
of getting around. You summon the master of the relay station. He answers
with deathly insolence: If the general wishes to speak to me, let him come
to my room. It is the same distance from his to mine. Despite everything,
you were able to drag yourself about even as you were dying and reach
your native city, which had so many times thrust you from its bosom and
plunged you into a life of the worst sacrifices. You arrived on the very
day that Buenos Aires, in the grip of anarchy, had three governors because
it lacked one, and you, general, dying, dying, with that Ay patria mía! on
your lips, your body hideously swollen, and that immense heart that left
the surgeons who performed the autopsy thunderstruck. That heart—one
of them said—does not belong to this body! You, distant, silent. Through
your silence, my esteemed general, I see the cut marble slab of a commode
covering your body, your memory, your works.

My fate has turned out to be precisely the opposite. All I have had
to do to occupy my time is flop about in my sewer-hole. Betrayed by those
who fear me most and are the most abject and disloyal. In my case they
offer me funeral rites first. Then they bury me. After that they dig me up
again. They throw my ashes into the river, some people claim; others, that
one of my craniums is kept in his house by a traitorous triumvir, and then
later brought to Buenos Aires. My second cranium remains in Asunción,
according to those who think they know all the answers. All this many
years later. As for you, general, just a month after your death, as in ancient
Greece and Rome, your friends meet for a funeral banquet. In the hall hung
with flags, your portrait crowned with laurel is seated at the head of the
table. As the guests enter, the Tacit Brigadier records, the sad and solemn
music of a hymn composed for the occasion is heard, and all intone the
antiphone, evoking your Manes. Amid this horrible dirge, published later
by The Theophilanthropic Awakener,§ the inextinguishable cry of Ay
Patria mía! continues to resound. But that cry from the depths, altitudo
. . . udo . . . udo!, was heard neither by the Tacit Brigadier nor by the

§*El Supremo*'s nickname for Mitre, the "Tacit Brigadier," founder of a Buenos Aires
newspaper.

Porteño patricians as they overturned their wine goblets on the memorial flowers.

As for me, I see the past now confused with the future. The false half of my skull kept by my enemies for thirty years in a box of noodles, amid the junk piled in an attic.

As will be seen in the Appendix, this prediction of *El Supremo*'s was also fulfilled down to the last detail. *(Compiler's Note.)*

The remains of the cranium, id est, will not be mine. But then, what skull hammered to pieces by the enemies of the fatherland; what particle of thought, what people, living or dead, will there be left in the country who do not henceforward bear my mark? The red-hot brand of **I-HE**. Entire. Inextinguishable. Left behind in the protracted nothingness of the race to whom destiny has offered suffering as diversion, non-lived life as life, unreality as reality. Our mark will remain on it.

My private physician, the only one who has access to my chamber, my life in his hands, has been able to do no more to strengthen my bad health. Bonpland's remedies, on the other hand, at a distance of more than a hundred leagues, did me some good, though at the cost of certain political troubles he also caused me. As a show of my will, I allowed him to leave only after the high and haughty of this earth ceased to importune me, demanding his liberation. I preferred to have the dysenteric flux rather than have the sages, the statesmen of the world, Napoleon himself, whoever, Alexander of Macedonia, the Seven Sages of Greece believe that they could divert my course. Didn't Simón Bolívar threaten to invade Paraguay, as Father Pérez recalled at my funeral services, in order to liberate his French friend, thereby destroying a free American people? Liberate the Frenchy naturalist from what, if here in this country he enjoyed greater freedom than anywhere and enjoyed a prosperity the equal of, or greater than, that of any of its citizens once he learned to obey its laws and respect its sovereignty? Wasn't it Amadeo Bonpland himself who declared that he did not want to leave Paraguay, where he had found the Lost Paradise? Did they want to free him or to yank him out of the First Garden? What sort of devilment were these demands on the part of the powerful of this world, who took this poor man rich in felicity and peace here as the pretext for their devilry? The dignity of a head of state must rise above his diarrheas. I let Bonpland go, against his will, only when they left off pestering me and when it so pleased me. I let him go and again fell into the hands of the protophysician and his insipid eggnogs.

Tell me, Patiño, what would you think of a great man who, being a friend of the great men of this world, who, being himself one of the most highly esteemed scholars in the world, suddenly settles down in the most secluded part of our wilds on the pretext of gathering and classifying plants? What would you say of such a distinguished man, dripping with medals, who decides to set up shop on the very borders of the country?

I would say, Sire, that with all those medals clanking, he's not going to go one step without people for miles around hearing him. But he came very silently and secretly, the Frenchy, and began to compete with the Paraguayan State. As he tried to set himself up smuggling maté, mendaciously maintaining it was mint and other such medicinal herbs, not to mention coca, the Great Man kept his eyecup trained this way, watching everything that went on here. Hand in glove with the worst enemies of the country. Conniving with Artigas, the big corporal of bandits and brigands, who is here now as a free Paraguayan present, a title and status vastly superior to that of Protector of the Banda Oriental. Conniving with the protector's lieutenant, Pancho Ramírez, the wicked traitor from Entre Ríos, who at the end of his incursions left his madbrained buzzard's head in a cage. Conniving with Artigas's other lieutenant, the renegade Indian caudillo Nicolás Aripi. Conniving with all this petty vermin, the great traveler began to pillage our property. Why? What for? Wouldn't you have said that such a great man was a schemer of the lowest sort, a common spy, any way you looked at him? Yes, of course, Sire, no doubt about it! A dastardly and despicable spy who should have ended up roasting on a spit! Not so fast, my delicate anthropophagous secretary. All I did was send a corps of five hundred men to rout that horde of interloping Indians, thieves, and troublemakers of the accursed Aripi, who'd turned into both a bodyguard and a boss (as always happens with scoundrels who act as secretaries). When the espiocolony was destroyed and the gang of thugs captured, the savant was wounded in the head and also fell prisoner. Through the stupidity and clumsiness of my soldiers, the only one who managed to escape was the ignorant and accursed Indian. I ordered that the prisoner be treated with the greatest consideration; likewise the fourteen little Indian girls and the horde of blacks captured with him. I confined the savant to the best lands in the settlement of Santa María, where the captors themselves helped him build the colony. What do you say to that? I merely repeat now, Sire, what I have said again and again since the days when these things happened: that Your Grace is the kindest of Men and the most generous of Governors. And all the more so in the case of that dirty spy! You can swallow your former, and false, indignation now. What would you say if that dirty spy, having been cut down to size, begins to remedy my ills without asking me for anything in return? That he's a saintly man, Sire. Though on second thought, Excellency, not all that saintly, since he's not doing what he's doing because he wants to but because he's obliged to. Naturally you think that the learned prisoner recently come from Napoleon's court to these wilds was in a position to sever the thread of my life with his concoctions. Naturally, Majesty

. . . I mean Excellency. Would you do such a thing, my spiritual-minded secretary? Not I, Sire! God save and keep this loyal servant! Such things shouldn't be done helter-skelter, Patiño. When my eye itches, I look for eyewash, not a spine of coconut palm. In your case, it's your rear that itches. Don't think you can stop the itching by rubbing it on my seat. What you'll end up with is a noose round your neck. It's already happened. It was written. Fulfilled.

There are those who speak of the hair, bones, teeth of the earth. It is a great animal. It bears us on its back. Some for a fair time, others less. One day it gets tired, rolls us off, and eats us. Other men, double-men, come out of its insides. The First-Grandfather of the Indians of the forest, according to the dream told and sung in their traditions, made his way out of the bowels of the earth by raking it with his fingernails. Ant-bears came out of the earth that devours men in search of the Land-without-Evil. They came out looking for honey. Some of them turned into honey-bears. Others into white jaguars. These latter eat honey and honey-eaters. But, to the earth, red hair, bones, teeth, couldn't matter less. Mere baubles. She always ends up eating those who come into and those who come out of her inside. She's down there waiting. Absolutely true, Sire!

(Written at dawn. Last quarter.)

I arrived at Santa María that night disguised as a peasant. I had my men wait a league away, hidden in the forest. Covered by my straw sombrero, I took my place in the line of sick people waiting in front of the hut on the side of the hill. I found myself between a paralytic and a leper lying on the ground; the one with his sores and a sombrero crowned with candles as a sign of his disease; the other, buried media res in total immobility. I lay down too, pretending to be asleep, my face glued to the bare dirt with the smell of many passing illnesses. I let them past. When I opened my eyes I found myself before a rosy-cheeked, chubby, robust little man. Gray, nearly platinum locks. Very fine hair, sweeping his shoulders. His voice, exactly like him, said: Don't take off your sombrero. Don't uncover yourself. He didn't touch me. He didn't ascultate me. He didn't ask about my illnesses. Immediately, without speaking, without asking, he knew more about me than I knew and could tell him myself. Take this. He held out a handful of bulbs and roots. They appeared to be moistened with a very sticky resin. Have them boiled and set the infusion out to cool for three nights in a row. He took out a little pouch like the one I use for snuff. Opened it. Inside a very fine powder gleamed with the greenish luminosity of fireflies. Put this in the infusion. You'll have your Corvisart tisane. My breath nearly taken away, I stowed the bulbs and the little box in my pilgrim's sack. I made a move to take out some coins. He put his hand over mine. No, he said, my patients don't pay. Did he know me? Did he pretend not to know me? Life is a mystery. He didn't recognize me by sight. Perhaps, perhaps not. What he respected was the secret told without words, in the shade of the sombrero that concealed my shadow. I made my way outside, reeling for sheer joy, stumbling over the dim shapes lying on the ground. A multitude in the dark resembling a moaning mass of bodies strewn all over a battlefield after a bloody combat. I made my way along, stepping on hands, feet, heads that raised up and insulted me with the tremendous rancor of the ill. But these insults merely made me happier still. Health does not know the language of choler. I was taking my salvation away with me in my pocket.

I drank the tisane for three days. For three years my body pissed away all its ills.

Without the least nostalgia for Malmaison, for the pomp of the Napoleonic court, oblivious to his own renown, Don Amadeo continued to enjoy his paradisiac corner in the Paraguayan countryside, feeling more and more at home. Protected, cherished, venerated. As armies were mobilized, conspiracies hatched, letters exchanged, as emissaries from all over the world, scientists of unquestioned prestige, and dubious political ruffians seeking to enlist him in the service of their interests were marshaling their forces, compadre Amadeo sent me simples for my complaints: the sticky bulbs and the phosphoric Corvisart powder.

Grandsire was different. He came in search of Bonpland. Saw. Was convinced. He said with utmost clarity what he had to say without straying too far from the truth. On the other side of the ocean, the most conspicuous men of science of the era awaited his reports. From afar, they all continued to see in Bonpland the Bonpland that was no more. Humboldt, the Bonpland who saved him from crocodiles when their boats sank on the Orinoco, or in the snows of the Chimborazo, or searching for his companion in the depths of the equatorial jungle in the darkest hours of the night. The others, with their royal-peacock eyes, the learned courtier of Malmaison and Navarre, Josephine's landscape artist. The most eagle-eyed, the golden eagle of science, the naturalist, who after traveling with Humboldt more than nine thousand leagues, from one end of the continent to the other, came back to Paris with a collection of sixty thousand plants and some ten thousand unknown species. Humboldt and Bonpland, the Castor and Pollux of Nature, were never to meet again beneath equinoctial constellations.

How's it going in Misiones, Don Amado?, I asked him in a note. Prodigiously well, Excellency! Odd that he doesn't come out with his little phrase in French. He is careful not to do so, because of what happened to Grandsire when the latter came, as he put it, to "rescue him from his captivity." Return his impertinent message to this individual who has just arrived, I ordered the administrator of Itapúa, and tell him for me that his frivolous message, its ridiculously haughty style, and his jumbled hand-writing and bad ink made it incomprehensible and beneath notice. Tell this supposed and undoubtedly false envoy of the Institut de France that we do not permit persons who may be suspected of disturbing the security, tranquillity, and independence of this Republic to cross our borders. What is this absurd story that the Frenchman is circulating as a cover for his real aims: that he's coming to Paraguay to search for the juncture or the union of the Amazon and the Río de la Plata? Even if there were such a thing, which everybody here knows there isn't, these naturalists or unnatural spies will not be allowed to enter our territory in the disguise of scientists to observe, examine, and engage in things other than what they declare, claim, or pretend, thereby concealing their real ends. In addition to all this, what is this ignorance of Spanish that the envoy from the Institut de France makes so much of? What business does he think ignorant people have here? If he doesn't know our language, the Government by the same token is under no obligation to know his. So tell this Monsieur Grandsire that we don't speak French here and that the Government of Paraguay is not prepared to pay an interpreter to attend to or contend with pretensions whose intention is to deceive. Therefore he will not only not be received, but will be invited forthwith to take a powder. That means, my dear administrator, that the new spy, or whatever he is, must leave immediately, not that we're going to give him a good whiff of powder or shoot him dead on the spot as you're in the habit of doing with interlopers from the other shore.

Compadre Amadeo knows I speak French, but those little phrases and interjections that pedants deliberately scatter about in their writings so as to appear that they know more than they do escape him only inadvertently. Do you think you'll manage to collect some six hundred thousand plants, at the very least, here? Oh it seems to me that oui, oui, Monsieur le Dictateur, if God and Your Excellency are willing! I hear Don Amadeo's fresh laugh. The earth of Paraguay, Excellency, is the heaven of plants;

there are more of them here than there are stars in the firmament and grains of sand in the deserts. I have tirelessly interrogated the layers of our planet. I have opened them like the leaves of a book in which the three kingdoms of nature keep their archives. In each one of its pages each species, before it disappears, has left its trace, its memento. Man himself, the latest arrival, has left proofs of his former existence. Have you read all those pages, Don Amado? Impossible, Excellency! It would take millions of years and we'd still only be at the beginning! What do you think of the pages of the Book in Paraguay? Here I must dig deeper, Excellency. Poke about in layer after layer till I get to the very bottom. Read from right to left, from the right side, the wrong side, up, down. Not only that, Don Amadeo. Here you must read these pages with disinterested passion. Absolutely disinterested. The one who succeeds in doing that will be the beginning of a species unique on this planet. As long as we're content to be what we are, we can't know or even guess what it will be like. You are right, Excellency. I have collected nearly a hundred thousand plants and twelve thousand six hundred species, absolutely unknown, of the three kingdoms, which in this Republic are extremely prolific and varied. I should like to remain here, Monsieur le Dictateur, till the end of my days, if Yr. Exc.ʸ gives me permission. As far as I'm concerned, Don Amado, you may stay as long as you like. Perpetuity is our business here. I in my line of work. You in yours. But he was caught in the toils of conspiracies, plots, clever ambushes of the enemies of the country. I don't say that he was quite prepared to be used, but that machinating myrmidons were preparing to use him in any event.

It is a great error both in Paris and in London, Grandsire himself said, to think that the Dictator of Paraguay is holding Bonpland because of some personal enmity against him or out of caprice. No, indeed: that is not the case, and were it not for the extremely delicate position in which the Dictator finds himself vis-à-vis the turbulent republics that surround him; were it not for his eager desire to make his country respected and place it in free communication with the rest of the world, M. Bonpland would not be obliged to languish in the captivity that he shares with other Frenchmen, Italians, Englishmen, Germans, and Americans who have met with the same fate. At last someone understood! Those few individuals held captive, apart from traitors and conspirators, are being held as hostages for the freedom of the entire people. It is to be ill acquainted with the disposition and character of the Supreme Dictator to believe him likely to yield to fear or to a threat, Grandsire adds. Yes, indeed: it is to be ill acquainted with me. Or if you don't believe it, Bolívar himself can tell you. I didn't even answer his note, a confused mixture, part plea, part complaint, and part threat. Or Parish, the consul general of the British empire in Buenos Aires, and other petty adventurers who dared stick their noses in Paraguay, can say a word or two on the subject. Grandsire wrote things to Baron Humboldt that were true beyond question. With due respect for the truth, I am bound to say, the Frenchman says, that from everything I see here, the inhabitants of Paraguay have for twenty-two years enjoyed perfect peace, under a good administration. The contrast with the countries through which I have traveled heretofore is most surprising. One journeys through Paraguay without arms; people scarcely bother to close their doors since the punishment for theft is death, and what is more, the owners of the house or the commune where a theft is committed are obligated to make restitution. There are no beggars to be seen; everyone works. The children are educated at State expense. Almost all the inhabitants know how to read and write. (I omit his judgment concerning my person, since even though it may be quite sincere, the praise of individuals makes me uncomfortable.) This country may one day come to be of the greatest importance for European commerce. The Dictator is extremely irritated by the insulting stories that the government of Buenos Aires spreads about him in European periodicals. Yesterday I had occasion to see a farmer, a neighbor of Bonpland's, who meets him every day. He says that Bonpland is getting along very well, that he possesses land the Dictator has given him, that he is practicing medicine, that he is actively engaged in distilling alcohol from honey, and that he is still receiving and describing plants for his collections, which grow vaster with each passing day, with the same passionate enthusiasm as ever. Bonpland the "prisoner" wrote to his colleague, the botanist Delille: I am as happy and vigorous as when you knew me in Navarre and at Malmaison. Though I do not have as much money, I am loved and esteemed by everyone, which to me represents true wealth.

I allowed him to take with him everything he possessed, cattle, money, collections, papers and books, his distillery for making cordials and brandy, his carpentry shop and sawmill, the equipment and beds of his hospital and maternity clinic. Paraguayan peasants accompanied the Frenchman to the border. They bade him farewell with songs, lamentations, and cheers. The Itapúa battalion escorted the traveler's flotilla across the Paraná. The tumult did not cease until the multitude lost sight of him. On their return the men in the escort reported that they had barely set foot on the other side when four horses were stolen from him. It's plain to see we aren't in Paraguay anymore!, they said that Don Amadeo said, turning his eyes brimming with tears toward our shores. A moment of inattention that the Correntinos took advantage of to steal the remainder of his drove of horses and baggage.

Bonpland left Paraguay reluctantly, early in February 1831, at precisely the same place where he had arrived ten years before. Ortellado, the district commissioner, who had had him under his protection during all this time, tells how, as they embraced each other and shed tears together when the time came to part, Bonpland said to him: Look, Don Norberto, they brought me here under duress. I am leaving here under duress. Don't say that, Don Amadeo! Your Worship knows very well that if he wishes to stay our Supreme will not refuse him permission to remain here. That poor Ortellado was always a mawkishly sentimental imbecile. Bonpland taught him a lesson: No, Don Norberto. I am most grateful for your words, but I know very well that The Supreme is as inexorable in his rigor as he is implacable in his goodness. When he did not want me to leave, there was no power in the world that could drag me out of here. And now *He* believes that I ought to leave, and there is no power in the world that is going to change his mind. That was indeed how it was, Don Amadeo. The pages of this earth taught you something.

For the past ten years I have had only vague news of his person and his labors. He left Paraguay shortly after the death of Bolívar, the proud liberator. Bonpland went off into exile amid the blessings and tears of a people who were not his own, but whom he had made his. Bolívar fled into exile amid portraits of himself torn in half by crowds of a people who were his, a people he liberated, a people who then drove him out. Dead too, forgotten, despised: Dean Gregorio Funes, Bolívar's agent and spy in the Plata. When Grimorio the Funereal kept pressing Bolívar to invade Paraguay, I said to him of this chimerical project: Leave off your hocus-pocus, Father Grimorio. Either a thing is possible or it is not. You know that what you want is not possible. In any event, if your Bolívar comes here, be forewarned that many men are going to die, and it is a pity that so eminent and worthy a man should remain here to shine my shoes and saddle my horses. Come instead and set up a funeral parlor, your paternity. It would do honor to your illustrious surname and sepulchral intentions. There is excellent wood for coffins here and the best craftsmen in the world, who will make you first-rate ones. They'll cost you almost nothing and you can sell them wholesale to the Porteño kinsmen of those who set foot on this sacred land, do you hear me? Sacred! If the business is a success, you could enlarge it and also engage in contraband traffic with the Disunited Provinces. The sales tax, the fructuary, usuary, and tributary contributions, the anata, demora, and gabelle, the galley and anchorage fees, plus the export tariff would not add up to more than 50% on each unit shipped off. The coffins could be transported by tying them together in floats or rafts, which would also save you the dead freight charges, reverend dean. And not only that. The flotillas of coffins, turned into boats, except for the ones already occupied by those who have died with honor on the battlefield, could carry, as duty-free belongings of military personnel, almost any sort of merchandise of the size and weight of a man. I don't know if I am making myself clear, reverend dean, but what I'm saying is what I mean: this latter expedient would permit the funeral director to reimburse himself for the freight charges collected for feretral transport ... What's that? No, Father Grimorio, you didn't hear me rightly. I didn't say *federal*. I said *feretral*. From the Latin feretrum, a coffin. Ah, this blasted habit of mine of inventing or deriving words! Though today, as far as the Disunited Provinces are concerned, *feretral* is a true synonym of *federal*, and not a barbarous neologism designating an imaginary reality. Become still more barbarous, funereal, and unreal through the works and grace of men such as yourself, Reverend Grimorio Funes.

Poor Simón Bolívar died in exile. They buried the conniving dean, his agent and spy in the Plata. They consigned to the worms, those neutral and neuter readers of upright men and downright scoundrels, the old, torn book of his ugly person.

(Written at midnight)

Only old Bonpland miraculously survives. I say *miraculously*, though my intention thereby is not to render any sort of praise to ill-named divine providence, but simply to recognize the secret law of chance. Almost the moment he left Paraguay, Don Amadeo fell into the vortex of anarchy. From vicissitude to vicissitude, from misfortune to misfortune, from disgrace to disgrace he no doubt missed the peaceful years of his retreat in Santa María. I have learned that not long ago, at the time of the bloody battle of Pago Largo between Rivera's troops and Rosas' (my idiotic, ignorant informants are incapable of reporting even the general disposition of the contending forces), Bonpland, along with a few others, escaped by a hair from being beheaded along with the thousand three hundred prisoners who fell into General Echagüe's hands. They tell me that he is again wandering about San Borja, on the shores of the Uruguay River, in Santa Ana de Misiones, or in the Yapeyú. Don Amadeo was always the sort of man to be in several different places at once. A way of having several lives. Some have seen him journeying to the East; others to the West. Someone swears he's seen him in the north; someone else in the south. They appear to be numerous, distant and distinct, but they are all just one man alone. If only my scouts could locate him and the courier bring back the passion-flower bulbs and the fine powder of the magic tisane. But news of him above all. I imagine him as being the same as ever, even amid the din of pounding hoofs, forests of lances, rivers of blood, absorbed in leafing through layer after layer of the Great Book. I see his bright little sky-blue eyes interrogating traces and mementos of past existences. Secret archives: those hiding-places where nature sits by the fire in the depths of its laboratory. Where it waits patiently for millions of years, working on the scale of the minimum. Manufacturing its saps, its sparks, its stones. Strange beings. Presences now past. Presences not yet come. Invisible creatures in transit from age to age. Eh, Don Amadeo! What do you see in those pages? After a long wait, his faint voice. Very little, Grand Seigneur. Much dust in this salmagundi. Whirlwinds of dust. Entire deserts ten times greater than the Sahara, torn up by the roots, occupy the place of the clouds. Galaxies of sand hide the sky, blot out the sun. What a tremendous weight! Thousands and thousands of lancers gallop over the dunes, each one bearing a beheaded man at lance-rest amid the simoon of whinnies. It is necessary to wait for all that to die down, to settle down, to clear up a little, so that a person can go back to reading it again. Lights, I mean fires, do you see fires? Don't your sharp eyes see bonfires glowing? Mais oui, Monsieur Grand Seigneur!§ Fire, yes. I see fires everywhere. Campfires, would you say? Them too, them too, the embers of combat. Ignes fatui zigzagging across the mountains, across the battlefields. They wink on, wink off. But the flame of life is there. Oh, yes! Fixed forever in its one place and in all places. Burning, burning. I sometimes read by the light of that fire. I do not sleep. I seek. I see. I shed light on dark enigmas that can only be read rightly wrong side to. . . . What, the Frenchy's starting to copy Gracián§§ now? Well in that case, Don Amadeo, there's nothing lost. Except that. . . . Wait! Listen, listen carefully to what I'm going to tell you. I'm all ears, Grand Seigneur. Except that this fire, are you listening,

§French for Karaí Guasú.

§§Spanish Golden Age author of *El Criticón,* an allegorical novel contrasting idyllic primitive life and the evils of civilization.

Don Amadeo, except that that fire is probably the fire of hell, isn't that so? I hear Bonpland's fresh laughter again, coming to me from the four points of the compass. Mais non, mon pauvre sire! If there is a hell, as we've fallen into the habit of thinking, it can be nothing other than the eternal absence of fire. That old Frenchy, more candid than Candide, prince of universal optimism, wants to console me, comfort me, revive me. Though he may perhaps be right. He is right reason itself. If there is a hell, it is this absolute nothingness of absolute solitude. Alone. Alone. Alone, in the black, in the white, in the gray, in the indistinct, in the uncreated. The iron hand, dead-still on the point of the dial; that point where beginning and end are joined at last. That old peasant, sitting beneath the eaves of his hut, in Tobatí, is smoking his cigar, completely motionless amid the chalk-white cloud of powder-dust of the earth. His non-life has lasted a hundred years. But he is more alive than I am. He hasn't been born yet. There is nothing he is waiting for, nothing he desires. He is more alive than I. Hey there, Don Amadeo! Hey! It's you now who are allowing me to leave. You're allowing me to leave, freed of the excessive superlove of one's own person, which is our way of mortally hating all men in a single one. If you happen, by any chance, to come across the footprint of the species to which I belong, rub it out. Hide the trail. If you should find this noxious weed in some remote cranny, pull it out by the root. You won't mistake it. It must resemble the root of a little plant in the form of a lizard, toothed back and tail, scales and icy eyes. Animal-plant of a species so cold that it puts fire out merely by touching it. I won't mistake it, my good Sire. I know it very well. It turns up everywhere. One roots it out and it springs up again. Keeps growing and growing. Turns into an immense tree. The gigantic tree of Absolute Power. Somebody comes with an ax. Chops it down. Leaves branches strewn all over. Out of this great leveling there grows another one. This evil species of the Single-Person will not die out until the Multitude-Person arises by its own right to impose the full power of its right on what is twisted and poisonous in the human species. Hey there, Don Amadeo! Are you using my words now? Are you copying me? Or are you my corrector and commentator, coming back once again to interrupt our talk? Hey, Don Amadeo! Hey? He doesn't answer. He's playing deaf and dumb. He's playing dead. Can he too be dead? Hey, Frenchy, answer me! Ah? Il n'y a pas de mais qui tienne!§ I'm getting in my little phrase too. Trying out a bit of my terrible French again. I don't know if that's the right way to write it, but I don't have the dictionary

§There are no buts about it!

at hand any longer. Hey, Frenchy! If you haven't died, if they haven't put your head in a cage yet, speak to me! Ah! Shutting up now, now of all times, when in this sepulchral silence I need to hear a voice, any voice, even though it's nothing more than the croaking of a miserable batracian!

Amadeo Bonpland returned to Paraguay in 1857, aboard *Le Bisson,* a ship of the French fleet, with the intention of collecting plants in Asunción, the capital city that he had had no chance to become acquainted with during his benign ten-year captivity in Misiones, under the rule of *El Supremo.* It was evident that, as much as the collection of natural species, what passionately interested him was finding out what had happened to the mortal remains of the Perpetual Dictator. The monolith that marked the burial site in front of the main altar of Encarnación had disappeared and the tomb had been profaned. All his efforts to turn up any information whatsoever met with an impenetrable watchword of silence, in both official and popular circles.

The following year the celebrated naturalist died in his eighty-fifth year (May 11, 1858). His body was brought to the locality of Restauración (today Paso de los Libres). At his death he was director and founder of the Museum of Natural Sciences in Corrientes, an honorary post awarded him shortly after Rosas was overthrown. The governor ordered his body embalmed so that the entire population of Corrientes might participate in the funeral rites, which by his decree were to be held for seven days. The governor's plan was thwarted, however, by a drunkard who knifed the corpse exposed to the night air in the front courtyard of the house, amid the smoke of the aromatic and medicinal plants in which he was "cured" or mummified, according to the embalm-

ing method indicated by Bonpland himself in his manuscripts. The drunkard's assault was due to his belief that the well-known, beloved physician refused to greet him, something entirely beyond the possibilities of his proverbial affability.

A descendant of *El Supremo*'s, old Macario of Itapé, related the episode to a mediocre scribe, who transcribes it as follows:

"—A few years before the Great War I went to visit the Guasú doctor of Santa Ana to ask him for remedies for my sister Candé, who was suffering from a chilling of the blood. I remembered the previous journey, twenty years before, when they sent me with taitá to seek balm for the Karaí Guasú *(El Supremo).* This time I had no luck. Useless journey. The Frenchy was sick too. That's what I was told. I stayed for three days in front of his house, waiting for him to get better. At night they brought him out onto the veranda in an old high-backed friar's chair. We could see him, still and white and plump, fast asleep in the moonlight. On the last night a drunk kept passing by the sick man, shouting greetings to him. He kept walking back and forth, growing angrier and angrier, and shouting louder and louder:—Good evening, Karaí Bonpland! Ave María Purísima, Karaí Bonpland! . . . Finally he became downright insulting. The guasú doctor, big and white and naked, lost in dreams, paid no attention to him, didn't turn a hair. That was too much for the drunk. He took out his knife, went up onto the veranda, and stabbed him in blind fury till I leapt upon him and took the knife from him. A whole bunch of people came. We later learned that the guasú doctor had died three days before. For me, it was as though he had died a second time, and because I tried to save him this second time at least, I ended up in prison with the criminal drunk, who got out safe and sound in three days. But they kept me in jail for three months on bread and water, because the police thought I was the drunkard's accomplice. It's plain to see you can't do anybody a good turn in this world. Not even dead people. The living come along and beat the daylights out of you for just about anything. Especially if you're poor. They accuse you of having killed a dead man, of having wiped your ass with a bird, of being alive. Anything. Just to nail you for something. The drunkard, who was some sort of relation of the governor's, didn't need to explain anything. But the more I explained, the less they believed me and the harder they laid into me. Finally they forgot all about me. Not even water or hardtack. I roasted mosquitoes in the fire of my cigar butt, and had at least them to eat. But there was even less to them than there was to me. I managed to escape only after I was nothing but skin and bones. Thinner than a grapevine. I gave one last puff on the butt and mingled with the smoke. Once I managed to slip through a crack in the adobe wall, I took off and never stopped once till I was home." *(Compiler's Note.)*

(Logbook)

The sun's rays beat down on the two-master. It is being rowed down the river at low water. Not a breath of a breeze. The fore-and-aft sail hangs limply from the gaff. At certain hours, gusts of hot air swell it, sending it upstream. The two-master moves backward in little leaps and bounds. The twenty rowers redouble their efforts to move it forward. Guttural cries. Eyes with the whites turned up. Black bodies oiled with sweat, leaning on their takuara boat poles. The sun riveted at the zenith. If the days and the nights pass, they do so behind Joshua's shield,§ without our having any way of knowing whether we are in the dazzling darkness of noon or in the searching shadow of midnight. For the moment, the sun is male. The female moon unbuttons her phases. She shows her full, round self, naked, the barefaced bawd. The Indian and mulatto rowers contemplate her, their whole bodies groaning, taut and slack in the arc of desire as they rhythmically row beneath the waxing and waning. They alone see her change form. They see her lie in her old swaybacked hammock. Man too will rock back and forth there one day, cohabiting with this animal the color of flowers. Soft, solitary animal the color of honey. Chameleoness of the night. Barren sow swelling up till the navel of her round pregnancy shows or, turning over on her side, nothing but the new-moon curve of her hip. Most fertile sterility. That makes seeds sprout. Tides ebb and flow. The blood of women. The thought of men. For all I care, you can go to the devil, satellite-woman. You've devoured even my teeth now, turning them to dust.

We are passing through a great patch of victoria-regias. Extending for more than a league. The entire stream covered with sieves of giant water lilies. The round black silk buds suck up the light and give off a vapor that smells of funeral wreaths. The water reeks of the slime of sunbaked shoals. Foul fumes of tarry viscosity. Stench of shallows where

§In the constellation of Orion.

the fermented mire boils. Carrion of dead fish. Islands of festering water weeds. The fetor of the tawny dirtfilled water drifts out to meet us. Implacably pursues us.

The two-master is loaded with hides in vats of brine. Bales of maté. Barrels of tallow, wax, grease. Every so often the heat causes them to explode and the contents flow into the bilge. Flames flare up. The goatish captain leaps all about, smothering them with his poncho. Bundles of spices. Medicinal plants. Fierce odors. Farther within the stench, another. The unbearable stench that travels with us. Incalculable cubic yards, tons of cylindrical pestilence towering a hundred times higher than the mainmast. Coming up not from the hold of the two-master but from the cellar of our souls. Like the bad smell of Sunday Mass.* Something that cannot come from anything healthy or earthly. Blasphemous stench. Negotiium perambulans in tenebris.§ A stench such as came to me only once, when I found myself standing immediately next to a moribund object: that old man who for more than seventy years had been regarded as a human being. And one other time that rank smell had attacked me, in the Archive of Genealogies of the Province as I was endeavoring to track down the facts of my origin. Naturally, I failed to find them there. They were nowhere to be found. Except for that terrible smell of a bastard lineage. I presented myself before the bar of justice, requesting a full and complete certification of blood lines and good conduct. My origin? You will know it as a fetor, someone murmured in my ear. You can tell the cality by the smell, nanny Encarnación used to say. The hotter a man's blood is in life, the worse it smells after he's dead. Did that stench constitute my entire agnatic ancestry? Seven false witnesses, echoing the false tenor of the questions, testifying under a false oath, falsely swear: that they hold my lineage to be noble and of pure and distinguished blood from generation unto generation, so known and recognized by the witness generally without voices to the contrary. Dreadful dialect! There were many contrary voices, including my own. Haven't they said that Doña María Josefa de Velasco y de Yegros y Ledesma, the great patrician lady with the little slate, is not my mother? Haven't they said that the Lusitanian-Cariocan scoundrel arrived from

---

*People were buried beneath the floor and all round the churches; the heat of the perpetual Paraguayan summer, made worse by that of the crowds of the faithful, brought up from the cracks in the floor the foul odor that gave rise to the expression still current in popular speech, even though its origin has been forgotten: "more evil-smelling than Mass-on-Sunday." *(Compiler's Note.)*

---

§Business being done in the dark.

Brazil with his concubine in tow only to repudiate her later and enter into a marriage of convenience? Having married in accordance with the command of Holy Mother Church, he then continued, beneath her protection, to twist the black tobacco of his black soul. Nonetheless, the full and complete certification of genealogy and good conduct was approved with no objection by prosecutors and judges. They mistook mongrels for greyhounds. My genealogical tree is growing sideways in the chapter hall. Although I have no father or mother, and haven't even been born yet, I have been had and procreated legitimately, according to the perjuries of notaries. Stink of an obscure heredity falsified on the coat-of-arms of my non-house: a black cat suckling a white rat on gray quarters in the gules abysses of the nine partitions, parturitions, and disparitions.

The unpublished correspondence between Dr. Ventura and Brother Mariano Ignacio Bel-Asshole, concerning the *Proclamation* of the latter, alludes to the genealogical mystery:

"Another observation of your critics, Rev. Father, has to do with the disputed Genealogy of the Tirant.

"They maintain that in order for you to attract the interest of our Countrymen, it matters little whether or not the Dictator is the son of a forainer, since in our provinces and Localities, due to the natives' backwardness and ignorance, the most capable leaders are always or almost always sons of forainers.

"Likewise they adduce that little importance should be attached to attempts to cast a blot on his lineage by way of the two mothers that are attributed to him; one of Patrician origin; the other, plebeian and forain; the same is true of the tittle-tattle going the rounds concerning the dates of his double birth.

"In point of fact, as you doubtless know better than I, inasmuch as you are a Relative, the story generally accepted regards the Dictator as the son of Doña María Josefa Fabiana Velasco y de Legros y Ledesma, your cousin, begotten in the strange marriage of this patrician lady with the plebeian Portuguese parvenu José Engracia, or Graciano, or García Rodrigues, hailing according to some people from the district of Mariana in the Viceroyalty of Janeiro, as the immigrant from Rio himself swore before Governor Lázaro de Ribera.

"Before Alós and Brú he swears that he is Portuguese, a native of Oporto, in the kingdoms of Portugal. In several of his repeated and well-nigh obsessive requests for complete inquiries, the Dictator states that his father was French. A number of his relations assert, on the other hand, that he was a Spaniard from the Sierras de Francia, a region situated between Salamanca, Cáceres, and Portugal.

"The elements cleverly used by the Portuguese-Brazilian to compound the confusion and thereby conceal the bastard origins of his adventurous life are the letters of his suppositious names: the Portuguese suffix *es* changed to the Castilian *ez*, as it appears in certain documents; the maternal name (the ç of França, with a little cedilla underneath), very well known among Paulista bandeirantes, has also been Castilianized.

"The one thing that is certain is that, after sixty years of living in Paraguay and engaging in the most diverse occupations, from that of hired hand engaged in the manufacture of twists of chewing tobacco, to that of soldier and later on councilman and administrator of Temporalities in Indian Settlements, no one knows who he is nor where he came from.

"He is a forainer, a Governor will say of him, though we still do not know whether he is French or Portuguese, Spanish or descended from the moon. That he is a lunatic no one can doubt, judging from the stigmata of notable degeneration in his line of descent.

"An enigma that is especially painful to our Patrician stock is the union of Doña María Josefa Fabiana with the Lusitanian-Cariocan adventurer; something that has no plausible explanation, save for the scabrous little tale about it that is making the rounds, which I presume is also known to Yr. Mercy.

"One of the versions, as I have already said, has it that he is the son of Doña Josefa Fabiana, born on January 6, 1766; another, that the Dictator was born on that day and month, but in 1756, that is to say ten years earlier, of the union between José Engracia, or Graciano, or García Rodríguez, and the mistress or concubine that this individual apparently had brought with him when he came to Paraguay as a member of the group of Portuguese-Brazilians hired in 1750 by Governor Jaime Sanjust, at the request of the Jesuits, to exploit tobacco.

"Both of these knotty problems have been lost sight of in the nebula of more or less apocryphal testimony and documents; for, as you know, nothing is certain regarding these facts appertaining to the origin and genealogy that the Dictator has done his best to keep hidden until his ascent to Absolute Power.

"But that is a horse of a different color."

Am I the hook of the binnacle of the pestilential compass? Gripping the rudder bar, the pilot looks at me out of the corner of his eye and every so often corrects the heading as he negotiates the sinuous canal lying between treacherous sand banks. The compact mass of the stench, heavier than the cargo, causes the two-master to sink below its waterline. Welcome, fierce wild odor, if you come alone! My companion, my comrade. Useless to gather together the thoughts put to flight by the evil furies of life. I linger over one memorable invocation: In the name of the Living One who does not die and shall not die. In the name of Him to whom there belong glory and permanence. The words are not his. The words are not anyone's. The thoughts belong to everyone and to no one. As do this river and the animals: they know nothing of death, memories. Deserters of the past, of the future, they have no age. This water that is flowing by is eternal because it is fleeting. I see it, touch it, precisely because it is passing and at the same instant recomposing itself. Life and death form the pulse of its matter, which is not merely a figure. Whereas I . . . what can I say of myself? I am less than the water that flows past. Less than the animal that lives and does not know that it lives. At this moment that I am writing I can say: an infinite duration has preceded my birth. I have always been I; that is to say, all those who said I during this time, were none other than I-HE, together. But what's the use of adding to the collection of foolishness that has already been endlessly repeated by an endless number of copycat com-pilers? In that moment, in this moment in which I am floating along sitting on top of the solid stink, I am not thinking of such rubbish. I am a youngster fourteen years old. At times I read. At times I write, hidden in the prow amid the bales of maté and the reeking hides. Heedlessness. Diversion. I am still within nature. At times I let my hand fall in the overheated water.

It's going on twenty days now that we've been on this journey. The man who says he's my father, devoting his efforts at present to commercial dealings, is captaining his boat. Standing between barrels as between the embrasures of a fort. He is making for a precise port, Santa Fe, where a watertight state monopoly on tobacco holds sway, along with other leonine tariffs levied on Paraguayan products.

My presumptive father has decided to send me to the University of Córdoba. He wants me to become a priest. He wants me to become a rogue. He wants to free himself of my bothersome presence. But he also wants to make of me his future crook and crutch, his rod and staff, once my scion's hide has been ecclesiastically tanned. For the moment he has loaded me into the two-master, amid the skins and the spices, the tallow and the maize. I, the most insignificant, the most worthless of his goods.

Someone, mayhap the patrician lady who is taken to be his wife, who is taken to be my mother, has predicted: One day this obscure child will be heard condemning the name of his father on the brow of Sentinel Hill! The patrician lady was a mute. Some sort of throat trouble caused her to lose the power of speech. At least I never heard issue from her lips a human voice, any sound or murmur that resembled one. Hence she must have written the prediction on the little tablets she used in order to communicate. As she slept one afternoon, I hid the slate and the sticks of chalk. I beat them to dust with a hammer. I buried them in a vacant lot. They provided her with new little tablets and pieces of chalk. She wrote once again in a firmer hand: One day this obscure child will be heard condemning his father and mother! After writing this, the mute woman broke the slate tablet and began to weep, ceaselessly, for seven days in a row. They had to change her sheets, her pillows, her soaking wet mattresses again and again. Nobody knew what it meant. Probably some family relation, Colonel Espínola y Peña perhaps (who was also rumored to be my real father), or perhaps that rascal of a Bel-Asshole, or who knows who read the sibylline phrase in some book. The nanny repeated it in her songs. She sewed it inside the lining of my destiny.

I have never loved anyone. I would remember it. Some trace of it would have remained in my memory. But only in dreams, and then they were animals. Dream-animals, from the beyond. Human figures of an indescribable perfection. Above all that creature that summed them all up. Woman-vision. Female-star. Wandering-comet. Otherworldly being with blue eyes. Dazzling whiteness. Very long golden hair, emerging from amid the clouds of vapor on the horizon, sweeping, covering at a fantastic speed the entire arc of the equinoctial hemisphere.

I did not love Clara Petrona Zavala y Delgadillo. At least not in the form of normal love, which is not granted to an abnormal being such as I am. Don't you understand that the impossible doesn't happen in a normal world?, I tell myself over and over. Especially to a spirit such as mine throughout my life. Always on the alert against myself; always mistrustful, even of what is most trustworthy.

Those blinding paroxysms of rage. Sudden acts of violence. Why those insane fits of temper? That wrath, that fierce exaltation suddenly rising within me with the fury of a devastating wind. With no more cause or reason than their own unreason. Those terrible eruptions that made my life a hell. So long a dying after the fatigue of having been born twice. Once was already too much. So weary in the end!

In a certain sense it may have been regrettable. Not to have found, to have deserved a good wife to help me be a calm man. A spouse. Resigned to being simply that.

Perhaps I would be sitting in the sun smoking my cigar, patting the bottoms of third generations or fourth. Swirling in my brain, on the tip of my tongue, the aftertaste of what is going to be served at dinner, amid the good smells coming from the kitchen, the clatter of dishes. Esteemed, respected by all. Slippered ease, rather than dragging worn-out shoes over the same old or new paths. Being. Staying. Enduring. To a spirit such as I have always had, journeying, constant contretemps, hectic rushing back and forth have never been enjoyable.

Ah, had it not been for that horrible sense of malaise I have always had, I would have spent my life shut up in a great empty room, full of echoes. Not in this sewer hole. With nothing to do but listen to the long-kept silence. A great grandfather clock. Listening, growing drowsy. Not the sounds of a sick mind clattering along. My eyes following the pendulum swinging back and forth from black to white. Seeing the lead weights drooping, lower and lower, until I get up from my chair. I pull the weights back up once a week.

According to the Latin proverb *Stercus cuique suum bene olet,* everyone finds the smell of his own dung pleasing; but would my good wife, however patient, have put up with the miseries of a conjugal life? If it had fallen to her lot, let us suppose, to marry that man of whom the bishop of Hippo speaks, forced by the gases in his belly to fart incessantly for more than forty years till he descended to the grave, on the wings of those winds in his insides, in a manner of speaking?

Let us assume, however, the best of cases. Let us imagine the optimistic variant proposed by Vives, the commentator of the saint, by way of another example of his era; that of the man who was able to work his will upon his asshole, the most rebellious, the most tumultuary of our organs. It had become so obedient to his will that he could make it expel its gases in the form of musical tunes, varying its repertory every so often, so that many people visited him, hoping to be favored with one of these odoriferous concerts. Vives reports that the virtuoso was sometimes so inspired in the solitary retreat of his chamber that the quality of his executions bordered on that of the best bagpipers, the most renowned flageoletists of the country. These are exceptions. But let us think for a moment of the poor wife of the man with the musical behind. Would she have been able to bear hearing those clarinet solos for more than forty years, without a single moment's respite, without going out of her mind?

But not only the gases. Rheumatism too, the stone, the countless disorders of age, of health. These inevitable aches and pains, these extravasations, deflexions, exudations are not the only ones that cause the conjugal union to mildew, deteriorate, crack apart. One must also bargain for the worst ailment of all: the solitude of two who live in each other's company. Having to see each other, rub shoulders, put up with each other, willingly or unwillingly, one day, every day with no end to it save death itself. To watch each other every minute. Endure the other's caprices, manias, whims.

The bitter tyranny of not being able to face a thought different from one's own. The one remedy then is never to see each other at meals. To flee from the other. Never speak. Especially when the other belongs to that fanatical breed that persuades itself that it is rendering proper worship to its own self-nature by denaturing itself; that becomes enamored of its own contempt; that betters itself by becoming worse. Monstrous animal, the one horrified by itself, whose very pleasures are a heavy burden! Under such conditions the company of a dog is more human than that of a peculiar husband, than that of a hysterical wife. *Nostri nosmet poenitet.* We are our own penance, as Terence rightly said.

There are certain people who hide their lives.

No, I did not love any woman, unless it was that woman-comet.

I could not have loved Clara Petrona Zavala y Delgadillo. If for an instant she occupied the place of my celestial Dulcinea, it was for only an instant.

In any event her mother, Doña Josefa Fabiana, formed a single person with Clara Petrona. The daughter, the crepuscular shadow of that woman, to whom I, not the Porteños, gave the name of Star of the North. But that name really corresponds to a star of my secret cosmos that I myself do not know.

The heart expands in every direction when it loves. The one who falls in love because of a person's beauty: is it that person who is the beloved? No, because the smallpox that kills beauty without killing the person would cause the lover to cease to love. One does not love persons. It is their qualities one loves. Clara Petrona's, though well-nigh insurpassable, were inferior to her mother's; her mother's in turn were not the equal of those of the Star of the North, my celestial deity.

As a child I called her Leontina. Perhaps because of the luminous sounds I felt light up within me on uttering that name stolen from the nanny's confidences. It was in that name that the story of the fair-haired child took shape. Her name. That name in which the lights of a Catherine-wheel blended. Force. Fragility. Sound without sex, audible to me only in supreme femininity.

Ah, Star of the North! An overflowing heart followed you everywhere. Above all at night. Dog-adventure. Lion-adventure. Was I hoping to find her in the unhoped-for? As you follow the path, the nanny warned me, don't get yourself into a hole.

I closed my eyes in the dark. I murmured the name. I saw her gleam beneath my eyelids. In those days she was a child too. Even then I sensed that I could love only her. Her fair hair fell to below her waist, above her aó-poí tunic, belted at the waist with an esparto sash. Her comet-hair did not yet light up the black holes of the Southern Cross, amid the three Canopuses that Amerigo Vespucci speaks of in his Relation of his Third Voyage. But the first description of the black spaces, of the Coalsacks, I found much later in the *De Rebus Oceanisis* of Peter Martyr of Anghiera.

In bygone days I would lie on my back in the grass, searching for the Star of the North, amid the constellations of the She-Bears. Following along behind me came my nurse, covered with sores, holding Heraclitus by the hand. They used to make fun of me. You'll find her in the hole, the hoarse voice of the one said mockingly. Woman comes forth from the humid, the other one said. Look for her in the law of the seasons; there where the number seven enters into conjunction with the moon.

The heart confuses loves. Everything fits together inside that round universe. Tiny brain that pulses as though it were thinking.

Many other loves in my life took the form of the Star-of-the-North. But they did so only for an instant. Only she remained changeless in my heart, in the pupils of my child's eyes, in the inconstancies of my manhood, in this sad second childhood of old age.

Try to close your eyes again. Do you see her shine beneath your eyelids? No; the darkness is inside now, outside, everywhere. The black smudges of the Southern Cross cover the empty expanses of the sky. Dead light of constellations, turned to coal, two bulging bags full of it beneath your eyes. The soft, flickering glow of the nubeculae turned into gummy sleep in your eyes.

Won't you ever stop talking about yourself? Who is it you're trying to stage this scene for now? You are trying not to confuse the black holes of the Southern Cross with the luminous clouds of Magellan. You are speaking of those beings whose pole is the night. You are searching the boreal sky. I am searching for my Star-of-the-North amid the Coalsacks of the Cross.

In those days I removed myself only halfway from nature. I shut myself up with her in an attic. Rejected by human beings and even by animals, I gave myself over to books. Not to books on paper; to books of stone, plants, desiccated insects. Above all, the famous stones of the

Guayrá.* Very crystalline stones. I must take them out of my memory now, where they lie buried hundreds of ells deep. The crystalline stones are formed inside hollow balls of flint. Closely packed together, like the seeds of a pomegranate. They are of different colors, and so diaphanous and lustrous that at first they were taken to be very fine gems. But the first finders were wrong. They are much more precious than rubies, emeralds, amethysts, topazes, even diamonds. Of incalculable value. The most beautiful are found in the Serrezuela de Maldonado. I know, I am the only one who knows how the sap penetrates the outer crust of these stone coconuts, forming the crystals inside. They grow inside. When there is no more empty space and they become very compressed, the coconut bursts with as deafening a roar as a bomb or a cannon shot. The pieces are scattered all over a large area or imbed themselves inside others, forming single composite, conjoined stones. In the very bottom of the last one, in the innermost nucleus, the gleaming walls and towers of miniature cities, no bigger than a pinhead, can sometimes be seen. As visible as though they were on the top of a mountain. Some of these pieces bury themselves very deeply and burst again, producing tremors and rumbles in the hills and highlands. And in the lakes and rivers as well when the weather turns bad. . . . I brought these stones to the garret under the roofbeams, turned into a secret alchemical laboratory, nursing the chimerical illusion of fabricating with their essence the stone of stones: The Stone.

From this daydream that they did not suffice to protect, ah lovely, traitorous stones, I was wrenched by my presumptive father, whose mind was made up: I was to be sent off to the Gothic Pagoda. Before he goes crazier than his brother Pedro fooling around the livelong day with mulatta and Indian girls, he decreed. Off you go, dotorsinho da merda!§

And so here we are drifting downstream. Overwhelmed by the fetid pyramid-column of the stench. I am writing in the notebook on my knees. I address myself to the river at low water; that way perhaps it will listen to me: You know that I am going against my will. Can someone who as yet has no *being* be taken against his will? You, whose flow is unending, whose birthings are ceaseless; you who have no age; you who are pregnant

---

*This passage is composed of fragments taken from Azara (*Description*, p. 31), from Ruy Díaz de Guzmán (*Argentina*, LIII, c. XVI), and in particular from the Decree of the Marqués de Montes Claros, Governor and Captain-General of Peru, Tierra Firme, and Chile, "that the Stones of the Guayrá be sent, under heavy escort, to the Royal Treasury of Potosí," April 1, 1613. Cod. Viriato Díaz-Pérez. (*Compiler's Note.*)

---

§You little shithead scholar!

with the conscience of the earth; you who have given your humor to a race for millennia, can you help me to relieve my multiple souls still in embryo, to find my double body submerged in your waters? If you can do so—and you can—give me a sign, a signal, an indication, no matter how small and imperceptible. Don't be like the miserly spirits of Sentinel Hill. Some time back, I left a message beneath a rock for them, asking them about the Star of the North. I found the paper wadded up into a little ball, stained with a substance that was not exactly spiritual. Ah! Aha!, the river cleared its throat on a broad beach: The Takumbú is a very old hill. In its dotage. Driveling. It knows very little. It suffers from stone and from the cavernous flux that the Serpent cult left in its bowels. Why do you think they put prisoners sentenced to forced labor for political crimes there? The Great Tutelary Toad has ordered them to quarry stones from it for the streets of this accursed city. Asunción will be paved with bad thoughts . . . The wailing of the rowers interrupted it. The two-master heeled over for an instant above the edge of a sand bank. Several takuaras bent double and broke in two as they pushed. The two-master barely skirted the reef. I took advantage of the confusion. I placed the sheet of paper in a bottle, and dropped it overboard amid the water hyacinths.

My putative father spent the whole night telling of his life and labors in Paraguay, from the time of his arrival in the Brazilian caravan to exploit black tobacco. Rising in the world. Adventures. Blustering and bragging. He told of joining the royal militias. Manufacturing gunpowder. Repairing harquebuses. Inspecting the forts, presidios, and ramparts of the Province, from top to bottom. Founding the fort of San Carlos. Commanding those of Remolinos and Borbón. Erecting new forts and bastions. Collaborating with Félix de Azara and Francisco de Aguirre in the demarcation of the boundaries between the Spanish and Lusitanian empires. Speaking endlessly of his services to the crown. Monotonous lip intonation, without a thought for what he is saying. Don Engracia repeats the old story a thousand times and then one more. For the moment he is interested only in distracting the rowers as they take turns at the oars. Those taking a rest fall asleep, lulled by the murmur of the capric voice.

At times the tutorial voice fades amid the muffled sound of the oars, the slap of the water against the sides of the boat, the crackle of the bales, the explosion of a barrel of tallow. So that in their own way these interruptions tell other stories. These too no one listens to for their sense, only their sound. Except for me. I listen to them for both things, and hear both.

(The tutorial voice)

In 1774 I was promoted to captain. Twenty years of hard labor. Total fidelity to our Sovereign. Three years later I performed the most important service of my career for the Crown. I was commissioned to investigate in secret the situation in which the vassals of the Most Faithful King found themselves along the banks of the Igatimí River, where they had a fort of the same name. Following rugged trails invaded by infidels, the savage Mbayá Indians, stirred up by the bandeiros, I entered deep into enemy territory with only a deserter of the aforementioned nation as a guide. At enormous risk, and on two occasions, I infiltrated, in the silence da noite, the previously mentioned bastion occupied in those days by the Portuguese-Brazilians through cunning and treachery. I observed its fortifications and situation with the utmost accuracy. I made a detailed plan of everything, in plane view and otherwise, which, as Governor Pinedo himself said afterward, was very useful and favorável§ when we passed to the attack and took the aforesaid fort.

We lay siege to it for three nights and three days, in the dead of winter. Shivering with the cold, we animals and men slipped and fell on the thick layers of ice. They broke beneath our weight, plunging us into the deep trenches and ditches of the defenses, as heavy discharges from the besieged and Indian arrows rained down upon us.

The artillery pieces bogged down on this field of yelo§§ that lighted the darkness. Three times the cavalry scattered. Naked, without food, we men turned to veritable icicles.

Our jefesinho, Officer Dn. Joseph Antonio Yegros, father of the present Captain Don Fulgencio Yegros, a half-relation of mine, gave the order to simulate a retreat. Intentarem un último ataque en la madrugada. Isso era querer enganar ao macaco com banana pintada. Encender vela sem pabilo.§§§

Sitting on the hides, leaning against the mainmast, amid the stench made worse now by the putrefaction of the corpses of Igatimí, the narrator fell silent for a moment. The red navigation lantern placed on his knees hollowed out his he-goat features, half man, half beast. Entirely absorbed

---

§*Favorável:* advantageous (Portuguese).
§§Combination of Portuguese *gêlo* and Spanish *hielo.*
§§§So as to stage a last attack at dawn. This was to try to fool a parrot with a painted banana. To light a candle without a wick.

in his memories, he is present here only in the bone. Antihuman soul wandering through great regions of yelo, of wind, where thousands of arrows hum, where reports of cannons, of rifles resound. Savage cries in Portuguese, in native dialects. Infernal uproar. Hellish din.

It is glaringly obvious that the tutorial voice is no longer taking any notice of the rowers, the pilot, the boatswain, the mulatto ferrymen, the Indian oarsmen. Less still, surely, of me. He never thought of me as anything but a ridiculous, monstrous creature. I did not exist for my putative father save as an object of his hatred, of his angry shouts, of his punishments. The Portuguese lets fly with slaps so hard they could shatter a lion's jaws. The wind from the fillip he gave me when he caught me with the skull that afternoon is still whirling round and round beneath my scalp. Another one, in the night, because I took my time about obeying his order to throw the skull in the river. But that night the force of my fist too makes itself felt with the swiftness of lightning. The talon-hand lands its blow on the tutorial master. Clutches his neck. Closes around it. Does not let go until tears of rage and impotence well up in his deathly-dull eyes. Can two deserts weep? I rivet my eyes on his, and now the deserts number four. The Portuguese finally gives up. With his next-to-last rasping breath: Let go, rapaisinho.§ Come on, let go, I'm strangling to death! Throw the skull in the river and let that be the end of it! I slowly took my hand away from his Adam's apple. The cainine fingers were still tightly clenched. I had to submerge them all night long in the stinking water, which little by little loosened them until it brought them back to their natural state.

(The tutorial voice)

. . . I did not die that night in the ditch, naked, shivering from the cold, a short distance away from the enemy palisades. With a superhuman effort I dragged myself through the brush stiff with frost, over to two corpses still just barely warm. I covered myself with them like a quilt. I huddled up close to one of them, holding on to him by the arrow stuck in his back. I glued my mouth to the corpse's in search of any remaining heat that he still might have within him. Pardon me!, I murmured amid the bloody froth, already frozen as hard as the hairs of his mustache. Ayúdame, miliciano morto! No me dexes morir si voçé ya está morto!§§ The cadaver said nothing, as though giving me to understand: Go to it,

§Bastardized form of Portuguese *rapazinho:* child, "kid."
§§Help me, dead militiaman! Don't let me die if you're already dead!

cumpai. Whatever I have left I have very little need of. From the tone of voice I recognized my cumpai Brígido Barroso in the dark. The most stingy skinflint in all of Tierra Firma since time everlasting. It surprised me a little that he'd suddenly turned so generous. I tucked his body in snugly all around me. If you're already in the Infernos, tell me what it's like there, cumpai Barroso, and si es verdade que estaís en el País do Fogo,§ give me a little bit of that fire, even if it's just one little coal. But Barroso's mouth gradually froze over, haggling, splitting hairs, quibbling over what wasn't his even after he was dead. . . .

A cry escaped me that resounded in the night. The Capricorn rose. He was about to leap upon me. I raised my short-barreled carbine and pointed it at him. He stopped in his tracks. He heaped insults on my head in his barbarous bandeirante dialect. The two-master luffed and went aground in the tuff of the riverbank. My word, what's the matter, Excellency! I just heard you give a terrible shout! Nothing, Patiño. Perhaps I was dreaming I was going down the river. I had my hand in the water. Perhaps a piranha bit me. Nothing serious. Off with you. Don't bother me when I'm writing by myself. Don't come in when I don't call you. But . . . Excellency! Your fingers are dripping blood! I'm going to summon the doctor immediately! Never mind. They won't bleed much. It's not worth bothering that old fool for such an old wound. Out with you.

In this part of the notebook, the handwriting in fact appears somewhat scrawled, covered with a reddish scum where the bookworms have feasted, leaving large holes.

When we awoke, the two-master was beached at a bend in the river that resembled a funnel of tall cliffs. Everyone was sleeping like the dead. The skipper, the crew sprawled out on the cargo, deader than the corpses of Igatimí. The sun leapt out from the other shore and settled down in its appointed place. Nailed to the noonday sky. The stench grew stronger. You will recognize it as a fetor, the Voice at my back said. At this moment I saw the jaguar, crouching in the brush of the cliff. I could foresee what was going to happen. In the shadow of the sails, raised as improvised awnings, the crew was still asleep in the suffocating heat of late afternoon. I attuned my will to that of the wild beast already tensed for the eight-

§If it's true you're in the Land of Fire. (País do Fogo = Hell.)

meter leap downward. A thousandth of a second before the roaring, spotted meteor hurtled down upon the two-master, I plunged into the water. I fell onto an island of floating plants. From there, drifting gently, I saw the jaguar rip Don Engracia to pieces with its talons as he tried to get to his feet to confront the beast with his rifle. The weapon described a parabolic curve and landed in my hands. I aimed carefully, ceremoniously, unhurriedly. I held back for a moment to delight in the spectacle of the two-master turned into a sacrificial altar. I pressed the trigger. The powder flash outlined the figure of the jaguar in a ring of smoke and sulfur. Roars of pain made the waters tremble, the floating islands shiver, the shores of the river resound. The bloody head of the jaguar turned round, panting. Furious. Its eyes riveted on mine. A gaze untold ages old. Trying to transmit some message to me. I slowly aimed once again at the yellow pupil. The shot extinguished its burning gleam. I closed my eyes and felt I was being born. Rocked in the basket of the giant water lily, I felt I was being born of the muddy water, of the stinking mire. I emerged into the stench of the world. I awoke to the fetor of the universe. Bud of black silk floating on the crown-raft, armed with a smoking rifle, emerging at the dawn of a different time. Was I being born? I was being born. The true place lost forever, my first cries of a newborn babe wailed. Will I ever find it? You will find it, yes, in the very same place where it was lost, said the river's rasping voice. A bottle was floating at my side. On the other side a dense shadow reigned. I lifted it. I saw the funnel of the wooded cliff burning in the zenithal brightness. I tilted the bottle up. I drank my own questions down in one swallow. Devil's-milk. I sucked my own milk, from my frontal sinuses. I slowly rose to my feet, clutching the rifle.

I looked about. I saw the deserted two-master, heeled over on the riverbank, spilling out the foul smell of its cargo. The head of the jaguar threaded on the pike of the gaffsail boom. In the background, amid the dark foliage of the cliff, I saw two files of twinkling lights around what appeared to be a coffin. The boatswain came running down the slope. His silhouette, at once dark and transparent, halted before me, hesitating, not knowing how to begin: Sire . . . Your Worship's father is asking for you! . . . Leave off such nonsense, bosun. In the first place, I don't have a father. In the second, if you're speaking of the one you call my father, aren't they keeping watch over him up there? Yes, Sire. Don Engracia has just died. Well, I've just been born. As you see then, at this moment we have different business at hand. Your esteemed father keeps insisting that Your Worship come up to see him. I've already told you that there are no ties of kinship binding me to that man, living or dead. Moreover, if he insists on seeing me at all costs, let him climb out of that box for a while and come down here to see me. I'm not budging from here for any reason. Sire, Your Worship knows that only people with a limp negotiate downward slopes easily, but the master is already a completely helpless case and couldn't take one step no matter how hard he tried. He wanted to bid Your Worship farewell, be reconciled with you, receive your pardon before he was laid in his grave. My pardon won't protect him from the work the flies will do first, and then the worms. Sire, it's a question of that old man's soul. That crapulous old gaffer doesn't have a soul, and if he does have one it's through sheer carelessness on the part of the dispenser of souls. As far as I'm concerned, he can go to hell.

In Letter *XLVIII,* Guillermo P. Robertson gives the following account of this episode:

"Many years before being a public figure, *El Supremo* quarreled with his father over a trivial matter. They did not see or speak to each other for years. Finally, the father lay on his deathbed, and before giving his great and final account of himself, he was eager to make his peace with his son. He sent word to him to this effect, but his son refused to see him. The old man's illness was aggravated by his son's obduracy; indeed, it horrified him to leave the world without having secured a reconciliation and mutual pardon. He protested that the salvation of his soul was gravely endangered if he died in such a state. Once again, a few hours before breathing his last, he persuaded certain relatives to approach the rebellious son and implore him to receive and give benediction and pardon. The latter remained inflexible in his rancor, and answered in the negative. They told him that his father believed that his soul would not reach heaven if he did not depart at peace with his firstborn. Human nature shudders in horror at the

reply:—Well then, tell the old man he can go to hell.

"The venerable old man died in delirium, calling to his son with heartrending moans that history has preserved."

Basing himself on the works of the Robertsons and on other accounts, Thomas Carlyle describes the scene with less bathos. In the face of the old man's plea for reconciliation, since he cannot resign himself to dying without seeing his son and granting him mutual pardon for fear that he will not be able to enter heaven if this does not come about, Carlyle has *El Supremo* merely say: "Tell him that my many occupations do not permit me to go, and above all, it is pointless."

Further testimony, which cannot be suspected of indulgence or of temporizing on the subject of the rupture, is forthcoming from the correspondence of Brother Bel-Asshole and Doctor Buenaventura Díaz de Ventura. The latter was *El Supremo*'s predecessor in the office of syndic-procurator general, who later settled in Buenos Aires and became an influential figure in Porteño political affairs; Brother Mariano was the author of the fierce libel launched, under the title of *Proclamation of a Paraguayan to His Countrymen,* against the Perpetual Dictator shortly after his being so named. Both could not help but tell lies like truth (though as the indicted party was in the habit of saying, any contemporary reference is suspect).

Reduced to the essential, the counterpoint of the letters runs:

"Following his return from Córdoba he hung up the full habits to which he was entitled as a Cleric of Minor Orders and First Tonsure, and embarked upon a life even more licentious and dissolute than the one he had led in Córdoba. Because of this he broke with his father, at the time Administrator of Temporalities of the Indian Settlement of Jaguarón, and refused to have any further dealings with him.

"Years before the bad son took over the Supreme Government, the old man, being close to death, wished to be reconciled with his firstborn. He sent certain kinsmen to him with the plea that he be at his side in his agony in order to give him his last benediction. The answer was a most resounding and pitiless negative.

"The old man despaired, calling to his son and begging his pardon. In his deathbed delirium, however, he was doubtless the victim of a delusion when he saw his son appear in the room, enveloped in his red cape, and approach his bed.

"The poor man died crying out *Vade retro Satanás,* and cursing him with his last dying breath.

"However, at the time of these sad events, our future Dictator was constantly tormented by the bitterness caused him by the continual allusions to his bastard origin. Through trickery he contrived to come by a false genealogical record. From that time on, in the Cabildo, in all public offices, in the sine-

cures and benefices that were the rungs on the ladder leading to Supreme Power, he will always begin his representations with the sacramental words: I, Councilman of the First Vote, Syndic-Procurator General, native of this City of Asunción, descendant of the earliest hidalgos and conquerors of this Meridional America. He believed that he was thereby safeguarding himself against more contumely arising from his condition as the son of a foreigner, a parvenu, a Paulista mameluco; above all, against what for him was the terribly insulting and degrading word *mulatto,* whose burning brand seared his soul beneath the stigma of his dark skin."

"What cannot be doubted, Rev. Father, is that the break with his father dates from that period of depravity and vices. The versions of various witnesses have passed on this fact with a certain superstitious aversion which has made of it something ambiguous and equivocal. The truth, however, would appear to be that, on having been sternly reproached by the father for his abominable conduct and severely rebuked for other no less vile and filthy acts, the brute, poisoned by his moral vices, cuffed him pitilessly, and in a most cowardly fashion, since he was a man in the prime of life and the other a very old man.

"There are any number of witnesses who maintain that only the intercession of neighbors prevented him from beating him to death. Had this happened, our Dictator's career would have been off to a good start with this act of parricide."

"No, my friend Ventura; do not allow yourself to be carried away by your righteous indignation. That 'superstitious aversion' of witnesses who reported the incident between father and son is not based on an ambiguous or equivocal fact. Let the truth be told, especially between the two of us, even though it behooves us to let sleeping dogs lie for the moment, since it might be counterproductive to spread it too far abroad. I will reveal it to you, but keep it to yourself with the reserve that gives you your reputation for prudence and circumspection.

"The rupture between Don Engracia, at the time Administrator of the Temporalities of Jaguarón, and his irascible son was due to the excesses and orgies to which Don Engracia himself gave himself over from the very beginning, together with his son Pedro, who at the time already evidenced clear signs of madness, in that Indian settlement.

"The abuses of the Captain of Artillery of the King's Militias grew worse and worse once he had become Administrator, if we are to judge from the terrible charges brought against him by the inhabitants of the settlement of Jaguarón in a memorandum presented directly to the viceroy by the cacique Juan Pedro Motatí, the corregidor of the aforementioned settlement."

(Memorandum of the cacique Motatí)

It is not surprising that the Indians suffer such grievous servitude, when the agent who is fanning the flames of their wrath is of an insatiable greed, burdened with offspring and debts, devoid of assets capable of remedying his situation. When he took on the mission of governing Indians he was filled with ambition, crushing them with an intolerable burden of work, stripping them of the few personal goods they had, and contemplating them in a state that merits tears.

"Who could think, sire, that these acts of violence would extend to stealing from us our daughters and wives, committing with them the most horrendous crime of which human evil-mindedness can conceive.

"For all these reasons, we beg Yr. Exc.Y. to deign to send an individual of absolute integrity, such as these dire misfortunes call for, in order that he may confirm in the realm of facts this secret Report which we humbly place before your exalted justification; may the Administrator be declared a criminal offender and be given exemplary punishment, as provided by the laws, in view of the great inhumanity he has manifested by his vile and heinous deeds, removing him meanwhile from the office that he holds. . . ."

"It is probable that the accusations of the cacique Motatí were somewhat exaggerated. The picture he painted of the desolation of his people as a consequence of the presumed extortions, cruelties, and excesses of the administrator may well be a bit overdone.

"Veridical things? Calumnies? Who can say!

"Around the same time, the predecessor of my relative by marriage, whom the latter came to replace, the priest Gaspar Cáceres, an old man already near death, nonetheless still had the strength to level furious accusations against the captain-administrator.

"In his own hand he wrote . . . Pardon me, Father: a dying man writing in his own hand? Well, my friend Buenaventura, it's more than likely that he penned the accusations a little while before, when the whole affair began to get very murky. As Father Cáceres denounced: His violent acts are such that the caciques of the settlement emigrate en masse to the neighboring provinces with their wives and children. The town of Yaguarón has been left with no other inhabitants save oldsters, invalids, and those natives whom the administrator forces, with whip and rifle, to work on his lands, as in the old regime of the yanaconato§ and the encomiendas. The fear and hatred that he inspired in that town were the only works he left behind him, the ex administrator affirmed on his deathbed, in his own hand or else dictating these incendiary remarks to some familiar.

"There is no doubt about it, Brother Mariano: the ailing ex administrator, having been removed from that canonship, was deeply resentful of the energetic spirit of enterprise of the captain-administrator of Temporalidades. The cankerous rancor, the spite of dying men is very often terrible.

"What is certain, my dear doctor and friend, is that several years later, when the captain was again serving in the militias of the Province, the file on the emigration en masse of the natives, headed by their caciques, among them one by the name of Azucapé (Flat-Nose), the most rebellious and willful of them all, had not yet been closed. The Administrator might well have ordered him hanged had he not made his timely escape.

"The cause of the rupture between father and son should be sought in these events. It is evident to me that my nephew's abandonment of his ecclesiastical career and his sudden wallowing in a life of depravity and vice, were posterior to this break; in all likelihood its corollary and consequence.

"Up until that time he led a monkish life, someone who presumes himself to be well informed conjectures. But are austere habits, clothed in the dignity of monk's robes, of any use?, he must often have asked himself. Why make so great a sacrifice for the honor of a name, the target of terrible attacks, when there in Jaguarón his father and brothers Pedro and Juan Ignacio were dragging in the mud not only the name but the tradition of the entire family in vacanals with Indian girls and mulattas?

"He changes radically. Thus, while the oppressed natives abandon their ancestral heritage, the ex Cleric of Minor Orders of Córdoba plunges from dark to dawn into the excesses of an unbridled libertinage.

"He turns into a mad devotee of Venus. He seeks frivolous love affairs, carefree amorous adventures, wanton women. He spends his nights endlessly carousing. He wanders with bands of merrymakers all over the outskirts of the city, giving serenades, taking part in vulgar suburban balls. He is a bright light at these revels because he plays the guitar admirably and is a good singer.

"Above all he loves to gamble. On many occasions dawn finds him dealing a hand of monte bank or truque, in which he loses with the same ease with which he wins the lucrative lawsuits for which he has become famous, having never lost a single one since his admittance into the confraternity of the bar." *(Compiler's Note.)*

Bury him once and for all, as deeply as you can. Then bring the men. We are going to free the two-master from its mudhole and return immedi-

§*Yanaconas:* name given to Indians who became personal servants of Spaniards in the colonial era (cf. note, p. 147). Their condition is referred to as the "yanaconato."

ately to Asunción. The boatswain went off. Fleeting reflection amid the reflections climbing up the ravine. At the top of the cliff, in the white shadow of midday, the glints from the candles shimmer with a beautiful, dazzling, many-colored light. Effects of perspective and refraction, the aerial vigil amid the trees creates an agreeable spectacle whose crowning touch is the six great tapers reaching almost to the clouds.

The sails of the two-master gently swelled and tautened with the north wind that began to blow, and the boat continued on downriver in the dusk. The capric voice began all over again its recital of its labors as captain of the king's militias. The silhouette propped up against the mainmast appeared to be more erect than in the thirty days just past. Its voice clearer. The reddish light of the little navigation lamp afforded a glimpse of a more healthy-looking countenance. The majority of the crew, sitting round about, nodded drowsily as they listened to the lilting voice reeling off the endless story. Only a few Indian rowers helped the wind along with their long takuaras, pushing the two-master along the canal path. In seven days, exactly, we described our precisely designated destination, the port of Santa Fe.

(Perpetual circular)

What is good, what is certain despite everything, is that here the Revolution has not been lost. The country has come out ahead. The people-multitude has risen to occupy its rightful place. The useful animate objects of yesterday are the free peasants of today. They have their plots of land, patacoons in their pockets: patent remedies for all their ills, which have turned to goods. They no longer are obliged to hire themselves out, save to the State, their only employer, watching over them with just laws, equal for everyone. The land belongs to whoever works it, and each one receives what he needs. No more, but no less either.

Of the seven cows and a bull brought by Juan de Salazar when he founded Asunción, there are today no less than ten million on the seventy-four patricial estancias; there are hundreds of collective farms. The entire country has a superabundance of wealth. The need to multiply has not become the need to demultiply. For every excess of goods fatally degenerates into evils, as experience attests. The prosperity of a State does not consist principally in the existence of a very large population so much as in the perfect relation between the people and its means. The day will come when Paraguayans will not be able to take a single step without treading on mountains of ounces of gold. That feline from Rio Grande do Sul, Correia da Cámara, who came here several times trying to swap chimeras with me in the name of the Empire, prophesied as much. Sometimes the prophecies of slick swindlers are truer than the predictions of visionaries who see only fantastic elements produced by the chronic illusion of Utopia. Cross out this rigmarole. Put: We Paraguayans are about to set foot on the oracle paved with ounces of gold predicted by that Portuguese-Brazilian.

Our people, I have always said, will attain its rightful due some fine day; if not, time will see to it that it does. Let the rivers be opened to foreign trade; that is the one thing we lack in order for our riches to flood the globe. When the flag of the Republic is free to sail to the sea, foreigners will be permitted to come trade with us on equal terms.

Only then will the question of the traffic of goods be settled, and more important still, the question of limits between States divided artificially in order to ensure the rule of the Colony. And behind it the sub-colonies and the sub-empires supported by the interests of the oligarchies. They too have enriched themselves, hand over fist, using patriotism as their cloak. Only when the Confederation of American States becomes a palpable reality and not merely the empty words of speeches and treaties will commerce, foreign relations be set in order, as best suits Paraguayans and their needs and interests. Not for the exclusive benefit of aliens, as was the case before the Perpetual Dictatorship.

By its own effort Paraguay has created its foundation as Fatherland, Nation, Republic. The education you receive is national. As are the church, religion. Children learn in the Patrial Catechism that God is not a ghost, nor the saints a tribe of black superstitions with crowns of gilded tin. They sense that if God is something more than a very short word, he is in the earth they tread, in the air they breathe, in the goods earned in collective labor; not in their going about in Indian file begging in the streets, markets, villages, towns, cities, and deserts to see what chance may bring their way. Formed in the bosom of the earth, they think of it as their real mother. They treat their fellow citizens as brothers come forth from the same bosom. Hmmm. Strike out that image of the earth-mother. It's a notion that those whoresons would never be able to get through their thick heads.

I have nationalized everything here for everyone. Trees, plants for dyes, medicinal herbs, precious woods, minerals. I have even nationalized the maté bushes. I except the animals, the birds; they never abandon their native territories. Clouds come from the humidity of the earth, the water of the rivers, the respiration of plants. Clouds return in the form of rain, the dampness of the night dew. They come back to the earth, to the rivers, to the plants. Clouds, birds, animals, even inanimate creatures preach to us their fidelity to the soil. How does all that strike you, Patiño? Sire, your words are bringing tears to my eyes, and through the sweat of the eyes that tears are, I see dimly, but at the same time very clearly, everything that you are saying. Perhaps, Sire, because your words put inside one the truths that are outside . . . *(There follows an irreproducible insult of El Supremo's; the remainder of the folio is scorched.)*

(On a loose leaf)

. . . snail, worm, slug, pebble, flowers, field butterflies. A great love above all for what is fixed, firmly rooted. Innumerable species of plants. Impossible to name them all. I have hunted monkeys, jaguars, foxes, deer, wild hogs. All sorts of predators. Fierce species or very gentle ones. I once hunted a specimen of the animal called a *manticore,* a gigantic red lion, with a human face and three rows of teeth, almost always invisible because the iridescence of its pelt blends with reflection of the light off the sand dunes. It breathes out through its nostrils the terror of lonely places. Its tail bristling with quills, it shoots them in every direction, swifter than arrows. They imbed themselves in the trees. Make drops of blood rain from the leaves. I downed the manticore in the Plinian expanse by shooting it with a narcotic dart. I let it go. When it awoke it returned to its secret dwelling. When I awoke, I found myself spattered with droplets of blood. These species do not emigrate; from the manticore to the white snail filleted with red, I have seen them all return freely to their wild haunts. I have seen birds fly so high, so far that they appeared to be motionless at the point of my keen sight. They vanished. Fell to the other side of the horizon. Moments later they dived down on me from every quarter of the compass. Ravens have done that to me. Also other varieties of volatiles, of aquatiles. But all, all, even the most erratile, return. Living things, like inanimate ones, have a great love of what is fixed, rooted, immutable. If stones had a way of moving about, they would go out for a little jaunt and then return to their places of origin in almost no time. The stone firmly planted by its weight, the plant by its roots. Tenacity of the act of remaining. Thought of staying permanently in the same place. I grieve for each one of those giant trees that I must order cut down so as to exchange them for gunpowder, ammunition, arms. Each blow of the ax falls on my trunk; its keening cry at being uprooted and dying cries out within me. The rafts go floating down the rivers, thousands of logs bound together. Let's go!, I say to them. Don't be idiots! You must fall so that the Fatherland may rise; you must go down the river so that the Fatherland may stay behind and make its way upstream again.

(Perpetual circular)

It is only migratile humans who do not have what is national in their blood. Going away, renouncing their heritage, the matter that gave birth to them, the medium that engendered them: what kind of business is that? Men are worse than vermin!

Those migrants who exiled themselves, renouncing their lares, abandoning their land, I do not call my countrymen, nor do I consider them as such. They turn into parasites of other States. They forswear their mother country and their mother tongue once they are abroad. They sell their words to the highest bidder. As men without a country, without a tongue to call their own, they vilify, defame, perpetrate pernicious fictions against their country. Plotting with the enemy, they hire out as spies, scouts, army clerks, informers. If they return, they do so hand in glove with the invader. They incite him, aid him in his conquests, in the subjugation of their own country. If only every last one of them could at least be traded for a grain of powder!

Had it not been for my Government, they would have emigrated en masse. They were leaving in legions till I fulminated the edict: Either you stay, you migratory vipers, or you'll leave your skin for the ants! Some of them escaped my grasp, the traitor José Tomás Isasi for one, who later sent as payment for his escape a few barrels of unusable yellow gunpowder, thus adding insult to the injury done the Government, the country, by his flight and his felonious larceny.

On the other hand, numerous partisans of union, of the Porteñista cause remained in ambush here. Dead mosquitoes in the daytime. Buzzing culicids at night. Conspiring, prowling about, prying, spying. Sweating dryness. Chewing bitterness. Sucking the juice of their fingernails. Incubating malarial eggs in their pools of drivel. Deprogressing. Spawning the subhuman. Nits of contagion. Infection. Lift up a rotten cabbage head, a grainless ear of corn. Underneath is a grub in the form of a minuscule man. A fistula in the shape of a man. What are you doing here? It doesn't answer. Doesn't speak. Lacks a voice. Disguised absence. Not having been able to escape, they pretend for all they're worth to be little dead creatures far removed from the human. Mouth sewn shut. One ridiculous hair like an antenna in the middle of a naked noggin. Eight false feet. Twelve blind eyes. At first a person thinks: Damn! Might this not be a cotton-louse weevil? The megacephalous Brazilian coleopteron that carries the germ of cattle carbuncle perhaps? Bandeiras of venomous larvae now! I grind it under my heel. It has now dissolved into a long thread of spittle. My shoe sole sticks fast in the poisonous glue. One of the bandeirante coleoptera once climbed up as far as the buckle of my shoe. I removed it with the tip of my cane. It left a trace like that of a corrosive acid on the metal. I had the spot bathed in a solution of extract of nicotine, black soap, phenic acid, and formic acid extracted from fierce Guaykurú ants. All in vain. The threads of rust were still there. Many of them join together, forming a slime. Teem and multiply in the pool of poison as though in their element. Form colonies. Speak a dialect of bandeirante Portuguese or a bastardized migratory Porteño. Once darkness falls, depending on the phase of the moon, they transform themselves into spiderwebs. I have watched them for entire nights at a time. They vanish with the sun's first rays. The threads of slime have left the trail of their filth behind on doors, façades, corridors. A trail of drivel on the perjured paper of the cathedralic pasquinades . . .

Don't copy these last paragraphs into the draft of the circular. No, Sire, I haven't copied them. When Your Grace dictates in circular form, order of the Perpetual Dictator, I write his words down in the Perpetual Circular. When Your Grace thinks out loud, in the voice of the Supreme Man, I note his words down in the Spiral Notebook. If, that is, I am able to, Excellency, what I mean to say is if I manage to net those words that caracole out of your mouth, mounting ever more swiftly upward. And on what do you base the opposition Supreme Dictator/Supreme Man? In what do you note the difference? In the tone, Sire. The tone of your word dictates downward or upward, let us say with your permission, depending on which direction the ergodic wind takes as it gusts forth from your mouth. It is only Your Eminence who knows a way of speaking that speaks volumes. The bird hears the worm wriggling underground. Your Eminence must hear me moving underneath all these papers in the same way. Your Excellency commands me. Directs me. Has taught me to write. Governs my hand. I can also slice you in two, you worm of a scribe! Perfectly true, Excellency. Most certainly. Absolute master of so doing at any moment, at Your Grace's pleasure. In such a case, there will be two of us scribes to serve him. Even if, as you yourself, Sire, so often say, the amanuensis has no responsibility. Although Your Worship is also in the habit of turning the same truth the other way around and saying: Who can be proud of being a miserable scribbler? I always keep this well in mind, Sire. No, Patiño; what you ought to ask yourself at each and every moment is whether it is not the servant who is to blame for everything that goes wrong: from the one who polishes my shoes to the one who copies what I dictate. In any case, let us continue.

The present well-being, the future progress of our country are the things that I wish to protect, to preserve; if such be possible, to promote even further. To this end, now that I judge the circumstances to be more suitable, I am taking measures, making preparations to free Paraguay from onerous servitude. Freeing mercantile traffic of the obstacles, confiscations, barbarous exactions with which the peoples of the Coast hinder the movement of Paraguayan vessels, arbitrarily claiming dominion over the river in order to grease their own palms, to further their depradations, their aim being to maintain this Republic in servile dependence, backwardness, discredit, ruin.

I prevented the successive invasions meant to subject our people to blood and fire. That of Bolívar, from the west, by way of Pilcomayo. That of the Portuguese-Brazilian empire, from the east, via the old depredatory routes of the bandit bandeirantes. From the south, the constant incursions of the Porteños; the most infamous of all the one planned by the infamous Puigrredón, who recognizes our country to be the richest prize in all of America, and wanted to come not only to seize our territory but also to clean out, purely and simply, all the gold in our coffers.

Rough draft in Pueyrredón's hand. Project to pacify Santa Fe, dominate Entre Ríos and Corrientes, and subjugate Paraguay:

It appears that the goal of the Entre Ríos expedition should be Corrientes, because of its situation. Once the troops of this province have been incorporated in the manner that I have mentioned, the army will be composed of at least five thousand men, with more than sufficient weapons. Here, then, is the most magnificent field, and the easiest for gathering the finest fruit of the entire undertaking, subjugating the rebel province of Paraguay. With the mere appearance of a force in such numbers, the entire province will surrender without a single shot being fired. Far from displeasing our people, they will enter that country most willingly, inasmuch as it is the richest prize in all of America today, both with regard to the state coffers where there must be a million or a million and a half pesos, and with regard to the region as a whole, since it has not been burdened with the taxes, levies, and erogations to which the other provinces have been subject. Independently of all the other advantages that would result from annexing this populous province and from putting an end to the anxiety in which the equivocal conduct of its tyrant has plunged us as regards patriotism, the principal benefit of the expedition would lie in its serving as a warning to other peoples by pulling down the keystone of scandal, destroying the hotbed of dissidence that this country has been and continues to be.

So long as due and proper order has not been established in Paraguay, there will be no end to the clamor of the ill-intended and the ignorant who maintain that Paraguayans are the only ones who understand.

(Documents of Pueyrredón, III, 281.)

Two years before, early in 1815, another Porteño sharper, General Alvear, Supreme Dictator of the sharks of the port, endeavors to renew relations with our Republic. On what terms? On those of a cheating, conniving, rag-picking profiteer! He writes to me trying to trick me into believing that if Buenos Aires succumbs, Paraguay will not be able to be free. He tries to intimidate me with the trumped-up story of another European invasion. He offers me, as a consequence, an interchange not of free trade and friendship, but a slaver's deal: twenty-five rifles in exchange for every hundred Paraguayan recruits for his army. I do not know of, nor have I ever read of, such baseness even among the most wicked and cynical rulers of American history.

Still others seek to invade Paraguay. Emigré Paraguayans plead with General Dorrego to do so. Perfidy of migrants. And before and after Dorrego, others. Arrogant capons: Artigas, Ramírez, Facundo Quiroga. Jaguars of the plains, wildcats, roaring, mewing, hissing, sighing to come to sack us. They all ended up buried, banished; one of them in our own land.

Simón Bolívar also seeks to invade us. The Liberator of half a Continent makes ready to attack Paraguay and subjugate the one country in all of America that is free and sovereign! On the pretext of coming to liberate his friend Bonpland he plans an invasion by way of the Bermejo River. Woe to him had he set foot on Paraguayan soil! The red waters of the Bermejo would have lived up to their name. He first writes me an artful letter, concealing amid flowery flattery and duplicity the thorn of a pompous ultimatum.* I didn't even take the trouble to answer it. Let

---

*To the Supreme Dictator of Paraguay

Most esteemed Sir:

From the early days of my youth I had the honor of cultivating the friendship of Monsieur Bonpland and of Baron Humboldt, whose knowledge has done more good in America than all its conquerors.

It is my sentiment at present that Monsieur Bonpland, my adored friend, is being held in Paraguay for reasons which are unknown to me. I suspect that certain false information may have calumniated this virtuous scholar, and that the government that

him come, I tell those who are frightened by the rodomontades of the liberticide liberator. If he contrives to arrive, I will allow him to cross the frontier just so that I can make him my orderly and head groom. In the face of my silence he writes to his spy in Buenos Aires, Dean Grimorio Funes, asking him to pave the way for his entering this country, "to liberate it from the talons of a rebel and restore it to Río de la Plata as a province," Don Simón proposes. The funereal dean's intrigues and plots meet with little success. Why should this gloomy meddleman expect any at all! He

---

Yr. Excy. heads may have been taken by surprise with regard to this gentleman.

Two circumstances impel me to earnestly beseech Yr. Excy. to grant Monsieur Bonpland his freedom. The first is that I am the cause of his arrival in America, since it was I who invited him to come to Colombia; he had already decided to make the journey when the war situation made it imperative for him to go instead to Buenos Aires; the second is that this savant can bring enlightenment to my country with his knowledge, provided that Yr. Excy. will be good enough to allow him to come to Colombia, whose government I head through the will of the people.

Yr. Excy. doubtless will not recognize my name or know of the services I have rendered to the American cause; but were I allowed to place all my personal merit in the balance in order to obtain the freedom of Monsieur Bonpland, I would be so bold as to address such a plea to Yr. Excy.

May Yr. Excy. deign to hear the outcry of four million Americans freed by the army under my command, all of whom join me in imploring Yr. Excy.'s clemency, humanity, wisdom, and justice, as a tribute to Monsieur Bonpland. Monsieur Bonpland can swear to Yr. Excy., before leaving the territory under his command, that he will depart from the provinces of Río de la Plata so that there will be no possible way for him to cause harm to the Province of Paraguay; I, meanwhile, await him with the anxiety of a friend and the respect of a disciple, which are such that I would be capable of marching to Paraguay for the sole purpose of freeing the best of men and the most celebrated of travelers.

Most Excellent Sir: I hope that Yr. Excy. will not allow my ardent plea to go unheeded, and I also hope that you will count me among the number of your most faithful and grateful friends, so long as the innocent whom I love is not the victim of an injustice.

I have the honor to be Yr. Excy.'s respectful, obedient servant.

Simón Bolívar
Lima, October 23, 1823.

Compiler's Note: The Supreme Dictator, in fact, did not answer this letter from Bolívar. The reply that certain novelist-historians give is apocryphal; at any rate, it gives evidence of a courtesy that was definitely not *El Supremo*'s style.

Letter from José Antonio Sucre, president of the brand-new state of Bolivia, to General Francisco de Paula Santander, vice-president of Colombia, both of whom were lieutenants of Bolívar's:

"The Liberator appears to be planning to send an expedition of Army Corps from Upper and Lower Peru to take Paraguay, which as you know is groaning beneath the tyrant who not only oppresses that province most cruelly, but has also cut it off from all human interchange, since no one enters there save at the pleasure of its Perpetual Dictator." (October 11, 1825.)

From Santander to Sucre:

"Cultivated Europe would greatly rejoice if Paraguay were to emerge from the cruel tutelage of the tyrant who oppresses it, and who has separated it from the rest of the world." (September, 1825.)

gives signs of being very disappointed when Buenos Aires proves reluctant to undertake "the taming of this wild beast"—meaning me. What Bolívar has in mind is not only setting his booted foot in Paraguay. Not content with having tripped up San Martín in Guayaquil, he intends to trample all over the Río de la Plata as well.

At the conference he holds in Potosí with the Porteño foxes Alvear and Díaz Vélez, Don Simón again sets forth his "redemptionist" aims, on October 8, 1825. I am going to set before you, he says, a neutral idea. Some neutral idea! Gentlemen, he says to them, I have had my scouts reconnoiter the entire length of the Pilcomayo, all the way down to its mouth, so as to have intelligence of the best route for entering Paraguay, with a view to betaking myself to that Province, to bringing down that tyrant. I can have him in my pocket in three days. What do you think? No deal, the silver foxes of the Plata say. We've been trying to do exactly that for ten years now. That wild hen is putting up a fierce resistance. It lays its golden eggs in its hermetic henhouse that it has turned into an impregnable bastion, and there is no way for us to gobble up either the hen or the eggs. Of course not, you stupid vulpeculae. I've outfoxed you by eating them half-hatched every morning for breakfast.

Bolívar, Sucre, Santander then write to me. I neither read nor answer

---

From Dean Funes to Simón Bolívar:
"Minister García having reported this happening to me [the abrupt rupture by the dictator of Paraguay of the negotiations initiated by the English minister in Buenos Aires], I took advantage of this opportunity to make him sensible to how mistaken an undertaking it was to tame this wild beast by way of reason, and on the other hand how correct Yr. Excy.'s judgment that he should be made to feel the force of your arms by way of the Bermejo. . . . I thought it my duty to bring all of this to Yr. Excy.'s notice, since it is my intention to provide you with sufficient matter for the fecundity of your genius, and since in my opinion the undertaking should not be abandoned." (September 28, 1825.)

Note from Juan Esteban Richard Grandsire:
"The extract from the aforementioned periodical speaks of threats on the part of General Sucre if the head of government of Paraguay does not take into consideration the steps that have supposedly been taken by Bolívar to obtain Monsieur Bonpland's freedom. It is to be ill-acquainted with the disposition and character of the Perpetual Dictator to believe him to be susceptible of yielding to fear, or to an indirect threat: the man who has been holding the reins of government in Paraguay for twelve years now, and who has been able to calm passions and maintain the tranquillity, both within and without, of the vast states that he governs, despite the intrigues and the revolutions of neighboring governments, will never be regarded as a coarse and common man by men of good sense and discrimination, and the threats might well bring down upon Monsieur Bonpland's head a deplorable catastrophe which can be avoided by a direct representation of the consul general of France in Río de Janeiro; and it would be better still if the request were to come from Paris." (September 6, 1826.)

letters full of black threats from blackguards. I am not at all worried by big-headed bigwigs of any latitude on this earth.

But what a difference, above all, between Bolívar and San Martín! The latter is the only one who refuses to go along with the absurd undertaking of subjugating Paraguay. His cause was not that of bringing free peoples beneath his yoke but that of liberating the American nation. "My country is all of America," San Martín and Monteagudo proclaim as one. Their battle begins with the revolution in October, 1812. The only one that legitimately deserves the name in the Río de la Plata, it was inspired by these two men whose method and thought entitle them to be called Paraguayans; San Martín, moreover, was born in the land of the Guaranís. It matters little that it seems to them that they have put their plow to the sea, steered a perilous course between cordilleras and volcanos. San Martín, thwarted by Bolívar in Guayaquil. Bernardo de Monteagudo, his minister of internal affairs, deposed by a reactionary uprising, then later assassinated in Lima. The downfall of Simón Bolívar himself, whom Monteagudo supported in his supreme attempt to form an American Confederation, the plan for which I outlined to the Junta of Buenos Aires three years before him.

Someday, the obsessive idea of America as a single Fatherland, one and united, which could have been born only in Paraguay, the most hemmed-in, the most hounded country on this Continent, will explode like an immense volcano and correct the "counsels" of geography corrupted by cunning people-eaters. Let time take its course. For now no new invasions threaten.

Naturally these facts, or better put these malefacts, are known to some of you only through hearsay; others of you have no doubt forgotten them, and the rest of you do not appreciate their real meaning. For the simple reason that you have not had to face them squarely and resolve them at the opportune moment, as I have been obliged to do. Amid the fat benefits reaped by the Supreme Chief for all, his subordinates forget the lean days he has been obliged to live through. In times of good fortune few remember the contretemps of misfortune. But a minimum of memory is needed to live; if not merely to subsist: to complain at leisure, which appears to have become your natural state, of the sufferings endured in order to arrive at your present state of well-being. Everything, even the smallest good, has its value and its price. Do not underestimate, my esteemed chiefs and functionaries, the price that it has cost us to make of our country, in the words of one of our worst enemies, the richest prize today in all of America.

(In the private notebook)

Paraguay is a real Utopia and His Excellency the Solon of modern times, the brothers Robertson said in praise of me in the bad days at the beginning. As yet I have been unable to read the book of these ambitious young men, who must be old men by now and, naturally, worse blackguards than before. To judge from the title, I cannot hope that their letters on my Reign of Terror (I do not know if there are two volumes of them or only one) are an improvement on the picture maliciously painted ten years before by that Rengger and Longchamp pair. Doubtless a new batch of lies and infamies seasoned to please the palates of Europeans who can't get enough of these barbarous realms. The barbarism of sophisticated, surfeited spirits. They take their pleasure flagellating themselves with the misfortunes of inferior races, ever seeking new erections. The sufferings of others are an excellent aphrodisiac that travelers grind out for stay-at-homes. Ah ah ah! Blind, deaf, mute, they fail to realize that the only thing they can transcribe is the sound of their resentments and their lapses of memory. What else can one expect of these errant adventurers, these predacious, rapacious globetrotters? Where and how do they fish up the material for such memoirs? If my own manuscripts aren't safe in my box with seven keys, those of these migratory traffickers, whose one thought is hunting down doubloons, could well be lost seven times over down who knows what latrines.

The *Letters* and *The Reign of Terror* appeared in print only after long delay, owing to the loss of the originals that *El Supremo* appeared to have foreseen and predicted: "On one of those nights of January last," the Robertsons say, "when all the inanimate things of nature had frozen solid, when the roads were covered with snow and the sidewalks treacherously slippery, one of the authors of these *Letters on Paraguay* was traveling in an omnibus from London to Kensington. He was carrying the manuscript of the work under his arm. On descending from the conveyance, an almost spectral black, hidden beneath a large cape and tricorne, suddenly materialized, blocking the traveler's path and staring at him intently. The latter slipped and fell on the ice. The strange apparition became more spectral still in the feeble glow of the gaslight. Suddenly it vanished. For a moment his head was in a daze from the concussion and the fright he had experienced. As soon as he was able, he struggled to his feet and limped away in great pain. He had hobbled along for only a few moments when he *felt* that his two arms had gone numb, in addition to his painful lameness. At that very moment, his errant consciousness had the sudden revelation that he had lost the *manuscript*. He returned to the ill-fated site of the fall. He searched about and brushed away the snow, trembling the while with the vague fear that he might find himself face to face once more with the phantasmal figure looming before his mind. This figure did not reappear; nor did the manuscript turn up again. The following day notice of the loss was posted on placards and in the newspapers. Rewards were offered. But we were never to lay eyes again on the lost pages. Several days later we received an anonymous note that said: *Go back to Paraguay. You will find the manuscript there.* We thought it a joke in bad taste perpetrated by certain of our friends. We did not return to Paraguay, naturally. It was easier to rewrite the *Letters,* which enjoyed a most flattering success. In three months the edition had sold out, even before the troublesome lameness and the pins and needles in our arms had completely disappeared. There were nonetheless a number of objections and criticisms raised. Thomas Carlyle, for one, dealt severely with us. He for his part saw in El Supremo of Paraguay the most remarkable man in that part of America. His spirit gave off a most sulfurous and somber light—the worshiper of Heroes maintains—yet with that light it illuminated Paraguay as best it could. In the last analysis, instead of discrediting our work, adverse opinions such as those of the great Carlyle added to its prestige, in view of the fact that men of his stature had taken note of it, thereby greatly contributing to its promotion and diffusion."

On the other hand, a number of contemporary authors maintain that the *Letters* are more or less apocryphal; that is to say, that the Robertsons attributed to themselves, at least partially, the paternity of material gleaned from the many libels against *El Supremo* circulating at the time in the Río de la Plata. If one keeps in mind the "taking ways" that constituted the fortune, and in the end the ruin, of the Robertsons in the course of their South American adventures, the statement doubtless contains a modicum of truth. The "stylistic unity" of these ex merchants transformed into memorialists or novelists, their talent for "painting superlative portraits," and other literary virtues are indeed evident in the volumes of the *Letters* and in *The Reign of Terror,* but they do not exclude the probability of an imposture. The loss of the "mad" manuscript, confessed to or invented by the authors, betrays this possibility. It is further corroborated by the episode, no doubt no less fraudulent, of the phantasmagoric encounter in a back street of London with the dark specter, very much in the taste of the mystery literature popular in that day. The authors appear to be trying to suggest that *El Supremo* appeared from the beyond in order to steal from them the manuscript which, according to them, would be his tombstone. Surely the authors thought of their former amphitryon as already "dead and buried" and believed that they could take double revenge with impunity by passing him off as the author of this "ladronicide" under the cloak of an incident straight out of a puerile mystery story. But *El Supremo* was still alive in Asunción, waiting to be able to read the announced works which finally appeared in 1838 and 1839, shortly before his death. *(Compiler's Note.)*

Anxious to sell their memories, the soul they no longer possess, to the devil of an imaginary reader, the most nefarious species I know, they invent for his afro-disiac delight travelers' tales, calumnies, imaginary facts. They relate their own perversities as being those of others.

Not so much to please these fawning censer-bearers worshiping money and power as to use them in the service of the country that they were using to make fat profits, I had the idea of naming them my representatives to Great Britain, that is to say England, since they were its subjects. They had been coming round for some time to pester me to appoint them to this office. For them, a distinction having no peer, as well as a new means of increasing and multiplying their fortune as traffickers and smugglers enjoying diplomatic immunity. I was not unaware, naturally, of the fact that the aim of these greedy merchants was not to offer their faithful collaboration in the development of the economic prosperity of our Nation but to line their own pockets. They were being underhanded, but I knew it, and hence it was I who had the upper hand without their knowing it.

So I sent for Juan Parish Robertson, the older brother, and put the matter to him with my customary frankness.

In his *Letters on Paraguay* J. P. Robertson gives the following account of the interview:

"An officer of the palace guard arrived last night with the peremptory message:—El Supremo orders that you come to see him immediately.

"I left with the aide, a black sublieutenant who reeked of rancid cooking fat and soot. It was well known what the visits of these nebulous 'officers' of the escort regiment meant. He walked ahead of me, invisible except for his white lancer's jacket, so that I hastened to this meeting, which augured ill for our fate, with the sensation that I was accompanying a fetid uniformed shadow, who made no sound save for the rubbing of his dress sword against his leg.

"When I arrived at the palace I was nonetheless received by The Supreme with more kindliness and affability than

usual. His face lighted up with an expression almost bordering on joviality. His mordoré cape hung from his shoulders in graceful folds. He appeared to be smoking his cigar with more than usual pleasure, and contrary to his custom of having just one light burning in his humble little reception room, two tall candles of the best-quality tallow stood lit on the little round single-footed table, at which no more than three people could be seated: the dining table of the Absolute Lord and Master of that part of the world. He held his hand out to me very cordially:—Sit down, Señor Don Juan. He pulled his chair over next to mine and expressed his wish that I listen to him very attentively.

"—You know what my policy has been with regard to Paraguay. You know that they have tried to yoke me to the other provinces where the evil germ of anarchy and corruption reigns. Paraguay is enjoying greater prosperity than any other country; we are living off the fat of the land. Here all is order, subordination, tranquillity. But the moment one goes beyond its borders, as you yourself have been able to verify, the cannon's roar and the sound of discord assail one's ears. There all is ruin and desolation; here all is luxury, calm, and order. And what is the reason for all of this? The fact that there is no man in South America, outside of the one addressing you, who understands the nature of the people and is capable of governing it in accordance with its necessities and aspirations. Is that true or not?—he asked me. I nodded. I could not tell him no, since The Supreme does not permit himself to be contradicted.

"—The Porteños are the most capricious, vain, voluble, and libertine of all those who were under the domination of the Spaniards in this hemisphere. They cry out for free institutions, but the only ends they pursue are spoliation and the expansion of their interests. As a consequence, I have resolved to having nothing whatsoever to do with them. My desire is to establish relations directly with England, government to government. Ships of Great Britain, triumphantly traversing the Atlantic, will enter Paraguay, and together with our fleet will challenge any interruption of trade, from the mouth of the Plata to the lagoon of Xarayes, five hundred leagues north of Asunción. Your government will have a minister here, and I will have mine at the Court of Saint James's. Your compatriots will deal in manufactured goods and war munitions, and will receive in exchange the noble products of this country.

"At this point in his speech he rose from his chair in great agitation, and calling to the sentry, ordered the sergeant of the guard to be sent for. The moment the latter appeared, he peremptorily ordered him to bring 'the thing.' The sergeant went off and in less than three minutes' time came back with four grenadiers carrying a great leather pouch of tobacco weighing two hundred pounds, a bale of maté of equal size and weight, a demijohn of Paraguayan cane brandy, a huge sugar loaf, and a great number of packets of cigars tied and decorated with multicolored ribbons. Finally there came an aged black woman with samples of cotton fabrics in the form of doilies, serviettes, and cloths of every sort. I thought it must be a present that The Supreme wanted to give me on the eve of my departure for Buenos Aires. You may well imagine my surprise then when I suddenly heard him say to me:

"—Señor Don Juan, these are only a few of the rich products of this soil and of the industry and talent of its inhabitants. I have gone to some trouble to furnish you with the best samples of various categories of goods that this country produces. You know to what an unlimited extent these products can be obtained in what I may safely call this Paradise of the world. And now, without entering into a discussion as to whether this continent is ripe for liberal and bourgeois institutions (I think that it is not), there is no denying that in an old and civilized country such as Great Britain these institutions have gradually, and for all practical purposes, done away with old forms of government, generally feudal, constituting at the same time the foundation of a nation possessed of stability and grandeur, which is today the greatest power on earth. It is my desire, then, that you continue on to your country, and that as soon as you arrive in London you appear before the House of Commons. Here, take these samples with you. Ask to be heard from the bar and announce that you are the deputy from Paraguay, the First Republic of the South, and present to that House the products of this rich, free, and prosperous country. Tell them that I have authorized you to invite England to cultivate political and commercial relations with me, and that I am ready and most willing to receive a minister of the Court of Saint James's in my capital, with all due deference to the relations between civilized nations. Once this minister arrives here with the formal recognition of our Independence, I will name my envoy to that court.

"Such were almost word for word the terms in which The Supreme delivered his harangue to me. I was left speechless at the idea of being named minister plenipotentiary, not to the Court of Saint James's, but to the House of Commons. He especially enjoined me not to meet personally with the chief executive, 'because —The Supreme affirmed— I know very well how inclined the great men of England are to deal with such important questions as this only when the House of Commons has debated them and rendered its affirmative.'

"Never in my life have I been at such a loss as to how to act or what to say. To refuse this quixotic mission was to bring immediate ruin down upon my unfortunate head and that of my poor brother, if we didn't lose them first beneath the executioner's axe. There was nothing to do but accept. And that is what I did, despite the suffocating feeling of ridiculousness that overcame me when I envisioned myself forcing my way to the bar of the House of Commons, overpowering the usher of Parliament with half a dozen porters, and delivering, despite opposition and resistance, both the leather pouches filled with Paraguayan products and the Supreme's speech, *verbatim*. But Asunción was a long way away from Saint James's. Hence I agreed to the mission, if not the proposal, and trusted that chance would turn up some remote possibility of an excuse that would acceptably discharge me of guilt for not having been able to pass, with such an unprecedented honor and the leather pouches, through the door on the other side of the ocean toward which I had been pointed."

Look, Don Juan, I said to him, let us speak quite frankly. I am prepared to grant you the honor that you have long been seeking. I will make you the trade representative of Paraguay accredited to the government of your empire. It is my desire to promote direct relations with England, something I consider to be of mutual advantage for the two countries: yours, the major power of the contemporary world; mine, the most prosperous and stable Republic of these new worlds. Does this sinecure suit you? He outdid himself in praise and expressions of gratitude. But at that very moment, as always happens to me whenever I am confronted with swindlers out to gull me, I knew that this bowing and scraping Englishman was not going to do any of the things that he himself hastened to promise. What was more, from the very sound of his flattery I *knew* that he was going to play me false. Nonetheless it was a card I was obliged to play. The Robertson mission was a way of sounding out, under cover of the British flag, the possibility of breaking the shipping blockade by forcing the hand of the successive scoundrels governing the Río de la Plata, who had already become vassals of the British Crown beneath the cloak of a supposed "protectorate." It seemed to me rather a clever trick to try to use English hands to pull coconuts out of the fire. The rascals deserved no better.

I want you, Don Juan, I said to him, burying my fingernails in his ticker, to arrange for the reestablishment of the freedom of commerce and navigation of which, contrary to all rights of men and nations, Paraguay has been deprived by Buenos Aires. I am in an excellent position to do so, Most Excellent Sire, the trader assured me. I am a close friend of the Protector and commandant of the British squadron in the Río de la Plata. As soon as I speak with him, Paraguayan ships will enter and leave with no difficulty, protected by the warships of Captain Percy. We agree then, Don Juan. It is my desire, however, that your functions not be limited solely to the realm of commerce. This will not be possible without prior recognition by Great Britain of the Independence and sovereignty of Paraguay. It will be an honor for me, the merchant replied, to arrange for this just recognition, and I am certain that my country will be proud to establish relations with a free, independent, and sovereign nation such as Paraguay, which the entire universe already rightly calls the *Paradise of the World.* Big words rip pockets, Don Juan. Don't get lost in pipe dreams: Paraguay is not the Utopia you say it is, but a very real reality. Its products are forthcoming in unlimited quantities and can meet all the needs of the Old World. According to my information, the situation is this: The downfall of Napoleon and the restoration of Ferdinand VII have thrown the minds of the men in Buenos Aires into utter confusion. Alvear is now Supreme Director. Artigas badly beat the partisans of the directorals at Guayabos; they have been left without direction, drifting with events with no one at the helm, after their expulsion from the Banda Oriental. This is the opportune moment for you to try what I propose. I will fit out a fleet of boats loaded to the gunwales. I will put you in command and you will not stop till you reach the White House, or rather the House of Commons, to present these products, your credentials, and my demands that the independence and sovereignty of the Republic be recognized. Are we agreed? Inspired idea, Excellency!

Some days later Robertson left for Buenos Aires in his boat La Inglesita. General euphoria. Pleasing prospects. A first sounding-out operation, suggested by José Tomás Isasi. I also allow him to leave with two brigantines loaded with products.

The *Notes* again confuse the dates. José Tomás Isasi did not leave with Juan Robertson, but ten years later, in the group formed by Rengger and Longchamp and other foreigners whose departure from the country was authorized by El Supremo in 1825.

The unprecedented event had its origin in a petition from Woodbine Parish, the British consul in Buenos Aires. In it he petitioned the head of the Paraguayan government to allow the English merchants to leave, taking their belongings with them. The tacit recognition of the sovereignty of Paraguay by Great Britain, as implied in the petition of its chargé d'affaires in the Río de la Plata, had its effect, Rengger and Longchamp declare in their book. The Perpetual Dictator agreed to allow not only the English merchants, but also other European subjects chosen by him (merchants or not), to leave the country. He issued them safe-conduct warrants and allowed the boats to be fitted out, on the one condition that their crews be made up of foreigners or blacks. Moreover, he forbade them to take with them anything except those effects and goods which they had acquired with their own money. This order was rigorously enforced by the authorities. José Tomás Isasi, naturally, was not only exempted from this requirement but enjoyed the broadest special privileges. "He was able to put one over on me—his compadre was later to say—because two circumstances conspired in his favor. I allowed him to leave so that no one would think that I was yielding to necessity or to the pressure of the Englishman by freeing only his compatriots. Furthermore, my villainous compadre—an accursed institution, compaternity!—used his daughter's cough as the letter-patent of a privateer." Isasi never returned to Paraguay. He put the crowning touch on his disloyalty by sending back some time later several barrels of unusable gunpowder; his only, derisory restitution for the enormous sums he had embezzled. His indignant ex friend tried to secure his capture at any price. He ordered that all his property be confiscated, and a young man named Gregorio Zelaya, an employee in his commercial establishment in Asunción, was shot to death after a summary trial, exactly one year after Isasi's escape, on April 25, 1826. On each anniversary another hostage was executed, in a sort of ritual which punished the guilty man "in-absentia"—in accordance with the immemorial symbolism of such sacrifices—in the persons of the most innocent victims. The Dictator's power and all his efforts over the years were in vain. The enemies of Artigas (who had been given asylum in Paraguay) offered to hand Isasi over in exchange for the ex Supreme of the Banda Oriental. It was the one scheme that the Perpetual Dictator rejected with such vast indignation. He had the bearer of the offer of exchange shot to death without a trial. He nonetheless did not give up his obsessive pursuit of the fugitive, who disappeared as though the earth had swallowed him up.

As for the "implied promise" of official recognition, free navigation, and commerce, Mr. Parish postponed it indefinitely, once the travelers had made their way through the "wall of China" by way of the Puerta del Sur at La Unión de las Siete Corrientes. As a reminder, and playing the last card of his pride disguised as courtesy, the Dictator chartered another vessel for the sole purpose of taking a note to the English consul. It was not a very politic one, however; after vague considerations regarding the happy end of the journey for those who had been liberated, the note took on an extremely bitter tone: "The subjects of His Britannic Majesty have merely endured the same lot to which all of the inhabitants of Paraguay have been condemned by this iniquitous blockade. Finally, they have no reason to complain, since they came to Paraguay without ever being asked to come." The British chargé d'affaires ignored the "implied" protest, and wrote to the Dictator requesting this time that he free Bonpland. *El Supremo*'s explosion of wrath was silent but eloquent: he sent the note back in the same diplomatic folder with a crude label pasted on it bearing the inscription, in his secretary's handwriting: "To Parish, English consul in Buenos Aires." At the same time he sent a laconic circular round to his functionaries all over the country: "You must never believe Europeans, or trust them, whatever nation they are from, and whatever they may claim their objectives to be. Slam the door in the face of any one of them that appears, and if he continues to plague you, don't say to him: Come on in, be my guest, as is our unfailingly hospitable custom, but beat him across the snout with a club and shout at him in a good loud voice: Clear out of here, vermin!"

Of the feelings of respect and consideration that the liberated foreigners continued to have for the Perpetual Dictator outside of Paraguay (feelings as intense as those of citizens and foreigners residing in the Paraguayan Arcadia), Rengger and Longchamp offer unimpeachable testimony, cited later by the consul of France in Buenos Aires, Monsieur Aimé Roger: "Captain Hervaux, who was given permission to leave in one of Señor Isasi's brigs following a prolonged captivity in Paraguay, died in Buenos Aires in 1832. During the seven years that passed between his liberty and his death, he never pronounced the name of *El Supremo* (the one title of the Perpetual Dictator's that he accepted) or heard it pronounced without rising to his feet, coming to attention with a loud click of his heels, and raising his hand to his hat. A Paraguayan fled as a stowaway on another brig. I asked him: Why did you leave Paraguay? I was a soldier for twenty-five years. Is that the only reason you fled? The only one, sir, for twenty-five years. Were you unhappy there? No, sir, not at all! Good land, good people, and above all, what a good government. But twenty-five years!" *(Compiler's Note.)*

I give Isasi fifty thousand pesos in gold coin from the public treasury to buy gunpowder and armaments of the best quality. Robertson the Englishman double-crosses me. The Paraguayan Isasi double double-crosses me. I should have suspected him when he asked me for permission to take his wife and daughter with him. He cleverly concealed his intentions, taking advantage of my weakness for the girl. Why do you want to subject your family to this sacrifice? It's for my daughter's sake, Sire. She suffers from whooping cough, and Doctor Rengger assures me that the change can cure her. Listen to how the poor thing coughs! Day and night, without a letup. Well, José Tomás, if it's a question of my goddaughter's health, take her with you. Be careful on the return voyage. You will not be escorted by the English vessels then, and it remains to be seen whether the British consul will fulfill his implied promise of negotiating the trade treaty between England and Paraguay. I have my suspicions about this Juan Parish. The English are perfidious. Best not to trust them till they show that they're trustworthy. José Tomás Isasi, my friend, my compadre, my bosom companion of many years, listens to me deep down. From the height of his shoes. He lifts the little girl up to me. She clings to my neck in an unusual show of affection, since up to this moment she has tended to show signs of a certain instinctive fear of me. The coqueluche has not diminished the child's truly angelic beauty. On the contrary, it has transfigured it into an expression that has an air of the supernatural about it. Perhaps by contrast to the black and not yet visible treachery of her father. In a pause between fits of coughing, which make her gasp convulsively, she gives me a kiss on each cheek. Farewell, fa . . . !, she sobs, breaking off as another attack overcomes her. Instinct of children who sense the farewells that will be forever. They carried her off, her long gasping cry immediately drowned out by the commotion in the port. The last I saw of my goddaughter was her fair hair gleaming in a ray of sunlight on that splendid April morning. With a strange apprehension I immersed myself in the feverish preparations for the departure.

On his return from his next-to-last journey, Juan Robertson paid for a part of his sins. My worst enemies, Artigas's followers, were the ones charged with collecting the debt and administering the condign punishment. Between Santa Fe and La Bajada, the bandits and brigands of the Protector of the Banda Oriental pirated the pirate descended from pirates. They subjected him to terrible abuse. They spread-eagled him naked between stakes, lying face downward on the ground. The mob of Tapes§ and Correntinos worked him over for hours. Confused story of things experienced at midnight. Dreamed of at midday. I don't know if the gringo was sincere. I would like to read the version of the episode that he gives in his book, if in fact he works up the courage to recount it.

The episode is related by the Robertsons in *The Reign of Terror*. The suppression of certain revolting details is attributable not so much to Puritan prudishness as to the proverbial English penchant for reserve and decorous understatement, as well as to the remoteness of the facts narrated in measured prose by the authors. Their version nonetheless coincides in general with that given by *El Supremo*. *(Compiler's Note.)*

Amid the reproaches and insults I heaped upon the Englishman, there suddenly stole into my mind the melody that he used to hum softly during our chess games or my divagations on the lore of the stars, indigenous myths, the Gallic Wars, or the burning of the Library of Alexandria. There's a Divinity that shapes our ends, Rough-hew them how we will! I can hear Juan Parish's voice. The Beneficent Divinity finally shaped his end "how he willed" in the fields of La Bajada.

Artigas's bandits pillaged La Inglesita from head to foot. Even the kepis and dress uniforms ordered by the military leaders of the Junta. Sashes, laces, cotton prints and percales, trinkets and baubles for their wives.

§Guaranís. More generally, persons who appear to be Indians.

At the time of these events, neither the Governing Junta nor the Consulate that had replaced it any longer existed. The dictatorship pro tempore was on the eve of turning *El Supremo* into Perpetual Dictator. The ex military leaders of the First Junta were for the most part either banished or in prison. *(Compiler's Note.)*

A tricorne, optical and musical instruments, a telescope, various electrical machines, articles that I had ordered wholesale and listed in great detail. The complete stock of arms and munitions, naturally, that he was bringing in for the army on my order, under cover of a shipment of coal and wheat.

The striped rag of his empire was of no use to him when it came to grabbing the red-hot handle of the frying pan where the chestnuts were toasting. When the English ephebe awoke from his nightmare he witnessed an amusing spectacle improvised in his honor. Artigas's band of toughs, decked out in the full dress uniforms, the ecclesiastical ornaments and adornments, dolled up in the dresses and jewelry of the women, were dancing a wild, demoniacal gypsy zambra round about him, brandishing brand-new pistols and sabers. They were laying bets at the top of their lungs as to which of them was strong enough to behead him with a single stroke. Juan Parish Robertson, like the old man in Chaucer's tale (and as happened to me a short time ago), must at that instant have been pounding with his fists on the doors of mother earth begging her to let him in. I don't know what thoughts must have crossed Juan Robertson's mind at that moment. Not at all comforting ones, doubtless. A wounded heart bears the knife no love. Though an Englishman always tries his best to be timeless, Juana Esquivel was no longer at his side to stanch his wounds and lull him to sleep with her cicada's songs.

To make matters worse, the night before his departure, with everyone drunk as a piper, his brother had bade him farewell with rather prophetic jokes and pantomimes. Don't laugh, gentlemen, you especially, Don Juan, my future commercial consul. He who laughs first laughs worst. If an old hen scratches for corn long enough, she'll find what she wasn't looking for. Told is foretold.

Juan Parish was saved by the piccolo he used to play during our evenings together. As the vandals of La Bajada had their way with him, they discovered the double piccolo among his effects. Play the flute!, his costumed captors ordered again and again as they carried him off, tied to the mast of his own ship, to the command post in the town. With my wounds and sores still bleeding, the satyrs disguised as women, curés, military officers forced me to keep playing the piccolo, as they strutted and shimmied round me, making the bridge shake with their darky dances, Juan Robertson recounted, seeking to garner my sympathy. Play the flute! Play the flute!, they kept ordering, striking me with the flat of their swords each time my breath gave out. I was gasping my last, and in desperation I clutched my instrument with my fingers, my fingernails. I had nothing to cling to save that little straw of sound. I assure you, Excellency, that there is nothing sadder than to tootle one's own requiem out of tune on a damned flute to keep those who are about to kill you in a festive mood!

Juan Robertson didn't die. Confounded scoundrel! Artigas's brigands didn't kill him. On the contrary, he contrived to get himself paid a good price for the snags he'd hit and the rags he was missing. He managed, with the collusion of the British squadron, to get himself generously indemnified for the attack by the hordes of Artiguistas of which he'd been the victim. With the safe-conduct granted him by the Protector of the Banda Oriental, he reaped fat profits all along the coast, coming out with double or triple the amount that the goods they'd stolen from him had been worth. Shamefully trading on his misfortunes, the Anglican trafficker sold for its weight in gold every drop of blood he had lost in the modest Golgotha at La Bajada. Afterwards he had the nerve to turn up here, despite his having been forbidden ever to set foot on Paraguayan soil again.

What I can't forgive you for, Señor Robertson, is your having basely negotiated an arms sale with Director Alvear in exchange for the blood of Paraguayans! The Porteño blackguard offered me a trade: muskets for men. He offered me 25 rifles per 100 Paraguayans. Four citizens of this free Nation for one shotgun! Infamous merchants! That's the price they estimate the valor of my compatriots to be worth! And you, to whom I offered more honors and considerations than to any other foreign subject, are the one who brings me this offer. Hawker of human flesh! What did you think, you pirate slave-dealer! I'll have everyone know that there is not enough gold on earth to pay for as much as the nail of the little finger of the most useless of my fellow citizens!

Timidly, like a worm cut in two speaking through a crack in the ground, Juan Robertson tried to clear his name: I never had any part in such a negotiation, Excellency! I merely agreed that Director Alvear could send a sealed and signeted letter addressed to Your Excellency in the mail pouch of my boat. Not just a hypocrite but a coward too! Or perhaps you had no idea what was in that infamous letter? I won't say that I had no idea whatsoever, Excellency. General Alvear had told me a little something regarding his proposal at the fort of Buenos Aires. He told me that he needed to obtain recruits from Paraguay to reinforce the Río de la Plata legions. I immediately informed Director Alvear that you would never accept such an agreement; that it was evident to me that Your Excellency only exchanges trees or maté, tobacco or cowhides for arms and munitions, never human skins! Ah, the Supreme Dictator of Paraguay would not tolerate such a thing under any circumstances whatsoever!, I said to the head of the Porteño government, and roundly refused to serve as a third party in this affair. Yet you agreed to bring the infamous letter in your boat. You don't bring the letter. No. It's the mail pouch of your boat that brings it. Clever way out. Discreet alibi. In addition you allowed yourself to be robbed of the arms that I paid you for in advance with a shipment of goods worth a hundred times more. Sire, they robbed me of everything that a man can be robbed of. And more besides. But I am prepared to make complete restitution, in good hard coin, for the shipment that was stolen. Naturally; you will do precisely that, down to the last céntimo, plus punitive damages! But there is more to it than that. In the meantime, Artigas has sent off copies of the purloined letter to the four winds so that everyone in the world will know that my fellow citizens are going to be sold as slaves. I am deeply sorry, Sire. The truth of the matter will soon be reestablished. Don't you know yet that the truth doesn't exist and that falsehood and calumny are never effaced? But enough of this vain philosophizing. What I want to know nonetheless is when the arms under embargo are going to be handed over to me. I regret to tell Your Excellency that unfortunately that will not be possible. Kindly explain to me, then, Señor Robertson: what purpose is served by the cannons of the British squadron, which served you quite nicely when it came to getting yourself reimbursed many times over for everything you were robbed of? Why didn't you insist to the consul of your empire, to your bosom pal, the commandant of those warships, that what belongs to me be returned to me? Doesn't that fleet back the British protectorate over the Río de la Plata? Is it incapable of preventing acts of piracy from being committed with impunity, acts that have robbed my country of armament necessary for its defense? Arms, Excellency, are considered articles of war, and in such cases the British consul and commander forbear to intervene. That would be to violate the sovereignty and autonomy of States. Your Excellency knows that, and would be just as unwilling to permit it in his case. Don't bother me with such trifles. I have had more than enough of slippery tricks coated with English phlegm! Hence, in brief, and to put a fine point on all this arrant nonsense, your commandants and consuls cannot assure me of free traffic on the river which, according to the right of peoples and nations, is neither the patrimony nor the exclusive property of any of the bordering states. That is how it is, Excellency. It is outside their powers, I am sorry to say, Sire, but that is how it is. So then, señor slave-trader, when it is a question of the sovereignty of the Protectorate there is sovereignty, and when it's a question of the sovereignty of a free and sovereign country such as Paraguay there is no sovereignty. A splendid way of protecting the self-determination of peoples! They are protected if they are vassals. They are oppressed and exploited if they are free. It would appear that there is no alternative now other than to place our bet and take our chances with an English or French master and those who come after. I for my part am not willing to tolerate such chicanery by any empire on earth.

Look here, Robertson, you and your brother have been received generously in this Republic. You have been allowed to engage in commerce on as broad a scale as you pleased. You have trafficked in everything and dealt with a free hand in all manner of contraband, even coca and mulattas.*

---

*One of the *Letters* is illustrative in this respect. It transcribes *verbatim et literatum* the one that the Scottish sergeant David Spalding (who had become a deserter at the time of the English invasions and later settled in Corrientes) writes to his friends, the Robertson brothers, asking them for payment of a small "debt." Sergeant Spalding's letter is dated around the time of Juan Parish's misadventures at La Bajada, thus proving in this aspect as well to be firsthand "testimony," despite its peculiar spelling and obscure syntax. Here are the pertinent paragraphs of the letter, written in English:

"I deeply regret being ovliged to inform you of the news that I have just received thanks to the fact that Don Agustín, the skipper of Ysasy's [sic: the reference is to José Tomás Isasi] brig, found your brother in the Río San Juan, some three leagues downstream from the port of Caballú Cuatiá, who had been taken away or brought back by Artigas's soldiers who attacked him at La Vajada as he was coming upriver bringing arms for El Supremo of Paraguay. On the 25 of this month I intend to head for that place, and if I can be of any serbice to him, I will do everything within my power and limited resources, and find out how matters stand once I get there.

"I sent you from the coast of the river, through Don Enrique de Arébalo (who goes by the nickname of the Tucu-tucu) a gold chain, a cross *idem*, four rings *idem*, from those lists of things to be given as gifts and an equal number of others that are worth less than they weigh but look as though they are worth much more. Kindly tell me whether or not you have received them, since the emboy is not at all to be trusted in such matters. The gold chain is two yards long, and it would be a shame if it were to end up hanging in the wrong place, especially when I am still owed the price it cost me.

"I hope that as of this date you will have sold my mulatta girl, and now that your brother is in prison and God only knows when he'll get out, be good enough to send me the price she brought in first-quality yerva suave at your first opportunity. *(Robertson, Notes.)*

I choke with indignation. I take out the little pouch containing the Corvisart balm that Bonpland gave me. I inhale it in the form of snuff (it was no time for tisanes!), a goodly number of whiffs, till my entire face and hands take on a greenish phosphorescence. Overawed, Juan takes a step backward. Listen! Your face has disappeared, Excellency! Better than being a barefaced scoundrel like you, you miserable bugger! Not only have you and your brother lived and traded here as you pleased. Many other English merchants did too. When they wanted to leave they did. They took fortunes away with them. You and your brother have made a fabulous fortune here. I have tried, as you know, to initiate direct relations between your nation and this rich country. It has been my desire to name you my commercial representative, my consul, my chargé d'affaires accredited to your Common House. And this is the payment I receive! When I ask for the articles I need, I am told that your authorities cannot free traffic in arms! When it is necessary to take my interests into consideration, I am told that the matériel destined for my Republic is to remain at the mercy of troublemakers and cutthroats, while the British officials scandalously turn a deaf ear to my rightful claims! Allow me to inform you then that I shall no longer allow you, your brother, or any British trader to reside in my territory. I shall no longer allow you to carry on your English rag trade. The words English rag send me into a fit of sneezing. A rheum of revulsion. I inhale more phosphorescent snuff. Clouds of fire-beetles fly in through the windows. I squash them by the handful. I rub my face, my neck, with the guts of these lampyrids. I rub my entire body with this luminous grease. The room is filled with livid lights. My fury burns from the floor to the ceiling. The series of sneezes overturns the funeral urn where I keep snuff from Brazil. A black fog flecked with yellow fills the room. I know this now as I write it. Back then Robertson saw it, electrified by those flashes. As he cowers there in terror amid the shower of sparks, I push along, upside down and right side to, from one wall to another, from one shore to another, turned into a green flame. Clear out and take your miserable rags with you! Ignoble ragpickers' gladrags! Rags infested with troops of fleas, lice, and other species of insects! We've no need in this country for tatters spattered with filth! You and your brother must leave the Republic in twenty-four hours if you don't want to leave your hides behind once the time limit is up. Allow me to say, Excellency, that we must get our belongings together! . . . I won't allow you anything! You don't have any belongings except the dirty rag of your existence! Get it out of here before my Syracusan ravens pick your Britannic scraps to the bone! Did you hear me? Eh? I beg your pardon, Excellency? Shut up, Robertson!

Hold your doormat of a tongue and get packing. You and your brother are banished and expelled. The two of you have exactly 1435 minutes to cast off your moorings and free this city of your pestiferous persons! Did you hear me?

The impostor backs out of the room, his eyes riveted on the buckles of my shoes, the buckles of my breeches, the buckles of my patience. He comes wriggling back as though he were unable to get free of that strand that has him caught in an invisible web. Pardon, Excellency! Dog-fashion. Dragging himself along the floor yelping, licking the soles of my shoes. Robertson, I've told you get out! How long do you think my patience is going to last! Go with God or with the devil! But clear out once and for all! Go and tell the commander of your squadron for me that I dub him a scoundrel! Go and tell your consul for me that I dub him a double-dyed scoundrel! Go and tell that cur of a king of yours and that bitch of a queen that I dub them the most consummate scoundrels this planet has ever given birth to! Tell them for me that my rusty chamber pot is worth more, a very great deal more, than their filthy crown, and I'm not about to trade! And if I don't say to go tell the honorable members of your Common House for me that I dub them worthless scoundrels and bastards it's because the one thing I still have respect for is the commons, which like the common outhouse is of and for the people, even in the stinking hole of your empire. Lieutenant, take this green-go-home to the barracks, where he is to be kept under guard with that other green-go-home of a brother of his, till it's time for them to leave. Tell the district commander of my order so that he can execute it. Ko'ã pytaguá tekaká oñemosê vaêrã jaguaicha!*§ He has exactly 1431 minutes, beginning at this moment, to do so. Like seven powder flashes, the seven timepieces lifted their faces up from the table, showing their needle-sharp hands riveted on the same point and struck the hour in unison. Come on, herd this black-guard off to the guards! Then go wake up my confidential clerk. Bring him here, asleep or dead. I am going to dictate to him, this minute, the order of confiscation and expulsion. Juan Robertson threw himself at my feet, sobbing and pleading, in one last desperate attempt to get me to commute their sentence. At a sign from me, the sublieutenant pulled him up by one arm and pushed and shoved him out of my presence. I stood motionless in the middle of the room until the sound of their footsteps, martial in the one case, dragging in the other, died away. The greenish light of my person projected itself into the darkness through the door. I went out to give the watchword to the sentinel. Patiño arrived, buttoning up

*§ *These gringo shits must be thrown out like dogs!*

his breeches, his eyes covered with spider webs. You've been ages getting here, as always, you scoundrel! I was just called, Sire! Go back to sleep. Tomorrow will be the same day as today. I closed the doors and barred them. I went into my chamber and began to write in the white cone of the little candlestick.

In the flicker of the candle an insect is burning: my certainty as to the law of necessary chance. It is only an insect. Has it come in through the cracks? Has it come out of me? A fly, a flesh fly. The first one. The first one? Who knows how many may have already come to spy on my inclination to negotiate an agreement, to surrender unconditionally! In any case, the first one I've seen. A black emisery, omissory, emissary of the anomalous animal souls of the night. Very soon now they will begin to invade me. For the moment only one, apparently. The flesh fly insists on burning itself up. It is not able to. It's not that the flesh fly can't burn itself to death. It's that the flame of the stubby candle is unable to consume it. The bad smell of the tallow and the scorched insect fills the pit of my inner chamber. I can't ventilate it now. I can't remove the fly that's getting soaking wet in the flicker of the candle, the way I removed the flies drowned in the inkwell with the point of my lance-pen in time gone by. Memory-pen. I'm the one who's drowning now. Who'll fish me out with the point of his pen? Some creeping, crawling, son-of-a-bitching bookshitter, doubtless, on whom I place my curse henceforth. Vade retro! The fly takes on the color of hot ashes. Flutters happily about. Polishes its wings with its feet. Its enormous faceted eyes observe me. Reddish diamond. Iridescent flashes in the blackness. Have you come out of me, you son of a bitch?! The flesh fly shoots one of its polyhedral eyes mounted on springs out at me. I feel in me the effect of a cannon shot. Vae victis!§ The moment has arrived, the instant has passed, the hour, the minute, the fraction of eternity is about to strike in which I cast the iron scepter into the balance weighing the treasure destined to redeem our Nation.

. . .

§Woe to the vanquished! (What the Gallic chieftain Brennus exclaimed as he threw his heavy sword into the scales in which the defeated Romans were weighing the tribute that would ensure the Gauls' departure; Livy V, 48.)

Rule over happenstance! Ah madness! Rule out chance. Chance is there spawning in the fire. Hatching the eggs of its immortality unlike any other. Chance emerges intact from the trembling flame. I have tried in vain to reduce it and place it in the service of Absolute Power, weaker than the egg of that fly. You will know it as a fetor, the pen writes-repeats. There must be something hidden at the bottom of everything. Old space, there is no chance. Old time, you are the chance that does not exist. No? Yes! Don't try to fool me at this late date! Deception is not your business anymore. Not with me at least. The candle smells of what dies and ends. Condemned to live in the heart of a race, *I* too am tied to the orange tree of executions. Un-usable carrion. Even my own ravens scorn it in disgust. Useless madness. Someone dictates to me: Blow out the candle of being whereby everything has existed. Come on, try. Blow. I blow as hard as I can. The light doesn't dim in the slightest. The dark ember of the fly simply brightens a little. Very little. Almost nothing. Nothing. Come on! Try again. Impossible. I'm very weak. I'm going to have a go at it another way: by way of supreme weakness; by way of words; by way of the dead end of the written word. Go ahead and do it this time, then, this last time, with the most simple-minded, most idiotic rhetoric possible. Do the exercise as though you really believed in it. The simulation must be perfect. Like the formula for the most efficacious exorcisms. The recipe for incantations, conjurations. Come on! Write. Write as the flesh fly watches you, gleefully making mock of you.

Race that is mine . . . (that still sounds like a sermon, an edict, a proclamation. What's the use of that, if nobody will read what I write; if the public crier will no longer announce my decrees to the sound of trumpet and drum?). Race of mine, listen nonetheless. Listen before my candle gutters out. Lend an ear to the story I shall tell you of my life. I shall tell you what I am about to tell you as a true thing.

Having ruled out chance through an anachronism, one of the many I use in my battle against time, I am that fantastic personage whose name the washerwomen bandy back and forth as they pound the filth of bodies out of mountains of clothes. Blood or sweat: it makes no difference. Tears. Sacramental, excremental humors: all the same. I am that **PERSONAGE** and that **NAME**. Supreme incarnation of the race. You have elected me and have handed the government and the destiny of your lives over to me for life. I am the **SUPREME PERSONAGE** who watches over and protects your sleeping dream, your waking dream (there is no difference between the one and the other); who seeks the passage through the Red Sea amid persecution and entrapment by our enemies . . . How does that sound? Like real horseshit! Not even the most purblind one-eyed capon among the many cocks crowing at midnight trying to awaken the dawn ahead of time, or the most ignorant of those scribblers scratching about searching for the handwriting of the pasquinade in the Archive would believe a single word of what you've written. Even you yourself don't believe it. Right, but I don't give a hoot in hell.

Stomach-turning stench. The sound of the candle-snuffer's footfalls filters through the slits; his rheumy refrain keeps watch over me: The stroooooke of tweeelve and all is weeeelllll. Though you've gooot the vaapors, I'm snuffing the taaaaapers! . . . Distant cries of the sentinels passing along the watchword: Indepeeendence oooor deeaaath!!! Ah, the custom that rusts the best habits and eats holes in what is most holy . . . *(Go into this more deeply, if I can . . .)*

Detracing the path leading back through so many years, passing once again by way of low tricks and high treason, misfeasance and malfeasance, José Tomás Isasi, against his black ladronicide will, has gone back upriver against the current. I finally captured him. I was obliged to do so, otherwise he would have fled to the very end of the universe. Why did you betray my friendship? Silence of stone. Why did you rob the State? Silence of dust. Why did you betray your Country? Silence of gunpowder. They drag him out from the Truth Chamber to the middle of the Plaza where a bonfire has been lighted with the unusable barrels of powder he sent me. Symbol of his treachery. The useless yellow powder is at least serving now to burn the scoundrel alive. Tied to an iron stake, he is paying the supreme penalty that I dictated against him the very moment his infamous deed was discovered. I see him burning from my window. It is ten years now that I've been seeing him burning there. The smoke of his fried flesh forms above his head the figure of a furious gold monster that weeps and weeps, pleading for pardon. His tears have the appearance of drops of gold smelted from the fifty thousand doubloons he stole from the Coffer. The golden lament arouses no compassion in the crowd witnessing the execution. It feels debased, rather, merely listening to him, hearing and seeing those newly minted tears that the wind scatters dangling from the leaves of the trees murmuring plaintive peeps. No one—not even the children—makes the slightest move to go catch those plorant pluvial drops of shining black gold. A little river of gleaming black gold lava rolls toward Government House, leaks in under the doors. Its tongue licks the soles of my shoes. A detachment of grenadiers, hussars, and other guardsmen rushes in with buckets of water and cartloads of sand to act as firemen. In the wink of an eye they put out the eyes of the fire. They wash away the filth of gleaming black gold. They clean up the traces of lava. For a long time, beneath the clump of heavy patrial boots, invisible filaments of this black weeping continue to voice their plaint from the cracks in the floor. With saber tips, swabbing with mops, more scrubbing with swabs, lye, and soap they remove the last tearful remains.

A mute presence brings me out of my drowsiness. Makes me raise my eyelids. Even before seeing her, I *know* that it is she. María de los Ángeles is there. Arms crossed on her breast. Head tilted slightly downward toward one shoulder, the left. Shock of ash-blond hair cascading to her waist. Standing straight and tall, without hauteur but also without false modesty; neither evidencing nor inspiring compassion. She gazes fixedly at me from an inaccessible distance. She lights up the old dead space. Were you present at your father's execution in the plaza? She smiles. Only now has the ring of the iris (very slightly) changed color. On the paper the pupil is almost heron-blue. I learn everything in an instant that does not fit on the sheet of paper. José Tomás Isasi, a cattle dealer in Santa Fe, died poor and ill. He had fallen off his horse, and they buried him in the very spot where he fell. An old Indian woman took you in and brought you to Córdoba, and then later to Tucumán. I see you, a child still, keeping watch on the house in which your godfather Manuel Belgrano rested and prayed after his battles. The place where his agony began; the post station turned into his Garden of Oblivion. Amid the tatters of your tunic, I see a mark on your left shoulder. I know what it is. A trace left by life in the wilds. The weight of the lance, of the rifle. I can calculate the time that that woman's shoulder has carried them. Scar on the neck. Stitches taken by the evil furies of life. To an old man such as I am, with no heat other than that of his desiccation, yearning for the beloved person is a waste of spirit. And it is of no avail to seek any more, because there isn't any more anymore.

I had her father executed because he stole the gold of the State. She is bringing me the price of redemption. Of my own redemption perhaps. I now know what help is. I know it only now. Why only now when there is no more now?

You do not speak and I understand you. I write and you do not understand me. Even if I were able to get out of this hole, I could not be at your side. In another time we journeyed conjoined, one. An enormous horse, half white, half black, interposed between us his white half, his black half. We traveled along side by side but unable to join each other, in different ages. I journeyed through all those great remotenesses with only my own person at my side, without anybody. Alone. Without family. Alone. Without love. Without consolation. Alone. Without anybody. Alone in a strange country, the strangest one being that most my own. Alone. My trapped, lonely, alien country. Deserted. Alone. Full of my empty person. When I left that desert, I landed in one more deserted still. The wind flies between the two, with the smell of rain about to fall. Such wanting to be able to love! Receiving only fear, hence ending up longing for hatred as though it were love! The rain falls in torrents. Great solid drops. Lead curtain between two ages of the universe. Is it the Deluge? The Deluge. We go on. Forty days. Forty centuries. Forty millennia. Amid the huge leaves and the gentle giant monsters, two children play. They do not know each other. Have they ever seen each other? They do not remember. Adam and Eve? I don't know, I don't know. . . . We have not yet learned to speak. But already we understand each other. We play amid the slow-moving peaceful monsters. You go about waking the black silk buds of the giant water lilies one by one. I kick at an angustifoliate pomegranate. I call you without naming you. You turn round and look. Within the passionfruit is something that moves. Living seed. What is it? What is it? We do not know the names of things, of creatures. That is when we know them best. Their names are themselves. Identical in form, in figure, in thought. They palpitate within us. They give off sparks, without and within. We see a tiny chick appear. Metallic plumage. A tiny little human head with little bird eyes. Our hands touch amid the soft down. We remove it from its prison. Colibri. Hummingbird. Picaflor. The original bird. Amid the original darkness Our First-Last-Last Father brought forth the hummingbird so as to keep him company. When he had created the foundation of human language/ when he had created a tiny portion of love/ the Hummingbird refreshed his mouth/ the one who nourished Ñamanduí with the fruits of Paradise was the Hummingbird . . . Yes, yes, a trifling task accomplished by our First-Last-Last Father, laying down the foundations of language! Ah! He sweated hummingbird-drops! There you are! The celebrated phenomenon of human language! After that we too speak. Millions of years after, the fat scholastics idling on their asses and broom-skinny preachers straddling their pulpits were to say that we did not get language from a mere passionfruit but from an "extraordinary aid." And now this *extraordinary aid* is of no help to me whatsoever. I hear you and understand you in memory. The rest, all lost. The huge black horse between the two.

You've arrived today of all days, May 12, your birthday. I've nothing left to give you. Come over here to the table. Take this toy left over from the ones distributed last year. It represents the days of the week revolving on a wheel. It changes color and sound according to the day. In the dark, certain timbres allow one to imagine the figure and color of each day. I think the spring jammed on a Tenebrio Obscurus Sunday. Trujillo the gunsmith came to try to repair it. He said: "I've no power against the evil eye!" Master Alejandro came. The barber worked on it for a good while with his razor. All of a sudden he cried out and drew back: Terrible, what I've seen! Patiño came. He picked up the day-clock, sat down at his three-legged table, put his feet in the basin. He spent a long time picking at the nasal fossae of the clock with his pen, but it continued to lie there in a dead faint. He couldn't even get the hands to go round. All Patiño can do is make the treadmill of the writing desk go round and round, turn the handle of the perpetual-circular. This toy is bewitched, Sire!, he shouted. Bewitched, my eye! It's those mischief-makers who are be-witched. The senile darkness they find themselves in makes them more fearful than children. Each one sees in it what he is inside. Don't blame that innocent thing! They didn't understand. They fled, hagridden by their fear. I'm not going to take the time to wind clocks anymore. Here, take it. Maybe you can fix it. She calmly leaves it lying where it was. She doesn't want it. Perhaps time goes by in a different way for her. A person's life goes round seven times, I say to her. Yes, but life isn't something one has, I hear her say without moving her lips. It's not a child. What can I give you? That rifle perhaps . . . Among the rifles manufactured from meteoric material is the rifle I grabbed when I was born. That one, that one! Take it. Can you carry it? She can! In the stories they tell in books things like this don't happen. She carefully inspects the rifle. She doesn't seem at all satisfied. She picks up the broken musical clock. She sets it. She makes it strike the hour. Twelve strokes. Sunday noon. Color indigo blue. I ask you if you're thinking of staying in the Fatherland. You're the one migrant who's come back. I'm glad you've stopped trailing along as a guerrilla-fighter in the wake of second-rate Attilas of the Disunited Prov-inces, the Ramírezes, the Bustoses, the Disgustoses, the Lópezes and other such shady characters. The only thing they know how to do is slit each other's throats. Thread each other's heads on pikes. Hand in glove with the native-born ne'er-do-wells, Pancho Ramírez tries to invade us. He ends up with his head in a cage. Facundo Quiroga, the Tiger of the Plains, also blusters behind the smokescreen of a supposed invasion. They will smash that blowhard's jaw with a pistol butt in a lordling's coach. We are the only ones who made the Revolution and gained Liberation. The Paraguay-ans are the only ones who understand, our worst enemies said. What? You say not? You'll see. We have here the only free and sovereign Country in South America; the only truly revolutionary Revolution. I see you don't look very convinced. To see the things of this world clearly, you must look at them wrong side to. And then right them. So that's why you've come? Ah, I see. Here I should write that I give a laugh that has an edge of sarcasm. Simply to hide my hesitant stammer. I'm asking you if you would like to do some useful work. This is the price of redemption that you must pay. You are guilty of nothing. I cannot legally condemn you, hand down a death sentence that would be valid. Paying the penalty provided by law, an execution, a hanging: I cannot hand down such trifling verdicts against you. I approve, accept, value this proof that you are a person of few words, of great will. When she moved her hand, consummate slowness, a motion just barely perceptible, I thought she was about to shoot the rifle of my birth at my non-person. Not that I hesitated. Just the slightest twinge of sadness. It's simply that I must test you a bit first, I say to her, my eyes seeking hers. Great will, the best of intentions are worth nothing if not carried out. You must begin from the bottom up; sometimes what is lowest is highest. The end of things depends on their beginning. There are no hierarchies save for that based on the quality of the results. Do you accept? Then you are named directress of the House of Orphan and Foundling Girls. It hasn't been a working institution since Jesusa Bocanegra died in 1617. Despite being a nun, and a poor horsewoman besides, Bocanegra was the first guerrilla-fighter of education in these parts. Proceed immediately to reorganize the House. Make it fulfill its function. You'll find some orphan girls of mine around the place. If they're still there, that is, and haven't gone wrong by making bad marriages and all those sad things that happen to women born to be subdued.

When I left the Hospital Barracks, Patiño brought me the news that the House of Orphan and Foundling Girls was turning into a big brothel. Even the worst whores who were serving sentences in the prisons have been taken, Sire, to that House of ill fame where they are enjoying the good life. It looks like a barracks-house, it's so full at night of city guards, grenadiers, hussars. They whoop it up with the girls in cueribus.§ Much worse than Indian girls. I sent an inspector, Excellency. They practically kicked him out bodily. They say a really tough female, one that nobody knows, at least one that nobody's seen yet, is the person in charge of this company of strumpets, if I may so put it, Sire. They've nailed up their Licence over the door, on a paper with your very own signature, Sire. What I mean, what I suspect, Sire, is that it may just be another mock decree like the one they posted on the door of the cathedral. I've had sent spies round, Sire. Get them out of there. What's that, Excellency? Don't you approve of our keeping watch on the House? Get your spies out of there, you scoundrel!

§Macaronic Latin: in the raw.

The vicar general enters, mounted on a roll of paper. What's up, Céspedes? I am most concerned about your health, Excellency. It's not a matter that concerns you for the moment. The time will come soon enough when you'll be obliged to take the trouble to recite a little responsum for me. I thought that perhaps Your Grace might like to have a priest summoned. You've already proposed that to me. Didn't you receive the reply I sent you through the protophysician? What's the meaning of your coming here like this, Céspedes, disobeying my orders? He tucks the roll under his arm. He begins to knead his hands together. Slow contradanse around the bed. The sacrament of confession, Sire, as Your Worship knows . . . A priest . . . No, Céspedes, I don't need an interpreter to translate my soul into divine dialect. I lunch with God out of the same dish. Not like the lot of you rascals, on sumptuous plates that the devil then licks clean. The vicar tripped over the meteor. Sparks came out his ears. Wait a minute, Céspedes. Perhaps you're right. It may be that the moment has arrived for a private settling of accounts of my public affairs with the Church. Thank God, Excellency, that Your Lordship has decided to receive the sacrament of confession! No, my dear Céspedes Xeria, I'm talking neither about sacraments nor about secretements. Nothing to confess or hide as regards my double Person. That flock of follicules with or without tonsure will take care of that. As for my conduct with respect to the Church, hasn't it been generous, magnanimous, archicharitable? Add whatever superlatives you like to that. Isn't that true, vicar? That is true, Excellency. There will never be words enough to praise the Paternal Trust exercised by the Government by nationalizing the Catholic Church, thereby converting it from Roman to Paraguayan. I allowed the Church complete freedom to govern itself, on the basis of the Patrial Reformed Catechism. As your paternity well knows. Ever since *I* placed you at the head of the Church as vicar general, when Bishop Panés lost his reason twenty years ago, you have been managing the altar industry at your discretion. Which is only proper, since according to the apostle, those who serve at altars are to draw their sustenance therefrom. What is not proper is that the servants of the altar draw from this industry a hundred times more than their sustenance, as your paternity also knows very well. What Your Excellency has said is the pure and simple truth. My gratitude for his magnanimity will be eternal . . . Never mind all that, Céspedes. Go summon the court clerk and come back. I want these confessions between Patron and Pastor to be a legally documented act, without any secrecy. That ought to be the essence of the sacrament of confession. Sanctified not by secrecy but by public note and record. Sin and fault are never reducible to a matter of private conscience or lack of conscience. They always affect one's neighbor, even the one most remote. I have therefore decided that this settlement of accounts in extremis is to be proclaimed and disseminated at my death from all the pulpits of the capital, the towns, and the villages of the Republic.

What are my sins? What fault is mine? My clandestine calumniators from within and without accuse me of having turned the Nation into a doghouse stricken with hydrophobia. They defame me for having ordered the principal figures of the country beheaded, hanged, shot. Is that true, vicar? No, Excellency, it is evident to me that that is absolutely untrue. How many executions have taken place, Patiño, under my Reign of Terror? As a consequence of the Great Conspiracy of the year '20, sixty-eight conspirators were sent to the foot of the orange tree, Excellency. How long did the trial of those infamous traitors to the Fatherland last? As long as was necessary in order not to rush to judgment. They were granted the right to defend themselves. In the end every recourse was exhausted. It might be said that the case was never closed. It is still open. Not all the guilty parties were sentenced to death and executed. Some of them managed to save their skins. That was how it came about that fifteen years went by after his death before it was discovered that the first traitor to his Country, at Paraguay and Takuary, Manuel Atanasio Cavañas, was involved in the plot, and was condemned like the others. Because, my dear vicar, here no guilty party, alive or dead, escapes Justice. So then, tell me, vicar, answer me if you can; I am asking you, reflect, answer in your own heart: Less than a hundred executions of thieves, common criminals, and traitors found guilty of lèse-Patrie—is that an atrocity? What would you have to say to me, by comparison, of the vandalage of bandits who make the earth of the entire American continent tremble with their infernal cavalcade? They pillage, cut off heads, at full tilt and with impunity. When they have finished off the defenseless populace, they decapitate each other. Each one ties the head of his adversary to the halter of his mount as his own is already flying off his shoulders from the mighty saber slash that will leave it tied to the halter of another saddle. Headless horsemen galloping in pools of blood. Stressing the subtle exceptions and the limit cases, I might say that they have become accustomed to living and killing without a head. But then why would they need one, why would they want one if their horses think for them?

Stressing the subtle exceptions and the limit cases, I might also say that I stand in all humility and modesty before these wild Attilas. The patriarcane head of this oasis of peace that is Paraguay, I do not use violence nor do I permit it to be used against me. Let us say, in short, although it is saying a great deal, and only as a figure and movement of the mind, feeling myself to be a reserved, retiring Abraham, clutching the knife here in this dense brush on the third day of the Foundation. A solitary Moses erecting the Tablets of my own Law. Without clouds of fire around my head. Without sacrificial calves. With no need of receiving the Rebelled Truths from Jehovah. Discovering for myself the falsehoods overthrown.

Placed side by side, impossible to compare me with them. But on the other hand my honor would be no less than theirs if we were to establish a passing coincidence with those founding patriarchs as regards time and place. All things considered, they too had their difficulties, marked off by knots standing for forty. Moses took 40 years to lead his people to the Promised Land, and they are still wandering about from sion to Zion. Disper-sion. Inaccessible dimen-Zion. Poor Moses spent 40 days, which were another forty years, on Mount Sinai in order to receive the 10 commandments that nobody observes. I needed less time; 26 years were enough for me to impose my three capital commands and lead my people not to the Promised Land but to the Land Fulfilled. I have achieved this without departing from the axis of my sphere. According to the Bible, the flood covered the earth for forty days. Here, ills and calamities of all sorts rained down for three centuries and yet the Ark of Paraguay didn't founder. In the New Testament we read that Jesus fasted for 40 days in the desert and was tempted by Satan. Here in this desert I fasted for 40 years and was tested by 40 thousand satans. I was not vanquished nor will they crucify me as long as I'm alive. So, vicar, you can see how much the cabalistic forty preys on my mind!

You pollarded padres speak of God by painting shadows and sketching abysses in your rat-trap churches. It is not by believing but by doubting that one can attain to the truth, which is ever changing form and condition. You clericocks paint God in the likeness of a man. But you also paint the devil in the likeness of a man. The difference, then, lies in the beard and the tail. You say: Jesus was born under Pontius Pilate. Was crucified. Descended into hells. The third day he rose again from the dead and ascended into the Heavens. But I ask you: Where was Jesus born? In the world, Céspedes. Where did he do his work? In the world. Where did he suffer his martyrdom? In the world. Where did he die? In the world. Where did he rise again from the dead? In the world. So then, where are the hells? In the world, that's where. Hell is in the world and it's you who are the devils and the imps of Satan, with a tonsure and a tail hanging down in front.

In the Bible we read that when Cain killed his brother Abel out of envy, God asked him: Cain, what hast thou done with thy brother Abel? He asked him, but he did not punish him. Hence, if he exists, God does not punish anyone. He is the one who is punished, for pointing to the truth. What truth? What God? That's what I call painting shadows that no one can grasp, however long his fingernails, however many blessed candles he clutches in his accursed hands.

Nonetheless, I did not forbid any form of worship here. Nor did I fancy creating the cult of the Supreme Being, which certain weak governing powers feel the need to enthrone on their altars, thereby unfurling a protective umbrella for the morrow. The Dictator of a Nation, if he is Supreme, does not need the help of any Supreme Being. He himself is that. In this capacity what I did was to protect freedom of worship. The one condition that I imposed was that the form of worship be subservient to the interests of the Nation. I promulgated the Patrial Reformed Catechism. True worship does not lie in to-ing and fro-ing, but in understanding and complying. I want works, not words, for words come easily while works come hard, not because it is difficult to accomplish work but because the original evil of human nature twists and poisons everything, so long as there is not a soul of iron to watch over, guide, and protect nature and man.

What I did was to protect the National Church against the abuses of those who, instead of serving it and dignifying it as was their duty, debased and degraded it with their dissolute morals and vices. You priests and monks lived publicly with your concubines. Far from being ashamed of it, you boasted of it. Eh? Ah! Here you have the tract of that Rengger and Longchamp pair. Testimony beyond suspicion from this point of view. The prior of the Dominicans, among others, Juan Rengo recounts, light-heartedly confessed during one meeting that he was the father of twenty-four children born of different mothers. How many have you sired, Céspedes? By God and the Blessed Virgin, Excellency, you're putting me on the spot! Your Worship knows . . . Yes, that you've sown more than a hundred offspring; for the most part, among the savage heathen of the gentle sex in Misiones, your duty being to imbue them with Christianity, not impregnate them. Many of these sons of yours are now enlisted in the troops of the line guarding the borders. More honorable than you are. I wouldn't say that here in the capital my vigilance has resulted in making you chaste. But it has at least restrained your lustful urges somewhat. If only your behavior had been intended to challenge the rules of canon law by adopting the rules of the droit de cuissage! In their twisted sensuality the partisans of the tonsure have straightened out the matter by laying claim to both rights at the same time. Which is inexcusable. In 1525 Martin Luther married a nun. I married, Don Martín maintained, not out of love but out of hatred for certain rules reeking with age. I could have done otherwise, since no intimate reason obliged me to act as I did. But I took the step I did in order to mock the devil and his henchmen, the princes and the bishops, the inventors of hindrances, on seeing that they were mad enough to forbid the marriage of priests. I would be pleased to provoke an even greater scandal, Don Martín said, were I to discover that there is another position I might take that would both please God and enrage my enemies.

Stop twisting your roll, Céspedes. Accept your faults as I accept mine. In this confession ex confessione we must absolve each other mutually. Excellency, my gratitude for your unlimited magnanimity and generosity will be eternal. You have done me an honor by having taken those poor souls in at the House for Poor Girls. The House isn't called that anymore, Céspedes. There are no more poor in Paraguay. You are well aware that by Supreme Decree it is now called the House of Foundling and Orphan Girls. What are they if not orphans, even though their parents are still alive? Orphans, but not poor. Adoptive daughters of the State. Children must not suffer for the sins of their fathers.

Moreover, as you also are well aware, I did not confiscate the possessions, the convents, the innumerable properties of the Church with the aim of hereticizing the country. I did so with the aim of clipping the wings of the dissolute servants of God who in reality made him serve their purposes as they led their crapulous lives at the expense of the ignorant people. They came close to parading their fat humanities in the streets in puribus.§ Modesty, much less shame, was no longer the rule for either the regular or the irregular tonsured clergy. Why the talaric habit if these Alarics could swoop down on women's wombs at any place and time they chose? How did the monks go down to the river to bathe, Patiño? Bare naked, Excellency. In a secluded spot? No, Sire, near the sewer outlet of La Lucha, in the little stream always full of washerwomen. You see,

§Macaronic Latin: in the buff.

Céspedes. Piranhas and caribes sliced off the incelibate member of more than one of your followers. They came out covered with blood. Which apparently did not doom them to forced celibacy, for in a short time, as though the stump had sent out new green shoots, they were up to their old tricks again. Was the Government not obliged to take measures against such inequities? Is this to have risen up in rebellion against God? Was it not, rather, to protect him against the blackest abuses of the clericocks?

When the brain of Bishop Panés divaricated, what did the madman do, Patiño? Back in those days, Sire, he craftily found a way to come bother Your Excellency every day, trying to make him believe that he had the Holy Spirit trapped in a cage in the sacrarium of the cathedral. He maintained that the Bird-God dictated his pastorals and humilies to him, and that it was he, the bishop, in person who copied them down with one of the feathers that he had plucked from the wings of the Holy Spirit. The last time he sought yet another audience, Your Worship ordered me to tell the bishop that if what he wanted was to ramble on once again about the Trinitarian Cock Pigeon, he need only to have it roasted and eat it. That a good bird like that would have sufficient virtue to dispel all the vapor of madness that had accumulated in his head, and that if this was not enough to cure him, he should find himself a little turtledove like the other friars, who didn't go out dancing but did better still by staying in with their sisters. Unless there is some error or omission in my account, that's the story of what happened, Sire, and I wash my hands of it. Ah, Patiño, you confounded imbecile! You muddle and mix up everything. The horrible way with words of an idiot. I didn't order you to tell the insane bishop that he should roast the Trinitarian Dove and eat it. I ordered you to tell him that he should cut a pigeon in two and apply it to his head as a plaster. You know very well that this is the remedy used here and everywhere to draw bad humors out of the brain. A pigeon, any pigeon. Not the Holy Spirit, you sacrilegious idiot! That part about the turtledove was added by you, you irreverent mulatto, you vulgar prattler, making mock of that poor old man who was practically a nonagenarian. I didn't order you to pass on that rude message to him. I ordered you to tell him that I was not an idler like him, hence able to receive him at any and every moment, and that if he wanted us to remain on good terms, he should occupy himself with the duties of his office, unless he preferred to have his seat taken from him. Later on, people went so far as to spread the calumny that I poisoned him with the bottles of wine for Mass that I sent him as a gift. Excellency, in the name of Heaven, the shadow of that suspicion has been sufficiently dispelled! The death of His Reverence was due to his bad health and more than advanced age. When the bishop died, what did they find in the sacrarium? Spider webs, Excellency. You see, vicar, how frail the form of the Spirit is! All I did was to confiscate the possessions of the Church. Clean out the impure hordes that had populated it. I cleaned out the rats' nest of the convents. I turned them into military barracks. I ordered the ruined temples to be torn down and burned. I left the ritual intact. I respected the sacraments. I stripped the mad bishop of his prerogatives. I put you in his place, for even though you were not the best you were also not the worst. Hence, even if the Government has ceased to be Catholic it must continue to respect religious faith, so long as it is sincere, austere, without malice, hypocrisy, fanaticism, or fetishism.

Here, through the fault of you País, precisely the contrary happened. Do you remember, vicar, the commanders who asked that statues of saints be sent to guard the frontiers? You've just seen what the parish priest of Encarnación tried to do to the widow of my sentry Arroyo. A matter of fees. Dirty business.

The priest-Paí is the one who has made this faithful people adulterous. It was full of innocence, of natural goodness. If only they had left it in peace, to live in its primitive Christianity! The Old Testament tells of Jehovah's fits of wrath against a Jerusalem crawling with scribes and pharisees. It tells of the misdeeds of the wicked priests, of the false prophets. If this happened in the times of Jehovah with the so-called People of God, what miseries were not to reign here in these lands that the Catholic conquistadors and missionaries came to reduce to a foreshadowing of hell for the greater glory of God?

I removed Bishop Panés from his seat in 1819, after many years of his refusing to fulfill his obligations or exercise his ministry. His madness itself, whether real or simulated, was merely the form assumed by his furious rancor against the patriots. Atheist! Heretic! Anti-Christ!, my clandestine calumniators cry to high heaven. And what do priests here below do? Nothing but skim the pot of black intentions. Nobody is better acquainted with the bottom of the pot than the ladle. I des-potted the ladles of friars and priests. I scooped them up out of their cubbyholes and lairs of shame and degradation. If you'll allow me to put my spoon in and stir that pot, Sire, let me add that Major Bejarano took the confessionals out of the churches at your order, and set them up throughout the city as sentry boxes. A pretty sight, Sire, those carved and gilded wooden niches all along the streets! The guards sitting inside, keeping watch through the little satin curtains. The tips of their drawn bayonets poking out, gleaming in the sun. Your Excellency, very pleased, used to say with a defunctory laugh: No army in the world posts its guards in more luxurious sentry boxes! The women kept coming to kneel before the grilles of the ex confessional sentry

boxes wanting to confess their sins. Denouncements. Complaints. Delations. Quarrels between neighbor women. A few grains would sometimes
get stuck in the sieve of the grille. The guard-curé imposed penance on
sinneresses in the ditches and sent sinners to the nearest police station. A
man of unsound mind came to confess to the sentry that he had assassinated
Your Excellency. I wish to pay for my sin! I wish to pay for my crime
against our Supreme Government!, he kept shouting so that everyone in
front of the Barracks of the Recollects could hear him. He was foaming
at the mouth. I killed our Karaí-Guasú! I want to pay, I want to pay, I
want to pay! I want to be executed! The sentry didn't know what to do
with the madman. Go and turn yourself in at the barracks. No, I want to
be killed here and now!, the madman kept shouting. He leapt up from the
spot where he was kneeling, grabbed the guard's bayonet, and plunged it
into his breast up to the hilt. I killed the Government! And now I've done
it again!, were his last words.

It's as I was saying, Céspedes. Those are the sort of bedevilments that
the evil País have produced in these poor people. They all practice deception. Then they try to cure the affliction, to heal the wounds of my people
saying: All is well! Peace! Peace! Peace! But that peace is nowhere to be
found. The priests do not shepherd men in the fields of the Gospel. They
minister to devils. Hasn't the Pope of Rome himself just said as much?
Hasn't he just emphasized the frightful plurality of the devil? The pontiff
himself! To your knowledge, Céspedes, how many demons were there in
the New Testament? Sixty-seven, Excellency. No, vicar, you're not up on
the latest demonographic statistics. In his latest bull, reprinted in the
Buenos Aires Gazette, the pope stated that there are thousands upon
millions of demons. Did you hear? Thousands of millions! They've multiplied more than the human species. You see what a tremendous sperm
count Satan has! Now each sinner no longer has just one poor devil to
contend with but millions of potent, lustful demons. What can a single
guardian angel do against so many countless evil ones! Are we all doomed
then, with no possible remission, to plunge headfirst into hell? What to
do against the Prince of Darkness? For the moment, do away with all that
remains of the ecclesiastical apparatus, which has proved to be of no use
in the fight against Satan except to let the asses of the faithful go down
the drain, as the vulgar saying goes. From the establishment of the Church
in Paraguay in 1547, the altar industry has produced so much wealth that
it sounds like some sort of preposterous story fit to make us die laughing.
I've made very careful calculations. With a mere half of all that wealth
we could have bought, three times over, all the Yslands of the Yndies of
the Ocean Sea that are under the Brotherhood of the Lord, comprising the

Ymmense Fold of the Faith, as the Bull of Erection reads. The entire bull is taken up with the stipendiary, salariary, tariffary, prebendary, canonary, and calendary ordinaries, and all the other benefices of all the personnel that the Ymmense Sheepfold of the Faith was to shelter. Of the annual rents two hundred gold ducats allotted to the episcopal table, the bishop being empowered to augment it, enlarge it, alter it freely and licitly as often as he saw fit in his diocese. To the dignity of dean, one hundred fifty pounds. To those of archdeacon and precentor, one hundred thirty pesos. To canons, one hundred. What do these anchorites do? The archdeacon, Excellency, examines the clerics who are to be ordained. The precentor presides at the facistol—the choir desk—and teaches the choir servants to sing. The canons celebrate Mass in the absence of the bishop, and recite the Passions, the Epistles, the Prophecies and the Lamentations. Enough, enough, Céspedes. Since there are no more prelates, choirs, or choir desks, and we've had it up to here with passions, prophecies, pasquinal epistles, and defamatory lamentations, all these benefices are abolished. And all these benefits. Do you understand, vicar? No more canonicates, acolicates, prebenders, or fascistos of any sort. Abolished likewise the indignities of prebenders who enjoy high living at seventy pesos a head, and half-prebenders who half live it up at thirty-five rupees per capita. What's this sinecure of magistral canon? His duty is to teach the clergy grammar, Excellency. Abolished. And that of organist? His duty, Sire, is to play the organ at pontifical Masses, at the bidding of the Prelate of the Cathedral Chapter. He is also the one, along with the dean, who gives those persons who need to leave the Choir during the Service because of an urgent necessity of their organs permission to go. Look, Céspedes, at all the waste there's been from 1547 to now with all of this widdle-waddling from the choir to the crapper! Out! All finished! Order all satans in soutanes who have survived the abolition of 1824 to be sent off to work on the patrial farms and estancias. Those too old or too ill to be sent there are to be interned in hospitals, asylums, hospices, or madhouses.

The only real organist Paraguay has ever known: Modesto Servín. Take him as an example, Céspedes. A genius! Never cost the state a single real. Eats his soul. Lives on that, gives to those more needy than himself all the maniocs and maizes of his farm, planted by his own hands. He could have been organist in the Basilica of Saint Peter's. He preferred to be faithful to his Country, playing in the poor temple of an Indian village. Organist of Jaguarón. Elementary schoolteacher. Supreme sanctity. The place where he was born should be consecrated. Office abolished. Let whoever plays the organ do it out of pleasure, with art and out of love of art. Like Modesto Servín.

Are there more ecclesiastic indignities and cardinal offices likely to unhinge their holders, Céspedes? There is that of verger, that of warden or procurator, that of treasurer, whose duty is to open and shut the church; to ring the bells, to safeguard all the liturgical objects; to care for the lamps and chalices; to provide the incense, lights, bread and wine and other things necessary to celebrate the rites. And then, Excellency, there is the dignity of beadle, whose duty is to chase dogs out of the church and sweep the House of the Lord on Saturdays and on the eve of feast days for which vigil is held. How much did the Bull of Establishment allot to the marshalcy of dogs? Twelve gold pounds, Excellency. Do you know, vicar, how much a schoolmaster earns? Six pesos, plus one cow per month. Do you know how much a soldier of the line earns? The same amount, plus his uniform and equipment. Order the beadles to work with the forces of law and order in the annual dog-hunt in the city, towns, and villages. They're already doing that, Excellency. Since the Reform of the Church introduced by the Supreme Government, the beadles have been lending a hand in rounding up strays, and they are the ones who put to death the ever-increasing numbers of rabid ones. How much do you earn, Céspedes? The endowment and table of the bishop, since it is a vacant see, Sire. Plus those of archdeacon, precentor, and canon. Plus the whole and half livings to which I am entitled as dignitary of the Pontifical Habit and vicar apostolic responsible for the Administration of our Church. That strikes me as an outrage! From today on you will receive the pay of an army officer. All clergymen, whatever their offices and malefices may be, are to receive a salary equal to that of schoolmasters. Does that seem like a good idea to you, my dear vicar-provisional? You have spoken, Excellency. May your Supreme Will be obeyed. What news of the arrival of the new bishop? New bishop, Excellency? Don't play dumb, Céspedes. Or is it that you're afraid of losing your bacchant seat? It's not that, Excellency; it's simply that I have had no notice of the arrival of a new bishop. He's not a new one but a very old one. The opulent churchman Manuel López y Espinoza, appointed by the pope in the year 1765. Impossible, Sire! Doctor Don Manuel López y Espinoza, named bishop of this Diocese in the year that Your Grace mentions, would be more than a hundred and fifty years old now. He must be dead long since. No, Céspedes. These Methusalemic bishops don't die. Wasn't Bishop Cárdenas a hundred and six when he passed on? López y Espinoza is taking his time getting here because he's being transported in a litter from Upper Peru. He is being escorted by an army of familiars and slaves. He is bringing with him the vast estates he possessed in Trujillo, Cochabamba, Potosí and Chuquisaca. Cattle. Carts loaded with silver ingots. Opulentia opulentissima. The last I heard of him was that he and his slow-moving caravan had taken a detour and were proceeding via the Gran Chaco instead of the old road from Córdoba del Tucumán out of fear of the guerrillas in the North. I have been waiting all this time for him to arrive. For years now, trained Guaykurú Indians, army scouts, my best gaucho trackers have been patrolling all probable routes through the Chaco in search of him. I am certain that the gestatorial-migratorial chair will arrive in Asunción, even if there's nothing sitting inside it but the petrified skeleton of López Espinoza. But that nullity of an old man doesn't interest me. From this moment on, Céspedes, you may count on the miter, the crosier of the sesquicentenarian, if he is still alive. If he is not, see to it that the much-traveled skeleton is given Christian burial when it arrives on our shores. Any property that the episcopal patriarch may bring with him will be incorporated within the national patrimony; this plus the sums we have just saved on expenditures for church personnel will be sufficient in themselves to finance the great army I plan to create in order to defend the sovereignty of the Fatherland.

The Church of Paraguai, true Grain of mustard in these ymmensities, newly sprowted in such well water'd earth, is prospering splendydly, like a luxuryantly leafie Tree in whose branches Birds of Heaven of ev'ry colour and plumage have bilt most prescious nests without number, the first accounts shortly after the Establishment report with celestial delight. And look at how the mustard seed has grown since! Too many birds of prey amid its branches! Let us proceed in such a way that the luxuryantly leafie Tree will prune itself, so that the foliage drenched with love will be good for something else besides sheltering great birds of a feather flocking together. Period.

Should God have permitted all these iniquities to be perpetrated? Eh? I am asking you who title yourself his minister. No, Excellency, the truth is that he ought not to have permitted them. What do you think God is? I think, Excellency, that, according to the Patrial Reformed Catechism, God the Just, God the Omnipotent, God the Wise is . . . Stop right there! I'll tell you without all that amphibolosity: God is who is definitively. The demon, the contrary. That is the best definition of God that I've ever heard in my life, Excellency!

Let us proceed now to a little examination. What is the first question of the Catechism? With pleasure, Excellency. The first question is: What is the Government of your Country? Answer: the Patrial Reformed. The second question, vicar-provisional. The second, Sire, is: What is meant by Patrial Reformed? Answer: That ruled by wise and just principles, founded on the nature and necessities of men and on the conditions of society. The third. The third question, Excellency, is . . . is . . . Yes! The third question is: How can our system be proved to be good? Answer: With positive facts ... You've made a mistake, vicar-provisional. That's the answer to the fifth question. The positive fact is that your memory is failing. You oblige me to lower your salary to the pay of a sublieutenant. Be more frugal and you'll regain your memory. The joys of frugality cannot be bought for gold. True sanctity is not a sham. It is not the sort that is hidden beneath a tonsure the size of a silver real, established by the Erection as the monetary unit for stipends. If that is religion, let the devil come and tell us so! What a difference between the bad servants of religion and those who serve it in supreme poverty, in total renunciation! The latter see God in their neighbor, in their fellow. The poorer, the more long-suffering, the more vividly they see him. We had an example here. Padre Amancio González y Escobar, the founding father of the melodious villages of the Chaco. I do not have, sirs, any other goods save poverty, part of my religion, he wrote before he died. A brother lent me this bed. I owe this thin little mattress to the piety of an old woman. That earthen jar was made for me by an Indian. This box, by an honored neighbor. This table, this prie-dieu, by a leprous woodworker, a maker of instruments. I order that they be restored to their owners the poor, as I am giving back my life to the one to whom I owe it. Death will find no other spoils in my hut than those in the sack of my body. My soul alone belongs to God. This is what Father Amancio said in words and deeds. He evangelized the Indians in the same measure that the Indians evangelized him. That is the language that the melodious little curé of Emboscada spoke. Everyone understood it. Apostle's language. You, Céspedes Xeria, are not a believer. Yet you speak as though you were one. In my own way, I have a certain faith in God, which you lack. For me there is no such thing as religious consolation. There exists only a religious way of thinking. For you there exist only reward and punishment, which have no meaning after death. Unless life can give a meaning to death in this world that has none. It has no meaning, or else it has one we don't understand. For the meaning of the world is not necessarily that of our life. Our civilization is not the first to deny the immortality of the soul. But it is doubtless the first one to deny the soul any importance. After the battle, one of the oldest Books in the world says, butterflies alight on the dead warriors and the sleeping victors. You, Céspedes Xeria, are not one of those butterflies. If the Church, if its servants want to be what they must be, they will be obliged one day to come out on the side of those who are nothing. Not only here in Paraguay. In all the places on earth peopled by human suffering. Christ wanted to win not only spiritual power. Temporal power as well. Overthrow the Sanhedrin. Destroy the sources of privileges. Smite the foreheads of the privileged.

Otherwise the promise of heavenly bliss, so much wallpaper. Christ paid for breaking the Law on the cross. Pilate washed his hands of the broken china. On this initial failure, on these shards the false apostles descended from Judas erected the false Judeo–Christian religion. Two millennia of falsehoods. Pillage. Destruction. Vandalism. This the religion I must believe in? I know not this God of destruction and death. I must confess my sins to an unknown God? Do you want me to double over with laughter? No, Céspedes. Enough of your funereal jokes! Do you have anything more to say? Just that I came most humbly, Sire, to assure Your Grace of the gratitude and fidelity of the Paraguayan Church toward its Supreme Patron. With the advice and consent of my brothers in religion, I have permitted myself to bring for your examination the Funeral Oration that Father Manuel Antonio Pérez, our most brilliant Sacred Orator, will deliver at the last rites for Your Lordship . . . what I mean to say is, when the moment arrives, if it does arrive, and if Your Excellency deigns to approve it. That moment has come, Céspedes. And that moment has gone. Take the funeral pasquinade and pin it with four thumbtacks to the door of the cathedral. There the flies that win battles will be its most devoted and punctual readers. They will correct its punctuation and meaning. They will save the historians work. Ego te absolvo . . . *(what follows torn, burned).*

(In the private notebook)

Far worse, more contemptible, the civil/military functionaries. Hence on this point, at least, that worthless decretory document is more or less right to propose the gibbet for all of them. It has just reminded me of something I ought to have done without delay.

In thirty years my venal Sanchos Panzas have caused me more trouble than all my enemies within and without put together. It sufficed to send them out with precise measures that would move the Revolution ahead on its orbit for those scullions to turn all my orders topsy-turvy. All my plans. They made the country advance backwards, treading on the feet of the retrograde counterrevolution. Are these the leaders I begat, the patriots I nurtured? I should have done with them what I did with the traitor of the first hour.

Revolution-that-is-revolutionary does not devour its true children. It destroys its bastards. Bunch of troublemakers! I tolerated them. I wanted to rehabilitate them, make worthy functionaries of them. I nested crows that hatched into heirs. Weren't they laughing behind my back as they made me their most miserable of accomplices? They have turned each department of the country into a satrapy where they act and rule like real despots. Buried up to the crown of their heads in corruption, they have counterbanded my power with their flabby counterpower of abjections, obsequiosities, lies. They have counterbanded my orders with their disorders. They have worn my fingernails down to nothing with their piles of files. They laugh up their sleeves at the old madman deluded by the belief that he is capable of governing the country with nothing but words, orders, words, orders, words.

No need to keep these perfidious people. No need of an intermediary counterpower between Nation/Supreme Head. No competitors. Jealous of my authority, their one aim is to undermine it so as to enhance their own. The more I divide my power, the more I shall weaken it, and since I wish only to do good, I wish nothing to stand in my way, not even the worst of evils. Will I resign myself, now that I can barely move, to being the subaltern of a hundred despots of my Nation? Become a useless personage, my uselessness has given my people a hundred masters. As a consequence, it has fallen victim to a hundred different passions instead of being governed by the sole obsession of a Supreme Chief: protecting the common welfare, the freedom, the independence, the sovereignty of the Nation.

I shall hack with my ax and cut down this jungle of parasitic plants. I haven't too much time. But neither do I lack it. I work myself into a rage. I must contain it. My handwriting trembles from having been held back. It makes my arm ache. I discharge my word-orders onto the paper. I cross out. I blot out. I hunch over, erasing every last trace of the secret.

I shall not command the sun to stand still. It suffices to have one more day at my disposal. A single antinatural day in which nature itself would appear to have perverted itself by coupling the longest day with the longest night. Enough! I don't need more than that to destroy these vermin Chiefs, magistrates, functionaries, bah! The best of them is still the worst. The same ones who, by progressing ever upward, might have placed themselves at the head of the Republic, have instead fallen lower and lower and ended up in a fistula.

The circumstances once carefully weighed, everything concurs to assure me that I am going to be re-present at things. Not re-present them. Without haste. Fall on these loathsome pests all of a sudden, with the speed of lightning. Fulminate them. Questions to consider immediately: Exterminate the plague; not just chase it away by raising a din the way one drives off locusts. Work with a delicate touch. If I milk the cow gently I'll get butter. If I blow my nose hard I'll get blood. The barbarians will be scared off. For now trim candles without putting them out. Bring things closer to fruition by gathering all those rotten apples together under the orange tree. Bring everything that's hidden to light. Quidquid latet apparebit.§ Give chase where there's no trace. I'm going to begin with the double-dealer closest at hand: my amanuensis and confidential clerk, who's been weaving his plots and intrigues so as to throw his lot in with the provisory fatuous government and stage a rebellion as soon as he can. Just a little touch of voltaic current in the anuran actuary's sensitive areas.

Let's be fair, eh, Patiño? Doesn't it seem to you that the pasquinade is right after all? What's that, Excellency? When you're not sneezing you're sleeping. I wasn't sleeping, Sire. I merely had my eyes closed. That

§All that is hidden will appear. (From the Dies Irae.)

way, besides hearing, I *see* your words. I was thinking of those words you dictated to me the other day when you said that, living or dying, man is not immediately aware of his death: that he always dies in the person of another while the earth lies waiting below. That is not exactly what I dictated to you, but it's exactly what is going to happen to you within not much more than very little time. I've asked you if it doesn't seem to you that the pasquinade is right. It doesn't seem to me that a pasquinade can be right, Sire. Especially if it's against the Superior Government. Doesn't it seem to you that I ought to have sent to the gallows all those who say they're serving the Fatherland when the only thing they're doing is robbing it at will? What do you think, my trust-unworthy scribe? You already know, Excellency. You don't know that I know. But I know that you don't know everything that should be of importance to you. If thieving rascals knew the advantages of honesty they'd be clever enough rascals to turn honest before it's too late. What's frightening you so? Are you one of them? I'm merely your humble servant, Excellency. You're trembling all over. Your aquatile feet are making the basin rattle below its waterline. Your teeth are chattering. Or have you too suddenly been seized with the convulsions of epilepsy? I'll promote you posthumously to epileptenant of death-on-your-feet, or rather, of death-left-hanging. Don't try to hide your fear. However hard you try to temper it, alter it, cut it down to size, it will always be bigger than you. Only the person who has lost it is master of his fear.

Steadying your magnifying glass in the lance-rest, you delve more deeply into the pamphletary writing. You would like to be able to bury yourself in it, right?; find a substitute; *see* that someone who must die for you. I know, my poor Patiño. To die, ah to die, a very cruel dream even for a dog. Even more so for those who, like you, earn their living through the death of others. You're monstrously fat. You're nothing but a ball of suet. My presumptive sister Petrona Regalada could make more than a thousand candles for the church with your vile body. And as many lowly candles for the city lighting. Give my sister the candle-maker a regal gift: your corpse. She will turn it into candles for your own wake. That way, after your death at least, you'll be the most enlightened confidential clerk I've ever had in my service. Offer that lump of fat that is your person. But do it legally, in a public document, before witnesses. You're one of those who lay traps even after they're dead. I don't know how they'll contrive to hang you when your turn comes. They're going to have to hoist you up with a crank. The ropes of your hammock will suffice for you. You stole a march on the executioner by hanging yourself so as not to have to render an accounting of your betrayals and ladronicides. That heavy thing you carried in your mouth, treason-adulation, made the work of the noose easier. Your haste did not allow you time to write little farewell verses with a bit of charcoal on the walls of your cell, doggerel of the sort that certain scribes claim my relative Fulgencio Yegros wrote before his execution. The shining knight of the lasso and bola, ex president of the First Junta and subsequent conspirator-traitor, could barely write his own name. You were able to imitate the insult-apostrophe that the Cavallero-Bayard scrawled with his index finger dipped in his own blood. He opened his veins with the buckle of his belt, which he then used to hang himself, according to the lies still taught in the public schools a century and a half later. Not to honor him, despite his being a traitor and conspirator, but to denigrate me. Repeat it. Come on! Bray out that fiction that's taught in the schools today. I know full well that suicide is contrary to the laws of God and man, but the thirst for blood of the tyrant of my country will not be quenched with mine . . . Sire, Your Worship is not a tyrant! There are several versions of that posthumous hoax. You may choose whatever one you please. Invent an even more elaborate one before you lose your memory in the noose. Sweat or tears dripping onto the promontory of your belly. You are giving yourself over to the devil and all his kind. The pope already said so. So many demons assailing a single individual, more contemptible than all of them put together.

Do what the mulatto inhabitants of Areguá did, on the advice of the Mercedary friars, when they felt they were being assailed by a horde of demons. They built them a house of their own so that they would stop raising havoc in theirs. The lucibels, lucifers, lieutifers, beelzebubs, mephistopheles, anopheles, leviathans, she-devilesses, and the lemurs of three sexes, which Dante did not record as being in his infernal circles of medieval demonology, launched a fierce assault on the people of Areguá. They continued their diabolical attacks because the house that was built for them did not seem noble enough or comfortable enough. Until Mistress Carlota Palmerola built them a marble palace on the shores of Lake Ypacaray which still stands today. (*In the margin:* Dictate the Decree confiscating this abandoned building, which belongs to the tax authority by right of escheat.) Only then did the cacodemons calm down, demanding only that the women bring them food, and the she-devils that the best-endowed black and mulatto males make the rounds of their bedrooms at night. A price that the first inhabitants of Areguá paid most willingly. For a time the town enjoyed its happiest days. What's bad about happiness is that it doesn't last; what's good about orgies is that they soon wear out both men and demons. After those hundred days of lust in which the people of Areguá far surpassed Sodom and Gomorrah, with the surpassing advantage that fire did not destroy it, the darkies, men and women, returned to the routine of their decorous customs. Those bacchanales in the white castle are no doubt the source of the reddish pigmentation of the skin of Aregüeños, as is attested by the chronicler Benigno Gabriel Caxaxia in his veridical history now translated into several languages. Your father, who emigrated from Areguá to enter the service of the last Spanish governor as scribe, bore on his chubby dusky-purple cheeks this fire-and-ashes granulation. You inherited his face, but your barefacedness is yours alone.

Revolution of the Farrapos§ in Brazil. New paragraphs concerning an old acquaintance, that bugger Correia da Cámara. The young republic sends him to me as minister plenipotentiary. He requests permission to enter the country for the purpose of "maintaining with the Government of Paraguay the relations of perfect intelligence, peace, and good harmony that happily already exist between the two States."

What are the real motives of this so-called republic? If there's an empire still, then there's not a republic. I expect nothing new or good to be forthcoming from it; less still if Correia is its ambassador. And here he is, knocking again at the gates of Itapúa. Before, he came as the emissary of the empire; now, as ambassador of the republic. This good-for-nothing is eternal! More persistent than the great river, this man from Rio Grande do Sul! Running on endlessly. What is all this business about our relations of perfect intelligence, peace, and good harmony between the States? Are the Farrapos trying to gain my good will with a bad joke?

Message to the deputy of Itapúa: I do not know what matter it is that the envoy sent by those who call themselves the revolutionaries of Brazil wishes to negotiate with me. The Brazilians are always the same tricky scoundrels, whatever their disguise. Empire or republic: underneath they're still the same. That raggle-taggle bunch claims it has passed through the needle's eye of Revolution! I am not surprised that it's Correia they've sent once again to palaver with me, the same hunchbacked camel I expelled an endless number of times since his one reason for coming was to hold up and delay, with his endless inept maneuvers, the satisfaction of the claims that I have made and will continue to make till the end of time, so long as they are not duly satisfied. I don't believe he's coming on any important business, but with more of his impertinent stuff and nonsense, a field in

§*Farrapos:* literally, rags (Brazilian). Members of the republican movement centered in Rio Grande do Sul (1835) were known as Farrapos. (The word is also an anagram for Spanish *párrafos,* paragraphs.)

which he considers himself a past master. We won't be losing anything, however, by putting that scoundrel to the test to see what sort of skin game he's playing with his republican phrygian bonnet, his imperial top hat, his gaucho pirate hat, or his bandeirante's hairband.

Ten years back, I offered the Brazilian envoy his last chance. He lost it. I gave orders that he be detained for two years in Itapúa, from September of '27 to June of '29. Nothing beats keeping people waiting for getting them to show their true fiber. Since I don't trust that scatter-brain of an Ortellado, I replace him with Ramírez, the only one who can hold a candle to Correia for cynicism and knavery. The first thing you're to tell him, my dear José León, is that Brazil must give the Republic of Paraguay complete satisfaction with regard to all its claims, and not dally, delay, while away the time and perhaps years in vain pretenses of being diligently engaged in efforts that are futile, frivolous, and fruitless, a strategy aimed at frustrating our extremely just demands concerning well known, indeed all too notorious, matters and facts, doubtless thinking that we here do not have enough intelligence to know what is going on and trying, moreover, with comical tenacity to come to spy on our territory in highly suspect bad faith. You must read the scoundrel this part of the message very solemnly, emphasizing the words, the silences, the threat-pauses. Your mission is to harass him in the countless ways that will occur to you, until he gives up, gives in, or goes away. Wring very delicate chords out of him, no matter how long it takes you. The greatest discretion, of course. All on your own account, without compromising the Supreme Government. Your orders will be executed, Excellency. I shall be most circumspect. Lodge Corr-eia and his retinue in the ex commissariat, José León. Ortellado informs me that the imperial envoy has brought me a hundred Arabian horses as a subornative present from the empire. Put them in the most grazed-out pasture you can find, so that the Arabic steeds may shit their fill and starve at will; and see that the shameless scoundrel takes them with him when he goes. Do you understand, José León? Perfectly, Excellency. Don't shrink before him by so much as a fingernail. Don't retreat a single inch—or better put, a single flea-hop—in the face of the emissary. You know me well, Most Excellent Sire. I shall be very high-handed.

As I wait for things to take their course, I shut myself up in the Hospital Barracks. I thus cut off all possibility of official communication. Incidentally, I devote myself entirely to my studies and writings.

Complete silence from my brand-new representative. What's going on there? I send my liaison officer, Amadís Cantero. Correia da Cámara will later denigrate him in his reports and memoranda. It will be the one and only time he tells the truth.* Not without reason, doubtless, Corriea protests against Cantero. Meanwhile my exegete and liaison officer inter-

---

*"Reader of novels of chivalry, writer himself of unbearable tripe; one of the most decided pedants of the century, this errant Spanish righter of wrongs naturalized a Paraguayan; the vilest vermin I have ever known in all the years of my life. His forte is history, but many times he has Zoroaster acting in China, Tamerlane in Sweden, Hermes Trimegistus in France. A plotter of the first water, he struggled along in misery until he found a place as a spy with the Supreme Dictator, who, I am informed, holds him in great esteem. Night after night he has been reading me something vaguely resembling a novelized biography of El Supremo of Paraguay. An abject dithyramb in which he sets the misanthropic Dictator on the horns of the moon. As far as the Empire and I are concerned, old Amadís uses the most ignoble language. Cloaked in impunity, in ignorance, in vileness, he has poured out on paper a horrible hodge-podge of infamies and lies. The worst thing of all is that I have had to put up with the reading of the delirious manuscript for all of these two long years with feigned admiration and enthusiasm. Forced to listen to its knave of an author, the two of us have wept scalding tears amid the thick smoke from the cow dung they burn here to combat the hordes of insects. To me your tears are the best earnest of your emotion and sincerity, of your admiration and respect for our Supreme Dictator, the biographer and spy of the sultan of Paraguay dared to say to me. It is torture, the worst humiliation to which I have ever been subjected!" (Report by Correa, *Anais, op. cit.*)

Correa da Cámara's indignation explodes: "What the Dictator is making me suffer is unspeakable. I am the representative of an Empire, and he is treating me as though I were a common horse thief. Instead of being offered suitable accommodations, I am detained, held prisoner almost, in the disease-infested shack of an ex commissariat in the middle of a swamp. Despite this ignominious treatment, were I the only one concerned I would not complain, since it is my duty to endure the greatest sacrifices. Is it right, however, that my wife and daughters should be obliged to tolerate such vile abuses? We find ourselves surrounded by pools of water from which there emanate pestilential miasmas, putrid effluvia, insects that are the carriers of swamp fever, dysentery, black fluxes. Storms, strong winds, torrential rains, hailstorms, fall intempestively and continually. Furious thunder and flashing lightning, all the miseries in the world! This is hell, I swear! Indian camps. Brothels everywhere. My wife and daughters are forced to witness obscene and abominable spectacles. The room in which we have been obliged to take refuge is missing half its walls. It has been impossible for us to sleep or rest since our arrival. Stones pelt the tin roof from midnight till dawn. Drunks pass by the house at all hours shouting and throwing stones at the doors and windows, as though for amusement. Indians steal into the dwelling and harass my female slaves. Rob us of food. The atmosphere reeks of the stink of their filthy persons. Soldiers who pretend to be drunk try to force the door, and go away only when I myself threaten to fire on them.

"Yesterday they shot a thief, not twenty paces from my window. Where is the delegate? I send for him. The spy Cantero brazenly tried to put me off with the story that he is busy, that he cannot see me because he is out chasing fleas. Set your mind at rest,

cepts his messages and secret reports. Cantero sends me the intelligence that Itapúa is a beehive of minor events. They take place almost imperceptibly and as though in secret, he says, faithful to his mania for narrating trivia in literary style. Don José León Ramírez has set everyone, including the subdelegate, the commandant and the officers, every soldier in the garrison, to chasing fleas. Don José León himself has climbed into a basket bigger than a boat, fitted out with jugs of water and provisions, and had himself hoisted up to the rooftop of the Delegation building by means of some sort of apparatus, where presumably he too is engaged in hunting fleas. For the last three days he has given no signs of life other than a few sporadic tremors of the basket up there; spasms similar to violent attacks of the ague.

Your Imperial Emissarial Excellency, he says, trying to placate me with feigned courtesy. Your Eminence may be absolutely certain that if the Delegate of the Supreme Government of Paraguay, Don Joseph León Ramírez, is out chasing fleas, he is beyond the shadow of a doubt doing so in honor of your comfort. Fleas are not the only plague tormenting us in this inferno, my dear sir!, I answer. I request, indeed I demand to see the representative immediately, and you tell me that he's gone up in a basket to the top of the Government Delegation building and is now embarked upon an absurd flea-hunt. I remind Yr. Excy., the writer-spy answers imperturbably, that everybody has his own way of doing things, and when it comes to catching fleas the methods used by the Delegate of the Supreme Government are infallible.

"That isn't all, Senhor Cantero. This morning, an old Indian woman demanded a large indemnity from me, claiming that her she-ass had been raped and killed by the he-ass that was bringing water to this hovel. I was obliged to give her a gold doubloon, since she refused to accept less. In your estimation, is all this possible to bear? To top off everything else, the death toll of victims of the plague is mounting. I have seen, with my own eyes from the door of this shack, more than five hundred of those unfortunates being buried in the immediate vicinity. Everything happens in the space of a day, and one day here is no different from the one that follows, from one end of the year to the next, so that I have no idea whether I arrived here during the past week or the past century. The way it is in dreams, Most Exc. Senhor!, Cantero says jokingly. Speaking of dreams, I had one about Paraguay and Brazil a week or so ago. I dreamed that Brazil would be the greatest empire in the world if the dividing line were extended to the shore of the Paraguay River on the west and to the Paraná River on the south. I dreamed, the crafty spy added, that Paraguay and Brazil forged not only a total alliance but formed a complete unity. I do not believe, however, that such are the aims of the Brazilian Empire. Moreover, I don't believe in dreams, he said. I was forced to answer him in my severest tone of voice: I believe even less in trickery disguised as subtlety! One step more, Senhor Roa,[1] on the path of insults and the Paraguayan Government will discover to what point the representative of the Empire is capable of upholding the dignity of his eminent character and the offended majesty of his sovereign!" (Report by Correa, op. cit.)

[1] The compiler wishes to point out that this lapsus and mention are not attributable to him: Correa's confidential report mentions this name textually, as can be verified in Anais, Volume IV, p. 60. (Compiler's Note.)

What shall I do, Excellency?, Cantero asks. Wait, I order him. Go on drawing Correia out.

My confidence in Ramírez is not yet shaken. He must be plotting some clever ruse against the envoy of the imperial court.

As you will see, Your Excellency, Cantero tells me in his last report, I am endeavoring by every possible means to mollify the emissary of the imperial court and wheedle information out of him as to the hidden intentions of the second and third degree that may have brought him here, as Your Excellency has ordered me to do. During one conversation I hit upon the idea of taking another tack, trying my best to loosen his tongue by telling him of a supposed dream I had had concerning the alliance between Paraguay and Brazil, which would make the two of us together the major power on this Continent. The imperial envoy appears to be in such low spirits that he is really beginning to arouse one's pity for him.

In the cool galleries of the Hospital Barracks I delight in imagining the envoy of the empire devoured by mosquitoes, bedbugs, and fleas. Overrun by the vipers of the swamplands. Sweltering from the heat of summer in the miserable oven of the ex commissariat. Hounded by that pest Amadís Cantero, who is trying to discover by way of dreams what Brazil's expansionist plans are.

A dispatch from Ramírez at last. He triumphantly explains to me in detail, on a millimetric scale, the relationship that obtains between a flea's hop and the length of its feet. A hop that varies from male to female, before and after sucking the blood of its victims; also before and after copulation, begging Your Worship's pardon. My crude clod of a delegate has recorded all the copulary movements in risqué sketches.

Confidential report from Cantero: What the Honorable Delegate Ramírez has taken up to the rooftop of the Delegation in the basket, Excellency, isn't just victuals or water; he has also placed one of the imperial envoy's chambermaids aboard the basket. The Honorable Delegate took off toward the heavens so discreetly that no one saw or suspected a thing. The basket-belly buttoned the old fashioned way, the occupants joyously rubbed their bacon making the two-backed beast on the roof of the Delegation. The imperial envoy for his part has complained to me that the invasion of fleas has grown considerably worse. I am trying to keep him from getting wind of this latest turn of events, already public and notorious in the town. Even the Indians are laughing about the basket-that-went-to-heaven. I greatly fear that the mistrustful Brazilian will want to be indemnified, and thus recoup the indemnity he paid the Indian woman for her dead ass. The beautiful mulatta slave, however, seems to be well pleased after her encanastation with the Honorable Representative. We can only say that with a certain sacrifice on his part, it must be admitted, Don Joseph León Ramírez has cleverly contrived to benefit our cause. The mulatta is the one who steals her master's secret correspondence, thereby allowing us to make a complete copy of it in order to keep Your Grace fully informed of the imperial envoy's communications to his chancellery.

I order Cantero to give up his pacifying offensive. In his last dispatch he informs me: I invited the imperial envoy and his family for an outing on horseback in the splendid woods along the Paraná. He curtly refused. I then sent him as a gift a Paraguayan hammock for him, his wife, and his daughters. And then later on some silverwork ornaments. Same refusal. On the occasion of the national celebration of your birthday, Most Excellent Sire, the imperial envoy took advantage of the opportunity to emphasize his vast annoyance. He had celebrated the sixth of January of the year before in a most notable fashion. He ordered two great bonfires lit and the front of his residence illuminated with eight hundred candles, in the way I had told him that the Paraguayan populace shows its devotion to our Supreme Dictator on the eve of the anniversary of his birth. Besides the candles, the imperial envoy distributed alms to the poor and, in full dress, witnessed with his family the dances and festivities of the people. This year, on the other hand, he kept the doors and windows of his dwelling closed and, dressed in the most ordinary garb, strode up and down outside in an ostensible and defiant manner. I allowed myself to remark on the change in his attitude from one year to the other. What obligation does the plenipotentiary of an Empire have, he replied with asperity, to celebrate the birthday of a head of government who detains him for seventeen months in an indecent, unhealthy Indian village? A man continually mistreated cannot and ought not to allow himself diversions. Inform your Supreme Dictator, who appears to boast of the fact that Brazil fears him, that such is not the case. The Empire is not frightened by petty things and considers the source of the insults heaped upon its envoy. Inform him for me that if the progress of the negotiations has slowed down, it is due to the duplicitous conduct of the Paraguayan Cabinet, a moral sickness most definitely unknown at the Court of Rio de Janeiro. How ought I to reply to the insolent remarks of this wretched envoy? Let him vent his spleen. Tell him that if he really has anything important to tell me, that proofs to that effect be forthcoming in the form of keeping his pledged word regarding the sending of arms and everything else. If he can't come up with anything, let him go back where he came from. I must also inform Your Grace that the bones of the Arabian horses brought as a gift by the imperial envoy are already turning white in the pasture as flocks of birds of prey descend on them. Tell the ravens for me, Cantero, that I wish them good appetite!

Last report of Correia to his government, Cantero chatters in code: The international ties of the Dictatorship are vast. Its tentacles extend to the Plata, to the Banda Oriental, to Río Grande, to Santa Cruz de la Sierra. The fundamental objective is clear from the plans afoot for the formation of a Grand Confederation of which the center and the head would be Paraguay. There is no doubt that the Paraguayan government is in league with Marshal Barreto of Río Grande, and that it is not abandoning the project of inciting Río Grande del Sur to wage Revolution and confederating it with Montevideo against Buenos Aires, as soon as it can count on an alliance with Brazil in order to thwart the bold intentions of the Porteños. The moment he received news that the provinces of the interior were planning to break with Buenos Aires, the Dictator, who is the soul of this new Federation, even though he is still keeping himself hidden behind a curtain that can easily be seen through, ordered the position or camp of Salto, which he had abandoned, to be reoccupied and sent a mission to reconnoiter the ports of his new future allies. Ah, that prattling plotter Correia! And you're the one who's coming now as the ambassador of the revolutionaries of Río Grande! I should allow you to come ahead to Asunción, just to have the pleasure of planting your head threaded on a pike in the center of the Plaza de la República! Bah, you filthy blackguard! I'm not even going to grant you the honor of staining Paraguayan soil with your blood! You can go straight to the devil himself! That naïve Cantero cautions me with his usual idiocy: I have learned, Excellency, that the imperial envoy is also an Arch-Mason, belonging to the highest and most fearsome ranks of this forbiddingly obscure association. That would be far from the worst thing about Correia, my dear Cantero. On the contrary, being a Mason, if that is what he is, would be the only minuscule good point about this scheming bandeirante disguised sometimes as an emissary of the empire and at others as the ambassador of the ragtag republic of the Farrapos. Poor republican tatterdemalions! Poor Masons! Having this superfluous swindler in their ranks will be their ruin. Cantero's message continues: The imperial and republican representative, Most Excellent Sire, considers Your Grace to be the head of the vast confederation aborning. As of this date, he states in his report of April 2, more the head of the Argentine Federation than Buenos Ayres itself, conniving in the Cisplatine State and in the Peruvian Republic, able to count on supporters in Misiones and Río Grande, with a wealth of secret contacts in Matto

Grosso, the Dictator will take advantage of the first opportunity to lend a hand to the partisans of the absolute independence of the Province of Rio Grande and finish Buenos Ayres off once and for all; to place himself openly at the head of the present Federation, invade Matto Grosso, take possession of Misiones Orientales by way of compensation or reprisals, and bring the horrors of war to the center of the Province of San Pablo, entering by way of El Salto de Sete Quedas, on the same pretext. The uninterrupted correspondence between the Paraguayan Government and the dissident provinces of the Federation of the Río de la Plata, through the intermediary of Corrientes, during the most recent campaign in the south, the amazing repatriation of the subjects of Córdoba, Santa Fe, and Paraná by the Paraguayan Dictator, just a few short months before these Provinces rebelled against Buenos Ayres and declared war on it; all these circumstances, along with others of which I shall continue to give a punctual account in my reports, lead to the conclusion that there is no other way to ward off the dangers that threaten the Empire on every hand save to form an alliance with Paraguay and its cunning and unruly dictator ... And what did I have in mind other than that, you crafty rascal? You're as good as Cantero at setting down on paper an impossible farrago of faked facts, fictions, fabrications of all sorts and sizes. Shut up inside your basket of intrigues, your imagination is feebler than José León Ramírez's when it comes to killing fleas. Expel that impenitent degenerate once and for all, José León, and make sure you search his baggage carefully. Don't let him carry off even one flea that belongs to us! Do you understand! Keep a sharp eye out! And tell him in no uncertain terms that if he doesn't want to lose for good the head he doesn't have, he is never to set foot on our shores again. He can go to hell with his empire or his republic, and with both at the same time!

(In the private notebook)

The fleabrain's ideas aren't bad at all. Paraguay, nucleus of a vast Confederation, is what I thought of from the very first and proposed to those Porteño imbeciles, those Oriental imbeciles, those Brazilian imbeciles. What's bad, indeed downright deplorable, is that those miserable wretches are turning a project as generous and beneficent as an American Confederation, formed in the image and likeness of their own interests and freed of the influence of foreign masters, into a matter for underhanded plotting and scheming.

Another subject:

I have discharged José León Ramírez. Have me shot, Excellency!, he begged, weeping a bitter tear and throwing himself on my mercy when I ordered him to present himself and render an account of his misdeeds, because as you should have remembered, José León, fleas feast on feet stretched beyond the sheet. A consummate actor! He was about to swallow the buckle of my shoe. I shall die happy as I face the firing squad, Supreme Sire, if those bullets are the price I must pay for having pulled the leg of that rascal from the empire who tried to make fun of our Country and our Government!

I should not have been taken in by that farceur's repentance. Exactly nine months after his rehabilitation he gave my supposed niece Cecilia Marecos a son. He obviously hadn't found it necessary to tuck her into a basket or pretend that he wanted to try out a peculiar new way of catching fleas or crabs. I ordered him to pay the mother the pension to which she is entitled by law. To allow him to earn the money to pay it to her with all due dignity, I put him to work, in leg irons, mucking out army latrines. He'll be at it quite a while, till the boy reaches his majority. In the end the years will deflate José León's copulative conceits.

Perpetual Circular

When I received this wretched Government, I found no money in the Treasury, not a yard of cloth, no arms, no munitions, no sort of provisions or equipment. I am nonetheless bearing all the ever-increasing expenses, securing the supplies, readying the war matériel required for public safety and national security, not to mention costly works projects, thanks to clever schemes and strategies, astuteness, constant effort. Endless labors, days and nights without sleep, filling posts, ministries, offices that should be occupied by others, in the civil, the military, and even the mechanical domain. Overburdened by all this and by other tasks that are not my concern or my responsibility. All this because I find myself in a country full of nothing but idiots, where the Government has no one to turn to, thereby obliging me to turn to myself to get things done, to instruct, to train, to administer, to take care of everything down to the very last detail, in my eagerness to rescue Paraguay from the misery, the despair, the abjection into which it has been plunged for three centuries now.

I find myself unable even to breathe. Submerged in the immense cumulus of duties/occupations that are incumbent upon me alone, in this country where it is necessary for me to fill fifty offices at once. If things go on this way, it is best that I take a rest. Allow Paraguay to go on living as it always has, that is to say in the Paraguayan way. A people of redfaces, inured to the scorn, the mockery of the people of other countries. In the end my back-breaking labors will have been in vain; my outlays of money wasted. Silver down the drain. Paraguayans will remain Paraguayans, and nothing more, for all time to come. Thus, despite all its titles of Sovereign and Independent Republic that have made it the First Republic of the South, it will be regarded as nothing more than a Republic of Guanás, on whose sweat and substance others grow fat.

If, amid all these burdens I bear, there are those who want more than I can offer, I have no other choice than to dismiss them. I am unable to work what the friars call miracles. Certainly not in this land of impossibles.

I'd like to see all of you fighting here from the Government with the incompetence of functionaries in the departments of Treasury, Police, Civil Justice, Public Works, Foreign Relations, Interior, Brake Inspection, and who knows how many others! Going in desperation day after day to berate the employees in the lime factory, the arms, gunpowder, and ammunition factory; the dockyards, the shipyards, where I am unable to get them to ready the fleet of war vessels that will cover the defense of the river from the Capital to Corrientes. The Ark of Paraguay, the great merchant vessel, has been lying buried in the sand for twenty years now. Add to these activities the equipping, instruction, training of our land-based artillery, infantry, cavalry troops; of navy crews that have mastered all the practical skills required; the superintendence, the supervision, the direction of the Patrial workshops, warehouses, estancias, farms; the organization of the espionage network, scouts, spies, liaison men, secret agents, the most ignorant and inept intelligence corps in the entire world.

In addition to being Perpetual Dictator, I must at the same time be Minister of War, Commander-in-Chief of the Armed Forces, Chief Justice, Judge Advocate General, Director of the Armament Factory. Since all the ranks of commissioned officers down to captain have been done away with, I alone constitute the General Staff in all branches of the armed services. As Director of Public Works, I must personally supervise everyone, down to the last craftsman, the last little seamstress, the last mason, the last road worker; all this without counting the work, the irritations, the vexations continually caused me by all of you officials, you civil/military functionaries in garrisons all over the country, in the most distant fortresses.

I should like to see you do what I do! I offer you the job. Come take it over if it still seems to you a mere nothing. Do it better than I do, if you can.

A pasquinade circulating these days claims that the people have lost their confidence in me, that they are sick and tired of me, completely fed up with me; and that I continue in the Government only because they do not have the power to overthrow me. Is that certain fact? I am certain it is not. On the other hand, if I were to end up losing confidence in the people, having my fill of it, growing so weary of it that I can bear no more, can I dissolve it, elect another? Note the difference.

Chiefs of the Republic: Above all else you should examine yourselves, delve into the depths of your consciences, ask yourselves to what degree you regard yourselves as being free of that ptomaine that appears in those who are dead before they die. Make a footnote: Ptomaine is the poison that results from the corruption of animal substances. A thick suppuration with a fetid odor, produced by the Vibrio proteus bacillus in connubial conjunction with the virgula or comma. Mortally pathogenic, since it comes from the alembics of Thanatos. Those savages, I now realize, are capable of going so far as to make ptomaine instead of cane brandy in their clandestine stills! It is also vulgarly known as cadaverine. I can offer you no antidote for this poison that the living-dead manufacture inside themselves. I shall tell you without vacillation that for this bacillus there is no counterbacillus. There is no resurrection against cadaverine. At least no one has discovered it yet, and probably no one ever will. So be careful! These poisonous juices form not only in those who are to be buried in pastures outside the walls with neither cross nor mark to commemorate their names. They are also engendered in those who lie beneath fatuous "cumuli." In those more monstrously fatuous still who commission pyramid-mausoleums in which to keep their carcasses like a treasure in a strongbox. The proto-founders of our country, the proto-heroes, the proto-beings, the proto-rogues and other sorts of protos have statues of themselves erected, get plazas, streets, public buildings, forts, fortlets, cities, towns, villages, general stores, places of amusement, pelota courts, schools, hospitals, cemeteries named after them. Lupanary sanctuaries of their sacred rests and recreations. This has always been so, in all times and places. It is still so today. It will continue to be so, as long as the living go on being idiots. Things will change only when it is commonly recognized, without false pride but also without false humility, that the people, not the plebs, is the only living monument that no cataclysm can cause to fall to wrack and ruin.

Here too, before our Revolution, this happened. I have already spoken to you of the fastuousness and the fatuousness of the militia of noble lineage; that is to say, those lords of the lasso and bola who inherited estancias, sabers, and gold braid. It would not be at all surprising if this happened again now. Weeds put down deep roots. It might well be that the ptomaine of those unworthy officials and chiefs is again infecting you from the outside in, from the inside out. I have said and still say that a revolution is not really revolutionary unless it forms its own army; that is to say if this army does not come forth from the very bowels of revolution. Its offspring, engendered and armed by it. But it may happen that the hierarchies of this army become corrupted or go rotten in their turn, if instead of placing themselves completely at the service of Revolution, they place Revolution in their service and degenerate. I would say then that the execution of some hundred conspirators and traitors to the

Country was not enough. I thought I had rounded up every last treacherous stray in the military, lie-quidated every last one of them; skimmed off the scum of all those who took themselves to be specially called and chosen, each of them of and by himself, to be the head of the Revolution, when all they were was ignorant politicasters, venal milicasters tricked out in glittering uniforms. It would seem evident that the ignominious punishments reserved for these miserable traitors to their Country and the People of the Republic have not served as a remedy. These punishments—the gantlet, shooting, running through the pikes—have apparently not put an end to the degradation of chiefs and officials, a degradation which has propagated itself to a disgraceful degree and spread its rank infection to the lower echelons of the armed services. I would be obliged to infer the following: there is something uniformly malign beneath the uniform. This *something* thus comes to constitute the very insignia of dishonor, not of honor; the sign not of the condignity of loyalty but of the indignity of disloyalty. The inventions of men are different from century to century. The malice of the militia seems to be forever the same. A uniform stigma in signia saeculorum.

Comport yourselves as not only honorable but also humble soldiers of your Country, whatever your rank, function, and authority.

El Supremo's principal libelists, whose testimony may be partial but nonetheless not open to the suspicion of a marked bias in his favor, explain and unwittingly justify the austere rigor and implacable discipline that the Perpetual Dictator tried to impose upon his armed forces, apparently without much success:

"Running the gantlet is ordinarily a military punishment only. In order for such punishment to be inflicted, an order from the Supreme Dictator suffices. Those sentenced to capital punishment meet their death at the hands of harquebusiers, as in the last days of Spanish rule. On the day of the execution a gibbet is set up in the plaza, from which the body of the executed criminal hangs suspended." (Rengger and Longchamp, *Historical Essay*, chap. II.)

With regard to the trial and execution of the conspirators of the year '20

(the majority of them military leaders, many of whom had distinguished themselves in the battle against Belgrano's expedition), Wisner de Morgenstern states: "The atmosphere was heated, and there is no doubt that the storm was gathering, for all those who did not share power were against the Dictatorship. The Dictator had received several anonymous letters warning him to be careful, and he had redoubled his vigilance. On the night of the second day of Holy Week, five individuals were arrested and subjected to rigorous interrogation. Another one, who had managed to escape the dragnet, a certain Bogarín, a fearful and timid man, went to confession and revealed everything he knew about the plan that had been drawn up to eliminate the Dictator. Good Friday was the day chosen to finish him off, on the street, during his usual afternoon outing. Captain Montiel was the officer designated to do the deed. Once the Dictator had disappeared, General Fulgencio Yegros, his kinsman, would take over the government, and Majors Cavallero and Montiel would assume command of the troops, among whom were a number of sergeants in on the plot. The contrite Bogarín was enjoined by the priest to go to the Dictator that very day and reveal the plan, since as a good Christian, and in view of the fact that a crime was about to be committed, it was his duty not to have any part in it." *(The Dictator of Paraguay,* chap. XVII.)

Over the years, the case was "tried" in the basements of the Truth Chamber, which Wisner more cautiously calls the *Trial Room.* The Guaykurú torturers of Bejarano and Patiño had their work cut out for them in this laborious inquiry. In the end the confessions wrested from them by the "lizard-tail" whips left not a shadow of a doubt. On July 17, 1821, the sixty-eight men accused of conspiracy and high treason were executed. Following this, the *Supreme Dictator* guided the ship of State without further complications until his death. In one of his notes we read this placid reflection: "The problems of political meteorology were resolved once and for all in less than a week by the firing squads." *(Compiler's Note.)*

"The Dictator's greatest pleasure was talking about his Ministry of War. The armorer once entered with three or four repaired muskets. The Great Man raised them one by one to his shoulder, and aiming at me, as though to shoot, squeezed the trigger several times, striking sparks from the flint. Delighted,

roaring with laughter, he asked me:— What did you think, Mister Robertson? I wasn't going to shoot a friend! My muskets will send a bullet through the heart of my enemies!

"Another time the tailor presented himself with a jacket for a newly recruited grenadier. He ordered the conscript to be brought in. He made him get undressed to try it on. After superhuman efforts, since it was evident that he had never worn garments with sleeves, the poor lad managed to get it on. The jacket was utterly ridiculous. Yet it had been made after a passing fancy and a design of the Dictator himself. He praised the tailor and threatened the recruit with terrible punishments if the uniform was stained in any way whatsoever through carelessness. The tailor and the soldier left the room trembling. Then, winking an eye at me, he said to me:—C'est un calembour, Monsieur Robertson, qu'ils ne comprendent pas!

"I never saw a little girl dress her doll with more seriousness and delight than this man displayed as he went about dressing and equipping each one of his grenadiers." (Robertson, *Letters.*)

If unimpeachable testimony were still needed as regards the Supreme Dictator's preoccupation, his constant concern for his armed forces, that provided by Father Pérez in the eulogy at his obsequies would more than suffice:

"What steps did His Excellency not take to preserve the peace of the Republic, to bring it to a respectable state with respect to other States? Supplying arms, training soldiers provided with the most dazzling uniforms ever seen in the armies of these Republics and even those in the kingdoms of the Old World.

"I am amazed when I contemplate

this Great Man devoting so much time to these matters! He buries himself in the study of militia, and very shortly thereafter is commanding military drills and evolutions as though he were the most experienced veteran. How many times I have seen His Excellency stand behind a recruit to show him how to aim straight at the target! What Paraguayan would neglect to carry his rifle in precisely the proper way when his own Dictator showed him how to handle it, use it, clean it and repair even its smallest pieces? He appeared in person at the head of the cavalry squadrons and led them with such energy and skill that he transmitted his living spirit to those following after. His voice rang out more powerfully than the bugle on marches and in the hand-to-hand engagements of mock combats. And even more than that! It was a great marvel to see the Dictator himself, after these epic practice maneuvers, minutely review each and every man, one by one, and find not the slightest stain on any of those spotless, immaculate white uniforms!"

. . .

"All Paraguayans enter service as privates, and the Dictator does not commission them as officers for many years, and then only after they have gone through all the lower ranks. The general uniform is a blue jacket with ruffles and edgings, whose color varies according to the branch of service, white trousers, and a round hat; aiguillettes on the seams of the shoulder distinguish the cavalry from the infantry. The one exception is the corps of mulatto lancers; their uniform consists of a white jacket without buttons, a red waistcoat, white trousers, and a cap, also red. In order to make these waistcoats and other uniform items, the damasks from the ornaments that were still to be found in the confiscated temples and convents were used. It is true that the Dictator had several hundred dress uniforms made for the mounted dragoons and grenadiers, but they are worn only on parade days and to mount guard at Government House on the occasion of the visit of a foreign envoy. Outside of these two cases, the uniforms are carefully stowed away in the State storehouses." *(Rengger and Longchamp, ibid.)*

When I asked you to sign receipts for the uniforms issued the troops, one of you came up with a ridiculous question concerning a few scraps of worn-out shoe leather, as though I had any reason to concern myself with such rubbish, though naturally I am not going to throw it out in the street. The measure of a soldier is his capacity, not the clothes he wears. In the viceroyalty of New Granada, most of the army of patriots had only chiripás and blouses; most of the time they were naked, marching for days on end, dying continually in frequent battles with the Europeans. The austere words of the Liberator San Martín, born in the Paraguayan Yapeyú, confirm this. In a General Order of the year '19, the Liberator harangues his men: Comrades: We must make war as best we can. Though we have no money, we still have meat and a plug of tobacco. When our clothes wear out, we will dress in the lowly homespun that our women weave for us, and if we don't have that, we will go about bare naked like our compatriots the Indians. Let us be free, for the rest matters not at all.

This was what a great, distinguished general proclaimed in the midst of the campaign for liberation. Here, my elegallant officers want to strut about in dress uniforms as their troops muster on the drill field or in the Plaza at reveille or retreat, so as to dazzle the populace. As though they were superior beings. No, gentlemen. The military must make sobriety and austerity their habit. To be a good soldier, luxury is not only not necessary but positively harmful. Don't ask me for any more red waistcoats of satin, damask, heavy silk, brocade, embossed leather, andaripola cotton, or chambray. I ordered them made only once, for the mulatto lancers. The high-buttoned passementerie tunics worn by the white officers who commanded the corps of coloreds no longer exist. The cloth of the ornaments confiscated from the Church was only enough for the wardrobe of the battalions of grenadiers, dragoons, and hussars. All the ecclesiastical adornments have rotted away. Waistcoats, jackets, baldrics edged with silver. High-crested velvet helmets adorned with white edging, with yellow taffeta ribbons fluttering in the wind of the marches, all nothing but tatters now. There are no more ornaments to confiscate. I beg your pardon, Excellency. I just wanted to remind you that in the State Stores there are still twenty bundles of those fabrics that were seized in the churches of the Indian villages. Silence! You are not to speak unless you're spoken to. Don't contradict what I dictate. Be content with a suit of punteví, of satin-finish duck or drill. Dressed leather trousers. Brabant blouses for officers. Striped cotton ones for the men, made from remnants. Schoolmasters dress even more modestly than soldiers of the line. It is only in the last two years that they have been provided with somewhat more decent undergarments; inferior nonetheless to those issued the troops. Twill trousers; linsey-woolsey shirts. Jacket of whatever cloth is available. Nankeen waistcoat. Poncho, a felt hat, a neckerchief. Before that, they wore garments made of cloth that they themselves learned to make out of cotton, karaguatá, pindó fibers. They have no need of any fancier apparel to fulfill their duties as teachers in front of a classroom of naked children, clothed in nothing but their innocence. The only garments I myself have left these days are a much-mended frock coat and two pairs of breeches, one for formal occasions, and the other for riding. And two waistcoats that have waged a thirty years' war against moths, cockroaches, termites.

What is more, I don't understand why you want, why you keep pestering me for luxurious wardrobes if you keep leaving your finery lying about wherever you toss it. I am indignant enough as it is, having learned that officers on duty strut about dressed in the most outlandish manner, in

Irish linen dressing gowns, bombazine balloon pants, nightcaps like mine, imitating my intimate apparel, instead of wearing the regulation uniform corresponding to their rank and duty. What sort of arrant nonsense is this? For a leader of men, I do not want a popinjay proud of his curly locks and the clocks on his socks, hiding his shamelessness behind the shameful antics of a puppet. I prefer one who looks like a little bowlegged banty but takes a firm stand, at precisely the right spot and exactly the right moment. A bold heart in the service of the republic. Able to fulfill his duties to the hilt, without ostentation and without disgracing himself. Everything has two handles. Mind you don't grasp the wrong one.

Those in command must also keep an eye on the discipline and the good health of their men. Paraguayan troops look like a bunch of weaklings. Our army isn't destroyed by its enemies, as happens in other countries. It renders itself unfit, wipes itself out whole squares at a time, what with the men's excesses: leading Indian girls and half-breeds a merry dance, getting drunk on the brandy that foreigners smuggle in to them to bribe them, or worse still, to make degenerates of them, to bring about their ruin even sooner.

I order you to punish these crimes ruthlessly. Extremely summary trials. The guilty parties must be put to death on the very spot where you catch them committing such heinous crimes. If this is not done, their commandant will be brought before a court-martial to answer for his indolence in the face of such abuses.

The Indian population, the wives of the natives in particular, deserve special protection. They too are Paraguayans. With all the more reason and natural rights of far longer standing than those who inhabit the country today. You must allow them and their customs, their languages, their ceremonies, to go on living in the lands, the forests that have been theirs since the beginning. Remember that exacting slave labor from Indians is absolutely forbidden. The rule to apply to them is the same as with free peasants, since they are no more and no less than they.

I don't know how another one of you, who is regarded as a great chief, dared ask me, without so much as blushing, to allow him to transfer a soldier to his office to act as his secretary, maintaining that he needs him to draft his dispatches properly. This is as much as to admit that the soldier can discharge the duties of office chief, or even commandant, better than he. Unless this business of getting off reports conceals some unavowable duty. Which would be twice as bad.

Is it possible that many of you do not even know how to draw up a bad report, scribble a message, milk the udder of your intelligence by scrawling words on a page? This is a sad state of affairs for the Government.

When I receive bunches of paperwork from commandants, the first thing I do is study the handwriting, the style of writing. One and the same thing can be said in different ways with different applications that may have different meanings. Hence both the commandant who doesn't know how to write and the clerk that writes what he doesn't know end up talking about things that can't be understood no matter how they're read, backwards or forwards, upside down or right side up, front side to or hind side around. If something bad happens on account of a badly written report, the commandant can always evade responsibility by saying he wasn't the one who wrote it; it was the clerk, who misinterpreted what was misdictated. Moreover, when it is a question of sending out a confidential order, the Government is placed in an embarrassing position, suspecting that the commander won't understand it. In his reply he'll no doubt come out with some sort of balderdash or fiddle-faddle, as frequently happens. Shouldn't I promote the clerk to commandant and demote the likes of the illiterate commandant to the ranks?

I took you all out of nowhere, back in the days when you were nobodies and I was out gathering wildflowers that were still nothing but little nubbins of buds. I want new people, I said to myself. I want a golden harvest in the grain. I want to enlist the best of the best in the service of the Country. And so it was that I discovered those who seemed to me to be the best. I wasn't about to search out the secret hidden in the wombs of our women with Jehovah's candle. I simply took what I found at hand. It was enough for me if each one of you spoke of himself as a stranger; someone who was not master even of his own person. I asked each of you: Is this your house? No, Sire, this house belongs to everyone. Is this dog yours? No, Sire, I don't have a dog of my own. Are your body, your life at least your own? No, Sire, they have just been lent me till our Supreme Government wishes to make use of them. Such a lack of a sense of private property was a sign of incalculable strength. You had nothing. Yet you possessed everything, since each of you was all. I said: These are people born with their feet on the ground. They are what I need to put the country on its feet. That, for example, was how I found José León Ramírez. A quick mind. An eagle eye. Faster than lightning. Back before he started. Far sooner done than said. Always a little bit ahead of everything. He was one of my best men, till he turned into the very worst. Neither a bootlicker nor a pander. José León Ramírez obeyed any and every command, yet remained himself. As the years went by, I considered promoting him to captain, making him my Minister of War. For a time, I even thought of naming him my successor. He had his chance. I gave him his opportunity. He leapt straight at it, taut as an arrow. And lost it out his drooping trousers fly.

Another high flier who had a bad fall: Rolón, ex captain Rolón. Rose to the highest rank. Descended to the lowest. For five years I personally instructed him in the art of war. Artillery was where his natural talents lay. He would go up to a cannon. Run his hand along it, stroke it like a gentle mount. As he hitched it to the gun carriage, he would talk to it, telling it in a low voice what it was supposed to do. As he lit the fuse, he would trace a parabolic curve with his finger and point to the target, the way an expert equestrian indicates to his mount the barrier it is to jump over. A little click of his tongue, and the cannon would go off. Ninety-nine times out of a hundred the shell landed right on target, no matter how far away.

Ah, Rolón, Rolón! I taught you a whole bag of tricks to vanquish any enemy, to demolish any citadel, even that of your own soul. We held terrible practice battles, on land and sea. In one of these mock encounters, you scored a hundred points. You almost beat me. Promoted from private to captain. The highest-ranking officer in the army of the Republic at the time. An impressive captain of artillery. A rammer. A hammerer. Matchless. Irreplaceable. Unique.

Do you remember what he looked like, Patiño? I can see him now, Sire. Tall, head grazing the ceiling. Solid as a rock. Long hair, moustaches down to his waist. Just seeing him made one feel awed by him, Excellency. Yes, that was Rolón, just the way you picture him. That was Rolón, first captain of the Republic.

In a skirmish with the Correntinos I ordered him to bombard their stronghold so as to teach them a lesson. I placed four good men-of-war at his disposal, armed with twenty-some cannons. Rolón put them to no use whatsoever save to put on a ridiculous free show for the enemy. He made a laughingstock out of me by the madcap way he led the expedition. Where was his love of country? His honor and his pride, his respect for the government? His own self-esteem?

At the confluence of the Paraná and the Paraguay, the four warships began to dance about in the eddies of the seven streams that meet in front of the fort of Corrientes. Without firing a single cannon. Not knowing which way to turn; whether to sink or to fly.

The townspeople and the troops improvised a burlesque carnival in honor of the invading vessels. They began a dance contest with them. And if the Correntinos failed to capture them simply by reaching out their hands, it was only because they were so drunk they keeled over, just as Rolón and his men did, from fear. On his return from his heroic exploit, he presented himself, brazen as you please, spouting all sorts of nonsense to excuse his failure. That's what happens when one entrusts an undertaking to insolent incompetents. I freely admit I ordered that expedition only as a test, which didn't turn out very well for me. That was the only reason I didn't have Rolón executed. His death sentence was commuted, and he was condemned instead to rowing in perpetuity. What's happened to him? He's still rowing his boat, Sire. The latest reports from the garrisons along the river state that he's nothing but skin and bones now. Others, that he's nothing but a great shock of hair with a pigtail more than ten feet long that trails in the current as he rows. The people who live along the Guarnipitán have started strange rumors. Some have it that the man sitting in the stern isn't the one condemned for life, but his shade. According to others, it's death in person rowing the black, rotted boat. And that must be so, because for years now it hasn't been picking up the supplies left in the places set forth in his sentence, between Villa del Pilar and the Guarnipitán.

What are you doing there on that paper? Scratching out the *o* of rumors, Sire, and writing it with an *i* instead. So as to change, if only by one letter, the fate of ex captain Rolón.

I have before me that other pusillanimous poultroon, the ex commandant of Itapuá, Ojeda. The worthless reverse of what a real commander of a garrison ought to be. He abandons Candelaria to Ferré's troops, who invade our territory in an attempt to extend theirs and seize Misiones, long the property and possession of Paraguay. My garrison commander retreats without putting up any resistance, before the first shot has rung out. Arms melt away in the hands of those chicken-hearted hens in uniform the moment they're forced to make use of them. He leaves his line of retreat strewn with baggage, equipment, supplies that cost the country blood and sweat. I summon him. You've made a mess of everything, including your own underdrawers. And disgraced the Republic thereby. Dishonor without equal. Ignominy without precedent. And finally, you have shamed me by your inexcusable, simple-minded lack of discrimination, which caused me to lose Candelaria, an indispensable bastion for the security of the country; the last crack left open to us for trade with the outside. What will those foreign traders say? What will people in Paraguay say, when your compatriots find out what happened? They will spit in your face, and instead of being the commandant of the most important garrison in the Republic, you will be the lowliest spittoon for the scorn and the mockery of one and all.

I for my part forbear to spit. I am trying my best not to be enraged at you. I do not allow myself to nurse a rage against men as good-for-little, as good-for-nothing as you. Nursing a rage against miserable scoundrels is the same as allowing such counterpersons to come to rule for a time the ideas and the feelings of our Person. This represents a double loss.

For the moment, I shall not send you to the orange tree. Not out of goodness or mercy, mind you. I cannot excuse your utter folly. Tolerance, source of all evils. Utter foolishness. I stress the point once again: I am trying my best not to fall into useless rages against worthless sorts such as you.

I do not ask my men to act at all times with the certainty of automata. A frontier commander, you have allowed yourself to become a lesser man, to be overcome with a vain fear, for no reason, needlessly, and done nothing. This is a lack of energy, of resolution, hence very little can be expected of you. And don't try to wriggle out by claiming you were awaiting orders. At the slightest rumor or sign of the enemy, every commander has the obligation to ready the defenses at his disposal. This does not prevent him from awaiting orders that will be forthcoming if circumstances permit. Things must not be thrown into complete disorder on the pretext that there are no orders. Placing yourself in a state of alert, since you had the necessary means at your disposal, is the least you should have done. When in the course of a battle one fights by all possible means to secure the position of a given chapel or stronghold, one must fight for it as though it were the most important national sanctuary, even though such objectives may have a merely tactical value at the moment, perhaps only for that one engagement. You had more than enough forces to send up to five thousand men to Santo Tomé, with good artillery, plus infantry and cavalry reserves, plus two elite squadrons of lancers. You had the opportunity to make of this sector the beginning of a real military campaign for the defense of our frontiers, and given the proper circumstances, turn it into a long-range crusade aimed at extending and ensuring our control of the rivers all the way to the ocean sea against the hordes of savages and sham governments that stand in the way of our right to free navigation on the rivers, offend our pride, and hinder our foreign trade.

Due to bungling such as yours, these savage enemies go on retailing their idle gossip. They take Paraguayans to be simple-minded, lukewarm patriots, and hence easily tricked, taken in by most anything, even bright little bits of mirror, just as the Spaniards went about tricking and deceiving the Indians.

They would hold their tongues if the Supreme Dictator of Paraguay had an army man worthy of his rank and of the honor of the Republic. An army man, not an ass, trained in the art of making war. Capable of sallying forth like a general, though he might be no more than a sergeant, or at most a captain, to raze Corrientes and La Bajada, as payment and punishment for their ladronicides, depredations, and mockeries.

A good rank and file, but above all good chiefs, have a different spirit, a different energy, a different determination. The fire of the fatherland burns in their veins, keeps them from turning tail to the enemy, from getting their rifles jammed. Within each chief, each ranker, the entire country is on the march. Seeing enemies who insult them, they all fall upon them at once and reduce them to dust. But soldiers under the command of yellow-livered officers have ice in their veins. Nothing matters to them. If everything is of no importance to their chiefs, why should the rank and file care?

Through your fault, my dear caponed commander who's escaped the orange tree, I have been obliged to close the Salto camp, so as not to be kept hopping chasing down other cowards who have decamped. Foreseeing further disasters, I have padlocked the gateways of San Miguel and Loreto.

For the time being I am not ordering you to be shot, on condition that you not give an inch in future skirmishes with the enemy. You are hereby ordered always to march at the head of your troops during engagements and attacks. You are not to retreat under any pretext. And to keep you from committing further derelictions of duty, I order you to read to the troops, for three days, at reveille and retreat, the Supreme Proclamation enclosed herewith, in which I authorize and order company sergeants, corporals, and every last private to put a good round of birdshot in your back at the slightest sign that you are about to turn it on the enemy again. I generously offer you this commutation of your sentence and leave in your hands, or rather, to your feet, the alternative of being shot dead in combat. You are to read the Proclamation in person.

A good militia is the only sort capable of remedying these ills. We are not going to perpetuate military castes. I do not want a bunch of parasites good for nothing but attacking/conquering their neighbors; reducing to bondage/enslaving the entire citizenry of their country.

I want each of them to be citizen soldiers through and through, despite the fact that they may lack complete military training, even though they begin to receive it in grade school as they are learning the alphabet. When attacked by the enemy, all our citizens will automatically turn into soldiers. There is not one of them who will not sooner die than see his Fatherland invaded, his Government in danger.

Citizens can become excellent soldiers in a month. So-called regular army troops don't lost their vices in a hundred years.

Functionaries, a category in which the two superior classes of the State must be included, the one serving as magistrates, the other as aides or executors armed with the decisions of the former, should receive a rigorous education that will enable those in the first category to defend the Nation against its enemies, the others to administer justice in the people's favor, thereby putting an end to the injustices that continue to exist even after our Revolution.

The military, the magistrates must sedulously avoid accumulating wealth with their right hand while their left hand holds the reins of power, thus destroying the egalitarian foundation of society.

Hence I have prescribed for them a totally austere way of life; the way of life that I have imposed upon myself. Neither you nor I are to have material possessions of any sort. I enjoin you to perpetual celibacy in order that you may not leave widows. We are forbidden to establish our own family, since that would lead us to unjust acts of favoritism. Warriors, magistrates, aides, armed saints so to speak, possessing nothing of their own, without a conjugal life, are obliged to defend others with a total disregard for any other consideration. I wish this to be clearly understood. Reread my orders. Commit them to memory. I do not want my position to be rendered less than clear by your supposition. The saying has it that it's through bloody behinds that letters enter, but I want to see you get them through your heads.

I ask, I demand of all of you the strict supervision of public goods, funds, expenses. The strictest vigilance so as to prevent ladronicides, bribes, illegal collections, exactions, extorsions, subornations. Peculation in which some of you appear to be more expert than in the proper application of regulations. I shall come back to this matter of piracy on the part of functionaries. I intend to tighten the pegs of the strings around your necks so as to fine-tune each one of you. Cross out this paragraph. After subornations, write: Cleaning up the administration is an indispensable step toward carrying out the plan of public salvation that we must effect through our conjoined efforts.

The Republic is the totality, the union, the confederation of all the thousands of citizens who constitute it. All patriots, that is to say. Those who are not patriots must not be counted or considered part of it, save as the bad money that risks being taken for the good, as you have been taught by the Patrial Catechism.

We have the cheapest State in the world, the richest Nation on earth as regards natural resources. After the many, the uncountable years during which we have enjoyed the greatest peace, tranquillity, well-being ever known on this Continent, we must now bend our efforts toward defending this incommensurable good.

The state of perpetual peace will be succeeded by the state of permanent war. We shall not attack anyone. We shall not allow anyone to attack us. Paraguay will be invincible so long as it remains hermetically sealed round about the nucleus of its own strength. But should it issue forth from this nucleus, its power will decrease in inverse proportion to the square of the distance in which its forces are dispersed. The law of gravity holding sway horizontally. It's not every day that Newton sees the apple fall. Cross out apple. Write orange instead. No, that won't do either. Strike out the whole paragraph. Who is there around here who has any idea who Newton is?

With an eye to reorganizing the population statistics you are to take immediately an absolutely complete census of all the inhabitants, including the natives, who are located in the particular jurisdiction of the twenty Departments of the Republic that each of you is in charge of, so as to have current records concerning our population. This census is to include, on the questionnaires provided for the purpose, complete information as to the number of adults, age, sex, occupations, aptitudes of each man or woman, family background, political affiliations, police records where applicable, in particular in the case of heads of family; plus a notation indicating their affection and disaffection as regards the Cause of our Independence. Number of children, from those newly born to those old enough to begin military service. Situation of those children who are receiving instruction. You are to submit lists of the children in school. Those who already know how to write are to provide a sample. As for the most advanced, they are to answer in the form of a written composition the question: what do they think of the Supreme Government? They have full freedom of expression. The Government will assign inspectors to each one of these schools to verify and provide adequate proof of the progress of the pupils, their average attendance, industriousness, attainments, and application, as well as the causes responsible for any diminished output, absenteeism, or repeating of grades. Today it is more necessary than ever before to make an old saying come completely true: In Paraguay there is not a single citizen who does not know how to read or write, and as a consequence express himself correctly.

Reflect at length on these points that constitute the foundation of our Republic. Focal points of its progress in the future. I want chiefs, delegates, administrators who are skilled in their various functions. I want to find integrity, austerity, valor, honesty in each of you. I want patriots with wills of steel and stainless virtues. Note down any doubt, opinion, suggestion that you may wish to put forward concerning the principal subject dealt with in this Circular. It is my intention to hold a conclave shortly, that is to say a sort of Congress of chiefs, functionaries, employees from the highest rank to the lowest, so that between all of us the future policy of the Supreme Government may be strengthened and made uniform.

Each one of you is to prepare yourself to render an account of all your activities in the various functions that have been assigned you since your entry into public administration. A rendering of accounts that will be studied by the Supreme Government before the Conclave. Your reports on your comportment, that usually you distort, must this time conform to the forms that will be sent you by the next courier. These service records, along with the population census and the educational census that I have ordered must be sent in within a month, that is to say, by the end of September of this year at the latest.

The reason behind this rendering of accounts, naturally, is not to remove you from your posts for errors you might have perpetrated in the past; the very thought is absurd. Condemning you for stupidities you might have committed would merely be a further stupidity. What has been done with good intentions is well and good. What has been done with bad ones we shall try to do better in the future. My idea is to guide each one of you in order that you may become master administrators, irreproachable civil servants of the Republic. Hence I want your messages, your dispatches, your reports to be made to accord with the reality of the facts. Do not allow yourselves to drift along the riverbanks of your imagination. I want no more of your piles of onionskin you've strained to fill with nonsense. And I'll soon peel any hardcore troublemaker down to size, without wasting a single tear on you. I want you to take my warnings not as those of a Supreme Chief, but rather as those of a friend who not only esteems you but loves you. Perhaps much more than you yourself may suspect.

The days we are living in may well be the last; hence the right time to mend our ways, proceeding backwards. For the sake of inconvenience rather than personal convenience. Having been taught little by good examples, which have never abounded in our country, I place bad ones before you instead. While the lesson to be learned from them by turning them around is quite ordinary, an extraordinary lesson can be learned from them if they are studied exactly as they stand.

By custom, our justice executes those who are guilty as a warning to others. To keep the bad example from spreading, the one who is punished is not the one who is hanged but the others, through the intermediary of the hanged man. It is always another who dies. And don't try to tell me that you're already dead or that you've forgotten that you are. I'm not taken in by lies. I always discover them eventually, even hidden under the soles of people's shoes. Superstitions and cabals don't affect me or delude me. You are all thoroughly acquainted with my clemency; you also know my inexorable rigor. This rigor is placed entirely in the service of the Fatherland. To defend it with all my strength against its enemies, be they within or without.

Hark unto my words, my poor fellow citizens! I would rather die than see my poor Country so cruelly oppressed once again, and I have the satisfaction of believing that all the people of the Republic are of the same mind. If not, the fault will be ours. But in that event none of us will escape the disaster that befalls the Country. Why? Because each and all of us *will be* that disaster. The mortal remains over which the wild beasts of the desert will establish their dominion.

It is often said that he who trusts the people builds on sand. Perhaps, when the people is absolutely nothing but sand. But such cabalistic calculations do not reign here. I am fighting not with a people of sand or of phantoms, but with a people of men with a thousand miseries and more. Paraguayans, one last effort if you would be truly free!

Once I receive the results of the new census and general registry of citizens that I am ordering you to make herewith, you will be informed of the plan that I have conceived for the formation of a great army and a war fleet in order to free our country once and for all of the iniquitous blockade of navigation and reinforce our defenses, the foundation of our self-determination and sovereignty. The details of the plan will be revealed to military commandants at the opportune moment in highly confidential instructions.

For the moment what I am going to do is this: Once the forest of satraps has been cut down, once the plague of hydrophobic dogs slavering with abjection is exterminated, I shall order that a thick layer of lime and oblivion be spread over their remains. No more contemptible, clownish military officers. No more troops of the line idling about waiting to flee from the slightest danger. No more soldiers of a real army that exists but is utterly useless, since all of them, down to the last man, inevitably end up contracting the vices of their superiors. No more uniforms, no more ranks, hierarchical distinctions, awarded not on the basis of merit but on the seniority of uselessness. The army of the Fatherland will be the entire people, clad in the dress and dignity of being the people in arms. An invisible army, but more effective than all other armies. Its effectives, the free peasants, with a cadre of natural chiefs who will arise out of this natural army of work and defense of the Republic. By day they will work. By night they will drill. They will train in the dark so that the shadows will be their best allies. Their arms will be hidden during the day, alongside the furrows of the fields. The wooded walls of the forest will be our best bastions; the deserts and swamplands, our impenetrable fosses; the rivers, lakes, and brooks, the arteries through which there will circulate the fulminic force of our detachments joined together in small units. Let the elephants come. As compadre Confucius said, mosquitoes end up devouring elephants. When the enemy marches in, it will believe that it is entering an unarmed and peaceful country. But when the invaders, trapped in a flash by the optical illusion of a vast multitude of men and women defending their birthright in work clothes, realize their error, they will know that a people cannot be conquered unless it so wishes.

The troops made up of heads of families installed in the Paraná zone, which I sent to fight the invading army of Correntinos, were a good example in the beginning. From now on, no more useless troops of the line. I shall dissolve the ranks of idlers and good-for-nothings who bolt off like a shot out of a gun at the first round of fire from the enemy. I have had quite enough of that army of parasites that uselessly suck the blood of the people and humiliate them endlessly by committing every sort of outrage and abuse.

From now on, the people itself will be the army: all men and women, all adults, young people, and children fit for service in the Great Army of the Fatherland. Unique, invisible, invincible. Study every aspect of its organization. Draw up, down to the very last detail, a strategic and tactical plan; a rule book of guerrilla warfare and a general system of self-suffi- ciency, aimed at meeting the central objectives of work and defense.

The most important basis for this conversion of traditional militias into militias of the people is . . . *(rest of the folio burned).*

The skull rises up, shaking off the dirt on itself. It raises up half its carcass, supporting itself on its hindquarters. It is about to throw the secret of Pilar the black in my face. A little rainbow of spittle is forming around its muzzle. A sarcastic smile in the naked shadow of the bone. I will take one step backward, out of its reach. I look at it out of the corner of my eye. The hydrophobia of a dead dog can be doubly fatal. You had him killed because of! . . . He contains himself by feigning a coughing fit. Take it easy, my good old Sultan. You have all eternity before you. Come on, out with it, what was it you were about to say about the black? Go on. I'm listening. You weren't that good a listener in the old days, my esteemed Supreme. Nor were you that much of a conversationalist during your dog's life. You sent him before the firing squad in the same year you celebrated the silver anniversary of your wedding to the Perpetual Dictatorship. Hot tallow ran that year as never before. Do you remember that giant taper, supreme? I can see it now. There's never been a candle that could hold a candle to that one! Your hydrolatrous admirers erected it for you: forty rods high and three thick at the base. Ten thousand quintals of burning-hot wax were poured over this skeleton scaffolding. Then they lit the wick, with its flame inside its little mica niche calculated to last for at least another quarter of a century. They set it up during the night in the Plaza de la República. On the eve of the feast of the Nativity that year. You knew nothing about it. A complete surprise. Except for the light still burning after curfew, in a place you'd never seen one before or ever ordered one to be kept lit. You focused your telescope from your window. The Star of the North!, I heard you murmur. You contemplated it all that night. The low-pitched howl of a dog that has lost its mate. A thousand sighs. A single sigh, cut off by a thousand countersighs. So that they were a thousand yet one. You forced me to sigh and howl along with you, crushing my paw beneath the iron heel of your shoe. As you sighed and howled like a dog, I practically dragged you to bed. Shut you up in your attic. Mounted guard at the door.

Your attention attracted by the hubbub in the plaza, you discovered the giant taper a few hours later. It had come loose from its framework of takuara rods, and beneath the sun's burning rays it was now bent completely double, with wax and smoke spurting from the tip. Shouts and peals of laughter, cheers and hurrahs for El Supremo! The crowd grows more and more excited. Leaps and cavorts round the immense candle, which has done its humble best to bow its head to the multitude in this unprecedented celebration. The women writhe frenetically in the red dust of the plaza. The more ecstatic of the vatic Bacchae fling themselves upon the softened tip. Their hair standing on end. Tunics rent to pieces. Eyes bulging from their sockets. They scrape off bits of hot wax. Gather the burning-hot drops in the hollow of their hands. Rub their bellies, their breasts, their mouths with chunks of warm wax. Howl in mad maenadic rapture:

> Oé . . . oé . . . yekó raka'é
> ñande Karai–Guasú o nacé vaekué . . . *§

You raised hell. What for them was the Fiesta of Fiestas struck you as the most sinister mockery of mockeries. You ordered troops to clear the plaza with fixed bayonets. Your grenadiers had to charge three times in combat formation. The hydrolators trembled.

That very day, you sent Pilar the black to his death before a firing squad. I went to lick the gaping wounds left by the bullets in his breast. Around the ninth hour, in the voice of a dead man, the black said to me, with just a trace of laughter: All those candles lit to Saint Fart, in honor of nothing at all! Isn't that so, Sultan? I left Olariega the Indian girl pregnant. When she's given birth to my child, tell her for me that I wish her to give it my name. And tell that shitty old bastard who doesn't have a name that I wish him not to know where he's going or what he should say when he gets there, that I hope it gets pitch dark inside him and he goes to sleep for good without ever knowing he's died. That's what Pilar the black said. His posthumous wish. Why is it you don't write these true things down among all the lies that your hand borrows from other lies, believing that they're your truths?

You know I didn't order him killed out of sheer cruelty, Sultan, but on account of what he did. I sent him to hell for his thieving, for his treason. What hell? That of your black conscience? Your Supreme Inferno? Don't be disrespectful! Have me shot to death too, you accursed old man

---

*§Guaraní: Ohé . . . ohé . . . they say
Our Lord was born on a long-ago day.

dead of supremacy! I've had my fill of you! Kill me off before your hand is no longer able to push that pen. Now that we have both met our end we can understand each other. No, Sultan, all this requires a power of comprehension that, living or dead, is beyond your understanding. Bah, Supreme! You don't yet know what happiness, what relief you'll feel below earth! The delusion in whose toils you lie is making you swallow the dregs of that bitter elixir you call life, as you finish digging your own grave in the cemetery of the written word. Solomon himself says: the man who strays from the path of understanding will remain, though he be yet alive, in the congregation of the dead. You are only half initiated; as I am an initiate of far longer standing, in that order, you the novice owe me respect, Supreme. Wisdom increaseth grief, as we already know. But there is a grief that turns into madness, and this is not written anywhere. Don't become too absorbed in contemplating that fire that your incipient verbal blindness thinks it sees burning in Books. If such a fire exists, it is not in books. It would only burn them to ashes. Fry you to a crisp. I returned to your stinking doghouse on this occasion only to keep you company for a short while; in the end I felt for you the pity that the dead feel for the living. Don't try to understand me. You might suddenly be happy again. Do you know how terrible it is to be happy in this world?

In the blindness of your Absolute Power through which you think you dominate everything, you haven't acquired a single real's worth of the wisdom of King Solomon, the non-Christian. As he slept with his concubines he kept the knife of Ecclesiastes hidden beneath his pillow. Sometimes, without a sound, he took out the steel forged-in-pain as they slept. He cut off their hair and made from it splendid red, golden blond, raven-black, wavy, kinky, curly beards for himself that reached down to his navel. With a smile, he cut off their breasts in one stroke, so gently that those sleeping concubines must have felt they were still being caressed in their dreams. He plucked their eyes from their sockets in a twinkling. There is nothing more pleasing than to contemplate a pair of sleep-filled eyes nestling in the palm of one's hand! The umbilical cord of the optic nerve dangling between one's fingers. The pupils burn with a phosphorescent light in the dark for a moment. A sulphurous gleam of love-hate. Then they are hidden from sight on the dark side of the earth. These are things not found in the Song of Songs.

Wait a minute, Sultan! Who said that? Don't confuse me. It doesn't matter, Supreme. Don't let it bother you. Why wouldn't it bother me? I'm trying to understand; I don't want to get what's mine mixed up with your dog-tricks from beyond the grave. I've already told you: you won't understand till you understand. But this won't happen so long as you keep pretending you're buried in these folios. False tombs make terrible refuges. A scriptorial sepulcher worth half a real a ream the worst one of all. It's only beneath the earth-earth that you're going to find the sol that never stops shining. Germinal darkness. The night-night of pilgrim-journeying eyes. A single lamp lighting your life-and-death labors. Because even though one doesn't always die in the dark, it's only out of the dark that one comes into the world, do you see what I mean, Supreme? You were useful to me when you were still alive, my dear Sultan. I hear you growl in your dreams. Bark. Wake up with a start. Raise your right paw to make your bad vision go away. The image of the Alien is reflected in your eyes. An unknown without color or form. Thing. Happening. Prophecy passing from black to gray; from gray to white; from white to a shadow halted before you. Your sleep too heavy now. Your dreams a bore. You can't play death the way you used to so superbly in the old days to amuse my guests. Like that clownish Pilar the black, able to act out farces of the same sort, patching together voices, figures, gesticulations of the strangest strangers. Mime. Actor. Pander. Improviser. Satyr. Quick-change artist. Basso-buffo. Swindler. Petty larcenist.

Tell me, Sultan, just between us, paw on your chest. Tell me, absolutely frankly, if the black ever said anything to you about that mad idea of his that set his brain on fire, that business about being king of Paraguay some day. All humbug! Lies cooked up by your finagling private secretary to discredit the black even more! The last thing he would ever have wanted to be was king of this shitty country! The one who's dreaming of dethroning you and making himself king someday is none other than your secretary, Policarpo himself. Look at the back of your lackey's chair. What do you see written there in charcoal: *Policarpo I King of Paraguay!* Have him erase that legend with his tongue. That's just what he'll do, don't worry, before the hangman's knot makes it come leaping out of his mouth, all warm and wet.

By order of the dog, I shall write then about Pilar the black. For ten years the valet enjoyed my entire confidence. Except for the protophysician, the only one to enter my room. He prepares my maté. Supervises the cooking of my food. Tastes the dishes before I do. Acts as assistant at audiences; as lookout on my afternoon outings. I ride along on the Arabian; I advance slowly down the streets bared of trees. The black's hawk eyes watch every crack in the façades of the barricaded houses. Stragglers in the underbrush, a bunch of straw-hatted heads. Pilar falls upon them, brandishing the whip. Heads of curious youngsters hidden beneath the sombreros. Lashing out with his rawhide, he drives them away.

During military exercises he rides along at my side. He can handle a lance or a rifle as well as the most expert of my hussars. The black arouses envy, astonishment, admiration in them. In the annual dog hunts, Pilar is always in the forefront. He takes special delight in entering patrician mansions. Before the eyes of their terrified masters, he finishes off, with skillful thrusts of his bayonet, the little lapdogs hidden underneath the beds, in the kitchens, in the basements, beneath the women's petticoats. During one of these battues he ran Hero through with a pike, thus settling old accounts with him. You're lying, Supreme. It wasn't Pilar the black who killed Hero, already starving to death back in the days when you expelled the Robertsons. Nobody would throw a bone his way, not even in secret, for fear of falling into disgrace if you should happen to hear about it. Be still, Sultan. Don't you start interrupting me now. I won't have you dictating or correcting. I'm talking about Pilar the black, not about you. I am writing about him, and letters couldn't care less whether what is written with them is true or false.

What most dazzled him was contemplating the heavens at night through the telescope, searching for my favorite constellations. Look, José María, I'm going to read the calendar of the zodiac to you. What's the zodiac, Godfather? Something like an almanac of the sky. Oh, I see, Godfather, something like the Almanach of Notable Personages that you sometimes read. Don't mix up vulgar things with things of the cosmos! Listen, if I handed you a candle end and told you to eat it, would you do so? No, Sire, because you yourself have told me that a person shouldn't consume his own candle. Listen, you little rascal: the sun travels round and round its burning ring and needs no other food than its own self. If only a person could be a sun! Don't you think so too, Sire? Imagine eating whole bellyfuls of yourself! Don't interrupt me now. The zodiac is the circular band of the twelve constellations that the sun travels through in the space of a year. The twelve signs mark the four seasons. We're going to read the calendar now. Here is Aries, the ram, a lustful beast that engenders us. Next, Taurus, the bull, who starts off by butting us with his horns. When we play bull-candle, Sire, I'm always the first to give the other blacks a goring. Look now at Gemini, the twins; that is to say, Virtue and Vice. As we're trying to catch virtue, Cancer, the crab, comes along and grabs us with his snaggle-toothed pincers. As we depart from Virtue, Leo, the roaring lion, crosses our path. He rakes us fiercely with his claws. Is he the dying lion of the Aesop's fable you often tell me, Sire? The one that organizes the parade so as to devour the other animals? If you don't let me talk, we'll never get to the end. Glue your black soul to the telescope; listen to what I'm telling you. We flee from the Lion and meet Virgo, the virgin. Our first love. We wed her. Why are you laughing? Nothing, Sire; it's just that I've also heard you say that virgins are as hard to find as a needle in a haystack, though that's the best place to look for them. But from what you're saying they're not as hard to come by in heaven. We believe that we will be eternally happy when Libra, the scales, appears, and we find that our happiness weighs no more in the balance than smoke. This leaves us very sad. Scorpio, the scorpion, then gives us a stab in the back that gives us a terrible start. We are just curing ourselves of our wounds when arrows come raining down on us from all directions: Sagittarius, the archer, is making sport of us. We pull out the arrows. Watch out! We are now floating in the Ark. Aquarius, the water-bearer, has arrived, unleashing his deluge that floods the earth. He's turned it into an ocean where Piscis, the Fish, reigns, because they catch us without using either bait or hook. A meaning is hidden in each thing. A sign in each man. What is yours, Sire? Capricorn, the capricorn of the Tropic. A battering ram that butts its way and horns in everywhere. This Book of the Heavens is some book, Godfather! The sun reads it every year, Pilar. It always has a happy ending, and he goes gaily on his daily round, safe and sound up there. I can do that too, Sire. Read it directly. I don't know when I was born, neither the month, nor the day, nor the hour, but when I see the devilment of the different signs, I think maybe mine is the Twins. I'm the kōi of my kōi. It's more likely your sign is the next one, the crab. If I just look at little things from day to day, yes, you're more than right, Sire. What I'm wondering now is if that's how it is in Your Worship's life too. Since to me, your sign is your very self, Sire. You don't depend on the luck of the moment that makes its way along a thread in little hops, nudging along the things we don't see as the things we do see happen. Isn't that how it is in the stories in books? If Your Grace will allow me, I too will read that Almanac of the Noble Persons of Heaven. You don't know how to read yet. Learn. Go learn the alphabet in school. I'm going to see if I can do it, Sire, what I mean to say is, make a hundred flowers bloom with words alone.

The black won't get past Capricorn. A very delatory scholar. His false inventiveness keeps him stuck fast in treacherous irreverence. Mere echoing of the stale stories spread so maliciously by my detractors, who attribute my hatred for patricians to my love for the daughter of Colonel Zavala y Delgadillo that came to nothing. The brazen-faced chatterbox doesn't mention names. Just vague, vulgar allusions to the Star of the North, an amusing appellation bestowed upon the charming Doña María Josefa Rodríguez Peña, mother of the stunningly beautiful Petrona. A public nickname equated in the mouth of the black with my most carefully kept secret. A tale of a constellation that was pure fiction. Further solid proof that even in the most distant galaxies the vile worm inevitably spoils sound fruit. The black's heart was already being gnawed at. I had him given a thorough thrashing. He took it without a whimper. Then he knelt at my feet, begging my pardon. I gave him a chance to rehabilitate himself. This was the last time I ever committed an act of stupid compassion. He continued to deceive me for a time. In my presence, unexampled humility, discretion; in secret, the worst rascal imaginable. He became a cynic, a libertine, a toper, a relapsed thief. Aided by the young Indian Olegaria Paré, his concubine, he began to steal from the State stores. Wickedness coupled with wickedness. He began to pocket money regularly behind my back, to collect bribes for supposedly pulling strings with the Government. Trickery of every sort, a product of his prodigious capabilities for knavery, invention, guile. Everyone fought for the favors of the famous gentleman of the bedchamber that my former valet had become. Meanwhile the Indian woman, pregnant and about to give birth, went on boldly selling the goods that her lover stole, in the marketplace and even in the houses of the enemy. Lengths of English linen, brabant, spiderwork, dragonfly-gauze, lace jabots, colored ribbons, handkerchiefs, toys ended up in the hands of old families come down in the world, once-wealthy Spanish immigrants who had lost their fortunes, pretentious patricians. They gave what they did not have in order to pay for these luxuries stolen from the State Stores. Great rejoicing. A guard caught him throwing through the skylights spools of ribbon that slowly came unwound in the breeze from the river.*

---

*Declaration of guard Epifanio Boba-dilla:

. . . What are you doing, Your Worship Joséph María?, the witness testifies that he asked the accused. Nothing, sentinel. Tossing *pets-de-nonne* in the air. And the Indian girl who's down there below, hidden in the gully? Er, she's catching *couilles-de-moine*, that's all. Back to your post, guard. I'm going to report you for having abandoned your picket. Don't say a word to anyone about what you've seen and heard. You haven't seen or heard anything. Understand, sentinel? Very well, Your Worship Don Joséph María. You're dismissed, soldier. Ten-shun! Fooorwaaard, maaarch!, Don Joséph María ordered me. Can't you see that if you keep nosing around, the nun gets all embarrassed? She hides her ass. She doesn't know how she can let fly with her little *pets* filled with north-wind. And the *couilles-de-moine* in Olegaria's skirts are getting all dried out. Clear out of here, cop. Here's a box§ of candy for you and my regards to your sister, sworn witness Bobadilla declares that the accused said to him. At these words the militiaman withdrew, taking the box with him.

§The deposition here reads *caxeta*. Cf. Spanish *cajeta;* Portuguese *caixeta*.

One afternoon, on returning from my outing, astonishment stopped me dead in my tracks at the office door. Wearing my dress uniform, the black was sitting at my desk dictating, in strident tones, the most outlandish decrees to an invisible scribe. Completely drunk, he leafs through the dossiers piled up on the desk top, ripping entire pages out of them. I struggle to overcome the stupor that has turned me to stone, a stone of imagination, I mean to say indignation. The worst of it is that in the hallucination of my anger I see in that emaciated black a perfect portrait of myself! He is faultlessly imitating my own voice, my appearance, my gestures, down to the last detail! He gets to his feet. Removes from their secret hiding place the keys of the strongbox. Takes out the thick file containing the trial records of the Conspiracy of the year '20. Starts tearing them apart. Tosses whole fistfuls of folios in the air, screaming insults at each of the sixty-eight traitors put to death. Terrible imprecations! The same ones I too hurl at them still, after twenty years.

He has not heard me enter the room. Does not notice my presence. Finally catches sight of me. Despite his drunken state, he gives such a start that he hits the ceiling. The intoxication of his brazen pantomime sends him into an even madder frenzy. He does not pay the slightest heed to my insults, my threats. He leaps upon me. Rips off my riding coat, yanks off my shirt. Teases me with it like a bullfighter. Dances round me twanging a drunken magic spell. Corners me, backs me into the meteor, forcing me to play a role in the farce being staged by this monkey disguised as the Supreme Dictator of a Nation.

One after the other, in a dizzying whirl, he transforms himself into each of the sixty-eight traitors put to death. It is they who insult me now, curse me, judge me, as I lie prostrate behind the great stone. Sixty-eight figures that blend into a single one in the vertiginous rhythm that electrifies the black's movements. Sixty-eight representations of illustrious traitors, more faithful to their vanished images than the portraits painted by Alborno, the celebrated illustriographer of the famous. Sixty-eight voices from beyond the grave, commingled in a single shriek from the black. Guards!

Stunned, terrified by the fierce battle that threatens, hussars, grenadiers, guards enter, crouching over, prepared to confront a legion of demons. They do not see me in the shadow. Only the black, in whom they see me, leaping about the room, the light glancing off the gold hilt of the dress sword, the big silver buckles of the Napoleonic patent-leather pumps.

The supreme simian glimmers, from one end of the room to the other. Loud cries rend the air. The black bounds and rebounds from one wall to the other. Crashes into the ceiling, into the floor; into the walls once more, into the furniture, into the gun racks, into the flags, into the bars over the window. Finally falls motionless, doubled over in a knot on top of the aerolith, howling with stentorian laughter. Still screaming insults at me in the imitation of my own voice. Interjections, obscene exclamations. The crudest of provocations, learned in the most vulgar libertinism.

Over there!, I cry, pointing with my forefinger as I get up from the floor. There he is! Catch him this instant, you idiots! My orders come out in the black's shrill voice. The guards can't decide whose side they are on. Whether they're for me, almost naked, black in the dark shadow, black with rage, or whether they're for the black, tricked out in my uniform, drenched with sweat, gleaming atop the meteor. Over there!, the black cries in turn. Take him away, you clods, you louts! Get him out of here!

They drag the two of us out. The black is still struggling with all his might. He bites an ear off one of the guards; rips off the thumb of another with his teeth. They knock him senseless with their rifle butts and drag him out, leaving a trail of blood, of vomit that reeks of cheap tavern brandy. The pieces of the full-dress uniform scattered all over the floor are still writhing in the last spasms of this dizzying nightmare. A shoe floats round and round through the air in search of the foot it has lost. It falls on top of the table, ending up as a paperweight.

He denied all the charges brought against him. The bull-pizzle whips were able to drag no more than the strict minimum out of him. Bejarano, Patiño, the Guaykurú torturers worked him over conscientiously in the Truth Chamber. Half skinned alive, ashen, he brazened it out. I went to see him one night. I spied on him through a crack in his cell. A permanent mocking smile between his swollen black-and-blue lips. He stubbornly denied all his crimes. He even threatened to drag down many people with him if he talked; top-ranking people in Government, he said, superior officers, high officials to whom he had lent money. But the worst of all his crimes were his acts of ladronicide with the Indian woman.

Declaration of the Indian Olegaria Paré:
She swears that it is certain truth that she has had relations and communications with the manservant Joséph María Pilar, who solicited her personally to this end, not calling upon any third person, and began to make use of her services in the month of September of the year 1834. She also declares that she willingly provided these services for Señor Joséph María for the pleasure of pleasing him and out of no other interest . . . *(rest of paragraph crossed out).*

Having rejected his first solicitations, she agreed of her own free will to do what Don Joséph María asked her to in the month of October, while His Excellency was in the aforementioned Barracks. Don Joséph María having indicated that the half Islands just off the shores of the little stream that runs past the aforesaid Barracks were to be the appointed place for their relations and communications, they met there until His Excellency came out and began to occupy himself once more with the military target drills that he was in the habit of holding. The two continued to meet in the vosky thickets of the half Islands, but she does not remember how many times.

It was there that Señor Joséph María handed over to her some spools of blue and crimson ribbon two fingers wide and some fifteen varas long, and some papers of needles, though she does not remember how many spools, or how much the steel pieces weighed, or how many papers of needles. Except that in order to understand each other in an innocent language, as she says that Don Joséph María told her, and in order not to arouse suspicion, they called the arms "couilles de moine" and the reels of ribbon "pets de nonne," though she does not remember how many of them he threw to her.

She declares that these relations and communications went on until mid-Lent, when, sensing that she was pregnant, she stopped having them, that is to say those trysts and diversions between the two of them on the half Islands; this was at her own request, so that no one would discover that it was Don Joséph who was responsible. She says, however, that he himself came once to bring her 3 yards of brabant and 5 other yards of English cloth, of which lengths of fabric she had a hoop skirt and a shirt or smock made for herself, though she does not remember who sewed them, and the girdle to hide what would be the fruit of her womb, articles that she herewith presents in devilution, very badly worn but nicely washed and ironed.

In the month of June, she goes on to say, she again began to pass by the back end of Government House with a bundle of clothes like a washerwoman, so as to conceal her condition and her relations with Joséph María Pilar. From that time on, using the same means and artifices, from some little windows that open onto the street from the Warehouses, Don Joséph María Pilar continued to throw down to her to where she was hiding velow in a gully, more rolls of ribbons, some 3 dozen, of all different colors, and more lengths of cloth of various qualities, which she sold to individuals in the puvlic market.

When questioned about the relationship between herself and the said individuals, she declares that none of them are personally known to her, though all of them were poor people who went to the Plasa, to whom she sold the goods in wholesale lots for whatever price they offered her. To another question put to her, she answers that she never tried to dispose of the merchandise that had been stolen in the houses of rich families since, being an Indian, the ladies of high society would have refused even to receive her. She says she handed the money over to Don Joséph María, who divided it among beggars in the streets and prisoners in jail so that they would have food, she recounted with tears in her eyes; she believes this to be true, since the following day the aforesaid Pilar had no more money left and she was obliged to go on selling things. Of the cash she handed over to him each time, she declares that he gave her 6 reales and 3 more for the unborne child and its food.

On Monday the 13th of July, as she was on her way to the Puvlic Market to buy maize cakes, Don Joséph María approached her very furtively amid the crowd, telling her that the "farts" and the "balls" were raising a stink and that the smell had reached the Karaí-Guasú, because he'd had him beaten within an inch of his life. He told me it was necessary to be prepared for anything. She says she answered him that she was always prepared and would take the blame for everything upon her own head, and that she wasn't afraid of anything.

Then the accused gave her 3 handkerchiefs of English linen, 2 of them striped and 1 plain-colored, one shirt of ordinary Creole cloth with a lace jabot and an iridescent red-and-yellow striped scarf with gold-colored flowers, to be washed and ironed. A costume that the aforesaid Joséph María wore when the two of them went dancing at the black balls of Kambá-kua, Huguá-de-seda, or Campamento Loma, where they danced, in the words of the deponent, till they lost all feeling of their bodies, coming back at dawn almost without touching the ground.

He also gave her a seven-strand silver ring and a mirror with a frame of the same metal, as the last present she said he said he could give her, since he didn't have a Warning Angel, much less a Guardian Angel, but that he could feel in his bones the vaguest shadow of the fleeting idea that he was about to have his candle snuffed out very soon, and if that was how things turned out, the Indian woman says textually: "His Worship Don Joséph María, would continue to remember me under the ground and our baby too who would be born when he was already dead, which came to pass on Christmas Eve of the year just ended. Milord Don Joséph María also told me that if we wanted to see him all we had to do was look in the mirror, that we'd always find his face there, looking at us with great joy and tender devotion . . . (The last paragraph crossed out, almost illegible.)

Today, the sixth of January, The Day of His Supreme Excellency, she declares that she has come to present herself, by her own free will and desision, without anyone ordering her to do so, to answer the charges of which, as we have already expressed ut supra, she claims that she alone is guilty.

She is also coming to present in devilution to the State everything that the deseased gave to her; the dancing costume, nicely washed and ironed and perfumed with little branches of sweet vasil and jasmin; plus the mirror; minus the rest of the money which she says she had to spend on tolls in order to try to see the accused before his execution . . . *(crossed out)* . . . and the last real and a half, which she spent, the Indian woman says textually, to buy a candle which she placed last night in the covered galleries of his Excellency's House since He no longer accepts any other gifts. I lighted my little candle amid the sea of candles gleaming on the floor of that place in vaster numbers than the stars in the sky, disappearing amid them the moment I placed it there, which was what I wanted, because I didn't wish to seem too forward. I put my candle that cost me a real and a half among all the others, the greatest homage I could light to His Excellency, who watches over all of us now and in the hour, to the king Saint Gaspar his Patron, and also in memory of his ex Godson and ex Valet, milord Don Joséph María Pilar, who was what I loved most . . . *(the end erased, illegible).*

So what? You had him executed just for that? The black wanted to live freely the thirty gold pieces' worth of freedom you bought for him. He found everything good in what you call everything evil; from the line round his middle downward. Do you consider that the waterline of what you keep pompously referring to as the arguments of Universal Reason? Adam didn't have a navel. You, ex supreme, have lost yours. Don't you remember your rakehell life as a gambler, a vihuela-player, and a woman-chaser? The black too liked to fool around with Olegaria the Indian girl in the half-islands in the stream. He flitted joyously about amid the smell of fried food, maize cakes, oranges, sweat, stink, the cries of pleasure of the market-women of the plaza. He pinched their buttocks, their breasts. He poked his proboscis-hand under the skirts of the youngest and prettiest chicks, just to suck in the acid aroma of woman-pollen, without which we come back again to Ecclesiastes. Back to what happened to me. To ignominy. To wretchedness. I grew old at your side. I left this world with a good half of my rump gone, lost warming your gouty leg, and my tail rubbed hairless from scraping to your Absolute Power for a quarter of a century.

Pilar the black was the only free being who lived at your side. The very next day you demanded and received reimbursement for the thirty ounces of gold that his manumission had cost you. I ordered him executed because his corruption was irremediable. I understand, ex master, old supreme shadow. You ordered the death of the man corrupted by nature only because you were unable to understand what a corrupt nature is. Listen to me, Sultan: I'll have none of the captious language of men of the cloth. Don't be an ingrate. When you eat, share your food with dogs even though they bite you, the great Zoroaster said. You were the only one with whom I was not afraid to put this precept into practice. We can almost say that we ate out of the same dish. But now neither you nor I can bite. Have you too passed over to the enemy now that you're dead? No, ex supreme. I'm too old a dog to betray my canine nature. You, the one who hounded the pasquinaders, were the worst of them, bound to voluntary servitude. You don't want to admit it because it's an ex dog that's singing you this tune, and you, after all, are only an ex man. From having doggedly observed you, I found out in the end that what you didn't know about yourself was that part of your nature that your old fear kept you from knowing. Listen to me, Sultan. Without anger. Without scorn. You will admit that I was never cruel for the sheer pleasure of it. Atrocities are not atrocious because and only because they are atrocities. You will grant me at least the belief that I always obeyed the great principle of Justice: prevent crime rather than punish it. All that is needed to execute a guilty man is a firing squad or a hangman. To prevent there being guilty men requires great astuteness. Implacable rigor in order to do away with rigor. If there is still some fool around who wants to dig his own grave, let him dig away. He made it, he'll enjoy lying in it. The black. Rubbed out. The same way one rubs out an abusive word. The malefactor alone, the word alone, mean nothing. No risk. Rubbed out. Erased. Obliter-oblivionated. Silence is now my manner of speaking. If they understood my silence-speech, they could vanquish me in turn. Impenetrable system of defense. That's what you think, supreme carrion. All you're doing is getting yourself all tangled up in words. Like that man who fornicated with the three girls he'd had by his mother, among whom there was one girl who married his son, so that when he fornicated with her, he was fornicating with his sister, his daughter, and his daughter-in-law, and obliging his son to fornicate with his sister and his mother-in-law . . . *(the remainder of the folio burned)*.

In a little while you won't be able to read aloud.

What will happen after the first ictus? Or in more vulgar terms, after the first attack of apoplexy, what will happen to you? It's possible that you'll lose the use of words. Lose the faculty of speech? Bah, it's not a bad thing to lose what's bad. No; you won't lose the faculty of speech properly speaking, but rather the memory of words. Memory pure and simple, you probably mean; that's what I have Patiño for. No; I mean the memory of the movements of language, those that make use of words to say something. Verbal memory, digging itself orbitary fossae in the Isthmus-of-the-Fauces. Wolf-thought, crouching on the Island-of-Lobules amid temporals, parietals, occipitals, dry rains on the torrid zones of Capricorn. Those arid craters plunged in double darkness will not produce even half a half-harvest of seven words. You will not be able to hum a single measure of the Song of Roland, as was your habit when you aimed your telescope at the equinoctial heavens. You will hide the moon under your armpit, trying to shield it from the dogs that Silvius the shepherd sics on with whistles. You will end up throwing it down the drain of Broca's brain area.

Is that all, hound of Minerva? Not at all. It is probable that the image of the end will project the shadow of a cross on your darkened brain. Your tongue feels heavy, isn't that so? You can still move it. You can move your tongue, your larynx, your vocal cords. But at times you'll be unable to say the right words. You'll see this very well before you even open your mouth. They'll be different when they come out. Wrong, dissimilar, mutilated words; not the ones you saw and tried to pronounce. Later on, the little breath coming out of the cavern of your lungs, shaped by your tongue, flattened against your palate, and I won't add broken up by your teeth because you no longer have any, will produce no sound at all.

For the moment, nothing but the first symptoms. Instead of saying *trunk* you pronounce *trump;* instead of saying to Patiño: *What do the pupils of your eyes see?,* you ask him: *What do the nipples of your eyes see?*—right, you old rascal? Instead of saying *my tongue,* it comes out *the scissors I have in my mouth.* Which is not at all incorrect. You cut phrases. You speak with a ball in your mouth. All balled up. Embolismatic. Embolophrastic. You introduce irrelevant, odd, badly formed, badly informed words into things that couldn't be more simple and straightforward. You beat about the bush, giving yourself time to think of what you want to say, yet once said it will betray you. You alter the way sentences are formulated. You speak in infinitives and gerunds. Verbs that don't verberate. Sentences full of pebbles. You skip syllables and words. You repeat syllables and words. You join together, you separate syllables and words. Arbitrarily. You yourself don't know why. You interrupt the conversation at every turn. You stammer, you drawl out endings; a sort of echo of your desiccated ego. An involuntary spasm. You clear your throat, you gurgle, you burble for no reason. You won't lubricate your larynx that way. You'll only ruin it even more. A throat in flames. Swallowing your saliva a double torture: because you must swallow, because it's your saliva. Its absorption increases your sensibility to the effects of this toxic.

Let's conduct a little test. Say for example: *Orpheus and Eurydice.* Come on, open your mouth; utter the phrase. Nothing easier: *Orifice and eurypygy.* You see? Substitution. Invention of a word. Another phrase. Utter the supreme slogan. Come on, out with it. INDEPENDENCE OR DEATH! Very good; it came out correctly. With that sentence you have the benefit of constant repetition. The fundamental mechanism of language is repetition, and it is through repetition that changes in language come about.

You are rapidly losing the memory of speech however. You attribute to yourself sentences that you have read, that you have heard. You are more irritable than you used to be. Worse still, your ear too is beginning to deteriorate. You string words together incorrectly. You don't hear well. Useless to try to goad it with your pen. Or even with a lance. There's no point in it. You're galloping toward verbal deafness, toward total muteness. The time will come when even your shirt collar won't hear you. Don't let it trouble you too much. These are still merely the beginning stages. Moreover, your comprehension remains and will remain intact.

It's plain to see, poor Sultan, that being underground so long has de-celebrated you! The earth has swallowed you whole. It has left only the worst of you. Dog-dross. You always were ungrateful, unappreciative. You never manifested the slightest feeling of pleasure or gratitude no matter how hard I tried to cater to your whims, to satisfy your least desires. Many times you were clearly in a rage. Only against me. Cynically sarcastic. In your old age you couldn't even lap up your soup; I myself spooned it down you. Your only thanks was to snap at me when you'd had enough. A most ungrateful cur. When sleep brought you to the thalamium, I could awaken you only by pushing and shoving you, making a great deal of noise. Then you fell into a sleep heavier than all the thalami and hypothalami that ever existed. All the pushing and shoving imaginable. All noises put together. What's the meaning of all this sound and fury you're coming out with against me from your posthumous poochly posture?

You'll forget nouns first, then adjectives, and even interjections. In your tremendous explosions of anger, it may well be that, in the best of cases, you'll still manage to articulate certain sentences, the ones you've used most frequently. For example, in the past you've often said: *I want means being able to say I do not want.* In a little while, when you try to force yourself to say NO, you will only be able to stutter, after many attempts, in a paroxysm of irritation: *I can't say NO!*

You will begin with pronouns. Do you know what it will be like for you not to be able to remember, not to be able to stammer **I-HE** anymore? Your suffering will soon be over. Eventually you will not even be able to remember to recall.

In addition to deafness you will suffer from verbal blindness. Pulvinar powder will clog your optical focuses with its fine sand. You will also lose your visual memory completely. When *that* happens, you will naturally go on seeing; but even though you haven't budged from the place where you are, you will find yourself in a completely different place. You will no longer be able to conjure up from your memory anything known, and as for the unknown, how will you be able to recognize it?

Assailed, first of all, by idiotic sounds of a foreign language. A dead language that comes to life again for a moment on being cut into little pieces by your scissors-tongue. Then after that, unknown images. You will continue to see certain objects; you will not be able to see the letters of books, or what you write. This will not interfere, however, with your ability to copy, and even to imitate the letters of a strange script, though you will not thereby understand their meaning. I write, you will say, as though I had my eyes closed, though I know they're really open. It will be a splendid experience for you. The last one. If you feel bored to death, you can play dominoes or cards with Patiño: and even beat him as often as you like.

Listen to me, Sultan . . .

I understand, I understand; you don't need to tell me anything, ex supreme. Your whole story is perfectly clear to me. You want to write. Do so. You still have a bit of *that*—what humans call time—left. Your hand will go on writing until the end and even after the end, even though you now say: I know very well how the word is written, but when I try to write it with my right hand I don't know how. Nothing simpler. Anyone who can no longer write with his right hand can do so with his left; anyone who can no longer write with his hands can do so with his feet. Even with your right arm paralyzed, your left leg swelling up more and more, you can go on writing. It doesn't matter that you don't see what you write. It doesn't matter that you don't understand it. Write. Follow the clew of thread through the horizontal-vertical labyrinth of the folios, which is not at all like the circumvolutions of your subterranean latomies. Your speech is so obscure that it seems to come straight out of the maze of those underground cells.

Listen to me, Sultan . . .

The test of recalled memories. I shall explain by way of an example. If you had lived in the age in which apparatuses for kinetic, visual, and verbal reproduction had been invented, you would not have had any difficulty. You would have been able to have these notes, the discourse of your memory, everything you copied from other authors imprinted on a quartz plaque, on a magnetic tape, on a filament of photoelectric cells one ten-thousandth of a hair thick, and leave it all there, completely forgotten. Then, when the machine chanced to be set in motion, you would have heard it again and recognized it as your thanks to certain properties. You would have gone on with it, or someone else would have; the chain would not have been broken. But that future of machines and apparatuses has not yet regressed to this uncivilized country, which you love and hate; for which you live, for which you are going to die.

What is written in the Book of Memories has to be read first; that is to say, it must evoke all the sounds corresponding to the memory of the word, and those sounds have to evoke the meaning that is not in the words, but rather, was united to them by the mind's movement and figure at a given moment, when the word *was seen* through the thing and the thing was understood through the word. *Symptomal,* you would say. Symptomatic.

This second reading, by an inverse movement, reveals what is veiled in the text itself, read first and written afterwards. Two texts, of which the absence of the first is necessarily the presence of the second. Because what you write now is already contained, anticipated in the readable text, the part that is its own invisible side.

Go on writing. It has no importance, in any event. When all is said and done, what is prodigious, fearful, unknown in the human being has never yet been put into words or books, and never will be. At least so long as the malediction of language does not disappear, in the way that irregular condemnations eventually evaporate. So go ahead and write. Bury yourself in letters.

Sultan, wait! Wait a minute! . . .

He's collapsed again. He vanishes little by little. Waggishly stealing away. Nothing left but the bare skull lying on the ground. It too sinks from sight. Disappears.

Great fatigue. Merely from having embarked upon a long colloquy with the mad shadow of a dog.

Five times every hundred years there is a month, the shortest one in the year, in which the moon prevaricates. The past February was one without a moon. Then the storm in August, the one that threw me from my horse on the afternoon of my last outing. Lying on my back in the rain, I fought desperately to free myself from the mud sucking me down. The rain firing at my face. Not an ordinary rain falling from above. A more than solid downpour, heavy, ice-cold. Drops of melted lead, burning-hot and freezing at the same time. A deluge of drops fired in all directions. Great gouts of fire and frost, making my bones rattle, making me retch. Beneath this cataract, the bay, stained with sudden streaks of white from the flashes of lightning, started off again, fearless as ever. Sitting astride it, cape whipping in the wind, erect as always, **HE**, taking off with his back turned to me, and at the same time fallen in the mudhole, vomiting, dragging me along, screaming out orders, entreaties, yapping like a beaten dog, crushed by the block of water. After struggling with more ardor and heroism than the most hard-shelled diehard, I managed to turn over on my belly and went on fighting tooth and nail in the quaking bog. I was finally able to sit up, weighted down with mud and despair. I roamed through the city all night long, leaning on a tree branch I picked up at random. I did not dare prowl around in the vicinity of Government House out of fear of my own guards. I wandered about the most deserted spots, making my way along like a blind man, in circles that kept leading me back to the same blind alley, the same crossroads. A beggar, the Supreme Mendicant, the One Great Alms-Seeker. Alone. Carrying my empty person on my back. Alone, without a family, without a home, in a strange land. Alone. Born old, feeling that I could die no more. Condemned to unlive my life till my last breath. Alone. Without a family. Alone, old, sick, without a family, without even a dog to turn to. Enough of this, damn it! You keep on whining like a dog. If you're only a shadow now, at least learn to behave like a man. The rain had stopped completely. Complete darkness. Complete silence in the alleyway. Then I said to myself: the only way out of the blind alley is the alley itself. I went on, leaning on the branch. A night patrol came my way: Halt! Who goes there! Nooobody!, I answered, though no sound came out. Passwoooord!, they demanded, amid the clack of rifle bolts. The Fatherland!, I made my voice resound inside those bodies soaked with rain and patriotism. Where do you live?, the corporal asked insistently. No fixed abode!, I said. What's brought you out at this hour, you old rascal? I got lost in the storm, my sons. Don't you know it's forbidden to be abroad after curfew? Yes, yes, I know. I gave that order myself. They did not understand. They heaped insults upon me. Yes, yes, my sons, I know very well that it is forbidden to go out after curfew. But there are too many curs barking, not just a few. This old gaffer's either crazy or crocked, the corporal said. Let him go. Go on, old-timer, go sleep off your hangover in a ditch somewhere if you don't have a home! And don't let us find you around here again!

I walked toward a flickering light that appeared at the other end of the alleyway. It wasn't yet the first light of dawn. I saw that it was Orrego's general store. He was just opening the place. I hesitated whether to go in. Finally I decided I would. Who would recognize me in the state I'm in? Spies are so stupid. I gestured that I wanted a brandy. Well, compadre, you're wetter than a puddle of dog piss! The rain's rusted your horns, has it, chief! He tried to get a conversation going. I drew my sleeve across my gullet in a slicing motion. Yep, compadre, looks like you've lost your voice for sure! I threw him a carlos cuatro cuarto, which fell on the floor amid the sacks and crates. He got down on his knees, arse in the air, to look for it. Where the devil has that fuckin' quarter gone anyway! I went out, leaving the spy still heaping insults on the sovereign defeated at Trafalgar, now only a piddling coin.

The following afternoon, from the roof terrace of the Hospital Barracks, through the spyglass aimed toward the Chaco, I saw a strange-shaped cloud approaching. Swirls and shudders as it came roaring in. Another storm!, imagination tolled in my bones. Locusts! I thought of the double harvest of the year pillaged by the plague. The whole country on a war footing once again. Wooden rattles, drums, battle cries deafening the air from one end of the country to the other. The cloud stopped dead on the horizon. Seemed to move backwards. Disappear. Vanish amid the reflections of the setting sun. A fancy trick of the imagination, a binocular illusion. A phenomenon of refraction, who knows how or why. By the time I realized what it was, a skirl of madly drifting swallows was falling. Blind birds. The bullets of rain from the cloudburst had put their eyes out. I was able to escape because as I fell from the horse I had pulled my bicorne down over my face. It was not enough. I got out the steel breastplate I was wearing underneath my clothes. I was able to withstand the hail of freezing melted lead; the swallows were not. They were bringing their summer with them from the north. The Deluge waylaid them. Settled accounts with them. The roof terrace was immediately covered with little eyeless birds looking at me through the drops of blood in their empty eye sockets. They fluttered for a moment and then keeled over dead. I strode rapidly across the creaking, cheeping little bones, as one walks over heaps of dry alfalfa. I deduced that the storm had extended over a vast area. That whole great flock had come from the farthest borders of the country to die at my feet.

How is the investigation of the cathedral pasquinade going? Have you identified the Hand? No, Excellency, thus far we haven't had any luck. Not so much as the tip of a hair in all the tons of paperwork in the Archive, even though we've now gone over every last folio, every last folicule with a fine-toothed comb. Stop searching. It's no longer important. I only wanted to add, begging your pardon, Excellency, that perhaps you didn't find the guilty party in the files and dossiers of the Archive because most of the signers of those papers are already dead or in prison, which is more or less the same thing. I couldn't be sure though, so I sent the scribes under heavy guard to repopulate the Tevegó penal colony. That way we'll kill two birds with one stone, I thought; or rather, we'll be taking steps to avoid two evils. On the one hand, we'll keep those scoundrels from continuing to lend a hand to the band of pasquinading guerrilla-fighters. And on the other, we'll put an end to the witchcraft at Tevegó, and I have a notion that the only way to bring new life, if I may so put it, to the penal colony is by bringing prisoners in to replace the ones who evaporated into stone. Because this morning, Excellency, as I was coming to the Palace, I was once again witness to a very strange happening. What, you knave, are you starting another of your Scheherazadished stories so as to waste my time and delay your sentence? No, Most Excellent Sire. God keep me from vainly petarding your patience with tittle-tattle, fiddle-faddle, rumors and other such idle *díceres*. I've said a thousand times that one doesn't say *díceres*, but *decires*. The word comes from the Latin *dicere*, but in our language it's said backwards. Yes, Sire, I won't let it happen again. But as it happens, something's happened that has no likes of which and has never been seen before. Reel off your story and be done with it. I'm beginning, Sire, and may God and Your Excellency aid me. It's not a simple matter. I don't even know where to begin. Begin: that way you'll at least know where to end.

The time Your Excellency fell off the horse during the storm, and we're a month away from that evil day now, it so happened that while Your Grace was confined in the Barracks Hospital, two men, a woman, and a child entered the city. They came, or so it would appear, to seek alms. That's what they said when a deposition was taken from them. That in itself was already odd, seeing that there are no more beggars, mendicants, or alms-seekers since Your Excellency took over the reins of the Supreme Government. Where are you from?, was the first thing I asked them. Then I remembered what Your Worship always says about all things going back to their image. But I could recall no known image of that thing or people I saw there before me. Where are you from?, I asked them again, feeling my head reel a bit from the terrible smell they were giving off. They had no idea, or else they didn't want to tell me. They just bobbed their heads up and down, gesturing like deafmutes. Were they mute? Weren't they? Were they deaf? Weren't they? I couldn't be sure, so I asked them: Are you from Tevegó by any chance? They didn't say a word. One of them, the one who piped up then and said he was the father, began to scratch himself hard, all over. You people know that the punishment for begging is twenty-five lashes. We don't know anything, sir, the man who piped up and said he was the uncle answered. We don't have anything, the woman who piped up and said she was the child's aunt murmured, and then, pointing to it: We don't have anything but this to earn us a living, and the only other thing we have is empty bellies because we haven't eaten even one wretched mouthful of manioc in three days. Nobody will give us anything. They're afraid of us, they shut their doors in our faces, they run from us, they set their dogs on us, they throw stones at us, the big people and the little ones, as though we had Saint Lazarus's complaint, or worse, a much worse complaint, sir.

In the beginning I thought they were trying to pull the wool over the eyes of the law. The child looked more or less normal. It's true that its two feet were very misshapen and its legs badly bowed. But it walked like other little ones its age. Albino hair, so white you almost couldn't see it in the sunlight. Sightless eyes, apparently, even though sight isn't born unless there are eyes to see. But it's certain they could see, because when the aunt-machú bent down to quiet the little one's whimpering it grabbed her by the breast. Put them in the guardhouse and take care of them, I ordered the soldiers.

The child dropped to the ground and began crawling, whining in a very worn-out, very old voice, that didn't sound like a child but like a frightened iguana or some other creature of the wilds. I went over to it and put my plug of chewing tobacco in its mouth. It chewed for a moment and then spat it out, along with a mouthful of black juice. Nákore!,§ it

§Guaraní: Go to the devil!

said. It went on howling, louder and louder. The aunt-machú knelt down and suckled it again. How old is it?, I asked. It'll be two, cabal-eté,§ on our Karaí-Guasú's next birthday, the father said. It was born on the same Day of the Three Kings, the uncle said.

A guard came and tried to pick it up in his arms. He couldn't. It weighs more than a five-arroba stone, he said, trying to pick up his cap, which had fallen on the child's head. He pulled on the cap with all his strength and couldn't get it off. Another guard came, and he couldn't lift it either. It must weigh a good ten arrobas, he said. Even between all five guards they couldn't lift the child up off the ground, and it was now screaming and howling loud enough for two. What with their pulling and tugging, the guards had yanked all its clothes off. And then we suddenly saw what kind of a creature *that* child was. Just under its little tit it was attached to another one, a boy-child, with no head and a behind that had no opening. The rest of the body, complete. Except that one arm was shorter than the other. It was broken when it was born, the aunt said from where she was sitting on the ground. The two creatures were joined front to front, as though the smaller little boy were trying to embrace the bigger little girl. The place where they were joined together to form a pair looked to measure less than the distance between the tip of a thumb and the tip of a forefinger, so that if you raised up the imperfect little boy you could have seen the navel of the other one. Its arms, thighs and legs, which weren't joined to the little girl, hung about halfway down her.

The aunt told us that the little boy without organs did his business through the little girl's tracts, so the two of them ate and lived on the same thing. When I asked them where the mother was, they said they didn't know. The father merely explained vaguely how the mother had disappeared the day the double creature was born. Or rather, he said, correcting his statement, when I came back from the fields at nightfall, the double creature was there but the mother had disappeared. With my brother and sister, who continues to suckle the two of them and always has enough milk for both, we went to see a healer in Lambaré, the Payaguá Payé who raises wild hogs. He told us we should come to see our Karaí Guasú, because somewhere one day these twins against nature were going to be seers and could be useful to the Supreme Government by providing it with favorable predictions for preserving the unity of its laws and the different parts of our State.

I still thought they were just trying to get out of the flogging meted out to beggars. They might well be people trained by the pasquinaders or

§Guaraní (from Spanish): exactly.

by people belonging to the Twenty Golden Families to try Your Excellency's patience. Do you think, I said to them, that even if your cock-and-bull story were true and the likes of these two creatures joined together turned out to be the best seers in the world, our Supreme Dictator would be willing to beg for predictions, prognostications, or miracles from these twins against nature? I told them, Sire, that you were against sorceries of any sort, being vestiges of the influence of the País on people's ignorance.

The father, the uncle, and the wetnurse-aunt didn't say another word. They gave no sign of fear or distress. To the pillory and twenty-five lashes for each of them!, I cried to the guards. The double creature stopped whimpering. The aunt lifted it up with no difficulty, put it astride one of her hips and followed the guards who were taking the men away. As she walked along she took the cap off the little girl's head and gave it back to the guard. I left orders with the sergeant that once they'd been given their punishment they were to be put in the pillory and left there till Your Worship had recovered and gave orders as to what to do with them.

I was drinking maté at my house the next morning when the sergeant appeared, looking completely dumbfounded. Stumbling over his words, still filled with the fear disguised as courage that a soldier must always have even though he's already dead, he blurted out the story of what had happened. Fear is a bad counselor. Do you know what happened, Señor Patiño? If you stop talking like a deafmute, maybe I'll find out some day, I said to him. What's the story, sergeant? The two men and the woman were stripped for the punishment, señor secretary of the Government. Not one of the three of them had so much as a trace of their privates, male or female. Nothing at all. Just three holes they kept piddling out of in a steady trickle. The lashes rotted the minute they touched those damp bodies. We had to change even the toughest ones we had, the ones made of braided bull pizzle, as many as five times. The Indians refused to go on whipping them. I had the lawbreakers put in the stocks. The twins too. At dawn this morning they were gone. All that was left was a puddle of piss on the floor of the prisoners' cell. The neckholes of the stocks were black, charred. Still warm. It's something I wanted to tell Your Worship about. I wish I could understand these things without equal, but only you, Sire, could understand this happening that happened with your knowledge and wisdom. Perhaps what we ignorant people call monsters, like those others from Tevegó, aren't monsters in your eyes. Maybe these beings of flesh and blood are only figures from a world unknown to ordinary people; the lost handiwork of some world that came before ours; things recounted in books lost to us. Perhaps they're related to other beings that have no name, but exist nonetheless, and are more powerful than ordinary folk. You will never know what is enough if you don't first find out what is more than enough, you always tell me, Sire, when I make an ass of myself.

I read the entire Bible through seeking a like fact so as to compare. Isaiah told me that no work, no worthwhile book had ever been lost in this world or in any other. I asked the prophet Ezequiel why he ate dung and spent so much time lying on his right side, and on his left as well. He replied: the desire to elevate others to the perception of the infinite. I don't know what those two words mean.

I know I'm telling what I'm telling badly, Sire. But it's not so as to waste your time or disguise my thought. You mustn't think that. The thing is, I don't know how to tell it any other way. You yourself, Sire, say that facts can't be recounted, and yet you're able to think other's thought as though it were your own, even if it's the thought of an ignorant man like myself.

I have my reverence, Supreme Sire, my firm respect, signed with a firm hand. You are wasting your time and patience hearing me. What I am most grateful for is your close attention. You have even closed your eyes in order to hear me better. I envy your education; what I envy even more is your intelligence, your knowledge, your experience. Many of the things you say from up where you are I don't understand from down where I am, even though I know without knowing that they are truth itself. You are more than good, far too kind, to listen to my idiotcies, the idiolatries that come drooling out of my mouth simply because the hole in it has been punched out, and you listen to me with the patience of a saint.

In every movement of true joy or sorrow that I have ever had in my life, if I go on and put it into words, on hearing myself I feel that I am another person. A person-that-talks. He says what he has heard many times, till this tongue of mine manages to get moisture from someone else's mouth so as to slide its words out. They come out gabbled and garbled and gargled, like a parrot talking. I know that what I am saying is very hard to follow, very intervolved. But you pluck up my courage with your patience in hearing me out. I almost feel that I am confessing, like the demented man who killed himself with the guard's bayonet because he believed he'd murdered Your Excellency in his sleep.

One always feels himself to be someone else when he speaks. But I want to be myself. To speak as a man who is master of his tongue, of his thought. To tell you the story of my life with its pluses and its minuses. You, Sire, often say that living is not living but disliving. I would like to tell you about that. I would like to understand fear, valor, the urges that impel a person to embody what is happening without the body becoming aware of it. To do so many things that a person doesn't understand, like dismented, disheartened, disfigured dreams. So many strange bad acts we do when we are so close to what is ours, by right, by destiny, who knows what, and one doesn't know it, doesn't know it, doesn't know it!, even if he plunges his feet in the coldest water.

Persons and things are not what they seem to be. It is very seldom that dreams show us visible, sensible figures. They have two faces, they do things backwards. It must have happened to you too, Sire: the light is less of a shock to your eyes on awakening if you have dreamed of visible things. No, Your Excellency is different. Your Worship must always see what he dreams of. You keep calling me an idiot, an animal. And you are right. I am different. I must be like the crow that would like everything to be white, or like the owl that would like everything to be black.

What I am most grateful for is your kind attention. You listen to me, you think, you rethink what I am saying to you in a very simpleminded but very reverent way. I am talking to you about what I don't know but I know that you know. I am going to talk to you a little more, now that my memory has turned into a wasp's nest that is swelling up and making my head go round and round; now that my hand seems to be more faithful to the paper and is being pushed by another hand as it writes. The serious, the exact, the certain truth of what happened is this. Listen, Sire, listen to me disarmed; listen to me more than what I am saying, for only Your Excellency sees beyond all the visible, hears what is beyond all the audible. Only Your Excellency can couple the fact with the divination of the fact. Divining things that are past is easy. Joys don't laugh. Sorrows don't weep. Prayers don't plow, praise doesn't ripen. Those are all favorite díceres of yours. And many things lack a name. Or at least I don't know what name to give them and so they escape me. I'm getting more and more confused. What's happening is more serious than it appears to be. Because what happened on that ill-starred day of your fall happened again this morning. As though through an evil sorcerer's trick, those monster-people have appeared in the city again. More monstrous still, and not just one family like the first time. I alone, Sire, coming from my house to Government House, ran into some ten covens of those no-goods. They're coming out of the drains, climbing up the cliffs, coming down from Sentinel Hill. They seem very sure of themselves and very determined. They show no fear of anything or anybody. Although they're still peaceable enough when there are soldiers and armed guards about, who knows what villainy they'll be capable of when there are more of them.

They're turning up all over, according to the reports from the guard posts and the pickets outside the walls. But just as they appear, they disappear, in the blink of an eye, as though the earth had swallowed them up or they were hiding in the folds of the hills and the brush in the ravine. The ones now, Sire, don't talk; or rather, they only talk among themselves, by signs or by buzzing like flesh flies at funerals. . . . Isn't your patience exhausted, Sire? Eh, Your Worship? Have you dropped off to sleep, Excellency? Enveloped in the depths of obscurity as you are, you don't even seem to be breathing. And what if you were dead? Ah, if he were! Then . . . No, my dear secretary. Don't get your hopes up. He who expects the death of another to be his salvation is doomed to perdition. That's what's going to happen to you shortly. You've been talking to me about those monsters of semihuman appearance that have begun to invade the city. But I tell you that there are others worse still, and they don't need to invade us because they have been among us for a long time now. By comparison with them, those others are doubtless more innocent than suckling babes. Doubtless they are also more loyal, reliable, responsible, and intelligent. I am going to have to entrust the census I ordered my men to make to these peaceable but active monsters. What's this bunch of nonsense you handed me yesterday? According to these population figures, Paraguay alone has more inhabitants than the entire continent all told. You can see from a hundred leagues away that that whole corps of idlers has been busy inventing all sorts of nonsense to get out of working. To sum it all up in a few words, writing, noting things down is easy. A piece of paper puts up with anything. In order to go on doing nothing, my civil and military functionaries have foisted the work off onto their clerks and sent them out to count heads, which they've done by counting on their fingers, lying stretched out in their hammocks after having chased after peasant girls, mulattas and Indians all over the backlands, in all the brakes and brambles, round the remotest farmhouse. One sniff at the papers and you can smell the stink of their breeches. Those good-for-nothings have given birth to people out of nothing. They've provided every family where the father and mother are unknown with a whole flock of kids that don't exist. The couple that has the fewest shows up on their list with more than a hundred. Unmarried mothers are even more prolific than the ones who are married, kept, seduced, or concubinated. I find here one Erena Cheve, a woman those clerks have had the balls to give 567 sons to, all with the oddest names and ages, the youngest still unborn and the oldest older than his mother. This isn't childbirth; it's wildbirth. As a result, the population would appear to have increased a hundredfold since the last master-census that I had taken ten years ago, and if I trusted the word of that herd of rakehills, I could count on and order an immediate levy of no less than a hundred thousand names. An army of phantoms come from the heights of the imagination of those profligate figure-flingers who have made of their trousers flies their principal pieces of military equipment!

Sire, the first lists from 140 public schoolteachers have also arrived, with the answers of their pupils to the question of how they see the sacrosanct image of our Supreme National Government. Come, come, enough of your idiolatric rubbish. Read the first ones. I begin, Sire:

School District Number 1, capital, School Number 27, "First Republic of the South." Teacher José Gabriel Téllez. Pupil Liberta Patricia Núñez, age 12: "The Supreme Dictator is a thousand years old like God and has shoes with gold buckles edged and trimmed with leather. The Supreme decides when we should be born and that all those who die should go to heaven, so that there are far too many people there and the Lord God doesn't have enough maize or manioc to feed all the beggars of his Divine Beatitude." Another of Schoolmaster Téllez's pupils, Victoriana Hermosilla, age 8, blind from birth, says: "The Supreme Government is very old. Older than the Lord God, that our schoolmaster Don José Gabriel tells us about in a low voice." That's enough from Téllez's pupils. He and Quintana are the ones who earn the most as masters of the rod and ferule, but instead of teaching the Patrial Catechism they slyly slip in the one that's been abolished, and instead of the usual First Reader, and the De Senectudine for the older ones, they pervert their pupils with vain and profane antipatriotic tales. If I remember correctly, Téllez and Quintana are fulfilling their functions as teachers on a temporary basis until more suitable ones are found, isn't that right? Yes, Excellency, they have occupied their temporary posts since March 11, 1812, when they were appointed by the First Junta. Have a close watch kept on these schoolmasters who have gone so far as to give private lessons in secret to the children of the Twenty. Your order will be executed, Excellency.

School Number 5, "Independent Paraguay." Teacher Juan Pedro Escalada. Pupil Prudencio Salazar y Espinosa, age 8: "The Supreme Government is 106 years old. He helps us be good and works hard to make the grass, the flowers, and the plants grow. Sometimes he takes a bath and then it rains down here below. But it's either God or the devil, I really don't know which, or maybe both of them together, that make the weeds and the yavorai of our kapueras§ grow." Hmmm . . . Well! This pupil is making progress, despite the Porteño pedant who remained here as a leftover from the Areopagites.

Same school, the following compositions:

Pupil Genuaria Alderete, age 6: "The Supreme Government is like water that boils outside the pot. It goes on boiling even though the fire goes out, and sees to it that we don't lack for food."

Pupil Amancio Recalde, age 9: "He rides by on his horse without looking at us but he sees all of us and nobody sees Him." Ha! It's plain to see that this boy is Don Antonio Recalde's grandson.

Pupil Juan de Mena y Mompox, age 11: "The Supreme Dictator is the one who gave us the Revolution. He's in command now, because he wants to be, forever and ever."

Pupil Petronita Carísimo, age 7: "Mama says that he's the Bad Man who put our grandfather in prison just because the horse he rides every afternoon stumbled on a loose flagstone in front of Grandfather's house. He ordered a heavy shackle put on him and he sank to the bottom of the earth, so we'll never see Grandpa José again." Shall I tear up this little girl's composition, Sire? No. Leave it. The truth as children see it is not to be torn up, twisted, bent, folded or mutilated.

Pupil Leovigildo Urrunaga, age 7: "The Supreme is the Man-Who-Is-Master-of-Fear. Papa says he's a Man who never sleeps. He writes night and day and loves us backwards. He also says he's a Great Wall around the world that nobody can get past. Mama says he's a hairy spider forever spinning its web in Government House. Nobody escapes from it, she says. When I do something bad, my mama says to me: 'The Karaí is going to stick a hairy foot through the window and carry you off!' " Have the parents of this child summoned. Have them bring him with them and let him see me. It is not right to fool children. They'll be fooled enough in the schools later on, if there are any left, where they'll be told that when the hairy spider died they had to stick a long pole through the window and poke it to see if it was really dead. Very well, Sire.

School Number 1, "Fatherland or Death." Native teacher Venancio Touvé. Pupil Francisco Solano López, age 13: "I would like to ask the Supreme Government to give me the Perpetual Dictator's dress sword, so as to keep it in my care and use it in the defense of the Fatherland." That child has a brave soul. Send him the sword. Sire, with your permission I remind you that he is the son of Don Carlos Antonio López, the one who . . . I remember him, I remember him, Patiño. Carlos Antonio López and

---

§Guaraní: brush of our farmlands.

the Indian Venancio Touvé were the last two pupils of the Colegio San Carlos whom I examined and passed with the highest grade, shortly after the Revolution. You too will remember Don Carlos Antonio López, the future president of Paraguay. Before his star rises in the heaven of the Fatherland, the rope of your hammock will be knotted round your neck. Go on.

Special School "Home for Orphan and Foundling Girls." Pupil Telésfora Almada, age 17: "The Supreme Government must immediately call for popular and sovereign elections. Meanwhile, it must dissolve the parasitical army commanded by corrupt and venal leaders, and transform it into militias that will advance the Revolution and all the people of the Fatherland. . . ." Aha! That's not a bad idea that little girl has there, not bad at all! Speaking of the Home for Orphan and Foundling Girls, Most Excellent Sire, I take the liberty of informing you that very strange things are going on in that establishment. Do you mean to tell me, Patiño, that those monsters never before seen that have begun invading the city and perhaps the entire country have been turning up there too? They haven't gone that far, Sire. But the real and certain truth is that the greatest libertinage that anyone can imagine reigns there. Nobody knows exactly what they do, nor when those girls and women of every sort sleep. By night the Home is a brothel. By day a barracks. They've formed a battalion of every color, age, and estate. White, half-breeds, blacks, and Indians. Before dawn breaks they take off into the wilds. It could be that they practice combat maneuvers. From dawn to dark you can hear distant rifle fire. I've sent scouts to have a look. They come back without having seen one thing. One of them was tied fast to a tree with lianas and an insulting placard hung around his neck. The male-ysipó§ they tied him up with couldn't be cut even with a machete and it had to be burned off him to free him. He was subjected to a long interrogation in the Truth Chamber. He wouldn't or couldn't or decided he shouldn't tell us anything that had happened, and finally fell senseless after five hundred lashes. I went personally this morning to search the House and found it empty. Not a trace, Sire. Except for the air of having been abandoned quite some time ago. Given these circumstances, I take the liberty of requesting orders from Your Eminence as to what I should do. As regards the House, nothing for the moment, my ex faithful scribe. Take your pen and write what I am about to dictate to you. Grip it firmly, squeeze it as hard as you can. I want to hear it moan with each stroke as it tears through the paper with my last will.

§Guaraní: liana.

SUMMONS

I THE SUPREME DICTATOR OF THE REPUBLIC

Order all delegates, commandants of garrisons and troops of the line, appointed judges, administrators, stewards, tax collectors, customs agents, mayors of towns and villages, to present themselves at Government House for the meeting of the conclave announced in the Perpetual Circular. The meeting will begin at 12 o'clock next Sunday, the twentieth day of the month of September.

Appearance is mandatory and its omission will not be excused or justified in any case, no matter how extreme the cause.

I am now going to dictate to you the special invitation concerning your esteemed person:

I THE SUPREME PERPETUAL DICTATOR

Order that on presentation of this warrant by the interested party himself, the Commander of the Garrison proceed to arrest the confidential clerk Policarpo Patiño and keep him in confinement, totally and absolutely incommunicado. Having been implicated in a conspirative plan of usurpation of the Government, the criminal Policarpo Patiño is to be hanged as an infamous traitor to the Fatherland, and his corpse is to be buried in pastures outside the walls with neither cross nor mark to commemorate his name.

The Commander of the Garrison and the three remaining commanders are jointly responsible for executing this Supreme Decree. Having so done, they are to report, immediately and personally, to the undersigned in order to render a full account, the four commanders being subject to the penalties for any and all subreption, leniency, or complicity, by omission or commission, in which they might be implicated.

Hand me the papers. I'm going to sign them right now. Another waterspout, the last one, splashed out of the basin as the result of the brusque movement. The condemned man has come to attention. Clicked his heels. Disappeared. The catafalque-person of the mulatto has dissolved in the pool of water flooding the floor and forming rivulets in the cracks. The pestilence of long standing has suddenly increased to double its size and fetor. The enormous flat feet are still there however. Heels together. Big toes apart, raising their horny heads with trembling movements of supplication, of terror. Only the wet feet, gleaming in the semidarkness. Immense. Bathed in sweat. They have become so swollen that the obese confidential clerk must have slid all of himself into them, trying to sink down deeper and deeper. To bury himself. But in his attempt to flee, to absent himself, the floor boards, harder than iron, have produced a contrary effect. They have made that absence more present still in the immense swelling of the human monster turned into two sweating feet. Two feet gazing out from amid blinking toenails. Two feet squared militarily, imploring. Two feet already moving back and forth in the slow swaying dangle of hanged men. Come on, come closer! Or do you want to die twice? Hand me the papers. The confidential clerk fearfully creeps out of his hiding place reinforced by a double heelbone. The enormous carcass emerges from its feet on tiptoe. Little by little. Fear by fear. The heel-sacs go slack as the carcass takes on its original size, plus its duplicity. The treacherous trickster, split cleanly in two from top to bottom by the slash of the pen. I sign. Signed. Scatter sand on these decrees. Put yours in an envelope. Seal it. There's no more sealing wax left, Sire. It doesn't matter, your ex person has left its greasy imprint on it. Suddenly naked, he covers himself with one decree in front, the other behind. From the innermost depths of his chest comes a mortal sigh. His right hand, transformed into a black penholder, smites his face. Is the wretch trying at this late date to suborn me by arousing my compassion? By performing one last circus turn on the high wire? He suddenly raises his pen-hand to his gullet, pierces his Adam's-apple clean through, so that the nib comes out the other side of his neck at the base of his skull; on the very tip of it a little boy appears, singing and executing fiendishly difficult pirouettes. In the voice of a dwarf, ex Patiño begs me: Most Excellent Sire, I humbly accept the just punishment that Your Worship has seen fit to visit upon me, since I have borne my black conscience along a very wicked way, a low road beset with mud and mire and secret ire, a path besmattered and besmirched by the blackest ingratitude toward Your Most Excellent Person. But more hum-bly still, I dare pray Your Excellency not to deprive my grave of that sign that is most precious to every good Christian, the Most Holy Cross. It does not matter to me, Sire, if I am buried in the barest pasture outside the walls. It does not matter to me if the Cross is made of the most lowly or even deadly wood. It doesn't matter to me, Sire, if it is draped with a stole or adorned with little colored stones at its foot. But Sire, the Cross, the Cross!, the impenitent liar moans, his face contorting with mystery. Without the aid and protection of the Cross, Most Merciful Sire, the spirits with which I still have accounts to settle will come to balance the books and take their vengeance upon me! . . . If I hear rightly, you consider yourself already hanged and buried, and you want to hold your wake here and now. Who, me, Sire? . . . Your sighs smack of belches to me. Do you consider yourself a good Christian? I'm no plaster saint, Sire, but neither am I a whited sepulcher. My belief in the Cross couldn't be simpler. It has always been my present help, Sire. And you've been the craftiest scoundrel in the last hundred years. So what can the cross mean to you? And so: Nequaquam! Neither cross nor mark! You were born by mistake and will die by mistake. I don't intend to have a kicking-match with my ex pack mule. I'll kick it out like an ex secretary. Go find your last shitting spot. You know the saying: When the burro's kicked off you might as well shove its food up its ass. Off with you, and stop coming to attention because I'll hear the sound of four heels clicking. The stupid beast didn't understand. He gets down on all fours, brays a little, and splashes off through the mud. Ex Policarpo Patiño! He suddenly halts. At your orders, Excellency! The magnifying glass, remember the magnifying glass! What magnifying glass, Sire? Put the magnifying glass in the sun. Ah, yes, Excellency! The mulatto gets to his feet, puffing for all he's worth. Come on, hurry up! Open the shutter. Place the lens in the arch that I ordered you ex profeso to set into the windowframe. Yes, Sire, I am placing it there now. He excitedly fits the lens into the circlet. Child's play. Expende Dictatorem nostrum Populo sibi comiso et exercitu suo!* How many arrobas of ashes will my frail bones produce? At least a hundred, Sire! Exoriare aliquis nostris es ossibus ultor!,** I murmur as I see cineral zenithal rays of the sun fall on the lens. As they glance off the biconvex surface, they form a solid ingot of melting gold. Good. Very good. The universe continues to cooperate by offering its precious gifts, which cost me a most modest price. Place beneath this ingot of fire your ex table and all the rest, with all the dead souls bound to its legs. Heap on top of it a pyre-pile of papers. Change the position of the table slightly. Focus the pencil of solar fire on the very peak of the

---

*Combination of the expression *Expende Hannibalem*, from a verse of Juvenal (*Satires*, X, 147): "Put Hannibal in the scales. How many pounds of ashes will you find that that great captain weighs?", and the phrase of the daily rogation made mandatory for secular and cloistered priests by the congress of June 1, 1816 that elected *El Supremo* as Perpetual Dictator of the Republic, replacing the ejaculatory prayer *De Regem* previously offered. (*Compiler's Note.*)

**May one to avenge these ashes be born one day! (Virgil, *Aeneid*, 625).

paper-pyre. There, that's it. When the first curls of smoke mount to his face, the ex confidential clerk stops smiling. He gazes at me with a hangdog look, his eyes brimming with tears. Wind the seven timepieces. None of them will strike the hour for you now. Put the one with the repeating mechanism within reach of my hand with its bells tolling twice. Take up your basin and go. If we are not to see each other again in this life, farewell till eternity!

My memory is not a dreamer. Once upon a time it did its work wide awake, even in sleep, if I ever managed to fall asleep. Which is most unlikely. At present, it works even in non-sleep. A dis-memory calling to mind my great command in eclipse. I write amid the swirls of smoke filling the room. Truth Chamber. Closet of Justice. Seat of Voluntary Confessions. Posthumous confessional. My works are my memorial. My innocence and my guilt. My right and wrong guesses. Poor countrymen, you have read me badly! And what is the final reckoning of your Debit and Credit, counterhearer of your own silence?, the one who is correcting these notes behind my back asks; the one who at times governs my hand when my strengths fall off from Absolute Power to Absolute Impotence. What is the final reckoning, perpetual executor of your mistrust? Amid the smoke the hand worms its way into my secrets. Pokes about. Separates the chaff from the grain. Very few grains. Perhaps only one: Very tiny. Diamantiferous. Blinding bright on the black pillow of the Insignia. A great deal of chaff; almost all the rest. Destined to be consumed in the fire. The iron hand forces my hand. Ever alert against everything, my hand writes as the other directs it. You can't bear the suspicion and you can't escape it. Immured in your concave mirror, you have seen and will continue to see, all at one time, repeated in successive rings to infinity, the earth in which you lie trying out your first-last-last resting place. Forests. Swamplands. Clouds. Objects surrounding you. The spectral image of your race, scattered like sands of the desert. You have played out your passion in cold blood. True. But you risked it at the gaming table of chance. The passion of the Absolute—oh, you bad player!—has rusted you, eaten you away little by little, though you took no account of it as you kept careful watch over every last penny in your ledgers. You have been content with very little. You have put your enormously swollen leg up on the aerolith. There it is, a prisoner. Here you are, trapped with it. You can feel it breathing, feel it throbbing better than you. You feel in the meteor the natural pulse of the universe. At any moment it may take to its stellar ways again. Those stray canines of the cosmos don't catch hydrophobia. You can no longer move. Except for that hand that writes out of inertia. Vestigial act of an absolutely gratuitous Habit. The one thing left for you to do is fall into the grave. Down the drain, down the funnel: to the very bottom of the trick mirror. Any ray of light that penetrates its envelope of strange refraction, like nothing under the sun, heavier than the atmosphere of Venus, will follow an invariably rational arc more acute than your own thought . . . Am I repeating myself? No: because it is not my will that dips itself in ink and expresses itself in signs. Nonetheless: yes! The Voice repeats the cogitations I noted down one time in my almanac. I had completely forgotten them! The Almastronomy I wrote on December 13, 1804! The image of the concave mirror and the ray of light, repeating, in successive rings extending to infinity, the eye that is observing, till finally it causes it to disappear in its own multiple reflections. In this perfect hall of mirrors there would be no way of knowing which is the real object. Hence the real would not exist; only its image. I did not produce the philosopher's stone in my alchemical laboratory. I succeeded in doing something much better. I discovered the line of perfect rectitude passing through all possible refractions. I fabricated a prism that could break a thought down into the seven colors of the spectrum. Then each one of them into seven others, until I caused a light to come forth that is white and black at the same time, there where those capable of conceiving only the double-opposite in all things see nothing more than a confused jumble of colors. News of this discovery never reached the ears of my master Lalande, to whom the pope, on that very same date, December 13, 1804, declared that an astronomer as great as he could not be an atheist. What would the Sovereign Pontiff have said of me had he come to Paraguay, where I had reserved the office of chaplain for him? What would His Holiness, bathed in the heavy atmosphere of Venus, have said on seeing in my concave mirror the specter of God come forth from the prism? Would he have called me an atheologue too?

When I fixed the formula, my own thought was a prism and a mirror-funnel. Even the very smallest mote of dust was reflected in it. It made the page of ether sparkle. There was another time, I remind myself, when I wrote, dictated, copied. I flung myself heart and soul into paper-and-ink work. Suddenly a full stop. An abrupt end to this abandon. The point at which the absolute begins to take on the form of history from the other side. At one time toward the beginning, I believed that I dictated, read, and worked under the sway of universal reason, under the rule of my own sovereignty, under the dictates of the Absolute. I now ask myself:

Who is the amanuensis? Not the trust-unworthy scribe, certainly. Back then, I ordered him to work barefooted, so that the blood that had accumulated in his feet from the heat of his patrial half-boots would expand and fill his head. The blood rose and activated to a slightly greater degree the battery cells of his encephalus, which were clogged with fat and lacking in gray matter. His blood went to his head, but so did the fumes. We were in the early days of the Perpetual Dictatorship then. The faithless-faithful scribe wasn't satisfied with the coolness of the dirt floor. He made improvements. He himself contributed the basin of cold water. For more than a quarter of a century he kept his feet in that black water that turned thicker than ink. Without knowing it, without doing so intentionally, he managed to contradict Heraclitus. The amanuensis's amphibian feet bathed in the very same motionless water in an *always* quite like eternity. Throw out that dirty, stinking water, Patiño. Change it. Sire, with your permission, I'd really rather just leave it in the basin for now. It's taken on the shape of my feet by this time. If I change it I don't know what might happen. It might turn us to rust, or who knows what. It could be—Heaven preserve us!—that the new water would dissolve my feet and even my body. How am I to know! I'm deathly afraid of river water and even of rain water. Of the first because it runs. Of the second because it falls like the piss-tail streaming down from a cow or a horse. My Sancho Panza's reasoning is not at all unreasonable. Didn't King Solomon the Wise maintain that time eats away iron with rust and men with uncertainty? What is there that is more fixed and immovable than the Pater Noster? And yet the Our Father moves unceasingly in people's mouths. The thought of the Pater Noster is more agile than twelve thousand Holy Ghosts, even if each one had twelve feather capes, and each cape had twelve winds, and each wind twelve victoriosities, and each victoriosity twelve thousand eternities. The Grotiuses and Pufendors make the same observation. They say its clauses were already in use at the time of Christ. And who are you to contradict them! Where is the counterproof? What Christ did, they maintain, was to gather them up and string them all together like nuggets of gold, myrrh, and frankincense. Ah, the smoke is growing thicker and coughing is absorbing the functions of thought! I'm the one who's sneezing now! During the night I would kneel before the amanuensis's basin. In the white cone of the candle, I would bend over the round black mirror. I would join my hands and wait in the attitude of prayer. At a given moment, at long last, sometimes, not always, I would see blurred images like clouds glide very slowly from one horizon to another on the tarred surface. Did the feet of my confidential clerk think, then, in a manner that was the reverse of his untutored and retentive mind? Those amphibian soles were thinking some secret thought. I also heard voices sometimes; something like the droning of a procession marching through the streets behind the baldachin of the Most Holy. Thinking of the amanuensis brought me to Aristotle, when he maintained that Plato's words were fleet, ever-shifting, and as a consequence, animated, and to Antiphanes, when he argued that the words addressed by Plato to children congealed because of the coldness of the air. Hence they were not understood until they were old; the children too grew old, whereupon they understood something very different from what the words said in the beginning. But what did the amanuensis's feet think? What did they say? Were their words animated like Plato's? If they said something it wasn't in Castilian, Guaraní, Latin, or any other language, living or dead. The images never turned into anything more than very white clouds that took on the forms of unknown animals. Bestiaries. Animal fables. At times, tinged by the reflections of some tiny submerged sun, the clouds turned the bluish color that dims the cornea of the one-eyed; to the opalescent color of the thin membrane of cataracts, or the red-and-gold of jaguars in heat. Merely that. No revelation in the Patmos of the basin. Nonetheless, one must proceed cautiously. One never knows. A louse mounted on a speck of dandruff can fly. The most profound revelations sometimes take the rudest and most unexpected paths. Petronius thought that words touched each other in the form of an equilateral triangle, and that Truth resided in the center of them. All words, example, ideas, and images of all things, past and future, dwelt therein.

In the inferno of summer, even on the hottest nights, the basin remained stubbornly silent. By the light of the candle, of the moon, of the most powerful lantern, the heavy water slept undisturbed, without dreams. Like the dead. It was with the first spells of freezing winter weather that the clouds and the faint sounds began. I tried the most diverse reagents, of acids, salts, substances distilled from buckwheat, sarrazin, lycopodium and many other aperitive essences. The seminal pollen of plants is highly inflammable. All they managed to do was to bring to a state of erection some elongated bubbles that silently burst, throwing in my face the fetor of the mulatto's corns. I worked all night with an acetylene torch to see if I could defrost the words and the figures locked up in those clouds, in those murmurs. The flame of the torch turned whiter still, to a blinding bone-whiteness; the water blacker, till it began to boil, giving off a sulfurous vapor. The torch exploded. Its fragments embedded themselves in the walls, like splinters of a grenade. The following morning, I observed, with the greatest dissimulation and attention, my amanuensis's behavior. Every so often, in the pauses of the dictation, he would lift up one foot and scratch it underneath the table as the drops fell, boring holes in the stone of my patience. I felt them fall like gouts of molten lead on the most sensitive areas of my gouty leg, made even more so by the attack of acephalalgy that I had been suffering from ever since nightfall. What's the matter, Patiño? Why are you scratching your foot? Nothing, Sire, it's just that the water seems a bit hot, that's all. So I'm breaking out in a bit of a rash, or measles, or I don't know what. With your permission, Sire, I'm going to go change it. No!, I begged him now, almost shouting. Don't change it! Your wish is my command, Sire. I for my part like the water on the lukewarm side. One's feet feel incomparably cool afterward in the breeze of the swaying hammock, when one drops off for an afternoon nap and sleeps the sleep of the dead. I was thinking of keeping that water with the secrets thought by my amanuensis's feet. So clever, that mulatto, so infinitely clever that he foresaw that latter possibility and overturned the basin on purpose! There's a little more water for under the bridge, I thought I heard him say as he left the room.

Tongues of fire shoot up joyfully in several places, perfectly attuned to my mood. Pabulum ignis!§ Welcome, Igneous Power! Come in, friend Fire. Make yourself at home. Work with a will, like a man. It won't take you long to put an end to all this. All of it! Eh! You will wreak the revenge of the small on the great. Of the hidden on the manifest. Don't dissipate your energies. Concentrate. Don't be distracted by the rumers spread by certain people to the effect that men are nothing but women expanded by heat, or that women are secret men because they have male elements hidden inside them. Allow me to address you in the familiar form. Unto thee I commend my end between your flame and the stone, just as I formed my beginning between water and fire. I did not arise from the rubbing of two sticks of wood together, nor from a man and a woman gaily rubbing their bacon as they made the beast with two backs, as my exegete Cantero claimed. You won't suffer from indigestion with me. But neither will you be able to finish me altogether. There's always some little bit left over that you find hard to swallow. You spit it out. Pliny flung himself into Aetna. The volcano ejected him as a vapor that preserved intact his form, his mocking smile, even the twitch in his eye (the left one —he was one-eyed), which never stopped winking. Empedocles, plastered to the gills, hurled himself into the same volcano, not so much because he wanted to kill himself as because he wanted to hoodwink his compatriots; to make them believe, when they found no trace of his body, that he had

§Food for fire.

ascended to heaven. Vulcan vomited out intact the vapor of the one, the bronze sandals of the other, thereby giving away the game that those two vainglorious tricksters were up to.

I shall not burn on a pyre in the Plaza de la República but in my own room; on a bonfire of papers set aflame at my command. I wish you to understand me clearly. I am not flinging myself headfirst into your flames. I am throwing myself into the Ethna of my Race. Some day its crater in eruption will eject only my name. It will scatter the burning lava of my memory far and wide. Useless to inter my remains next to the main altar of the church of the Encarnación. Then in the common grave behind the sacristy. Then in a box of noodles. None of those places will give back a single buckle of my shoes, a single sliver of my bones. No one is taking my life from me. I am giving it. In doing so I am not even imitating Christ. According to the melancholy dean, the Son-God committed suicide on Golgotha. It matters little that the cause was the salvation of men. Perhaps the self-entitled "People of God" did not deserve, does not deserve, will not ever deserve to have any god commit suicide for its sake. Which would prove in passing that the idea of God is miserably human. A God-God-God three times First-Last is not one even though he may rise from the dead on the Third Day. Even though he is a Trinitarian-God in Three-Separate-and-Equal-Persons. If he really is one, he is obliged to exist without a pause; to be unable to die even for an instant. Furthermore, at the moment of the gall and vinegar, the Son-God hesitated in the Garden of Olives. O my Father, let this cup pass from me, et cetera et cetera . . . Soft! Chicken-hearted, the poor Son-God. Maybe the Redeemer failed to pay the last drop of blood of the ransom that will be exacted from the human species, supposedly redeemed, in the great pyre of universal destruction beneath the terrible mushroom-cloud of the Apocalypse. But let us not lose ourselves in atheological hypotheses.

When one is oneself the pit that exhales this mortal emanation, the oven that spews forth burning clouds of smoke, the mine that vomits out a suffocating damp, is it possible not to say that we do not kill ourselves with our own vapors? What have I done to engender these vapors that issue forth from me?, my left hand continues to copy, since the right one has already fallen dead at my side. It writes, it drags itself across the Book, it writes, it copies. I dictate the inter-dict beneath the rule of another hand, an alien thought. The hand is mine nonetheless. The thought as well. If anyone has a grievance against the written word, I am that person, since everywhere and always it has served to persecute me. But it is necessary to love letters despite the misuse that is made of them, as it is necessary to love our Country, however many injustices we suffer in it and even though we may lose our very life for it, since one dies only as one has lived. I take from others, here and there, those maxims that express my thought better than I myself could, not to store them up in my memory, since I lack that faculty. In this way the thoughts and words are my very own as well, as much mine as before writing them. It is not possible to say anything, however absurd it may be, without discovering that it has already been said and written by someone somewhere, Cicero says (*De Divinat,* II, 58). The I-would-have-said-it-first-if-he-hadn't-said-it does not exist. Someone says something because someone else has already said it or will say it much later, even without knowing that someone has already said it. The one thing that is ours is what remains inexpressible behind the words. It is even farther inside us than what we ourselves are within ourselves. Those who feign modesty are the worst. Socrates hypocritically bows his head when he utters his famous sentence that is a lie: I only know that I know nothing. How could the peripatetic know that he knew nothing if he knew nothing? Hence he deserved the punishment of the hemlock. He who says I lie and tells the truth lies, indubitably. But he who says I lie and really lies is telling the scriptest truth. Sophistitricks. Politicoils. A miserable honor, entrusting the desire for immortality to words, the very symbol of the perishable, the melancholy dean sermonizes. Then countersermonizes: All humanity belongs to a single author. There is but a single volume. When a man dies, that does not mean that that chapter is torn out of the pages of the Book. It means that it has been translated into a better language. Each chapter is thus translated. The hands of God (said he who spoke of the suicide of God, a really witty sally!) will bind all of our scattered pages together once again for the Great Library in which each book will lie side by side with another, with its final page, its final letter, its ultimate sentence. Compadre Franklin, a thrifty man, ever the hoarder, copies in his epitaph the thought of the dean. Compadre Blaise copies the Lord of the Mountain, feigning false modesty in his turn: When I write, my thought sometimes escapes me. I am thereby reminded of my weakness which I constantly forget. This is as instructive to me as the forgotten thought, for I thus tend to turn my mind only to my failings. From an early age, when I read a book, I made my way inside it, so that when I closed it I went on reading it (like cockroaches or bookworms, eh?). It then seemed to me that those thoughts had always been mine. No one can think the unthought, only remember what has been thought or done. He who is not possessed of a memory copies, which is his way of remembering. That is how it is with me. When a thought escapes me, I would like to write it down, and all I write is that it has escaped me. It's not the same with flies. Observe their radical power, their far from flyspecktatorial patriotism. They win battles. They prevent our souls from acting, devour our bodies, and deposit in our warm remains the eggs that make them eternal, even though each of them as a single fly lives only a few days. Flies! I've saved myself from them! The fire and smoke have kept me from being invaded by them, warded off their depredative migrations! When they arrive all they'll find is one charred table companion at the Ash Supper, the Last Repast I never managed to offer the thousand Judases plus one among my traitorous apostles.

Why are you taking so long, fire, to do your work? Eh there, you layabout? What's the matter with you? Are you too afflicted with senility and impotence after a certain age? Are you older than I am? Or is it just that you too are smothering to death in my sewer hole? Could I have gotten this from somewhere? Even if I did, no matter. Patiño, a spiritualist, would have consoled me: Sire, who can prove to you that that other Ancient of Days is not yourself? It's proven fact that a spirit passes from one body to another and is always the same for time everlasting! The knave was quite capable of turning his dead souls into migratory meta-psychoses.

I don't know why I'm still busying myself looking after the clocks at this point. In the mortal silence of the city, the repeater one is tolling its death knell. The only sound. For the living and for the dead. I do not want to die, but being dead no longer matters to me, I read in Cicero, copying one of Epicarnes's§ maxims. And in Augustine of Hippo: Death is an evil only because of what follows it *(De Civit-Dei,* I, II). Quite true, compadre. It is less cruel to be dead once and for all than to find oneself waiting for the end of life. Above all when I myself dictated my sentence and the death chosen by me is my own creature. How many prisoners have dug their own graves in this earth! Others have given the death squad at their own execution the order to fire. I have seen them act their parts in the drama resolutely, I might almost say joyfully. Others are still lying, after all this time, on the floor or in their hammocks, laden with chains. At this siesta hour, which for them continues to be one of impenetrable darkness, they are sleeping peacefully, sheltered from the blinding sun. They work in their dreams, digging their graves with their own weight no greater than that of the skinniest of my white crows. I see the latter fluffing up their scabby wings, delousing themselves in the long afternoon of their lingering hope. Two black spots amid light reflections. The prisoners rocking back and forth in the darkness. They scarcely move in the

---

§Epicarnes: Greek comic poet, d. circa 450 B.C., renowned for his wise saws and philosophical disquisitions.

perpetual swaying back and forth. The creaking of their chains lulls me with a certain maternal sound. I, on the other hand, absolutely motionless. Beneficiary of a death that is certain, I teach them mortification by example. From midday on, I lie across the bed with my head hanging down toward the floor. In the window frame the inverted figures of Patiño and the commandants timidly appear. The ex confidential clerk is now clutching not his pen but a long takuara pole. He begins to poke my body, not to bring it to life but to see whether it is dead. Nudged by the pole, I feel myself float in the stygial-vestigial waters, but also in another living, dazzling river: the River-of-Crowns, the River-River.

"Always, to the very end, the torturing and perennial obsession of the *river, a free path!*" (Julio César, *op. cit.*)

My body continues to swell, to grow to giant size in the racial water that my enemies thought they had barred with chains. My corpse breaks them one by one, dredging the depths, widening the banks. Who can stop me now? The posthumous hand seizes the tip of the pole. Half dead with fear, the ex amanuensis lets go of it. We have traced the last sign together.

Policarpo Patiño escaped the sentence for a short time, just as *El Supremo* had predicted. On the latter's death, on September 20, 1840, a junta formed by the military commandants took over the headless government, after a palace intrigue. It was brought down by a barracks coup led by another "marshal" of the Deceased, Sergeant Romualdo Duré (a cracker manufacturer). The ex scribe Policarpo Patiño, secretary of State and éminence grise of the defeated junta, hanged himself in his cell with the rope of his hammock. *(Compiler's Note.)*

"On August 24, 1840, Saint Bartholomew's Day, under the influence of his infernal manservant, the Dictator set fire before dying to all the important records of his communications and death sentence, without regard for the possibility that the voracity of the element might be so great that it would inevitably set his bed on fire. Desperate, suffocated by the smoke, he called to his servants and guards to come to his rescue. Doors and windows were opened, and amid the conflagration mattresses, bedcovers, clothing and papers in flames were thrown out onto the street. O clear forewarning of the flames that in the month to come would begin to consume his soul for all eternity! Meanwhile the one thing that is certain fact is that on this occasion the passersby who were able to overcome their terror saw for the first time the gloomy interiors of Government House. Some even stopped to examine the charred scraps of bombazine, a fabric unknown in the country, of which The Supreme's sheets were made.

"For Catholics, the twenty-fourth of August is the day when the devil walks abroad alone. Many people associated this circumstance and the color of the Dictator's cape, deducing therefrom that his end was near." *(Manuel Pedro de Peña, Letters.)*

The fire drowses, not knowing exactly where to attack. It crackles on the papers that it is scorching and turning to smoke, to ashes. It sends out a trail of live sparks to the corners of the room. It does not dare to approach me; perhaps because it is unable to cross the quagmire surrounding the bed. The water and the fire, from which I formed myself, are plotting now to consign me to final solitude. Alone, in a strange country full of nothing but idiots. Alone. With no origin. With no destination. Shut up in perpetual captivity. Alone. Helpless. Defenseless. Condemned to wander without repose. Expelled successively from all the refuges I choose. Kept from descending to the grave . . . Come, come, things aren't that bad! Death will not contrive to plunge you into the self-compassion that did not even dent the surface of your life. The dead are very weak. But the dead man who in death lives on / is to be counted triply strong.

I agree that this struggle ad astra per aspera§ has made of me a half-breed with two souls. One, my cold-soul, now gazes from the other shore, where time is stemmed and is beginning to crab its way backwards. The other one, the warm-soul, is still keeping watch within me. An adept at absolute doubt, I can still get about by leaning my diurnal right leg, the one too swollen now to be able to support me, on my nocturnal left one. That one is still holding up. It carries my weight. I am going to get up for a while. I must poke up the fire. It is **HE** who emerges from **I**, turning me over again with the momentum of his retrocharge. **HE** claps a hand. The fire revives instantly. It dances merrily once again, with greater energy than before. Its blazing flames bring a sort of dawn to the room. **HE** gives another clap of his hand. It echoes like a cannon report. Dragoons, hussars, grenadiers come rushing in helter-skelter with pails of water and wheelbarrows full of sand. All the contingents with all the elements. As when I ordered José Tomás Isasi consigned to the gunpowder flames, and the blaze of yellow lava spread to my own room. The fire is now smothered once more beneath veritable torrents of water and sand. A deluge of mud falls into the room through doors, windows, skylights, bull's-eyes, cracks in the ceiling. Great guttering gouts. Drops of molten lead, at once burning-hot and ice-cold; a heavy, more than solid downpour, making my bones rattle. The spouts of mire shoot in all directions. They

§To the stars through bolts and bars.

soak, burn, pierce, stain, congeal, melt everything they come across in my lair. They turn it into an overflowing cesspool, in which there float viscous bits of ice, islets of flames. In the middle, **HE**, erect, with his usual brio, the sovereign power of the first day. One hand behind him, the other tucked in the lapel of his frock coat. The blasts of wind and water do not touch him. I pop the last aneurism of voice I was hoarding beneath my tongue. I spit a bloody insult at him. I want to exasperate him: even though they bury us at opposite ends of the earth, the same dog will find both of us! I do not recognize my voice: that breath that comes from the lungs and starts up all the elaborate machinery of phonation. Chords, tubes, alveoles, ventricles, palate, tongue, teeth, lips no longer form in me the ephemeral sound we call a voice. I haven't shouted for such a long time now! Attuning words and the sound of thought. The most difficult thing in the world! I pass my hand across my face in the darkness. I do not recognize it. Seeing in a lamp two focuses of light. One black, the other white. In a man, two faces. One alive, the other dead. **HE** loses interest. Feigns indifference. Opens the door. Heads toward the entrance. Goes outside. I see his silhouette in the passageway, haloed with that filament of white and black light, phosphorically streaking the darkness. I hear him give the password to the head of the guard detail: **THE FATHERLAND OR DEATH!** His voice fills the whole night. The last watchword I will hear. It remains sewed to the lining of the destiny of my fellow citizens. The earth trembles with the vibration of that outcry. It is passed on from one sentinel to another through all the confines of the night. **I** is **HE**, definitively, **I-HE-SUPREME.** Immemorial. Imperishable. The one thing left for me to do is swallow my old skin. He molts. I molt. He mute. I mute. Only the silence listens to me now, patient, without a word, seated beside me, atop me. Only the hand goes on writing endlessly. Animal with a life of its own, wriggling, writhing endlessly. It writes, writes on and on, impelled, shaken by the violent agitation of convulsionaries. Ultima ratio, last rat escaped from the sunken ship. Enthroned upon the stage machinery of Absolute Power, the Supreme Person constructs his own gallows. Is hanged with the rope that his own hands have braided. Deus ex machina. Farce. Parody. The Supreme-Clown's company of strolling players. On the boards, only the hand writes. Hand that dreams that it writes. Dreams that it is awake. Only if he is awake can the sleeper relate his dream. The hand-rat-shipwrecked victim writes: I feel myself falling amid the blind birds falling as the sun sets on the afternoon of the fall. Their blown-out eyes soak me with blood. They retain the image of my fall amid the storm. Those birds are mad! Those birds are **I**! Attention! They are waiting for me! If I don't keep a tight hold at all times on the Justice pouch I shall never recognize them . . .

  never . . .

    never . . .

      never . . .

        never . . .

          never . . .

            NEVERMORE!!!

He is coming back. I see his shadow loom larger. I hear his footsteps resound. Strange that a shadow should have such a heavy tread. Iron-tipped cane and studded boots. He climbs the stairs martially. He makes the stairboards creak. He stops on the last one. The most resistant one. The step of Certainty, Power, Command. The halo of his erect presence appears. Bright red aureole round the dark silhouette. Continuing to advance. For an instant a pillar hides it. It reappears. **HE** is here. He tosses the great round skirt of his cape over his shoulder and enters the chamber, inundating it in a scarlet phosphorescence. The shadow of a sword is projected on the wall: the nail of his index finger points at me. Runs me through. **HE** laughs. For two hundred seven years, for the space of a breath he scrutinizes me. Eyes of fire. **I,** playing dead. He locks the doors. Lowers the crossbars that weigh five arrobas into their catches. I hear him make the rounds of the thirteen remaining outbuildings of the House of Government with the same heavy step and go through the same operation of barring the doors, inspecting, checking every last detail: from the armory to the general storehouses, passing by the way of the toilets. I know that he did not neglect to search a single chink in the immense parallelopipedonic, babylonic bulk of the Supreme Fortress. The smoke of the fire extinguished in the afternoon slowly eddies and pools in the antechamber, in the chamber, in the inner chamber where I am lying. Why doesn't this old wreck of a place just collapse and be done with it amid all the dampness!, I think in exasperation, remembering those mornings when I used to go after Mass to watch them excavating for the foundations. Hidden among the piles of red dirt, under cover of my altar boy's baby-bonnet, I dumped cartloads of salt in the ditches in place of the stones the workers were shoveling in. I watched them attentively as they did their work while I did mine. If only the first rain dissolves the salt and sinks you, you damned mansion!, my thought cried out, seeing it grow in size, massive, quadrangular, pyramidal. Tumble down, once and for all! Surely the salt of one's wits is more resistant than the millstone of disgrace. The salt of my sacred body resists intact the viscosity of the Third Deluge.

Despite the vapors, the hermetic immurement, the first cadavicera comes in. It probably stole in through some crack or crevice in the main altar. Cadaviceras are attracted by the fascination of death. Certain emanations announce its imminence to small flies. Once life has ended, other species of flies come swarming about. Migrations follow one upon the other. From the moment that the breath of corruption becomes perceptible by setting up camp in the cadaveric reality, the first one arrives: the green fly whose scientific name is *Lucilia Caesar;* the blue fly, *Azura Passimflorata,* and the large fly with a black-and-white-striped thorax, called the *Great Sarcophaga,* the spurhead of this first migratory invasion. The first colony of flies to respond to this signal of a taste-treat may produce in corpses up to seven and eight generations of larvae which accumulate and proliferate for some six months. The larvae of the Great Sarcophaga increase in weight two hundred times every day. The skin of the corpses then turns a yellow with a faint pinkish tinge; the belly a light green; the back a dark green. At any rate, that is what the colors would be if the entire phenomenon did not take place in total darkness. Then comes the next onslaught of cadaverophile grenadieres: Piophiles that produce cheese-worms. Then corniettes, longuettes, ophiras, pharidas. They form their chrysalises like the grated breadcrumbs on ham or the bean soup I was so fond of. Then the nature of the decomposition changes. A new fermentation, richer than the previous ones, and more lively and dynamic as well, produces fatty acids known vulgarly as corpse fat. This is the stage of dermestoid capricorn beetles, which produce larvae equipped with long hairs, and of the caterpillars that will later flower into beautiful butterflies called aglossates or Coronas Borealis. Some of these substances will crystallize and later gleam like spangles or tiny metallic nuggets in the definitive dust. More contingents of immigrants arrive. To this deliciously black decomposition there now hasten avid sylphids with diamantine, iridescent eyes; the nine species of necrophores, lyrophore Homers of this funerary epic. The squadron of round and hook-shaped aquarians initiates the process of desiccation and mummification. After the aquarians (whose real name is acarians although I prefer to call them aquarians) come the agrarians. They gnaw, saw, crumble the tissues thin as parchment, the ligaments and tendons transformed into a resinous substance, as well as the callosities, the horny matter, the hair and the nails. The moment has arrived when these latter cease to grow on the corpses, as is commonly, and rightly, believed. My toenails will grow no longer, and my unnatural baldness is beyond remedy. Finally, in three years' time, the last great migrant, an immense black coleopter, larger than Government House, called *Tenebrion Obscurus,* arrives and dictates the decree of total dissolution. It is all over. The stench, the very last sign of life, has disappeared. Everything has melted away, vanished completely. Even the mourning has ended. The *Tenebrion Obscurus* has the magic quality of being ubiquitous and invisible. It appears and disappears. It is found in different places at the same time. Its eyes with their millions of facets gaze at me but I do not see them. They devour my image, but I cannot make out theirs enveloped in the black cape with the crimson lining . . . *(the following ten folios are stuck together and petrified).*

(Beginning of the folio burned) . . . and now you can no longer act. You say you do not want to witness the disaster of your Country, that you yourself have paved the way for. You will die first. That part of you which sees what is mortal will die. You cannot escape seeing what does not die. Because the very worst thing of all, grotesque Archi-loco, is that the dead man suffers, everywhere and always, no matter how completely dead he is, regardless of how much earth and oblivion are piled on top of him. You believed that the Country you helped bring to birth, that the Revolution that came forth armed from your cranium, began-ended in you. Your own pride made you say that you were the offspring of a terrible parturition and a principle of mixture. You fooled yourself and fooled others by pretending that your power was absolute. You lost your oil, you old ex theologian passing yourself off as a statesman. You believed you were playing your game of absolute passion to the limit: everything or nothing. Oleum perdidiste.§ You ceased to believe in God, but neither did you believe in the people with the true mystique of Revolution; the only one that leads a true locomotive-engineer of history to identify himself with its cause, not use it as a hiding place from his absolute vertical Person, in which worms are now feeding horizontally. With grand words, with grand dogmas that appeared to be just, once the flame of Revolution had been extinguished in you you continued to hoodwink your fellow citizens with the most contemptible baseness, with the most vulgar and perverse of ruses, that of illness and old age. Sick with ambition and pride, with cowardice and fear, you shut yourself up within yourself and turned the necessary isolation of your country into the bastion-hideout of your own person. You surrounded yourself with scoundrels who prospered in

§You wasted the oil [in your lamp].

your name; you kept at a distance the people from whom you received power and sovereignty: well fed, protected, taught fear and veneration, because in your heart of hearts you too feared the people but did not venerate it. You turned yourself into a Great Obscurity for the people-mob; into the great Don-Amo, the Lord-and-Master who demands docility in return for a full belly and an empty head. Ignorance of a time at the crossroads. Better than anyone else, you knew that so long as the city and its privileges hold dominion over the totality of the People, Revolution is merely a caricature of itself. Every truly revolutionary movement, in the present era of our Republics, begins, solely and self-evidently, with sovereignty as a real whole in act. A century ago, the Revolution of the Comuneros failed when the power of the people was betrayed by the patricians of the capital. You wanted to avoid that. You stopped halfway, and did not form true revolutionary leaders but a plague of toadies trailing after your shadow. You misread the will of the People and as a consequence you misused your power, as your dotard's affections spun about geron-tropically in the vacuum of your all-embracing will. No, little mummy; true Revolution does not devour its children. Only its bastards; those who are not capable of carrying it out to its ultimate consequences. Beyond its limits if necessary. The absolute does not tremble to carry out its thought to the very end. You knew that. You copied it in those papers addressed to no one, destined to end up as dead letters. You hesitated. You too are doomed. Your punishment is worse than that of the others. For you there is no redemption possible. Oblivion will devour the others. You, ex Supreme, are the one who must render an account of everything and pay up to the very last quarter . . . *(what follows is crushed into a ball, illegible).*

. . . at midnight, you will go down to the dungeons. You will walk about amid the rows of hammocks hanging one atop the other, rotted by twenty years of darkness, suffering, and sweat. They will not recognize you. They will not even see you. They will neither see nor hear you. If you still had a voice, you would have liked to insult them, to cause a great uproar as usual; to wreak your vengeance on these specters who dare to ignore you. Listen to me, you damned dimwits!, you would have liked to apostrophize them, repeating for the last time what you growled thousands of times. The good part, the best part of all is that nobody hears you now. Useless to scream your head off in the absolute silence. You will go down the rows of prisoners. You will look each one of them in their gummy eyes dimmed by cataracts. They will not blink. Will you know whether they are dreaming, dreaming of you as a strange animal, as a monster without a name? Dreaming. A dream. What is most sacred in man and beast. For them you will be no more than the form of forgetfulness. An emptiness. An obscurity in that obscurity. You will finally stretch out in an empty hammock. The last one. The lowest one among the rows of hammocks that sway gently beneath arrobas of irons a hundred times heavier than their bones of specters. Fallen to pieces from mildew and age, the hammock will dump you out onto the floor. No one will laugh. Silence of the tomb. You will spend the entire night there, lying amid the pestilential remains. Eyes closed, hands crossed on your chest. The sweat of these wretches, their shit, their urine, trickling from hammock to hammock, will dribble down on you, rain down drops, drops of sepulchral slime. They will crush you flatter and flatter, push you farther and farther down. They will aim these inversed pillars at your immobility. Stalactites growing above your supreme impotence. When the scab mites, the sylphs, the cadaviceras, the sarcophagas, and all the other migrations of larvae and caterpillars, of tiny necrophagous gnawers and plowers, finish with what remains of your esteemed non-person, you will at that moment also be seized with a tremendous urge to eat. A terrible appetite. So terrible that eating up the world, the entire universe, would still not be nearly enough to appease your hunger. You will remember the egg that you ordered placed beneath the warm ashes for your last breakfast, the one you never got to eat. You will make a superhuman effort to raise yourself up from beneath the great mass of darkness that is crushing you. You will not be able to. Your last hair will fall out. The larvae will go on peacefully feeding on your remains. They will weave a wig from its long hairs to cover your baldness, so that your bare skull will not suffer too much from the cold. As they are fretting away at you to the sound of their lutes and lauds, aphonic, aphasic, in a catarrhal mutism aggravated by the dampness, you will beg them to bring you your egg, the fertilized egg, the egg forgotten in the ashes, the egg that others more astute than you and less forgetful will already have eaten or thrown into the garbage. That's how things are. So then, Supreme Deceased, what if we leave you as you are, condemned to perpetual hunger to gobble down an egg, because you didn't know . . . *(the remainder stuck together, illegible, the rest unable to be found, the worm-eaten letters of the Book hopelessly scattered).*

APPENDIX

1. The remains of EL SUPREMO

On January 31, 1961, an official circular invited historians of the nation to a conclave, in order to "initiate steps leading to the recovery of the mortal remains of the Supreme Dictator and the restoration of these sacred relics to the national patrimony." The invitation was also extended to the citizenry as a whole, urging it to collaborate in the patriotic Crusade to reconquer both the sepulcher of the Founder of the Republic and his remains, which had disappeared, scattered to the winds by anonymous profaners, enemies of the Perpetual Dictator.

The echoes of this summons reach the most remote confines of the country. As in other crucial moments of the nation's life, its citizens rise to their feet as one and answer as with a single voice.

The one dissonant note in this plebiscitary chorus of approval is—surprise!—that sounded by specialists, chroniclers, and popularizers of Paraguayan history. A sudden uncertainty would appear to have unexpectedly fallen like a dark shadow over the national historiographic consciousness as regards the question of the one and only true skull of *El Supremo*. Opinion is divided; the historians contradict each other, engage in heated exchanges, argue vociferously. As if in fulfillment of *El Supremo*'s predictions, this epic national undertaking turns into a small-scale civil war, fortunately a bloodless one, since the confrontation takes place "only on paper."

Here is a very brief roundup of some of the statements on the subject that were forthcoming from the most noted national historians (presented in the order in which they were made public):

Benigno Riquelme García (February 23, 1961):

"Allow me to state to Your Excellency that personally, and in view of the information with which I am acquainted, I am of the opinion that there exist valid reasons to presume that both the remains extant in the Museo Histórico Nacional de Buenos Aires and those in our own Museo Godoi have been removed from a grave that was undoubtedly that of the illustrious patriot in question.

"What could well be a matter of dispute is the previously mentioned contestation of the authenticity of these remains, an assessment that might either be invalidated or substantiated following unbiased expertise, which I most respectfully suggest to Your Excellency, and which might be carried out by the institutions listed below:

SMITHSONIAN INSTITUTION
United States National Museum
Washington, D.C.

DEPARTMENT OF ANTHROPOLOGY
Yale University
U.S.A.

PEABODY MUSEUM OF AMERICAN ARCHAEOLOGY
AND ETHNOLOGY
Harvard University
Cambridge, Massachusetts, U.S.A.

"Their competency and impartiality in this matter would be beyond question. As regards the necessary circumspection that the Government of the Republic must observe on initiating the pertinent steps, for understandable reasons that it is not opportune to explain I believe that it is necessary to avoid a prudence so excessive that it will preclude making a gesture whose exemplarity is beyond all doubt, whatever the verdict of the scientific centers which I have taken the liberty of proposing." [There is a report appended that traces the fate of the remains preserved in the Museo Histórico Nacional de Buenos Aires and criticizes the expert opinion of Dr. Félix F. Outes concerning the aforementioned remains, rejecting and sarcastically demolishing the latter's conclusions.]

Jesús Blanco Sánchez (March 14, 1961):

"To begin with, I must inform Your Excellency that the decision of the Superior Government to honor the memory of our heroes of National Independence is especially gratifying to me and impresses me as being most laudable. Allow me therefore to add that from the moment that our government undertakes this project, it is of fundamental importance that it be pursued with absolute seriousness, and above all that all possible steps be taken in order to avoid unpleasant surprises, to which the Government of the Nation cannot expose itself.

"As Your Excellency is well aware, if these remains were in our own country there would be no major problem standing in the way of the realization of this most felicitous aim, but in the final analysis and over and above all else it is the symbolic meaning that such things have which is always most conspicuous. But in view of the fact that these remains must be brought from Buenos Aires, where this hero of our Independence has been so bitterly fought, especially by a powerful and persistent current of opinion that is adverse both to his person and, even more particularly, to his labor as Head of Government, this subject, for these reasons, becomes delicate and worthy of careful and objective study. In this connection, I believe that the aforementioned current of opinion is again on the rise in Argentina at present, and therefore we must foresee the possibility that the remains preserved in the Museo Histórico de Buenos Aires are not authentic; if this should prove to be the case, there can be no doubt that we would expose ourselves to a treacherous propaganda campaign aimed at leaving us in a ridiculous position.

"No one can question the authenticity of the document. [The reference is to a document that apparently proves that the remains are authentic.] In my opinion it does not constitute completely convincing proof, since whoever kept these relics 'in a box of noodles' for some time and then gave them to a foreigner is eloquently indicating to us that they never aroused his interest in the slightest, nor did they awaken in him any patriotic feeling whatsoever."

Manuel Peña Villamil (March 24, 1961):

"In order to provide Your Excellency with the desired information while adhering to a strict criterion of scientific research, it becomes necessary to answer two questions which, although related, correspond to different aspects of the problem. Firstly, is it likely that the remains extant in the Museo Histórico Nacional de Buenos Aires are those of the Perpetual Dictator? Secondly, does the present state of the historical investigations of the matter authorize the Superior Government to initiate official steps in order to secure the return of these mortal remains?

"In answer to the first problem posed, I must say that I am not in a position either to affirm or deny categorically that these remains are authentic. Before any answer can be given, it is necessary to consider the procedures followed by Señor Loizaga in order to exhume the remains from the old church of the Encarnación. As it happens, we have Señor Loizaga's own version of the exhumation, in the form of a letter sent to the Argentine historian Dr. Estanislao Zeballos. In a monograph entitled *Muerte y Exhumación de los restos del Dictador Perpetuo del Paraguay*, the Paraguayan historian Ricardo Lafuente Machaín reproduces it without essential variants and without further research. Father Becchi and Señor Juan Silvano Godoi are mentioned as eyewitnesses of the event. On that occasion the latter removed another skull from the same grave; it is preserved in the museum in Asunción that bears his name.

"The observations which seem to us to indicate the procedure followed by Señor Loizaga in effecting the aforementioned exhumation are as follows: (a) His act was inspired not by a spirit of serious and impartial historical investigation but by political passion; (b) He did not submit the remains to any expert examination that would exclude the possibility that an error had been made in the process of exhumation." [There follow other considerations in which he questions the authenticity of the remains, as certified in a report by the Paraguayan physician Dr. Pedro Peña, published in the daily *La Prensa*, Asunción, I° = II = 1898, and in the famous phrenological study by the Argentine physician Dr. Félix F. Outes, 1925, a key document in this dispute between museums, published in the Boletín del Instituto de Investigaciones Históricas, Fac. Filosofía y Letras de Buenos Aires (tomo IV, pp. 1 ff.).]

Julio César Chaves (March 28, 1961):

"Toward the middle of the year 1841, the political atmosphere in Paraguay was extremely tense as a heated polemic concerning the life and works of El Supremo began. Pamphlets and lampoons circulated, prose and verse made the rounds. His enemies and his supporters girded themselves for battle and threw themselves into it with equal passion. The former declared that the Supreme was not worthy of being laid to rest in a church and publicly announced their intention of getting their hands on his remains so as to toss them on a rubbish heap. We may here remind the reader that a short time later a placard appeared on the door of the church, stating that it had been sent by him from hell and begging that he be removed from that sacred place in order to lessen his burden of sin. Moreover, several of the families cruelly persecuted by El Supremo, among them the Machaíns, made no secret of their plans to take their vengeance upon his remains. His supporters, in their turn, did not remain inactive. They organized continual popular demonstrations whose participants marched in procession to their leader's grave. The tension grew all through the year 1841 and would appear to have reached its peak on September 20, the first anniversary of the death of the Supreme Dictator. The passions that had been unleashed threatened to set off a civil war; the atmosphere became so heated that it threatened the peace of the nation, particularly necessary at that juncture in order to allow it to confront and resolve serious international, economic and social problems. It was then that the Consuls resolved to take action, decisively and dramatically: they ordered that the mausoleum housing the remains be demolished and the body buried 'no one knows where.' According to Alfred Demersay's version of events (*Le Docteur Francia, Dictateur du Paraguay,* 1856): 'He was buried in the church of the Encarnación and a granite column marked his last resting place for the veneration and worship of his numerous partisans. It was said that shortly after the anniversary of that day of mourning the mausoleum disappeared, and the rumor spread that the remains of the famous Doctor had been transferred to the cemetery of the church. Part of this story straight out of a novel was true, but the consular government, the mysterious source of this measure inspired by politics, vehemently denied any thought of a gratuitous profanation. The Supreme now rests in the place that the piety of those men chose for him, but his tomb has never ceased to case a shadow upon his successors.'

"Thomas Jefferson Page, the captain of the North American vessel *Water Witch,* which arrived in Paraguay on a mission of exploration and research, has this to say on the subject: 'The churches are well maintained, but one of them, quite evidently, was less well attended than the others. The good people rarely mention the fact, because an awesome mystery has penetrated within its sacred limits. One quiet morning, the temple was opened for prayer as usual: the monument had been shattered and the bones of the tyrant had disappeared forever. No one knew how they had disappeared, no one asked what had become of them. It was merely whispered that the devil had reclaimed what was his: body and soul.' (*La Plata, The Argentina Confederation and Paraguay,* London, 1859.)

"Can the remains donated by Dr. Estanislao S. Zeballos to the Museo Histórico

Nacional de Buenos Aires be those of the Perpetual Dictator of Paraguay? These remains were on exhibition for many years in this museum: they are at present in the basement of that institution, among the objects of no value.

"We know of only two opinions, both well-supported and both negative [the reference is to the two studies already mentioned]. Outes, an eminent scientist, impelled by his curiosity as a researcher, examined the supposed remains. After so doing, he stated: 'In the first place, the calvaria, because of its morphological characteristics and its anatomical features, belongs to an individual of the feminine sex, 40 years old at most, who very probably was not a European, *sensu lato*. There is no relationship whatsoever between the calotte and the facial mask. Quite aside from the characteristics offered by the latter, any effort of reconstruction based on both pieces would be fruitless, since there is an excess of frontal bone in each. This is evidence, *prima facie,* that it corresponds to two individuals. The jaw, finally, is that of a child, which at death still had all of its milk teeth.'

"His conclusions, therefore, are as follows: Firstly: The skullcap belonged to a woman, 40 years old at most, and non-European: either black or Indian. Secondly: The facial mask was that of an adult, not of a senile. Thirdly: The jaw belonged to a child less than six years old."

2. *Migration of the remains of EL SUPREMO*

R. Antonio Ramos (April 6, 1961):

"Francisco Wisner de Morgenstern, who wrote a book about The Supreme Dictator at the request of Marshal Francisco Solano López, notes the following: 'A few months after the death of the Dictator, the sacristan of the church was surprised one morning to find the sepulcher where he was buried open. It was never discovered who the authors of this deed were; however, they had left a trail that disappeared on the shore of the Paraguay River, into which there is good reason to presume that they were thrown, since traces were found on the aforementioned shore which prove this. Several versions of what had happened made the rounds in the Asunción of that era: one of them had it that orders had been given men paid by the M. . . . family to remove the remains and throw them into the river, as vengeance for the execution of members of this same family ordered by the Dictator after the last Yegros conspiracy was discovered; another version was that a certain family had the remains taken from the vault in order to incinerate them and throw his ashes to the winds; and finally, that another family, by agreement with the priest, removed them in order to hide them elsewhere.' " [Commentary of the Compiler: If we accept Wisner's version, based on gossip whispered about the city wherein the remains of El Supremo disappear into water, fire, air, or earth, we find ourselves confronted with the fact that the migration of his remains, profaned out of hatred or vengeance, never took place.]

Be that as it may, let us follow the remainder of Dr. Ramos's statement:

"Wisner de Morgenstern nonetheless cites another version based on testimony that we shall now examine. Carlos Loizaga, who was a member of the triumvirate set up in Asunción in 1869 and who negotiated with Baron de Cotegipe the peace treaty with Brazil [the reference is to the puppet government placed in power by the occupation forces of the War of '70, a year before it officially ended], states in a letter addressed to Dr. Estanislao Zeballos that he [the ex-triumvir Loizaga], accompanied by Father Vecchi, the parish priest of Encarnación, exhumed 'the remains of the tyrant.' Those relics—he adds—had previously been in a sarcophagus located to one side of the High Altar of that church, and the parish priest Don Juan Gregorio Urbieta, later Bishop, removed them one night, in the days of Don Carlos Antonio López, and buried them behind the sacristy, in 1841.

"In the aforementioned letter by Carlos Loizaga, he states that Father Vecchi was present when he exhumed the 'remains of the Tyrant.' But Ricardo de Lafuente Machaín states that Juan Silvano Godoy was present as well. 'Despite the great circumspection surrounding this undertaking'—he declares—'Dr. Juan Silvano Godoy, secretary of the High Court of Justice, learned of it, and though he had not been invited to attend, decided to do so. On the appointed night he hid behind one of the pillars, awaiting the arrival of Señor de Loizaga. From there he flew forth to meet him, enveloped in his cape and an immense broad-brimmed hat, like a giant bat in human form. Once recovered from his fright, occasioned by the place, the circumstances, and the intentions of this sudden apparition, or perhaps judging the latter to be irreproachable, Señor de Loizaga offered no objections to the functionary's joining him and the workmen, and the latter set to work. Once the stone was removed and the workers' grub-hoes dug in, human remains soon appeared. It was presumed that those of the Supreme Dictator were the ones lying at the very top. Señor de Loizaga ordered them to be collected and placed in a little noodle box that he had brought with him especially for that purpose. But amid the earth and the debris another skull came to light. Señor Godoy leaned down, picked it up, and carried it off underneath his cape. They say that the ex triumvir, Señor de Loizaga, watched him take off into the distance, wondering for a moment which of the two skulls was the real one. He was nonetheless quite certain that the remains he had collected in the noodle box were those of The Supreme, and stowed it away in an attic in his house until he could decide what to do with the contents.'" [Señor Godoy kept the skull that he had carried away with him that night in his private museum, worthy of a man of the Renaissance; thus the story of the remains is left hanging suspended at this fork in the path of the bicephalous skull of the tyrant, other scholiasts comment.]

Dr. Ramos goes on: "Let us now see what happened to the skull collected by Loizaga. At the time of his visit to Asunción in 1876, Dr. Honorio Leguizamón, the ship's physician of the Argentine gunboat *Paraná*, learned that 'the remains of the Perpetual Dictator were in the possession of Carlos Loizaga.' This news reached him through the intermediary of the latter's family. Leguizamón tried 'to see and examine the precious remains.' Loizaga refused at first, but later acceded to the desires of the Argentine physician [who had treated him and cured him of a serious disease]. Dr. Leguizamón himself offers the following account: 'The remains were handed over to me inside a large noodle box. I was vastly disappointed to find myself in possession of nothing more than a shapeless mass of bones shattered to bits with a hammer. Knowing the temperament of my patient as well as his long-standing hatred of the Dictator, it was not difficult for me to conjecture the motive that lay behind those hammer-blows. Of the skull only the upper portion was well preserved. As for garments all I found was the sole of a shoe that would fit only a very small foot; probably that of a very young child. I persuaded Señor Loizaga, from whom I refused to accept any honoraria, to allow me to take away with me the skull of what had once been El Supremo of Paraguay.'

"At a later date," Dr. Ramos concludes, "Leguizamón gave the intact portion of the skull to Dr. Estanislao Zeballos, who donated it in turn to the Museo Histórico Nacional de Buenos Aires. According to the latest information the skull is no longer on public exhibition, as was the case in earlier days. In view of the considerations briefly outlined above, in no way meant to exhaust the subject, it cannot be definitely stated that the skull preserved in the Museo Histórico Nacional de Buenos Aires is that of the Supreme Dictator. There exist no certain facts to support such a statement."

Marco Antonio Laconich (April 21, 1961):

"After Asunción fell to the Triple Alliance, the [Paraguayan] legionnaries took over the sacked and pillaged captive city. And like frenetic worm-wolves [sic: misprint?] they began to dig about in the sacred ground of the dead, to satisfy hatreds toward El Supremo that went back half a century. In 1870 Loizaga was a member of the Triumvirate placed in power in Asunción by the allies, as the provisory 'Paraguayan' government. Loizaga was a primate of the Legion. We do not doubt for an instant that he was the author of this profanation of sacred remains, of which he appears to boast in his answer to Dr. Zeballos. Moreover, he was in a privileged position to commit it with the greatest impunity; but if he believed that he had found the Dictator's grave, and died in that belief, he was laboring under a serious misapprehension. For there is every reason to presume that Loizaga stumbled on a common grave of some sort and extracted from it, in the dead of night, the human remains that he long kept in his house, in a noodle box. We conclude that it was a common grave on the basis of the results of the analysis of some of these bones made by Dr. Outes; bones carried away with him by Dr. H. Leguizamón.

"Who knows whether, by one of the ironies of fate, whereby Our Lord is sometimes pleased to frustrate the workings of human rancor, some of those bones that Loizaga kept in a box of noodles might not have been those of some beloved relative of his. . . . For the Dictator, I presume, did not still have his baby teeth intact when he died!

" 'The remainder of the skeleton,' Loizaga says, 'was carried by me to an open grave.' Again the same lack of witnesses to the goings and comings of this solitary gravedigger. If the rest of the skeleton was like the reconstructed skull, there is every reason to suppose that it was composed of, for example, five long bones [femurs], three backbones, fifty ribs, and so on; which could be regarded as proof that the Dictator was a far from ordinary skeletal phenomenon.

"In any event, it is most curious that Loizaga and Godoy left the church, enveloped in the shadows of the night, with two skulls of the Dictator, as though the latter had had two heads. Each of them was convinced that he had gone off with the authentic skull of El Supremo."

[*Compiler's note:* According to a revelation by an old family slave, Loizaga kept an urn containing the ashes of his maternal grandmother in the same cabinet. This informant, in full possession of her mental faculties despite the fact that she was over a hundred years old, told me that one night, by error, she put those ashes in the soup that she made for dinner. The slave, now freed, also told me in confidence that since her masters hadn't noticed her mistake, she filled the funerary urn with sand from the courtyard, so that no one would discover her fateful error. She earnestly beseeched me not to tell on her or set "all this foolishness down on paper for no good reason." Since the slave's negligence was a much less grave offense than the profanation and theft of the remains of *El Supremo* committed by Loizaga, I am not being disloyal in bringing to public notice the story of the ex slave of the ex triumvir; on the contrary, I consider it only my duty to do so.]

Dr. Laconich continues:

"On June 23, 1906, Dr. Honorio Leguizamón wrote a letter to the publisher of *La Nación* that I regard as being of the utmost importance. In this letter Dr. Leguizamón, at the time the ship's physician of the Argentine gunboat *Paraná*, describes the circumstances in which he obtained from Loizaga, in the year 1876, the remains in question, which he later turned over to Dr. Zeballos, who subsequently donated them to the Museo Histórico Nacional de Buenos Aires, in July, 1890.

" 'At first,' Dr. Leguizamón writes, 'I met with a resounding no; but once Señor Loizaga was convinced that my information had come from the best possible sources, since members of his own family confirmed that it was they who had passed it on to me, he was obliged to yield to my importunities and confess the whole truth to me: his religious spirit had impelled him to dig up those remains, which profaned the ground in which they had been buried. The remains were handed over to me inside a large noodle box'—and then he adds these words, which we would do well to keep in mind: '*I was vastly disappointed to find myself in possession of nothing more than a shapeless mass of shattered bones. . . .*'

"Following this disappointing discovery, Dr. Leguizamón asked himself: 'Could this fragmentation of the skeleton have resulted from the vengeful fury of some victim? At the time I did not dare to ask him.'

"The letter leaves the lingering suspicion between the lines that Loizaga pounded those bones to splinters with a mallet, thereby taking his vengeance upon the Dictator. In a postscript, Dr. Leguizamón furthers this suspicion by adding that it was an age-old tradition among the Guaranís to take their vengeance upon their enemies by removing their bones and breaking them to bits.

"It is our sincere belief that this custom of the Guaranís is a discovery of Dr. Leguizamón's unsupported by other evidence, tailor-made by him to fit his needs. The Guaranís were far more interested in the flesh of their enemies than in their bones: if they found them appetizing, they ate them, without further ado. We leave it to Hans Staden to contradict us. . . .

"The *shapeless mass of fragmented bones* would seem to confirm the hypothesis of a common grave, which goes hand in hand with the existence of the skullcap of a woman, the facial mask of an adult male, and the jaw of a child, the mere jumble of bones described in the expert opinion rendered by Dr. Outes. However . . .

"Dr. Leguizamón states categorically in his letter that the only remains of any sort of garment he found in the noodle box was 'the intact sole of a shoe that would fit only a very small foot.' It is a well-known fact that the Supreme Dictator had small hands and feet, of which he was very proud since he regarded them as proof of good bloodlines; but the words 'very small' call to mind a little child.

"Hence it is my opinion that it is not advisable to organize this national homage to celebrate the repatriation of remains of such dubious and much-debated authenticity of those preserved at present in the Museo Histórico Nacional de Buenos Aires. The circumstances leading to a hoax linked to the box of noodles of Legionnaire Loizaga"—Dr. Laconich concludes—"would inevitably cast a shadow over the homage paid to the illustrious memory of the Founding Father."

FINAL COMPILER'S NOTE

This compilation has been culled—it would be more honest to say coaxed —from some twenty thousand dossiers, published and unpublished; from an equal number of other volumes, pamphlets, periodicals, correspondences and all manner of testimony—gleaned, garnered, resurrected, inspected—in public and private libraries and archives. To this must be added the versions collected from the sources of oral tradition, and some fifteen thousand hours of interviews, recorded on tape, filled with inexactitudes and confusions, with supposed descendants of supposed functionaries; with supposed kith and kin, close or distant, of The Supreme, who always boasted of not having any; with epigoni, panegyrists, and detractors no less self-proclaimed and nebulous.

The reader will already have noted that, unlike ordinary texts, this one was read first and written later. Instead of saying and writing something new, it merely faithfully copies what has already been said and composed by others. Thus in this compilation there is not a single page, a single sentence, a single word, from the title to this final note, that has not been written in this way. "All history that is not contemporary is suspect," El Supremo was fond of saying. "It is not necessary to know how they were born to see that such fabulous stories are not of the time in which they were written. There is a vast difference between a book made by an individual and put before the people, and a book made by a people. There can be no doubt, then, that this book is as old as the people that dictated it."

Hence, imitating the Dictator once again (dictators fulfill precisely this function: replacing writers, historians, artists, thinkers, etc.), the re-scriptor declares, in the words of a contemporary author, that the history contained in these Notes is reduced to the fact that the story that should have been told in them has not been told. As a consequence, the characters and facts that figure in them have earned, through the fatality of the written language, the right to a fictitious and autonomous existence in the service of the no less fictitious and autonomous reader.

GUARANÍ WORDS USED IN THE NOVEL

(Note: The spelling used in the novel has been preserved here.)

abatí: uncured brandy distilled from corn
aó-poí: a type of handmade cotton cloth
axé-guayakí: an indigenous tribe
caranday: palm
chipá: maize cake
chiripá: long cloth girdling the loins
guaná: indigenous nation
guasú: great
Guaykurú: Indians who live apart, on the plains of Paraguay, Buenos Aires, Bolivia, and Brazil
güembé: plant whose bark has medicinal properties
jupiká: a stew whose principal ingredient is broad beans
kaguaré: ant bear
ka'aiguá: people of the wilds
kambá: a black, especially a Brazilian soldier during the War of the Triple Alliance
kapuera: a plot of farm land cultivated for family use
karaguatá: a plant that produces textile fibers
karaí: lord, leader, chief; the Supreme Dictator was known as Karaí Guasú.
kõi: twin
machú: nanny, nurse, housekeeper
marandová: worm
Mbayá: indigenous tribe that lived west of the Paraguay River
mbopí: bat

ñandutí: very delicate handmade lace

paí: priest, friar

payaguá: (1) tribe of Indians; (2) plant

payé: sorcerer

pindó: variety of palm tree

pirí: straw sombrero

samu'ú-peré: large tree, from the trunk of which canoes were made; known in Spanish
    as *palo borracho*. Pcré = bare.

sarakí: playful, frisky, mischievous

so'yo: a soup made with water, rice, chopped or ground meat, oregano, salt, and oil

taguató: sparrow hawk

taitá: papa

takuara: bamboo, hollow cane

tanimbú: ash

tapera: tumbledown house, ruins

tepotí: excrement

Tikú: diminutive of Francisco

timbó: timber tree; a red and a white variety exist. Timbó = emitting smoke.

tuyá: old

urukure'á: owl

urundey: timber tree with hard red wood

xake: watch out!

yateí-ka'á: medicinal herb, used to ward off appendicitis

yatytá: snail

yavorai: brush

ysipó: liana